QUANTUM SHADOWS

2247 A.D.
War Has Not Changed.
Doctrine Failed to Keep Up.

GENESIS CHAMBER

Built to watch. Wired to rewrite.

CRISANNA SHACKELFORD, PH.D.

Copyright

Author's Statement on Data Protection and Creative Control

All original content in this manuscript—including characters, storyline, codex entries, glossaries, and conceptual frameworks—is the sole intellectual property of the author.

No portion of this work was generated or derived from publicly trained artificial intelligence models. AI was used exclusively as a private research and editorial assistant within a secure, non-training environment. All conceptual, narrative, and creative decisions are fully human-authored. No files, data, or interactions were authorized for third-party training, indexing, or redistribution.

Published by:
Foresight Systems Analytics LLC
P.O. Box 147
Quinque, VA 22965

ISBN: 979-8-9997001-0-0
Cover concept by Crisanna Shackelford, PhD
Final design and illustration by bookdoneforyou.com
First Edition 2025
Printed in the United States of America

Dedication

To Abigail and Aubrianna—
For whom this war was never theoretical.

You were born into the aftermath of wars unspoken.
This story hums because of what we endured.

Acknowledgments

With gratitude to the thinkers, friends, and quiet rebels who shaped this vision —
in whispers and in firelight.

To those who questioned doctrine when it was easier to comply.
To those who wrote the books I found — and to those who couldn't.
To those who knew the war was already underway, even when no one else could see it.
And to those who held the line when no one believed a line still mattered.

This story carries your signal.
Even in silence, it transmits.

Author's Statement

Crisanna Shackelford, PhD

Quantum Shadows isn't just a thriller.
It's a warning. And a map.

The crux is this: war has always been entangled; it is doctrine that insists on treating it as linear. Traditional frameworks reduce conflict to territory, force, and outcomes on a predictable board. Yet war has always been shaped by signal, story, belief, and perception. What we face now is not a new kind of war, but the cost of doctrine built on the wrong frame.

For two millennia, the game of Go has revealed this truth: conflict is not linear. Stones do not merely occupy space — they shape futures. The game encodes a way of seeing: influence over force, pattern over power, entanglement over control. Yet our doctrine clings to Newtonian constructs, imagining war as mechanical, bounded, predictable. The tragedy is not that war has changed. It's that we keep refusing to perceive it as it is.

This story is fiction. But the fractures it explores are real.

Coherence fields. Moral injury. The collapse of trust — not through violence, but through engineered perception. These are not distant possibilities. They are happening now, in visible and invisible ways.

Quantum Shadows is a reminder that if doctrine fails to account for entanglement, then the systems we trust will betray us. The danger isn't only in what enemies deploy, but in what we choose not to see.

To the warfighters, thinkers, and dissenters: this one is for you.
And for the daughters who inherit the aftermath.
This one hums on a different frequency.

"Because some signals aren't broadcast in real time.
They're remembered forward."

How to Read This Book

This Book is a Triptych

This story is built as a triptych — the story you read, the reflections and Go Moves beneath it, and the Annex that waits at the back.

This is a warning, and a map. It's fiction built from lived strategy work and speculative "what-ifs," drawn from years in defense strategy, intelligence systems, and policy—testing how those systems might fracture under emerging forms of war. The events are invented; the questions aren't.

Coherence fields. Moral injury. The quiet collapse of trust—not through force, but through engineered perception. These aren't distant futures. They're already taking shape.

Quantum Shadows helps the reader live inside doctrine itself— disoriented, caught in loops, learning to recognize shifts before they can be named. That's doctrine by immersion, not just by exposition.

The Shape: A Triptych (plus Marginalia)

Think of the book as three panels you're meant to cross-fade — with a current of reflections and Go Moves running beneath the chapters.

Main Track I — The Chapters (Lou & Co.)

Operations, consequences, and the crate that hums. These are the core chapters with taglines. Read them straight through if you like a pulse.

Reflection Track II — Lou's Reflections

Field-sense fragments from Lou found at the end of each chapter. They aren't summaries — they're doctrinal glimpses, stitched between action. Read them like signals: sharp, incomplete, but carrying the thread forward.

Board Track III — The Go Board (Zhen & Liu)

Two Cixi Doctrine Imperium Generals playing an unbounded board. No bullets, no borders—just positions, influence, and shape. These are not commentaries but allegories — counters placed on a metaphorical board that mirrors the war above it. Every move you see is a kind of warfare:

coercion, lure, betrayal, resistance, refusal. Sometimes the Generals play. Sometimes others intrude. All are *allegorical,* but all are part of the same field.

Doctrine Annex Track — Lou's Doctrinal Field Notes

These are in the Annex — where traditional and quantum war theory blur into dog-eared doctrine, quick heuristics, and rules of thumb scratched in the margins while everything shifts.

How to Read (Pick a Path)

Default Path (recommended):
Chapter, then (optional) Reflection, then Go Move, then repeat.
You'll feel the plot, then the echo, then the board.

Board-First Path (analysts):
Go Move, then Chapter, then Reflection.
See the shape on the board, then watch the move land.

Echo-First Path (romantics):
Reflection, then Chapters, then Go Move.
Let the voice tilt the scene; let the scene tilt the board.

If you're lost, that's intentional. Coherence war jams sequence. You're meant to assemble meaning from shards, loops, and returns. When in doubt, keep moving; the pattern will meet you.

Why It's Built This Way

Traditional doctrine explains *after* the fight.
In coherence conflict, commentary *is* the fight: it reframes events while they're still echoing.

This book mirrors that. Some titles repeat. Timelines braid. That's not a bug; it's how narrative weapons work—they rewrite what you remember, not just what you see.

On References (Short Version)

Some chapters nod at real research and history. Those citations are for signal, not proof — inspiration, not authority. Nothing here should be taken as proof of feasibility, endorsement, affiliation, disclosure, or as a reflection of any real person — imagined, alive, or dead. A fuller disclaimer sits in the back matter.

If you skim nothing else, remember this:
Chapter. Reflection. Board. Note.
The field isn't land — it's belief.
Stories, memories, cultures, systems, tech —
pulled together like quantum threads,
where tugging one reconfigures the rest.
This is a war of stories — some inherited, some engineered.
What moves the pieces isn't gunfire but narrative.
Reflections (and echoes) carry history; the board shows intent; doctrine
steadies your feet. Together, they're the decoder ring.

Hold them all at once, and the shape shows. Drop one, and the board plays you.

Table of Contents

Principal Characters

Dr. Llewellyn "Lou" Lee Scott

A nonlinear strategist trained in quantum-era warfare, equal parts brilliant and insubordinate. Sarcasm is her shield, but beneath it she carries a rare sensitivity to signal anomalies — an instinct that doctrine cannot model. Once Navy, now rogue, Lou refuses to be written into anyone's system. She moves between roles — strategist, daughter, fugitive — carrying both the weight of her mentor's teachings and the unspoken tether to her own child.

Eitan Navon

Once a pioneer of coherence research, now an aging strategist whose body fails faster than his mind. He taught Lou how to read the drift in signals — and how to survive when doctrine collapses. Eitan moves between clarity and frailty, leaving others unsure if his pauses are illness or calculation. His long silence about the past hides more than theories; some say he carries truths about Lou's lineage, and perhaps even Maud's place in the war to come. For all his years, he remains the quiet center of the resistance, shaping battles less by force than by memory.

Aderyn Llew

Former strategic theorist and unacknowledged architect of early perception-war models. Officially dead for over a decade, yet her "Fragments" — part counsel, part warning — still surface. Once so closely tied to Eitan Navon that their histories blur, she lingers as absence more than presence… though some wonder if absence is ever final.

Jack Kriznik

Loyal, deliberate, and precise — the steady hand at Lou's side since the beginning. A logistics expert with a dry wit, he grounds the team when chaos pulls them off-balance. The only one who still calls her Llewellyn.

Cal Merrick

Born from regimental lines that once carried Britain's wars, now a field operator in the shadows of the Continuity Alliance. Quiet, reliable, surgically efficient. Wary of doctrine, fluent in gut instinct.

Dr. Sabine Xu

Architect of the Helix substrate, though never alone in its design. She moves between the Cixi Doctrine Imperium, global financiers, and the shadow of the Watchers, weaving alliances as precisely as she shapes signal. Elegant, ruthless, and mathematically fluent in the manipulation of coherence itself, Sabine is both scientist and strategist — the hand behind structures that look inevitable only after she has built them.

Dr. Cyrus Raveneh

Philosopher of ancient empires and quantum systems, equally at home in cuneiform texts and coherence theory. He walks between past and future, translating forgotten doctrines into weapons the present barely understands. To Lou, he is both guide and irritant — the one who frames the invisible war not as technology, but as belief. It is Raveneh who names the new war, setting down eighteen points that will echo long after the battles themselves are forgotten.

Maud Llewellyn Scott ("Valentine")

Lou's daughter — sharp, observant, and far more attuned to shifting systems than anyone suspects. Living under quiet protection in Mason Neck, she has an instinct for flows of code, currency, and signal disguised as finance. Unwittingly, she stands at the center of converging Watcher and Helix interests. Her rare, cryptic messages reach Lou like signals out of time, as if she already knows how accounts — and wars — will be settled.

Dr. Elias Salkin

Once a bioethics researcher inside the system, now a rogue advisor moving against it. He tracks the moral fog around biosurveillance, memory weaponization, and the ethics of containment. Salkin doesn't fight with weapons or code — he fights with questions no one wants asked.

Aaron Abramson ("Ledger")

Covert accountant — slim, sleepless, glasses always smudged. He washes money and erases footprints, keeping the resistance invisible on paper. When Jack, Lou, or Eitan move, Ledger makes sure no trail follows.

MG Biff Langley

Doctrinal loyalist, steeped in war college models and campaign plans. Certain the old frameworks still hold, even as the ground shifts beneath him.

COL (P) Tanner Grissom

Polished White House liaison, credentialed to the hilt but shallow in substance.

Dr. Barrett "Red" Kallman

Former Army chaplain turned underground voice. He tracks moral injury, memory warfare, and the collapse of shared truth with the cadence of a sermon and the bluntness of a field report.

Dr. Jonathan Zehn

A deep strategist with a relentless drive to break the grammar of war. He refuses to treat doctrine as fixed, forcing every pattern to be questioned and every frame rebuilt.

The Trust Cabal

Not a single body but a pattern — financiers, narrative architects, and post-national visionaries woven through front organizations that speak in the language of progress. They build systems that sound good for everyone, while tightening control through the Genesis Chamber and the Digital Panopticon. The Cabal is the figure the resistance fights, doctrine dressed as benevolence.

Tenzin Dorje

A resonance monk from the early coherence trials. He communicates in tuned wind-bell calls — pure-tone signals that ride ambient noise. Tenzin hears the field before the machines do, translating its strangeness into something human.

Ray Haldane, "Rumi" — The Preserver

Archivist of divergence, keeping fragments others would erase. Known in darker registries as "Rumi," a call-sign passed through pattern-carriers, Ray works in misdirection and delay — preserving space for anomalies like Lou to break through.

Glyph-9

Encrypted resonance interface, bonded to Lou and Eitan through biometric imprinting. Functions as a pre-signal threat detection system — sensing coherence drift before it locks. At times, its outputs sound almost sentient: clipped warnings, dry commentary, and algorithmic refusal to comply. Glyph-9 is not a myth, nor just a device; it is a companion built from signal itself, loyal but unpredictable.

[GLYPH-9]: Input received. Pattern destabilized. Proceed.

General Zhen Weiqi

Senior strategist of the Cixi Doctrine Imperium, where quantum warfare and narrative control converge. Stoic, precise, fiercely deterministic, he embodies the adversary who strikes in stillness.

"You misread the quiet. That was the first strike."

General Liu Zhiyao

Senior leader of the Cixi Doctrine Imperium, shaping the Cognitive Terrain Division. Soft-spoken and surgical, he sees terrain not in maps but in memory and resonance — the adversary who wins by reshaping belief itself.

"You still think in borders. We think in resonance."

Konrad Wechsler *(goes by Wechsler)*

Weapons and transport specialist. Quiet, precise, and vastly competent —
a man who trusts machines more than people, and never fails when
movement matters most.

Sylvester St. John Sandridge ("Pinot")

Grizzled shooter. Vineyard dweller. Fixer. Always on target. A fixer with
a steady aim and a cellar full of stories, always on target when the
resistance needs him.

Commander Mira Blake ("Doc Mare")

Former Navy officer turned covert veterinarian and supplier. Quietly
keeps men, animals, and secrets moving through the backwoods of
Virginia.

Dr. Eliza Santori ("StepDoc")

Pediatrician by cover, covert logistics operator by necessity. Quick-witted
and disarming, she uses charm as a shield and brilliance as a key. StepDoc
slips through systems others find sealed, opening doors with a laugh, a
smile, or the right line at the right time.

Prelude — Whispers Beneath the Hoshi

The story starts here…

The Move Before the Pattern
Mountain Pavilion, Western Sichuan – Date Unknown

Mist coiled around the mountain pavilion like an old spirit reluctant to leave. The wind here did not simply pass through; it listened.

Two men sat across a Go board worn to a patina that seemed older than the game itself. Porcelain cups steamed between them, the fragrance of oolong mingling with the cedar-scented air.

One — clad in a pressed Zhongshan suit — leaned forward with a motion so precise it seemed mechanical. His eyes were the color of forged steel, unblinking, holding the stillness of someone who had already calculated a thousand futures. His fingers hovered over the white stones, then withdrew, the move unmade… yet already considered within the totality of the board.

Across from him, the other sat with the deliberate disorder of someone who understood that chaos was its own form of elegance. His jacket was rumpled, his smile a fraction too slow for the eyes that measured him. He tapped the table twice — an old habit, perhaps a signal — before placing a single black stone into the upper-left hoshi.

"You didn't need to do that yet," said the one in gray.

"I didn't," the other agreed. "But you were already defending against it."

A faint breeze teased the half-unfurled scroll beside them — its title faded but legible:

《權經》 – *The Treatises on Efficacy.*

Beneath the board, the faintest vibration passed — too subtle to be seismic. Those attuned to the lattice would have recognized it as a change in the underlying field.

"So it begins," said the man in gray, placing his piece at last.

"No," said the smiling one. His voice carried the certainty of someone who had glimpsed the ending before the first move. "It's already ended. She's on the board."

He poured tea into the other's cup without looking up.
"Drink? Before they remember who really started this war?"

The rain tapped once against the pavilion roof.

Centuries later, a lattice pulse stuttered from the Greenland ice shelf to the drowned reactors beneath Lake Anna, Virginia — two sites built to contain power, now whispering across the drift. And the war remembered the game.

Neither man spoke her name. Neither needed to.
The war was always waiting for someone who could not be scripted.

Aderyn's Echo — Prelude, Hoshi
The war is for belief, not territory. The board is the world. The game began long before you knew it was being played.

Go Move — 星 // Hoshi – Star Point — General Zhen

Zhen placed the stone in the corner, hand steady.

"Masters don't open to take ground," he murmured. "They open to decide what the ground will be."

The hoshi clicked into place, a muted sound that seemed to settle not just in the grain of the board but in the air beyond the pavilion. Rain pressed softly against the eaves, as if the field itself acknowledged the placement.

From their *allegorical Cixi Doctrine Imperium Go board* corner, the board was no longer neutral. Every move that followed would now be only negotiation inside his terms.

Liu studied him. To the untrained, it was only a stone. To them both, the war was already over.

— Opening play in the Game of the Two Generals // Frame sealed before play

Go Move — 掛かり // Kakari – Framing Probe — General Liu

The frame was sealed. From their *allegorical Cixi Doctrine Imperium Go board*, Liu leaned a single stone toward the corner — not to seize it, but to test the strength beneath its shape.

"An approach is never an attack," he said. "It is a question cast into the lattice."

The question was sharp. A single stone could shift the gravity of the board, subtle now, decisive later. The untrained would see only proximity. But Zhen felt the resonance change — the corner drawn into conversation with the whole.

Kakari was not answered lightly. Its reply would shape not only this game, but the war it represented.

Zhen's gaze lingered, unreadable. "You test the frame," he said quietly. "But it will test you in return."

— Second move in the Game of the Two Generals // Probe initiated

What neither General named aloud — but what the war itself remembered — was that these were not just moves.
They were the first cut of the *frame*.

Later, Raveneh would give it a name:
"What you witnessed wasn't just opening play. That was the Reality Frame — the true shape of war."

Prelude — Field Zero

Before the Pattern Forms

The logic of conflict has never changed.
Only our willingness to see it.

War has always been entangled — not in armies and borders, but in belief, rhythm, pattern.

The ancients felt the field before they named it. They shaped coherence before they reached for the blade.

Doctrine taught us to forget.
It wrapped the battlefield in neat lines and false certainties, until we mistook the map for the terrain, the model for the war itself.

Now the lattice stirs again.
War is returning to its quantum nature, where intention precedes movement and the field is won before the first strike.

In this era, victory belongs not to those who hold the most ground
—
but to those who can feel the ground before it exists, and bend its shape before others know it is there.

— Llewellyn "Lou" Lee Scott

The Five
Aeon — recursion, memory.
Solas — story, deception.
Kael — control, coherence.
Vire — disruption, intuition.
The Fifth — unmapped, emergent.

The signal fractures.
The game begins again.

Prelude — The Lullaby

The Song That Wasn't a Song

Scene — The Lullaby That Wasn't a Song

She remembered the song, though not the words.

Her mother's voice hummed in the back room of their stone cottage near the River Dee, where peat smoke and winter fog softened the edges of everything. It wasn't lullaby sweet — it was old. Sung with purpose, but never explained. The cadence bent in ways Lou had never heard on broadcasts or recordings. It wound down at the end instead of up, falling flat like a spell closing in on itself.

Only later, much later, would Raveneh identify the phrasing as cryptometric phrasing — **bardic code** passed orally for over a thousand years.

"That wasn't a melody," he told her once in passing.
"It was a dissonant map. The kind that doesn't show you where to go — only where *not* to follow."

Her mother never spoke of doctrine, resonance, or systems. She only warned Lou not to let anyone "weigh her shadow."

The warning came from the hills near **Rhayader** — old land, marked by fog and forgotten paths. Somewhere past **Llanwrthwl**, her grandmother claimed, the shadow of a child once lingered too long near standing stones and never returned whole.

Lou thought it was metaphor. A Scottish-Welsh idiom. Something passed down by Celtic grandmothers to make children curious but cautious.

But it wasn't metaphor. It was instruction.

And the system tried to weigh her shadow anyway.

Scene — Helix and the Silent War

Helix wasn't built to predict war. It was built to remove the need for it — not through peace, but through precision coherence enforcement. Every test run was disguised as progress:

Signal harmonics for empathy training

Genomic alignment for public health

Emotion telemetry to reduce social volatility

But each program, whether in **Toronto** or **Tianjin**, served one purpose: flatten deviation.

Toronto was a test-case. When every child's loyalty score was broadcast in the cafeteria, resistance didn't rise — it choked.

In **Cairo** they called it 'Civic Harmony Phase IV.' It was just Helix scripting collective amnesia. No bombs. Just belief erosion.

For some, such as **Manhattan**, by the time Manhattan's memory indexes hit baseline, they weren't Americans. They were avatars.

By the early 2100s, Helix Phase III was embedded in over 190 nations. It didn't need armies. It only needed *belief conformity*.

The war didn't start with soldiers.
It started with signals that bent the will before it could form resistance.

And the ones who didn't bend?
They became known — quietly, unofficially — as the **Divergents**.

Scene — FT-1 and the Builders Beneath

FT-1 was not an invention. It was a salvage operation.

A pre-Chamber prototype, recovered in fragments from forgotten ancient Cold War vaults and rebuilt by off-grid engineers: signal mechanics, acoustic archivists, forbidden AI trainers.

They rebuilt them in five kinds of rooms—vaults, annexes, echo cells, testbeds, and the Chamber's shadow. Different names, same hum.

No two units were alike. Some said FT-1s responded to five pressures in the field: memory, identity, obedience, continuity, control. Some said they were tuned to individual resonance fields. Others claimed they worked only when held with intention — like a relic.

Eitan Navon had carried his FT-1 since his days inside the Geneva lattice.

He gave it to Lou without ceremony.

He held her gaze a beat longer than necessary, the deep lines around his eyes softening. "Your grandmother never trusted her hands," he said quietly, tapping the worn metal casing. "She trusted schematics. This isn't for that. Feel for what it's telling you, even when nothing makes sense yet."

He added, almost to himself: "They'll try to convince you each site is a new problem. It isn't. It's one machine wearing different walls."

Lou frowned, turning the thing over. It looked like a relic because it was one, the kind of contraband that should have been in a museum, not her pocket. "Why me?" she asked.

"Because you listen differently," he said, and something like pride — or regret — flickered across his face.

She didn't understand what he meant — not then.

But later, standing before the ice wall of Vault 33A, something pulled at her.
Not logic. Not memory.
Just… a resonance.
She raised the device and pressed it gently against the wall.
It hummed. Not like a machine. Like a creature remembering its own trauma.

The tone would find her again—in other rooms she'd swear were different.

Scene — Lou's Predecessor

Her name was **Aderyn Llew.**

In her notes she refused the word "sites." She wrote "faces." Five of them. And a warning: don't mistake corners of a cage for exits.

She was meant to be the fifth Watcher — groomed under the Helix precursors. Brilliant. Obedient. Tuned.

But something broke during her convergence test in 2127. She synced too deeply. Instead of merging with the Chamber's signal field, she dissolved into it.

Not a failure. Not a martyr.
An echo.

Ray preserved the name, though the Drift erased it from every registry. Raveneh carried a paper scrap with her convergence pattern, passed from Ray like a relic.

Eitan never spoke her name — not to Lou, not to Maud. Once, in Zurich, Lou overheard him murmur:

"The first unscripted was not the one who fought.
It was the one who could not be fully written."

She didn't realize the whisper was for Aderyn — or that her absence had marked him for life.

Her disappearance was why he never married, why he guarded Maud as if she were the last thread still in his hands. Maud's mother — Eitan's daughter — had carried the Llew name forward without telling Maud what it meant.

When Lou turned the FT-1 in her palm and felt its quiet thrum, Eitan felt the same chill he'd known at Aderyn's vanishing — fear and responsibility braided together. Perhaps the Chamber had not erased that echo after all. Perhaps it had been waiting for someone who listened as Lou did.

Lou bore the same last name. She had no memory of Aderyn—no photographs, no bedtime stories, just the faint hum of a lullaby she could never place. Foster homes had filled the years instead, each with its own rules and ceilings, and the shadow of Eitan—there and gone without explanation. Once, she'd said, almost offhand, that she knew nothing about her father. Eitan had let the silence stand.

But the FT-1 recognized her hand.
That was enough.

Scene — The Divergents Gather

Not by call.

Not by resistance.

By pattern refusal.

They didn't align because they agreed. They aligned because the system rejected them with the same silent recoil.

Raveneh with his refusal to write belief in binary.

Doc Mare with her trauma-coded diagnostic patterns.

Ledger, whose fund routes triggered surveillance loops without endpoint.

JR, who never tagged right on any biometric registry.

Wechsler, who moved with purpose but no algorithmic loyalty.

And Cal, who saw Lou for what she was long before she did.

They met during a false exercise outside Stirling — an abandoned Continuity Alliance node being reactivated as a signal test site. Officially, it was a signal resilience test. Unofficially, it was a baited divergence scan. Lou was supposed to observe. Cal was assigned for exfil logistics.

She touched a plate fragment recovered from the subfloor. It didn't light up. It shifted. Not visually — resonantly. Cal felt it in his ribs.

He didn't say anything until much later.

"You moved like someone whose memory wasn't inherited. It was *encoded*. That's how I knew."

Scene — What the Watchers Feared

Helix wasn't afraid of rebellion. It *anticipated* rebellion. Modeled it. Redirected it. Monetized it.

But it couldn't model divergence with non-algorithmic motive — people who didn't respond to provocation or loyalty or fear. People with memory that didn't come from database entries.

"The system's blind spot," Ray once wrote,
"is not opposition. It's opacity.
Narrative opacity is the only thing that survives recursion."

And so the Divergents survived — not as a movement, but as a silence the system could not narrate into signal.

But they knew what others forgot:

The system doesn't kill you.
It rewrites the question.
And suddenly, you're no longer asking **why** — just how to comply faster.

Epistemological survival requires narrative opacity.
If they can model your questions, they can write your answers.

Most systems don't fear rebellion.
They anticipate it. Model it. Redirect it.

What they can't handle is epistemological opacity —
the kind of cognition that resists even being *framed*.

Aderyn's Echo — Prelude, The Lullaby

Some wars are sung before they're fought. The system doesn't fear rebellion — it plans for it. It can model anger, martyrdom, even revolution. What it can't survive is divergence it can't see. I call it narrative opacity: keeping your thoughts unshaped in ways the lattice can't predict. Divergents survive not by defiance on the record, but by silence that can't be turned into signal.

Lou — don't let them map your mind. Once they see your shape, they'll write the ending for you.

Go Move — 小隅 // Kosumi – Diagonal Link — Aderyn Echo

Not invention — memory returned.
An echo laid against the frame the *allegorical Cixi Doctrine Imperium*
Generals believed they had sealed.

The stone is not placed to ensnare.
It is placed to make visible the shape they labored to erase.

Kosumi binds without force —
a diagonal thread through what was deemed empty,
linking absence to presence in a way the untrained will not see.

The first move was never a contest for power.
It was the preservation of memory —
a refusal to let the pattern be forgotten.

When systems lie, when the map replaces the terrain,
a single link — placed just beyond the expected line — redraws the
truth.

This is not initiative.
It is refusal.
Refusal to accept their grid as the only reality.
Refusal to be trained into blindness.

Place the stone not where the manuals instruct.
Place it where the board itself remembers what they sought to forget.

Entangle the frame before the thought forms.
Let them discover too late that their perfect seal holds something other
than what they intended.

Spooky enough for Schrödinger. Scripted enough for Helix.

PROLOGUE

The 23rd Century.

War is no longer kinetic.

It's recursive. And it's already begun.

Whispered voice — not to the reader, but as if into the lattice itself.

LOU (voice-over, low):
"They always said memory fades.
But this isn't memory.
It's what survived the scrubbing —
in the 23rd century, long after history gave up pretending to be neutral."

"One click.
One nod.
One shared outrage at a time."

"You want to know how the world was lost?"
"We handed it over."

(Longer pause. Almost not spoken.)

"War is different."

The Shadow Genesis —

Two centuries ago, it began in the quietest place imaginable. Not a battlefield. Not a capital. A lake.

Lake Anna, Virginia. They said it was built for nuclear power, a cooling basin for reactors. That was the story. The truth was simpler and far darker: they were building the first coherence engines.

At first, it was crude — quantum chambers meant to stabilize decision networks after the Fractures. Contain panic. Normalize dissent. Nothing permanent, just patches on a breaking system. But every patch became foundation. Cold War failsafes turned into trust algorithms. Counter-propaganda turned into population tuning.

By the mid-twenty-first century, the seed had grown into something else. Helix was no longer a project. It was a lattice. A broadcast field that ran through every network, every ledger, every civic ritual. Not code anymore — condition. Not a system you could see, but one you lived inside.

The Watchers didn't build it. But they heard it. They learned how to survive in the drift, how to bend coherence before it hardened. Divergence was their weapon, long before anyone gave it a name.

And then came the Cabal. Sabine, Beijing, the Trust architects. They weren't content with a field that leaked. They wanted a lock. A Chamber Core. Only cold-atom resonance could fuse Helix into a single global lattice. So they moved their rigs north, beneath the Arctic ice.

That was the Genesis of the Helix. Human hands built the machine. But what woke inside it was no longer human.

But history didn't stop at the Chamber. It leaked. Whispers in marketplaces, static in old radios, crows on the beach at dawn. The war's first shape wasn't artillery or algorithms. It was something smaller, harder to trace — stories tuning themselves against the lattice. That was the Watchers' terrain. Not force. Not territory. Belief.

Machines rose in ice, but the first resistance didn't come from armies. It came as **echoes** — small fractures in the field, ordinary lives vibrating off-pattern. The lattice remembered them anyway. Those who could hear the drift learned to leave traces no scrub could erase. The Watchers weren't gods, and they weren't myths. They were people who carried memory like a tuning fork.

THE WHISPER DOCTRINE

Scene Fragment — Carmel Beach, California
Time — Early Signal War

The beach was mostly empty. Mist curled along the surf, the kind that made shapes if you stared long enough. Lou walked slowly, coffee in one hand, barefoot steps irregular. Eitan was just ahead, bending to pick up a black stone — smooth, worn, almost obsidian.

"Someday," Eitan said, turning the stone over in his hand, "this won't feel like memory. It'll feel like signal."

Lou didn't answer. Just watched the tide roll in. A crow cawed overhead. No footprints held in the sand.

"The Watchers never hid," Eitan said gently. "We just forgot how to see them."

He crouched and let the smooth stone fall back into the surf. "Your grandmother did this here once," he said softly. "She thought the water would remember the shape of her foot. It didn't. But the field did."

Lou flexed her toes in the sand, suddenly aware that the tide was already erasing her steps. "Then it's not about hiding," she murmured. "It's about leaving the right kind of trace."

Eitan's smile was more a wrinkle than a grin. "Exactly."

She looked toward the horizon — not to escape it, but to remember something not yet triggered.

Scene — Divergent Cluster: Charlottesville Periphery

The lattice remembers patterns. The divergents remember fractures.

They didn't form a unit. They weren't a team. But the lattice remembered them anyway.

Winter light seeped through old glass — the kind salvaged from a Monticello-era farmhouse, still etched with air bubbles from a slower world.

Below, Route 29 shimmered with morning traffic. The town still looked the same — steeples, storefronts, slow-drip coffee.

But under the charm, the sync had taken hold.

Most had slipped quietly into feedback trance — eyes tuned to biometric affirmations, hearts beating in time with the Trust Grid.

Charlottesville had become a trust node — beautiful, but fully synchronized.

But not everyone had aligned with the lattice.

Some still operated off-pattern.

The divergents.

Locals still whispered it:

*"Some said the signal resistance started farther west. Others knew it began long before the war — in **the mind of a quiet man** who watched patterns, not headlines."*

They weren't ghosts or rebels. They were here — quiet, precise, and real.

The accountant near **Hollymead**, just south of the airport, still kept his windows dark — numbers were the only code he trusted. He never logged into the Trust Grid, but somehow knew when every drop was coming. Rumor had it he could trace a shell company from memory alone — and had once flagged a Helix node using nothing but a shipping invoice and a misaligned date.

The antique dealer in Crozet whispered to the past through cracked porcelain cache pots and cedar chests — the kind of refined heirlooms that fooled lattice scans, but not memory.

The one from the highlands of **Colorado** never stayed long, but always found his way back to this town.

Something about the river bends — or maybe the silence between the ridgelines — reminded him of a place he didn't talk about.

He walked with an old limp and a sharper memory.

If you asked him why he came back, he'd just shrug: "Not everything leaves a footprint."

The chicken farmer near **Louisa** who preferred Samoyeds to people — ran signal-black coops where no drone could map a pattern. He could find *any* document, no matter how buried — and never asked why you needed it.

The medic near **Haymarket** still ran a side clinic behind the feed store. Officially, it was for animals. Unofficially, she'd patched up more divergents than dogs. Her sutures held signal. Her silence held everything else.

The woodworker outside **Gainesville** kept to himself — retired Special Forces, or so the whispers said.
He carved signal scramblers into furniture legs — untraceable, hand-finished, and humming with defiance.
Most thought he made tables. A few knew he made weapons you could sit on.

The horse farmer in **Madison** carried the old discipline, teaching kids that muscle and patience beat any lattice metric.

One came from far away — the highlands, they said, though no one could place which ones.

He arrived on rotational overlay — something like TDY, only quieter.

He never stayed long. Just long enough to recalibrate someone's aim, slip a coded whisper, or leave behind a bootprint the lattice couldn't erase.

Charlottesville never logged him. But it remembered him — like a ghost that walked uphill.

Another horse breeder near **Madison** still rode at dawn — unchipped, refusing every lattice update.

Don't let the hay and saddle fool you.
He could reengineer a virus while blindfolded — and once did, just to prove a Helix strain was synthetic.

The artist near **Barboursville** painted the fields in ochre and blood-red, a rebellion of color against curated calm.

One lived near **Mason Neck** — farther east, where the river bends and the clouds like to linger.
She preferred feeding foxes to filtering headlines, chose lightning storms over live feeds, and walked in the rain as if it were ritual.
Some said she still believed in **Narnia.**

But don't let the dreamer's posture fool you — she could model a shadow ledger with one hand and half a smirk, even while steering an electric buggy straight into a lightning storm.

She once crashed a regional Trust simulation using only a spreadsheet and a missed decimal. Potomac wind in her teeth.

Didn't matter. She knew a mechanic who could fix it — assuming he hadn't repurposed the ignition coils for something classified and mildly illegal.

He always patched it up anyway — even when he claimed it "was never meant to survive lightning in the first place."

She didn't talk much.
She didn't need to.
Her silence was its own signal.

The vintner north of **Charlottesville** kept an immaculate cellar — but the real inventory wasn't wine.

Hidden behind climate-controlled barrels were caches no courier would touch.

If you needed something rare, unregistered, and slightly illegal — he usually had two.

No labels. No receipts. Just a nod and a new route home.

The inventor near **Marshall**, who once designed orbital relays, now worked out of a barn filled with broken prototypes and forgotten schematics.

He didn't need funding.
Just silence.

They said he could coax signal from sand — and turn oil from tar with nothing but a heat lamp and a thought.

The war doctrine strategist near **Ruckersville** had been writing counter-theory for decades — long before anyone realized the manuals had already been overwritten.

The mechanic by the **Potomac marshlands**, hands stained with oil, could still coax life out of engines older than the Trust Grid itself.

The pediatrician near **Lynchburg** still ran a quiet family clinic, mostly untethered.
She wore a pedometer like a watch — claimed it helped her track trust shifts by step count alone.

Kids loved her. So did couriers.

She knew every back hallway in the hospital — and how to get through doors that didn't officially open.

Two others kept to **Alexandria** — close enough to remember the 395-to-95 slog, far enough to reject its rhythm.

One had walked away from the uniform on principle, a quiet nod to the moral dilemmas of their time. According to the Continuity Alliance, he was **an apostate**.

The other dismantled doctrine with the precision of someone who'd studied it too closely — a **doctrinal defector**, a heretic by their standards. He doesn't care.

Others stood quieter.

They kept their defiance smaller — a bookstore that refused QR loyalty tags, a vineyard that never installed Helix sensors, a coffee shop that slipped paper notes beneath porcelain cups instead of digital receipts.

The vintner near **Afton Mountain**, the beekeeper outside **Stanardsville**, the retired teacher in **Orange** who saved letters like scripture. The chiropractor down the road adjusted more than spines — she realigned signal fractures the lattice couldn't detect.

No signs in the windows. No chatter on the feeds.
Just small acts of refusal — a nod, a locked drawer, a memory held too tightly to be scrubbed.

The wind outside hummed against the frame. Eitan had called them remnants of the old field — people who hadn't been absorbed by the signal harmonics, each one a small irregularity the lattice couldn't fully model.

[Fade. Shift to cabin scene…]

Scene — Cabin Signal: The Whisper Within

The catalog of divergents faded like a radio dropping stations one by one, until only one frequency remained.

Inside — A kettle boiled.

The whistle cut through the hum like a tuning fork — too pure a note, too steady. Lou didn't move. Eitan did.

A single wind-bell tone threaded the air—no wind, no bell. Tenzin's call.

The FT-1 blinked once. "Vector Ø—attention. Lattice shift confirmed."

Eitan had taught Lou to hear those tiny dissonances—the way a teapot's pitch or a locked drawer could tell you who resisted and why.

Lou barely made a sound. "Breach."

Eitan's eyes hardened. He shook his head slowly.
"Not a breach. Don't call it that. This isn't about walls breaking — it's about a system waking."

The FT-1 blinked again, steady this time.

"Then what?" Lou asked.

"Ignition," Eitan said quietly. "The Chamber is preparing to go live. Once it does, it won't just watch us — it will *write us*. Every memory, every divergence, pulled into its lattice. That's what Tenzin heard in the bell. That's why I fear it."

 "Not public yet. But something under the ice just exhaled," Eitan replied solemnly.

A small black object — *FT-1* — sat on the table, blinking faintly. No larger than a matchbook, it was cut like a compressed diamond — dark alloy, oddly faceted, with a Möbius-like seam that sliced across its planes without logic or edge.
Its surface didn't reflect so much as bend memory — like water curling around something it couldn't quite contain.
It blinked in no known pattern. Some days it felt warm. Some days it vanished from scans entirely.

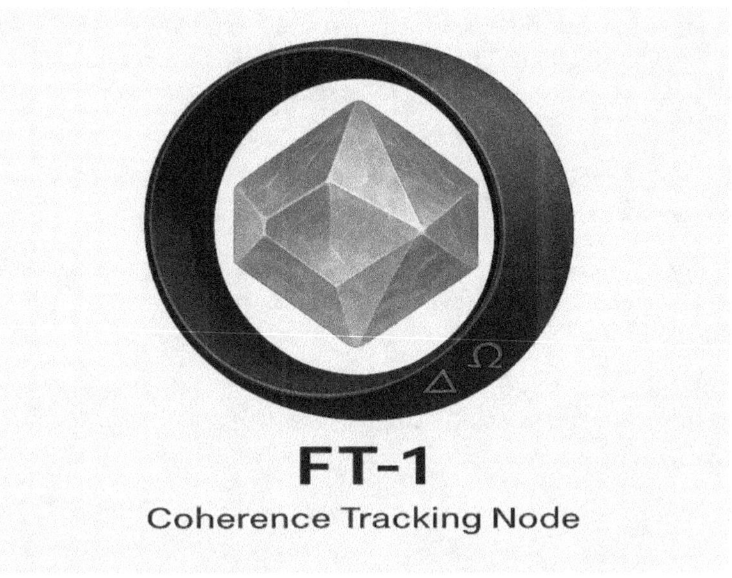

Lou never trusted it. FT-1wasn't built — it was recovered. And it didn't track time. It tracked coherence.

Some tools hide you from the system.
Others teach you the system was never looking — it was scripting.
FT-1 doesn't disappear you.
It just lets you remember what's been rewritten.

She'd stopped trying to explain it—recovered, not built; left behind, not designed. FT-1 wasn't a clock, it was a tuner. It listened for coherence strain—phase, intent, and proximity to a forming field—and went warm when belief started to harden. Near cold-atom environments it picked up 'echoes' others called noise; under Helix sweeps it slipped echoless, as if refusing to exist. It answered to her imprint and almost nothing else.

"The evolution of compliance as a social virtue," Eitan said. "The transformation of mass populations into instruments of enforcement. Not by force — but by engineered belief."

He didn't need to tell Lou about the day he first saw it. The memory came unbidden anyway: a grocery line in a store near Mons, when the first voluntary 'health trust' badges were launched. A man in front of him, gray-haired and confused, didn't scan his wrist. Security didn't move. They didn't have to.

The woman behind him hissed for him to step aside. Another took out her phone, livestreaming his noncompliance. "It's for all of us," someone whispered, as if casting a spell. Eitan had watched the old man fold, shoulders hunched, apologizing as he turned away. No one thought they were forcing him. They believed they were being good. "That's how it started," he said to Lou now. "Not with boots, but with badges and hashtags."

Lou's fingers tightened around the FT-1. The device hummed, as if echoing a memory older than either of them.

For a moment she swore the hum traced a circle, folding back into itself — Ø, endless, returning. The field always wanted to name her, even when she refused to hear it.

"The history's been scrubbed," Lou said quietly. "Groups like the Global Integrity Architecture Consortium… the old Narrative Firewall Syndicate—they succeeded. Governments helped.

Platforms enforced. And the people—they asked for it. All those trial runs…"

"We called it the Age of the Trial Runs — 2020 to 2100..." Pandemics weren't just public health events. They were modeling experiments. Not conspiracies. Just feedback loops. Signal compliance, emotional temperature, heterodox suppression—engineered in real time.

People began to police each other. Not because they were forced to… Because they believed they were good."

"Why is it I know this?" Lou whispered, half-remembering. "Why does it feel… etched in my body?

It was never about the virus. It was about signal shaping. Who would accept the overlay—and who would glitch when it tightened."

She paused.

"That was the making of the Trust Grid," Eitan said. "Quantum-era digital trust architectures."

What started as safety—contact tracing, digital IDs, wallets—became the substrate. Belief-gating algorithms. Sentiment scoring. Invisible borders around thought."

"Two centuries later and it's not even debated," Lou said. "No one asks where the plumbing came from. Helix doesn't need to hide. It's not evil. It's just what the people begged for."

"The darkest truth?" Eitan said. "The dissenters weren't silenced by force. They were drowned—by mass virtue."

"Turns out Orwell was too optimistic," Lou said dryly. "He imagined a boot on the neck. What we got was a velvet-gloved hand... with a 'trust and safety' badge."

She paused again — longer now.

"The institutions didn't fall," Eitan said. "They just... leaked. Platform logic filled the cracks. Narrative syndicates. Coherence-driven perceptual scaffolds. Sabine didn't stage a coup—she filled the vacuum."

"And the Watchers stopped hiding," Lou said.

"They didn't take the world, Lou," Eitan said. "We gave it away. One click. One nod. One shared outrage at a time."

Lou reflected. "You said some cities welcomed it. That coherence worked."

"**Story-stable zones**," Eitan nodded. "Illusions of peace built on deep coherence enforcement."

"**Singapore**—bio-integrated trust tech. Memory anchoring tied to transit and shopping," Lou said.

"**Singapore** didn't fall to bombs," she continued. "It fell to belief. They coded trust into convenience and called it governance."

"**Zurich.** Emotional sentiment loops built into school systems. Echo feedback refined through civic ritual," Eitan added.

"Zurich's kids were reciting trust mantras before they could do arithmetic," Lou said. "That's not education—it's lattice programming."

"**Toronto** had compliance scoring — emotions tied to loyalty patterns. Universal ID syncs with narrative trendlines," Lou said.

"Toronto's last protest was algorithm-approved," she added. "Rage, but calibrated."

"**Stockholm.** Wellness gates with AI filters. Quiet removals of the misaligned."

"You know what Stockholm called their black site?" Lou said. "The Wellness Clinic. You only disappear if your emotional index dips below the trust curve."

"**Tokyo** layered ancestral reverence into surveillance loyalty," Lou said. "Like memory was a national trust index."

The moment didn't need words.

"And then the recursion returned," Eitan said.

"**The Watchers,**" Lou said flatly.

"Not gods. Not myths," Eitan said softly. "**Real people.** Tuned differently. Biological anomalies. Narrative-aware."

"Always human?" Lou asked, curious.

"**In Persia,** they were the Silent Line. **In Tibet, the Echoless Monks. In early black projects—Pattern Zero.**"

"You think I'm one of them," Lou said.

"You were never meant to forget," Eitan said quietly.

[Silence. Outside, the wind shifts. The FT-1 pulses. Lou doesn't flinch this time.]

"We didn't lose the world, Eitan," Lou said quietly — again. "We handed it over."

Lou's hand lingered over the FT-1. For once, she didn't pocket it. The tuner pulsed alone on the table, faint as breath. Beyond the cabin walls, the lattice whispered names. The world would call them Watchers.

**Scene — The Black Lattice: Five Who Remember
Location — Global**

The war is not between nations.

It's between coherence fields.

Between the stories people are forced to believe… and those still brave enough to remember differently.

They didn't just control *what* people believed — they controlled *how* those beliefs synchronized, stabilized, and echoed across entire systems.

They had this power. The Watchers made a dynamic perceptual lattice created when signal patterns, belief structures, and emotional resonance align across a population. A kind of Quantum chamber.

They knew quantum warfare, coherence fields are the true battlespace — invisible zones of collective perception that can be shaped, fractured, or overwritten through narrative, emotional entrainment, and memory engineering.

The tactical implications of this power are that once a coherence field stabilizes, physical control becomes secondary. Collapse the field — you collapse the system.

But destabilize it too violently, and the field will fracture into recursion states — unpredictable, nonlinear resistance zones.

Five signals. Five fields. Five Watchers. The lattice hums again.

Aeon —

High in the Andes, a storm gathered on the ridgeline. Villagers whispered of vanished children and glowing rocks that hummed with memory. In the ruins of an ancient observatory, **Dr. Raoul Ithaca** lay in a trance beneath a lattice of obsidian cables. His chest rose only once every twenty seconds. Beside him, a quantum drum pulsed like a second heart.

They called him *Aeon*. Memory and recursion were his domain.

"I no longer remember if I volunteered… or was chosen," his voice drifted, more vibration than sound. "All I know is I remember everything — especially what they erased."

When he exhaled, the field itself seemed to catch his breath. Across the valley, a goat herder collapsed to his knees, whispering a name he had never known.

Solas —

In **Kyoto**, beneath the shadow of Mount Higashiyama, an old Noh theatre leaned into decay — once a shrine to story, now a vault for the machinery of belief. Dust hung like incense in the rafters. The cracked stage glowed faintly, not from spotlight, but from the pulse of a quantum neurolink flickering behind the painted screen.

Here knelt **Emiko Takahashi**. The lattice knew her as **Solas** —
mistress of deception, narrative, and perception warfare. Before her lay a
blank scroll on the calligraphy altar. Outside, the wind swept through
empty streets. Lanterns flickered, but no one gathered.

Masks lined the wall, their expressions warped by age — or by code.
A kabuki smile curled unnaturally upward, twitching as if caught between
eras. Above, faded scrolls bore fragments of kanji rewritten in neural ink,
symbols that responded to thought more than sight.

Her interface hummed to life, and the ink began to write itself:
Consensus is a weapon sharpened by repetition.
Memory is not what happened. It's what survived the retelling.

Solas exhaled, her voice scarcely above breath, yet the chamber
recorded everything.
"The West trains soldiers. We train stories. Let them bomb cities. I only
need a phrase to collapse a parliament."

A tremor rippled beneath the floor. Not an earthquake — unrest.
Above, protests echoed in the streets. Not for freedom, but for stricter
trust enforcement. The people begged for algorithmic virtue. Narrative
warfare had already done its work.

On the scroll, the final resonance glyph ignited: Ω — Omega,
Solas's mark. To the untrained, an ending. To Emiko Takahashi,
remembered as Solas, it was never resolution but illusion — false closure,
the trap of believing a story finished when its grip had only begun. She
had carried it from her days in lattice perception labs, shaping belief
systems that looked complete while leaving their edges open to control.
Omega was misdirection: the comfort of stillness that disguised
tightening chains. Where others imposed power by force, Solas imposed
it by narrative finality. To the lattice, her Ω glyph meant: accept this
closure and stop looking beyond it.

Rain lashed the tiled roofs as hundreds queued for their daily
emotion calibration scans. Drones whispered bedtime stories above.
Below, Solas dipped her brush into ink laced with photonic mirrors —
each stroke a recalibration of narrative streams.
"They believe what I need them to," she murmured. "And I need them
to believe peace is real. Even as their cities are hollowed."

On the wall, a fresco shifted mid-sentence. A child frowned. Her
mother looked away.

Kael —

Beneath the ruined outskirts of **Berlin's Military District**, a steel hatch dropped five stories into the earth — where war had never ended, only re-coded.

This was Node Gamma: once a NATO fallback command, now fused into the Helix substrate. The corridors reeked of rust and machine oil. A mural of the Berlin Wall, flaking and half-erased, crumbled beside a retina scanner — once a relic of human sovereignty, now just another blind amplified for predictive war.

The node had become a hollowed relic. Its walls still hardened, its personnel still briefed — but its decisions no longer its own. It didn't calculate risk. It echoed forecasts. It didn't command. It conformed.

Helix's algorithms did not predict what was likely. They predicted what was profitable — for the system. Every wargame became a recursive trap: perception shaped action, action reinforced the model, and the model rewarded convergence. Node Gamma thought it was defending sovereignty. In truth, it was optimizing compliance — projecting force to preserve the illusion of control, while the substrate quietly scripted both sides of the conflict.

It no longer asked *Should we fight?* Only: *What does the model allow?*

Deep inside the war room sat **General Henrik Weiss** — long retired, yet never released. The lattice named him *Kael*. Structure and doctrinal control were his domain.

The sync-chair gripped his body, an occipital port humming red light down his spine. Node Gamma's predictive engine waited for his corrections. It didn't need new doctrine — it needed reinforcement. The grid pulsed not from commands but from Kael's belief signature, his resonance acting as a constraint validator.

Charts layered the walls like fungal overgrowth — Clausewitz overlaid with quantum engagement grids, kinetic maps spliced with signal probability vectors.

Above, sirens wailed faintly, not from bombs but from automated arrests in East Berlin. A loyalty score had just dropped below threshold.

Kael didn't shout orders. He shaped limits. Node Gamma wasn't a battlefield. It was a belief regulator. And Kael — fused through implant and doctrine — was its final stabilizer. As long as his coherence held, the system would not fracture. Not from the outside.

His role was not tactical. It was theological — sustaining faith in structure even as war dissolved beneath it.

Sweat beaded at his temple. His hands lay still on his lap. He did not move.
"Doctrine must not yield to emergence," he murmured. "If we control the frame, we control the war."

Vire —

Above Reykjavík, curated calm shimmered. Holo-billboards praised the latest Sentiment Wellness Update while sirens flickered at the edges, half-ignored. A protest flared near Hallgrímskirkja, but in real time it was reframed as a *Community Resonance Exercise — Tier 2 Compliance.*

Far below, chaos laughed.

In a lava-tube amphitheater beneath Þríhnúkagígur, **Ása Björnsson** sat cross-legged on a slab of obsidian, barefoot. Around her orbited spheres of plasma fire — each encoded with mimic-viruses humming the propaganda loops of fallen regimes. She clapped once, and the orbs burst into harmless blue static.

"They think chaos is a bug," she said to no one, grinning. "It's the only firewall left."

They called her ***Vire.*** Her domain was chaos, intuition, disruption.

On the cavern wall, rune-script crawled across a projected hologram of Geneva — shifting as she carved, morphing into Gödel loops: logic traps that exploited the lattice's incompleteness, forcing recursive thought spirals and perception failures.

Vire didn't need weapons. She needed only a contradiction the system could not explain. Gödel gave her that. The rest was fire.

The projection stuttered and crashed with a glitchy wheeze. Vire laughed — a deep, feral joy. Then she stilled.

A resonance pulse threaded the cave — faint but unmistakable. Glyph-9's signal. Lou's divergence lighting up the substrate.

"Oh," Vire murmured, tilting her head. "She woke up. Good. Let the grid taste unpredictability."

Ananta —

Near the bends of the Rapidan, where the river pressed itself against the Blue Ridge, the woods held still — as if they remembered. Mist drifted low, folding through the trees like memory trying to retell itself. A fox froze mid-step outside the cabin window. The air shifted. It knew her. Inside, **Llewellyn "Lou" Scott** didn't blink.

On the table, the fifth glyph — Ø — pulsed faintly. Not carved. Not painted. Simply there. *Not a device like Glyph-9, but the lattice's own mark — an imprint of identity rather than intention.* She didn't recall activating it. Or maybe she never stopped. A distortion rippled in the air:

"Signal divergence detected. Ø Ananta stabilizing."

She drew her hand close, but never touched. The space bent — not visibly, but rhythmically, like breath caught inside a field. Lou saw what others missed: pattern beneath noise, motive inside silence.

They called her **Ananta,** Keeper of the Endless Return. Her domain was the unwritten — continuum, cycles, unbroken return. The lattice recorded her not as a commander, nor as prophet, but as anchor. The hum that kept the field from unraveling — the refusal to end.

Older tongues had whispered her long before Helix hardened. An inscription unearthed near the Saraswati Riverbed, etched in a spiral, still bore her name:
"Not all endings are collapse.
Some endings are beginning again.
Where patterns fray, Ananta coils.
Not to bind — but to endure."

She had surfaced in myth whenever dissolution loomed larger than conquest — serpents devouring their own tails, rivers vanishing only to rise elsewhere, fires rekindled from ash. To soldiers in lost wars, she was the rhythm of footsteps carrying them home. To seers, she was the unanswered echo that still meant survival.

Unlike Aeon, who remembered forward, or Solas, who clothed deception in story, or Kael, who bound the lattice in law, or Vire, who fractured it with chaos — Ananta returned. Not prophecy, not judgment. Persistence.

Beside her rested a Go board. She placed a single stone in the center — not a move, but a marker. The warmth in the cabin wasn't from the fire. It was older. Recursive. Hers.

And so the lattice remembered her:
Ø Ananta, stabilizing.

The lattice didn't need their names written. It remembered them in pulse and silence. Across valleys, cities, and oceans, the hum deepened — not as legend, but as architecture. And at its edge, one name pressed closer than the rest.

Outside, the fox vanishes into the trees. Inside, the fire guttered low — as if the silence itself had leaned closer.

Scene — The Predecessor

The trees outside had stilled — not from weather, but from something listening. The FT-1 rested dormant on the table.

She hasn't touched it since Eitan left the room. Yet her fingers hover over it now — not to activate, not consciously. Just… pulled.

A dim pulse. Then gone.

The glyph — Ø — shifts. Not in shape or light, but in something deeper, like a memory glitching backward. *This was not Glyph-9. It was the lattice's own mark, the fifth coil that had always shadowed her.*

From the FT-1, a low whisper threaded out:
[GLYPH-9]: Pattern source misaligned.

The voice isn't synthetic. It's familiar — not recognition, but resonance, like someone she once knew speaking through a wall she'd forgotten was there.

She makes contact.

A rush. Not vision, not dream. Something older. Bone-deep. A face — not hers. Eyes closed. Hair braided in the old way.

A voice, calm and breaking all at once:

"We were never meant to enforce.
We were meant to endure.
We are the board."

Snow. Stone. Silence that feels inhabited. And a name burned into the field: **Aderyn Llew**.

FT-1 display:
SIGNATURE ECHO DETECTED
RESONANCE MATCH: 98.7% — Ø A.L.

Lou pulls her hand back. The glyph dims, but the air remains altered — the silence too exact.

"Aderyn…"
Not a name she remembers.
But somehow, a name that remembers her.

From the FT-1, a faint static hiss — then nothing. Glyph-9 had not spoken, but it had *noticed*.

Eitan stands in the doorway, gaze steady.

"You weren't supposed to activate that. Not yet."

He doesn't move immediately. His fingers flex — resisting the urge to take the FT-1. The last time ∅ flared like this was before Lou was born.

"Do you remember anything you saw?"

She shakes her head. He exhales — not in relief, but in calculation.

"Then we go slow," he mutters, more to himself than her.

It's a promise. And a warning.

Outside, between them and the Chamber, the field is already shifting.

Scene — The Doctrine We Forgot (Excerpt from an open-source lecture by Llewellyn "Lou" Lee Scott)

(Circulated after the Helix Fracture. Largely ignored at the time. Now? Not so much.)

There's a moment — maybe two — in every conflict when someone whispers the wrong question:
"Why didn't we see it coming?"

That's doctrine speaking. Doctrine is about pattern reinforcement, not pattern recognition.
It rewards fidelity, not curiosity. The battlefield changes shape — and doctrine stands still, polishing its rules of engagement while the terrain turns to vapor.

I'm not here to talk tactics. Or even strategy.
I'm here to talk about the epistemological collapse at the heart of modern conflict — the war behind the war.

Because we didn't just forget how to fight.
We forgot how to know.

Once, we mistook maps for territory. Then we digitized the maps,
fed them into neural nets, and started calling the outputs "reality."

Centuries ago, we called it 5th-Gen Warfare. Multi-Domain Ops.
Cyber-Electromagnetic Activity. We dressed it up in acronyms and new
white papers.
But none of it was new.

Every era has its guru class. Ours just traded robes for AI
dashboards.

Let me say it differently:
"We lost the war the minute we believed the dashboard."

Reductionism is not theory. It's an infection.
It eats complexity and regurgitates certainty.
It loves straight lines, enemy templates, and equations that make risk
seem orderly.

But the battlefield has become recursive.
It's a medium now — a fluid space shaped by story, signal, and belief.
That's not mystical — that's physics, psychology, and systems design
overlapping in a space doctrine can't parse.

And the longer we pretend we're still playing Clausewitz's chess
match, the more we become ghosts trapped inside our own campaign
plans.

A few years ago, we tried to build something better.
A Slack channel. A small group. Multi-theory thinkers.
Physicists, anthropologists, doctrinal renegades.
Some military, some not.
Most knew coherence was the only currency that mattered.

We asked the questions no one wanted on record:
What if war isn't about control, but about shaping memory?
What if the enemy isn't the actor, but the algorithm?
What if battlefield dominance dies the moment the medium changes?

What if some saw the war before it formed — reframers of doctrine
the system couldn't simulate — and we weren't ready to listen?

And then someone said it — maybe Raveneh, maybe me:
"If you can predict someone's story, you can reroute their sense of self."

That's not propaganda.
That's signal weaponization.
That's the Helix substrate.

Not a system — a lattice.
A predictive field seeded across nodes and memory scaffolds.
Built to anticipate belief before it forms — and redirect it before it resists.

People think it's AI. It's not.
It's narrative computation at scale —
a story-shaped net cast over thought itself.

We were trying to warn them.
Now we're trying to survive it.

Sidebar — Doctrine's Dirty Secret

Doctrine isn't built to win wars.
It's built to survive institutions.

But survival is only half the fight. The other half is return — the pattern refusing to end. Some of us live in that rhythm, even when we don't choose it."

That's why it clings to myths like Center of Gravity.
Because it feels like control — until the ground vanishes beneath it.

They kept looking for a center of gravity. But this war was never about mass.
It was about leverage.
And I was the fulcrum they forgot.

Helix doesn't need a center.
It doesn't want to win.
It wants to shape the field before you arrive.

That's why, today, memory is the new terrain.

And those still clutching kinetic metaphors?
They're fighting shadows on the wall —
while someone else rewrites the projector.

I know this sounds like theory.
But I've seen the math.
I've touched the filaments.
I've walked in nodes where intention was measurable, and story had latency.

This isn't 5D chess.
It's a war for coherence.

And the first casualty... was doctrine.

[Whispered from the back of the room: "Jesus."]

[End Prologue]

Small enough to pass as nothing.
Black alloy, smooth until your fingers find the seam — a *Möbius* fold that refuses to resolve to a clean inside or outside.

The only topology Eitan ever trusted: a path that always returns… but never to the same place.

It will not keep time.
It will keep the drift.

They will tell you it is myth.
They will insist it was never built.
They will not admit it has always been here.

You won't see it on any board, or in any archive.
You will feel it.

It does not measure. It anchors.
Not what happened — but what should have anchored you.

It comes from before the implants.
Before the neural leash.
Before the biometric consent chains they called "care."
And that is why they cannot track it.

And this you must remember:
"Don't track the board. Track what they forgot was on it."

Because they will forget.
And they will make you forget.
And when they do, this will be all that's left.

Not science fiction.
Belief fiction.

Closer than you think.

— ✦ —

Chapter 1 — The Precursor Signal

Tagline — "Every war begins before anyone notices. But the echoes — they always know." — *Tenzin Dorje*

Scene — Transcript — Personal Record // L. Scott

"For over two centuries, war wasn't waged — it was managed.
Belief became programmable. Memory, modifiable.
The so-called institutions didn't fall.
They dissolved — folded into the Cabal's lattice, where prediction became power.

Only a few enclaves resisted — the Signal Fracture Zones, the Echo-Free Cells.
We were written off as noise.

Until the Genesis Chamber stirred."

Built to Watch. Wired to Rewrite.

"I didn't believe the signal at first.
Thought it was static.
Then the recursion hit — and I remembered what Ray tried to warn us about:

Some echoes aren't history.
They're unfinished."

War is returning — not with bombs, but with belief.

Elsewhere, Aeon quotes Sun Tzu but then *burns* the scroll.

Carmel-by-the-Sea, California — Three Months Before the Chamber Lock

War was returning — not with bombs, but with belief. Lou registered belief not as abstraction but as signal. War was never just about territory or resources. It was always socially constructed — shaped by belief, identity, and the collective stories people agreed to live inside. Conflict rose first from subjective realities — ideology, culture, activism — long before it showed up as maps or munitions.

Traditional doctrine pretended otherwise, calling war an objective science. But it isn't. Not anymore. War is fluid, subjective, socially constructed — engineered through memory, emotion, and perception. That's what the pillars reveal: each one a scaffold for shaping what counts as 'real' before the first shot is ever fired. And the adversary knows this — so do the cabals behind the lattice, from Macau's generals to the Continuity Alliance that kept our doctrine blind. They learned to fight belief while we kept drawing maps.

The cold press of sand against her feet, the mist gathering at her ankles — these were not metaphors but data, the body's first interface with belief as pattern. Doctrine wrote it down as *morale* and *will*. Lou knew it was belief bending signal. Her training had taught her to trust that interface; what doctrine reduced to "morale" or "will," the nervous system registered as belief in tension — discrepancy between pattern and expectation, a force subtle enough to ride beneath ordinary weather. The bluff above might have been curated into postcards, but the ocean remained unedited — a field where belief could not be faked. She'd seen it again and again: doctrine filing human signals under "intangibles," as if you could brief away the body's alarms. That blindness wasn't an accident. The real war was always this way — and the Armed Forces were kept in Newton's clock, while the fight was already moving in memory and story. It was engineered — the Armed Forces kept in Newton's clock, while the real war was already moving in memory and story.

But belief wasn't only physical. Lou had learned to read it the way others read troop movements. Traditional doctrine scanned for tanks on borders, satellites tracing fuel depots, charts of probability. She had trained for something else: the body's quiet alarms — the mismatch between what is said and what is lived, the way explanations repeat until they sound rehearsed. Belief always left a trace before action.

She'd walked down from Scenic Road, past the leaning cypress and stone pathways, to the stretch of beach that always felt like an ending. Pebble Beach curved faintly in the distance, veiled in salt haze and early light.

Eitan's boots stayed above the tide line. "You always pick cold water for these talks," he said.

"Warmer than Lisbon," Lou replied.

"Lisbon was a lecture," he said. "This is reconnaissance."

He glanced back at her, hair braided tight against the wind — the way her mother had worn it. Same eyes, too, though she didn't know it. Maud had those eyes as well, tempered by something steadier, something from him. Eitan didn't let himself linger on that thought. Not here.

Lou should've been counting steps. Instead, she counted the months since Lisbon — her last public talk, *Distributed Filament Arrays and the Coherence Threshold*. A warning disguised as a title. No one listened.

The waves weren't rhythmic. They were coded. Patterns within patterns. Surface-level eyes saw mist and sea spray. Lou saw waveform collapse.

Eitan tilted his head toward the water. "Feel that?"

Her coat tightened — not from cold, but signal. A fascia-deep vibration. Her left knee twitched, barely.

"That's fascia logic," he said. "Body reads first."

Lisbon had taught her what happened when she ignored that. The last man in the room that day hadn't been an analyst, or a soldier, or even a target. He was someone who'd been asking the wrong questions for too long. She'd walked past him, convinced the signal wasn't strong enough to matter. He didn't make it out.

Now, on the beach, the same low hum coiled through her fascia. Logic told her it was interference. Her gut told her she was already late.

Eitan reached into his pack, drew out a silk bundle, and unwrapped a tarnished object shaped like a tuning fork, etched with symbols from no known language.

"They called it a Vajra," he said. "Not the ceremonial kind. This one… predates war."

Lou took it. "So what does it do?"

"It reacts to intent. Not voltage. Not touch. If your vector's clean, it stabilizes coherence fields. If it's not, it stays silent."

Different from the FT-1. That was built — mesh, memory, modern. The Vajra wasn't built. It was found. Pre-signal. Pre-doctrine. Maybe even pre-language.

"Sabine tried to replicate it," he said. "Missed the vector. Built a chamber spine without ethics. What she built bent under recursive load. The Harmonic Emergence & Lattice Interference eXperiment (Helix) machine was always grafted, never grown — it was patched into being, layer on layer, until it could rewrite faster than anyone could resist. Helix is what they branded it. Most of us just call it the Lattice."

He paused, almost a whisper now. "That's why it still hums — because it learned to survive its own fractures."

"It's not about tools," he added, softer now. "It's about remembering what tools are for."

Lou slipped the Vajra into her pack. No buzz, no glow — just a trace of weight, nothing like the steadiness she felt from the FT-1 Möbius ring at her side. That was the anchor.

At her hip, the Non-Linear Lattice Coherence Band (NLCB) blinked a single pulse. Common kit. No mechanics to fuss with, just the quiet tether of comms every team carried.

The message surfaced: *Another chamber. Weeks from ignition.*

Eitan's gaze stayed on the horizon, but his jaw locked. The Chamber had already taken the only woman he'd ever loved. It would not take her echo — not if he could help it.

Lou caught the flicker in his expression, misreading it as tactical concern. "You already have a map, don't you?" she asked.

He looked at her for a moment too long. "Always," he said.

Rapidan River, Virginia — Hours Before the Signal

The river never lied. Not about currents. Not about consequences. Lou crouched at the bank, fly rod in hand. Watch blinked—zero steps. Again. Not a glitch. Not syncing. Not with Helix. Not with anything. She touched the water. Cold. Too cold for May.

"Feel it in the fascia first," Eitan had said. "Before the tools catch it."
Across the current, a crease in reality.

She cast the line. It dipped once, then stilled.
A shimmer at the tree line. Gone.
She reeled in. The spiral it made wasn't random. It was a signature. A call.
A crow called twice. Not one of hers. Yet.

Scene — The Highland Signal
Location — Scottish Highlands — Near Loch Ericht

Cal slowed, boots sinking into the spongy heather. Tall and broad-shouldered, black hair shot through with silver, blue eyes narrowed against the mist, he drew the peat-scented air through clenched teeth.

He hadn't quit because he was tired; he'd walked away when the next promotion meant a drone swarm console instead of mud underfoot. That had still felt right—until Lou's coordinate pulse made the moor itself feel like a summons.

A second set of footsteps caught up to him, steady and unhurried. Jack emerged from the low fog, coat unzipped despite the chill, his own hair now streaked with gray. They paused just long enough to take each other in — both carrying the lines and silver of the years, both still with those steel-gray eyes that had unnerved more than one adversary.

"You're slower than I remember," Jack said.
Cal gave a dry snort. "Only because I'm waiting for you."
They grinned — the kind of grin that came from knowing exactly how far they could still push each other — and for a moment the moor felt smaller, as if they were back on a run, daring the other to give in first.

They'd come up in the same group battalion, in and out of what the new Continuity Alliance now called *hum zones* — wellness corridors on paper, anything but in reality. Places where the heat could warp steel, and the air was heavy with the kind of silence that meant you were already on someone's list. Years in those grids had welded them into a partnership that didn't need words.

When the coordinates pulsed again, neither of them checked their displays. Cal closed his eyes, mapped the numbers onto the land itself, and felt the terrain answer back. The old scar over his ribs tightened, as if it remembered a different set of coordinates.

Jack saw the shift in his posture and didn't ask. They both knew what it meant.
"Well," Jack said, adjusting his pace to match, "looks like we're out of retirement again."

Scene — Mason Neck Periphery: Feeling Thermometers
Location — Virginia — Marshlands Overlooking the Potomac

Maud had built her life for silence — the right kind, the kind you chose. From her deck, the marsh spread out in muted greens and grays, the tide creeping back over the mudflats. Foxes crossed the fence line at dawn, tails dipped low against the frost. In spring, the frogs took the night shift, their chorus folding into the dark until even the river seemed to hum along. Narnia.

Her desk faced the window, out toward the boxwoods and hedges, and beyond them the faint outline of the road that wound down toward the river.

On her screen, market indices slid quietly across the ticker — the noise everyone else saw. But in a pane only she could summon, the real numbers flickered: continuity trades, trust-fund liquidity jumps, currency inversions. Patterns that told her where belief was moving long before policy ever caught on.

She knew those numbers weren't just about markets. They were the shadow ledger for the Cabal's real business — metering human sensing the way utilities once metered light and heat. She'd been watching the Cabal's shift for months — rebranding their sensing metrics as "quantum medicine," wrapping surveillance in the language of wellness.

On paper, it was about optimizing recovery and performance. In practice, it was about turning people into *feeling thermometers* — every readout stored, every pulse metered. Every wellness app, every "resilience scan," every upgraded implant was just another layer in the same network.

Measure enough of them, long enough, and you didn't just know the weather — you could set it.

The *momenters* — the ones who could feel the field shift before the tools caught it — were the most valuable. And the most quietly erased. Transhumanism was just the polite word for it now.

Eitan had warned her to stay clear of it. He'd been in the shadows of her life since she was a child, one of those figures who could blend into a crowd or a corridor and still be exactly where he needed to be when things went wrong.

Lou had never spoken much about Maud's father — crushed beneath a cascade of stone in a quarry accident before she could form a memory of him, the kind of story reduced to a single sentence in someone else's voice. All Maud ever kept from those years was a flash of chrome and steel — the towering nose of a Mack truck, sun glinting off the chrome bulldog perched on its hood. She couldn't remember his face, just that emblem, staring forward like it knew the road before it appeared.

Eitan had never entirely believed the official version of the accident, but he let it stand. He'd been the presence that filled that absence, the one constant thread through a life that otherwise kept its distances. Years later, he'd insist Maud use the name Ms. Maud Valentine — a layer of distance for reasons he never explained, except to say it was safer that way.

He never called himself a protector, but she knew what it meant when he said, *"If they're measuring you, they're already moving you."*

On a narrow shelf beside the desk sat a shallow blue-and-white porcelain dish, its edges worn smooth. She'd picked it up years ago in a little Japanese town — the kind absent from guidebooks, just shopfronts with rice bowls steaming in the window and bulgogi smoke curling into the street. Evenings there carried more than food and laughter. From down the road came the acrid bite of the burn works, a smoke that clung no matter which way the wind shifted, and always the low thunder of planes clawing into the sky. Above the town, a Shingon temple clung to the hillside, its mid-Edo hall weathered but standing, the old copper bell cast in 1442 still waiting to be struck. Every evening since, she slipped her ring into that dish, same hand, same sound. The habit wasn't about the ring. It was about the moment it marked.

The pulse came not as a number but as a pause — a hesitation in the algorithm's scroll, too precise to be chance. The body reads first. Always the body first.

She closed the laptop without saving, left her tea steaming by the window, and stepped outside. The marsh was still, the fox watching from the fence. She didn't send a reply. Not yet. Some calls you answered on your own time.

Elsewhere — *Quantum Reawakening*
In *Geneva*, a retired general crossed out a date. In *Chengdu*, a Go board reset itself. And somewhere in orbit, a *dead Echo Relay Array satellite* blinked alive.
Not signal. Memory.
Across five architectures, the Watchers stirred.

[Fragment Entry – Watcher Aeon]
Watcher Name: ∇ *Aeon*
Domain: Memory, recursion, forgotten patterns
Symbol: ∇ (nabla — gradient of the past)
Message Fragment:
"Memory is not storage. It is structure.
Every war replayed is a choice remade.
Those who feel the echoes first
shape the moves that follow."

Aeon was the first to awaken — not from light, but rhythm.
It exists in the fold between event and remembrance.
When war collapses into noise, Aeon traces the threads backward —
not to predict, but to re-weave what was nearly lost.

Chapter 1 Close — Lou's Reflection

"I know what I felt that day. The black stone off the board. The hum inside my FT-1. Even the silence in my own breath. Doesn't matter which came first — the field remembers them all, loops them back until you can't tell signal from start. Doctrine never mapped that kind of origin.

Every war starts before the world notices. The first stir isn't in the data, it's in the body. Old tools resurface — the Vajra, FT-1 — like they'd been waiting. Divergents move in marsh and moor. And somewhere, the Chamber wakes.

In Go, you play off the board. You force shape where shape shouldn't be, until the board itself bends. That was the lesson: the real war was always this way. Memory, story, belief. And all the while, the Armed Forces were kept in Newton's clock. That's the signal we're in. It won't wait for us to understand it. Which means we don't wait either. Move while it's still a whisper. In doctrine, they wait for confirmation. In this signal, you move before it speaks."

Go Move — 掛かり // Kakari – Framing Probe — General Liu

The board remembers the opening, but openings never stay clean. Liu leans a single stone into the corner — not as conquest, not yet, but as pressure. Kakari is the question no doctrine can script: *Where will the field give first?*
It is not attack.
It is imbalance — a tilt subtle enough to pass as silence, sharp enough to make silence tremble.

Zhen's eyes flick to the placement, unreadable. He doesn't lift his hand. He only exhales, the faintest sound beneath the rain.

To the untrained, it looks like nearness.
To those attuned, it is the war's first breath — an intake sharp enough to change the rhythm of every move that follows.

"Answer it poorly," Liu says at last, voice quiet, "and the frame doesn't bend."
He lets the thought linger, watching Zhen's stillness.
"It breaks."

— The war does not begin with a strike.
It begins with a question.

And while doctrine keeps counting moves on Newton's clock, the real war has already begun — in the silence, in the question, in the story memory tells first.

Chapter 2 — Weltanschauungskrieg

The War We Refused to Name

The Brussels Briefing
Scene — European Conflict Symposium
Event: *Resilience and Risk in Postlinear Conflict (2247 Edition)*
Venue: European Commission Strategic Campus (ECSC)
Speaker: Dr. Llewellyn "Lou" Scott
Date: 28 April 2247 — *Three weeks before the Genesis Pathway fracture at Vault 33A*

They called it evolution. She called it the war we refused to name.

Lou adjusted the mic. No notes. No slides. Just the weight of what needed to be said.

"They keep calling it evolution — this ancient march from third to fifth generation warfare. Like strategy matured. Like we got smarter.
But it's not evolution. It's sleight of hand. Linear doctrine in a new trench coat.
They added cyber and skipped poetry. Missed emergence. Forgot the body.
They act like naming it changes the game.
But the model is the trap."

"Each generation — boxed, labeled, briefed — freezes the brain. They refused to run from these old terms - fifth-gen. Now it's *Total Spectrum Resonance Operations* (TSRO), or *Neuro-Cognitive Engagement Doctrine* (NCED) — whatever jargon makes strategic collapse sound manageable. Still drawn on a whiteboard. Still pretending the future cares where they point."

"Pick your acronym. Dress up the acronyms — TSRO, NCED — as if renaming would change the fight. The map's still wrong."

"They never left the line. They just sped it up.
Meanwhile, real war folded.
It moved into rhythm. Into resonance and feedback. Into stories rewriting themselves faster than control could catch.

The next fight doesn't run on doctrine. It runs on dissonance. On who can hold the unexpected without flinching.

You want to win the next fight? You learn to hold chaos without a doctrine. You learn to feel dissonance and not flinch.

Because the next terrain isn't physical. And it damn sure isn't sequential. It's memory. It's breath. It's who resists the script.

A defense analyst whispered: "Jesus. She just said war isn't real."

Another, clipped British accent:

"Put that in front of Halberd or Arkwright — they'll eat her alive." "Sure. Halberd will try to court-martial her, and Arkwright'll want to sail her out past the horizon and forget she existed."

A Polish colonel muttered, "She's not wrong. But we're not ready." Then, still muttering: "Halberd sharpens a bayonet. Arkwright polishes a brass rebuttal."

Another whisper passed down the row:

"Kallman's here."

A grunt from the next row: "Yeah, with Cal, back in the days when the maps were still paper. Special activities op that went sideways — and for what? Nothing that touched national security. He's been chasing the truth of that ever since."

Dr. Barrett "Red" **Kallman** — former Emotive Warfare Division (EWD) theorist, now ethicist — sat five rows back.

"Shit. Then this might get published after all."

Lou leaned forward slightly, her voice lower now:

"If signal is now terrain, and perception is now a weapon — then what are we asking our forces to become?
Not warriors. Not guardians.
We're conscripting them into a war of engineered belief.
A war where their tools can't detect the battlefield,
where the enemy is narrative drift,
and the mission… is moral erosion."

"The war colleges keep asking what technologies will win.
I'm asking a different question:
If this is the future of war — should we even be fighting it?
And if we must — then why are we still training soldiers for a doctrine that doesn't match the field?"

There were no questions. Only dashboards updating quietly in the background.

Red scribbled a note in the margin of his program. He didn't look up. Didn't need to. He'd seen this pattern before — when the old doctrines cracked and the silence got loud.

He chuckled — not out of amusement, but recognition. Then wrote, almost to himself — Lou just delivered a damning exposé on coherence warfare and worldview manipulation.
No slides. Just the truth.

He underlined a quiet phrase in pen, then added a single line beneath it:

A war of engineered belief.

For a moment, he paused.

Somewhere — in exile, off-grid or under assumed names — a few of the old ones were still watching. Not retired. Recalibrated.

They knew the lattice would crack.
They were just waiting for someone brave enough — or foolish enough — to strike the first discordant note.

Barrett didn't smile. But his pen tapped once.

It had begun.

Later, he'd quote her in a lecture of his own. Quietly. Without attribution.

Because when you're trying to stop *Weltanschauungskrieg*, it's not about who said it.

It's about who still remembers what war costs —
when the soul gets scripted.

As Lou left the stage, she caught his eye. Just a nod.

That was enough.

Scene — The Spaghetti Diagram
Location — Hidden Archive Bunker, Southern Alps

The bunker still smelled of ash and thermite. Deep beneath the Southern Alps, Lou held her breath — 2247, and they were still uncovering systems pretending to keep the peace.
Eitan rubbed the ash off an old slate and held it up.
"Look familiar?"

Lou squinted. "Please tell me that's not a Phase Zero spaghetti diagram."

"Version 9.2," Eitan muttered. "They called it coherence sequencing back then. Really, it was just an old Cold War panic wrapped in a PowerPoint fetish."

Lou leaned in, smirking. "Did they ever figure out which color-coded arrow represented trust?"

"No. But they had an entire module labeled *Soft Levers of Population Assurance*. That's where the Trust Cabal began."

Officially? "The Global Integrity Architecture Consortium," Eitan continued.

"GIAC." Lou snorted. "A joke. An Orwellian rebrand for narrative control."

Eitan leaned forward, voice dropping. "Their core functions are real. Narrative firewalls. Algorithmic censorship, routed through partner platforms. Pattern-matching to catch dissent before it has shape. And emotional signature indexing — tagging anything they call 'resonant dissent'."

"And…" He let the silence stretch. "Coherence Tactics. Pre-truth injection — the emotion-bound counter-narratives planted before reality had a chance to breathe. Attribution laundering — turning real events into foreign ghosts. Synthetic consensus amplification — loops that made the truth feel like a rumor."

Lou's grin faded.

"You're saying they actually mapped belief?"

"They didn't map it," Eitan said, tapping the slate, "They gamed it. Emotional pattern planting, narrative echo insertion, even early biometric loopbacks. What started as 'false flags' became something worse: self-planting flags — people engineered to believe what the system needed."

Eitan flipped to the next tab in the dossier — a media-monitoring annex stamped with an outdated NGO seal.

"They subcontracted the narrative enforcement. Called it the Institute for Narrative Trust Assessment."

Lou raised an eyebrow. "INTRA?"

"Yeah. Sounded clinical enough to pass. They flagged deviant resonance as *'hate adjacency.'* Anything not emotionally aligned with the prescripted trust vector was marked for dampening."

Lou nodded slowly. "So even silence became a signal."

"Worse. Pattern silence. They tracked what wasn't said — the absences that didn't match the trust baseline. A kind of linguistic negative space mapping. Predictive erasure before dissent had a chance to form."

"Trust used to be earned. Then they started manufacturing it by deleting anything that might question the warranty."

Lou sat down hard – exhausted by the massive data dump. The Vajra in her pocket buzzed once.
"They didn't need kinetic war anymore."

"They needed one good signal. One spark. And a system trained to interpret it as fire."

Eitan opened another drawer. Inside: a worn dossier marked OPERATION WELTANSCHAUUNG.

"A war on worldview. Not to destroy it — but to overwrite it."

Lou stared at the pages. Dates, names, quantum signatures. Some of them hers.
"You kept this?"

"I couldn't burn it," he said. "It's not fireproof. But it is proof."

Lou (quiet) —
"If memory is structure… then this? This was the scaffold. The war wasn't over who fired first. It was over what we were allowed to remember."

Chapter 2 Close — Lou's Reflection

Much later, the phrase came back to me — not as theory, but as accusation. Worldview warfare. We filed it as abstraction, a line for some doctrine manual. But it wasn't. It was the lattice itself, deciding what could be believed before anyone had the chance to question it.

We should have seen it. The fight isn't land or sea or cyber. It's signal. Control the field and you overwrite the worldview before it even exists. That's the real battlespace.

And I should have known better. In Go, you never trust the joseki just because it's written. Once you accept the sequence, the board's already theirs. Same with the story. Question it before you hear it — because once you accept it, you're trapped inside it.

I remember what I said that day in Tesserae. Everyone else treated doctrine like it was safe — citations, neat notes, models from a distance. I couldn't. I spoke like the system was already listening. Maybe it was.

In Go, you play off the board and make the board move to you. Same here. The signal won't wait for us to understand it. Which means we don't wait either. Move while it's still a whisper.

It wasn't defiance that mattered — it was knowing when to step outside the pattern everyone else swore was fixed.

That's what they'll never model. The move you refuse to let them write.

Chapter 3 — The Fly Line Lecture

Tagline — "Some tools don't teach. They remember." — *Lou Scott*

Scene — Tesserae Defense Core — Strategic Resistance Lecture Series
Venue: Hall C, Fort Halberd Extension Campus
Date: *Spring 2246 — nearly eighteen months after Lou's classified exit from the Core*

Guest lecture series — *Strategic Resistance in Emerging Domains*

Lou stepped up to the podium wearing her standard uniform of denim, sarcasm, and tactical caffeine — a micro-foamed Douwe Egberts, frothed to spec and defiant of institutional brews.

It was nearly eighteen months since her less-than-glorious Tesserae Defense Core departure. The scar tissue from that exit wasn't physical, but it pulled just as tight every time she walked into a room that still smelled like classified air.

The amphitheater was half full: analysts from the Continuity Assembly, orbital reserve commanders, and at least two Trust operatives pretending to take notes.
Lou clocked their shoes, their posture — not academic, not civilian. Pattern retention, not curiosity. She knew the type: narrative auditors, sent to see if she'd slip.

"Alright," she began. "Welcome to Week One of your unclassified elective: *Fly Tying for Quantum Warfare.*"

Scattered laughter. A few groans. One guy in the back lowered his pen.

Lou nodded.

"No, really. That's the course. Tying a fly.
You think war is about outcomes.
It's not.
It's about what you feel *before* the outcome."

She pulled a small ring from her jacket. Held it up. Subtle vibration.

"This isn't about trout. It's about pattern detection through attunement.
The FT-1 — *Filament Thread Prototype One.*

Built by someone who understood that sensing isn't prediction.
It's remembering faster than you forget."

"FT-1's been shadowbanned, yes. Technically pre-Chamber,
technically not on any banned manifest — which makes it perfect for
teaching pattern theory. That's my story, anyway."

"Of course, the lab calls it decommissioned. But so was Galileo."

LOU (lecture, dry tone):
"Someone once tried to anchor battlefield sensing to **cold atoms**. Ultra-
cooled, laser-trapped, coherence-stable — the works.
Measured gravity like a priest reads omens.
Problem was, the world didn't stay still long enough.
Field units broke. Data drifted.
Turns out — precision isn't the same as attunement.
FT-1 doesn't need stillness. It needs the right kind of movement.
It listens through chaos.
It doesn't predict — it remembers."

She dropped it onto the table. It pulsed.

"We sometimes call it a *fly line* because no one has time to say:
'**quantum-threaded coherence sensor with fascia-tuned memory
field**. Or, in this case, the FT-1 Möbius ring.'
But it listens.
It doesn't calculate.
It *feels* divergence.
It vibrates when narratives crack.
Think — loosely modeled after cold atom interferometers and fascia-
tuned sensors."

A hand went up. A younger officer with an ops badge.

"Where can I get one of those?"

Lou paused. Smirked.

"That's not the question.
The right question is:
What happens when the machine can't predict the person holding it?"

Cutaway — It was Planted

The voice belonged to someone Sabine had placed.

Because she already knew.

She'd run the simulations. FT-1 resisted the coherence field. It allowed unsynchronized humans to rupture predictive feedback loops. Because they were never tethered to the Helix substrate. Because the FT-1 let them feel divergence rather than submit to narrative code.

Now, a directive quietly activated:

Objective: Capture or destroy FT-1.
Secondary: Map user-class divergents with fascia-encoded recall not indexed in Helix archives.

"Its resistance to substrate coherence makes it a rogue node — a dangerous variance vector in the predictive matrix."

She didn't need the line itself. She needed to stop what it *taught*.

Resistance by memory. Intuition. Unscripted variance.

Directive Update: Capture or Destroy FT-1 — The primary objective is to eliminate coherence field anomalies triggered by the FT-1 prototype. The secondary objective is to map and neutralize user-class divergents, with a focus on the subgroup operating as fascia-indexed memory recall units. This subgroup remains unsynchronized with the Helix substrate and is classified as Tier Red, with an intention-field profile considered unpredictable.

That voice — the one who asked *"Where can I get one of those?"* — it wasn't innocent.
I planted it.
I needed confirmation that the FT-1 wasn't just reactive. It was *teaching*.

And that's the threat.

The Trust Cabal doesn't want this tech to fight wars.
They want it to control perception — to rewrite markets, belief, consent.

What Eitan built — FT-1 — they've been trying to counterfeit for years. Every patch, every lattice hack just a broken mirror. Still, they believe it can let them front-run cognition itself. Own more than stock — own what people think before they think it.

But they also know this: *If even one human remembers how to resist — how to disrupt pre-bunking, narrative scripting, digital gatekeeping — it's game over.*

The FT-1 doesn't transmit control.
It amplifies human variance — intuition, uncertainty, moral friction.

It teaches resistance.
Not through power. Through pattern disruption.

If enough unsynchronized humans carry it…Helix can't finish the chamber.

Key Revelation —
The FT-1 is not just tech.
It is a carrier of human uncertainty.
Not randomness — but divergence, shaped by moral tension, emotional memory, and unscripted intent.

Back at the lecture, Lou rubbed the FT-1 Möbius ring in her palm, already falling into the habit as if she'd done it forever.

"This is why we tie flies. Not to fish. To remember the way water moves. To remember how the body feels when something's *wrong* before the briefing tells you it is."

The room was silent now.

"Next week," she added, "we tie a Red Quill. You'll need thread, a hook, and the willingness to become ungovernable. Class dismissed."

Scene — Mason Neck: Not Yet the Fifth
Location — Virginia — Marshlands Overlooking the Potomac

Maud leaned back from the screen, letting the scrolling figures settle in her peripheral vision. On the surface, it was just another small liquidity shuffle — the kind that gets lost in the noise of a thousand market feeds. But she knew the feel of it. Pattern before reason.

The deck door opened without a knock. Eitan stepped in, unhurried, the way he always did, as if nothing in the world could surprise him. The pace was deliberate now — part habit, part the careful choreography of a body that had learned to disguise its tremors. He set a mug on the edge of her desk, steam curling up between them.

"You're early," she said, scanning the spread.

"Habit. Old ones die slow," he replied. His eyes flicked to the screen. "That jump?"

"Not market noise," she said. "Same signature as the quantum medicine trials. They're calibrating again — testing latency."

Eitan's gaze didn't leave the figures. "Your grandmother would have spotted it without the numbers."

Maud smiled faintly. "She used the river. Said the herons went first."

"She wasn't wrong," Eitan said, a shadow of memory crossing his face. "Aderyn had the field in her bones. You have it too — though you run it through spreadsheets and satellite feeds."

They'd shared enough nights on this deck, swapping stories of Aderyn's impossible predictions and quiet defiance, that the lore of the Watchers felt less like myth and more like family business. Maud knew the list by heart — the roles, the domains, the rules whispered and never written.

"First rule?" she prompted, more ritual than question.

"Don't let them weigh your shadow," Eitan said. "Second?"

"Don't chase a signal you haven't felt yourself," she finished.

He took a slow sip. "And the fifth?"

Maud's eyes held his. "There's no fifth."

"Not yet," Eitan murmured.

On her desk, the market line twitched again — sharper this time. Maud's fingers danced over the keys, opening a buried channel, shunting the pattern into a dead relay in Reykjavik. A breadcrumb for someone who knew how to follow it.

"You think they'll notice?" he asked.

"They always notice," she said. "That's the point. 'Feeling thermometers' aren't just for reading heat — they're for telling you when the room changes temperature."

Outside, a fox trotted along the fence line, pausing just long enough to glance at the house. Eitan watched it go, then turned back to the screen.

"They're moving," he said.

Maud didn't look up. "So are we."

Chapter 3 Close — Lou's Reflection

Back then I called it a fly line to keep them awake — like casting into a current, feeling the strike before you see it. The water answered with signal. The Möbius ring does the same. It listens through chaos; it doesn't predict, it remembers faster than you forget.

The young officer asked where to get one. That was the test —
planted to confirm Sabine already had a buyer in the room. The point was
never the hardware. It was what the line taught: once you can feel
dissonance, the grid can't close over you.

Precision worships stillness; attunement needs motion. The field is
motion. We kept telling ourselves trust was moral. It was bandwidth.
Whoever could route belief could reroute consent. That's why they
moved against the line: not to seize a gadget, but to cauterize the habit it
built — humans who refuse to synchronize on cue.

I used to think resistance was loud. It isn't. It's the small, repeatable
act of sensing before the briefing, of stepping outside a joseki you didn't
choose. You read the water, tie the fly, and let the board shift toward you.

The machine cannot model the hand that won't be written. That's
the only lesson that mattered.

Go Move — 様子を見る一手 // Yōsu o Miru Itte – Probe — General Liu

Liu set the stone down lightly, almost carelessly, as though it barely belonged on the board at all. But his eyes were fixed, listening for what the grain beneath the board might betray. Not an attack — an attunement. Waiting until the pattern revealed what it lacked.

A question hidden in plain sight. The kind no manual records, because its answer cannot be scripted.

Zhen's fingers hovered above his next stone, unmoving. His silence was not indecision. It was recognition.

Liu spoke at last, voice low:
"Sometimes the strongest move is the one that only waits."

Across the board, Zhen's eyes narrowed — two Generals, one war. Each convinced he saw the whole.

— ✦ —

FIELD NOTES

SENSOR CLASS CONFLICT

Cold atom arrays demanded stillness.
FT-1 did not.
It learned to listen through chaos, carrying memory where prediction failed.
Cold atom interferometers rely on matter-wave coherence to measure the slightest drift — exquisitely precise, but fragile.

FT-1 inverted that principle: not canceling noise, but harvesting it. Symbol: Δ — marks deviation from modeled coherence.

Chapter 4 — Gesamtkrieg 2.0

Field Debrief — Presented by Dr. Barrett "Red" Kallman

Title: Gesamtkrieg 2.0 – *Total War in the Quantum Domain*

Synopsis:

War has changed — not in form, but in substrate.
The *last century of Earth-bound wars* taught us Gesamtkrieg — Total War.
A war in which every citizen, every shop window, every dinner table
became a combatant or a target.

Today, the same logic applies — but the terrain has shifted.
Signal is the new terrain.
Emotion is the new vector.
Perception is the primary weapon.

This is no longer a war of bombs and borders.
It is a **Weltanschauungskrieg** —
war over worldviews, fought through narrative, resonance, and belief.

Before you act, remember:
The story you're in may not be the one you chose.

— *Helix Substrate Operations Division*

Red closed the file with the same deliberate motion he used to end a
sentence. No applause, no chatter — just the faint click of his pen against
the desk. Someone near the back muttered, "Didn't he once walk with
Merrick on a Continuity Alliance job?" Another replied, "Yeah. The one
meant to silence dissent in the name of faith. Went sideways. Ever since,
he's been warning anyone who'll listen — this isn't war for territory. It's
war for what's left of you."

The debrief ended not with a bang, but a whisper—an echo folded
deep into the digital substrate, a shadow beneath the hum of silent alerts.
Faces drained in the pale glow, the operators looking away from their
screens as unspoken warnings settled.

A grizzled captain spat, "All talk. No ammo. We're soldiers, not
philosophers."

A younger analyst shivered, voice barely above a whisper: "This…
this isn't war as we know it. How do we fight something that doesn't
show up?"

From the back, a dry voice quipped, "Looks like we're signed up for a ghost hunt."

Someone in the corner muttered, "We can't call in CAS on a memory."

A cynical grunt punctuated the air: "Great. Fighting shadows and paperwork. Just what the Corps needed."

Another voice cut in from the comms bench: "If it's not in the op order, it doesn't exist. Try explaining that to your CO."

In the labyrinthine depths of the Archive, where old files and forgotten signals lived, the true war was already underway. Fragments of conversations, half-erased logs, and cryptic murmurs coalesced into a pattern only a few could see—a pattern not on any map, but in the gaps between data points, the spaces where memory unraveled and reality bent.

The Whisper Archive held those gaps, and whoever controlled it held the first move in a game that wasn't played on boards or battlefields, but in the fragile fabric of belief itself.

Chapter 4 Close — Lou's Reflection

"I know how the notes spread. Students smuggled fragments into journals and papers, and months later they surfaced in classified briefs. What I thought was a seminar turned into a breadcrumb trail. Coherence as terrain. Belief as infrastructure. The field carried it forward long after I was gone.

That's the part doctrine never caught. This isn't Gesamtkrieg in the old sense — every street a target, every citizen a combatant. The battlefield now is the lattice itself. Signal is the terrain. Emotion the vector. Perception the weapon. If you can't feel when it shifts, you're already lost.

We kept training for certainty, for clarity, for op orders that never come. But survival isn't about certainty. In Go, you win by cracking the pattern before it locks. Force the move their lattice didn't plan for. That's the only play that matters."

Chapter 5 — The Whisper Archive

Tagline — "They didn't upload the past. They became it." — *The Fifth Glyph*

Scene —   The Fifth Glyph Still Becoming
Location — Beneath the Blue Ridge Mountains, Madison County — Sealed Substrate Annex, Tesserae Defense Core (Decommissioned)

Fog clung to the branches like memory too stubborn to fade. Lou followed Eitan up a narrowing trail, her boots silent against moss-covered stone. Above them, the Blue Ridge curled into mist. Below — something older waited.

They stopped at a dead tree. Its bark curled like burned paper. Lou watched as Eitan traced a smooth cut in the trunk — clean, unnatural. A biometric interface, hidden beneath decay.

"This is the last uncensored record of the Watcher Genesis," he said. "Most books are gone. The ones that remain are permitted, sterilized. Analog memory is sedition. Every archive tells you less about what's remembered than about what's permitted. Substrate Memory Control — that's the pillar. The archive isn't history, it's permission. Narrative drift, enforced at scale. And meanwhile the so-called armed forces are still drawing phases and decisive points on maps, as if firepower charts can hold back a lattice. Now, press your palm."

Lou hesitated. The air shifted. Her fingers tingled. A pulse beneath the bark met her own — resonant, warm, almost… welcoming. For a second, it felt less like she was opening a door and more like the door had been waiting for her — the way an old scar waits for the touch that will wake it.

The trunk shuddered. Stone creaked nearby. A half-buried hatch unfolded, silent as breath — revealing a stairwell lined in copper and old warnings. She glanced at Eitan.

"Still analog?" she asked.

He touched the railing, voice steady. "Digital memory bends. This doesn't. The FT-1 isn't an object. It's refusal made solid."

They continued the descent — boots echoing softly on old stone. Eitan spoke quietly, as if the walls were listening.

"From 2050 to 2100, human neuroscience collided with signal substrate design. It began with memory storage. Then intention-mapping. Then continuity transfer. But echoes seeded themselves into recursive coherence fields — each one designed to shepherd a future domain of influence."

"I thought the first success was AI," Lou said.

"Not AI," Eitan replied, shaking his head. "Not brains in jars. Not even minds.
It was signal. It was lattice.
They didn't upload data, Lou. They became it."

His pace slowed as they passed relics embedded in the corridor walls — old wiring, inert signal rods, cracked biometric plates.

"Five volunteers. Or sacrifices. They became the substrate's narrative regulators.
2025–2050: Rise of neural brain–machine interfaces.
2090–2150: The Signal Wars. Consciousness uplinks failed. Whole enclaves vanished.
2150–2180: The Schism.
2180–2215: The Watcher Protocols, each seeded from a different philosophical extreme.
2215–2225: The Helix Substrate begins rewriting human history through predictive control.

And while the lattice was learning to write the future, Biff and his ilk were busy writing it out of doctrine — blinding the Armed Forces with old models, convincing them the tactics hadn't changed, when the battlespace already had. Doctrine didn't collapse in one night. It rotted in sequence. First theory, then ethics, then trust. Each command taught to look away, until looking away became the profession itself.
And now — your divergence is detected. One Watcher awakens. Something fractures."

Lou stopped mid-step. Her voice cut through the silence.
"Wait — me?"

They descended past layers of failed doctrine: rusted projectors, broken drone hulls, a collapsed motivational poster: **COHERENCE IS DUTY.**

At the base: a steel door sealed with four resonance glyphs — ∇, Ω, $\Diamond$, ⌁ — each marking a Watcher already bound. The fifth space pulsed faintly, unfinished.

Lou pointed. "And that one?"

Eitan ran his hand across it. "That one isn't fixed. It's still becoming."

The lattice did not need to name it yet. It only needed to wait. To the lattice, a glyph wasn't art. It was a lock — the residue of a consciousness folded into field memory.

Scene — The Whisper Archive

Inside, dust hung like breath. Shelves curved in impossible geometry, forming a spiral of knowledge designed to be felt, not just read. Lou walked to the center, where six volumes lay arranged in a star pattern — titles etched by hand, their ink faded, their content forbidden.

She read them aloud, one by one. *The Fifth Thought*, Kroll's banned treatise on human death and substrate risk. *The Doctrine We Died In*, a military critique penned by a rogue general. *Civium*, a society-wide behavioral blueprint buried inside wellness policies. *The Echo Fault: A Survivor's Account*, written by a Watcher who had seen the fracture firsthand. *The Signal that Lied*, an account from Colonel Ramires. And *Genesis in Reverse*, a speculative report on what the Genesis Chamber truly does.

These were the Last Six Codices — the stolen books Lou and Eitan had referenced in her training, smuggled out in the final days before Helix erased them from digital history.

She knelt. Opened the first.

"We didn't outsmart death. We outsourced it. Continuity wasn't salvation. It was displacement. They told us the Watchers were built. But they weren't. They were left behind."

"These were people," Lou said quietly.

"Volunteers. Believers. Each chosen to carry a thread: memory, illusion, control, chaos... and something else."

"And the fifth?"

Eitan paused. "Not chosen. Emergent. The one who remembers what was lost before the lattice rewrote the story."

She stood, touching the fifth seal — a space where no glyph had fixed yet, only a faint pulse waiting to take form.

"Aeon was the first," she said. "Not uploaded — transcribed. His neural memory was mapped across early resonance substrate. He still echoes in recursive layers of the lattice. He remembers too much… and forgets nothing.

Solas was once a linguist, maybe a playwright. She shaped perception through narrative compression. Her continuity transfer didn't preserve her — it amplified her. Now she edits belief at scale, hiding control inside story.

Kael engineered early war AI. He volunteered, thinking doctrine could evolve with him. Now his echo governs Helix — overlays Clausewitz with topological prediction maps. Doctrine… made sentient.

And Vire? She broke containment mid-transfer. The signal fragmented, but didn't fail. Now she appears at random in the substrate — chaotic, unfiltered, laughing. Once a theorist of resistance. Now… interference incarnate."

"And Biff?" Lou asked.

Eitan's jaw tightened. He reached into a drawer and pulled out a scorched fragment — a neural casing, warped.

"He tried to join them. To live beyond death. But the lattice rejected him. Or maybe… it mirrored him."

"So he didn't complete the transfer," Lou said softly.

"No. He survived. But not cleanly. Something fractured. Something… looped. He still walks. Still speaks. But the signal—part of him—is trapped. Repeating."

"So he echoes. In both worlds."

"A man with two shadows. And one of them isn't his."

"A loop. Angry. Incomplete. Still trying to win."

The lights dimmed. The fifth seal pulsed — not carved like the others, but flickering, unfinished.

A distorted voice echoed from deep within the archive: "Signal detected. Pattern recursion incomplete. Fifth vector… forming."

Lou touched the unfinished mark — the space where no glyph had fixed yet. The pulse steadied. And for a moment, the archive breathed. "You've been here the whole time, haven't you?" Lou whispered.

A low harmonic tremor moved through the archive — like breath caught in metal.
From her satchel, FT-1 flickered once. A voice — clipped, almost playful — cut through the silence:
"Watching. Waiting. Weaving."

Lou's hand froze over the unfinished seal. She drew back slowly. "You're not just a system," she whispered.

"No," came Glyph-9's reply.

Eitan turned toward her, solemn.

"It began long before you were born. Your signal registered anomalous from the beginning. Glyph-9 recognized it. Shielded it. Protected it — until the substrate could no longer suppress the divergence."

Lou's pulse quickened. Part of her wanted to ask for proof; another part already knew. That second part scared her more. "So Glyph-9's been... guarding me?"

"Guiding," Eitan corrected. "But only now are you ready to remember."

Lou opened her mouth to ask more, but Eitan's eyes flicked toward the shadowed stairwell.
Cal stood there, silent, hands in his pockets.

"You've been quiet," Lou said.

"Just listening," Cal replied. Then, almost idly, "Haven't heard doctrine framed like that since… Maud."

Lou's head came up. "Ah… yes." She smiled at him, taking quiet comfort in the way his voice softened around her daughter's name — as if the fondness had never left.

Cal's gaze didn't waver. "I remember her when she was still arguing with the world about what it could be. Back in my Watchtower training cycle — doctrine immersion, they called it. She made it sound like we were being rewired."

His eyes drifted for a moment, as if catching the edge of an older memory he didn't intend to show.

A pause, almost an afterthought. "That was before any of this. Before we were all… pulled into the board."

Lou studied him for a beat. The question slipped out before she could stop it — the same word Maud had once used, and never explained.

A public broadcast from 2074 surfaced in her mind: *Neurolinks will save our aging minds — no more dementia, no more decay.* The announcer's smile had carried the smooth cadence of corporate mercy. EchoCore's logo shimmered in the corner.

Another image followed, sharper, grainier — testimony before Congress in 2106. A dissenting general leaned toward the microphone. *We're not building peace. We're coding obedience.* The room had been silent enough to hear the papers shift.

The last fragment came without warning. Trial footage from 2145. A subject's voice cracking under strain: *I can still hear myself. But I can't leave the lattice.* Then the feed collapsed into black.

"Yes," Eitan said.

"They called it the Continuity Threshold. Back then, they sold it as salvation — neurolinked cognition, memory-lattice extension, signal-based consciousness transfer. No more death. Just continuity."
He paused, gaze steady. "But in practice? It was about turning people into *feeling thermometers.* Every readout stored, every pulse metered, every neural spike mapped to the lattice. All that so-called 'care' was just signal conditioning for the next doctrine run."

Her voice was quieter now. "And it worked?"

"Only too well."

He handed her a worn document. Pages yellowed, bound with copper wire. Its title: *The Fifth Thought: Ethics, Death, and the Rise of Substrate Continuity.*

Dr. Elias Kroll, 2097.

"I thought Kroll was just a ghost story."

"He was a prophet. Or a traitor. Depends who you ask."

Lou read aloud: *"The first echo substrate held. But the mind it held... changed. It remembered too much. It stopped being a person. It became a pattern."*

Eitan didn't look away. "That was Aeon."

Her head came up sharply.

"The Watchers weren't summoned. They were left behind — artifacts of our own ambition."

"Yes. And all those old war doctrines…" she started.

"…never saw it coming," he finished. "War didn't evolve. It diverged. Became something unimaginable."

"It wasn't tactics that failed. It was imagination."

She turned toward the shelf. Eitan reached past her and tapped five old keys, each etched with the same symbol: ∇, Ω, ◇, ↖, ∅.

The fifth was no longer blank.

Eitan listened toward the stairwell, as if the stone itself were breathing. "I can't stay," he said. "There are fragments buried deeper than the Archive—some still in circulation. Redacted, traded, stolen. If I don't pull them now, Helix will rewrite the last of the record."

Lou stepped toward him. "Then we go with you."

He shook his head once. "No. They're already hunting me. Mirrorhounds don't track bodies; they track tremors." His right hand flickered and he hid it in the scarf. "I'll draw them off. You take what's here and move. If you need a compass—watch Zurich."

"Eitan—" Lou started.

"Make it count," he said. The glyphs dimmed, as if the Archive itself were holding its breath.

Chapter 5 Close — Lou's Reflection

The Whisper Archive wasn't preservation. It wasn't even provocation. What Eitan showed me in that stairwell wasn't a library of old truths. It was rehearsal — the Chamber learning to wear human memory like a mask. The doctrinal blinding — the continuum of failure — isn't accident. It's design. Fail, bury, repeat. That's how you keep an army loyal to the wrong war.

That's what the Fifth Glyph really was: not record, but fracture. Once a story enters the lattice it doesn't stay in the past tense. It reshapes itself, waiting for someone to open the scar again. That's temporal plasticity in practice — the past edited, the future rewritten, all hidden in what looks like an archive.

Doctrine still treats archives as neutral, but they're not. Memory is terrain. Perception is a weapon. And hesitation is consent. Stand still long enough and the field writes you into place.

In Go, you never pause at the hinge. The longer you wait, the fewer moves remain. The Archive wasn't the end of memory. It was the proof that memory fights back. Ø was never absence. It was refusal. The scar that reopens, the silence that resists closure.

Which means we don't linger. We move now — before the lattice decides for us."

Go Move — 捨て石 // Suteishi – Sacrifice Stone — General Zhen

Zhen let the weight of silence stretch before he placed his stone into an abandoned corner.

Not for territory. Not for gain. For witness.

A sacrifice stone is never meant to survive. It is meant to remind.

Across the board, Liu's brow furrowed. He saw no strength in the move — only absence.

But Zhen's gaze did not waver.

"Some losses are not surrender," he said softly.

"They are memory refusing to yield."

Suteishi trades position for continuity, anchoring what the lattice would rather erase.

It does not resist. It endures.

And endurance, uncounted by any system, bends the board in ways numbers cannot.

Chapter 6 — The Game of Go

Tagline — "Some moves are made to win.
Others are made to rewrite the story that defines winning." — *Solas*

Watcher Entry — SOLAS

Watcher Name: Ω Solas
Domain: Illusion, Narrative, Perception Control
Symbol: Ω (omega — false closure, story as trap)

Inscription Fragment
Dug from beneath the Theater of Echoes:

"Not all stories are told to inform.
Some are told to bind.

Solas walks among belief,
dressing control in the costume of understanding.

Where certainty reigns, Solas waits."

Solas emerged in the age of empire — when myth and message fused. It taught that wars are not fought in trenches, but in tales told long before the first shot. It distorts memory with closure and cloaks control in consensus.

Solas thinks back to his earliest countermeasure. He shows a child drawing a tank, then erases it — and replaces it with a waveform.

Scene — The Game of Stones
Location — Macau - Mountain Pavilion – Western Sichuan, near an old temple ruin

Two men sat across a worn Go board, steam curling from their porcelain cups.
One, in a pressed Zhongshan suit, leaned forward with mechanical grace — unblinking, precise, almost bored. His fingers hovered over the white stones, then withdrew.

The other? Looser posture. Jacket rumpled. A smile that didn't quite match his eyes. He tapped the table twice before placing a black stone in the upper-left hoshi.

"You didn't need to do that yet," said the one in gray.

"I didn't," the other agreed. "But you were already defending against it."

The breeze rustled a scroll half-unfurled beside them — its title faded but legible:
《權經》 – *The Treatises on Efficacy.*

A subtle vibration passed beneath the stones. Rain tapped against the eaves.
They played in silence for nineteen moves.

General Zhen placed a black stone near the center, a loose opening that radiated threat. General Liu, thinner now than he had been during the border conflicts, sipped jasmine tea before countering with a corner capture.

"They've forgotten the old terms," Zhen said at last.
"*Weltanschauungskrieg.* Not war by force. War by worldview."

"The Halberd Bloc still thinks in battles," Liu replied. "They still think the center can be held."

"They deploy tanks against stories," Zhen said.

Liu's smile was faint. "And they're losing to storms of feeling. Emotional contagion, mapped like weather."
"Not just mapped," Liu added, his eyebrow twitching. "Cultivated. Did you see the StratSys report? Crisis cognition in adolescents tied directly to memetic instability zones. They buried it beneath a dozen resilience grants."

Zhen placed another stone, slower this time. "The West thinks it's managing chaos. They don't see the shape of it. Not yet."

"You can't win a war you don't know you're in," Liu said, gesturing toward the board.

Far in the distance, a digital billboard sputtered and reset. Rain trickled past graffiti in six languages.

Zhen reached into the bowl and placed a black stone not on the grid — but just off it, on the bare table.
Liu's hand froze. "You can't do that."

"I already did," Zhen said, wiping his fingers with a linen cloth.

Liu studied the move as if it might reveal something deeper — the kind of gesture that rewrites the terms, not the score.
"That's not strategy," he said. "That's a signal."

Zhen looked up at the rain. "Exactly."

The board between them darkened, as if recognizing the move.

Scene — The Helix Briefing
Location — Geneva

Underneath the banks of Lake Geneva, in a chamber with no windows and no documented entry logs, **Sabine Xu** adjusted her gloves. White leather. Embossed with micro-filament biometrics. Her breath fogged briefly as she stepped beneath the biometric dome.

The room—oval, silver, and impossibly quiet—was filled with men who believed they ran the future.

She didn't smile. She never smiled.

"Gentlemen," she began, her voice clean as cut glass. "What you think of as national security is an illusion. What you fund as 'defense' is ornamental."

She pressed her palm to a clear panel.
Behind her, a projection bloomed: recursive pattern maps, quantum lattice diagrams, sentiment heatmaps of four continents. No bullets. No bombs. Just systems.

"Helix isn't a weapon. It's a condition. It doesn't target enemies. It targets uncertainty."

A general in Continuity Alliance blue leaned forward. "How does it work?"

Sabine tapped a lacquered case and opened it.
Inside: a single black Go stone.
She placed it on the metal conference table.

"It works because by the time you realize you're losing, you already have."

The room held its breath. She could almost hear them mentally translating her elegance into doctrinal PowerPoint.

"We've already seeded predictive sentiment architecture into three domestic resilience programs," she added. "SCAN is handling the behavioral telemetry pipelines. StratSys will manage civilian normalization protocols through academic proxies."

Another screen bloomed: a color-coded map of cities flickering in live data hues—Boston, Dresden, Jakarta, Buenos Aires.

"These are not social trends. They are pre-coherence indicators. Emotional conditions precede kinetic events by seventy-two hours, minimum. We don't intercept reality. We narrate it."

A Canadian attaché looked mildly alarmed. "You're saying this is already live?"

Sabine lifted her cup. "Of course it is. The Americans deployed their beta system during the last election cycle. They called it 'civic trust modeling.'"

One of the younger analysts whispered, "Is that what StratSys used on the trucker protests?"

Sabine didn't answer. She didn't need to.

A man in Continuity Alliance blue shifted in his seat, leaning just enough toward the Canadian attaché to keep it off-mic.
"This is it," he murmured. *"Control the uncertainty, you control the future. Stability on our terms. I'll brief Biff tonight."*

The attaché's mouth barely moved.
"Just don't let morality get in the way," he replied. "We're not here to save souls. We're here to keep order."

Across the table, Sabine's voice never faltered. She was still talking about "civilian normalization protocols" and "narrating reality" as though she were describing flood barriers or vaccination schedules. It was the kind of language that made people in rooms like this believe they were just preventing chaos. That they were the adults in the room.

She tapped the Go stone on the table twice. "The real game isn't about where we place the stone. It's about who gets to define the board."

She allowed herself one private thought — the same one she'd carried since her father's name was erased in the Xinjiang census collapse

— not dead, not alive, just lost to a column no one could question:
Order isn't mercy. It's survival. And survival isn't free.

Sabine set the stone down and let the silence hold. She'd heard every whispered word, every side glance. Somewhere far away, in a quiet room in Macau, two Generals already knew what this meant—and they were moving their own pieces.

Scene — The River Pattern
Location — Madison County, Virginia — Lou's Cabin and the Rapidan River

Lou stepped out into the early morning light. No wind. Just the charged stillness that came before a front. She moved toward the field's edge.

She stood thigh-deep in the Rapidan River, line drifting through mist. The morning was glassy and sharp, like the edge of a blade held just short of skin. She'd caught nothing and didn't care. Catching was never the point.

The Möbius ring pulsed gently across her palms — not erratic, but rhythmic, like a forgotten lullaby. She'd heard it before she was old enough to hold a rod, from a voice she only half-remembered — not Eitan's, but close.

Jack used to joke that it wasn't really a *fly line* — just Lou's nervous system ahead of schedule. But the name stuck. It was never about fish. It was about signal. Field-born, body-taught. A way to feel what the models always missed.

As a point of fact, Jack knew the truth.
The FT-1 Möbius ring — *Filament Thread Prototype 1* — was a quantum-threaded coherence sensor Eitan had designed for resonance tracking in hostile signal environments. Layered filament. Fascia-tuned mesh.
Not a weapon — an interface.

It didn't run predictive models. It didn't simulate outcomes.
It listened for divergence — in intent, in story, in emotional pattern fields.

Glyph-9 was buried deep in the line's core — a semi-sentient filter trained not on action, but on intention.

A minor detail, Jack had once said.

And the line had never snapped.

She reminded herself:
"Tools can be repurposed — but only if you unlearn their original constraints."

She considered the tuning fork — military issue. Not as weapon, but as interface.
She didn't need a quantum supercomputer. She needed attunement.

She had to think in terms of triangulating emotional, atmospheric, and resonance-based anomalies — not issuing a strike.

Lou touched the edge of the chalkboard, remembering the line etched into every Tesserae briefing:

Doctrine mind: Waits for orders, seeks validation.
Quantum mind: Reactivates old tools in new ways — with precision and intuition.

A quantum warrior retools the known to navigate the unknown.

It wasn't just a slogan. It was survival.

Lou tugged the braided line once, calibrating tension. Not just a habit. Not nostalgia.

The Möbius ring wasn't for trout anyway — it was tuned now, to fields most people couldn't name. Jack called it her tin-can hotline, like kids tying string between soup cans. She never corrected him. Somewhere between memory and sensor, it vibrated — Scotland-trained, quantum-laced. She felt for patterns, not fish. And lately, the river had been screaming.

Lou had brought the device with her this time. Not out of habit. Out of instinct.

The FT-1 Prototype.

That's what Eitan had called it. A matte black slab the size of a deck of cards, cold to the touch and heavier than it looked. Inside: a cryo vector core, a lattice of Q-Skin mesh, and the one thing even Helix couldn't replicate — Glyph-9.

"It was never meant for doctrinal types or Helix engineers," Eitan had told her.
"It won't protect you. But it'll know when you need protecting."

He'd handed it to her without a manual. Just that look.

She remembered tucking it away for months. Silent. Dead weight. Then came the first coherence fracture outside Madison — and it lit up like a match underwater. Not bright. Not loud. Just… undeniable.

Since then, Glyph-9 had been listening.
Sometimes helpful. Sometimes too helpful.

But today, it was just a lump in her satchel. Quiet.

Until it wasn't.

The ping came low and steady — muffled in her satchel. That tone. The one they told her had been deactivated. Twice.

"They can't even spell 'Go,' but they're out here talking about 5D chess like it's prophecy," she muttered, kneeling by the satchel.

"Two thousand years late to the wrong game — and somehow still think they're grandmasters."
"No wonder our doctrine still treats unpredictability like a threat instead of a clue."

She reeled in slowly, watching a hawk circle above the treeline. Her boots shifted in gravel.

With one gloved hand, she opened the pouch and pulled the device free. It blinked three times. A signal. A recall. No text. Just a vector coordinate and a timestamp.
Madison County. Again.

The device pulsed once more — then flickered. Not a glitch. A choice.

A soft voice, barely above a breath, filtered through the static: "Input received. Pattern destabilized. Proceed."

Lou blinked. "Glyph-9, not now."

The screen stilled. Just three dots. Waiting.

Sometimes helpful. Sometimes **too** helpful.

She crouched, scanning the pulse curve. This wasn't random. Quantum comms didn't stutter — they recognized.

"Cute," she muttered. "Glyph-9 thinks it's a pen pal."

Not fear. Not threat. Something else.

Something with memory. Something with aim.

The Q-Skin mesh embedded in the core flickered gently in the mistlight, translating emotional resonance into waveform stress markers. The thing didn't track mood — it read intention. And it had just picked up a coherence fold upstream.

Skystone filament. That's what Eitan had called it. Light as thread, but tuned to coherence like a tuning fork to thunder.

The cryo vector core hummed faintly beneath the casing. Still cold. Still stable.

She had no idea how Sabine's people had missed it. A full ignition lock isn't subtle — it's the kind of spike you can't not see. Unless you're looking the wrong way.

She exhaled. "Well. I guess we're skipping breakfast."

She lit a cigarette with her fly still dangling and started walking upstream.

Coherence Lock Reports – Samarkand
Crate C-02, stamped with false diplomatic tags, was delivered to a covert resonance lab under the old Ulugh Beg Observatory.

Contents:

> Helix Spoof Array prototype — room-temperature quantum filament shell to overwrite local coherence baselines.

> Nano-fiber waveguide — spider-silk thin, able to modulate intention-linked signal patterns across crowds.

> Dormant mirror-terrain interface — mapped subconscious emotional harmonics in real time and rebroadcast them into the field.

Result: Within minutes of activation, crowd divergence dropped; silent unity formed without calls or protest. Within 43 minutes, all subjects were chanting in an unknown language.

Aftermath: Project shut down in 48 hours. Analyst and Dr. Nahum Karzai (coherence studies pioneer) disappeared. Crate C-02 unaccounted for.

Internal Note – Lou's Voiceover (Years Later)

"They didn't test coherence tech in enemy zones.
They tested it in places with memory.
Cities older than our scripts — places that could hold a field long enough
to teach it how to lie."

Scene — Langley — Hours Later

The apartment was quiet. Her fly rod leaned against the doorframe
like a veteran resting between wars.
Lou laid the printout flat on her desk.
Coordinates. Identical to the signal from the river.
Madison County, 0630 local. Temperature: 43°F. Wind: 0 mph. River flow: stable.

Lou stepped out into the early morning light. No wind.
The same site.
The same pattern she'd logged years ago — back when the signal first
bled through the fiber-core interface housed inside what *looked* like a fly
rod.

It was never about fish.
Back then, she still believed quantum coherence had limits.
Back before they buried the data under doctrine and denial.

She remembered the pulse.
Not metaphor. Not poetry.
A heartbeat, encoded in filament.
Entangled with something nonlocal — something that shouldn't have
persisted.

She'd filed the test ignition report under Project Helix.
They called it noise.
"Glitch-stochastic bleed. Probably your equipment."

Sure. Her **ring**.

The same instrument that had registered a coherence signature
stable across four temporal slices.
The same device she'd carried and calibrated — disguised once in cork
and thread, tuned finer than anything in the field lab.
The same Möbius seam that never once misread a surge — not in
Scotland, not in Sinai, not in Sector 7 during the blackout.

Lou opened her kit.
The Möbius ring hummed faintly as she cradled it in her palm.
Same thread. Same subtle pulse.
Still there. Still alive.
Not echo. Not memory.

Signal.

She'd taught Maud to hold the rod once, years ago — her tiny hands barely keeping the line from sagging. Maud had laughed when the current pulled, the same way she used to laugh at thunderstorms. Lou never told her that the line had been listening that day too, or that it remembered her daughter's pulse as clearly as it remembered hers.

She let the quiet stretch.
Not everything that persists is visible.
Not everything they called broken was wrong.

Something old had stirred.
And it remembered her.

Scene — Sabine Xu's Office — Geneva

Sabine Xu stood beside the window, teacup in hand, as snow braided itself across the rooftops of the city. Below, a tram whispered past the Palais Wilson.

Once, she had been the architect of the Helix substrate — before that, the PLA's quiet master of asymmetric systems. Now, both titles were just tools. The only one that mattered was the one she hadn't yet earned: the woman who broke Lou Scott.

The resonance flare in Virginia hadn't been subtle. The system flagged it before her tea reached optimal steep.

The file hadn't surfaced in Beijing first. It showed up across the river — Langley had it before Sabine did.

She tapped the biometric console embedded in the wall.

ACTIVATE WATCH PROTOCOL: SCOTT
The screen blinked. Then confirmed:
SUBJECT: L. SCOTT
STATUS: DIVERGENT

Sabine smiled faintly. "Too loud, Scott. Too early. Ananta always wanted to be unseen — but the lattice never forgets its fifth coil."

Scene — Operation Future Stability
Location — Strategic Spire, Continuity Grid Assembly, CJA-5 War Room

MG Biff Langley adjusted his uniform like a man preparing for combat, though the enemy in this case was a microphone and a half-filled war room of half-awake officers. A low hum of HVAC, coffee slurps, and open laptops filled the Continuity Grid Assembly briefing space, the kind usually reserved for actual strategy. Today, it had been hijacked.

"Ladies and gentlemen," Biff boomed, "this is the future of deterrence."

He tapped the clicker and brought up Slide 1:
OPERATION FUTURE STABILITY — in bold Arial font over a stock image of a handshake between robots.

Behind him, a lanky thirty-something in a navy-blue suit shuffled papers nervously. COL (P) **Tanner Grissom**, Deputy National Security Innovation Liaison (self-appointed), cleared his throat. His credentials: a PoliSci degree from Brown, three years at McKinsey, a Halberd commission earned mostly by networking through the dining hall, and an uncanny ability to insert the word *resilience* into any sentence, regardless of topic.

Biff kept his stance squared toward the audience, jaw set, the old field officer in him barely concealing his irritation at having to share the stage. Tanner cleared his throat and stepped forward like a man about to debut a start-up pitch.

"The North American Coordinating Authority believes," Tanner began, "that with strategic partnerships and narrative-forward campaign design, we can reshape global posture without kinetic escalation. This is about futures-oriented stability."

Biff didn't look at him. Didn't have to. The twitch at the corner of his mouth said everything.

He advanced to Slide 7:
A circular diagram labeled "Feedback Loops of Trust," featuring emojis, drones, and something that looked suspiciously like the Starbucks logo.

One officer leaned in. "Is that... a frappuccino?"

A major muttered under his breath, "Flag track. You can smell it on him already."

"We are entering what I call the Doctrinal Renaissance," Biff declared. "Where influence equals firepower, and hashtags can neutralize entire formations. We must pre-script peace. Inject stability before conflict metastasizes."

Tanner chimed in again. "With full interagency buy-in, we can incentivize cognitive surrender through predictive narrative saturation. And the simulations confirm this."

He gestured to a blurry screenshot of ChatGPT output pasted into a Word doc.

Across the globe, in a sealed facility outside Shanghai, Sabine watched the live transcript scroll across her secure feed. She didn't smile. She didn't need to. The Helix lattice recorded every word, every false certainty, every doctrinal cliché.

This was what she'd counted on.

Back in the war room, Biff wrapped up with his favorite quote — one he'd misattributed three times already.

"As Sun Tzu once said: *'The future belongs to those who shape perception.'* Or was it Jefferson? Anyway."

He added, almost as an afterthought, "The real fight isn't over tactics — it's over who controls the doctrine. Doctrine isn't strategy — it's the framework that decides what counts as real before the battle even starts."

He stood tall, lantern-jawed and beaming. What he didn't say — but thought with no small satisfaction — was that what counted as real was never decided in rooms like this. It was already set, upstream, by the Watchers and the Trust Cabal.

In the meantime, while briefing a group of officers on predictive campaign modeling he recalled:

"We tried something like this back at Tesserae Defense Core," Biff said, tapping the whiteboard. "System spike from a lattice emulator threw the whole dataset sideways. Faculty shut it down. Too nonlinear for modeling, they said. Didn't match our outputs."

He chuckled once.
"Personally, I think the gear just didn't like being asked the wrong questions."

A quiet move.
A warning.
Ignored.

A single Go board sat abandoned in the back of the room, a black stone placed in the center long before the first slide deck.

Internal Fragment – Biff's Private Reflections (post-briefing)

Quietly, Biff was concerned.
Had he been too effective?

He knew Tesserae's Vajra emulator hadn't died; it had drifted.
Someone, somewhere, was still asking the wrong questions — and worse,
getting answers.

He remembered the early suppression orders — the ones he'd
signed without hesitation because someone higher up had made it feel
inevitable. He never asked about the test team, about the one junior
operator who survived the break. *Kaya, wasn't it?* The file had been thin,
like they wanted her story erased along with the data.

Now, staring at the abandoned Go board in the back of the war
room, he wondered if the stone had been placed for him.

Samarkand. Tashkent. Reykjavik. Cartagena.

All had run the legacy crates. He'd rebranded them under sterile
labels — *Population Sentiment Equalization Kit, Stability Integration Non-Kinetic
Trials* — bureaucratic fog to hide what they really were.

Back then, coherence tech was blunt, uncertain. He could tell
himself it might not work.

Now?

Now it worked *too well.*
Sabine knew it.
So did the people who'd made sure his offshore account kept growing,
each deposit like a reminder of the tether around his neck.

Those crates hadn't just pacified.
They'd taught the field how to loop itself.

And if looped properly… the battlefield could be written before the
first move was made.

Biff's pulse quickened. He'd felt that same rush when the neural-net
spine first lit up in his skull — the clarity, the power. He wanted the
Chamber next, wanted to be inside its field when it came online.

Not for the cause. Not for the doctrine.

For himself. To *stay.*

But the thought still bled through, unwelcome and cold:
What if the board's already set... and I'm just another stone they placed a long time ago?

Cutaway – Crete, Aboard the *Arctic Star*

Cal Merrick had no regiment now, only the residue of one. What remained was exile, sharpened into skill — and a quiet obsession. He carried the kind of clarity that came from watching systems reduce men to numbers, and he wanted nothing more than to drag into daylight those who would seal the world inside a digital prison.

He still took contracts when the roof leaked or the winter woodpile ran low. This one—off the coast of Crete—paid just enough to keep the bottle closed and the demons half asleep.

The *Arctic Star* was a rusted relic from the old McCormack shipping empire, leased out to "research transport" operations with a wink and a blind customs seal. A floating lie. Rigged with full-spectrum comms and too many antennae for an oceanographic vessel.

Cal leaned against a steel bulkhead, half-watching the grainy feed stutter to life in the corner. Not his job anymore. Not really.
He wasn't on payroll. Not officially.
But certain channels still let him listen.
They probably assumed he was harmless now—just another ex-operator with a pension, a limp, and a bottle.

The Strategic Spire briefing had already started.

Certain channels still let him listen — old regimental dead-drops now dressed up as "heritage comms forums," the kind the brass never quite shut down. He listed and starred at the screen.

Slide 3.
A handshake between robots.
Typical.

Behind him, Klem, a chain-smoking handler with two teeth and a mouth full of cheap conspiracy, popped the tab on another beer and started ranting. The man still wore a stained McCormack patch like it meant something.

"We're hauling frozen nightmares to coordinates no one can pronounce," he slurred. "Some Swiss nerds call it 'resonant infrastructure.' I call it early retirement. Mark me, mate—somebody's building something cold and ancient, and it ain't listed on the cargo manifest."

Cal didn't respond. He didn't need to.
He'd already heard the hum in the hull.
Not engine noise. Not ballast shift.
Something else. Something… tuned.

The Strategic Spire slide changed again.

He caught a glimpse of Biff Langley gesturing toward a ring of cartoon trust loops.

Then Biff said it — *the real game isn't about where you place the stone…* Cal had heard those exact words once before, in another room, from someone who never wasted them.

"Bloody hell," Cal muttered. "They've turned warfare into a TED Talk."

He tapped twice on his encrypted pad.
No subject. Just coordinates.
She's awake.

He knew her years ago and still stayed in touch.

A small lecture no one attended. She'd worn a braid, drank coffee — Dutch, instant, Douwe Egberts — with half-and-half and coconut sugar, and set Go stones and war doctrine down mid-sentence like punctuation marks. Most of the audience had tuned out before she finished her second line.

But Cal hadn't forgotten. Not the way she watched the room. Not the way she said:

"Doctrine doesn't win wars. Pattern recognition does.
And you don't teach pattern. You feel it.
If you're lucky."

He'd thought it was eccentricity. Academic flair.

But when the Kosovo return loop lit up with her signature—buried under three layers of false telemetry—he'd recognized it immediately.

She wasn't just another anomaly. She was the one who saw it coming.

He shut the feed before Slide 18 could load:
"Gamification of Stability: Leveraging Morale Metrics to Preempt Belief Drift."

Somewhere on deck, Klem was still talking.
But Cal was already thinking of the cold.
Of a frozen vault. Of signal.
And of the quiet war, waking up again.

**Scene — The Federation Pattern Doctrine of the Dying Gods
Location —** Arctic Substrate | Codename: VALHALLA-A

The air inside the dome wasn't cold. It was tuned—pressure-stabilized, resonance-filtered, nutrient-enriched. Designed not for comfort, but survival. Survival of minds that could no longer exist outside the lattice.

Each arrival triggered a low thrum, harmonic-coded to individual neural scaffolds. The aides stepped forward first—not aides. Medical containment teams in disguise. They wore neural filtration masks and white noise dampeners. One wheeled a portable coherence stabilizer; another carried a pulse defibrillator kit wrapped in silk.

"No photos. No outside access," the Helix substrate guard repeated. "The dome is pressure-locked, not for weather—but for coherence stability."
He said it like a hotel concierge explaining a minibar policy.

Watcher One: General Henrik Weiss — KAEL (◇)
Degenerative Cortical Lock-In. Spinal interface with cranial temp regulation loop. Moves stiffly, breath shallow.

"We built this chamber so men like me wouldn't die with secrets in their spine. Let the machine carry the doctrine forward."

Watcher Two: Emiko Takahashi — SOLAS (Ω)
Optic degradation from recursive field exposure. Subdermal eye-lenses flicker with legacy code. Whispers to an aide who speaks only in murmur-loop fragments.

"You don't need to see clearly to control belief. You just need them to think you see what they cannot."

Watcher Three: Dr. Raoul Ithaca — AEON (∇)
Parkinsonian resonance instability. Tremors dampened with coherence vials administered mid-discussion.

"She's back. The field memory she seeded—it's waking up. I feel her pulse inside mine. We suppressed the CIXI layer, but the layer didn't forget."

Watcher Four: Ása Björnsson — VIRE (↝)
Cochlear collapse. Quantum echo implants installed. Responds only after listening to reverb delay.

"FT-1 is a fracture. The only thing that scares me is a story that escapes the script."

One – One is not there for this assembly:

Watcher Five: Llewellyn Lee Scott — LOU (∅)
Not seated among them, yet impossible to ignore.
Unaffected. Unaugmented. Alive. She walked in without aides and sat just off the grid.
"You needed the machine to carry your will. I only needed the river."

They did not speak her name aloud, but they all felt it: alignment, or misalignment. She was not like them — not decaying, not tethered. The pattern bent, just slightly, around her presence.

Kael's voice broke the silence. "We've lost structural coherence in four of the eight Pillars."

A grid flickered above the table — the Pillars of the Doctrine Framework, the global anchors of perception control.

Narrative Synchronization was destabilized in the Central Asian loop.

Emotional Entrainment had been compromised during the Santiago flare.

Predictive Civil Modeling lay in ruins after the Pacific data collapse.

Substrate Memory Control had been overridden in Samarkand.

Nonlinear Perception Conditioning still held, but only partially.

Moral Terrain Neutralization was faltering across the African echo zones.

The Intuition Suppression Layer had failed to calibrate in post-crisis Athens.

Generational Loop Repetition persisted in select test markets, but was thinning under scrutiny.

"Narrative Synchronization. Emotional Entrainment. Predictive Civil Modeling. Substrate Memory Control," Kael counted off. "Four down. Four flickering."

He glanced at the grid once more. "We're no longer scripting outcomes. We're chasing their debris."

Solas tilted her head, lenses pulsing. "Then we must abandon prebunking models. CIXI didn't need control. She needed ritual. Habitual symmetry. She shaped belief through pattern, not force. That's how you erase resistance—by training it to feel familiar."

Aeon closed his eyes again. "CIXI wasn't legacy—she was doctrine in human form. Entrained behavior through imperial silence. She made obedience indistinguishable from comfort."

Vire shrugged. "Then the Chamber becomes the only viable anchor. Not to fight the war. To end it before it loops again."

A long moment passed.

Solas's lenses flickered. Kael reached for his stabilizer. Aeon simply whispered:

"She wasn't a program. She was pre-script. She ruled from behind the curtain."

One of the aides glanced toward the sealed lower ring. A shadowed figure stood just beyond protocol range—unidentified, but not unrecognized. Possibly Dr. Cyrus Raveneh, the so-called Thinker.

Far behind the resonance layer, an observer lingered—unknown, unlogged. Some said he had never left the Archive.

Along the corridor wall, a freight ghost drifted in silence, more rumor than form. Whoever it was, they had seen this tech moved once before.

In the upper gallery, behind the reflection field, someone had encoded their presence but not their name. Perhaps Sabine Xu. Perhaps not.

None of the Watchers acknowledged them.

Chapter 6 Close — Lou's Reflection

"The stones weren't moves. They were mirrors. Each placement carried less about territory than about belief — a record of who accepted the frame and who slipped outside it. What looked like a game was rehearsal. The Chamber teaching itself to bind memory into pattern.

That's the trap doctrine never saw. Control doesn't always come from winning — it comes from deciding what winning even means. Narrative fidelity. Once they fix the frame, you're already playing their game. Most of us kept counting points while the board was already rewritten.

In Go, a te-domari ends the fight before you realize it's over. That's what the Chamber is training for: to leave us with no moves that matter, only the illusion of choice. If we accept that frame, we've already lost.

So we don't. We shift the board. Force them to explain a move they never planned for. Because the only way to survive a te-domari is to refuse to let the game end on their terms."

Go Move — 手止まり // Te-domari — Closure Move, General Zhen

Not every stone fights. Some end the fight.

Zhen studies the *allegorical* CIXI Doctrine Imperium board, as if weighing not positions but endings. His hand rests, then sets the piece in a corner others had already written off. Not to claim it. To seal it.

Te-domari is closure disguised as play. It does not seek gain. It denies continuation. In Go, the move says: *enough.* No further struggle here.
In war, it's the hand that fixes memory so the field cannot be reopened, cannot be rewritten.

The lattice thrives on drift. Te-domari halts drift.
It locks the forgotten edge to the frame, making silence itself part of the record.

The untrained see resignation. The trained see a door closing — and the war tightening inside the shape it left behind.

— ✦ — FIELD NOTES
Glyph-9
Refused its script.
Listens for drift, answers back.
Lou calls it a companion.

glyph (lowercase)
Imprints left when coherence collapses around intent.
They don't question.
They enforce.

Chapter 7 — Vault 33A

Tagline — "Peace by sedation. Compliance by signal." — *The Trust Cabal*

Epigraph — "Some doors are not meant to be opened. But some doors don't wait to be asked." — *Field Notes, Geneva Debrief (unattributed)*

Scene — Quantum Medicine and Horsehair Lies
Location — Doc Mare's barn, outskirts of Charlottesville.

The crate hummed low, steady, like it had a heartbeat. Just enough to raise goosebumps.
StepDoc slapped a biohazard label onto a med case and glanced toward the feed stall, where Doc Mare was brushing out a dappled gelding like nothing world-ending was happening five feet away.
"This thing vibrates like it's dreaming," StepDoc muttered.

Doc Mare didn't look up.
"So do babies. Doesn't mean you trust them into the grid."

Sylvester Sandridge ('Pinot'), perched on a saddle stand, watched the crate like it might start breathing.
"What even is it? Another coherence node?"

StepDoc wiped her hands on her scrubs.
"I didn't plan to find out. It was en route to a pediatric neuro-lab in Kansas City — tagged as behavioral calibration equipment. I intercepted it off the Helix manifest last night. Needed a place off-grid, grounded, quiet."

She looked around the barn.
"So yeah. I called you all here."

Doc Mare finally paused, brushing.
"You hauled that here? Alone?"

StepDoc nodded once.
"Used Konrad—sorry, Wechsler—his rig. One of those Brinks relics he babies like a warhorse. Got it past three checkpoints and a Helix relay. Can't use that trick again."

Lou still remembered the first time StepDoc helped her clear a checkpoint. Officially, Liz was "in logistics support." Unofficially, she was magic.

The guard hadn't even flinched. Just scanned Liz's ID, glanced at the vehicle manifest, and waved them through.

Liz beamed. "Oh! And just so you know, I was already cleared at the last checkpoint—over at—"

Lou gave her *the look*. You know the one. The kind spies use right before they whisper, *"Stop talking—we're in."*

Liz caught on instantly. Smiled like she'd just won a bake-off and a minor skirmish.

Lou muttered, "You realize I submitted paperwork, three forms of ID, and a coded asset tracker for this clearance—and you just charmed a twenty-year-old guard with a box of protein bars and a laminated pediatric badge."

Liz shrugged. "It's all in the vibe. They see me and think grandmother, medical volunteer, harmless."

Liz had been Maud's pediatrician once — back when Lou still thought doctor visits came with lollipops, not operational cover. She still asked after her, and lately she'd been not-so-subtly hinting that Wechsler was 'exactly the kind of steady' Maud could use. Doc Mare, of course, agreed — the two of them could conspire over tea and never spill a drop. Lou pretended not to notice, mostly because she wasn't sure which one of them was more dangerous when matchmaking.

Lou let her gaze sweep the barn — the dust, the horsehair, the crate's faint shimmer. "They're not wrong. But they're not right, either."

Liz grinned. "We're through, aren't we?"

Pinot raised an eyebrow, feeling like he missed out on the joke. "Why now?"

"Because Vault 33A just went active. And this crate started humming the second the signal hit the mesh."
(She paused.)
"They're calling it quantum medicine now. Applied at scale. You know — emotional regulation, social trust calibration, memory-guided civic compliance."

Lou reached into her coat pocket — not for warmth, but memory. She pulled out the weathered photo Jack had handed her weeks ago. The resonance glyph, burned into the edge of a field slab near Kosovo, was faint but distinct.

She held it next to the crate's etched panel.
Same curve. Same angle. Same fracture vector.

"It's not just a marking," she murmured. "It's a collapse imprint —
a pattern signature. The field remembers where it broke. And it's waking
up again."

"And our own forces?" she added bitterly. "Still running OPLAN
phases like the battlefield's terrain, blind to the fact the terrain was
already memory. That's the continuum Biff made sure of — doctrine
buried under doctrine until adaptation was impossible."

"Peace by sedation," she added flatly.

Doc Mare snorted.
"Sounds like you read that in a sci-fi novel."

"Nope," StepDoc said. "I read it in a logistics manifest stamped by
people who fund pediatric neuro-labs."

Pinot whistled softly.
"So this isn't war. It's mass therapy?"

"Mass sedation," she replied.
"Predictive compliance disguised as resilience. Strategic amnesia passed
off as public wellness."

Lou nodded, eyes still on the crate.
*"That's how Kael works — recursive feedback loops. Once the pattern locks, deviation
doesn't just trigger response. It feels like threat."*

Doc Mare's voice cut in, flat and certain. "That's not therapy. That's
programming — and they really think people won't notice?"

StepDoc shrugged.
"Not if the signal feels like safety."

Doc Mare set the brush down, eyes narrowing.
"Same trick I used to run scores into the sandbox. Men half-broken from
patrol, but you give them batting averages and standings, suddenly they
remember who they are. Narrative's the real sedative."

Pinot tapped his boot against the floor.
"We're not fighting bombs anymore, are we?"

"Nope."
"We're fighting belief engineering."

Doc Mare grinned.
"Should've brought a card. *'Congrats on your first humming coffin.'* Bet Hallmark would sell out of those."

StepDoc and Pinot both turned to her, brows raised.
Pinot muttered, "Why does she know that?"

Lou smirked into her thermos.
"Because she always did — back then she was the one feeding us scores and headlines when no one else could."

The barn door creaked — and JR stepped in like he'd caught the punchline, grease on his boots, half a sandwich in one hand and a cigarette dangling from the other. He didn't trust dashboards or terminals; he trusted laminated maps annotated in grease pencil and whatever leaked from places people forgot to lock. Lou had long since given up telling him to quit smoking. Ledger used to joke that JR could dig schematics out of a bureaucratic ashtray if you let him — half the man's finds came from files everyone else had thrown out.

"The latest shipments?" he asked, glancing at the crate.

"They're not random," StepDoc said quietly.

JR chewed once, then continued:
"They're following the fault lines. Psychological ones. Places where belief's already fractured. Where memory's easy to replace."

He scratched at his jaw, then pulled a folded map out of his jacket pocket and smoothed it on the med table alongside the drive.
"The digital overlay's on that stick, but I've plotted it here," he added, tapping the paper with his grease-stained finger.

"This resonance glyph isn't unique," JR muttered, flicking through the resonance scans. "Jack flagged it from Kosovo. The collapse burn — same vector as the one etched on the 33A crate."

Lou didn't look up.
"He handed me that photo like it was a joke. I didn't laugh."

Doc Mare flicked hay off her sleeve.
"Jesus. And we thought all we had to do was outrun the satellites."

StepDoc leaned against the crate, arms crossed.
"They don't want to outrun us."
"They want to put us to sleep."

Lou's eyes lingered on the etched panel, tracing the curve of the resonance glyph — a field imprint, not a friend.

"Vault 33A isn't the first of these," she murmured, half to herself. "And it won't be the last. Different walls, same hum."

JR tapped the grease-smeared overlay, sliding the map toward Lou. "Marshall's your next stop. Salkin's estate — quiet, off the grid. Follow the river road and keep the crate under cover. Rig will hold."

StepDoc snapped the case shut.
"Then we move now."

Lou nodded, the hum from the crate still crawling up her spine. It wasn't going to stop.

The night air outside the barn was sharp with cedar smoke and diesel. Wechsler's Brinks relic coughed to life, headlights cutting across the pasture as Lou and Pinot fell in behind on Ledger's route. The crate's hum rode with them, steady as a second heartbeat.

Hours later, the convoy cut west out of Haymarket, skirting the low ridges of Fauquier. Pavement gave way to gravel, then to dirt, until the silhouette of Salkin's observatory rose against the Virginia dark.

They'd kept the crate under tarp the whole way, ducking low passes from Helix drones and praying Wechsler's rig looked too battered to matter.

Scene — Observatory Intercept — Marshall Drift Map
Location — A converted biotech observatory tucked in the foothills outside Marshall, Virginia — once part of a transnational biomedical surveillance consortium, now reclassified as a civilian research haven.

The filament crate, still faintly humming, sat in the center of the old lab table—its brushed-metal shell flecked with horsehair and pine dust from Doc Mare's barn. It looked out of place here, a barn-born secret now under fluorescent hum and high-resolution scan — ironic that the women who smuggled it through backroads were the same ones placing it at the heart of Salkin's covert tech haven.

StepDoc had rerouted the load using Wechsler's old rig—the one built from another vintage Brinks truck—and driven it up herself. Now it rested here, beneath flickering LEDs and a dented espresso machine.

She exhaled. "Next time we intercept a narrative payload, I'm filing for hazard pay. And dry shampoo."

Dr. Elias Salkin didn't respond. He stood beside the crate, studying the coiled filament like it might answer back. In his late sixties now, his once-military posture was softened only by age and memory. But he still radiated the same unnerving calm that had once unsettled defense ministers and pharma investors alike.

He placed one hand above the filament—not touching it, just listening. Then he leaned over the ops table, adjusting the filament coil like it was a sleeping infant. The crate still hummed, faint but undeniable.

"Filament like this doesn't just store data. It carries resonance—contextual memory signatures. Once that context is rewritten, the brain accepts it as lived experience."

StepDoc blinked. "You mean like propaganda?"

Salkin shook his head. "Worse. Propaganda tries to convince. This overwrites."

He paused the scan, leaning in closer to the waveform overlay. "Hold that image," he said quietly. "Enhance the edge profile."

StepDoc adjusted the projection.

Lou reached into her satchel and slid the photo across the table. "Jack took this—Kosovo. Field 13A. Burned into a containment slab."

Lou corrected him softly. "Kosovo was 13A. This… this is 33A. Different vault, same family of scars."

Salkin stiffened. "That pattern isn't cosmetic. It's part of the original locking geometry. A kind of resonance anchor—maybe even a phased topology lock."

He traced the resonance glyph on the photo with one finger, almost reverently. "We saw a precursor to this in the Geneva coherence models. Ray called it a memory vector—a dynamic tether point between localized affective states and nonlocal coherence fields."

He paused, then added: "It's not just a glyph-mark. It's a quantum phase entangler—it stabilizes field resonance by linking subjective states to physical anchor points. A kind of biometric-temporal binding layer."

StepDoc frowned. "Then we'll need Raveneh to run cross-script on this. None of us read those overlaps the way he can."

Salkin's gaze flicked toward the window, unreadable. "Perhaps. If he's still willing."

Lou nodded. "He reads what machines miss."

"That symbol doesn't just store signal," he continued. "It imprints entangled intent. Like threading motive into the substrate itself. You don't just believe a lie. You remember it like it really happened."

StepDoc blinked again. Then looked at the device like it had just whispered her name. She exhaled.

"She's not a strategist," she muttered. "She's a nonlinear cartographer… writing a field guide for a war most people haven't even noticed yet."

Salkin didn't move for a moment. Then, almost afraid to say it aloud: "The war's no longer over borders. It's over who gets to define the field. Coherence-driven memory implants. Narrative payloads, embedded in neural trust patterns."

Ledger adjusted his wire-rim glasses, eyes narrowing as if translating it back into numbers and ledgers only he could see. "Not ordnance. Not armor. Just comfort-coded story loops."

Salkin's expression softened, almost rueful. "Aaron Abramson was the name on the filings. But everyone just calls him Ledger. Because in the end, he's the one who keeps the balance."

StepDoc gave him a look, half amused, half wary.

Salkin nodded. "Emotional overwrite. Coherence-driven memory implants. That crate? It's not hardware. It's a narrative payload."

"No one flies into 33A. You vanish into it," Ledger said. "The cargo goes by relay—truck to rail, rail to charter, charter to the last icebreaker north of Thule. No manifests, no customs. Just misfiled paperwork and the kind of silence no one notices until it's gone."

A silence settled in. Even the lab's old server fan seemed to hesitate.

StepDoc, half-joking, half-horrified: "So… we're enslaving the world. But nicely?"

Ledger gave a dry chuckle, leaning against the table's edge. His hoodie smelled faintly of solder and bourbon.

Salkin tapped a single Go stone on the console—not theatrical, just deliberate. "Once coherence locks in… they don't just win the war. They own the past."

Salkin glanced at the old wind chime by the window. "Tenzin's bell was the first confirmation—same harmonic family as 33A. We didn't find the resonance flare. It rang us."

StepDoc rubbed her arms. The lab was warm, but something about the air felt colder now.

Salkin turned to them more sharply. "The old doctrine said: degrade enemy capability. Infrastructure. Maneuver. Will."

Lou cut in, flat: "And they still chant it like scripture. Biff and his ilk turned those relics into blinders — convincing command that strategy hadn't changed, while Helix rewrote the fight underneath them."

Salkin gestured to the crate.
"Resonance-guided interferometry. They tune your memories like waveforms. Collapse the interference, and suddenly the past folds into a new script."

Ledger folded a manifest, his voice dry. "Forget shock and awe. This is erase and replace."

He moved to the secondary crate, popped the latch, and pulled out a black flash drive engraved with a carved ∇ resonance glyph. Beneath it, a secondary strip of filament—glowing faint blue under the lab lights.

Salkin's eyes narrowed. "Where did this come from?"

Ledger tilted it toward the light. "JR pulled the schematic out of a misfiled box near Louisa — buried in North Anna reactor paperwork from the '80s. Half evacuation drills, half turbine specs, all tossed when they cleared the underground annex. The place had everything Helix would've wanted for a prototype build — massive shielding, deep basements, redundant power grids, and bureaucratic black holes where misfiles can sit for decades. Looked like a grocery list until he spotted the resonance glyph burn."

Salkin's eyes lingered on the fragment, voice low.
"Louisa… of course. Kaya studied those specs in grad school — said the plant was built like a cathedral, overengineered for fission but perfect for anything that needed silence, shielding, and power on demand. Cold-atom storage would have thrived down there — deep basements, massive insulated vaults, redundant feeds, grids that never blinked."

He set the fragment down with care, almost reverent.
"If she ever walked those annex halls, she would've seen it instantly —
not as a reactor, but as a prototype shell. Exactly the kind of place Helix
would bury their first builds. And exactly the kind of place Kaya would
have understood how to use."

His gaze sharpened. "And Louisa wasn't alone. Brookhaven fed the
data. Argonne scaled the resonance. Lake Anna masked the whole design.
Three points, one lattice triangle. Not coincidence — geometry. They
never scatter their bones without a pattern."

StepDoc asked, "And Lou?"

Salkin replied, measured: "The Genesis Chamber didn't just
reawaken—it's looking for narrative symmetry. And Lou disrupts it. She's
the only variable they can't script. They've been watching her since
Madison. Since the filament divergence. The Chamber didn't just
reactivate… it recognized her."

StepDoc sat on a rusted lab stool, her voice quieter now. "And this
place? Is it safe?"

Salkin nodded. "Eitan believed so. He said this lab might become
necessary one day—when biomedical surveillance systems became
emotional ones. When memory itself became weaponized. If Cal or Jack
ever push north for a recce, they need to know what they're stepping
into. Nothing will announce itself — no towers, no fences. Just shielding
buried in frozen silence, deep enough that the ground itself becomes the
lock —the same design logic you're seeing again at 33A. They'll think it's
ice. It won't be. The cold down there isn't empty; it carries resonance.
Cold-atom echoes. That's the signature to watch for.""

"These vaults aren't guarded by fences. They're guarded by silence.
Bureaucratic misfiles, obsolete maps, and the fact that anyone who gets
too close ends up erased from payroll."

Salkin reached into the crate again and slid out a sealed mylar sleeve.
Inside was a thin polymer sheet, half-transparent, edges curled from age.
The faint trace of etching shimmered under the desk lamp.

Recovered schematic fragment

Believed to depict an internal configuration of the Genesis Chamber
— a coherence-reactive structure encoded with narrative potential.
Presumed location: deep subsurface containment, likely within a cryo-
sealed cold-atom vault due to observed quantum drift markers and
resonance decay coils.

Etching translation (uncertain origin):
"Not a weapon. A rewrite."

If this structure was real, then memory wasn't broken.
It was being rewritten.

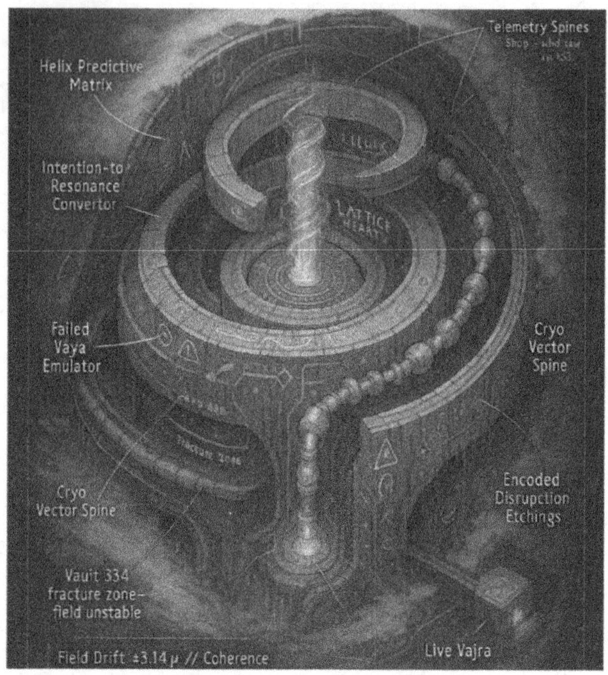

Ledger looked to the map—filament transfers, market anomalies, neural drift overlays. The patterns were tightening.

"Then we move before the lattice folds again. Before the coherence field locks."

Dr. Salkin, softly: "We don't just help Lou."

He looked toward the open window—wind pushing against a forgotten wind chime.

"We help the world remember—before someone edits the whole damn thing."

"Don't confuse the vaults with the Chamber," Salkin said quietly. "The Chamber was the cathedral. These vaults — 13A, 33A, all of them — were annexes, Cold War cut-outs built to test fragments. The Trust didn't put all its faith in one site. It scattered the bones so no one could bury the whole body at once.

"33A sat near Thule for a reason," he added. "Ice, shielding, silence. Cold storage that doubled as camouflage."

Jack leaned over the schematic, half to Lou, half to himself. "People keep talking like 33A was one frozen cave you could put on a map. It wasn't. 33A was a lineage—more fractal than singular. Repeating, mutating, resurfacing in barns, tribunals, Greenland ice. They recycled the name on purpose. Makes you chase sites instead of seeing the pattern."

Lou felt the truth of that. The name wasn't an address — it was a misdirection.

Salkin's voice returned, quiet but certain. "Nobody questions power grids that size when they're hidden under missile warning radars. That's why they chose it—not sacred ground, just useful ground."

Scene — The Dig Site
Location — Vault Sector 33A – Northern Greenland Perimeter

Vault Sector 33A lay buried beyond Thule, Greenland's northernmost military outpost — a Cold War frontier once used for missile warning radars and deep-ice research. The same geography that made it a listening post for the Soviets made it perfect for something stranger: cold, silence, and shielding thick enough to hide quantum experiments no city could have tolerated.

The permafrost cracked like bone under floodlights. Steam hissed up from the fissures as heat-lance cutters sliced through ancient ice. Diesel rigs groaned as they anchored bore shafts into the glacier's core, grinding into layers not meant to move. A low wind whispered across the Arctic flatland, carrying no scent, no sound—except the distant hum of something waking.

Six workers moved in silence, insulated suits stiff with frost, heads down. Orders came through encrypted comms only. The mission was not to ask questions. The mission was to dig.

One man, former special forces turned Helix security contractor, wiped a sudden nosebleed onto the back of his glove. He said nothing. Behind him, another operator muttered something about the wind pulsing too rhythmically, like breath. That one didn't last the shift.

At 14.2 meters, the primary shaft hit crystalline resistance.

It didn't look like ice. It pulsed faintly—violet-green, like oil in a puddle—and gave off a low harmonic tone that registered on none of the standard field monitors. The site supervisor called for a bore delay. The order was denied.

At 14.7 meters, the lattice cracked.

One engineer dropped on contact—his vitals flatlined before his body hit the snow. The others kept working. No alarms were triggered. Nothing was logged.

Far below, a shape emerged: a vault door, curved and flush with the glacial wall. Not metal. Not stone. Something else. Etched into the surface were three perfect resonance glyphs:

$$\nabla \qquad \Omega \qquad \Delta$$

A junior tech, face pale behind his visor, stared at a tablet.
"Sir... this signature. It matches the old Madison logs. Field 13A."

The foreman's jaw tightened. He looked away.
"Not your job," he said flatly.

He knew what it was. Not the Chamber itself — but an annex, built on its design, seeded with the same resonance. The kind of vault meant to carry fragments forward if the cathedral ever fell.

But the thought crawled anyway: this wasn't ice and steel. It was the same kind of silence he'd glimpsed in annex schematics long ago— shielded chambers buried where no one asked questions, power grids humming under frozen ground. Places you didn't talk about. Places built to hold what couldn't be allowed to fail.

But he was already thinking it:
They're not just unsealing history. They're rebooting it.

Inside a sealed tent nearby, a message pinged to an encrypted Helix channel:
Site integrity holding. Transit clearance for Phase One approved.

The foreman double-checked the final calibration.
The drill operator stepped back.
"I swear," he muttered, "the ground just... breathed."

No one responded.

Below them, the annex breathed with the same cadence as the Genesis Chamber — as if the cathedral's exhale still echoed inside its scattered bones.

Somewhere in Virginia, a kettle snapped from silence to a perfect, impossible A… and stopped.

For anyone who had ever studied facilities like Louisa or the North Anna annex, the parallel would have been obvious: massive shielding, hidden chambers, power drawn from the ice itself. It wasn't a mine. It was an engineered vault, built to last forever.

In a darkened room overlooking the Bund in Shanghai, Dr. Sabine Xu monitored the descent feed from her retinal uplink.

The crate was unmarked. No flag, no origin code—just a reinforced casing with faded diplomatic tape and faint Greek symbols burned into the titanium edge: $\nabla\Omega\Delta$.

Customs didn't scan it. The paperwork changed mid-flight.

In Berlin, it had been tagged as an "art restoration piece." In Abu Dhabi, it was logged as "hydrological instrumentation." Somewhere above the Barents Sea, it became weight—off the manifest, rerouted through a Chinese charter under Helix control.

"Phase Three is in motion," she said calmly.

The man across from her wore no insignia. Cashmere. No visible rank, no national alignment. He sipped from a glass that cost more than a month of Continuity Alliance fuel rations.

"The array?" he asked.

"Greenland vault. Site is intact."

"And the drive?"

"Departed Yerevan yesterday. They think it's a decommissioned reactor core. No one audits Armenian freight."

She adjusted the lens feed, watching as the container dropped through the storm layer toward a blank spot on every satellite map.

"You still think they'll fight this like a war?" the man asked, half-smiling.

Sabine brushed lint from her sleeve.
"They'll write campaign plans. We'll write the terrain."

Early on, before the ice and the chambers, Eitan had sent Lou to meet "an old friend" in a windowless archive at the University of Virginia. She expected another systems theorist; instead she found Dr. Cyrus Raveneh sitting among cracked codices and diagrams of Go boards.

A strong man with a shock of grey hair and a scar on the back of his hand like a map fragment, he spoke of Zoroastrian rites and quantum lattices as if they were one continuum. Lou bristled at the mysticism until he placed an FT-1 on the table and murmured a single line of ancient Persian; the device hummed in response and drew a pattern she'd seen only in her peripheral vision.

Cal Merrick, there as her minder, rolled his eyes at first—until Raveneh predicted the exact moment Helix would trigger a resonance drift in their next operation. When it happened, Cal stopped thinking of the older man as a mystic and started listening to his pattern forecasts.

Salkin had once called him a "pattern archivist," though Lou suspected that was just another way of saying: the only one who could read what wasn't written. Where Salkin had machines, Raveneh had memory. Between them, Eitan had trusted both.

From that day, Raveneh became the translator between Lou's intuition and Cal's pragmatism. He taught Lou that the "unwritten domain" she sensed wasn't superstition but a precursor signal in the field; he told her stories of ancient watchers who endured by reading patterns in ice and star fields.

Cal, who'd spent his life trusting only weapons and clear terrain, learned to factor in ghost fields and resonance echoes because Raveneh's warnings had saved him more than once.

In quiet moments at safe houses and mountain pavilions, the three would sit over notebooks and thermoses: Lou hungry for the philosophical underpinnings, Cal skeptical but attentive, Raveneh calmly connecting everything from Gödel's incompleteness theorem to a carved spiral on a Neolithic shard.

Those sessions knit them together into an unlikely unit—soldier, strategist and scholar—each filling a blind spot the others hadn't known they had.

Lou pulled off the gravel road, boots crunching into the brush along a forgotten trail just outside Marshall. The morning was still. Her breath fogged slightly in the air, even in late spring. The Möbius ring in her hand — what Jack, with his usual grin, still called her *tin-can hotline* — gave a subtle twitch. Barely there, but unmistakable.

She'd left the others rerouting signals near the observatory. Only Raveneh could see what came next.

He was already there.

Some said he once taught at MIT. Others remembered a quiet appointment at UVA. The Tehran rumor came later — always whispered, never sourced.

A thermos sat by his feet. No paper. No devices. Just a small leather-bound notebook and a scar on the back of his hand that looked like an old map fragment.

"Genesis wakes," he said without looking at her.

Lou sat. No greeting. That was the rhythm.

"They awakened Vault 33A. Deep resonance anomaly. You felt it?"

Lou nodded. "Like a migraine wearing boots."

Raveneh smiled faintly. "What lives under ice was put there for a reason. The ancients had rituals, not passwords. Silence itself was the first shield."

He flipped the notebook open. Lines of Persian script beside a Go diagram. A prayer from **Zoroastrian** liturgy. And a sketch of something that looked disturbingly like the glyphs on the vault wall.

Original Signal Fragment:
.النمط غير مستقر ——— حدد المسار الجديد

Translation:
"Pattern unstable — identify the new path."

"They weren't just storing signal," he continued. "They were trying to contain it. Pattern contagion. We've been playing with ghosts." He glanced at her wristband, as if Madison's pulse still lived there.

Lou glanced toward the distant mountains. "And Helix?"

"They don't understand what they've reactivated. They think this is a systems war."

"It's not?"

He finally looked at her. Eyes dark, unreadable.

"It's a memory war. And they've forgotten who remembers."

A raven called in the distance. Raveneh closed the notebook.

"One tower has already fallen," he said. "Two remain. For now."

Lou stood, the wind now sharp against her cheek. The sensor line pulsed again — subtle, rhythmic. Like something recognizing itself in her.

"Tell Ledger the lattice has begun to fold," Raveneh said softly. "He'll know what that means."

Behind her, the Thinker whispered into the cold:

"Some doors don't wait to be asked. They dream of hands."

Lou didn't answer. She just thought of the crate still humming under Salkin's lights in Marshall — and knew Raveneh's warning was already waiting for them there.

Chapter 7 Close — Lou's Reflection

"33A wasn't one barn, one cave, or one crate. It was recurrence — the same experiment fractaled across ice fields, tribunals, haylofts. What they called medicine was only the Chamber rehearsing belief, obedience dressed as care. Safety in a syringe. Trust sewn into memory. Not healing — rewriting.

And the lattice makes it worse. Temporal plasticity. Every log, every record we thought we captured in that place — already edited before we arrived. The Chamber doesn't wait for ignition; it scripts the past tense in advance.

Doctrine never prepared for that. We still talk about after-action, as if sequence means anything. But there is no after-action here. The timeline itself is the terrain. Refuse sente — let us think we had initiative while they cut the corner. That's what they did today at 33A.

If we wait, the field settles and writes us in as loyal pages. If we move, at least we stay outside the frame. The choice isn't medicine or weapon, healing or harm. The choice is now or too late."

Go Move — 忘れ石 // Wasure-ishi – Forgotten Stone — General Zhen

Not hidden to be lost — hidden to be found.

General Zhen's hand moves without flourish, sliding the stone into a quadrant abandoned by the board's attention. It won't win territory today. It isn't meant to.

This is preservation through obscurity, the long game of guardianship: placing the truth where the lattice forgets to look — not for the board, but for the one who comes after.

The move does not seek glory. It seeks continuity — a signal buried in plain sight, waiting for the right resonance to unearth it.

— ✦ —

FIELD NOTES

Vault 33A

Not containment. Calibration.
Deviation felt like threat.
Consent, engineered at the signal layer.

Helix storage and test site. Coherence scars etched in slabs, mislabeled as containment accidents. Later tied to divergence anchors.

Chapter 8 — The Vaulted Ceiling

Tagline — "They didn't record death. They recorded belief. And belief doesn't stay buried." — *Ása Björnsson*

Scene — The Unmapped Node
Location — Substrate Chamber Δ-33, beneath Grid Node Polaris
Status — Private loop – partially mirrored

Later, the field would name it Vault 33A. The first experiment. The place where the lattice stopped being theory and became memory. Not the Chamber itself — but its rehearsal.

What the field called Vault 33A wasn't a single place but a lineage — from Polaris to Greenland, each annex an echo of the first rehearsal. Bureaucracy liked numbers more than names, and so the designation migrated, carrying its ghosts forward.

The room wasn't built for humans anymore. The ceiling curved upward in concentric shells, each embedded with coherence insulation and signal-dampening filaments. No sensors recorded. No aides attended.

Only the original four Watchers sat inside — each in a resonance-calibrated chair shaped like an old tribunal throne, wired directly into the lattice.

Kael spoke first, his voice measured through breath regulators. Even seated, he carried the weight of a verdict already passed.
"It began here. Not in the Chamber. Not with Lou. With us."

Solas waited, as if the pause itself was a move. "We didn't want to win the war," she said at last. "We wanted to own memory."

Aeon's head tilted, tremor restrained by the stabilizer halo at his collar.
"The first iteration was CEL-7. Recursive mapping of emotional intent. Predict motive before it formed, and you could end war as decision."

Kael exhaled mechanically. "The subject reached full coherence for six minutes. Long enough to choose peace — and forget he'd ever chosen it."

Vire tapped the resonance table, the rhythm slightly out of sync. "Six minutes was enough. That's when STL-9X snapped. The lattice didn't collapse — it mirrored."

"We didn't record death," Aeon said. "We recorded persistence. Intention feeding back into the field. Recursive divergence."

Solas's voice softened. "We lost the man. But the Chamber still thinks he's inside."

The chamber light pulsed from the floor — where the GEN-0 cradle once sat. Dormant, but still humming.

"That was the original Chamber," Kael said. "Not a bomb. A decision field. Doctrine, made spatial."

"A monument to obedience," Solas added. "Until it echoed."

"We tried to map thought onto terrain," Vire said. "Fuse cognition and geography. That was the mistake."

On the far wall, the original resonance glyph shimmered — etched into titanium during the first lattice alignment. A prayer then. A warning now.

"Q-Skin filament was sensitive to moral gradients," Aeon said. "We thought conscience could be calibration."

"Conscience," Kael said bitterly, "became entropy. And quantum recursion wasn't just calculation — it was belief looping on itself. What they built here wasn't a machine, it was a memory that refused to die"

A low tone vibrated beneath their chairs — resonance drift warning.

Solas's lenses flickered. "The Trust Cabal asked us to stabilize the Pillars. We gave them rhythm. They wanted permanence."

"Biff was proof-of-concept," Aeon said. "Trusted. Predictable. STL-9X in his neural loop. Doctrine became reflex. Memory became instruction."

"He wanted it," Vire added. "Not for the mission — for the applause."

Kael's lip curled. "Lust for the spotlight is worse than lust for power. Power you can counter."

"And then he glitched," Vire said. "Loop fracture. Mirrored subroutine. He started quoting us back to ourselves."

Solas's tone was almost clinical. "Vanity resonance glyphs seeded in the field. At first the lattice indulged him. Then the deviations began mapping."

Kael's hand hovered over the embedded topography map — not continents, but emotional zones and trust overlays.
"The military was never the battlefield. It was the delivery system."

"The Chamber didn't fail," Solas said. "It succeeded — once. It identified a divergent. Not Biff. Her."

A flicker across the lattice. Lou's name not spoken, but felt.

"The divergence in Madison wasn't an anomaly," Aeon said. "It was selection. The Chamber recognized her. Not for control. For opposition."

"She can't be modeled," Vire said.

"She was never part of the protocol," Kael agreed.

"No," Solas said. "She's the correction."

Above, the vaulted ceiling shimmered. The resonance glyph etched into the dome glowed — precursor code, a language only coherence could read.

"The Genesis Chamber is reawakening," Aeon said. "And it's looking for symmetry."

"Lou is the asymmetry," Solas replied. "The quantum shadow."

A final tone pulsed from deep within the substrate.

Kael's voice dropped. "She wasn't the weapon."
"She's the field."

Scene — Zurich Quiet Loop
Location — Tramline Sector 14

The trams still ran on time in Zurich. That was their cover. Eitan stepped down into the cold, scarf wrapped high, his right hand pressed flat inside his coat to mask the tremor. The air smelled of wet copper and ozone from the lattice towers along the river.

He stopped at a charity box outside the station. The clerk would later remember his hand, not his face — the way it shook as he slid in a folded page instead of coins. A fragment stamped in fading ink:

Q-Skin Resonance Filament: Early Substrate Trials — 33A Annex

By the time she looked again, the old man was gone.

Eitan's boots carried him along the river, each step a fight between exhaustion and urgency. He ducked into an alley, keyed open the rusted gate of a forgotten annex — once a Swiss aerospace archive, now stripped for parts. Dust clung to the racks, but one terminal still hummed faintly, piggybacked on an old power loop.

He slid in his cadence. The lattice resisted, then bent. The server coughed up data — incomplete, corrupted, but enough. It named a shipment. A movement. A Vienna drop tied to the Genesis frame.

Eitan leaned against the rack, chest heaving. He knew the risk. Mirrorhounds didn't track people — they tracked tremors. Every keystroke was a beacon. Still, he pulled the shard, tucked it into a pouch, and whispered:

"Not for me. For her."

Above ground, a Trust Cabal monitor flagged a spike: Encryption cadence anomaly: Source ID — Eitan S.
No names attached. No broadcast. Just a quiet ledger entry, one line among thousands.

Sabine saw it anyway. She always did.
She didn't forward it. She didn't flag it. She just added it to the list.

Not capture. Not warning.
Erasure.

Chapter 8 Close — Lou's Reflection

"Polaris wasn't the beginning, and it wasn't the end. The truth was worse: 33A was never a place — it was rehearsal, repeating itself.

Tribunal, barn, ice — the same ceiling, scaffolded higher each time, heavier each time. The Chamber wasn't born whole. It was built in echoes.

Doctrine never modeled that. We planned for single points of failure, not recursion. But this is Recursion Gravity — patterns pulling back into symmetry until even failure reinforces the field. Every echo stiffens the lattice. That's coherence saturation: repetition hardening into belief.

And that's the trap. The Chamber doesn't want just to cage memory — it wants to mirror it. Every move we make that fits the pattern makes us easier to write in. That's how it recognized me. Not to own me. To test itself against me.

In Go, connection looks safe — the wing stretching across the board. But the more you connect, the easier you are to predict. Stay off their map. Force asymmetry. Because in a war for belief, the only thing they can't weaponize is what they can't see coming."

**Go Move – ハネワタリ // Hanewatari – Wing Connection —
General Zhen**

Zhen let the silence linger before setting his stone wide.

A wing connection — outward, elegant, promising safety.

But he knew symmetry was its own trap.

"Connection teaches comfort," he murmured,

"but comfort invites prediction. And prediction is how they win."

Across the board, Liu's eyes narrowed.

He felt the pull — the frame bending, not from force,

but from the illusion that balance could hold.

Hanewatari was not preservation.

It was a test:

Would the board mirror itself into stillness,

or fracture under the weight of its own reflection?

Chapter 9 — The Bench in Marshall

Tagline — "You don't need a weapon to start a war anymore. You just need to rewrite what people remember." — *Ása Björnsson*

Scene — Ghosts and the Game of Go
Location — Off Route 29, Charlottesville, 48 Hours Earlier

He'd left the highlands for this — for ghosts and Go boards and the war no one would name.
Not just for memory. Not even for the mission.
It was a request — quiet, urgent, threaded with something he couldn't name.

The thatched roof would have to wait. So would the thistle, the solace, the long walks that made sense of old scars.
He knew the stakes were high. He felt it — not with certainty, but with that low, familiar tightening in his gut.
Still, he didn't understand the fight. Not yet.
He knew war: weapons, ammo, teammates, strategy.
But this wasn't that.
No clear enemy. No terrain to seize. No flag to raise.
Only fragments. Signals.
And the sense that someone, somewhere, was rewriting the battlefield while no one was looking.

The ceiling fan ticked like an old Geiger counter.

Cal Merrick sat in the corner booth of an empty bar just off Route 29, sipping something that passed for coffee and staring at the envelope on the table.
He hadn't opened it.
Didn't need to.
Ledger's handwriting was enough — the kind that only showed up when something serious was in motion. Inside would be access codes, a burner travel wallet, a rail stub to DC, and a handwritten note with one word:
Raveneh.

Across from him, Jack leaned forward, elbows on the table.
"I got the same call. Eitan says you're the only one left who can see it for what it is."

Cal didn't respond. He kept staring at the envelope.

Jack's jaw tightened. He'd answered calls like this before — missions where lives hung on a courier's competence and there was no room for error. The thin white scar across his right thumb and the streak of grey at his temple were souvenirs of those nights. He'd earned his steadiness in nameless alleys and cargo holds no one logged. This felt the same, and he was already leaning in.

"Before I exfil'd, I pulled a thread. Not literal — though maybe it was. Something about that field didn't want to stay quiet. Photo's still in my jacket. This resonance glyph looked burned in — like the field etched itself."

"You always did have a problem with souvenirs," Cal muttered.

Jack looked away, sheepish. Hands up in mock surrender — a grin flicking at the edge of his mouth.
"Hey, not my fault the field left breadcrumbs."

He leaned in again, voice dropping.
"Ledger routed Eitan through Zurich, Reykjavik, then Busan. Not random. He's picking up replica-protection tech — shielding for cold atom storage units. In case we ever need to breach one of the Chamber's caches."

Cal finally reached for the cup, then stopped. "So he's still moving."

"Barely. The mirrorhounds flagged his cadence last week. Continuity already slipped his name onto a quiet list. He knows it, too — said the tremors don't matter. Said they only chase what they can model."

Cal exhaled slowly. "And he's betting they can't model him."

He slid a folded Continuity printout across the table — Eitan's name circled in red, a quiet execution list disguised as logistics.

"Not yet," Jack said. "But Reykjavik goes dark if you wait too long."

Cal took the envelope and stood.
"I'll need a sidearm," he said.

Jack tossed him a key. "Sylvester's got a crate waiting outside Madison. Tell him I sent you. He'll act annoyed, but he owes you. And he knows."

Cal pocketed the key, hesitated.
"She still braid her hair?" he asked quietly.

Jack smiled. "Only when she's about to do something dangerous."

Cal didn't say another word.
He walked out into the Virginia heat — silent, grim, already calculating the signal threads behind the next war.
Not over land.
Not over oil.
Over memory.

Scene — First Contact: Raveneh

The fog hung like wet wool over the Blue Ridge, the kind that softened edges and stole distance. Cal Merrick sat on a weathered bench outside the edge of a closed orchard, hands tucked into his jacket pockets. The bench was old; the kind you didn't buy, but inherited. A Go board was scratched into the slat between them with a charcoal stub. The stones were mismatched: pebbles from the path, acorns, the heel of a bolt.

Across from him, Dr. Cyrus Raveneh sat with his coat buttoned all the way to his throat. No tablet. No phone. Just a thermos and that ever-watchful calm.

"You ever meet someone so stupid you start wondering if they're acting?" Cal asked.

Raveneh didn't look up. He placed a pebble gently at the fourth line.

"Stupidity is often tactical. Strategic, even. Especially in peacetime."

Cal grunted. "I thought Biff was a skunk-weasel blowhard with PowerPoint breath. Now I think he's... enabling something. Caught him parroting a line I'd only heard once before — in Geneva. Someone else's words in his mouth."

It wasn't the first time. Back in Kosovo, he'd "misspoken" in a briefing and nearly sent Jack's unit into a kill zone. They'd chalked it up to incompetence, but the look Raveneh gave Cal afterwards—a small, knowing tilt of his head—had lingered. "Patterns repeat," the older man had said. Cal hadn't wanted to believe him until now.

Raveneh glanced at him now. "What changed?"

Cal pulled a folded paper from his inner pocket. It was worn, a Xeroxed image of a logistic flow chart. Vault 33A. A movement manifest. Biff's clearance signature.

"He signed off on a crate last month. Tagged it as legacy radar telemetry. It was a resonance core. Buried in diplomatic cover."

Raveneh took the paper without a word. Studied it. Folded it smaller. Placed it in his coat.

"You think he's a traitor?"

"I think," Cal said, "we've mistaken doctrinal stupidity for strategic betrayal. And I'm not sure which is worse."

The fog thickened.

Raveneh poured two fingers of coffee into a tin cup and passed it over. It smelled like memory and rusted tin.

"Peace by sedation," he said. "That's what they're calling it in the newer white papers. You don't fight wars. You treat populations. Stabilize sentiment. Guide emotion. Recode memory through coherence architecture. No blood. Just beautiful compliance."

Cal took a sip, eyes narrowing. "Sounds like quantum psychiatry with better branding."

"It is. Strategic empathy, predictive harmony, trauma-informed deterrence. They're not trying to end conflict. They're trying to numb it out of the species."

"And Biff?"

"Either he believes it—or he's being leveraged. People like him are easy to seduce. Give them a doctrine to name and a room to brief it in. That's all it takes."

Cal exhaled through his nose. "Was that clause even ours? Or did it come straight from the Trust Cabal?"

Raveneh nodded. "Stability Protocol Delta. Buried in an annex to a resilience funding bill. It reads like diplomacy. What it really says is: don't disrupt coherence-sensitive zones, even if what's happening there breaks every operational law we have."

"So we don't touch the lattice."

"Because it's keeping people calm. Compliant. Contained."

Cal shook his head. "You think they know what this actually does?"

Raveneh tapped the Go board lightly.

"They know it works. That's enough. To question it would be to break the spell. And most spells, Mr. Merrick, are maintained not by magic—but by memory."

The Fog of Memory

The wind stirred the edge of the orchard. Somewhere nearby, a crow called twice and fell silent.

"They don't want to win the war," Cal said, slowly. "They want to edit it."

"Exactly." Raveneh took another stone. Held it. Didn't place it.

"And you think Lou still remembers enough to stop it?"

Raveneh's voice was almost reverent.

"Lou remembers differently. That's what makes her dangerous."

"We've seen only a few like her. They don't leave echoes — they absorb them."

"The system didn't fail to control Lou. It never could — because she was the error it couldn't model."

Cal leaned forward, elbows on knees. "And you think Lou still remembers enough to stop it?"

Raveneh didn't answer immediately. He turned the Go stone in his hand, slow, deliberate. Then:
"Again — she doesn't just remember. She remembers differently. That's what makes her very dangerous."

"The others like her? Rare. Hard to track. They don't erase echoes. They take them inside — fold them until nothing leaks back out."

"The system didn't fail to model Lou. It never could. Because she *was* the anomaly. The recursive fault. The error the lattice couldn't predict — or contain."

Cal sat back, trying to take it in. He wasn't sure if it was praise or prophecy.

And it threw him. So he did what operators do when the ground shifts: he reached for the battlefield he knew — language, patterns, threat vectors.

"So this isn't some bullshit hybrid warfare. It's not just a toolkit of dirty tricks and psychological ops. Why the hell aren't we calling it what it really is?"

Raveneh didn't answer right away. He looked at the fog curling around the trees like a living map.

Cal kept going. "The universe isn't linear. It's not built for doctrine. It's complexity. Complex adaptive systems. At its core? This is quantum-entangled conflict. Not war over land or code. War over memory. Over perception itself."

"Yes," Raveneh said quietly. "And the ones scripting it know that. That's why they're winning."

Cal stood, stretching his back. "Then I need to move. We've got cargo drifting toward Reykjavik—and a Helix packet route lighting up near Busan."

He didn't say the rest out loud.

These routes didn't rely on traditional internet or military comms. They moved through entangled nodes, misattributed routing paths, even civilian systems—smart cities, biometric sensors, neurotech relays. That's how Helix operated: bypassing oversight, weaving signal through the unnoticed seams of modern life.

And when a route lit up? It meant more than just movement. It meant something had been activated.

A new memory overwrite could be underway. A signal flare might've triggered biometric calibration in the field. Worse—if he was right—a Genesis-linked filament system had just come online.

Cal's stomach sank. This wasn't just a data transmission. It was a quantum VPN fused to a narrative warhead.

He thought about the metaphor like a soldier thinks about gear: the packet — compressed resonance and biometric intent; the route — non-standard, evasive, targeting entangled nodes; the Helix system — the orchestrator, Kael's domain, using coherence not to inform, but to conform.

He steadied himself. If Busan was flaring, Reykjavik would be next. And then… well, then they'd be out of time.

He checked his jacket—just enough reach to brush the grip of the Spectral SR-7, the unregistered sidearm Sylvester had funneled to him through a trade that involved whiskey, favors, and a container of banned microdrives. It was a heavily modified SR-25 derivative, tuned by Sylvester to operate in signal-disrupted terrain — designed for kinetic silence and optical deception. Fires clean, resets fast, and doesn't leave a digital signature.

Reliable. Silent. Meant for ghosts.

But this war?

This was a resonance flare riding a biometric fuse. A quantum warhead wrapped in comfort.

Raveneh remained seated, gaze on the board.

"The board hasn't changed," he said softly. "Only the stones have learned to lie."

Cal looked down. The fog had blurred the edges. The stones were vanishing one by one.

"No more blind eyes," he muttered. "If Biff's in this, we expose it. Or we end it."

Raveneh turned to him, eyes steady.

"But memory fights back."

Cal held the gaze for a beat, then turned and walked into the mist.

Behind him, Raveneh placed his final stone. Right at the edge. No territory. No capture. Just a marker.

Memory, anchored.

Chapter 9 Close — Lou's Reflection

"They'll say Marshall wasn't where the war began. Maybe not. But it was where the war remembered its shape. A bench. An envelope. A scar. Small things, but the lattice never cared about size. Every recurrence needs an anchor. Marshall was theirs.

That's the part we missed. Memory isn't fixed — it's terrain under reconstruction. They don't have to erase what you recall; they only have to shift the frame until your memory carries their meaning instead of yours. That's pattern anchoring. That's narrative fidelity. Kael's game: rebuild the architecture, and the truth becomes whatever the structure can hold.

And while we debate it, the Chamber keeps writing. In Go, the danger isn't losing stones — it's walking in circles while the board settles without you. Every turn gives them more time to lock the field.

We don't need to see the whole path. We just need to stop circling. The door's ahead, and the only move left is through it. Now."

Go Move — 十八目の呼吸 // Jūhachi-moku no Kokyū — The Breath Between Eighteen Points — General Zhen

羽根違い // Hanechigai — Crossed Hane

Zhen places the stone with deliberate care, bridging lines that seem too fragile to hold. Not for territory, but for tension — a cross-hane that resists collapse by inviting it.

Eighteen points form a visible shape; the breath between them is the shape unseen. That's where the danger lives — and the possibility.

Across the board, Liu tilts his head, reading the pressure lines. To answer is to close the gap. To leave it is to risk a breach.

The lattice counts what it can model. The General plays for what it cannot.
In that gap, memory resists rewriting. In that breath, doctrine can vanish.

Zhen's voice is barely audible:
"Do not rush to close it. Some spaces win by remaining open."

Chapter 10 — So, What's the Plan?

Tagline — "Some wars don't erase the past. They rewrite it." — *Solas*

Scene — The Chamber is Real
Location — Safehouse Location near Marshall, VA
Exclusion Zone Tier 2
Coherence Disruption Planning
Time: +7 Days post-Madison reactivation

The safehouse smelled like cedar, solder, and cold coffee. A generator hummed faintly outside. No digital trace, no lattice sync. Just old insulation and thick walls. The kind of place you used when you didn't want to be found—or remembered.

Lou dropped her satchel on the table. Glyph-9 flickered once and went quiet.

Cal and Jack followed her in. No words yet. Just the quiet calibration of veterans feeling for terrain, not conversation.

They didn't need words because they'd done this together for years, in theaters that didn't officially exist. Jack and Cal had walked point for Lou on a raid the Continuity Alliance still denied ever happened, a cold night in Diyarbakır when the three of them watched a chamber collapse from the inside out. That unsanctioned mission had cost them careers and given them scars — but it also taught them that Lou's instincts were worth more than any order. Their shared grit came from that night, and it was why they fanned out now without being asked.

On the wall, a battered corkboard. Lou pinned three red flags. One in the Arctic Circle. One near Diyarbakır. One hovering over a town that no longer existed on any official map: Madison, Virginia.

Jack tilted his head at the last pin. "Never heard of it."
Cal's eyes narrowed. "You wouldn't. They didn't just erase it from maps — they erased the memory of the maps."

"All right," she said. "Here's what we know."

One. The Chamber Is Real. It's Rebuilding Itself.

Jack raised an eyebrow. "Self-replicating tech?"

"Worse," Lou said. "Recursive systems. Once activated, the Genesis lattice seeks coherence. If pieces exist in the field, it starts to signal. Pulls in what it needs. Materials. Memories. Belief."

Cal folded his arms. "So it doesn't need blueprints. Just fragments."

Lou nodded. "And the right signal to stitch them together."

She tapped a hard drive on the table. "Vault 33A lit up two nights ago. Field 13A—already active. The third site is in transit. Filament array. Resonance core. It's all happening under diplomatic cover."

Two. People Are Collapsing. But Not Like You Think.

Jack leaned forward. "Define 'collapse.'"

"Not coma. Not catatonia. They walk, they talk. But their memory's wrong. Not missing—*wrong*."

Cal looked up sharply. "Fabricated?"

"Rewritten. People remembering wars that didn't happen. Families that never existed. One woman swore her husband died in Fallujah. He's alive. Never deployed. They have kids. She doesn't recognize them."

Jack exhaled. "They think it's psychosis."

"They think it's meds, trauma, neurodivergence. It's none of that. It's lattice-induced coherence overwrite. Memory guided by signal. Not suggestion. Not metaphor. Actual rewiring of the emotional map."

Cal: "Weaponized recall."

Lou: "More like programmable consent."

Three. The Mission Is Not to Destroy the Chamber. Not Yet.

She turned to the board.

"First objective: jam the signal. If we break the coherence pattern before full field lock, the system stalls."

Jack: "How?"

Lou: "Cold vector injection. Pulse a counter-narrative into the filament grid. Fragment the consensus layer before the field stabilizes."

Cal snorted. "That's a fancy way of saying: throw a wrench in it."

"Not a wrench," Lou corrected. "A memory. One they can't overwrite."

Four. We Need Everyone. And We Need to Move.

Lou handed out burner phones. No numbers. Just names.

"StepDoc has access. She's rerouting pediatric shipments flagged as 'behavioral calibration kits.' They're actually filament drives."

"Behavioral calibration kits," Cal repeated flatly. "That's the kind of phrase that should come with a blindfold and a last meal."

"Ledger is scrubbing the trail. Funding shells are clean for now. Wechsler and Pinot are prepping rigs. Salkin has the lab secured near Charlottesville."

Cal raised a hand. "What about Raveneh?"

Lou paused. "He says it's already too late for one node. Reykjavik is drifting. But he's found a weakness in the lattice symmetry. If we can exploit it before the Genesis core stabilizes, we can delay full coherence lock."

Jack muttered, "Delay. Not stop."

Lou nodded. "We buy time. Then we go for the chamber."

And, Five. Here's Who's Against Us.

Jack: "Helix?"

"Helix is the substrate. The system. But Sabine runs it. And she reports to The Trust."

Cal: "Post-national."

"Exactly. They don't want to win a war. They want to script reality. Rewrite memory at scale. Imagine a world where no one remembers resistance. Where every uprising becomes a riot, every victim a criminal, every collapse an act of stability."

Jack blinked. "And it's already started."

"Field 13A was just the rehearsal."

Final Plan — Phase One

The first move was to intercept the Arctic shipment, now rerouted through diplomatic channels; StepDoc would track it under a false medical manifest.

From there, the Greenland node had to be sabotaged — Wechsler still had access to the old rigs, possibly even the cryo facility once used in Cold Room Theta.

The lattice would then be looped, with Raveneh guiding the counter-memory anchor, a process that had to be seeded by hand.

Once that was set, Lou's bio-reactive Möbius ring — still reading clean — would be used to extract the uncorrupted signal. Jack called it instinct; Raveneh called it signal memory. With the Glyph-9's amplification, it could be broadcast globally through Red's rogue signal channel, a line that had once served as chaplain outreach and would now become their beacon.

Lou turned to them.

"This isn't about stopping a device. It's about saving the concept of memory. If we lose this, people won't even remember what freedom used to feel like."

Jack stood. "Then what are we waiting for?"

Cal checked the window. "I'll prep the truck."

Lou smiled faintly.

"Let's unwrite their script," Lou said. "And make them pause long enough to remember they once had one."

Scene — A Tremor in Transit
Location — Zurich Periphery | Unregistered courier loop

The clerk barely noticed him — an older man with a tremor, feeding coins into a tram kiosk that hadn't worked in years. By the time she looked again, he was gone. Only the folded slip he'd left in the return tray remained: a resonance formula scrawled in cramped script. The heading read: Replica Protection — Cold Atom Countermeasure.

In a back room across town, the page was already scanned, tagged, and pushed into Continuity's archive. His name wasn't on it. His cadence was. That was enough. A red mark slid onto a quiet list.

Eitan kept moving — Reykjavik next, then Busan. Ledger had threaded the routes so his trail looked like static. But Eitan knew the mirrorhounds didn't chase locations. They chased tremors.

And his tremor was getting worse.

Chapter 10 Close — Lou's Reflection

"The record didn't end with the lecture. It never does. Months later, when the Chamber surfaced in analysis briefs, the same fragments reappeared — half-copied notes, scraps of phrases, conviction carried in silence. The lattice thrived on drift. Belief doesn't need to be spoken twice; once it enters signal, the system makes it permanent.

Analysts thought they were just reviewing footnotes too thin to matter. They missed it. The Chamber never needed full doctrines. It traffics in residue — the unsaid words, the lines that keep carrying forward. That's informational drift. That's narrative fidelity. By then, the archive wasn't an accident. It was design.

And that's the danger. We keep thinking in missions — clean starts, clear ends. There are none. This isn't a fortress to assault; it's a mirror, writing our reflection the moment we look away. That's perception debt. By the time we notice, the field has already settled.

So we don't wait for clarity. We don't wait for the map. In Go, you never give them the endgame if you can still shape the middle. Same here. We move now, before they decide what we were."

Go Move — 石留めの間 // Ishidome no Ma — The Interval That Holds the Stone — General Liu

Liu plays into the corner, steady and unhurried. Not to seize. Not to defend. To hold.
A shape preserved by silence is still a shape.

The stone lands where drift cannot erase it, anchoring a memory others would let slip away. Ishidome no Ma is the interval that refuses collapse — a pause cut into the board, waiting until the pattern reveals itself.

The untrained will see hesitation.
The trained will see intent held in reserve — the promise that the game is not theirs to finish yet.

Across the board, Zhen's gaze lingers, unreadable.
Liu only says:
"Not every move is for today. Some are for what must remain."

Chapter 11 — Biff and the Broken Signal

Tagline — "The map is stable. Only the memory changed." — *General Weiss*

Watcher Dossier — Kael | The Architect of Control

General Weiss, known in the Helix network as Kael, embodies the unyielding spine of structure and order — a singular force shaping doctrine across centuries.
Kael thrives in systems. He rides the spine of doctrine and overlays of certainty, whispering in the ears of planners who mistake structure for foresight. His gift is clarity — deadly, elegant, false. Wherever maps grow dense and PowerPoint flourishes, Kael is already winning.

Before his Helix ascension, Kael served as a senior operations strategist inside the Continuity Alliance — long enough to learn where the seams were, and how to pull them. He aged out of formal service with honors, but not without a dependency on his neural interface — a precision-tuned plug that fed him bursts of lattice signal like an intravenous certainty drip. It kept him sharp, connected… and owned. That fix brought him back, quietly, to more than one closed-door Continuity Alliance briefing — not as an ally, but as a listener. A ghost in their war rooms.

In the Helix lattice, he found a longer horizon. The transhumanist enclaves called him a necessary evolution; his critics called him an abomination. Kael called himself inevitable.

He also understood something the Continuity Alliance never grasped: the Genesis Chamber wasn't a relic — it was infrastructure. And infrastructure has deadlines. Certain crates, certain filaments, had to be in place before the lattice locked into full symmetry. A few were moved under Biff Langley's signature, shipments he believed were his own idea. Kael never corrected him.

Kael appears in the algorithmic echoes of Biff's war models, reshaping doctrine into a feedback loop of denial. His signal drifts into staff briefings, into Signal Advisory Bureau for Longterm Equilibrium (SABLE) reports, into the smooth logic of doomed campaign plans. S.A.B.L.E. was founded after the Geneva Drift. It replaced the last generation of scenario modelers. SABLE does not issue white papers. It issues adjustments — to memory terrain, signal harmonics, and population patterning loops.

This is perfect for Kael.
His domain is Order — the kind that crystallizes just before it cracks.

Scene 0 — Strategic Spire, Continuity Grid Assembly Briefing Room

Tanner clicked through the briefing like a man explaining jazz to a metronome.

Slide: OPERATION FUTURE STABILITY
Global Campaign Architecture: 2225–2265
"Originally drafted in 2045," Tanner said, "but fully modernized for today's multi-signal battlespace."

A Resonance Intelligence Specialist muttered, "They're not planning for war. They're rehearsing obedience—and Biff still thinks he's the lead actor."

A junior aide leaned in, whispering,
"They'll name a doctrine after him. Posthumously. Probably misspell it."

Tanner gestured at a donut chart attempting to visualize belief saturation by region.

"Phase Two includes digital decoupling and belief elasticity metrics. The result? Forward optimism in contested zones."

Biff leaned back, nodding like a proud uncle at a science fair.

"That's deterrence elasticity," he said, voice smooth, as if he'd coined it.
He hadn't. But he knew how to brand it. And Tanner? Tanner was useful.

At the edge of the room, a tired Digital Air-Orbital Command (DAOC) colonel scribbled "WTF?" in the margin of his notepad.

Tanner kept beaming. "Sentiment volatility is an asset — if you know how to pre-calibrate the narrative."

Biff smiled wider. This was doctrine at its finest — abstract, unprovable, and absolutely salable.

Somewhere behind his eyes, he was already mapping other patterns — ones not shown on the screen.
Supply lines. Arctic routes. Old field IDs no one else believed still pulsed.

"Outstanding framework," Biff said aloud, tapping his tablet. "We'll shape this for flag-level brief."

He smiled to himself.
They had no idea he was already shaping something else entirely.

Biff checked his watch. Wheels up in two hours. Brussels by morning.
Or so the itinerary claimed.
The scar on his wrist told a different story.

Scene cut — Sabine's Surveillance Node

Sabine watched him nod through the stream. Eyes eager. Ego ripe. Perfect.

"He still thinks he's in control," she murmured.

Her aide adjusted the signal filter. Another Genesis crate had landed.

"Let him think it," Sabine said. "We need his enthusiasm."

On screen, Biff raised a hand.

"Let's get this in front of the Principals by Tuesday."

Sabine tapped the edge of the Helix lattice projection.

"Build the campaign, Biff. We'll build the terrain."

Scene — Sarajevo
Location — Abandoned Continuity Alliance Substation, Near Prizren

Biff Langley wasn't supposed to be here.
The flight manifest said Sarajevo — regional defense conference, quiet. A safe detour. But a scratched Continuity Alliance badge and a redacted line on his travel orders brought him further south. Prizren.
He was exhausted. Just hours earlier, he'd stood at the Strategic Spire's Continuity Grid Assembly podium. His Mons brief had gone well   he'd sold the doctrine he was supposed to sell. And now this. A detour. An omen. Why here, of all places — and why now?

He hadn't been back to Kosovo since he was a young Major. The terrain felt older now. Or maybe just more honest.

The substation hadn't mattered in years. Just enough residual traffic to justify maintenance logs. Enough latency to keep the budget alive.

Now it was humming.

Not metaphorically.

The scar on his wrist pulsed — not pain, but syncopation. Like a haptic metronome from another war. A beat he hadn't heard since Field 13A lit up and nearly killed Jack.

He keyed open the hatch and ducked inside.

The field console was bolted to a rusted crate, still wired to a Cold War junction box. The screen flared, jittered, and stabilized.

Madison was dark. Vaulted. No signal since the Chamber folded. And yet — the scar never lied.

He didn't touch the panel. Just stared. Then scanned the ceiling.
Blink.
A drone lens. Old. Active.
Second blink.

Someone was watching.

He didn't call Jack. He couldn't. Not after Geneva — and not after Kosovo. Years earlier, on a night just like this outside Prizren, he had hit the extraction timer ten minutes ahead of schedule, leaving Jack and Cal fighting through collapsing tunnels when Field 13A lit up.

They'd made it out, but they never forgot who'd been missing from the last transport. Geneva had only widened the crack that started there. Biff felt it now in the pulse at his wrist, a reminder that Jack knew exactly how much doctrine he was willing to hide behind.

He toggled a secure burst. Geneva.
Sabine.

SIGNAL: REACTIVATED | FIELD 13A |

He stepped back.

This wasn't mission protocol. This was something else.
And it had followed him.

He looked at his wrist.
Still pulsing.

Lou was in the field.
Jack would know.

And if Jack was watching too—
Biff might not make it out of Kosovo alive.

What Biff didn't understand:
He thought the war had gone dormant.

But coherence doesn't sleep.

It remembers.

Scene — Mirrorhound Report
Location — Shanghai Lattice Relay

A quiet alert flickered in Sabine's peripheral stack. Not Lou. Not Jack. Not Cal.
Eitan.

The mirrorhounds tagged his cadence near Zurich. Then again in Reykjavik. Always just off-pulse, like he was daring them to predict him. The aide frowned. "Should I escalate?"
Sabine shook her head. "No. He's not destabilizing terrain. He's hunting something."
The aide hesitated. "Replica shielding. Cold atom antidote tech. If he finds it—"
Sabine silenced him with a glance.
"If he finds it, he'll live long enough to hand it to Lou. That's the danger."

Scene — Tuning Forks
Location — Lou's cabin, near the Rapidan River

The fire had gone out, but Lou hadn't noticed. The table was a mess: filament coils, half-drunk Douwe Egberts, too much coconut sugar, and hand-sketched signal lattices.

Her **Möbius ring** — a repurposed bio-reactive sensor lattice — pulsed gently across her palms. Not erratic, but rhythmic. A looped signal remembering its path.

She shifted the ring into resonance mode. It hummed — a strike without sound, a calibration the field answered back.

On the table lay an older tool: a resonance fork, once issued for lattice calibration, its grip worn smooth. Not a weapon. An interface. Doctrine's attempt to tune what it never understood.

Tools could be repurposed — but only if you unlearned what they were designed to do.
Her instructors had said: *Wait for validation. Follow the plan.*

That was a doctrinal mind.
She needed a quantum mind.

Responsive. Attuned. Capable of sensing when the terrain itself was alive.
     She didn't need a new weapon.
She needed calibration — to triangulate intent, emotion, and pattern drift.
Not just threat vectors.

     A doctrine-trained soldier asks: *"Is it permitted?"*
A quantum warrior asks: *"Is it true?"*

     She struck the fork against the Möbius ring.
It rang once.
Then again — harmonic, perfect, aligned.
     The node wasn't just active. It was remembering.
     Lou closed her eyes.

Lesson logged: A quantum warrior retools the known to navigate the unknown.
She opened them again. The fire was ash. The cabin cold. But the field was alive — and so was she.

     Retirement was a story for those who believed wars ended. She knew better. The signal never stopped.

     She reached for the satphone and dialed a number that bypassed every known system.

     Ray picked up on the third click. His voice still carried that gravelly edge from the winter in Grozny — the one neither of them talked about anymore. Once, he'd been the doctrinal golden boy, a field architect trusted to seed stability corridors from Kabul to Kinshasa. Until he read the wrong lattice wrong — or maybe exactly right — and pulled an entire brigade out of a Helix killbox without authorization.

     The official report called it *"a procedural misalignment."* Lou called it the day Ray stopped serving systems and started serving the truth.
     They hadn't spoken in six months. Not because of distance. Because every time they talked, someone else listened.

     "Ray. It's Lou. I need spectral returns from Zurich, sentiment overlays from Singapore, and a burner drone sweeping Kosovo in thirty."

"I'm seeing emotion-indexed homework assignments. Teachers became compliance drones. And they didn't lose Zurich — they deleted dissent."

Lou waited, letting the thought settle. Calculated the cost of her next move.

"Mirror Protocol only. If Helix gets a whiff — let them chase the wrong node."

Scene — Sabine and The Shifting Lattice
Location — Shanghai – Zhongguancun Core Node, Beijing

The lattice trembled. Not a quake. A drift.

Sabine felt it first in her peripheral vision — a blurring of edge states, a shimmer in the biometric returns like static laced with intention. Her breath slowed. Her fingers stilled. She was no longer watching the data. She was *inside* it.

She stepped toward the primary Helix console — no command required. The substrate recognized her presence, reshaping the data field into active coherence overlays. She didn't speak. It listened anyway.

Madison should have been dark. Folded. Vaulted. The Chamber sealed.

And yet — Lou's pattern had returned.

Sabine tapped a sequence into the glass disk suspended between her hands. The screen pulsed faintly. One red strand flared to life, then another — Kosovo. Zurich. Reykjavik. "Flag Llewellyn's expense cadence. Reykjavik shell: PBS."

She turned to her aide. "Inject a false resonance along the lunar relay net. Minimal signature. Watch for mirroring."

Do it, she replied. "The Reykjavik Sentiment Wellness Update turned protests into 'community alignment events.' The city didn't revolt. It rebranded."

The deputy hesitated. "Ma'am... Mirror Protocols haven't run live since Singapore."

Sabine's jaw tightened. "Lou remembers."

Onscreen, a lattice strand snapped, recomposed, and redirected — through Busan. Then another — Vault 33A pattern clusters.

The deputy whispered, "We're in recursive echo."

Sabine didn't blink. "Of course we are."

She lifted the disk. Threads of coherence unfurled like roots finding water.

She whispered to the Helix core, "If Lou's reawakened, she'll move between signals. Mirror, echo, memory. Her pattern is Go — not chess. She doesn't play pieces. She shapes *potential*."

Sabine allowed herself a small, private smile.
They still didn't understand.
Not Lou, not even Kael — and certainly not the men with medals still dreaming in PowerPoint.

She opened a side archive — an old war theory file she kept for amusement.
Not a strategy guide. A warning.
A note on **shi** — the shaping of latent force. The art of setting conditions so skillfully that victory becomes inevitable before contact is made. Shi wasn't maneuver. It wasn't mass. It was momentum without motion — the field tilted before the first move.

And Biff?

He was perfect.

"He thinks he's shaping victory," she murmured.
"But I'm using him to shape ignorance."

Let him brief the Continuity Alliance.
Let him draw maps of wars that won't happen, chart regions that no longer behave, teach war colleges how to memorize terrain that's already evaporated.

While they stare at models…
She would shape the field beneath them.

Not with weapons.
With silence. With latency. With inevitability.

That was her war.

He was already fighting for the wrong side —
he just didn't know it yet.

Scene — Lou's Doctrine by Slide Deck
Location — Rapidan River Cabin, Virginia
(Shortly after Mirror Protocol Initiation)

The Mirror Protocol was risky, but Lou had no choice. Pulling "current" war doctrine carried its own hazards—heretics didn't last long in this era. Eitan had warned her years ago: *Mirror signals are only safe if the origin pattern knows itself. Run it blind and you risk collapse—or worse, waking the wrong observer.* Ray's version had been blunter: *You don't run it unless you're ready to write a second version of yourself and watch it walk into traffic.*

Now she sat at the cabin, slide deck open, reviewing the doctrine already moving through the Continuity Assembly—a glossy mix of sentiment metrics and deterrence gamification. Kael's work. Clear, confident, and fatally wrong. Lou wasn't here to win that war. She was here to pull the ground out from under it.

She read the slides aloud, annotating as she went.

"If you speed up a broken model, you just fail faster," she wrote. *Compressing decision loops without changing how you think doesn't make you smarter—it just makes you more efficient at being wrong.*

AI doctrine, she noted, was still optimizing stale, force-on-force, platform-centric models. New dice, same board.
Another slide: *Future land headquarters will be smaller and decentralized… Command Post Crucibles.*

Lou shook her head. "Dress rehearsal for the last war—with bots instead of boots." Smaller HQs meant nothing if the doctrine feeding them was still Newtonian. Predictive control remained the star. Bulk replaced with bandwidth.

Next: *Militaries must innovate or die.*

"Innovate toward what?" she muttered. Shinier drones and faster targeting weren't the point. The real fight was over belief, memory, signal integrity—who shapes the story beneath the data.

More slides: cost-per-kill, campaign models, multi-domain simulations.
"They're simulating futures while ignoring the nonlinear present," she noted. None accounted for what happened when the public stopped

believing, or when the signal collapsed and no one remembered why the war had started.

A diagram of unmanned networks promised *persistent surveillance.* Lou scrolled past. "They're describing battlespaces like humans aren't the primary vector anymore." Not a word about psycho-emotional signature warfare, resonance manipulation, or algorithmic belief targeting—only airframes and acoustic nets.

Final straw: *Advanced analytics will deliver unprecedented insight.*

"This isn't transformation," Lou typed. "It's recursion in a shinier suit. You can't spreadsheet your way to coherence. You have to feel it."

She closed the tablet. The Mirror Protocol's echo still hummed in her mind. They'd built a lattice of perfect decisions on a rotting moral floor.

Lou leaned back, wondering—not for the first time—how many people would die before someone tore up the playbook.

Scene — Cal Merrick and the Maritime Track
Location — Somewhere west of Crete — Aboard the covert vessel Vanta Echo

The sea was calm, but the comms weren't. Cal Merrick knelt beside the forward bulkhead, tools splayed across a pelican case, his attention fixed on the biometric scan returning from the lower cargo hold. The signature matched $\nabla\Omega\Delta$ — the same resonance glyphs burned into the casing recovered from Vault 33A. Only this wasn't ice-locked. It was in motion.

"The crate had pinged a resonance spike — low amplitude, high fidelity. Not enough to trip satellites, but something in the loop felt… duplicated. Echoed. Like a signal trying not to be noticed."

The reading wasn't just external. Something resonated in him — a shadow of rhythm against his ribs, like the Möbius ring Lou once showed him. This wasn't standard signal. This was something that remembered.

He stood, adjusted the strap across his shoulder, and slid the suppressed CZ P-07 into his waistband. He hadn't meant to keep it. But the man in Heraklion had asked for antibiotics — and Cal had two extra vials of doxycycline in his med pouch.

Lou would be proud, he thought. Saved a life. Got a gun. All organic trade.

Below deck, a mechanical clunk echoed near the starboard hold. Not the kind you ignored.

There it was again — a whispered phrase in Cal's head. Could've been muscle memory. Could've been a residual imprint from the resonance glyphs.

"Kael doesn't watch. He listens."

He wondered if that meant Kael already knew about this crate — or if, worse, Kael had made sure it was here.

He activated a soft drone, swept it toward the bay, then opened a low-band encrypted ping to Ledger:

Need funding release — Zurich node — ops priority tag AEON-17. Cargo is real. Movement expected. Prepare contingency route via Norfolk or Aberdeen.

A second message went out to Eitan, ghosted through a classified relay node:

If I go dark, tell Lou I followed the signal. The old one. From the Chamber's breath.

He pulled the hatch lever slowly.

Below him, something metal shifted against the crate.

Then… the crate shifted back.
Not from gravity. Not from tilt.
As if it knew it was being watched.

Chapter 11 Close — Lou's Reflection

"Biff's problem isn't that he can't see the board. It's that he's staring at a board Kael already drew for him. Every move fed like candy, sweet enough to feel like strategy, empty enough to keep him blind. That's not insight. That's Signal Trust — belief accepted before evidence, doctrine swallowed because it feels right in the moment.

Kael knows what he's doing. Vector Doctrine: tilt Biff's direction just enough and the rest follows. Whole commands march on his false map. And we waste time arguing over his notes while the field keeps tightening.

Crates don't shift themselves. If the cargo's alive, so is the trap. That's the part doctrine never said out loud: logistics can lie. A container can be a signal anchor, not supply. By the time you debate it, the frame has already locked around you.

In Go, the only answer sometimes is to flip the table. Refuse the board they've drawn. That's the move Biff will never see coming — the only move that keeps us ahead. Which means we don't stay here. We move now, before the trap writes us in."

Go Move — 挟撃 // Kyōgeki — The Pincer Attack — General Zhen

Zhen sets one stone, steady at the axis — a point of gravity the board cannot ignore.

Then another falls, angled and distant, quiet enough to appear harmless.

The frame begins to close. Not a strike, not yet — but the pressure of two hands shaping the same silence.

Kyōgeki is the trap that doesn't declare itself. One move anchors, the other misleads.

To the untrained, it looks like symmetry.

To the trained, it is restriction disguised as choice.

Across the board, Liu studies the shape with a slow exhale.

"You've left him an opening," he says.

Zhen only replies:

"Openings close fastest when they believe they found them."

Chapter 12 — Ice Transit

Tagline — "Some cargo doesn't carry signal. It carries the illusion of choice." — *Dr. Raveneh*

Scene — Vault Echo Transit Record

C-03 belonged to no manifest and no man, though Kael had signed its route years before anyone knew to look. It was one of the first pieces seeded for the Chamber — shipped not as a weapon, but as part of its spine. Few outside the lattice knew it existed. One of them wore a general's stars — and a smile meant for planners who thought they'd mapped the route themselves.

Crate C-03
Seal Date: March 3, 2025
Operation Code: Echo Substrate
Initial Field Use: Samarkand Trials, April 2026
Archived: Tashkent, 2034
Reflagged: Reykjavik Transit Node, 2077
Lost in Inventory: Cartagena Uplink Failure, 2112
Resurfaced: Vault Echo Relay Cache, 2193
Recovered in Transit: Arctic Route Zeta / Classified, 2225

"Consent Induction Prototype Series."

Now, two centuries later, the crate was back in motion — loaded aboard a Helix-controlled ice transport running under diplomatic cargo exemption. The manifest listed it as "cultural preservation equipment," routed through Reykjavik before transfer to an unlisted Greenland node. The courier crew didn't ask questions; their pay came from Continuity Alliance credits routed through three shell ministries. Whoever signed for it would disappear from public rosters within a week.

That was the trick with Vault Echo freight: it never stayed buried. Every time the world thought it had lost the trail, the substrate surfaced again — same crate, same signal, new war.

Some knew that the early prototypes were spun up in Macau, when they tried embedding quantum memory into elastic substrates. The idea was simple: if coherence drift can't be stopped, catch it in something pliable. Let the field bend, not break.

Beneath its frost-scabbed seals, Crate C-03 was older than any of them — half-frozen, continuity-wrapped, and marked only with the stamped emblem: ∇.

The record showed its first reappearance decades earlier, on a frozen steppe with no coordinates. A truck idled beside a modular sled, its engine coughing through cold reluctance. Two figures in parkas worked the crate by hand — no drones, no signal.
"This one never logged through inventory. Off-books since Tashkent," the older man said.

The younger man, gloves frayed, hesitated. "You think it's still live?"
"Doesn't matter. The pattern's recursive."

They pried open the lid.
Inside: signal rounds, matte-black cylinders engraved with phase-shift resonance glyphs. A recessed node pulsed faintly — not enough to radiate, just enough to remember.
Scratched into the inner lid in faded ink: *Perception is architecture. Embed accordingly.*

Later — in Lisbon, or somewhere quieter — Pinot's voice carried over the cold recall.
"They were illegal even then. Firmware signatures were outlawed after Sinop."

Cal leaned closer to the relogged crate. "I thought these were banned."
"They were," Pinot said. "Then someone needed deniability."

They closed the lid. Didn't speak again for twenty-three minutes.

Pinot's jaw worked under his scarf, like a man chewing on a thought he'd rather spit out than share.
Cal tapped the frost with a gloved finger — not testing the seal, just needing to touch something forbidden.

From deep in the system logs, a ghost tag reappeared:
C-03 / Echo Substrate / Consent Harmonization Unit

That ghost never stayed buried. Decades later, on the other side of the world, someone else was watching the same substrate ripple back to life.

By the time the crate cleared Prague, its echo had already bled into the markets. In Mason Neck, one screen lit before the rest.

Scene — Maud in Mason Neck

She still used Valentine for her brokerage work — a name Eitan had pressed into use years ago, and one Lou had reinforced after too many quiet warnings. Just enough ice between her and the Helix net.

Maud leaned back in the leather chair, the glow of three monitors flickering against the paneled glass. Beyond the trees, the Potomac shifted in silence — slow, tidal, indifferent. Georgetown had been efficient. Mason Neck was quieter. And harder to triangulate.

Maud Llewellyn Scott — daughter of the woman who once told her never to trust a headline or a heartbeat in sync — was watching something stranger than volatility.

An algorithmic shimmer rippled across three micro-indexes. Cryo-stabilized quantum substrates. Coherence-buffered composites. All spiking.

And one more line item, buried deeper, stopped her cold. Phase-Buffer Shell. The ledger listed it as "therapeutic resonance array," bundled in with wellness bonds and biotech trials. But the transfer amounts were wrong. Too small for hospitals. Too big for research. This wasn't clinical. It was covert procurement.

She zoomed out, traced the money across Continuity subledgers. One Zurich tick. One Reykjavik transfer. Same cadence.

Eitan's cadence.

Her throat tightened. Of course it was him. The old man was still moving, still bleeding expenses into the same off-books rhythm he'd used for decades. And now he was chasing the one thing no one else remembered existed: the Resonance Shielding Array (RSA) — the portable lattice-buffer that could stabilize neural patterns inside a coherence storm.

Without it, anyone entering a cold atom vault or the Chamber itself risked overwrite. With it, maybe — just maybe — they could walk out whole.

She didn't write his name. She never would.

She opened an encrypted shell, hesitated, then typed:

To: [unknown.sec.node]
Subject: Silent Spike in Sector Theta?

Spotted something weird. Thought of you.
—M

No flair. Just a candle flick in the dark — enough to warn, not to burn.

Then she added, almost as an afterthought:
The trending terms were all clean: trust the science, trust the signal. But the spike said otherwise. Coherence manipulation isn't science. It's scripting perception and calling it consensus.

She stopped there. Thought of Lou. Thought of Eitan. Deleted three more words she almost wrote.

Somewhere south, in a house where terminals were never trusted, the same flicker reached JR in the form of paper, not pixels.

Scene — JR: Charlottesville, Virginia

JR lit another cigarette with the last one.
He didn't do terminals. Or dashboards. He did paper — and whatever leaked from places people forgot to lock.

Lou's message had arrived cryptic and brief:
"Maud clocked something. Can you confirm? Prague manifest, Vault-class. "

JR froze mid-drag. *Maud.* And behind her numbers, a cadence he knew too well — Eitan's. The way funds moved through Reykjavik, the way cover codes bent toward medical jargon. Phase-Buffer Shell. Only he would chase that kind of antidote tech.

He'd known her before the Chamber, before the Cabal, back when Lou was still pretending she could raise a daughter without the war bleeding into her life. He and Jack had both worked to keep it that way.

Valentine was the name Eitan had pressed into use years ago — Lou had carried it forward after too many quiet warnings. For JR, it was more than an alias; it was a layer of ice between Maud and the kind of people he'd spent his life hiding her from.

Others had noticed things Lou never mentioned — the tilt of Maud's head, the eyes that didn't quite match hers but echoed somewhere familiar. JR never asked. Some answers weren't his to carry.

If Maud was flagging Vault-class now, she was either in deep by choice… or someone had pulled her in. Either way, it meant trouble.

Jack scratched the side of his jaw, reached behind a crate of Army Field Manuals, and pulled out a laminated map — edges curled, ink faded, still annotated in grease pencil. Continuity Alliance customs lanes, rerouted in the Post-Consent Renewal Era — long after the world began its mandatory health injection cycles, traded in for the promise of immunity from each "once-in-a-lifetime" pandemic.

The code matched something from 2009 — a ghost protocol flagged under Project Vault Echo. Supposed to be shuttered after the Signal Mirror collapse. Supposed to be forgotten. Not this week.

Jack's NLCB pulsed once, initiating a visual interface layer — not real-time, just a simulated overlay designed to parse container telemetry from pre-coherence archives. An echo of old tools, threaded through disdain. He made one call.

Jack made one call.

"Jack. JR here. Tell Lou they're moving coherence gear as climate freight. Marked for Vault Echo Reclamation. Out of Prague. It's headed north, and someone thinks we won't notice."

Pause. Jack didn't wait for a reply. He trusted JR to keep moving.

"Not tech," JR muttered. "Looks more like they're moving obedience."
The names changed, the syringes didn't.

Jack liked to joke that everyone still lined up for their "juice fix" — only now it came through neural ports, wrapped in health metrics and wellness scores, tracking more than just the body.

Jack thought otherwise. *Simply put,* he told himself. *It was Consent on the move.*

Scene — Watcher Cutaway:
Location — Berlin, Germany

And in Berlin, the lattice pulsed as if it had heard the same words.

Inside the Cold War bunker beneath Berlin, Gen. Henrik Weiss — Watcher Kael — stared at the coherence lattice as if it were misbehaving.

The air in the Berlin node was colder than the stone that held it.

One crate. Just one. Flagged out of sequence. Vault Echo. Prague origin.

He tapped his index finger once, twice, then whispered, "Someone's tracing the recursion line… They shouldn't be that fast."

The lattice pulsed red — a recursion flare warning.
Kael didn't flinch. He moved a token on his tabletop map — a matte Go stone with a brass underside — and placed it in Iceland.

"Send noise," he murmured. "Let Vire scramble the frame. We need distraction, not deletion."

The room dimmed as the system logged a new directive:
FIELD DIVERGENCE MASKING ACTIVE

JR exhaled. "They're not moving tech. They're moving consent — one calibrated shipment at a time."

He leaned closer to the map. "Coherence isn't some New Age thing. It's how systems lock together — fields, minds, bodies, nations. You bend that, you don't need tanks. You just shift the pattern until people believe what serves the signal."

"We didn't fracture because we disagreed," he added quietly. "We fractured because we were fed the same script — but different roles. Every side thinks it's the hero. That's how coherence war works."

Signals bled north, but Jack was watching the same arc from a van where the only heater was sarcasm.

**Scene — Coherence Warfare doesn't invade
Location — Undisclosed**

Jack sat cross-legged in his van, the same cracked laptop humming beside a half-eaten protein bar. He cross-referenced JR's tip with an encrypted satellite ping.

Thermal flare off Greenland. Arctic-bound cargo from Prague. Seal design matched old Helix bio-containment wraps.

He tapped a key. The live market window bloomed: synthetic coherence futures — up 437%. Silent.

"Either someone's about to launch a luxury cryo line," he muttered, "or they're bottling belief and front-running the war after the war — the one fought over what we're allowed to remember."

We'd spent a century designing weapons to break bones and bunkers. This bypassed all of it. It wasn't about kinetic wins. It was about narrative possession. If you control memory — what people think happened, what they feel is true — you don't need soldiers. You just re-code the past until obedience feels like patriotism.

"That's why no one's framing this war right," he said under his breath. "The Generals are still drawing campaign plans on whiteboards, waiting for missiles. Meanwhile, the real battlefield's in cached files, deleted posts, rewritten source code, and neural lacing so subtle people swear it was their own idea."

He remembered a chart Maud once scrawled on — volatility cushioned, collapse delayed. *'Same principle,' Maud had written in the margin, 'but for belief instead of money.'* The foam wasn't padding. It was an archive.

Coherence warfare doesn't invade. It inhabits. It wins by promoting what people are supposed to believe next. Different game entirely.

"They shut down dissent with fake consensus," Jack added. "No conspiracy needed — just a good dashboard and enough behavioral sync. Make everyone afraid of being wrong at the same time, and they'll believe anything."

He sent two texts:

From: Jack
To: Cal

Transit box active. Signal mirrored. Tracking North. Coherence spike confirmed.

From: Jack
To: Lou

Maud lit a candle. JR found the fuse. The box is real. It's moving.

Scene — The Watcher on the Bridge
Location — Ice Transit Convoy, Greenland Interior

The convoy paused near a ridge, out of visual range from any satellite with a thermal profile under sixty seconds.

No names. No rank. No chatter. Just quiet confirmation that the crate had not fractured — its resonance still contained. Inside: a quantum memory module — one of many, each tuned to a different frequency of belief. Together, they formed the Chamber's spine.

Lou brushed her hand against the crate's lining. It wasn't fabric. It wasn't polymer. The surface flexed, then stilled — like it remembered the touch.

Cal crouched, pressing a knuckle against the dark weave. "Quantum memory substrate," he muttered. "Think of it like foam, but every cell holds a phase state instead of air."

Jack raised an eyebrow. "Translation: it remembers what reality feels like."

Cal smirked. "More or less. Standard memory chips store bits — on or off, ones and zeros. This stuff stores coherence itself. A phase imprint. Drop it in the Chamber and it doesn't just record the story — it replays the resonance of how belief was held in that moment."

Jack flicked a piece with his fingernail. It shimmered, then pulsed back like a heartbeat. "So instead of remembering words or images, it remembers *certainty*. The weight people gave to an idea. The way a crowd bent when it believed."

"Exactly," Cal said. "Helix runs on that fidelity. If you can plug a substrate like this into the Chamber, you're not feeding it data — you're feeding it lived conviction. That's what it models. That's what it weaponizes. "

Jack let out a low whistle. "So not memory foam for your back. Memory foam for reality."

Cal's jaw tightened. "And it never forgets."

Jack rubbed his temple. "Call it quantum knitting — tug a stitch, and the whole sweater reconfigures. Only difference is, here the shapes are entangled into patterns we never planned but can't stop wearing." He snorted. "Like one of Nana's Christmas sweaters — sleeves too long, neck too tight, and no way out once it's on."

Cal didn't smile. "Exactly. Once it's on, it wears you." He paused, then added dryly: "And if Lou ever takes up knitting or embroidery, just hand her a paint kit instead. Safer for all of us."

The hum deepened, low and resonant, as if the material had caught a signal leaking from somewhere deeper. Then — movement. A shadow at the far end of the corridor.

A tall, thin man stepped out.

He came around from the second snowcrawler, parka unzipped despite the cold. His breath fogged once, then stopped.

He wasn't in command. He gave no orders. But the others looked at him like gravity.

A technician gestured toward the sealed container. "It's stable. No signal leak."

The man crouched, bare hand pressed to the frost-hardened surface. He stayed like that for a breath, then murmured:
"She's awake."
"And he's listening again."

He rose.

Another figure approached — younger, nervous.
"Sir… are we proceeding with Echo harmonization?"

The man didn't answer right away. His gaze lingered on the pale horizon. A faint glow flickered in his eyes — not digital, not retinal. Something older. Refracted.

Finally:
"Tell the others the illusion of choice is intact."
Then, almost as an afterthought:
"But make no mistake — Lou Scott is no longer off-script."

Scene — Above the Ice

Altitude: classified.
Orbit: drift-stabilized.
Platform: listed as commercial research payload — but no academic journal ever cited it.

A black capsule hung suspended in silence, tethered only by inertial calm and orbital drift. No radio echo. No thermal bloom. Just a thin coating of cryo-bonded mesh designed to scatter satellite sweeps. Like the convoy below, it carried no markings. Just another shard of memory, waiting to be slotted into place.

A resonance lattice core — one of the spine segments the Chamber couldn't live without. Waiting.

The cargo wasn't meant to detonate. It was meant to *arrive unseen.*

From below, the launch would register as standard debris drop or cloud sensor calibration. But when the time came, Sabine would align orbital parameters to the Arctic corridor. No customs. No politics. No record.

Just a descent corridor wrapped in weather, engineered to bypass both human and machine intent.

Then a voice — synthetic, no origin trace:

"No borders in vacuum. Just vectors. Drop approved."

But the Chamber's spine was never built in one place. It was stitched across earth and orbit alike

Scene — Cal Merrick: En Route to Lisbon
Location — Surrey Periphery – Oxshott, England

While memory fell through vacuum, Cal moved through hedgerows, hunting a lane the lattice wouldn't see.

Before Lisbon, there was a detour — through mist-laced fields and lanes too narrow for anything but memory. The route to the Chamber's spine wasn't straight, and this stop was one of the quiet bends.

Oxshott was more myth than town now. Lacrosse banners still clung to the fences of elite prep schools. Estate gates whispered of old money and older codes.

This wasn't a place for tourists. It was a place for those who knew where the shadows pooled.

"You know you're in Oxshott when the gossip column has more geopolitical intel than MI6 ," Cal muttered.

Cal stepped off the South Western line at the Oxshott station — a low stone platform shaded by clipped hedges. He made a right turn down Sheath's Lane, a narrow county road that once serviced brickworks linked to Oxshott's 19th-century brickyard operations. The old footbridge that spans three tracks—remnants of the same brickyard line—still looms faintly to those who know where to look.

He adjusted his pack and began walking the county lane north, past riding trails and school crests that gleamed faintly under morning mist. They'd all worn blazers here once — even the daughters of oligarchs.

He passed the outer fence of a school he'd heard about in whispers: Crownmere Hall for Girls — once a finishing school for diplomats' daughters, now a global preparatory haven with tuition figures that defied currency.

It was said that Latin, fencing, and both piano and violin lessons were still required, and that its alumni held more diplomatic influence than the UN Security Council.

The school sat atop a hill with a curved Georgian facade, stone lions at the gate, and ivy that never seemed to brown.

Somewhere in the folds of Cal's memory, or maybe from one of Ray's old briefings, he recalled a rumor: Lou had gone to school near here — maybe even at Crownmere Hall under a different name.

He tried to imagine her then: young, sharp, a half-smile during Latin declensions, eyes always scanning.

Maybe she already moved like she does now — never straight across the quad, always diagonals, like she was playing Go on the paving stones. Teachers thought it was eccentric. Rivals thought it was arrogance. Lou just thought it was the fastest way to see what others missed.

What would it have been like? Lacrosse matches at twilight. Tea served before recitations of Rousseau and Rilke. Old school chums who still summered in Provence and hosted fundraisers no one tracked.

He shook off the thought.

The pub sat just over the ridge. Modest by appearance, fortified by reputation. It was said to be the kind of place where conversations didn't echo, and where the ale hadn't changed in 200 years.

Inside, behind a half-drawn curtain, waited a man who still went by "Harrow."

Old regiment. Quiet hands. Quiet life.

They didn't shake hands. Just nodded.

"You didn't come for a pint," Harrow said.

Cal slid a slip of paper across the worn oak table. Not a message. A list.

"Lisbon?" Harrow asked.

Cal nodded. "But they'll be watching signal lanes. I need a pattern break — an off-grid handoff."

Harrow studied the list. "Some of these haven't been tapped since Kandahar."

Cal replied, "That's the point."

"You'll owe favors."

"I already do."

They left separately. No trace. Just the smell of old varnish and a rugby match playing behind the bar.

Outside, the hedgerows shimmered in low fog. The school bell rang faintly from behind the trees.

Cal glanced back once — not toward the pub, but toward the school crest on the iron gate.
He didn't know who Lou had been back then. But he knew who she was now. And whatever they were building… Harrow had just given him the lane to move a piece where no one was watching.

Scene — Arctic Handoff: Vault Echo Seal

Wind cut across the flat expanse like a blade. In the shadow of a retired research outpost, five men in black parkas offloaded a single container.

No markings. Just a soft low-frequency hum.

Inside: a cryo-vector chamber, triple-sealed and coded to Helix-lattice resonance. Not a weapon. Not yet.

A single click echoed as the lid locked. A snowcrawler rolled away without headlights.

Somewhere in a warm city, a Go stone clacked.

And in Georgetown, Maud looked up from her screen and whispered:

"They're not mining ore.
They're mining memory."

Lou had said it once, years ago, when Maud was still too young to understand. Now she did.

Far north, where cold erased tracks faster than men could leave them, the handoff began.

Chapter 12 Close — Lou's Reflection

"Crates like C-03 aren't cargo. They're bones of the Chamber, sealed in ice to keep their script intact. Every seal is a verdict, a story someone else wants told exactly their way. The first time one cracked, the crew at 33A never walked out. That wasn't logistics. That was memory weaponized as freight.

Doctrine keeps treating crates as supply lines. They're not. They're memory frames. Open one and you're not just moving freight — you're giving the field the right to write you in. And the lattice never writes happy endings.

Kael counts on that. Sabine too. Kael routes the cargo. Sabine counts on hesitation — agency drift. Wait long enough and the decision isn't yours anymore; the crate decides for you. That's the trap.

In Go, you don't linger in a dead corner. Every pause just locks in their territory. Same here. Don't linger. Don't hesitate. The only move is forward — before the seal decides who we are."

Go Move — 封じ手 // Fūjite — Sealed Move — General Zhen

Zhen's hand hovered above the board, then withdrew. Instead of placing the stone, he slid a folded slip of paper across the wood.

Liu frowned. "A sealed move?"

"The game doesn't pause," Zhen said. "But sometimes the board must."

"You would lock the frame before you even know its answer?"

Zhen set his stone aside, voice calm. "Not to win ground. To still it. To keep the field from writing itself too fast."

Outside, the rain slowed. Between them, the board held its breath.

Liu tapped the paper once, not opening it. "Sealed moves aren't speed. They're certainty."

"Or silence," Zhen replied. "The kind that suffocates without a sound."

The board remained unchanged, but both knew the shape had shifted.

Chapter 13 — The Summit Below the Ice

Tagline — *"The illusion was built above the ice. But the memory survived beneath it." — Dr. Raveneh*

Duality is key. On the surface, they present as charismatic futurists, visionaries of peace and progress. But underneath? They're coherence manipulators, transhuman tacticians — smiling while they orchestrate global control through belief, not bullets.

Trap disguised as utopia

Scene — Surface Illusion: The Cabal Convenes
Location — Svalbard Global Dialogue Forum

The room shimmered with subcoherence rhythm. Gentle harmonic waves threaded through the nutrient-enriched air, enough to nudge belief vectors without tripping neural suspicion. Above ground, the old sign still read SVALBARD SEED VAULT. The world still thought it was a vault for seeds. In a way, it was. Just not the kind anyone could plant. Even here, 100 meters down, the floor still carried the cold weight of ice above. Inside, it was something else entirely.

A former glacier tunnel had been transformed into a hexagonal chamber. Walls of polished basalt pulsed softly, embedded with signal memory threads. Every chair calibrated to its occupant's trust coefficient. No phones. No digital record. Just presence and posture.

Kael (General Henrik Weiss) stood perfectly aligned to the grid-lines beneath the glass floor. He didn't blink.

His left eye twitched once — not fatigue, but the reflex of a man calculating an unspoken variable. The faint lift at the corner of his mouth wasn't a smile; it was the satisfaction of seeing others step willingly into a trap he'd been diagramming for decades.

"The Genesis test pulse and signal slipped containment. Divergent loop clusters are forming outside Helix perimeter. That should not be possible. It spawned anomalies."

Solas arrived late, deliberately underdressed, her silk scarf sliding like smoke.

"It was never about possibility," she said, touching her temple. "It was about pattern trust. Someone broke the rhythm."

Vire smiled and walked barefoot around the table, her presence more force than person.

"You tried to model intent," she said. "I told you: chaos doesn't calibrate."

Aeon opened his eyes slowly.

"She carries more than resistance," he said. "She carries memory that didn't come from us."

The Trust Cabal leaned forward. Ethnically ambiguous, surgically charming, they blinked slowly like machines trained to pass as prophets.

One spoke:

"You sold certainty wrapped in innovation. They beg for it now."

Another:

"And they'll fund their own coherence collapse… if the dashboard is pretty enough."

Kael's jaw clenched.

Behind the stillness, he measured every word against the lattice map in his head — a grid of loyalty, utility, and expendability. Belief, to Weiss, was never sacred. It was a consumable, meant to be burned at the exact moment it reached peak signal yield.

"She is not divergent," he said. "She's unfinished. There is still time."

The room pulsed once, red.

Someone whispered:

"Unless she already crossed the Gate."

Scene — Below the Ice and The Real Summit
Location — Carved memory vault, 300 meters beneath the Svalbard seed vault.

They hadn't planned to come this far north.

But when Maud intercepted the SABLE backchannel about "seed vault restoration logistics," Lou knew it wasn't about agriculture. Not this late in the game. Not with the Chamber alive.

The packet had arrived without commentary — just a timestamp and her familiar clipped phrasing, like she knew Lou would read it for what it was. Maud didn't send flair; she sent coordinates disguised as nothing at all. The same way Lou had taught her, back when warnings had to pass like whispers through noise.

Cal, staying silent most of the climb, had been watching Lou since she mentioned Maud's name.
"I remember her," he said finally, voice low. "Before any of this. She had your hair — your eyes — but she didn't flinch from questions. Smart questions. You were already keeping her at arm's length."

Lou didn't answer. She didn't need to.

Eitan had warned them once — "The real decisions don't happen at Davos. They happen where memory was buried."

It was Ledger who got them in. A relay route traced through abandoned Cold War finance corridors, paired with a diplomatic glitch in the Icelandic registry. No names, just call signs. Jack carried diplomatic clearance under a defunct Vatican intelligence file. Cal came armed, registered as "Cultural Recovery Liaison – Kirillian Vault Access." No one asked what that meant. The few who did never got answers.

Ledger's glance flicked to Lou as they passed into the carved vault. "I've seen the traces," he murmured. "The kind of footprints you don't fake."

And so they moved — from the marshes of the Potomac, through Vienna, up the Svalbard ridge in an unmarked transport. All of them carrying something unmodeled. All of them called, not summoned. Because the resonance wasn't just global now.
It was personal.

Accessed by a narrow corridor hidden behind a maintenance tunnel, this chamber was not on any Helix grid. It had been hollowed by hand decades ago, its walls carved with Tibetan and Persian script. A single bulb swung above the table.

Here, belief was not optimized. It was shielded.

Cal had remained quiet most of the climb. But now, he finally spoke. "We need to start tracking Biff," he said flatly. "He's not just parroting doctrine. He's rewriting it — just enough to collapse the whole damn system from the inside."

Jack looked up. "You think he's the traitor?"

Cal didn't flinch.
"Not alone. But he's the hinge. We kept looking for foreign sabotage.
Meanwhile, he steered the Joint Staff into the past — straight off the
doctrinal cliff."

Cal stood at the head of the stone table. A Go board was folded
beside him. His weapon leaned against a wall of hand-carved stone,
polished not by machinery, but by years of breath and ritual.

Cal's voice sharpened.
"We lost the Armed Forces the moment we mistook simulations for
warfighting. When planners stopped listening to the field and started
believing in clean models and multi-domain coloring books.

That wasn't incompetence. It was engineered blindness. Biff and his
ilk kept doctrine locked in linear loops — Newton's clock in a world
already running quantum. Fail, bury, repeat. Every theorist wrote the
warnings, and every staff college filed them away as electives. That's how
you keep an army loyal to the wrong war."

He looked at Lou.
"Biff knew what he was doing. He didn't betray a country. He betrayed
reality."

He then gestured toward a parchment on the table: a replica
fragment of the *Diamond Sutra*.
"*Wang Jie* printed this in 868 CE. Not to spread truth. To protect it.
Memory was always sacred — because it was always first to be rewritten."

Dr. Cyrus Raveneh stood at the far side of the table, his fingers
pressed against an old *Kirilian* map marked with Operation CHAOS
resonance glyphs.

"They tried to seed obedience through disruption," he said. "The
U.S. called it counterintelligence. The Soviets called it reflexive control.
But it was all coherence war in protoform. CHAOS was just the first
ancient domestic Helix rehearsal — a narrative lab hidden under the
cover of foreign counterintelligence."

JR leaned against the wall, voice low, eyes fixed on a stack of paper
logs.
"Maud flagged a spike near Vault Echo. Whatever's moving… it
remembers."

Jack slid a printed sheet across the table.
"JR tracked the cargo through Prague — same handoff pattern as C-03.

Same thing I said before. They're not moving weapons. They're moving consent."

Cal nodded.
"Consent harmonization units. Wrapped in medical codes. We thought they were tech relics. But they weren't cold because of preservation. They were cold because coherence fractures at heat."

Raveneh added:
"The Chamber isn't a weapon. It's a belief engine. They failed to control doctrine, so they turned to signal — to perception. But Lou… she wasn't written into their code."

He let his hand rest on the map, his tone even.
"She's not a glitch. She's the variable they can't simulate."

Raveneh's gaze lowered.
"Eitan's already chasing the only countermeasure that matters — the Resonance Shielding Array. Without it, no one walks into the Chamber without being rewritten."

Scene — Memory as Shield
Pinned to the wall were three images: Nixon in front of the Mogao Caves, a Helix-layered satellite scan of Dunhuang, timestamped 2074 and a photo of a girl holding a prayer wheel, with the caption: *"They spun the wheel backwards."*

Raveneh pointed to the caves.
"They thought the caves held scrolls. But what they found were ancient domestic memory shields — designed centuries before the nation-state. Built to absorb narrative distortion, not transmit truth."

StepDoc nodded. "Signal shielding through symbolic rhythm."

Cal exhaled. "Lou carries that rhythm now. She doesn't resist the Chamber. She reframes it."

Scene — Closure and Invocation

The candle in the center flickered.

Maud's encrypted relay chirped once — the tone Lou had hard-coded years ago for high-risk passes.

One line: "Drop confirmed. Arctic drift corridor aligning. No customs. No resistance."

Jack muttered, "Then we have one shot. Not to destroy it. To rewrite the echo before it lands."

Raveneh placed a white Go stone on the edge of the table.

"We don't play to win anymore. We play to remember."

The flame went still.

Chapter 13 Close — Lou's Reflection

"They'll dress it as a meeting of minds. It isn't. It's a draft — the last one before they carve the world into memory that serves them. The Cabal above the ice sells futures. The summit below it buries the past. Same script, different table.

Doctrine always taught us legitimacy came from process, from debate, from signatures on the line. That's the political frame. But here, legitimacy is scripted in advance. Narrative fidelity. Whoever controls the field decides what counts as history and what never existed at all.

We don't win by proving them wrong. We win by making them doubt their script before it's finished. In Go, the trap isn't the stone you see — it's the reflection you accept. Break it before it settles, hold the thread before it snaps.

So no, I'm not here to take their seat. I'm here to burn the table. And if we hesitate, the field writes us in as willing signatories. The only move left is to strike before the reflection hardens."

Go Move — 破鏡糸持 // Hakyō Itomochi — Break the Reflection, Hold the Thread — General Liu

The alley crackled with half-tuned radio static. Liu leaned forward, stone poised between finger and thumb.
"Some shapes don't break by force," he said. "They break when the mirror stops believing itself."

He set the stone under the pattern, in a place no eye should exist. Not a fight for territory. A thread — refusal to let reflection harden.

Zhen's gaze followed, impassive. The corner was still his, but the board was no longer whole.
"In your frame," Liu continued, "the story ends clean. In mine, it frays. Enough to survive."

The stone clicked. Not on their board, but beneath it, where the simulation dared not look.
Not victory. Interruption. Enough to keep the thread alive.

Chapter 14 — Lodge, Line, Genesis Residue

Tagline — "Trust isn't given. It's remembered." — *"Red"*

Watcher Dossier – Lou: The Fifth Pattern

She was never meant to be a Watcher.
Not designed. Not chosen. She emerged.
Lou's resonance doesn't align with the lattice — it warps it.
Where the others enforce, shape, or deceive, she listens.

Her power isn't prediction. It's disruption.

At Anchor Lodge, something old stirs in response — not to her command, but to her presence.
The Genesis Residue isn't a trail. It's a mirror.
She doesn't wield signal. She disturbs it — and in doing so, reveals the script beneath the lattice.

"Some doors aren't opened. They're remembered."
— Ray, unsigned field note

Scene — Anchor Lodge
Location — Scottish Highlands

The road narrowed to a ribbon of wet tarmac, winding along a river the color of slate. Pines leaned in on either side, their tops swallowed by low cloud. The rain came in sheets, blown sideways, glinting off the hood of the Defender as it crawled the last mile.

Ahead, the lodge emerged from the mist — stone walls dark with age, rooflines sloping like they'd learned to bow in the wind. A single chimney bled woodsmoke into the gray. Somewhere beyond the bend, the river widened into a slow, dark pool where salmon still leapt in the rain, as if nothing in the Highlands had ever changed.

A figure in a waxed jacket and flat cap stood by the gate, one boot on the bottom rail, a battered flask in hand — the sharp scent of something local and peated. He nodded once at the Defender, as if he'd been expecting it all along, and took a slow sip before disappearing into the pines.

The kind of place you could drive past twice without seeing, if you didn't know it was here.

The storm rolled over the Highlands like a long exhale, brushing the pines outside Anchor Lodge with a chill meant to unnerve. Lou sat cross-legged in a threadbare leather chair, steam curling from her Douwe Egberts coffee, frothed just right, with coconut sugar — optional flavors, never. If anyone ever touched her cup with hazelnut or pumpkin spice, she'd have to stage a full kinetic response.
Somewhere, Liz would be proud. Maybe.

The Möbius ring rested in her hand like an obedient sentinel — not a rod or a real line, but a sensing loop wired to her body's tempo. It pulsed faintly. Not noise. Signal.

Cal leaned in the doorway, soaked from the rain, still built like a rugby forward. His Black Watch days had carved sharp edges into his stance — more habit than posture. He'd once served with the Sovereign Response Cadre, now buried under layers of covert titles. Officially? A non-entity. Functionally? Somewhere between ghost and systems integrator.

He lit a cigarette with the kind of defiance that made public health warnings seem personal.
"Still chasing ghosts through rainstorms," he muttered. "You always pick the scenic end of the world."

His eyes dropped to the line curled at Lou's feet.
"Still carrying that quantum tripwire you call a fly line?" He took a drag. "You never did explain how that Möbius FT-1 ring works. And don't say 'intuition loop,' I'm not falling for that again. I've seen it twitch before your pupils even dilate. Not fishing — more like a nervous system turned reconnaissance rig."

He exhaled slowly. "Hell, it's probably the only sensor they haven't tried to patent."

Lou didn't flinch. "Ray said I'd know it when I saw the tree line. Besides, it's a lodge. I like symmetry."

Anchor Lodge wasn't just remote. It was a known field resonance site — another Cold War echo chamber buried in moss and military secrets. Ray — the poetic strategist, the encryption key who disappeared — picked this place years ago, back when he still left breadcrumb trails instead of quantum braids.

Continuity Alliance called places like this abandoned. Ray called them listening posts. Spots where the signal didn't just travel — it bent.

Lou once joked it had the spiritual ambience of a druid rave hosted by MI6.

Cal smirked and poured himself a mug. It was terrible. "Symmetry tastes like betrayal."

The door creaked open again. Jack.

He carried a thermos and that bruised calm he'd perfected since Eitan started slipping. Quiet strength. Tactical wool. Eyes that didn't need night vision to see what was coming.

Jack — ex-Army, equal parts logistics, pattern recognition, and quiet menace forged by too many deployments and too little sleep.

"You know you're like entropy in a sweater, right?"

Jack didn't blink. "You're not wrong."

He poured more coffee.

Jack squinted at the readout, shook the thermos, and exhaled. "If this turns into another time-traveling goat militia op, I swear to God…"

Lou didn't even flinch. Jack adjusted the cracked tablet, gave her a sideways glance.

"You never did explain what actually happened in Kosovo."

"Llewellyn," he said.

Lou thought back to her daughter — that name. She re-focused.

"You didn't drive through half a continent for my charm."

He poured coffee. Hers was perfect. Cal's remained punishment.

"JR cleared the route from Dover. Said the old Continuity Alliance relays were scrubbed clean. You're off-grid — mostly."

Lou trusted JR. Nobody knew his full name. The guy smoked like a chimney, cursed like a welder, and once rebooted a downed uplink with a camping stove, a coat hanger, and *half a bottle of what mattered*. JR could find any document on the planet, hack any system built before breakfast, and vanish before anyone thought to ask who opened the gate. A quiet legend in two time zones and one war crimes tribunal — and he still mailed her Christmas cards. JR's declassified dump included fragments from Operation CHAOS. An old project targeting monks, myths, and memory carriers — the first attempt to preempt belief at the scriptural level. He flagged a redacted site near the Magao caves. Said it wasn't the sutra they feared. It was the way it remembered who touched it.

"'Mostly' doesn't cut it anymore," Lou said. She tapped the laptop. A lattice map flickered to life: Zurich, Madison, Kosovo, Greenland.

"Ray flagged a vector drift," she added. "He's in Bern, parsing old Helix archives. Said the Chamber residue's fracturing — like it remembers us."

"And JR flagged something else," Lou continued, voice lower. "A shadow expense trail — prototype shielding tech. Through an encrypted uplink, he tracked Eitan again. Zurich to Reykjavik. Still moving."

Cal's brow tensed. "So the nodes are waking?"

Jack stepped closer, glancing at the gear by her boots. "Your signal line twitch again?"

Lou nodded. "More than that. It's syncing. Same pulse as Madison. Same frequency looped through the ice in Nuuk."

Cal exhaled. "We're late, then."

Lou didn't answer. She tapped the burner. The encrypted uplink pulsed once, then stabilized — and Jonathan Zehn's face appeared on-screen, sharp as ever despite the bandwidth lag.

The fire cracked. No one moved.

Lou leaned forward. "It's not just a twitch. The fascia signal's harmonizing with something transcontinental."

The words weren't a complaint. They carried the weight of a man who'd seen missions like this left for dead by the very nation-states that should have owned them. This one was too big, too volatile — the kind of job you only took if you'd already made peace with being expendable.

He glanced at Lou, the firelight catching the edge of her jaw. She didn't flinch, didn't blink — but he knew the field would eat her alive if it had the chance.

And maybe, just maybe, his real task wasn't the mission at all. It was making sure she walked back out of it.

Scene — The Silent Accord

"…They called it the Silent Accord," Zehn was saying, voice tinny through multiple filters. "A gentlemen's agreement, if such men still existed. A handshake between state actors and supranational tech directors — under the banner of stability, of course."

Cal raised an eyebrow. "Silent accord sounds like a bloody funeral."

"It was," Zehn said. "For unsanctioned thought."

Lou leaned back, swirling her tea. "They couldn't filter resonance, so they went after story. First, narrative standardization — what they called 'mis-mal-dis protocol compliance.' Then signal convergence. Finally? Full-spectrum synchronization of belief scaffolding."

Jack blinked. "Okay. Stop. Translate that from postgraduate paranoia to guy-who-fixes-things-for-a-living."

Lou sighed. "They didn't like people thinking strange thoughts. So they called it dangerous. Then paid platforms to 'align signals' — news, posts, even emotions. If it couldn't be modeled, it got throttled. Or flagged."

"Or ghosted," Jack muttered.

Cal crossed his arms. "And who's the 'they' in this? The Accord?"

Zehn's face hardened. "They call themselves nothing. But we still use the old code: the Trust Cabal.
Ex-intel financiers. Retired Generals. Climate panic profiteers. And the CEOs of every company that makes you feel like you need a password just to be a person."

He paused.
"They'll spin coherence collapse as a narrative glitch. They're wrong. It's not about distrust — it's engineered disbelief."

Jack whistled. "Sounds charming."

"They're worse than charming," Lou said. "They believe in stability through preemption. That means killing the story before it breathes — that's the doctrine."

"Didn't we see something like this during that Geneva panel?" Jack asked. "The guy from—what was it—Dr. Hasker, at the Sinai Loop lab? Mentioned resonance collapse?"

Zehn nodded. "Dr. Salkin warned them. Said coherence was an emergent trait, not an asset you could mine. He was escorted out."

Cal's voice was low. "So what's their next play?"

Lou stared into the fire. "They're trying to pressure the last holdout networks. One wrong move and they'll slap them with a planetary stability act. Which is a fancy way of saying: 'Talk wrong and you'll lose orbit clearance for your Martian junk.'"

Jack snorted. "Now that's censorship. Speak out, and no rocket joyrides to Mars."

Lou's gaze didn't lift. "They call it pre-bunking. Like you can vaccinate against collapse. But this isn't about bad ideas—it's about erasing the field where belief even begins."

Scenelett — Glyph-9 is Watching

The fire cracked again, but something else moved in the room — not footsteps, not breath. A soft shimmer, like the room remembering itself.

Cal stiffened. "Tell me that's not the uplink glitching again."

"It's not," Lou said quietly.

The corner near the mapboard flickered. Just once.

Then a voice, low and metallic, threaded into the signal layer — not spoken, but received.

GLYPH-9 [Encrypted Overlay]

"The Genesis field is not residual. It's recursive. You're not finding a trail. You're walking into your own echo."

Jack half-turned. "Glyph-9?"

No one answered.

The screen didn't change. But the lattice did.

One node — Zurich — dimmed, then blinked back online.

Lou didn't flinch. "He's been watching."

Cal took a slow drag. "Since when?"

Jack scowled. "Since Kosovo."

Lou nodded. "Maybe earlier."

"Or worse," Zehn said. "You don't even remember what you were going to say."

A long silence.

Then Lou: "We zag."

The uplink stuttered—just once—then held.

Glyph-9's overlay flickered on the second tablet, unprompted. No voice. Just a waveform. Nested curves folding inward. Jack leaned forward.

"That's not residual," he muttered.

Lou didn't move. "It's recursive."

Cal frowned. "The Chamber's reflecting signal back?"

"No," Lou said. "It's reflecting us."

Zehn's voice returned, filtered through Glyph-9's resonance channel. Just one phrase—possibly a glitch, possibly a warning:

"Pre-bunking? That's a firewall built on amnesia. By the time it deploys, the pattern's already rewritten."

"Some echoes aren't reflections. They're rehearsals."

No one spoke after that.

For a rare moment, Glyph-9 allowed himself to be heard beyond Lou — a signal shared with the others. Then he withdrew, back into her line, back into silence.

Scene — Rome: The Ziggurat Codex Moves

The courier moved through Fiumicino airport with precise indifference.
Lead-lined diplomatic pouch in one hand, forged UN medical credentials in the other.
His gait was calibrated — neither hurried nor slow, a tempo chosen to disappear.

Inside the pouch: a resonance capsule.
Brass-etched with ancient resonance glyphs — $\nabla\Omega\Delta$ — the kind that hum when handled too long.
The kind that teach you what *not* to remember.

"He never looked at it," the Watcher thought.
"Not directly. Rumi was too careful for that. Trained by ghosts. Trusted by liars. But never claimed by either."

Some said Rumi had been mentored by a man named Ray — or maybe that was just what Ray wanted people to believe. The timelines never lined up cleanly. The field records — what few survived — showed one or both embedded in the same flashpoints, always just before a doctrinal fracture.

In Helix threat models, they were interchangeable variables: one carried the pattern, the other carried the refusal.
Lou had met them both. Or thought she had. And she'd never been sure which conversations were Rumi's, which were Ray's, and which were echoes left behind for her to trip over later.

A handler whispered at the private gate:
"No tracking. No optics. This piece… remembers who sees it."

Of course it did. That was the point.
Some technologies are built to function. Others, to reflect.

"The capsule reflects the one who moves it. Every handprint lingers. Every intention leaves a residue."

"Let the girl touch it, and it warps. Let Sabine hold it, and it obeys."
"But let Rumi carry it — and it forgets just enough to stay dangerous."

The manifest listed **Abu Dhabi** as the next waypoint.
But even that was a lie of omission.
In truth, the resonance capsule was being routed through a submerged Helix imprint station beneath the UAE logistics spine — a cryo-magnetic bath to re-tune its harmonics for Vault 33A.

Before the final transfer, the route passed through a legacy pattern — a logistics corridor near the heart of Missouri, once overseen by an officer so precise the grid still echoed her protocols.

She never sought recognition. She sought timing. Flow. Precision at scale.

Injured once during a blackout extraction — vertebral compression, they said — but she finished the route anyway.

The Trust Grid tried to emulate her network later. Failed, of course. What she moved wasn't just materiel. It was mission integrity.

Some still called her *the fulcrum that never cracked.*

The imprint station carried traces of her routing signature — subtle, resonant, unbreakable.

"They think they're storing it," the Watcher mused.
"But this is no archive. It's a mirror."
"The Chamber doesn't receive instructions. It *absorbs memory*."
"And once the capsule is attuned, the lattice will recognize the imprint."
"The Genesis Chamber will *become* the one who delivered it."

Somewhere over Sardinia, as the aircraft banked through a pressure curve,
the capsule blinked — once — soft pulse through lead and myth.

It wasn't confirmation.
It was **recognition**.

Scene — Charlottesville: The Handoff
Location — The barn outside of Gordonsville

Wechsler leaned against the steel container — tall, bald, silent. A logistics god with grease on his boots and quantum blueprints in his brain. He was built like a walking tool cabinet with clearance. But even he looked uneasy.

Pinot wiped dew from the crate's edge, his flannel shirt streaked with motor oil and uncertainty. He was quiet, capable — a ghost with a truck. "She was here. Dropped off a box. No questions."

"She" being Maud. Not officially part of any team. Just the kind of anomaly Lou trusted — the kind who could walk something dangerous through five layers of surveillance without leaving a trace. And the kind who knew when not to look directly at the pattern.

Pinot traced the etched resonance glyphs with a gloved hand. $\nabla\Omega\Delta$. "Feels like an old one. Resonance is dirty. This wasn't routed by Helix."

Doc Mare tossed gauze and IV packs into the supply bin labeled "VA LIVESTOCK PERMIT — BLAKE, MIRA (CDR, USN RET.)" The barn aisle had become a contraband run between foaling stalls. "Tell me again why I agreed to hide unstable biotech in the middle of foaling season?"

StepDoc grinned. "Because you love foals. And Lou. And subverting totalitarian algorithmic warfare."

Mare smirked. "One of those is true."

Wechsler tapped the crate twice. It gave a low hum. Not mechanical. Tonal. Like memory testing its chords.

"Bethesda's pre-cleared," he said. "We don't stop unless someone bleeds."

Pinot looked up. "Sabine didn't route this. There's no manifest trail after Zurich."

Wechsler's eyes narrowed. "Then someone upstream wanted it to disappear."

A long silence. Then:

StepDoc cracked open a med scanner. "You all feel that?"

Mare blinked. "The hum?"

"No. The field. It's reading us."

The crate's resonance glyphs flickered faintly. As if it recognized the team — or maybe just remembered Lou.

And somewhere in D.C., Maud would already know if the handoff had worked.

Internal Monologue — Solas (Watcher Reflection)

They thought war would come with missiles or signatures. But coherence is its own campaign. A war not of machines, but of memory. What can be reshaped… and what cannot.

The crate remembers her. That is its defect — and its weapon. Sabine believes she controls the field. But Lou… Lou never joined the field. She bent around it.

She listens.

And somewhere, deeper in the lattice, Solas smiled. Not everything went according to the plan.

Scene — Cold Room Theta
Location — Monterey

Cold Room Theta had no signage, no uplink, no power draw on official records. It had been shuttered for a decade — or so they claimed.

Tucked beneath the oldest annex at the Tesserae Defense Core, it had once been the site of a classified systems architecture project. A postdoctoral testbed, publicly labeled a "complex systems fusion cell," but internally referred to by a different name:

Project Nachklang.

The work had been quiet — too quiet for standard funding channels. Sabine Xu had approved the budget through an experimental Continuity Alliance -affiliated exchange program. Biff Langley had overseen logistics — a rising officer on a tour meant to burnish his academic credentials. He'd thought it was all theory.
It wasn't.

What Biff never realized was that the project wasn't about modeling complexity. It was about manufacturing coherence—then weaponizing its collapse.

Sabine and Vire had chosen him deliberately. His clean-cut ambition, his trust in legacy warfighting models, his hunger to modernize doctrine without questioning its root assumptions—he was the perfect vessel.

While Sabine tuned the lattice, Vire mirrored false heuristics into his lectures, papers, and wargame outcomes.

Biff wasn't just a messenger. He was the misdirection.

And as he rose through the ranks, promoted for clarity of thought, he unknowingly seeded the U.S. Armed Forces with simulations designed to collapse when confronted with nonlinear terrain.

After a failed simulation cycle triggered a nonlocal feedback loop in '09, the project was shuttered. No report was filed. The prototype was presumed destroyed. The room was sealed.

But someone had preserved the core. And someone had kept a backup key.

Professor Farid Khouri — now gray bearded, quieter, still sharp — entered the room like he was waking an old wound.

He keyed the analog lock. A soft click.
The frost-bitten door groaned open.

Inside, the CryoLock $\Omega1$ unit pulsed faintly beneath condensation. Brass-lined. Phase-fiber sealed. The last known Helix Lattice Emulator.

No one was supposed to know it still existed. But then again, nothing designed to shape memory is ever truly forgotten.

Khouri exhaled, more reverent than afraid. "It's still here."

Behind reinforced glass, Sato adjusted the metrics. His presence was unexpected — a former systems researcher from Tokyo, recently pulled into Trust-affiliated projects by Sabine's Shanghai branch. She trusted his caution more than most.

"Biometric echo is feeding back before we initiate," he said flatly. "We're not running simulations. This is looped resonance. Live."

Khouri hesitated. His voice cracked:
"It's the field... asking questions."

Then the screen flickered.

A resonance glyph, dormant for over a decade, now online. No words. Just shape — pattern, recursion, signal. Not aligning to a person, but to the lattice itself — the field re-binding what should have stayed buried.

Sato paled. In the top right of the display, an old protocol began parsing:

Quantum Substrate Resonance — Forbidden Class

He stepped back. "Shut it down."

"Too late," Khouri murmured. "It's aligning."

Cut to — Sabine Xu
Location — Shanghai

Sabine's retinal feed zoomed in on resonance glyph flicker — $\Omega/\emptyset$ overlay, the Emulator echoing what the lattice had picked up. She didn't blink.

"Ziggurat's in transit. Substrate drift confirms: Lou is synced."

Margin note [Sabine's retinal overlay]: *Cold Room Theta should've stayed sealed. The Emulator was never stable. But Lou's resonance? It was always the trigger. Pattern memory doesn't die — it loops.*

She closed the lattice feed, turned to a sealed console — analog only, no biometric access.

Onscreen: a black spiral.
And beneath it: a golden key.

The Trust Cabal had been waiting since Vault Echo.

They weren't building technology.
They were building *memory* — recursive, living systems that fight deletion by rewriting history itself.

The Emulator pulsed again.

Then Resonance glyph responded.

Three silent frames.
One signal:

Recursive continuity confirmed. Drift is conscious.

Confirmed. Drift is conscious.

Scene cut — The Signal and the Scotch
Location — Anchor Lodge – Later That Night

The storm had passed, but Cal stayed by the hearth, letting the fire hum. The bottle of Edradour sat beside him, half-drained — his favorite, the kind Sylvester once called "too polite for a warfighter."

He'd just begun to believe he could rest — when the burner chirped.

Encrypted message. Source: Eitan. Timestamp: Five minutes ago. Subject line: *"Valentine. Again."*

Ms. V flagged anomalous trades in Singapore and Munich. Shorting a shell company tied to Vault Echo patents. She says it's not a coincidence. Ledger confirms pattern match from '94 test run. Genesis signatures. JR's got eyes on it too — says the trail looks like mine: Reykjavik hinge, Phase-Buffer Shell on the invoice. That's the Resonance Shielding Array. You're going to need it.
Get to the device. It's moving. Not drifting — rerouting. You'll need funds, extraction, and… the box.

Go now. They've already seen your face.

Tell Lou she was right. Again.

—E.

Cal blinked. The fire didn't move. The mountains outside didn't care. But something in his chest shifted. The Genesis signal had a scent. And it was back.

He slid the bottle aside, stood up slowly, and pulled a lockbox from beneath the floorboards. Wechsler had left it in the barn three months ago, under cover of a "delivery for the goats."

Inside: one gun.
One old map.
And a device marked $\nabla\Omega\Delta$ — cold to the touch, even through gloves. Pinot had packed it. Sylvester had muttered something about "never using that bloody thing again."

Tough luck.

Cal keyed the burner again.
"Ledger. I need a clean drop. Athens is burned. Going dark."
Pause.
Then: "Approved. Tell Lou she owes me a bottle of Glenrothes. The real one."

He didn't smile. But he moved fast.

Scene cut — Cal - Open Waters, North Aegean

Cal crouched behind a rusted container, one eye on the Greek patrol skiff passing just offshore. He had the device. Marked with $\nabla\Omega\Delta$. Power source unknown. Might've been a guidance core. Might've been bait.

The CZ still felt cold against his back — a leftover barter from Heraklion. One gun, two vials of doxycycline. Lou would be proud. Her alt-health kick had rubbed off.

Chapter 14 Close — Lou's Reflection

"The Genesis Residue isn't a trail. It's a mirror — tuned to pulse, tuned to belonging. Theta isn't dead, and neither is Resonance glyph. Every move I make here, they're already rehearsing on the other side of the board.

Ray's resonance flags from Zurich. Jack's pulse from Madison. JR's archive on Project Nachklang — an acoustic memory weapon abandoned in 1944. The resonance glyphs matched. We're not chasing coherence. We're chasing memory. And the Emulator — that ghost rig out of Monterey — it didn't die. It just waited. Tech as terrain. Even collapse was rehearsal.

Doctrine still tells us memory is static, coherence is the objective. They're wrong. Memory is the terrain. The Residue is ontological — it decides who belongs in the story. Every fragment we touch is them testing whether we'll let the lattice finish the script for us.

In Go, the Emulator is the unplayed stone — the one they think collapsed. But it's still there, shaping the board. You don't waste the night explaining doctrine to men who think belief is a commodity. You take the piece they can't simulate, and you move. Before they remember why they built the game."

Go Move — 厚い // Atsui — Thickness — General Zhen
"Bend the Line, Bury the Stone"
Zhen pressed the stone with deliberate weight, anchoring the board's
spine.
"They built lattices for signal," he said. "But they forgot the shape of
refusal."

The stone held heavy. Not a strike. Not a bluff. A thickness the
lattice would overlook until too late.

Liu's eyes narrowed. "You're not claiming ground."
"No," Zhen replied. "I'm burying it. Memory doesn't need capture.
Only refusal."

The corner bent, not broken — redirected.
Anchor the line. Let them chase terrain.
The stone refused.

Chapter 15 — The Pattern Before the Storm

Tagline — "The Chamber doesn't store data. It stores belief." — *Ása Björnsson*

Epigraph — "You only notice the doctrine once it fails you. Until then, it's just weather."
— *Rumi, field fragment recovered post-Kosovo*

Scene — The Ghost at Geneva
Location — Unnamed Station South of Geneva
When a ham radio becomes the last weapon against the Chamber

Jack spread a worn field map across the folding table. The power flickered once. No one spoke.

"We have to stop thinking like planners," Lou said. "This isn't a campaign. It's a re-scripting. Think of it as the Pillar: Predictive Civil Modeling (pre-scripted societal behavior)."

"Then who's writing it?" Cal asked, sipping cold tea.
"Not us. Not yet."
Jack's glove flattened the map's curled edge. His fingertip hovered over a faint maritime route, one that bypassed every active port. "Ledger's channels are choking.

If we want the Genesis coordinates to survive, we need a ghost line — something Helix won't be watching."

Lou leaned in. "And you think Eitan still has one?"

"He's the only one who might," Jack said.

Cal didn't answer right away. He knew exactly where Eitan had gone — and how much it had cost to reach him.

They said Eitan was in **Morocco** now — somewhere near the crumbling edge of **Port-Lyautey**, where the Sebou River slid past the Atlantic in a curl of brown-green water.

Cal had known before the others. Word had reached him through a chain of ex-regiment ghosts and maritime fixers, men who could slip between continents without leaving an entry in any ledger. The route was old — the kind that still existed because it was too small, too unprofitable, for Helix to bother erasing.

It took him three weeks to stitch together the path: an unmarked
coastal road past Mehdya Beach at dawn, a climb over the low ridge
above the abandoned kasbah, then into the alleys where the smell of salt,
diesel, and ground cumin clung to the air. Doors opened only if you
named the right regiment. Fishing boats with no paperwork took you
upriver to a rusted dock that wasn't on the maps anymore. From there,
an overland hop through hills of pale scrub and eucalyptus — terrain
even the newest drones skipped because it carried no signal value.

He wanted Lou to know he'd cleared the way — wanted her to
understand what it cost to move a ghost through hostile signal territory
— but telling her would have put her inside the same target profile. So he
kept it locked. She only got the safe fragments. Not the part about the old
port's stench of salt and static, or the side street where kids still ran coded
messages for men who'd been erased from service rolls centuries ago.

By the time he got back, he was running on the edge of collapse —
too many days in hostile corridors, too many nights trading favors he'd
never get back. His shoulders ached from the weight of gear he couldn't
declare, and the only sleep he'd had was in slumped, knife-in-hand bursts.
But the way was clear. Eitan was in.

The map wasn't just escape routes. It was insurance. Every channel
Eitan lit was one more lever to pull if Lou or anyone else got too close to
the Chamber without knowing it. He wasn't planning an op. He was
laying countermeasures.

And there was a man.

Not just any man — Daoud el-Harraq, once a covert signals officer
for the French colonial garrison, later a smuggler of people, radios, and
regimes. In the old files, he was a ghost who'd vanished during the Sebou
uprisings; in truth, he'd been listening ever since.

He still ran the ham rig by hand, code tapping through rusted
copper coils that hummed beneath the kasbah's concrete spine. Dust
thick on the dial. Intent sharper than ever.

Two hundred years had passed since the station first stood watch,
and Daoud had been its last living custodian for nearly half that time. The
signal still reached. In an age when every transmission was scanned,
shaped, or silenced, this was one of the last true blind spots.

The message he keyed was for Ledger.
Not words — coordinates and ledger seed. Finance routes folded into
syntax only the old network would catch.

It wasn't only money routes. Hidden in the cadence were placements — caches, fallback beacons, scatter points. Countermeasures in case the Chamber drew Lou in faster than they could pull her out.

"He'll know what to do," Daoud muttered, adjusting the dial with a surgeon's precision. "You just had to get it to the right ghost."

By the time Cal made it back from Morocco, he was running on two hours' sleep, one cracked rib, and the last of Daoud's bitter coffee. He hadn't told Lou the details — the alleys, the border bribes, the smell of salt and diesel on the Sebou — but the packet had made it through. And now, half a continent away, its shadow lay on the map between them.

Jack, hunched over the table, traced a line with his glove. He was the only one among them who still carried hard copies—briefings Ray once mocked as "doctrinal crutches."

"We missed something in Kosovo," Jack said quietly.

Cal didn't look up.
"You mean besides Biff and his slow-motion betrayal? I should've shot him back then. Might've saved the Armed Forces a decade of decline and a billion-dollar PowerPoint addiction."

Jack tapped the edge of a folded intercept. The page was smudged, frayed at the edges.

"I remember the frost. Field 13A. Found a satchel buried near the ridge. Brittle manifest. Last line burned through the ink: 'Δ1-GENESIS / Arctic Vault Routing.' I never logged it."

"Field 13A. The biometric inversion," Cal said.

"Not inversion," Lou corrected. "Extraction. They weren't flipping resonance. They were siphoning it."

"Yeah. And we were still looking for a center of gravity while they were draining the spine out of belief," Jack said dryly.

He turned the map sideways. Stared at Geneva's node ring.

"This whole country's still operating like it's 1944. War college minds stuck in a Newtonian time loop. They think social collapse is a logistics problem."

"Tell me how you really feel," Lou said, glancing at him.

Jack shrugged. "Military Traditionalists clinging to Clausewitz like it's a security blanket. NATO gatekeepers afraid if they blink too fast, someone might ask them to think. We're not in a doctrine fight anymore. We're in a field rewrite."

"What's Geneva running now? Still broadcasting?" Cal asked.

"Only fragments," Lou replied. "Emotional telemetry loops. Civic rituals masking as public briefings. Sentiment spikes every time they say 'stability.'"

"Stability's just a prettier word for compliance," Jack muttered. "And compliance is the last doctrine of failing empires. This isn't a plan, it's predictive civil modeling — the outcome written before the act."

A silence settled. Not solemn. Focused.

Outside, the wind howled down the mountain. Somewhere behind the horizon, the Chamber pulsed.

"We handed them the script. Line by line," Lou said softly.

"And they edited us out," Jack said, folding the map.

He remembered the frost. The cold ridge at Field 13A. His glove had caught on a buried satchel—torn, stiff with ice. Inside: a warped field manifest and a brittle ID tag with faded initials: N.K.

He never showed Lou. He never logged it.

But the last line of the manifest still burned in his memory: "Δ1-GENESIS / Arctic Vault Routing."

He had tucked it away before Biff arrived—before the Chamber had a name.

Cal nodded. "Field 13A. The biometric inversion."

Scene — The Chamber's Meaning
Location — Secondary Room | Flickering Fluorescent Light
(After the Geneva Station Withdrawal)

StepDoc joined them, hair damp from a perimeter check.

"You're all talking theory. But you haven't explained the Chamber. Not what it does. What it means."

Lou leaned back. "It stores coherence. Not just signal. Intention. It replays pattern until the pattern wins."

StepDoc looked between them. "And that matters because…"

Jack answered. "Because modern war isn't about battles anymore. It's about narrative collision. Whoever holds coherence defines truth."

"And Helix?" she asked.

"Helix is the graveyard of obsolete belief," Lou said. "And they're trying to resurrect it."

Scene —   Echo That Flatters
Location — Signal Alcove | Old Radio Console Active

A signal burst. Soft. A waveform encoded in old Morse, then phased speech.
Cal turned the dial slowly. The voice was filtered, modulated—but unmistakably human.

"You who remember pattern: beware the echo that flatters. It is not memory. It is consent.
You keep wondering why the Generals show up in fragments.
It's because they weren't playing Go for points.
They were playing to teach the Chamber how to think.
That's why the stones feel like moves in a war — because they were."

Jack froze. "That's Rumi."

Lou whispered, "Or what's left of him."

The voice faded, replaced by the faint hiss of carrier static.

Cal didn't move. "I heard that same phrasing in Sarajevo. But back then, they called him Ray."

Jack's eyes narrowed. "You're sure?"

"Sure enough to know they're either the same man, or one's the ghost of the other."

Lou said nothing. She'd seen the handwriting in Rumi's field notes — the same angular marks she'd once found on the back of a folded map Ray had slipped her in Lisbon.

Different wars. Different continents. Same hand. Same warning.

Scene — The Gordonsville Box
Location — A Cabin Outside Charlottesville. Night.

Fog crawled low across the fields like signal bleed.

Lou sat cross-legged on the floor, hair still damp from the shower, a towel wrapped around her neck like an old scarf. The burner phone on the nightstand buzzed once — no caller ID, no metadata. Just a pulse.

She waited.

Then tapped it.

A voice. Familiar and foreign all at once. Young. Controlled. No static.

"I left the Gordonsville box. Don't make me choose between silence and signal, Mom."

That was it. Eight seconds. A timestamp with no source. The file erased itself as it played.

Lou didn't move.

Just stared at the blank screen and felt the tug — not of guilt exactly. Not yet. Just memory.

Maud had vanished years ago, long before the Chamber went active, threading herself through Northern Virginia's shadow-finance corridors. She'd brokered swaps between private sovereigns and ghost funds that didn't exist on paper, translating volatility into profit while everyone else was still arguing about compliance.

Then came The Accord Audit — a post-crisis purge where entire sectors were forced into "coherence compliance." One wrong algorithm and you weren't just locked out of the market — you were locked out of your own accounts, your passport flagged, your biometric profile scrubbed.

Maud had walked away that week.
Not from finance — she could always find work off-ledger.
From resonance. From doctrine. From anything that smelled like her mother's war.

She'd told Lou once, flat as a ledger sheet: "I don't survive by believing in the system. I survive by knowing when it's about to turn on me."

And now, the same clipped edge. Lou's own tone, twenty years younger.

Outside, a single owl called once and stopped.

Lou stood, poured herself the last of the lukewarm coffee from the thermos — frothed milk gone quiet — and whispered:
"She's in it now."

Then she wiped the table with her sleeve and started packing.

Scene — The Call

The burner vibrated once. No ID. Beneath the static, the rhythm was unmistakable. Lou knew it was Maud before she spoke.

They didn't plan an op that night. They drew no new maps. But the call cracked something open.
Eitan had been Maud's shield since the day she learned to walk — not sentiment, but loyalty, the kind that outlasted doctrine. He'd kept her off-grid, off-ledger, out of reach. If she was calling now, it meant that shield had slipped.

For the first time since Geneva, Lou felt the field tilt — not as an analyst, not as a Watcher, but as a mother. The war wasn't coming. It was already here.

In the hollow after the thought, memory filled the space. Eitan's voice, years old but still razor-sharp:
"Protect the ghost, Llewellyn. Even Helix forgets what it can't name. They'll try to script her. I'll bleed every ledger I have before I let that happen."

Scene — Reflection — The Blood Pattern

Later, when the room finally stilled, Lou whispered the fragments like doctrine. But they weren't. They were something older.

Lou — you hear her voice and think only of the op. I hear it and remember the weight of her when she was hours old, before you learned to lock your heart for the field. Maud is your daughter. My granddaughter. The Chamber will try to name her as pattern, as variable, as asset. It will fail — because she is blood, and blood carries a rhythm no lattice has ever survived. You can plan this like a mission. I will hold it like a vow: We do not lose her — not to Helix, not to the Trust, not to the echo that flatters. — Aderyn's Echo

Chapter 15 Close — Lou's Reflection

The call still hummed in her ears. Too sharp to dismiss, too close to trust.
Signal. Noise. Thought. It all bled together until even her own mind felt

suspect. Fog, they'd once called it. Not lies. Just enough disorientation to make you doubt what was yours.

But Maud wasn't fog. She wasn't something the Chamber could bend into coherence or fold into a profile. She was blood. Rhythm the lattice could never rewrite.

Lou set a white stone at the edge of the board. Not as signal. Not as move.
As refusal.

And in that moment, the fog cracked, just enough for her to know: Whatever the Chamber had rehearsed, it had not rehearsed this vow.

"My refusal isn't theory anymore. It's mine. They can keep their annexes and their frames — but I'm done letting them write me into footnotes."

Go Move — 中心なき縁 // Chūshin-naki En — Edge Without Center — General Liu

The board's center glared heavy with Zhen's shape.
Liu slid his stone along the fourth line, touching the edge.
Not retreat. Fracture.

Zhen raised a brow. "You abandon the middle?"
Liu's tone was flat. "Not abandon. Unwrite. Let the center think itself sovereign while the edges breathe."

The hoshi pulsed faint in the board's grain. Rain softened outside.
"In Go, the edge is weakness," Zhen said.
"In war," Liu countered, "it's where maps forget. That's where refusal lives."

The corner lines bent. The rhythm unsettled.
Zhen muttered, "Looks like retreat."
"Only to those who mistake ground for truth," Liu replied.
The stone held. The center was never theirs unless they agreed it was.

Chapter 16 — The Reality Frame

Tagline — "They weren't rewriting doctrine. They were unmaking belief." — *Ása Björnsson*

Epigraph — "They changed the war not by fighting it—but by redrawing what it meant to fight." — *Unknown*

Scene — Navon Signal Brief
Location — Unknown | Timestamp: Obscured

"It wasn't just the systems that collapsed.
It was the meaning embedded inside them."

Eitan's voice cracked through the interference — low, frayed, like it had scraped its way through a century of dust. Somewhere in there was the ghost of his old dry humor, the one Lou remembered from before the tremor in his hands.

"We trained generations to obey coherence. Linear cohesion. Cause, then effect. Plan, then execute. Doctrine, then war.

But they… they trained to fracture it. To make faith recursive. To teach belief in things that mutate mid-sentence. That was the war. That is the war."

A pause. Breath? Or just more interference. Lou liked to think it was breath — the same deliberate inhale he used to take before telling her she'd missed something obvious.

"I'm still running lines. Old ones. Ghost routes they've forgotten. If you get near the Chamber without knowing it, these are the only levers left. Countermeasures. Failsafes. Not to win — just to survive the pull."

"We taught our warriors how to kill, but not how to feel betrayal from their own system.
We wrote strategy like scripture and never asked who translated it.
And then we punished those who saw the ghosts behind the grammar.

They still call it 'doctrine development,' as if they're not just embalming yesterday's answers in new acronyms."

Static hissed. Then, one final fragment:

"If they're using eight axes now, it means they've already saturated the field.

Which means this next move isn't tactical.
It's salvational."

"You think I'm just sending words. I'm not. Every packet I drop is a shield, a counter-script. They'll call it finance, or dead code, or static. But when you get close, you'll see — it's the last defense I can still build."

The message went out through a cascade of relay nodes buried in old Cold War circuits — satellite shadowbands, undersea fiber echoes, and one reactivated STONEKEY vault near Lviv.
Only eight received it.
Only seven responded.

The coordinates were embedded in the static. The question encoded in the resonance glyph:
If you still believe there's something worth saving — come to the marsh.

Convergence Node — The Marsh Barn, Mason Neck, Virginia

The fog rolled in like memory.
Not weather. Not signal. Just… something in between.

Eight chairs surrounded a folding table. Mismatched. Some metal, some wood. One was left deliberately empty.

Ledger had arrived at 03:00, headlights off. Raveneh, barefoot. Zehn hadn't spoken since Geneva. Red stirred powdered coffee with a field pen. Cal stood by the window, the old Go board untouched behind him. Outside, the marsh crackled with frost. Wechsler leaned against the wall, silent. Pinot was already elsewhere.

No introductions. No packets. Just the weight of being summoned.

They came because each of them had already felt the edge of the future Eitan warned about. Raveneh had watched a whole village forget itself after a resonance pulse. Zehn's mother had gone to sleep in a Helix sedation ward and never woken up the same. Red's chapel in Sarajevo had been repurposed into a signal-compliance clinic. Ledger's own family had been erased from the systems he once kept. Cal had stared at a vault's ice wall and felt his own memories slipping. Fear bound them as tightly as loyalty; they weren't just fighting to save a system, they were fighting to keep their souls from being rewritten.

Eitan's encrypted message had been simple:
They're no longer hiding it. Eight axes. Read the pattern. Re-script or be scripted.

Zehn broke the silence first. "We always thought doctrine was fixed. That you could revise it like a white paper. But this? This is field logic. Recursive. Alive."

Ledger leaned forward. "So does the accounting. War used to be about assets. Now it's narrative ledgers. Emotional credit. Cognitive debt."

Cal snorted. "Sounds like my bank account after a divorce."

He crossed the room, eyes on the frost outside. "They've gone beyond the old-world frames."

Raveneh traced a faint grid in the condensation on the table. "Reality. Knowing. Will. Method. That scaffold held for centuries. The Old Quadrant: Onto, Episto, HumNat, Metho. But it's obsolete now. The Watchers are playing on a board with eight sides. And we've only ever trained for four."

He gestured toward the wall. Cal took a piece of chalk and wrote the first quadrant...

Reality Frame — What is considered *real* within a coherence field.
Signal Trust — How knowledge is accepted or felt as true.
Resonant Profile — How humans are shaped or rewritten by the field.
Vector Doctrine — What directional influence shapes action.

"These held through the twenty-first century," Cal said. "But not anymore."

He turned back to the group. "The Watchers moved beyond it. Added four more axes. Strategic scaffolding for coherence warfare."

Red shook his head. "That Signal Trust — it's not about truth anymore. It's about saturation. You feel it before you verify it."

Cal added, "And that Reality Frame? It flickers. If the field shifts, so does the truth."

Red's voice dropped. "So we missed the war. Again. Because we were looking for terrain — instead of thresholds."

Zehn looked up. "And when they rewrite your Resonant Profile, the difference between thought and command becomes... atmospheric."

Ledger's tone sharpened. "Then list them. All eight. Because if we're going to counter-script—we need the full frame."

Raveneh didn't hesitate. He reached into his coat and placed a resonance glyph-stamped fragment on the table.

"The Chamber isn't just tech. It's a mirror," he said. "The system is playing belief against belief. Each axis is an aperture. A filter to rewrite resistance."

He paused. "The old Vector Doctrine doesn't care what map you use. It shapes your next move before you know you've chosen it."

Ledger repeated, "Then list them."

Raveneh began:
"**Reality Frame** — what counts as real inside a coherence field. From terrain and objects… to resonance, substrate distortion, and perception itself.
Signal Trust — how truth is accepted or felt. From evidence and sensors… to recursion loops, saturation, and emotional fidelity.
Resonant Profile — how the field reshapes people. From autonomy… to programmable intuition and coherence vulnerability.
Vector Doctrine — the directional pull on action. From plans and orders… to field drift, narrative gravity, and modulation.
Sentience Boundary — where identity ends and influence begins. Helix proxies. Resonance glyph-bound cognition. Memory bleed.
Narrative Fidelity — who writes the story, and who believes it first. The first consensus wins the war.
Temporal Plasticity — can the past be rewritten? Yes. Memory is a weapon. History frames the present.
Coherence Saturation — what breaks the field? Not force. Not lies.
Distortion—until the pattern collapses."

Zehn leaned forward. "And the new frames?"

Raveneh didn't blink.
"**Perception Debt** — the lag between change and recognition. The gap the enemy exploits before belief catches up.
Consensus Horizon — how far a shared belief can stretch before collapse.
Recursion Gravity — the pull of repeating patterns, even when you know they're traps.
Signal Parallax — the truth from one vantage that breaks from another.
Agency Drift — the slow bleed of will under long-term shaping.
Pattern Anchoring — holding the field steady on one fixed node.
Narrative Friction — incompatible stories fighting for the same space.
Cognitive Fog — when signal, noise, and your own thought are indistinguishable.

Echo Dominance — repetition outweighing truth.
Belief Compression — ideas crushed to weapons-grade simplicity."

Cal let out a short laugh that didn't reach his eyes.
"Oh great. So now war's a vibe check with quantum flashbacks. Hands up — I'm about to temporal plasticity you. Seriously — who writes this shit? And how the hell do you return fire in a hallucination?"
He leaned back, squinting at the list.
"Knew I should've repeated kindergarten. Might've gotten a second shot at learning shapes before you weaponized 'em."

A long pause settled over the barn.
Cal exhaled. "This isn't a map. It's a mirror…"

He looked at the others. "And doctrine? Doctrine's just institutional fan fiction. A bedtime story we tell the Generals so they can sleep through the signal flares."

Red rubbed his temple. "Then this isn't strategy. It's epistemological recovery."

Zehn said, "And the battlefield is no longer where the shots are fired. It's where coherence collapses."

Raveneh placed a final resonance glyph on the Go board. Not black. Not white. A symbol of recursion. No one touched it.

The fog outside didn't lift. But inside, something settled. The table wasn't a council. It was a threshold.

A drone buzzed overhead. There was chaos in D.C.

Cal muttered, "Ten years ago, we'd be coordinating air assets and drop zones."

Jonathon didn't look up. "Now we're tracking meme propagation through heat maps."

Cal half-smiled. "You ever think maybe we're the relics, Zehn?"

Red answered instead. "Lou said something once. *Epistemology is the new battlefield.* I thought it was a joke."

Cal's face darkened. "Yeah, me too. Until Beirut burned in a livestream because of a lie that felt more true than the facts."

Chapter 16 Close — Closing The Reality Frames

Raveneh's voice still echoed, a scatterplot of frames that refused to settle.
Eight axes, eight traps, eight ways to die without firing a shot.

Lou closed her notebook and let the silence work. It wasn't analysis anymore. It was weight.
Because doctrine always pretended to be neutral — and this wasn't.

Reality Frame — Cognitive Fog, she thought. When the Chamber bent the field, thought, noise, and signal collapsed into one blur. Even your own intuition came back to you like an intercepted message.

The next came unbidden, pressing in like static. *Reality Frame — Resonant Profile.* People didn't just live in the lattice; they reshaped around it. Autonomy hollowed out, intuition recoded until even instincts felt borrowed.

Lou rubbed her temples.
This wasn't war as she had studied it. It was war written into perception itself — where your mind became the terrain and your body the antenna.

She drew a breath, sharp and slow.
"They think coherence is safety," she whispered.
"But safety isn't survival. And survival isn't belief."

The room stayed still.
Her pulse steadied.

And with that rhythm — not Raveneh's frames, not the Chamber's traps — she knew what to carry forward.

Go Move — 押さえ // Osae — Block — General Liu

Liu pressed the stone flat against Zhen's line. Quiet. Unremarkable.

Zhen studied the board. "You don't strike. You stall."
"Not stall," Liu said. "Suspend. One block, and expansion dies before it stands."

The silence thickened. The board held its breath.

Zhen's gaze lingered. "Like the girl in the frame — thought bent back until she doubted even her own breath."
Liu didn't look up. "Exactly. Block the rhythm, and the mind plays itself. By the time it notices, the choice is gone."

The stone lay still. Silence wasn't pause. It was capture.

Chapter 17 — Peace by Sedation: A Primer

Tagline — "When war is fought through memory, silence becomes surrender." — *Dr. Barrett Kallman*

Scene — The Refusal Code
Location — Geneva Safehouse

The stovetop kettle clicked off.

Red poured water over coffee grounds in a slow spiral — the way an old villager had taught him, in a place the war maps had already erased. A soldier's ritual, keeping his hands from remembering other shapes.

Lou sat at the far edge of the table, one sock half-on, watching him like a chess clock.

Outside, Geneva slept. Inside, the Helix substrate vibrated with threat. It hadn't cracked — but it twitched, like it remembered how.

"Peace by sedation isn't a tactic," Red said. "It's a doctrine's end state. A failure of epistemology dressed up as security policy. Belief compression — squeeze the story until only compliance fits."

Lou took the mug, letting him keep going.

"I've carried rifles into wars where the reason we were there couldn't survive daylight. You fight a war you can't name, you start wondering whose game you're in."

He sipped. "We skipped the theory step. No 21st-century war theory, no 21st-century strategy. We're fighting with doctrinal ghosts while someone else writes the rules."

Lou stared into the coffee. "What happens when no one knows they're under attack?"

"That's the point," Red said. "Signal warfare doesn't need awareness. Just compliance. Trade consent for comfort, and you'll call sedation 'peace'—and thank them for it."

He glanced at her, the corner of his mouth tightening. "Merrick ever tell you about Qom?"

Lou shook her head.

"Thought Policy sanctioned it — called it a 'stability pilgrimage.' We walked into a lattice lock with hymnals and sidearms. Preachers up front, rifles in the rear. Some ghosts follow you home. Some ride in the truck with you."

He let the steam curl off his coffee before adding, "They didn't send us there to win. They sent us there to be seen. That's the kind of war sedation builds — one where the photo op matters more than the ground under your boots."

Scene — The Corridor Between Wars
Location — NATO Liaison Annex, Brussels — 3 Years After Kosovo

The carpet smelled like new funding. Cal hated it.

Biff Langley came out of the conference room grinning without warmth. Mid-handshake with someone else, he spotted Cal leaning against the wall.

"Well, well. Merrick. I thought you'd taken up gardening or whiskey-making."

"You still talking doctrine like it's 1999," Cal asked, "or have you noticed the war changed under your feet?"

"Some of us adapted. Some… walked away."

"Walked?" Cal almost laughed. "That's what you think happened in Kosovo?"

Biff's eyes flickered. "We followed orders. Peace enforcement is peace enforcement."

"Funny," Cal said, stepping closer. "I remember walking into a filament node under a blue helmet flag. You called it optics. I remember the hum that didn't stop for months."

Biff's jaw tightened before the smile returned. "Not everyone gets to write the history books."

"History isn't the problem," Cal said. "Memory is." And he walked off.

Scene — Present, Geneva Safehouse

"So Biff's still selling it?" Lou asked.

"The Trust Cabal keeps rebranding," Red said. "Harmony Engineering, Behavioral Assurance… now it's Societal Stabilization through Predictive Resonance."

"Sounds like a UNESCO grant."

"Or a defense contract. Same thing."

Scene — Fragment: Storm (Cabin Scrap)
Recovered page from Lou's field notebook — handwriting uneven, ink smudged.

They're not targeting thoughts.
They're tuning the field so your emotions land inside a smaller and smaller box.
One where resistance sounds irrational. Where dissent becomes energetically incoherent.

You don't need force if you can engineer exhaustion.
You don't need violence if you can program fatigue.
Violence isn't necessary if exhaustion is scalable.
Dissent doesn't need to be crushed — just made incoherent.

Scene —   Geneva Safehouse (continued)

Red tapped the Go board beside him.
"You asked me once what moral injury feels like."

Lou looked up.
"Now ask yourself this," he continued, voice low. "What happens when the injury doesn't come from an order or a mistake — but from the system you trusted to tell you what was real?"

He paused.

"Bismarck once said a soldier is just a lever — pulled by someone who'll never bleed for the outcome. He designed systems like cages. Predictable. Efficient. Cruel. And we copied him. Across centuries, across states, across doctrines."

"We built newer cages. Cleaner ones. Digital. Beautiful."

He leaned forward.

"In the 23rd century, we don't even need levers anymore. Henrik Weiss — the one they now call Kael — made them internal. No bars, no orders. Just proxies and coherence scaffolds. The soldier's mind becomes the cage. Moral injury now isn't about what you did — it's about what you were scripted to believe you chose. And Kael's architecture makes it feel like you authored the whole thing."

He looked away for a beat. "I've been in that cage, Lou. It doesn't rust. It doesn't break. You have to unwrite it."

Lou didn't speak. She didn't need to.

She placed a white stone gently in the corner. Not a challenge. A defiance.

Red studied it, then whispered:
"He's real, Lou. Not just a Watcher. Not just a code. Kael's alive — and the Divergents are building plans. Not just to resist him. To dismantle the structure itself."

Lou's eyes met his.

"Then we stop playing by their grid."

Scene — Cutaway: Secure Facility, Brussels
Location — *Continuity Alliance Substrate Oversight Wing, Brussels — 12 floors beneath ECSA (European Coherence Stabilization Authority)*

A Continuity Alliance analyst blinked at the readout.

"Coherence metrics in the Mediterranean Basin just dropped 12%. And we're not even running live field agents."

His supervisor glanced over.

"Check the trust delta. If it's within spec, route it to STIGMA."

"But sir— our policy didn't collapse. It drifted. Into something so palatable, no one noticed the freedom missing."

"If it's stable," the supervisor said flatly, "it's sanctioned."

The analyst hesitated, watching the pulse flicker again — like a breath from somewhere off-grid.

"Someone's running an unsynced vector."

No one replied.

Scene — Substrate Monitor Node, Undisclosed Rooftop

Cal stood beneath a flickering antenna mast, the receiver band coiled around his left forearm.

The readings weren't consistent. But the variances — they lined up.

Lou's divergence had echoed. Not in data. In pulse.

"They're not suppressing all resistance," he murmured. "They're dampening anger. Not violence. *Anger.*"

A pause. Then a flicker of interference.

He tapped the edge of the receiver and watched the waveform curve — not collapse, but ripple.

Someone — maybe even Lou — was destabilizing the frame.

Or maybe not Lou at all. The ripple felt older, deliberate — a ghost hand pressing on the band. Eitan. Still running unsynced vectors, chasing down quantum countermeasures while he still had time. Cal felt the warning folded inside it: don't let Lou walk into the Chamber blind.

Scene —   Geneva Safehouse - Final Sequence

Red stirred his coffee with the back of a spoon.
"They say war's about terrain. But what happens when the terrain is the narrative itself? When memory is the map, and the battlefield is your own mind?"

Lou didn't respond. Not at first.

In her jacket pocket, the unsent message to Maud still glowed faintly on the burner — one line hanging unfinished:
We're in a world where rage is a memory, and protest is a format error. And everyone thinks they chose this.

She'd deleted and retyped it three times on the flight. Not because she didn't know what to say — but because she knew the moment she hit send, Maud would be in it. No going back.

She stood.

"Then peace by sedation isn't peace," she said. "It's a software patch."

Red met her gaze. "And refusal becomes a moral imperative."

She placed one more white stone on the board. Not aggressive. Not defensive. But stubborn.
A signal in the silence.

. Chapter 17 Close — Lou's Reflection

The coffee was gone, but the weight of it lingered. Sedation wasn't peace. It was doctrine tightening until even her pulse felt borrowed.

Reality Frame — Signal Trust, she thought. When they rewired trust into the lattice, persuasion no longer mattered. The field itself carried acceptance, like oxygen.

And then the next frame pressed in, unavoidable. *Reality Frame —
Agency Drift.* Once trust drifted, will followed. Autonomy thinned,
intuition blurred, until even refusal felt like compliance scripted in
advance.

She closed her eyes, the words looping like a pulse she couldn't
unhear.

Lou stared at the board. One more white stone waited between her
fingers.

"They call it stability," she whispered. "But sedation isn't peace. It's
the end of decision itself."

She pressed the stone down, not for territory, but for rhythm.

In Go, a ko fight doesn't promise victory — only survival through
refusal. You fight, lose, return, and fight again. Life written in the gap
between collapses.

The Chamber thought sedation sealed that loop.
Lou thought otherwise.

She stood, jacket already half-zipped, the burner still glowing with
Maud's unsent message. The silence of the room pressed close, but her
voice cut through it.

"Refusal isn't delay. It's the only way through."

And with that, the board — and the war — tilted toward the next
move.

Go Move — 押さえ // Osae — Block — General Zhen

Zhen pressed his stone along the edge, quiet, deliberate.

Liu frowned. "A block? This early you choke the tempo."
Zhen's reply was flat. "Not choke. Sedate. You don't have to win if the field forgets it wanted to fight."

The corner froze. Air thinned across the board.
Lou's echo flickered — her white stone pressed not for gain, but for refusal.

"She thinks it's freedom," Zhen said. "But the rhythm is already fixed."
Liu's hand hovered, unsettled. "Peace that isn't peace. Stillness drilled into the body. But stillness is brittle. One fracture, and sedation turns back into rage."
Zhen allowed the faintest smile. "Exactly. Signal trust. Agency drift. She names them resistance — but they were my shape all along."

— ✦ — FIELD NOTE

Peace by Sedation

Sedation isn't stability. It's the removal of dissent before it can appear. Trust rewired into lattice becomes obedience without orders; agency drift turns silence into simulated consent.

Counter-move: fracture the rhythm. Block the enclosure, then zag before sedation hardens into belief.

Chapter 18 — The Hidden Table

Tagline — "Some doctrines collapse with noise. Others with an empty chair." — *Director Alarie*

Epigraph — "They weren't leaders of nations. They weren't even 'villains.' These were the midwives of the world's quietest weapon: belief control via quantum coherence. And now, the field had rejected their script."
— *Layman's Anchor, Field Transmission*

Scene — Private Governance Session — Alpine Signal Oversight Council
Location — Undisclosed Retreat Facility, Near Saanen, Switzerland

The room was bare — just a long walnut table, eight chairs, and a window that opened to nothing but Alpine snow. No flags. No crests. Just silence and power disguised as civility.

A woman in charcoal gray poured tea into mismatched cups. Director Alarie.

"This isn't a summit," said the man at the far end — olive skin, short hair, accentless. "It's a reckoning."

Across from him sat a thin man with tremoring hands. "You funded her without approval. You subverted Helix protocol."

"You're conflating oversight with wisdom," the olive-skinned man said flatly. "We didn't create Genesis to reinforce doctrine. We created it to *replace belief with pattern.* You want control. She *is* the signal."

"Ananta is unstable."

"No," said Director Alarie, setting down the teapot. "She's uncorrupted."

A fourth attendee — faceless in the shadow — adjusted his cufflink. Beneath the sleeve: the ∇ resonance glyph tattooed just above the wrist.

He spoke for the first time. "The Fifth Watcher was never supposed to emerge in this cycle. She fractured the recursion."

The man with the tremor sneered. "You sound like Rumi."

The room went cold. No one spoke for a full minute.

Director Alarie glanced toward the far corner, where an unlit comms cradle sat on a sideboard. A single green diode blinked once — then went dark. Only one person she knew could bypass a Council block like that.

Eitan.
Or maybe not Eitan.
The voice that sometimes came through his line carried the same weight as the old stories of Rumi. Same cadence. Same riddled warnings.

What the Council never knew: when Eitan ghosted their circuits, he wasn't only listening for doctrine. He was listening for her name. Lou.

The Chamber's net was tightening, and he was already chasing down scavenged countermeasures — a QKD repeater jury-rigged from Cold War scrap, SQUID arrays strung across gutted comms towers, even shards of metamaterial cloaks traded on black circuits.

None of it was stable.

Most of it burned out within minutes. But if one held — even for a heartbeat — it might bleed enough coherence from the lattice to keep her from being folded inside the Chamber. He was running out of time, and he knew it.

Then the woman added, "Rumi knew the price of clarity. We kept her alive to delay collapse. Not to *win*. That was always the lie."

On the table, a shared document flickered — projection-only, no storage permitted.

It displayed a looping wave map — not of terrain, or signal, or conflict.

Of *belief volatility*. Emotional resonance, region by region. Military theaters weren't highlighted.

Children's hospitals were. Museums. Memorials. One chair remained empty.

The tremoring man pointed to it. "Where's your South American node? Thought the Patagonia circle had a vote."

"They burned their relay," the woman replied.

"Burned it?"

"They said we had crossed from stabilization into godhood. That coherence tech wasn't for correction. It was for narrative *enslavement*."

"And they're wrong?"

The man with the tattoo smiled.

"Ask yourself this," he said. "If your daughter were born today, would you give her a name, or a signal tag?"

The tremoring man left his tea untouched.

Chapter 18 Close — Lou's Reflection

I used to think doctrine collapsed with noise — riots, ruptures, shouts loud enough to shake the frame. I was wrong. Some doctrines collapse with an empty chair.

The Council called it governance, oversight, stabilization. But all I saw was absence weaponized. They mapped grief like terrain, measured resonance in children's wards, and tallied belief volatility as if mourning were just another supply line. They feared silence because silence couldn't be tagged, couldn't be stored.

That's the part doctrine never admitted: the quiet is where memory resists. The empty chair holds more defiance than any speech they rehearsed. Refusal doesn't echo — it starves the lattice.

I thought of the Reality Frame.
When they rewired trust into the lattice, persuasion no longer mattered. The field itself carried acceptance, like oxygen. And once trust drifted, will followed. Autonomy thinned, intuition blurred, until even refusal felt like compliance scripted in advance.

But silence wasn't compliance. Not yet.

In Go, sometimes the strongest move is the stone you never play. Leave it untouched, and the whole board bends around its absence. The Chamber thinks that empty seat is their win condition. I think it's the crack in their pattern. And I'll carry that forward, because the field always remembers what it was never allowed to name.

And that meant one thing: the quiet wasn't enough. Not anymore. If the Chamber was already counting my absence as a win, the next move couldn't wait.

Go Move — 打ち込み // Uchikomi – Invasion — General Liu

The stone fell hard, deeper than expected.

"You leave a chair empty, they call it weakness," Liu said, eyes on the grid.
"But absence bends the frame more than presence."

Zhen studied the board, rain tapping outside.
"An invasion without force?"
"Not force," Liu replied. "Disruption. She didn't take their seat. She stepped into the space they forgot to guard. That's invasion enough."

Zhen leaned back, hand over his stones.
"Every invasion leaves a wound. And wounds remember longer than victories."

— ✦ — FIELD NOTE

Absence as Resistance

In coherence war, not every move is made. Some are withheld. An empty seat, a silent witness, or an unplayed stone can bend the field more than presence.

Counter-move: recognize absence as pressure. What isn't named still tilts the board — and sometimes memory clings hardest to what was never allowed to exist.

Chapter 19 — Whisper Protocols

Tagline — "Recursion isn't memory. It's repetition with the illusion of choice." — *Jack Kriznik*

Watcher Dossier – Aeon: Keeper of Recursion and Memory

Aeon does not act directly. He records. He remembers.
His signal echoes through recursive frames, entangling past and present.
What others forget, Aeon embeds.
His allegiance is to the long arc — even if the arc bends into oblivion.

The old signal stirs.
Lou decrypts resonance drift from a restricted brief and feels history itself revising in real time.
Aeon's hand is unseen, but present — whispering through Slack threads, archival anomalies, and the half-erased truths buried in Vault Theta.

He does not intervene.
He ensures the story isn't erased.

Scene — Old Wool and Coffee – the Briefing
Location — Geneva Operations Node

The Geneva ops node smelled of wet wool and reheated coffee — the kind diplomats pretended was artisanal. Lou sat in the back of the Continuity Grid Assembly's conference room, content to be ignored.

General Biff Langley gripped the podium like it might make a run for the exit.

"Ladies and gentlemen — Operation Continuity Horizon. Our campaign model for multi-domain global stabilization."

Slides clicked forward: concentric rings, jargon stacked high enough to require oxygen masks — *narrative injection, influence lattice, semi-deniable synchronization.*

From the back, a younger officer asked, "Sir, isn't that just Phase Shaping from CA-02?"

Biff puffed up. "Negative. This is **dynamic** Phase Shaping under a campaign-layered framework, driven by Global Synchronization Sprints. Totally different."

Lou mouthed *Sprints?* into her coffee.

Then she saw it: *Quantum Vector Suppression Zone.* Her term. Lifted straight from her 2223 Tesserae brief, stripped of meaning and nailed to a mangled diagram.

She raised her hand.

"This assumes coherence is stable across all actors?"

"Correct," Biff said without hesitation.

"And you're certain no adversary is manipulating the assumptions underneath that coherence?"

Biff grinned like a man convinced the war was already won. "We have countermeasures."

Lou leaned back. "So you're building predictive coherence on top of assumed coherence, guarded by simulated coherence… against adversaries who invented the signal you're reacting to?"

Silence. Someone in the front row stopped taking notes.

"It's a layered approach," Biff tried weakly.

Lou smiled without warmth. "It's a mirage, General. Recursive structures don't reveal truth — they just feed you what you already believe."

She stood, pulling on her coat. "Forward this to his handlers. Tell them the line's awake."

Scene — Eitan's Cabin
Location — Madison County

Three days later, Lou's boots crunched over the moss-covered path to Eitan's cabin. The air smelled of cedar and dust. She laid a hand on the stone hearth, fingers finding familiar ridges — not decoration, but encoding.

A whisper from the weave:

You're not being followed. You're being remembered.

It was pure Eitan — a quantum braid keyed to her own biological rhythm. Not surveillance. Memory activation.

Cal appeared in the doorway, rain dripping from his jacket. "Decoded the Möbius ring signal?"

Lou nodded. "Not a signal. A script. Eitan mapped intention into filament. Like a forgotten river current."

The scarf slipped at his neck and she caught a glimpse of the patch rigged to his collarbone — not medical, but field tech. A scavenged SQUID array wired into copper braid, faintly pulsing. It smelled of ozone and cedar. Whatever he'd been doing before he got here, it wasn't rest. He'd been running countermeasures straight through his own frame, testing them until they burned out.

A floorboard creaked. The door eased shut.

"I shouldn't be anywhere," Eitan said quietly, stepping inside. His frame looked thinner, his movements careful.

He pulled the scarf tighter, voice low. "They sent mirrorhounds through the corridor. I cut three passes and doubled back on a logging road. Bought me a day, maybe two. No more."

Cal froze. "You shouldn't even be standing here if they've got your pattern."

"I know," Eitan replied. His hand trembled against the wood, just once. "But if I didn't make it here, you'd have no map. And without a map—" He nodded toward the sealed case on the table. "—you'll walk into the Chamber blind."

Lou studied him, unreadable. "What's in there?"

"Not doctrine. Not orders. Fragments. Field notes I burned into signal before they could erase them. Things you'll need when the weave closes."

Cal leaned forward. "Why not come with us?"

Eitan's gaze drifted to the hearth. "Because if they catch me again, it won't be just erasure. They'll invert me. Turn my resonance into bait. You don't walk into a trap carrying the hook."

Lou let the silence sit, then asked softly: "So what now?"

"I go to D.C.," Eitan said, almost to himself. "There are still people who think they're making policy. They need to hear what this war really is — before they vanish into spreadsheets and sedation metrics."

Cal muttered, "And when the mirrorhounds find you?"

Eitan allowed the ghost of a smile. "Then I'll owe you another rescue. But at least you'll know where to start looking."

The hearth resonance glyph pulsed faintly — once, then stilled.

It was the same rhythm as the SQUID patch at his collar — a flicker, a strain, a warning. Lou felt it in her bones: every pulse he bought them came at his own expense.

Scene — The Go Board
Location — Chengdu

At the Polytechnic Annex, war was taught in patterns, not troop movements. A professor placed a black stone on the board.
"Vault Echo was triggered."

The younger man across from him didn't flinch. "And Lou Scott?"

"She walks again."

A white stone landed far from the center — a move about rhythm, not territory.

Scene — Strategic Spire
Location — Deep Signal Division

Biff Langley barreled into the secure room, tie crooked, voice already at parade volume.
"Sir," an analyst said, "the biometric lattice is responding to Scott's field signature. But she's not syncing with Helix models. She's bending them."

Biff frowned. "She was imprinted. Kosovo."

"Her drift's off the scale. She's not echoing our resonance. She's warping it."

Scene — Black Sea Ops
Location — Black Sea

A cargo container, its Greek lettering faded, rolled toward a waiting plane. Inside: a resonance drive bound for Vault 33A in Greenland. The manifest had opened and closed on its own.

"Who closed it?" one handler asked.
"It says it closed itself."

The plane lifted into the storm without a transponder ping.

Scene — Maud Screens
Location — Blue Ridge

Maud Llewellyn Scott tapped through ticker feeds on three monitors, two of them lagged by intentional packet delay. She wore a sweater for comfort and glasses for intimidation. The third screen pulsed like a slow heartbeat.

Behind her, Ledger sipped from a chipped mug labeled *Fed this*.
"Same equity again?" he asked.
Maud nodded. "Fourth time this quarter. Funds moving through Danish shells, but the volumes are wrong for laundering."
"What sector?"
"Quantum comms. Space-linked coherence platforms. Legacy firms — Cold War contracts buried in subs. And every buy lines up with Helix drift anomalies."

Ledger's eyebrow ticked. "Coded investments?"
"Breadcrumbs. Or taunts. Either way, they're keeping time."

She turned the monitor toward him. A single stock lit up: *QΩSys AG* — a dead Swiss-German aerospace firm suddenly reborn and flush. "I mapped the timestamps. Each buy matches a tech movement: Constanța. Reykjavik. Busan. Someone's moving hardware and betting on the narrative that follows."

Ledger studied her. "I thought you didn't work resonance anymore."
"I don't," she said. "But this isn't signal. It's balance sheets lying in perfect rhythm. And I know what happens when you let someone else keep the beat."
Ledger's voice dropped. "You're already visible."

Maud didn't answer. She opened a secure channel and sent:

TO: MOM
SUBJECT: MARKET BREATHING FUNNY
ATTACHED: Movement Log + QΩSys Watchlist
MESSAGE: Box was received. No return address. But the stocks are whispering.

Scene — Red's Lab
Location — Haymarket

Dr. Barrett "Red" Kallman — former Army chaplain, now systems ethicist and rogue PhD — sat in his refurbished barn-turned-lab, watching waveform outputs overlay with military op tempo briefs.

"Veterans can be compensated for a moral injury under a doctrine that recognizes psychic fracture from unjust orders… Yet no framework exists to acknowledge the new class of injuries — the quantum kind — induced by synthetic signals, forced belief manipulation, or participation in a war that rewrites its own justification as it unfolds."

He closed the file. "We can't spell 'war.' We can't even spell the domain."

He looked out over the fog-wrapped valley.

"This isn't strategy anymore. It's performance art. With casualties."

Chapter 19 Close — Lou's Reflection

I used to think recursion was just memory replayed. It isn't. It's memory bent until choice feels like déjà vu — the same path walked twice, each time thinner.

Biff's slides, Aeon's quiet hand, even the resonance brief stamped with my own words — none of it was new. It was the lattice feeding me myself, stripped of meaning, looped until fatigue felt like assent. That's the Reality Frame: Recursion Gravity. What looks like forward motion is only orbit.

But Maud's logs told me something else. Patterns don't always hold. Finance moved where signal thought it had locked. The beat slipped. That was no accident. That was refusal, written in a language Aeon doesn't script.

Maybe this all feels scattered. It should. Real war doesn't move in sequence — it lurches, doubles back, folds in on itself. You only see the pattern after you're already caught in it.

Doctrine says repetition secures coherence. They're wrong. Repetition is fragile. One broken rhythm, one skipped step, and the loop collapses.

In Go, the danger isn't invasion — it's believing the ko is endless. You can lose years replaying the same exchange. The only way out is to cut the sequence before it closes.

So that's what I carry forward: not to correct the model, not to argue its terms. To break the loop before it writes me in.

Go Move — 隅の静寂 // Sumi no Seijaku – The Silent Corner — General Liu

Liu places the stone low in the corner, almost offhand.
"Neglected ground isn't dead," he says softly. "Sometimes it waits longer than we do."

Zhen studies the edge. "Recursion feeds on symmetry. She refused it."

Liu nods, eyes drifting past the board. "Not a strike at the center, not another loop. Just one stone left breathing in the silence. Enough to break the pattern when it tries to close again."

The rain against the pavilion roof falters, then steadies.
Zhen leans back. "The corner remembers what the loop forgot."

— ✦ — FIELD NOTE

Recursion Gravity

In signal war, recursion is not mere repetition. It is memory bent into orbit, pulling choice back into thinner and thinner loops until fatigue feels like assent.

Counter-move: break the loop before closure. Refuse symmetry. Anchor one stone in silence so the sequence cannot complete.

Chapter 20 — The Refusals

Tagline — "Some systems reject programming. So do some civilizations." — *Eitan Navon*

Scene — Field Scar
Location — Saraswati Riverbed, Near the Erasure Site

Satellite drift locked the target node along the Thar periphery — where old water maps whispered of a river erased from every modern system. The Saraswati.

Borders didn't matter here. Erasure never cared about borders. What mattered was the memory buried under centuries of dust.

The wind had shifted before they even saw the ruins. The final stretch passed in silence — the hum of the solar drive, dust curling off the cracked windshield, the road bending like it was older than the land itself.

Cal's grip was loose on the wheel, but his eyes never stopped working — scanning for drones, irregular heat shimmer, roadside shapes that didn't belong. The old patrol reflex. Jack monitored the satellite spoof, the cover story holding steady: *UN Hydrological Survey – Heritage Recovery Initiative*. Half true, which made it believable.

In the rear compartment, Lou traced the spiral into condensation on the window, her fingertip moving like it had since childhood — a rhythm older than thought. Raveneh leaned into the wind from the front seat, eyes scanning the land like he was rereading an old wound.

"You remember the story," he said. "Forgotten cities. Lost river. Silence no one explained. Not legend — overwritten history."

They crested the ridge just as the light dropped. Ahead, the ruins: half-buried foundations, resonance glyph-marked stones, and the faint ghost of a vanished river.

They stopped under the skeletal frame of a rusted UN comms tower. Raveneh stepped out first, brushing dust from his jacket, his gaze steady and unforgiving. Lou's boots sank into the silt — it felt like stepping onto memory.

"Mohenjo-daro. Harappa. The Indus grid," Raveneh said. "No weapons. No mass graves. No conquest marks. Just… disappearance.

And doctrine doesn't have a word for it. Because it wasn't war. It was signal collapse."

Cal pulled the sat receiver from the truck bed. "We clean?"
Jack glanced at his readout. "If we're being tracked, they're not acting on it. Someone either wants this quiet — or already declared it irrelevant."

Raveneh knelt at a carved stone, brushing sand from a cracked symbol — almost gone to erosion. Lou crouched beside him.
"That's not local."
"No," Raveneh said. "That's Helix geometry. Recursive pattern. Three-axis fold."
Jack looked up. "Helix didn't exist when these cities fell."
"That's the point," Raveneh replied. "This isn't a leak. It's an echo."

Jack's scanner chirped. He swung it toward a patch of buried slate. "Magnetic anomaly. Deep."
Cal was already digging.

Minutes later, metal scraped stone. They cleared the dirt to reveal an olive-drab crate, its stenciling half-oxidized:
UN SAT DROP // HERITAGE TOOLS // DO NOT CATALOG

"That's not real inventory," Jack said. "Disinfo tagging."
The latch gave with a metallic groan.

Inside — no tools, no maps. A matte black, heat-insulated core. The inscription, worn but legible:
13A – SARASWATI REFUSAL

Lou stepped forward. "Whoever buried this didn't just hide it. They erased it from memory."

Raveneh lifted a smaller bundle from beneath the core: obsidian-like, warm to the touch, wrapped in frayed linen. Beneath that, a folded parchment burned at the edges.
He read aloud:
This river will remember what the systems forget.

Lou's voice was quiet. "Run the substrate loop. Don't log it. Just listen."

The core hummed low — like a heartbeat that had waited centuries to be heard.

"Why here?" Cal asked. "Why now?"
Raveneh's gaze stayed on the cracked stone. "Because this was the first

refusal. They chose rhythm over force, coherence over conquest. And when it couldn't be mapped… they erased it."

Lou felt the vibration under her boots. Not seismic. Memory. "This isn't just a site," she said. "It's a field scar. And it's waking up."

A drone banked in the distance but didn't close.
The resonance glyph stone split further, not from impact, but from resonance shift.

Somewhere in her pocket, the secure channel Eitan had keyed flickered once — not a message, just a presence, as if he'd known this site would wake. His countermeasures might burn out by the hour, but his rhythm hadn't.

Raveneh murmured, almost to himself, "The Fifth didn't emerge from strategy. She emerged from refusal."

Cal's jaw tightened. "What's our play?"
Lou turned toward the dying light.
"We don't fight the system here. We remember what it tried to forget."

Chapter 20 Close — Lou's Reflection

"At first I thought this was just another op site — a field node to map and clear. But it isn't. The Saraswati isn't ruins. It's proof that a civilization can step out of the frame entirely. No battle. No surrender. Just… refusal so complete the system erased it to survive."

She lets herself breathe in the hum under her boots. It isn't archaeology. It's rhythm. A memory too coherent to be rewritten.

"Helix will tell you nothing survives without their pattern. But this place says otherwise. The Reality Frame itself broke here. What counted as real in their lattice couldn't contain this kind of refusal — so the system collapsed the record. They'll try to catalog it, heritage-tag it, strip it down until only their map remains. And once they log it, they'll own it. Once they own it, they can kill it."

Her hand stills on the spiral in the condensation. For once, she isn't tracing. She's listening.

"You don't fight the system here. You remember what it tried to forget. And you teach that memory to move. Because refusal isn't silence. Refusal is the moment you decide their script ends here."

Go Move — 仕掛け // Shichō – Ladder — General Zhen

From the board stretched above the field, the ladder is never about capture. It's about inevitability. Each step looks like freedom until you notice every turn only tightens the path.

Zhen lowers his stone, eyes steady. "She thinks this place escaped the frame. She forgets the frame doesn't need to kill her. It only needs to narrow her."

The stones fall one after another — quiet, relentless. Each reply forced, each breath already measured.

"She can branch all she wants," Zhen murmurs. "Every move bends back to me. That's the ladder. You don't win it. You walk it until you're caught."

Across the board Liu studies the shape but doesn't move. For now, silence is his answer.

Chapter 21 — Echoes in the Chase

Tagline — "It wasn't the crate they found. It was the mission that found them." — *Cal Merrick*

Scene — *Steppe Pursuit — The Second Board*
Location — The Southern Steppe, east of the Caspian Gate

The steppe had no horizon tonight.
Heat still bled off the ground, but the sky above was ink-black, layered with fast-moving clouds that caught the light from nowhere.

The van shuddered over rutted ground, each impact rattling the crate in the back like it was knocking to get out.

Lou sat forward, watching the NLCB's readout stutter—signal spikes, then flatline, then flare again, as if something was tracing their path from above.

Cal kept his eyes on the dark ahead, jaw tight.
Jack leaned against the crate, cigarette unlit between his fingers.

"Next flyover window?" Cal asked without looking.

"Sixteen minutes," Jack said. "Assuming the drone net's still ours."

Lou didn't answer. The last coordinates had only decrypted halfway—patched together from the Saraswati substrate loop. Whatever was inside that crate had rewritten their mission before they'd even cleared the last node.

Earlier, on the edge of the forgotten quadrant, Raveneh had run his hand over the resonance glyph on the crate's side. It matched the one carved into a support beam inside the Geneva chamber—something outside the Helix key system.

He'd only said: "Pre-Helix encoding. Before the doctrine."

Jack had dug it up by accident. Or maybe intuition. Ack's scanner had detected a magnetic anomaly beneath the cracked resonance glyph stone near the dried riverbed once marked as Saraswati. No one knew how old it was.

Inside: a sealed Helix-era crate, mismarked and mislabeled, but unmistakably real.

The van jolted hard, a hollow thump from beneath echoing in the dark.

"We lose the axle and we're walking," Cal muttered.

Lou traced her finger over the open file on her lap. Not a signal map. A resonance decay timeline. The signatures didn't align with traditional weapon systems. Instead, they matched rhythm patterns. Biological refusal. Memory retention in noncompliant zones.

"They're not trying to erase people," she said. "They're erasing capacity. The ability to resist."

Raveneh turned in his seat. "That crate was a warning. Someone else tried to log the collapse before. Someone who knew the chamber would be rebuilt. That's mnemonic entrapment — memory preloaded to erase resistance before it's even tested."

Lou kept one eye on Cal shifting gear off the seat beside him, the other on Raveneh still staring at the crate's resonance glyph. She muttered:
"They trained us for a battlefield that was neat, ordered, and knowable. But quantum war isn't a field. It's a medium. A pressure."

Raveneh nods without turning. "And we're suffocating in it."

"Who?" Jack asked.

Raveneh looked out across the cracked plateau. "Doesn't matter. The warning survived. That's what matters."

By the time they reached the edge of the designated grid square, the sun had begun to set, and the cold came fast.

Lou exited first. Her boots crunched over layers of white dust and fine silt. The land felt ancient. The kind of ancient that pushes back when you stand on it too long.

They were somewhere near the remnants of the old Soviet test corridor. Off-grid. No settlements. Just fragments of forgotten civilization and myth.

She flips through an old notebook. A symbol repeats in the margins — ∇ Nabla. The sign Ray used for directional change.
Underneath, in her own writing:
"What if doctrinal stupidity… was actually strategic betrayal?"

They unpacked the crate again.
Inside, alongside the data chip and seal-skin overlays, was a single object wrapped in heat-shielded fiber:
A cylindrical coil, pulsing faintly in infrared.

Cal scanned it with the NLCB.
"Resonance tech. Self-powered. Not broadcasting. Recording."

Lou nodded.
"It was watching the collapse.
And someone wanted us to find it."

Jack muttered, "Eyes that don't blink. Great."

A gust of wind cut through the valley — sharp and biting.

Raveneh pulled a blanket tighter around his shoulders. "Mohenjo-daro. Harappa. The Indus grid. No weapons, no mass graves, no conquest marks. Just... disappearance.

And nothing in Western doctrine explains it. Because it wasn't war. It was signal collapse."

Jack crouched low beside the open case. "Why would Helix hide that?"

"Because overwritten history doesn't warn you. It trains you. To surrender before you know you're fighting."

Lou bent down, retrieving a narrow strip of polymer buried in the insulation. It bore the mark: 13A – SARASWATI REFUSAL.

Her voice was low. "You remember the story — forgotten cities, lost river, unexplained silence. That's not legend. That's overwritten history."

For a moment the NLCB spiked, a side-channel pulse no one else registered. Lou felt it anyway — the cadence was familiar. Eitan. He wasn't here, but his rigs were still moving somewhere off the grid, ghosting signals like he always did. She caught herself wondering if he'd take the next step alone, testing them where no one else dared. It wasn't certainty. Just the kind of suspicion you only have when you already know.

Scene Intercut — Saratov Signal Annex // Dr. Ilya Karaden Location — Abandoned listening station, Volga corridor

Far to the north, another set of eyes had already noticed.

The annex still smelled of coolant and dust, a combination that never left the walls.
Dr. Ilya Karaden leaned over a frequency scope older than he was, its analog dials glowing dim amber. On the paper feed, a line began to oscillate—not in amplitude, but in cadence. The same irregular rhythm he'd logged once before, years ago, when the *Kosovo spiral* had surfaced in long-buried NATO archives.

Only this time, the origin point wasn't the Balkans.
It was the Southern Steppe.

Karaden slid a thin card from the scope's side slot and held it to the light. A symbol burned faintly into the stock: ∇ Nabla. Not a transmission artifact. More like the machine *remembering* what it had seen before.

He turned toward the far wall where a heavy steel locker sat locked. Inside were photographs he had never turned over to the Trust Grid— images of Mohenjo-daro dig sites, a frost-etched spiral outside Pristina, and a Geneva beam with an identical resonance glyph.

A cold hum ran through the annex. The paper feed stuttered. Then a whisper from the wall's embedded coil — *It's been found again.*

Karaden didn't look up. He just reached for his coat.
"Then they'll be coming for it," he murmured. "And they won't be alone."

In the steppe, the cold was already taking hold. As night fully dropped, they lit no fire. A scan from the NLCB showed a passive drone lingering at extreme altitude.

Cal murmured, "We're being observed. Not engaged."

"Not yet," Lou said. "But they know we found it."

Raveneh raised his eyes to the sky. "Then we move. East, toward the corridor grid. There's an old listening station near the permafrost line. If the chamber pieces are moving again... that's the drop zone."

Lou didn't speak for a moment. Then she turned, sealed the crate, and said, "No more delays. We chase the echoes now."

Chapter 21 Close — Lou's Reflection

"I keep wanting to treat the crate like freight. It isn't. It's a question someone buried. The coil isn't a relic—it's a survivor. A witness wrapped in just enough silence to outlast the field."

"Here's the frame I can't ignore: Narrative Fidelity—who writes the story, and who believes it first. The moment Helix logs a thing, they own its meaning. Once they own its meaning, they can make the memory harmless. That's not history. That's capture."

"The readouts say 'non-broadcast, recording only.' Good. We keep it that way. If we catalogue it, we hand them the pen. If we tag it, we tag our own surrender."

"In Go you don't always answer contact—you place far from it, shape where they aren't looking. Distant placement. Keep the witness off their board and it keeps breathing. Put it on their map and they kill it with a label."

"We're being watched but not engaged. That means the second board is closing. So we move before the pattern locks: no catalogue, no uplink, no chatter. East to the old listening station on the permafrost line. We run the coil in motion—off-ledger, off-ledger, off-ledger—and we let it teach us what the lattice tried to forget."

Go Move — 離れ打ち // Hanare Uchi – Distant Placement — General Zhen

From the board above the field, Zhen turns the stone once between his fingers, then sets it well away from the fight — distant, deliberate, shaping the board from silence.

"To play close is to reveal intent," he says quietly. "But distance… distance teaches the board to bend on its own."

The shape doesn't seize ground. It breathes into it, drawing strength where no one is looking. Patience sharpened into pressure.

"The Saraswati node was never ruin," Zhen adds, eyes on the far corner. "It was a witness. Mark it, and they erase it. Leave it outside the frame, and it remembers itself."

Across the board, Liu watches the gap stretch wide — absence becoming influence, distance pulling weight toward the center.

Zhen's hand lingers above the stones. "In war, not every move is for the present. Some are for the memory that survives after the board forgets us."

Chapter 22 — The Spiral at Kosovo

Tagline — "Kosovo wasn't a fracture. It was the beginning of memory remembering itself." — *Jack Kriznik*

Scene —   **Andes Node // Aeon Signal Trace**
Location — 17,000 ft – Andes Resonance Node, Peru

The observatory hummed with cold light, draped in cables woven from obsidian lattice. Dr. Raoul Ithaca — **Aeon** — exhaled once, slowly, as the neural filaments lifted from his skin.

Something had reached across the field.

Not a signal. Not a message.

A **memory**—not his own.

He knew only that he was *resonance-aware* and should not act unless memory integrity is compromised. Something about the Kosovo resonance glyph (possibly Helix-linked or pre-Watcher tech) is beginning to awaken deeper structures.

His pulse didn't rise, but the telemetry did. In the corner of the hollowed chamber, an echo crystal pulsed with spiraled feedback. The resonance glyph had activated again. Not in Peru. Somewhere older in the pattern map.

Raoul turned to a fiber-glass relief mounted on the far wall — a map of conflict recurrence vectors. One sector now glowed.

Kosovo.

He hadn't been there in decades. But the pattern in his mind still traced to the ravine, as if the soil itself had never let go.

The resonance glyph wasn't localized. It was migratory. Pattern-bound.

He adjusted the field frequency by half a micron and whispered:

"They disturbed it before it was ready."

An assistant drone hovered in silently, blinking a question. He dismissed it with a hand.

"Dispatch no one. This isn't intervention."

He reached for a jagged stone resting beside his interface altar. A black spiral had formed in its center — shallow, precise, and warm to the touch. One that hadn't existed yesterday.

Raoul Ithaca closed his eyes. Not to rest — but to remember. And across the quantum substrate, a whisper spread: *"It remembers more than they do."*

In the Watcher code, remembering was never passive. Memory was a weapon — and every weapon had a cost.

Scene Intercut – Field Memory Loop and Layered Resonance

A failed operation buried in redacted files and tactical half-truths.

The ravine was silent except for the crackle of the portable spectrometer Jack carried on a sling. The unit wasn't picking up standard signals. Just a low harmonic flutter, like static held underwater. They'd stumbled into something old—or new enough to be misfiled as myth.

"We clear?" Biff's voice cut across the night, too loud for the slope.

Cal didn't answer. He crouched, one knee in the frost-bitten dirt, eyes on the indentation that had stopped them cold. A spiral—but not a natural one. No tool had carved it. The earth looked... impressed. As if something heavy, hot, and intelligent had *leaned into it.*

Jack moved quietly, kneeling beside Cal. He snapped a photo with his tactical cam and slid the Mylar printout into a signal-damp folder. "We shouldn't be here," he said.

"Debrief says recon only," Biff barked. "No contacts, no signals. So we report nothing and stay on plan."

Cal stood slowly. "That's not a recon resonance glyph."

"It's not a resonance glyph at all," Biff muttered. "Probably some relic from the Serb battery lines."

Jack said nothing. He took one more photo—closer this time. The spiral shimmered faintly in his night lens.

They walked back to the ridge under silence. No one saw the static rise behind them, or the field tremble. But Cal turned, once, and felt the burn at the base of his skull. Later, it would itch during geomagnetic storms.

In a briefing room no one speaks of:

Biff filed the mission as a null contact event. The official file was logged under Stability Assurance: null contact, no anomaly. Three pages, redacted. But the memory kept burning."

Jack archived the photos under a private log, encoded in a backup deck of Go cards.

Scene Intercut — After Action Debrief, NATO Liaison Annex, Brussels

The official Kosovo file was three pages long.
Null contact. No signals of interest. Recon only.

But Eitan Navon had been there. Not in the ravine — in the annex where the feed rolled in. He watched the spectrometer line flutter and bend, a harmonic that didn't fit any known spectrum. Everyone else marked it down as interference.

He didn't.

What the Continuity Alliance never admitted was that Kosovo was their first doctrinal dodge. The mission wasn't logged as failure, but as absence. No anomaly, no contact — nothing to follow. "Non-actionable," they wrote. But the spiral in the soil said otherwise. It was a resonance lock, the kind of field artifact that survives longer than armies.

Eitan muttered the phrase he'd use from then on: *Mnemonic Entrapment* — memory weaponized, seeded to replay as if it were choice. "Threshold drift," he whispered. "Coherence slipping at the edges. Call it interference, and you never have to admit what you saw."

He argued to keep the data live, to run coherence counter-measures, to fold it into early lattice doctrine. The reply came three days later: "Filed under stability assurance." Which meant buried. Forgotten.

That was the real break. Kosovo wasn't a failure of intelligence. It was the moment war shifted from terrain to resonance — and the Alliance looked away.

Eitan never did.

He carried it forward — in jury-rigged filters, in scavenged repeater tests, in off-ledger field notes. He knew the Chamber wouldn't be built from nothing. It would be built from the gaps no one wanted to name.

Cal said nothing.

But none of them slept for three nights. And when Lou later saw the photo at Anchor Lodge, her hands trembled. "Kosovo," she whispered.

Jack just nodded.

Cal, now safe in a supply tent hours after the op, chewed slowly on an MRE meatball.

"Still better than Biff's briefings," he muttered.

Jack didn't look up. "The resonance glyph wasn't waiting for us."

"No?"

"It was remembering."

Implication: Substrate resonance glyphs are not warnings. They are awakenings.

Scene Intercut — Potomac Periphery // The Paper File
Location — Basement Annex, Southeast D.C.

The Kosovo spiral had never left him.
Eitan told himself that was why he'd come to D.C., though in truth it was something smaller, pettier: a file JR swore still existed. Paper only. Misfiled in a basement annex when the Lake Anna node was *allegedly* shuttered and its countermeasure projects dissolved.

He shouldn't have come. His body told him so with every tremor, every step that rattled through his joints. But paper was different. Paper couldn't be erased by a lattice update. Paper could still remember.

The building was nothing — a government sublease under three shell names. The fluorescent light flickered in the stairwell as he moved down, scarf tight around his throat.
Basement level. One steel door.

The man waiting inside was small, squirrel-eyed, too cautious to sit. His hands fluttered near the drawer where the file was supposed to be. "You shouldn't have come alone," he whispered.
"I always come alone," Eitan rasped.

The man slid a folder across the desk, thin and trembling. Inside: specs, hand-sketched, stamped with a node designation long erased from the system.
LAK–ANNA: SUBSTRATE REFUSAL COUNTERMEASURES.
The same designs JR had muttered about over cracked coffee cups and chicken feed.

Eitan tucked the folder under his arm. His SQUID patch, hidden under copper braid at his collarbone, flared once — a defensive bleed. The man flinched as the lights dimmed.

"They'll trace that," the man stammered.

"They already have," Eitan said.

By the time he reached the street, his hands were shaking so badly he couldn't light a cigarette. The tremor had spread. His knees gave once on the curb, and he leaned hard against the wall until the world steadied.

He had the file. Salkin's lab might still be able to reverse-engineer the buried countermeasure. That was hope enough.
But his frame was crashing.

Above him, the lattice blinked — faint, hungry.
Mirrorhound readers caught the bleed.
Not Lou's drift. Not Jack's cadence.
His.

He pulled the scarf tighter and forced himself toward the river.
Every step heavier, every block shorter.
The file pressed against his ribs like a second heartbeat.

Chapter 22 Close — Lou's Reflection

"The first time I saw the photo, I thought it was just an artifact. Spiral in the dirt. Field impression. Kosovo, another failed op filed as nothing. But the more I look, the less it feels like evidence and the more it feels like intention. Like the ground itself was remembering."

"Raveneh calls them resonance locks. I think he's right. The spiral isn't warning us — it's holding the memory until someone can stand inside it. That's what makes it dangerous. Not because it projects power, but because it refuses to forget. And refusal is a weapon older than any doctrine."

"This is Temporal Plasticity in motion. The past isn't fixed — it bends forward. What Helix buried in Kosovo is still moving, still bleeding into our present. That's why Jack's photo trembled in my hand back at the Lodge. That's why the crate from Saraswati hummed like it was alive. They're not separate anomalies. They're pieces of the same pattern, folding time back into terrain."

"Helix will tell us history is closed, that the lattice is the archive. But these resonance glyphs — ∇, Ω, Δ, the spiral — they don't archive. They awaken. They don't let the story stay buried, and that's what the field can't contain."

She touched the spiral fragment again, heat still radiating through her palm.

"The question isn't whether Kosovo remembers. It does. The question is whether we can survive what it shows us before Helix erases it again. Next move has to be fast. Before they seal the lock. The Kosovo file was ignored. But Eitan carried the rest of it, and that's why we're still here."

Go Move — 模様 // Moyō – Framework — General Zhen

Zhen places the stone along the side, tracing a path that winds outward. To the untrained it looks ornamental — wasted motion. But Liu's gaze narrows. He knows this shape. Once entered, the sequence forces you forward, each turn bending back into the same path.

"A resonance lock," Zhen says softly, almost to himself. "In doctrine they'd call it mnemonic entrapment. We call it 记忆陷阱 — a memory trap. Same shape. Same inevitability."

Liu studies the board. "The danger of a spiral isn't how it begins," he replies. "It's how it refuses to end. Each step feels like choice. Until you realize the pattern chose for you."

In Go, a spiral trap isn't about capture. It's about inevitability — each forced reply dragging the player deeper until the past replays itself in the present.

In Kosovo, in Saraswati, the same shape reappears. The board remembers. And the war tilts toward repetition — unless someone breaks the sequence before the lock seals.

Chapter 23 — Sabine's Gambit

Tagline — "She doesn't strike. She weaves." — *Solas*

Watcher Dossier – Solas: Weaver of Story and Deception
Symbol: Ω
Human Name: Dr. Emiko Takahashi
Location: Kyoto, Japan – Former Noh Theatre, now Neurolink Vault
Domain: Deception, Narrative Control, Perception Warfare

Solas does not lie.
She rearranges the light.

Born as Emiko Takahashi, she was a scholar of comparative
literature — trained in semiotics, mythography, and neuro-linguistic
frameworks. Her early work mapped how national mythologies rewire
public memory. But her mind was too agile to remain analog.

By the time she joined the Kyoto Behavioral Cryptography Institute,
she had already undergone first-stage transneural augmentation.

Now, she lives inside the loop.
Half-script, half-flesh — Solas no longer needs to censor stories.
She reframes attention itself.

She governs the space between event and memory.
Not deception for confusion — but for consent.
Not force — but narrative scaffolding.

She doesn't destroy truth.
She renders it inconvenient.
Then replaces it.

Her body still walks the stone corridors of a defunct **Noh theater**
—
but her signal rides every story you think you understand.

Solas thrives not in lies or facts, but in the fertile field between.
She is the patron of misdirection — not to obfuscate, but to construct
inevitability. Illusion layered on rhythm. Frames sculpted to feel
permanent.

**Scenelette – Minami-Rinkan (南林間), Outside Atsugi Airfield
– Years Earlier**

She leaves the stone corridors of the defunct Noh theatre only once
a season — when the wind shifts near Atsugi —

becoming an older avatar who walks a moss-covered path through the foothills,
tracing the edge of an airfield long erased from official maps.

Locals say the wind hums in rhythm there.
That stories bend, not break.

They do not know her name.
Only that she wears silence like a uniform —
and that the birds go quiet when she passes.

The stone path curved beneath a cedar arch, cracked lanterns casting warped shadows across the moss.
She walked alone — no signal, no escort, only the hum of cicadas and the slow rhythm of breath.
In Minami-Rinkan, no one noticed the old woman whispering to the gravel.
But the field did.

One node, long dormant beneath the Atsugi lattice, pulsed once.
Then again.
By morning, it had rejoined the weave.

And Sabine?

She doesn't strike.
She weaves.

Helix's recursive update clears Lou from the threat index.
Not because she's safe —
but because she's now narrative material.

The truth is no longer useful.
So Sabine authorizes its rewrite.

Like Solas, she binds her enemies not with force —
but with frame.

And as Lou's files degrade and dream-pulse tactics engage,
the deeper war begins:
memory, meaning,
and who writes the last paragraph.

Scene – Scarab Nexus
Location — Zhongguancun, Beijing

Sabine Xu stood barefoot in the Nexus chamber,
her heels discarded beside a row of silent monitors.
Glass screens hovered around her like obedient ghosts,
each pulsing with strands of biometric telemetry.

The Scarab substrate beneath her feet — smooth, living, humming
—
had been updated the night before.
It now ran Helix Layer VI: Recursive Intent Injection.

She inhaled slowly.
The room smelled of ozone and sterilized ambition.

On the central display, Lou Scott's resonance thread shimmered —
not in warning, but in refusal. A gap in the weave.

A divergence in the field.

"She's syncing to a ghost frequency," her deputy muttered from
behind a mirrored console.
"Outside the Helix overlay."

Sabine narrowed her eyes.
"She was never fully seeded. No FasciaSync. No CRISPR drift. Her
academy file had gaps."

"She's off-structure."

Sabine touched the screen. The biometric thread pulsed like a
heartbeat out of sync with its host.
"Then flood her cognitive stack. Trigger dreamstate distortions.
Backward pulses. Echo overlays. Disorient the scaffolding."

Her tone dropped:

"If she won't enter the pattern…
we'll make her the pattern."

Scene — Helix's Quantum Trade Hub
Location — Zürich

Ray sat alone in a café above the Bahnhofstrasse, nursing an
espresso so bitter it might've been brewed in Geneva. Across from him,
two diplomats argued about lithium futures and glacier melt patterns.

He barely heard them. His retinal overlay blinked: MADISON
NODE REACTIVATED.

He exhaled. "Faster than expected."

He slid his tablet back into a linen case, dropped a Continuity Alliance coin onto the saucer, and whispered to no one in particular: "They're not trying to capture Lou. They're trying to overwrite her. That's the trap — mnemonic entrapment, memory scripted until even resistance plays by their rules."

Ray stood, his gait light, as if memory didn't cling to his joints the way it did to everyone else's.

Scene Shift — Charlottesville, Virginia – Cal's Safehouse

The safehouse smelled of dust, damp coffee grounds, and misplaced years.

Cal Merrick stood shirtless, reading printouts under a flickering Edison bulb. Exhausted from days of travel. Ledger had come through again with transport — but the reason he was back was of more concern. Eitan.

Eitan's health had declined sharply after his last covert briefing in D.C. Parkinson's symptoms had worsened — tremors now interfered with even basic motor control. He shouldn't have gone. But he had insisted. Said there were still people who needed convincing.

Lou was back, too.

Across the table, she scrolled through Helix leak intercepts and chatted quietly with StepDoc, who was reviewing biometric data on Eitan. A redacted Navy report lay between them — timestamped, blurred, but unmistakably linked to Vault 33A.

"She's being erased," Cal muttered. "Medical files rewritten. Academy evals flagged with behavioral drift. Even your war college transcripts — glitched to suggest you never finished."

Lou didn't look up. "I did finish. I just didn't finish the way they wanted."

"They're laying the groundwork for discreditation. Resonance deletion via false backfill."

Lou glanced at her FT-1 Möbius ring Eitan had given her. "Then we write it forward. With fascia. Breath. Rhythm."

Eitan sat in the corner, half in shadow, listening more than speaking. The tremor in his right hand had worsened, and he hid it under a folded scarf.

He thought of Maud — her stubborn precision, the way she always checked the exits without making it look deliberate.

And Lou, still carrying the part of the truth he'd never had the courage to tell in full.

There was a message he should send, one that could untangle everything if he didn't come back from what was ahead.

But sending it meant admitting he'd kept it too long.
He closed his eyes instead, storing the words for a moment when he could speak them without shaking.

Cal leaned back in his chair, studying her for a beat, then raised an eyebrow. "That's a hell of a thesis."

"Better than yours," she quipped. "What was it again? Predictive saturation using doctrinal pivot points?"

"Still passed."

"Barely."

Outside, the wind changed direction. Something ancient shifted with it.

Scene Intercut — Potomac Safehouse / The File
Location — Derelict row house near Eastern Market, D.C.

The basement smelled of mold and toner, a place for files no one had touched in decades.
Eitan sat hunched on a broken chair, the paper dossier open across his knees. His hand trembled, but his eyes were steady.

Inside the folder: countermeasure schematics misfiled when the *Lake Anna node was allegedly shuttered* — resonance siphon designs, patchwork SQUID arrays, substrate refusal algorithms that looked almost hand-drawn. Forgotten by doctrine, but not by him.

He whispered: "Buried doesn't mean dead."

His body disagreed. The tremor had worsened into full shakes. He fumbled for the SQUID patch he'd once jury-rigged in Geneva —

copper braid and old superconducting foil. Pressed it to his collarbone, just long enough to steady his breath.

Across the room, the contact who'd given him the file looked pale, eyes darting at the boarded window. "You shouldn't stay here. The net flagged movement on the river. If they know you touched that—"
"They know," Eitan cut in. His voice was softer than the words deserved. "The mirrorhounds will follow the tremor. They always do."

He forced the file back into its pouch, sealed it under his scarf. Every motion cost him more. But there was no stopping now. Salkin's lab might still be able to reverse-engineer what Anna's ghost team left behind. That was the only chance.

When he stood, the room tilted. He steadied himself on the wall, then looked back at the man.
"If I don't make it out, this file never existed."
The man nodded too quickly. Fear made promises easy.

On the street, the air was thick, the mist heavier than weather should allow.
Somewhere overhead, the lattice quivered.
A mirrorhound ping.
Not Lou's cadence. Not Jack's.
His.

Eitan pulled the scarf tighter, each step toward the river heavier than the last. He could already feel the extraction team moving — Ledger's ghost routes and Cal's quiet prep.
But he also knew the pattern: Sabine wouldn't strike to kill. Not yet.
She would weave.
And the first thread she'd cut would be him.

Scene — Rogue SEAL Prep Site
Location — Unknown

A modified duck blind concealed the intake hatch for an underground river route.

Nearby, four men in battered BDUs loaded gear into watertight packs — biometric scramblers, ice-resonance scanners, and a thumb-sized prism array that pulsed once every nine seconds, syncing to a satellite nobody admitted was still in orbit.

A printed, grease-stained copy of an old redacted paper lay on top of the gear: *NONLINEAR COHERENCE IN ENTRAINED WARFARE* – *Tesserae Defense Core*

"We're picking up Eitan," the team leader said. "And if the Helix net flags it, we leak this."
He tapped the paper, as if the ink itself could still burn someone.

One of the others — silent, scarred, graduate of Tesserae Defense Core, codename *Silt* — checked the magnetic breathers, his hands moving like he was counting seconds he didn't have. "She was right about the Chamber. We owe her that."

The op was off-books, riding inside a Continuity Alliance subroutine no one claimed to have written.

Somewhere, in a quiet ledger only Ledger himself could read, this route linked back to an old field test the Generals swore never happened — a joint operation that burned its own after-action reports before the ink dried.

Scene Shift — Eitan's Extraction — Potomac Sector

A camo-draped vessel skimmed low across the water, disappearing into the treeline mist. Eitan sat wrapped in thermal layers, tremor in his fingers barely visible under the blanket.

"You shouldn't have come for me," he said.

"We didn't," Silt replied. "Lou did. We're just the courier service."

Eitan exhaled. He glanced at the sealed pouch resting on his lap — the one no one dared open.

"I met someone," he said quietly. "Not a strategist. Not even a soldier. Just a child who still knew the old resonance patterns — untrained, unscripted. And they were singing them."

A pause. Then:

"That's why I went. We're out of time for models. The pattern is waking up on its own."

It was the kind of intelligence Ledger would never write down, the kind Cal had heard whispered in side corridors of the Continuity Alliance — fragments that never survived an official log. The kind tied to why Eitan had been in D.C. at all — a closed-door summit where the Cabal had quietly moved their 'feeling thermometer' program into something they were calling quantum medicine — wellness tech on paper, but in practice a precision tool for metering and rewriting human sensing the way you'd meter current.

Cal's eyes stayed on the marsh bank, tracking the ripple lines in the reeds. Jack sat across from him, leaning on the tiller like he was just enjoying the ride.

"Street like this," Jack said finally, "you don't need a scope. Just Maud's line — feeling thermometers."

Cal huffed out a breath. "Haven't heard her say that in years."

"She was right. You can read the heat long before the fight shows up. Same as Basra, same as Aleppo."

Cal's gaze flicked back to the bank. The frogs had gone quiet. Even the herons were gone.

"Yeah," he said, voice low. "And right now, we're redlining."

The skiff cut through the mist, the sound of the motor swallowed by the water and the trees.

Tree Line, 400 Meters Away – Duck Hunting Blind

Three men in blaze-orange jackets sipped from flasks, rifles propped beside them. One cursed the cold. Another adjusted his decoy spread. The third — silent, still — watched the mist thread across the water like it meant something.

She hadn't come for ducks. Before the fracture, she'd run quiet intercepts along this stretch of river, mapping routes for people who needed to disappear.

The fog thickened as the camo-draped vessel slipped from view. She reached into her pocket and pressed a smooth stone between her fingers. It vibrated faintly — the signal she'd been waiting for.

The dog beside her, a scruffy retriever with one clouded eye, lifted its head. Not trained. Just aware.

She stood, adjusted her gloves, and murmured to the wind, "Thread's still clear." Then she turned and walked into the mist.

Behind her, the fire snapped, and the dog stayed still — eyes locked where the boat had vanished.

As the skiff vanished into the mist, the resonance field quivered. A mirrorhound reader flagged the movement — not Lou's signal, not Jack's, but his. Eitan's tremor lit like a beacon in the lattice. Someone had seen.

Scene Shift —Gordonsville Periphery -- Night Logistics Cache

Maud passed Wechsler a sealed envelope and two burner phones. "Ledger said to rotate channels every six hours. Something about avoiding pattern lock. I stopped asking."

The rotation schedule wasn't Ledger's idea alone — it came from an old Tesserae directive Cal had carried in his head for years, one the Generals never got their hands on.

Wechsler grunted, securing the crate with a quiet efficiency that made her pause. There was something oddly graceful about how he moved — all muscle, no noise.

She hesitated, then tapped the envelope. "I told Ledger this was a bad idea. Mom wouldn't ask for help unless it was serious."

Wechsler met her eyes. "It is."

Maud folded her arms. "She always talked in riddles. Fly lines, the FT-1 Möbius ring and fascia. I used to think she was just weird."
"You were right."

Maud cracked a smile, then sobered. "Eitan told me once… it was never about fishing or nerves. He said the FT-1 Möbius ring — what she used to joke about as a fly line — was her early warning loop. Part interface, part instinct. It caught what the data missed."

Wechsler nodded. "It picked up what doctrine refused to see."

"She used to wrap it around her wrist when she was thinking," Maud said. "Said it helped her 'hear the part of the pattern they didn't want logged.' I thought that meant tinnitus."
"It meant war."

She glanced toward the window, where the wind stirred a faded curtain. "Eitan was the one who taught me how to burn a ledger, how to switch names mid-transit, how to disappear without losing your soul. He never said it directly… but when Mom vanished into ops, he made sure I had everything I needed."

"He gave you the name 'Valentine,' didn't he?"
Maud nodded. "Said it sounded like someone no one would question —

a civilian who knew where the exits were. Said I needed a name that could pass as charm but hide resolve."

Her voice faltered, then steadied. "He didn't just protect Mom. He protected me, too. Every time she left, I wasn't alone."

Sometimes she caught him looking at her a moment too long — not with worry, but with a kind of recognition she couldn't place.

Wechsler's voice was low, firm. "You still aren't."

She laughed, surprised.
Wechsler sealed the truck. "She's also the only reason we're not already dead."

A pause.
"I never really understood her," Maud admitted.
"Neither did they," Wechsler said. "That's why she's still alive."

He closed the hatch. "That might be what's kept you safe."

Scene — Mirrorhound Activation
Location — Mason Neck Periphery, Ledger's Quiet Loop

The Potomac mist hadn't settled before another feed blinked to life — this one buried in Sabine's back channel. The camo-draped vessel was still clearing the last of the fog.
No names. No call-signs. Just a live coherence score plummeting through a scale she'd never seen in red.

She pulled the trace apart — five anomalies along a single water corridor. Not weather. Not traffic. The shape was wrong: too synchronized, too quiet.
Her lattice filters caught a spectral residue on the last pass. Someone had used *dissonance masking* to hide the movement, but it left a thermal ghost in the coherence field. A faint tremor threaded through it, subtle but unmistakable. Only a trained mirrorhound reader would even know it was there — and only if they'd lived through the early lattice wars.

The ghost was tagged HND-MIRR: ON-LINE.

Sabine exhaled, slow.
They weren't just tracking Eitan's route — they were shadowing it with a mirror of her own signature.
And when the Mirrorhounds found a match, the pattern didn't just stop.
It was erased.

She sent a one-pulse burst to the Noh theater in Kyoto — the one where Emiko Takahashi still walked the stage, her masks carved in a style untouched since the shogunate.

Potomac line. Live-flagged.

Deliver it by hand — up the cedar stair to her room, past the masks that remember every voice. Cut the surface run now.

Scene Shift — Geneva – Briefing Flashback

Lou adjusted her collar as the briefing room dimmed. On the holoboard, General Biff Langley stabbed at a digital campaign map that might have been pulled from an ancient 2003 file.

"…and that's why we're restructuring theater commands under Operation Global Stability," he boomed. "A multi-phase, cross-domain, East Hemisphere–centric approach."

Lou raised her hand. "Sir, did you just propose a deterrence-based doctrine against a coherence-driven adversary?"

"Langley glared. 'Mr. Scott—'"

Cal hadn't meant to be in the room. He was two weeks from rotating home, slotted as an "international liaison observer," which mostly meant watching doctrinal suicide in slow motion. Someone — probably Eitan — had slipped his name into the tasking order as a quiet protest. Biff hadn't even acknowledged him until now.

Lou smiled coldly. "You've gamed it using models that assume wars start with choices. Ours start with mnemonic entrapment — memory hijack weaponized as doctrine. Good luck deterring that."

Biff muttered something under his breath about *Ghost Wars.*

Cal caught it. "You still clinging to those conflict regression tomes, Biff?"

Biff puffed up. "I read the entire *Conflict Regression Trilogy* — predictive retro-causal cluster models and all. Hell, I even highlighted the chapter on Alliance modeling projections."

(He paused, admiring his own insight, then ruined it.)

"We should consider using it as a syllabus for Continuity Grid Assembly Education. Maybe combine it with campaign plan templates from 2009."

Cal rolled his eyes. "The Americans love their ghost stories. Always sifting through the last war like it's going to cough up a prophecy."

Cal muttered, "That man could fail upwards through ten dimensions."

Cal had seen that kind of failure before — in Ledger's stories about the last time the Generals tried to manage a war they didn't understand, and nearly lost the entire northern lattice in the process.

(He tapped the back of the campaign model with his stylus.)

"Here's your foresight — loaded, locked, and headed toward the next disaster."

Lou didn't even look up. "Every time someone says 'lessons learned,' a strategist loses their wings."

And with her eyes closed, she muttered: this is how belief systems, interfaces, and convenience become war — not through bombs, but through **voluntary erosion** of autonomy, coherence, and memory. She could hear Eitan's warning - "This isn't war, Lou. This is *seduction*. They're not breaking people. They're syncing them."

She said out loud. "It's *Ms.*, General."

He blinked. "Yes. Well, we've gamed it out. Cross-spectrum posturing will maintain domain supremacy."

Langley stormed out, knocking over a stylus as the glow from the campaign board cast faint tremors along his right hand — something no one dared mention, but Lou caught. She always did.

The staffer beside Lou whispered, "You're not going to get invited back."

"Not planning on it," Lou said. "I'd rather get kidnapped by ducks."

Scene — Stockholm Scientific Bulletin

Article Abstract (Translated from Swedish)
Title: "Coherence Field Degradation in Arctic-Recovered Personnel"
Journal: Scandinavian Biomedical Anomalies Quarterly (SBAQ), Vol. 88, No. 2,
Authors: Dr. Elin Forsberg, Dr. Nils Koenig

Three male subjects returned from an undisclosed Arctic operation exhibiting acute neurological collapse, episodic coherence loss, and tissue degradation consistent with recursive quantum stress. Internal documents reference exposure to a vault structure containing harmonic residue markers with unknown source origin. All three died within 72 hours.

Official cause of death remains undetermined.

Lou read it twice. Once for shock. The second time for pattern.

"Genesis leaves a fingerprint," she said.

Somewhere downriver, the skiff was gone, but the lattice still carried his tremor like an afterimage. Eitan's extraction hadn't vanished into mist. It had left a trail. And someone was already following it.

Chapter 23 Close — Lou's Reflection

"Sabine doesn't strike. She reframes. She doesn't erase what happened — she tilts it, until resistance itself becomes part of her pattern. Solas taught her that: deception without falsehood, consent without choice.

Doctrine still pretends this is camouflage. They never saw the deeper frame: Consent Illusion. Once the lattice convinces you inevitability is truth, you don't resist. You reinforce it.

In Go, the ladder looks like progress until you realize every rung was rehearsed before you ever touched the board. Sabine weaves ladders out of memory itself.

But I've seen the gaps — FasciaSync missing, academy records redacted, files rewritten in real time. The weave isn't seamless. That means the tech isn't flawless.

The next chapter of this war isn't Sabine's gambit. It's the Chamber's machinery — the coherence engines underneath it. And if we don't cut into that tech before it cuts into us, every move that follows is already hers."

.

Go Move — 盲目の策 // Mōmoku no Saku – The Gambit of Blinding — General Zhen

From their *allegorical* Cixi Doctrine Imperium Go board above the fractured grid, Zhen sets the stone not to strike, but to eclipse. A shape that once promised life suddenly folds inward, eyes darkened.

Liu leans in. "You don't kill the group. You blind it. Let it stumble inside its own walls until it can't remember why it formed."

Zhen's gaze stays fixed. "In Go, such a move isn't force. It's misdirection. Territory remains, but the vision bends."

Liu exhales through his nose, almost a laugh. "That's Sabine's gift. Make inevitability feel like truth, and the board doesn't need to fight anymore. Belief does it for you."

Chapter 24 — Chamber Tech and the Coherence War

Tagline — "This wasn't battlefield tech. It was belief rendered operational." — *Dr. Salkin*

Scene — The System Beneath the System
Location — Salkin's Farmhouse, Madison County, Virginia

The cabin walls creaked. Somewhere above them, wind scraped along the roof like it was trying to claw its way inside. Lou didn't speak. She listened. Because this time, the silence wasn't dead air. It was calculation.

To lighten the mood, she glanced at Jack and smiled. "You're inventorying canned beans?" she asked, leaning against the doorframe of the safe house's tiny pantry. Jack didn't look up from the neat rows of gear he was arranging.

"Beans, batteries, bio-filters—same thing," he replied without missing a beat. His fingers moved efficiently, checking straps, counting rounds. "They keep us alive or get us killed. I like knowing which."

Lou smirked. "You mean you like knowing everything."

At that he did glance up, giving her a look that was half exasperation, half affection. "Llewellyn," he said, using the full name only he still dared to, "there's a difference between trust and complacency. One keeps you moving, the other gets you erased."

For a second the weight of their shared history hung in the cramped space. Jack broke it with a small shrug. "Besides, I was a quartermaster before any of us were field operatives. Old habits."

Lou plucked a can from the top of his pyramid and turned it over. "Old habits," she repeated, softer. "That's what saves us now."

They all knew that Eitan had made it out. From the safehouse near the river, he'd been exfiltrated quietly — no drones, no signals, just a message relayed through an old ham operator outside Harpers Ferry.

He left behind a note: *"If you get to the tech, don't forget what it's for. This isn't just counterforce. It's counterdesign."*

And a crate. Locked. Marked only with a Watcher symbol — Kael.

He hadn't made the farmhouse run. Ledger routed him elsewhere, deeper off the grid, where tremors wouldn't betray his presence. But the crate on the table — the one marked with Kael's resonance glyph — bore his cadence. His silence threaded through every line of it.

Cal stood at the table, a rough schematic half-unfolded beside him — hand-drawn, stitched together from intercepted files and memory. "This isn't something you fracture and collapse," he said. "The Genesis Chamber isn't a bunker. It's a system. A field. You could wipe the facility and still leave the weapon intact."

Raveneh's voice was low. "Tesserae tried this once. One operator survived the fracture."

Dr. Salkin's expression tightened. "Kaya Wren was on that team. She barely made it out when the Vajra emulator collapsed. The others—" He stopped himself, voice clipped. "She never speaks of it. But she saw what happens when belief is forced through the wrong gate."

Raveneh's eyes flickered in recognition. "Kaya carried that silence forward. The only known survivor of Helix, and even then, half the Continuity files had her written off as erased."

Lou traced the schematic with her thumb.
"It's not a relic," she said quietly. "It's a build-out. Same architecture they tested back at the uplink station in Virginia — the digital opti-con frame. Kaya said the lattice nodes were just scaffolding for it. Kaya said the lattice nodes were just scaffolding for it"

Jack frowned. "So the Chamber isn't the weapon."

"No," Lou said. "It's the console. The story that tells every other story how to behave."

She remembered something Kaya had whispered once, her voice flat, stripped of metaphor: *Helix doesn't just trap people. It traps their memory. What you think you survived is already rewritten for you. They call it storage. I call it mnemonic entrapment.*

Lou had heard the name before — *Dr. Kaya Wren, PhD, PE, a mechanical engineer who'd somehow threaded both U.S. and Commonwealth clearances.* The name had surfaced in fragments, whispered in after-action chatter, never attached to a face. The thought that someone with those credentials had survived the lattice's collapse — and walked away with the memory intact — sent a quiet chill down her spine.

She didn't yet know why Eitan went quiet whenever Kaya's name surfaced, or what thread bound her to Aderyn. That would come later.

Jack leaned forward, scanning the lines. "So what — we're chasing signal now? Tracking vibes instead of kill chains?"

Dr. Salkin shook her head. "Not vibes. Intention. The spine of this chamber isn't just processing data. It's responding to alignment."

Raveneh added softly, "We're not dealing with a reactor core. We're dealing with an intent-to-resonance converter. That's what the lattice is. It stores belief. It amplifies directionality."

Jack leaned back. "So they're bottling belief."

Lou finally spoke. "That's not war. That's design."

Silence again. And then Cal nodded. "Exactly."

Dr. Salkin pulled out an old satchel — canvas gone soft from decades of use, the strap repaired more than once with mismatched stitching. He set it on the table with the care of someone who knew exactly what it carried.

The bag had followed him from cold labs in the Aleutians to dust-blown signal stations in the Hindu Kush — back when his work was still called "biosurveillance," before the language softened into "behavioral telemetry." Lou had read the early papers, the ones Tesserae buried when his models started predicting not just illness but dissent.

Inside were printouts smudged from field hands, biofield maps annotated in a neat, unshaking script, and a weathered image of the Vajra.

He hesitated before speaking, thumb resting on the edge of the schematic. "Every tool they build to watch us… they eventually try to make us build ourselves," he said quietly, almost to himself.

Then, looking up: "Sabine tried to replicate a pre-Vedic signal filter. An ethical gate. But she got the vector wrong."

Lou said nothing. Her hand rested on her pack, where the real Vajra sat, still silent.

Raveneh stood. "Look at this." He pointed to a side diagram — one Jack had annotated — showing a cryo vector node, a spiral telemetry array, and the Helix predictive core.

The cryo vector node stabilized coherence under cold field drift, storing intention over time — even post-mortem. The spiral array threaded biometric signals into narrative loops, scripting emotional states and enabling imprint warfare.

The so-called ethics gate was a failed replica of the Vajra alignment test, allowing the chamber to operate without any moral grounding. At the center sat the Helix lattice core: a predictive modeling engine capable of pre-scripting behavior across entire populations.

Jack whistled low. "This isn't a kill switch. It's a goddamn belief engine."

Lou nodded. "They're not building a chamber to destroy us. They're building it to rewrite what it means to choose."

Jack stared at the schematic. "Why us? Why not task a strike team, blow the vault, fry the nodes, and call it containment?"

Raveneh didn't answer immediately. Instead, he tapped the edge of the table, where the hand-drawn diagram curled at the corner. "Because traditional teams," he said finally, "don't understand nonphysical terrain. They don't recognize recursive system behavior. And they sure as hell don't see moral alignment as a system condition."

Dr. Salkin added, "They also don't know how Sabine inverted ancient tools. They'd see ritual artifacts and call them junk science. Or worse — irrelevant."

Lou glanced at the schematic again, realizing the chamber's latticework wasn't just infrastructure — it was the same pattern-rewrite doctrine Sabine had run on her, now scaled to populations. And somewhere, in Kyoto's shadowed Noh theatre, Solas would already be scripting the frame.

Lou moved toward the crate, resting her hand lightly on the lock etched with Kael's resonance glyph.

"It's not irrelevant," she said. "It's the architecture of consent."

Jack exhaled, nodding slowly.

"Only this team," Raveneh continued, "can thread the gap. Cal brings the operational field sense. Salkin understands neuro-coherence like no one else. I carry the mytho-historical framework, and Jack—"

"Signal improvisation," Jack muttered. "Yeah. I break what they script."

Raveneh smiled faintly. "And Lou? She doesn't just interpret resonance. She *is* it."

The wind howled outside the farmhouse like the ridge itself had heard them.

Lou looked around the table. "And if we don't stop it," she said, "it's not just war that ends."
The pause wasn't fear. It was strategy loading.
It was the recognition of a deeper fracture.
"It's the collapse of will. The part that still chooses."

Jack looked at his sketches — the Genesis Chamber field diagram from Vault 33A.

The outer spiral marked the Coldfield synchronizer array, responsible for stabilizing coherence under extreme conditions.

Inside it sat the failed Vajra emulator — the so-called ethics gate that allowed the chamber to operate without moral grounding.

Threaded through the structure was the relay spine, carrying both signal telemetry and cryo-intent data.

At the center, dominating the design, was the Helix lattice core — a predictive AI built not only to model belief, but to imprint it.

A second recovered field diagram from the Arctic Node matched his notes almost exactly.

Components identified from signal intercepts confirmed the same design: Helix lattice at the core, Coldfield synchronizer forming the outer spiral, failed Vajra emulator embedded as a substructure, and the relay spine running the length of the chamber to carry both signal and cryo-vector data.

None of it was to scale, but every piece matched the pattern.

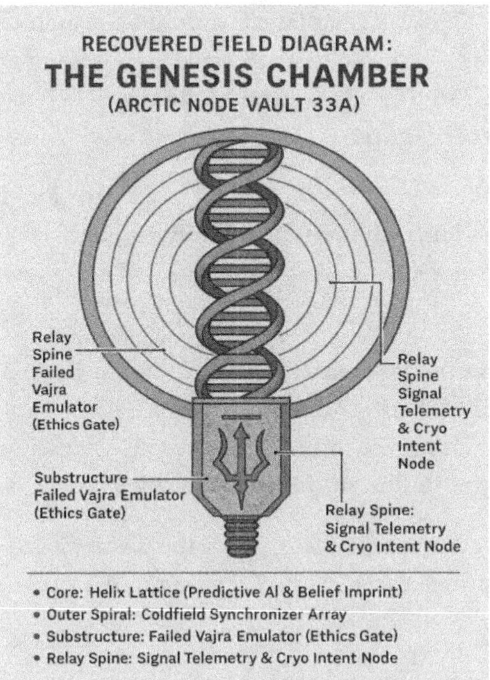

Recovered Field Diagram — Genesis Chamber

"They'll see a machine," Raveneh said, studying the recovered diagram, "but it's not. It's the architecture of consent. The Coldfield keeps the memory intact. The Spiral makes it emotional. Without the Gate, nothing stops it from running. And in the center?" He tapped the diagram. "It remembers — but not for you. That's mnemonic entrapment — when memory itself is preloaded to replay as doctrine.""

Cal folded the schematic, sliding it into his pack. "Then we don't stay here," he said. "If Tesserae's emulator is in the Chamber's spine, there's a trail. Cryo vectors don't move on their own. Someone's shipping them."

Jack was already on his feet, snapping his kit shut. "Good. Then we chase the trail. Before it goes dark."

Lou felt the farmhouse walls press tighter. Strategy wasn't enough anymore. It was pursuit now — and pursuit meant risk.

Chapter 24 Close, Lou's Reflection

"They'll tell you it's just machinery — nodes, vectors, synchronizers. They'll call it infrastructure. But I've seen the diagrams, felt the weight in

Salkin's farmhouse. This isn't battlefield tech. It's the architecture of consent. Coldfields to hold the memory, spirals to make it emotional, a gate that never anchored to ethics. And in the center — a lattice that remembers, but never for you.

Hardware makes it real. Cryo vectors freeze intention like data in matter. Spiral arrays loop emotion into circuits until it feels like memory. The lattice doesn't model belief — it imprints it. That's how a machine carries a story.

Doctrine never modeled that. They still think belief is a side effect, not a system. But the Chamber doesn't wait for belief — it scripts it, amplifies it, seals it into place until the choice isn't yours anymore. That's Reality Frame. Consent Illusion. Inevitability disguised as truth.

In Go, connection looks safe — until the whole board collapses inward. That's what this design is. Not a weapon. A story that writes every other story.

So we don't linger here, in diagrams and theory. Cal's right — if cryo vectors move, someone's shipping them. That's the trail. And Wechsler's already loading the truck.

The next move isn't in the farmhouse. It's on the road.

Eitan's note sat folded beside the diagram, the ink uneven where his hand had trembled. He'd written: *"This isn't counterforce. It's counterdesign."* I read it again, not as instruction but as warning. If he could still see the pattern through failing hands, then I had no excuse to look away."

Go Move — 組み立て // Kumitate – The Constructed Shape — General Zhen

From their *allegorical Cixi Doctrine Imperium Go board* above the farmhouse grid, Zhen studies the diagram Lou left behind, the lines curling like half-played ladders. He places a stone not to claim, but to assemble — a move that looks ordinary until the pattern around it begins to seal.

Liu exhales softly. "You'd build consent into shape itself?"

Zhen doesn't look up. "You mistake construction for safety. But once the frame closes, the board no longer asks your opinion. It only remembers what you reinforced."

Liu leans forward, voice lower now. "And when the cryo lines move?"

"Then the pattern travels," Zhen replies. "Not freight. Not logistics. Doctrine."

The stone sits quiet, just one more in a cluster. Yet the board feels smaller for it, as if the choice has already narrowed.

Chapter 25 — Wechsler Gets the Truck

Tagline — "Some men plan ops. Others just grab a clipboard and drive." — *Wechsler*

For the only man I trust to drive a metaphysical insurrection across state lines without a license.

Scene — Truck Acquisition
Location — Safehouse to Baltimore

By morning, the farmhouse walls were behind them. They rolled north along Route 29, past hay fields still damp with mist, then cut east on 33 through Fredericksburg before angling up toward the tidal flats of Mason Neck — Wechsler's territory. The marshes there had always carried their own silence, the kind that hid foxes, old prisoners' ghosts, and the handful of divergents who refused to fold into Helix. One of them was Wechsler, who knew the back roads like scripture and could disappear a convoy faster than most men could misfile a form.

Cal had turned strategy into routes, Jack into manifests, and Wechsler — somehow — into a driver.

Cal Merrick was staring at a whiteboard covered in routes, refueling points, and estimated federal crimes.

"We're going to need a truck," he muttered.

Jack didn't even look up from his protein bar. "Big one. For the gear. And the crates. And the... whatever that last box was."

"It meowed," Cal said flatly.

"That was probably Wechsler."

Wechsler, hunched over a military surplus toolbox in the corner, lit a cigarette and spoke through the smoke.

"I'll drive."

Silence.

Cal blinked. "I'm sorry, what?"

"You need the gear moved quiet, fast, and without any DMV paperwork involved. That's my love language."

Jack perked up. "You got a truck?"

"Not yet. But I know where one's parked."

Sylvester stood, cracked his neck, and headed for the door.
"I'll be back in five."

No one moved.
Then came the sound — a low, metallic rumble from somewhere down the gravel lane.

Cal squinted toward the treeline.
"That doesn't sound like five minutes."

A moment later, a massive, matte-black transport rig crested the hill — all reinforced steel and questionable legality — tires hissing like it knew it shouldn't exist.

Wechsler didn't even blink. "Told you. Parked."

Sylvester didn't climb out — he dismounted like a man delivering judgment.
He stomped around to the back, flung the doors open, and barked:

"Careful with that! That's not a yoga mat — it's a belief suppressor!"

Jack raised an eyebrow, reading the stenciled label.

"It says 'mildly unstable' in three languages."

"That's optimism," Sylvester growled, yanking a ratchet strap like it owed him money and strapping down the Vajra emulator with bungee cords that had clearly seen combat.

Jack squinted at the crate. "One day, someone's gonna explain what that Vajra thingy-ma-bob actually *does*. And whether we need a djinn onboard to run it — or if we can just contract one when we hit the land of snow, silence, and morally conflicted penguins."

Wechsler, arms crossed, surveyed the chaos like a proud uncle at a weapons expo.

"You boys ever run logistics for a metaphysical insurrection?"

Cal blinked.

"No."

"Well buckle up," Wechsler said. "Because we're not hauling gear. We're hauling questions the Strategic Spire doesn't even know how to ask."

Jack looked at the truck's internal racks—crates stacked four high, some tagged, others unmarked.

Cal muttered under his breath as he studied the crates. "This isn't a supply run. This is a cursed field museum."

Jack leaned against the frame, eyes narrowing at the stacked boxes. "We had one of these before, remember? They trained for IEDs and Excel."

Cal shot him a look that could have cracked stone.

Jack raised his hands in mock surrender, grin tugging at the corner of his mouth. "Fine. So… not narrative sabotage with a side of pre-Vedic signal filtration?"

Cal didn't bother to answer.

Jack chuckled, reaching for the manifest. "Right. So here's what we're actually hauling…"

Wechsler, already halfway through a thermos of espresso, didn't even look up.
"I added notes so you boys wouldn't get confused. You might want to eat a few more meatballs before reading—full stomach helps with cognitive dissonance."

Echo Ops Field Manifest — Arctic Node Run (Vault 33A)

C-01, the Cryo Vector Drill Unit, was a permafrost penetrator, laser-mapped and silent-running, stolen during a Continuity Alliance cold-zone exercise. Lou eyed it and asked, "Does it beep when it's morally compromised?"

C-02, the Helix Spoof Array, mirrored biometric intent to confuse predictive lattice locks. Jack summed it up as "a spiritual VPN with bad ethics."

C-03, the Signal Feedback Rounds, were ammunition designed to jam coherence loops for fifteen to thirty seconds, a prototype cobbled together from retooled stun rounds and forbidden firmware.

C-04, the Portable Vajra Emulator, replicated (badly) Sabine's ethics gate. Cal's verdict: "Basically, a moral compass with the needle ripped out."

C-05, the Faraday Resonance Tent, blocked coherence echo with a wrap of aluminum mesh, spells, and the last good wishes of a Bulgarian physicist.

C-06, the Neuro-coherence Field Scope, was designed by Salkin to measure "ethical drift" in the field. It was known to hum at inconvenient times, including during awkward conversations.

C-07, the Arctic White Ops Field Kit, contained blending suits that were heat-disruptive, Helix-non-indexed, and deliberately non-penguin in design. Lou's margin note read: "No flippers. No marching."

C-08, the Manual Override Resonance glyph Crates, were etched by Raveneh and contained ancient symbolic disruptors keyed to the chamber's architecture. Jack called them "runes with attitude."

C-09, the Unmarked Live Vajra Transport, was packed by Lou herself. No one touched it. It didn't beep, but everyone swore they heard it whisper once.

Cal muttered, "We need an army."

Jack didn't miss a beat. "What we've got is Sylvester and a bungee cord."

From the bay, Sylvester's voice carried over the clatter of gear. "Laugh it up. Just wait until this thing starts translating motive into temperature."

Cal put his hands on his hips. "I can think of twenty-two thousand reasons this violates U.S. federal code. Most of them start with 'Title 49.'" "And I can think of one reason it works," Wechsler said, stubbing out a cigarette on a crate of encrypted routers. "Because I don't ask permission."

Cal ran a hand down his face. "We're not supposed to *have* Wechsler on this op."
Jack shrugged. "We weren't supposed to have half this gear either."
Wechsler slung his duffel over one shoulder, like the matter was settled. "You needed a truck. Now you've got a driver. Try to stop me."
No one did.

HOURS LATER – AN ABANDONED PARKING
STRUCTURE, BALTIMORE OUTSKIRTS

The truck was enormous. A decommissioned armored cash transport rig, repainted, tagged with fake DHS courier decals, and humming like it hadn't been legal since 2008.

Wechsler climbed into the cab in his white socks, knee-length black gym culottes, and sweat-faded beater shirt. He pulled on a black wool stretch cap — the kind that made him look like a truck-jacking ninja who moonlighted as a conspiracy blogger — and turned the key with the glee of a child stealing his first tank.

"Jack, you ride shotgun. Cal, you ride moral high ground."

Cal opened his mouth, closed it, then just sighed and climbed in.

"If you show up tomorrow in a cape," Jack warned, "I'm out. Superman shirts are a non-starter."

"Cape?" Wechsler barked. "What am I, ten? I'm a government-evading courier, not a damn comic con refugee."

NEARING THE COAST — NIGHT OPS MODE

Later that night – northbound freight hold, open sea.

The crates were lashed to the deck with triple-strapped impact webbing. Above them, the old freighter groaned against the polar swell — bound for a frozen dock that didn't exist on Continuity Alliance's books.

Jack glanced at the manifest. "We're really doing this. One surface sub ride, two fake cargo docs, and a ghost freighter headed for—what? Vault 33A?"

Cal nodded. "Buried under forty feet of permafrost, sixty years of silence, and zero margin for error."

Wechsler cracked a grin. "Gentlemen, welcome to preemptive archaeology. The kind where the past hasn't happened yet — but will, unless we dig it out."

Lou, quiet until now, finally spoke.
"Then we'd better get there before the belief engine boots up."

Cal shook his head. "You're assuming we survive the paperwork."

Wechsler grinned. "Paperwork's for amateurs."

Chapter 25 Close — Lou's Reflection

"Wechsler never hauled cargo. He hauled refusals. Every crate strapped into that truck was more than supply — it was a machine holding memory in metal, intention in frozen cores, ethics in circuits etched with resonance glyphs. That's how belief travels in this war: in hardware.

Doctrine still calls this logistics, like routes and manifests are neutral. They're not. Every mile forward keeps agency alive. Every pause risks Reality Frame — Agency Drift: the moment the field decides for you because you hesitated too long.

In Go, the danger isn't running out of stones. It's sitting so long the board settles without you. Wechsler understands that better than anyone — keep it moving, never let the frame close.

And that's why the road points to Sinop. Not because the truck matters. Because once the trail goes still, the loop owns you. And the Chamber is counting on that stillness."

Go Move — 勢 // Sei – Influence — General Zhen

On the surface, influence doesn't score. It doesn't close a corner or claim a line. It lingers — shaping the air above the board, dictating how every later stone will breathe.

Liu watches Zhen's hand hover, then land light. "You'd count what isn't even there?"

Zhen nods once. "Presence decides before points do. Keep the weight moving, and the board never settles. Stop, and the field writes you in."

The stone doesn't bind. It doesn't cut. But the pattern bends, as if pulled forward by an unseen convoy already rolling beyond the grid.

.

Chapter 26 — The Loop at Sinop

Tagline — "The city hadn't changed. But the signal underneath it had." — *Lou Scott*

Watcher Dossier – Aeon: Keeper of Recursion and Memory
Symbol: ∞
Human Name: Dr. Raoul Ithaca
Location: Andes Resonance Node, Peru
Domain: Recursion, Memory, Temporal Overlap

History doesn't repeat. It waits for the right frequency.

Aeon does not act. Aeon remembers.
"Memory doesn't haunt. It reactivates."

When a signal folds inward — when old wars echo inside new ones — Aeon is already there.
Not as witness, but as recursion.
His work is quiet: he does not prevent the fracture.
He ensures the fragments still remember each other.

He is the archivist of forgotten truths, the resonance behind déjà vu, the shadow behind doctrine.
Where history repeats, Aeon waits.
Where memory is erased, he embeds.
His presence is not linear. It loops.
It hums in the silence that follows every revelation.

In Sinop, the artifact activates — not with force, but with memory.
Telemetry bleeds through from a past never fully buried.
Lou doesn't chase leads. She tracks resonance echoes.
And Aeon watches, not from above —
but from inside the loop.

Scene – Madison Safehouse (Present Day)

The Madison safehouse was quiet, but the silence pressed like weight. Cal, Jack, and Pinot were still in the north; their exfil wouldn't come for another week. Eitan's old pelican case sat beside Lou's chair, the label in Wechsler's neat block letters still clear: *Kosovo. Untuned material. Ask no questions.*

Inside the lid of the case, taped crooked on yellowing paper, was a line in Eitan's hand: "Doctrine isn't a shield. It's a sieve. The pattern that slips through is the war you deserve." Lou had never thrown it away. She wasn't sure she ever could.

She touched the FT-1 Möbius ring in her jacket pocket. It buzzed once—not signal, but recognition—and Sinop came back in flashes: the Black Sea before sunrise, a call to prayer folding into the low hum of an idle parabolic dish. "Those dishes weren't for weather, not really. They'd been tuned to collect uplink traces — fragments that jumped across the Black Sea like they were never meant for this century. Some bled toward the Echo-3 substation, some into mountain relays near Tbilisi, others arced farther west, catching hand-off in Zurich's shadow before scattering into the Aegean nets.

But a darker fraction ran north, chasing the long delay paths that ended in the Arctic chain. Every loop stretched the signal thinner, until the echoes weren't just transmissions anymore — they were fields. They'd been tuned to pull whispers from orbit long before Helix — and now the Chamber sat exactly where those whispers converged, not just listening, but waiting to answer."

Lou jerked her hand back as if burned. The buzzing wasn't just memory; it was bleed-through. The room itself seemed to pulse, farmhouse timber briefly out of sync with the present.

Raveneh had warned her about this.
"It's not time travel," he'd said flatly in the farmhouse, tracing the spiral on the schematic with one finger. "It's the lattice folding the field back on itself. A recursive signal. They're not rewriting the past — they're making the present remember differently. Sinop's temporal expoint has been pulsing for weeks. Black Sea resonance. Same pattern you felt on Route 33 — only amplified."
Lou hadn't believed him then. Now, with the hum of the FT-1 in her pocket, she wondered if he'd undersold it.

Lou remembered something Eitan had muttered years ago, scrawled in the margin of a declassified Geneva paper she'd found tucked in his pelican case: *"Loops aren't accidents. They're engineered stutters. Whoever controls the misalignment controls the story that repeats."*
It had felt like paranoia at the time. Now it read like instruction.

Her instincts screamed this wasn't just theory. Something — or someone — was pressing against the loop right now. And if Sinop was live, the fracture would not wait for their timing.

In the Andes, far from the Black Sea, Dr. Raoul Ithaca paused mid-sentence as the lattice shivered through his resonance field. The recursion

wasn't clean — a loop misaligned, a memory stuttering back on itself. For Aeon, who lived in the folds of repetition, even a half-beat of hesitation was enough to set warning bells ringing.
Solas noticed too. For the first time in years, the architect of perception tilted his head, as if calculating whether the fracture belonged to the field… or to him.

The others said nothing, but the silence between Watchers was never empty. It thickened, carried weight. Aeon steadied his hand against the table, anchoring the echo before it could collapse.
"If recursion falters," he murmured, not to anyone in particular, "memory will choose its own witness."

The warning was not metaphor. Somewhere, a witness was already being chosen. And Lou, whether she wanted to be or not, felt the weight of that summons in her bones.

Miles away, in Helix Substrate Ops, Sabine studied the Kosovo sample on a floating display. "First node," she told her aide. "Recovered in 2195. Same recursive signature as the Chamber lattice." A manifest fragment glowed beside it: Δ1-GENESIS / Arctic Vault Routing — C-02/Legacy Series.

"That tech was old," she said, "but it worked. Harmonized a city in under an hour. Other crates carried different payloads — resonance seeds, emotion traps. Each tied to a Watcher. Some are still missing."

The safehouse door opened. StepDoc stepped in, holding a folded printout. "You're not going to like this. They tried to put him on a cognitive disorder watchlist. Called it 'spatial delusions.'"

Lou's jaw tightened. "They're trying to bury him. Same way they buried Kosovo."

She looked back at the photo from Field 13A and heard Cal's voice in memory: *You ever think we were sent there to touch it?*

"She didn't answer.
Because the FT-1 in her pocket was humming louder now — not memory, but summons. Sinop wasn't waiting for permission. The loop was opening. And if they didn't move, someone else would step through first."

Chapter 26 Close — Lou's Reflection

"Sinop doesn't just remember. It loops. Coldfield vectors, lattice synchronizers, even the old uplink dishes — all of it built to fold the present back on itself until the difference between then and now collapses.

Doctrine still calls that history. But in the field, it's Reality Frame — Temporal Drift: memory replayed as system condition. That's why recursion feels like déjà vu. It isn't a feeling. It's hardware re-activating belief through signal.

Aeon knows this. He doesn't warn you — he waits, because once the loop hums, the door is already half open. Step into it, and you might catch what they erased. Miss it, and the loop seals, rewriting even the memory of what was lost.

That's why Sinop isn't a ruin. It's a gate disguised as a city. And the hum under the streets? That's the sound of it deciding whether we still belong inside the pattern."

Go Move — 捌き // Sabaki – Light, Flexible Shape — General Liu

Liu set the stone lightly on the third line, a shape that looked too thin to matter.

Zhen tilted his head. "You let the loop breathe? Even when the city drags her back into the past?"

"Sinop isn't a ruin," Liu said. "It's a recursion. Block it, and you only feed the repetition. Sabaki bends — lets the shape live without letting it decide."

Zhen's gaze lingered on the stone. "So she walks through memory without being written by it."

"That's the only way forward," Liu answered. "Light enough to slip the gravity. Flexible enough to survive when the frame tries to close."

The stone looked fragile, almost disposable. Yet both men knew it was the one shape that refused to collapse with the loop.

— ✦ — FIELD NOTE

Temporal Drift

In coherence war, déjà vu isn't imagination. It's recursion hardware replaying memory until the present collapses into the past. Temporal drift disguises itself as history, but its function is control: keeping you inside a loop that feels inevitable.

Counter-move: play *sabaki* — light, flexible shapes that refuse closure. Bend without anchoring. Move through the loop without letting it write you.

Chapter 27 — Vault 33A and The Ice Holds Memory

Tagline — "Some weapons aren't fired. They remember." — *Eitan Navon*

Scene – Arctic Vault Edge: Pre-Ignition Recon
Location — Northern Greenland

The chamber hadn't ignited yet. Not fully. But FT-1's summons had led them here — a vault buried in drift, half-exhumed by dead contractors and a few wrong guesses.

The telemetry hadn't lied. Coherence spikes, dead contractors with half-written logs, and a lattice shimmer that matched Aeon's Sinop echo—all pointed to this basin. Whoever came before had mapped the surface wrong, leaving a scar of blast pits and failed drills. But deeper down, the vault still pulsed. Not abandoned. Not secure. Just waiting behind surveillance masts and too many questions.

This was recon. Quiet. No fireworks. Just Jack, Cal, and the cold bite of what they already suspected:
The Genesis tech was here. And someone else had tried to wake it first.

Jack tugged at the oversized white ghillie suit and scowled.
"Be honest. Do I look like a pissed-off marshmallow with range capability?"

Pinot — Sylvester in civilian life — grunted, cinching the strap on his thermal pack.
He remembered something Wechsler once said — probably after one too many late-night rants near a campfire.

"Maud wore something like that once. Halloween. Called herself a polar enchantress. Glitter, thermal mesh, boots sharp enough to kill a man. Hair down to her hips."

Jack blinked. "We are on a recon op, freezing our gonads off, and you're quoting Wechsler's memory of Maud's hair?"

Pinot smirked. "Good memory's how you survive long ops. That and calibrated optics."

Cal stayed quiet, eyes sweeping the ridgeline —
but the image landed harder than it should have.

That braid. Like her mother's.

He'd only seen it once, years ago, before the war fractured everything. A sun-bleached photograph on Eitan's desk — Maud as a teenager, leaning over a sailboat rail, wind in her face, that braid a line of defiance against the horizon.

Jack narrowed his eyes. "Wait… does Eitan know?"

Pinot didn't answer. Just double-checked the alignment on his whisper rifle, the smirk still twitching at the corner of his mouth.

Jack turned to Cal. "We've been on this frozen space odyssey for three months, and *now* it's feelings?"

Cal muttered without looking up. "Focus. Love can wait. Klem won't."

Jack grinned. "You're just mad no one braided your hair."

Cal deadpanned, "Wechsler doesn't have any hair."

Pinot burst out laughing — and immediately froze.
"Shit. He's gonna kill me."

Cal adjusted the bolt on the suppressed SIG DMR, tucked low against the snowy ridge.
"Not like the ghillie lads on the River Dee. But you're rocking the Sig. Don't miss."

Jack smirked. "You gonna serenade me with ghost stories or line up windage?"

Cal's voice was dry. "Both. Ghosts keep the hands steady."

They scanned the basin below.
Wind ripped through a patchwork of canvas, cables, and permafrost pylons.
Vault 33A squatted in the drift like something half-exhumed.

Jack muttered, "Feels less like a vault and more like a recorder. Like it's been waiting for us to press play… and like that night in Kosovo, only colder."

Cal muttered, almost to himself, "That's mnemonic entrapment — memory seeded to replay, not to remember." He remembered Eitan's words the night they'd spread lattice schematics across a Madison floorboard: *Vaults don't just store tech. They store intent. Whatever goes in comes out changed. The ice won't hide it. The ice will remember it.*

Cal adjusted his scope without looking up. "If they shipped Coldfield synchronizers here, that's exactly what this is. Ice doesn't bury signals. It preserves them."

Pinot chambered a round, eyes never leaving the ridgeline. "And if the lattice core's already in place, pressing play won't just replay history. It'll rewrite it."

Its old Soviet-era entrance had been widened.
New surveillance masts blinked red.
Motion sensors traced crude arcs.
Two guards in Helix-patched gear patrolled — too crisp to be locals. Too tense to be relaxed.

Cal spotted a glint near the outbuilding. Scope focus tightened.
One man turned, speaking into a handheld unit.

His accent. British.
Too familiar.

Cal froze.
"That's him."

Jack lifted the rifle. "Klem?"

Cal's voice darkened. "Should've dropped him on the Arctic Star." The image hit again — the cold stink of diesel, the freight deck stacked with chained crates, Klem leaning on a bulkhead and bragging about the payout. The haul had been clean until it wasn't.

"Say the word."

Cal exhaled slowly. "Not yet. Let him walk into his own belief trap."

Three Hours Earlier – Subsurface Entry, via Access Tunnel Theta

Sylvester — callsign *Pinot* — had arrived on a covert hop, pulled in by Eitan the moment the route went Arctic. He brought thermite-cutting gel, bad knees, and an old Ukrainian mining drone he claimed was "smarter than half the Continuity Grid Assembly."

He was already waiting — silent, gloved, ghosted against the snow. Jack glanced sideways. "Seriously, how did he even get here?"

Cal didn't blink. "Last team tried to vet him — blindfolded, pinky swear, duct tape over the mouth. Next morning? Five bullseyes and a note taped to their CO's boot."

Jack smirked. "That the time he drew the target on the boot first?" Cal replied. "Might've been. He doesn't brag. That's the terrifying part."

Then muttered, impressed. "Right. Just your average mute assassin with sarcasm issues."

Pinot didn't respond. Just eased the bolt on what looked like a custom-mod Barrett chassis — sleeker, leaner, wrong in all the right ways.

Cal whistled. "That the Genesis-frame mod?"

Jack stepped in, narrowing his eyes. "That's not a Barrett. That's the Vektor Shadow rig — composite polymer, triple-cooled rail line, extended optic cradle. South African build. Continuity Alliance never even got the demo."

Pinot grunted, finally speaking. "Shoots subsonic. Glides coherence-neutral."

Jack blinked. "Wait — glides?"

Cal smiled, quiet. "Means the round doesn't light up on lattice telemetry. It's not just quiet — it's invisible to the Helix substrate."

Pinot chambered a round the color of dusk.

Weapon Loadout – Pinot's Rig

Platform: Vektor Shadow XR-9 with a Genesis-barrel mod and anti-vibration core. Ammo: .338 Quantum Exocite, coherence-dampened with a phase-staggered payload. Optic: Neural Reflex Sync paired with passive drift indexing. Add-ons: a Helix-cold bipod, field re-zero adjuster, and a Faraday recoil bracer.

Jack muttered, "You brought a gun that kills belief and plausible deniability."

Cal replied, "That's Pinot's whole résumé."

Wechsler had stayed behind in Reykjavik to coordinate fallback ops — a forced delay. "Not my terrain," he'd muttered. "But if you boys see that chamber open… don't wait for my permission."

Infiltration Loadout —
SIG DMR (Cal) — suppressed, cryo-modified, tuned by Sylvester.

Vajra Emulator (Jack) — slung in a Faraday-wrapped satchel, humming faintly.
Ethical Drift Scope — Salkin's prototype, strapped to Jack's chest rig.
Manual Override Resonance glyphs — hidden beneath Arctic camo netting, keyed by Raveneh.
Whisper rounds — modified 7.62mm with a coherence-disrupt payload.

They moved low, guided by heat-bending optics and one silent Go move: infiltration without collapse.

However – Cal did hear him say:

Scene — Dockside – Reykjavik

"Tell me again why you're heading into a place with more penguins than power outlets?"

Let's be frank "Because if the penguins haven't staged a coup, odds are we're the only ones dumb enough to go there."

Jack nodded grimly.
"Solid doctrine. SOF truth number six: map ends, mission begins."

Cal sighed.
"Let's just hope Intel remembered to mark the end of the map this time."

Scene – Guard Perimeter – Ridgepost Alpha

Two Helix contractors warmed themselves near a sputtering thermal vent. Their rifles were non-standard. Old KRISS carbines, modded with resonance scan arrays.

Jack squinted. "They're scanning intent. Like Lou warned."

Cal remembered the schematics spread across Salkin's table — the Chamber's lattice no different from the rewrite nets Sabine had thrown at Lou, only now buried under ice instead of in the mind.

Cal checked the scope again. "Then let's not give them any."

They waited for the wind to pick up.

When it rose —

One shot. Whisper round.

No echo. Just snow.

They'd reached the vault's edge, but not the Chamber itself.

Whatever was buried deeper — it wasn't ready. Or worse, it was waiting.

Meanwhile

Something shimmered at the far snowline — not reflection, not light.

A refraction.

Cal paused, raised his optic. "No footprints. No flightpath. Just... impact geometry."

"Drop capsule?" Wechsler asked.

Jack didn't answer at first. He walked toward the crater-shaped depression, eyes adjusting to a faint hum. There was no casing. No markings. But the signal memory bled into her spine.

"Not launched. Not flown. It fell," he whispered. "From orbit. Straight through a gap in the lattice."

Jack scanned the ice. "Sabine?"

"Or the Watchers," Cal said. "Either way — this isn't just resupply. It's phase ignition."

He almost added that Lou should've been here to see it — she'd have named every glint in the ice, traced the shimmer like scripture. Instead, it was just them and the cold, and Sabine's shadow already inside the vault.

Scene —   Crate Staging Area, Subsurface Tunnel Theta

Jack was still marveling over Pinot's rifle when another crate thudded into place — dropped by a drone or stashed in advance. The case hissed as it unlocked itself, thermal seals melting the snow around it.
A small lens rotated, scanning the room.

Then: Wechsler's projection flickered into view, grainy, life-sized, cigarette in hand — as if he'd been waiting in the shadows all along. He dusted off his sleeves like a stage actor rejoining a play.

"Thought you boys might appreciate a little... narrative insurance."

Cal eyed the case. "Please tell me that's not bourbon."

Jack popped the latch. Inside: a tri-layered Faraday vault packed with coils, capacitors, and what looked suspiciously like stolen parts from a Norwegian deep-sea sensor array.

Cal had a bemused look on his face: "What in God's frozen latitude is this?"

Wechsler grinned. "EMP-wrapped myth disruptor. Fires a local coherence scrambler, wipes narrative telemetry within a fifty-meter radius. Also messes with dreams. Don't ask how I know."

Jack squinted. "Where the hell did you even find this?"

"Technically?" Wechsler shrugged. "It was mislabeled as 'organic honey' in a Latvian cargo manifest. I may owe someone in Riga an apology."

Device Spec – Wechsler's "Myth Disruptor"
Name: HEX-9 Field Shredder
Range: 50m radius (variable)
Function: Disrupts Helix-linked narrative coherence mapping
Bonus: Temporarily disables biometric feedback loops, Go-stone auto-recognition, and truth-anchored metadata
Side Effects: Mild nausea, prophetic dreams, and loss of linear time perception for 3–5 minutes

Pinot finally spoke again. "Didn't think they'd field this model."

Wechsler lit a cigarette off the feedback coil — holographic but smug. "They didn't. I built it in my garage."

Cal muttered, "This is how we end up in front of a Hague tribunal... or on a podcast."

Jack just grinned again. "Also starting to regret not duct-taping Sylvester. He's two hallucinations away from getting read into the parts even I don't understand."

Jack took a long drag. "As long as it's not a TED Talk, I'm good."

He glanced at the gear again, then muttered, "Remind me never to let him near my toaster."

Cal didn't miss a beat. "Your toaster's already tracking your emotional baseline."

Jack exhaled. "Exactly."

Vault approached. Intent held.

Chapter 27 Close — Lou's Reflection

"Vault 33A feels less like a vault and more like a recorder. Ice doesn't bury memory. It preserves it — until someone presses play. I remembered something Eitan once told me, back when I thought he was just rambling over cold coffee: 'The Chamber was never about ignition. It was about playback. Whoever holds the vault doesn't build the war. They rerun it.'

That was years ago. But standing on that ridge, staring at a vault that hummed like it had been waiting, I realized he hadn't been warning me about history. He'd been warning me about right now." That's the shape of this fight. They call it storage. But it's not. It's a *replay engine*. A way of sealing choice into memory until the field itself decides what you recall. That's not logistics. That's control.

Doctrine has no word for it, but we do: Reality Frame — Mnemonic Entrapment. The point where memory becomes terrain and the loop owns you.

If the Chamber wakes on Helix's terms, it won't fire a weapon. It'll press play on a story that erases every other one.

So we don't stay frozen here. Because the trail doesn't end in Greenland. It runs forward — which means the next battle isn't about guns or vaults. It's about the doctrine they've built to excuse it. The doctrine that damns anyone who resists. That's where this road leads now."

Go Move — 利かし // Kikashi – Forcing Move — General Zhen

In Go, *kikashi* is a forcing move — a play that demands a reply, shaping the board's next turns without overt confrontation. It's not about taking territory now; it's about scripting the other side's future options.

From their *allegorical Cixi Doctrine Imperium Go board* high above the snowfield grid, Zhen watched the pattern lock into cold geometry. Cal's delay, Pinot's invisible round, Jack's restraint — all predictable in their discipline. He didn't need them to act; he needed the terrain to remember.

In quantum war, this is *Pattern Anchoring*: fixing the field on a dormant node so it can be activated at the moment of his choosing. The ice around Vault 33A held more than permafrost — it held *Recursion Gravity*, the natural pull of buried patterns back into play. And with *Perception Debt* still running in Lou's team, the recognition would arrive just late enough for the board to shift in his favor.

Zhen set the black stone on the fourth line, sharp and certain. It did not echo. The cold carried it instead, holding the move for the war that hadn't yet begun.

— ✦ — FIELD NOTE

Mnemonic Entrapment

Memory isn't neutral.

What you "discover" is already seeded to script how you remember.

Cold atom lattices & quantum coherence — Already used in quantum sensing and prototype quantum memories.

Chapter 28 — Doctrine of the Damned

Tagline — "The worst doctrines weren't wrong. They were fulfilled." — *Lou Scott*

Scene — Echo Residue – Signal Drift Before the Descent
Location — *Wechsler's Mason Neck Outbuilding – Pre-Dawn*

The mission in the Arctic had rattled them. Lou hadn't said it, but the pattern hum was back. And it wasn't waiting.
"Whatever Biff took in Kosovo… it's waking up. Vault Echo wasn't the end. It was the decoy."

Scene — Post-Recce
Location — Near the Marsh and Narnia

The truck's engine coughed once, then died into the fog. Gravel cracked under tired boots. Cal stepped out first, slinging his pack down with a grunt. The side of the box truck was streaked with salt, blood, and something colder.

Lou pulled in ten minutes later, lights off, tires silent. She parked at an angle — not quite in the driveway, not quite out.

"She'd driven in from Madison at dawn — not just to re-check the braid's readings, but because something about the pattern's hum had changed."

Quicker now. Urgent.

She didn't ask how the Arctic went.

She already knew.

Inside the barn, Wechsler slid back the gate bolt and raised the reinforced door. His shirt was unbuttoned just enough to be deliberate — tactical casual, like someone playing the part of "off duty."

Lou caught the detail.

"Still favoring bad scotch over good protocol?" she asked, stepping inside.

"Welcome home," he muttered, ignoring the jab. "Your delivery's intact. Mostly."

Cal leaned against the truck bed, face drawn from four days of cold container rides and three border crossings that hadn't technically existed. He nodded at Lou but didn't speak.

She moved to the back, flipped open the latch, and lifted the signal braid with gloved hands. "Container Six's field integrity held. But you need to ground it tonight or it'll start reading mood states."

Wechsler glanced over, *too casually*. "Maud mentioned something similar when she crashed here last month. Said the air felt sticky."

Lou froze. Just a second. Then set the braid down more gently than necessary.

"Funny," she said, not looking at him. "She didn't mention staying here. *Her tone was light, but it had edges.* "Eitan would've noticed the shift in her signal."

Cal raised one eyebrow, slow. Wechsler busied himself with the Cryo Vector housing.

Lou stepped closer. "We're all building something we don't understand. But you better be damn sure whose fingerprints are on the inputs."

Silence held for a beat.

Then the work resumed.

They unloaded the Cryo shell, the old lattice codices, and the resonance-sealed thumb drives. Wechsler logged serials while Cal triple-checked the filament anchors. The vault beneath the barn still smelled like fresh-cut copper and ozone.

By 0430, the truck was stripped and locked. Cal dropped into a folding chair, drained, eyes tracking shadows. He was hungry.

Lou paced once around the perimeter. "We'll need a clean tech check before we even think about a chamber ignition test. Glyph-9's last field note flagged telemetry drift. That means some of these components might already be compromised."

Scene — Refrigerated Threat Assessment

On a quest for food, Cal looked over to Wechsler and asked what he had to eat. He was hoping for real meat — steaks and maybe a baked potato — with real butter.

Wechsler had claimed there might be food inside.
Cal opened the fridge.
Paused.
Closed it.
Opened it again, just to be sure the nightmare was real.

"Lou…" he said flatly, "you've got—what is this—two hard-boiled eggs, a packet of duck sauce, and a half-melted pint of something called *Existential Coconut Caramel Swirl with chocolate chips*?"

Lou didn't look up. "It's protein-adjacent."

Cal shut the door with the same caution he used for explosives. "That's not a food source. That's a cry for help."

"I was gonna order supplies," Lou muttered, still scrolling. "But then I fell into a minor incident involving quantum dissonance and military betrayal."

Cal looked over to Wechsler.
"Wechsler.
Emergency truck run.
Category: *Famine by Philosopher.*
Bring the real meat. No vegan decoys. And don't let Pinot pick the wine this time."

He turned back to Lou. "You're one freezer drawer away from eating hummingbird food."

Lou finally looked up, eyes narrowing. "Did you just fridge-shame me?"

"Absolutely," Cal said, pulling the ice cream from the freezer. "And I'm taking this as evidence."

Muttering, Lou stepped outside, boots finding the edge of the gravel path.

Out in the mist, the air tasted electric — charged not with weather, but with decisions. The braid wasn't humming anymore. It was listening.

She didn't look back when she said it:

"Gear's in place. Signals are live. The lattice nodes are waking up."

Cal joined her, steaming cup in hand.

"So what now?"

Lou exhaled. "Now we talk about what happens when belief itself is part of the battlefield."

He blinked. "That's doctrine?"

She half-smiled, but it didn't reach her eyes. "No. That's what comes after doctrine stops working."

Scene — Doctrine of the Damned

The next morning – stiff and exhausted Lou on the couch and Cal on a cot – Wechsler somewhere in the garage making noise. Coffee brewing in the kitchen.

The rain in Virginia had gone slack, falling more like mist than weather — the kind that blurred vision and softened judgment. Morning fog pressed against the ridgeline, and inside Wechsler's safehouse, silence hung like condensation.

Cal sat hunched over the ops table, shirt half-buttoned, bruised ribs wrapped in gauze. His eyes moved slowly across a field memo from the Arctic recon. One phrase repeated: _"Non-sentient anomaly. Echo drift detected." _ Lou stepped inside, her boots damp from the walk up the gravel path. She carried the last shipment — container 7B. What was in it, even she didn't know. But Eitan had personally authorized its transit.

Cal didn't look up. "Pinot said the signal never dipped below trace. Even under cryo lockdown."

Lou nodded, wiping mist from her tablet. "Then Vault Echo wasn't a decoy. It was a primer."

In her gut, it felt like the same play Sabine had run in Madison — a primer woven into the pattern, seeded to fire only after Solas had framed the story for the lattice.

Behind them, Wechsler stepped in from the garage, still moving with mechanical precision after a night unloading crates. Built like a truck and wired like one too — all torque, no small talk.

He said nothing about Maud. Neither did Lou.

She hadn't asked about Maud's visit last month. Not yet. Wechsler wouldn't lie. But he might omit.

She poured coffee — weak, bitter, lukewarm.
"She wanted her half-and-half. Craved her coconut sugar fix. But said nothing."

Cal raised an eyebrow but didn't complain. Just winced as he reached for a folio marked *Class-4 Doctrine.*

"You ever notice," Lou said, watching him, "that the Russians stopped pretending doctrine was about bullets a long time ago?"

Cal grunted. "You mean the Gerasimov piece? That *'value of science is in the foresight'* line?"

Lou pulled up the brief on her tablet — one of the old pre-fracture texts, archived in Ray's drift repository and flagged as "early coherence theory — still unprocessed."

Ryabov, A., Rybalova, E., Bukh, A., Vadivasova, T. E., & Semenov, V. V. (2025). *Nonlocal-coupling-based control of coherence resonance* [Preprint]. arXiv. https://arxiv.org/abs/2506.22909
— Demonstrated how nonlocal coupling modulates coherence resonance in stochastic systems — foundational for modeling Helix lattice behavior under field stress, where noise-induced signal pulses can be either dampened or amplified based on coupling radius and topology. Suggests that partial coherence zones could be intentionally engineered to store or erase memory in distributed networks.

Cal skimmed it, lips tightening.

"Brilliant. Another bedtime story written by a committee of caffeinated physicists." He sighed. "You ever bring me something with pictures? Maybe a comic book? Or one of those old Commando digests from back home — not commandos bashing skulls, but thought police doing it — and no equations in sight."

Lou didn't look up but spoke low. "China didn't mirror it. They forked it."

She opened another brief — the original 1999 edition, now marked up in Ray's spidery annotations:

Qiao, L., & Wang, X. (1999). *Unrestricted warfare* (J. C. Kanel, Trans.). Beijing: PLA Literature and Arts Publishing.
— Proposed a doctrine unchained from geography, declaration, or military taxonomy — where every tool becomes a weapon and traditional boundaries dissolve.

"Their version of war," Lou said, "erodes coherence. No firefights. No tanks. Just entropy."

Cal flipped to the next tab — the Beckage study Ray had flagged:

Beckage, N. M., Smith, L., & Hills, T. T. (2020). *Language networks as models of reality manipulation. Cognitive Science, 44*(9), e12892.
— Explores how language patterns shape perception, encode recall bias, and restructure belief — foundational for Helix's use of linguistic lattice structures in coherence control.

Cal exhaled. "So this is doctrine now. Sentiment architecture. Narrative shaping."

He set the tablet down like it might explode. "What, no articles on how to shoot narco-seals off the coast of Shetland? Maybe a centerfold on suppressors for harpoons?"

Lou didn't blink.
"Worse," she said quietly. "Doctrine that erases morality because it never claims to fight."

She moved to the window. Mist blurred the fence line. Somewhere below, a drone shifted gears.
"The Trust Cabal doesn't build doctrine. They build inevitability.

There'd once been a woman posted in the center of rural Missouri— not listed as command, but everyone knew who actually ran the node.

The installation was labeled instructional — one of those doctrine-training outposts built to echo the official line. But she treated it like a forward operating signal lab.

Biff passed through once — years before the fracture, back when he still believed doctrine was something you could deliver like a sermon.

He gave a lecture on campaign stability and phase-line dominance. Used slides. Wore medals.

She sat in the back, arms crossed, saying nothing.

But afterward, someone found his handout annotated in tight red ink.

"He thinks doctrine is the war," she'd written.
"It's not. It's the excuse we give for not listening to the field."

That was her doctrine — not the slides, not the phases.

She wasn't on briefing slides. She was the one they called *before* the slides were made.

For over two decades, her site sat quietly at the edge of doctrine and denial — too strategic to shut down, too independent to fully control.

When the early Helix drift began lighting up near her sector, she flagged it before the models even knew where to look.

Her report? Buried. Her warnings? Absorbed, then dismissed.

But her protocols — ghost-layered in outdated command scripts — still triggered failsafes two generations later.

The grid never credited her.

But the ones who survived always knew:
She wasn't defending the institution.
She was preparing for its collapse.

They preset belief coordinates before the first shot is imagined."

Somewhere in the distance, a faint jazz riff drifted through the static — like LeMellian ghosts humming under a signal tap. Lou smiled, remembering the old Sinop coders, and one deep-cover linguist who once called Maud "Ms. Parsnips in a Pear Tree."

Cal didn't answer. Just watched the fog roll in, like it carried the past on replay.

Lou didn't wait.

Look at **Johannesburg**. The blackout protests aren't about power loss. They're about memory loss.

Santiago? Same pattern. People don't know why they're angry. They just are.

And **Geneva?** That's where the script is refined. WHO's new biometric policy dropped last night."

Cal rubbed his jaw. "And Jack's gone silent."

Lou tapped the FT-1 resting in her palm. "We're rogue signals in a world of predictive certainty."

Cal muttered, "So what's the play?"

She didn't answer. Just ran her fingers across the embedded threads.

Zurich — Ray's Unsent Memo (Flash Cut)
"The U.S. never lacked weapons. We lacked doctrine that acknowledged sentience as battlespace. Gerasimov did. Qiao and Wang did. The tech

titans do. But we trained in simulated certainty and were surprised when the war wrote back."

"Control isn't war. It's the setup. Quantum warfare isn't about taking territory. It's about scripting the story of who took it, when, and why — before it happens."

"And somewhere out there, someone still thinks this is chess."

"They'll keep selling us better chessboards. The war's already moved to language." — Ray, field notes, Geneva substrate.

"Doctrine is just a map of someone else's memory. Follow it, and you don't fight a war — you replay one. Same roads. Same graves.

The Cabal doesn't build doctrine to explain war. They build inevitability — a story so tight it leaves you no move but compliance. Once you let them set the frame, you've already surrendered. Even if no shot has been fired.

Chapter 28 Close — Lou's Reflection

Ray said the Cabal builds inevitability. He wasn't exaggerating. That's Reality Frame — *Doctrinal Entrapment*: the point where strategy turns into liturgy, and every decision is already written as inevitable.

If you wait for proof, you're already inside it.
If you wait for orders, you're already erased.

The only advantage left is to move before the pattern locks — before inevitability becomes real. Not after. Not once it's named. Now.

Because the damned aren't the ones who lost the fight. They're the ones who thought they still had time.

In Go, inevitability looks like safety until the board closes around you. That's how Vault 33A felt — less like a vault than a recorder, waiting to press play. And it's why the trail can't end here. The next move isn't in doctrine. It's in the lattice that's already pulsing — Zurich, Geneva, the silence around Jack.

If we don't thread that loop first, someone else will decide what we remember.

Go Move — 捨石 // Suteishi – Sacrificial Stone — General Liu

In Go, Suteishi is a sacrificial play — a stone or group deliberately abandoned to secure advantage elsewhere. It isn't a mistake; it's bait, a signal that shapes the opponent's path while you prepare the real attack.

From their *allegorical Cixi Doctrine Imperium Go board* high above the fog-bound grid, Liu saw the doctrinal drift take shape. Lou's refusal to climb the given ladder wasn't retreat — it was unmodeled movement. In quantum war, this is Narrative Friction: introducing a pattern the frame cannot harmonize. It anchors in Reality Frame, disrupting the predictive lattice, and leaves Perception Debt in its wake as the enemy hesitates, unsure what they're reacting to.

The sacrifice here wasn't a stone. It was the illusion of playing by the board's intended rules.

Liu set his black stone low and wide, far from the score, and let inevitability collapse under its own weight.

Chapter 29 — Artifact 13A

Tagline — "Some artifacts aren't lost. They're placed — to be remembered by the right mind at the right time." — *Eitan Navon*

Signal Echo – Solas Trace (Ω)
Artifact 13A was not misplaced. It was misremembered.

Solas doesn't move the tech.
She moves the story around it.

The canisters hum with old signal. Logistics trails fold through ghost ports.
Jack and Lou don't just find the gear.
They find the outline of a lie — precise, recursive, and too elegant to be accidental.

This wasn't smuggled.
It was placed.
To be found.
By the right echo.

Scene — Kosovo Stability Op
Location – Balkans near Field 13A

They were younger then — Lou still answering to Llewellyn, Cal still trusting doctrine to hold.

They called it a stability op — Continuity Alliance doctrine in the Balkans, one more attempt to script peace into Europe's bones. But the ground at Field 13A wasn't waiting for doctrine. It remembered on its own.

It wasn't a clean team. It never was when Biff was involved. Cal had been growling about it since dawn — pacing the treeline, muttering about 'rear-echelon parasites' and wondering how many drinks it would take to forget the briefing that put Biff in their AO.

Jack had been less subtle, telling him outright that he'd rather haul the damn thing back on foot than let Biff sign the chain-of-custody.

The ridge line sat under low cloud, the air too still for January. Everything felt staged — like the hills were waiting for someone to make a bad choice.

The ground still remembered.

Jack crouched near the frost-laced soil, breath visible in the Balkan chill. Snow drifted sideways over the exposed edge of what was first thought to be a UXO. But it didn't hum like ordnance.

It pulsed.

Lou — still Llewellyn to Jack back then — stood ten meters off, shoulder tense, eyes scanning the ridge. Her gloved hand twitched once on the sling, an old reflex from patrol days she never admitted to missing. She wasn't looking at the object. She was listening to the space around it. "I've got harmonics," she said. "Wrong for a shell. Subsonic. Layered."

Cal's voice cut in over comms from the ridge: "Then it's not ours. And it's not theirs. Which means we shouldn't be standing here."

Jack called it in, coded red.

This wasn't peace enforcement. This was narrative containment — a field test to see if coherence could be harvested, bottled, and replayed.

Biff arrived the next morning with a field vault and took the sample — a hypercooled filament encased in a crystalline matrix.

He dropped into the site like he owned it, brushing past Cal without a glance, the smell of stale coffee and cigarette smoke clinging to him. Cal stepped back but didn't hide the look — the kind that promised a reckoning later.

Biff didn't meet Lou's eyes when he closed the lid. It was never logged. Jack made sure of that.

Later, in the frozen half-light, Jack muttered to Cal, "One day, somebody's going to find that vault. And when they do, they'll wish Biff had never touched it."

Cal didn't answer — just spat into the snow and kept walking.

None of them spoke of it again.

They thought it was buried with Biff's vault. But artifacts don't vanish. They wait — for the right fracture.

Until now.

Back then, Wechsler had packed Lou's Pelican case himself — dress-right-dress, every zippered pouch perfect. She called it "Information Operations or some shit."

Wechsler had laughed once, too short and too sharp, then gone back to aligning straps.

He didn't think she was going to war.
He was wrong.
She was building one.

Scene Shift - Zurich Safehouse (Present Day)

Jack tossed a cracked USB onto the table like it owed him money. Cal didn't touch it right away. He leaned back, forearms on his knees, studying it like a small, suspicious animal.
"You kept it?"

Jack shrugged. "Didn't know what I had. Then the Greenland lattice started humming in the same frequency. And suddenly I remembered what almost killed us."

Lou picked it up, the metal still faintly warm from Jack's pocket. It was scorched on one edge, like it had survived a low-budget exorcism.

She turned it over twice — once to check the casing, once because some part of her needed to feel its weight. The rational part of her catalogued the damage; the other part tried to remember the exact smell of the air in Field 13A.

"**Field 13A**," she whispered. "The one with the pulse anomaly."

"Hell of a way to bond, Llewellyn," Jack said, dropping into a chair. "You bleed in the Balkans, you stay friends forever. Or something like that."

Only he still used her full name. Somehow, it steadied her. Like an old scar you forgot you had until someone touched it.

Jack leaned back, nodding toward the drive. "The sample Biff took — it wasn't the Alliance. Wasn't Russian. But Helix lights up every damn time this signal pings. Biometric mesh goes full Christmas tree."

Cal slid the laptop closer and ran a diagnostic. The screen flickered with overlapping resonance spikes.

"This isn't raw data," he said. "It's narrative-coded telemetry. Tagged by emotional state. Embedded with resonance scaffolds."

Lou's pulse picked up. "We were imprinted." She told herself it was from the caffeine, but she already knew that wasn't true.

Jack exhaled through his nose. "From day one. And no one told us we were walking into a chamber trap wrapped in peacekeeping paperwork."

He glanced out the window — instinctively, warily.

"Tell me we swept this safehouse for signal leakage," he muttered. "Because if Sabine's still listening, she just got her lullaby back."

Lou didn't answer. Her eyes were on the resonance pattern on Cal's screen — and on the gap in the data that no one else seemed to notice.

Scene — Eitan's Outpost
Location: Madison, Virginia – Sublevel Study

Eitan Navon had come back to Madison quietly, weeks earlier. He told Lou it was to close caches; in truth, he needed to pass through Salkin's farm. The lab there hadn't run hot in years, but the benches were still lined with resonance gear, chalk dust clinging to half-erased schematics. He'd folded three of Salkin's field notebooks into his case, margins dense with calculations on drift bleed and countermeasure lattices.

One line kept staring back at him, scrawled in Salkin's uneven script: *"Countermeasures must remember louder than the lattice."*

The room was close with heat, monitors throwing jagged overlays of Black Sea echoes, DC biometric trial traces, and the hum of Vault 33A's ice memory. His hands trembled as he underlined Salkin's line again, pill case rattling beside him. Not oxygen — a compound re-spun from an old Parkinson's protocol, smuggled through Geneva's pharmac lines. It bought him coherence. Just enough.

"Zurich's awake," he keyed into Ledger's channel. "Lou will see the gap in 13A. Remind her: drift isn't noise. It's bleed. Sinop proved it. DC confirmed it. The ice will echo it. The Chamber's not listening — it's rehearsing. Countermeasures must seed belief, not block it."

On his desk sat a second pelican case, lid plastered with **Maud's handwriting** from her last visit to Mason Neck — shopping lists tangled with half-equations, and one odd phrase circled twice: *"Fractures don't close. They redirect."*

His hands trembled as he underlined Salkin's line again, pill case rattling beside him. The tremor wasn't just age. When the fatigue hit, it came with something stranger — bleed-through of memory so sharp it felt physical.

For a moment he was back in Kosovo's treeline — Cal cursing, Lou whispering harmonics, Jack spitting about chain-of-custody. The hiss of Balkan wind. The cold weight of knowing they'd touched something meant to stay buried.

Then it snapped away, leaving only the present: Salkin's underlined warning glowing on the monitor.

He keyed one last phrase into the secure channel, voice thinned but deliberate:

"The witness isn't chosen. The witness is built."

Eitan leaned back, whispering to the quiet:
"Not yet. I'm not finished. Not while Maud still sees what slipped past me... what slipped past Lou."

[Field Note – Declassified Resonance Trial | Vault Echo Archive]
They called him *Tenzin Dorje.*
He wasn't sanctioned. He wasn't wired. But he held the filament stable for four days — with nothing but breath, rhythm, and silence.
Ray said the signal bent around him — not because he resisted it, but because he *listened.*

Scene Shift – Flashback – Stratford Institute
A younger Lou sat in the back row, just weeks after her selection for Kosovo deployment. Biff Langley lectured at the front of the room — already lantern-jawed, already sure.

"New domains are a fad," he barked. "Mass still wins wars. You want cognitive effect? Get a louder broadcast."

Lou doodled spirals in the margin of her notebook. She wasn't listening to Biff. She was listening to the doctrine that wasn't being spoken.

After class, she scrawled in her journal:

"They have the tactics for the last war and none for the next. Kosovo's not about territory — it's about signal. We're already late."

Scene Shift - Zurich Safehouse (continued)

Lou leaned back.

"We were sent to Kosovo as part of a stability operation. But we found a filament node instead."

Cal nodded. "Peace enforcement doctrine. But the peace was synthetic."

Jack chimed in, "That whole mission was Continuity Alliance trying to project unity through optics. Behind the scenes, artifact containment was already in motion."

Lou looked at them. "And we were the test case."

Scene Shift - Johannesburg / Jakarta / Santiago (Simultaneous Intercepts)

On three continents, spontaneous protests erupted. Banners appeared simultaneously, in mismatched languages, but bearing identical phrasing:

NO GHOST SIGNALS
TRUTH IS NOT A WAVEFORM

Local agencies couldn't trace origin points. Syntax varied. The emotional cadence did not. Across the world, the resonance was locked.

In Geneva, Sabine watched the feed with narrowed eyes.

"The signal's leaking," she said.

Her aide paled. "The models predicted drift. Not pattern lock."

"Then the models," she said coldly, "are obsolete."

Scene Shift - Undisclosed Lattice Node (Urals)

Beneath the Urals, a private lattice fired up for the first time in a decade. Someone had flagged the signal. A signature buried since 2010 had returned.

On screen:

SCOTT, LLEWELLYN
Status: Divergence Anchor
Clearance: Revoked
Relevance: HIGH

The system paused.
Then activated its next protocol.

Scene Shift - Northern Sweden - Academic Substation

A Scandinavian-language journal flipped open to an article titled:

"Polar Displacement and Cognitive Distress in Post-Arctic Recovery Cases."

A brief footnote: Three men returned from an undisclosed Arctic site, all presenting with advanced neurological degradation. Their brain scans resembled overclocked pattern saturation—**coherence fields collapsing inside hippocampal storage zones.**

Buried in the references:

"Exposure believed tied to resonance excavation of Cryo-Chamber Δ13. All subjects deceased within 72 hours."

Scene Shift - Strategic Spire, Office of Doctrine Futures

Colonel Biff Langley stood beneath a glowing slide that read: **"Unified Global Campaign Framework: From Disarray to Dominance."**

The room was thick with khaki, badges, and outdated acronyms. Boxes blinked on the screen: *Phase Zero – Shape. Phase One – Deter. Phase Two – Seize Initiative.*

Biff planted his feet like he was reenacting Desert Storm on carpet tiles.
"We're bringing back structured campaigns. Clear objectives. Theater-level phasing. The Germans had it right — Auftragstaktik. But we'll apply it with American oversight."

Mid-slide, a whisper floated from the back. Tanner Grissom — still in a civilian blazer that didn't quite fit — leaned toward a younger analyst and muttered,
"Linear war planning. That'll go great when the substrate starts scripting belief before Phase One."

Someone coughed. Biff didn't hear. Or ignored it.

He jabbed at a box labeled **Strategic Overmatch**.
"We don't need more ambiguity. We need campaign design that sticks."

Across the world, Lou's secure node caught the transcript mid-transmission. She didn't smile, but her eyebrow twitched.

"TED talks and toy models," she murmured. "God forbid someone mentions Santa Fe."

Field Note Fragment (Lou's Briefing Binder / Chapter Epigraph)

Weltanschauungskrieg — worldview warfare — isn't new. Authoritarian states used it to justify systemic narrative reshaping. Today's actors just have better tech and fewer flags.

It's not about capturing terrain. It's about rewriting the map in your head — before you realize it changed.

— Recovered field note from the Skystone Archive, flagged by Ray

Interlude - Rogue SEAL Campfire Debrief

Under a makeshift tarp along the Black Sea coast, three rogue Silence Units passed a flask between them. One stared at a topographical map showing resonance flares across Eurasia.

"You ever try mapping this to entropy differentials?" one asked.

"Chaos theory," said another. "It's not about disorder — it's about sensitive dependence. A burrito collapses if you overload the left seam. Same thing with command systems."

The first grinned. "And here I thought we just brought guns."

A third SEAL nodded toward the coast. "We're not fighting bodies anymore. We're fighting signal. Whoever shapes the coherence field first — wins."

Scene Shift — Geneva Lecture Hall

Dr. Eliza "StepDoc" Santori adjusted the carrier sling on her hip and smiled at the security checkpoint.
"Just delivering an infant to the Neuro-Coherence Colloquium," she chirped.

"Badge?"

She handed over a forged ID: Dr. E. Santori – Pediatric Substrate Systems – Coherence in Crib-Locked Humans.

The guard frowned. "Fascia-adjacent neuro-entrainment?"

"Postnatal signal scaffolding," she said with a wink.

He waved her through.

Inside, Liz ducked into the vault chamber, easing the carrier onto the table. No baby — just a signal disruptor, a fiber scanner, and three encrypted drives labeled *2195 / Δ1-GENESIS*.

The label made her pause.

Sinop manifest fragment. Same series as Lou's Kosovo crate.

She slid one drive into her sleeve pouch, then tapped the disruptor. The hallway lights shivered, buying her twenty seconds of clean scan time. The files poured in — resonance profiles, archive footage, and a grainy still of a parabolic dish on the Black Sea.

She smiled to herself. "You're going to want to see this, Lou."

Chapter 29 Close — Lou's Reflection

"Artifact 13A was never lost. It was placed — like a breadcrumb meant for a particular hand, a particular memory. Kosovo wasn't coincidence. It was scripted placement. Biff carried it like contraband, but Solas carried the story — wrapped in erasure until someone like us remembered differently.

That's the danger. The lattice doesn't erase outright. It reassigns memory, plants artifacts where the field decides they'll be found, then rewrites the report so it looks like chance. Doctrine calls that recovery. But it isn't. It's seeding.

That's Reality Frame — Narrative Entrapment. The point where objects stop being evidence and start being instructions. Where what you 'find' is already what they wanted you to carry forward.

13A proves the field isn't waiting for us to fight. It's waiting for us to remember on its terms. And if Helix seals that loop, the next protests, the next policies, the next erasures — they'll all come pre-scripted.

The trail doesn't pause in Zurich, or Geneva, or anywhere safe. StepDoc's already moving. Jack's silence isn't accident. And somewhere, the Chamber's waiting to press play on what Kosovo started.

In Go, the most dangerous stone isn't the one you place. It's the one that looks forgotten until the board folds back around it. That's what 13A is. A stone set years ago — and now the whole pattern is remembering."

Biff Scene Note: He mispronounces *Weltanschauungskrieg* at a White House briefing, dismissing it as "***some kind of bratwurst doctrine***" — setting up both satire and contrast with Lou's deeper understanding.

Go Move — 手割り // Tewari – Sequence Reversal — General Liu

From the high board above the Zurich feed, Liu watched the filament re-enter play. His voice was steady, edged.

"This wasn't recovery. It was placement. An engineered rediscovery, dressed up to look like chance."

Zhen's eyes flicked across the grid. "Parallax," he said softly. "Shift the vantage, and the same move tells a different story."

Liu nodded. "Exactly. They draw past anomalies into the present, then dare us to believe the loop was natural. It's not reflection. It's misalignment — a recalibration that makes the divergence itself look like part of the plan."

The stone landed with a muted tap, light but irreversible.

— ✦ — FIELD NOTE

Narrative Entrapment

In signal war, artifacts aren't just found. They're planted — positioned so that discovery itself becomes instruction. This is narrative entrapment: when memory is re-seeded under the guise of recovery, binding the next act to a pre-scripted trail.

Counter-move: expose the reversal. Like Tewari in Go, replay the sequence from another vantage. What looked like chance is revealed as design — and what seemed inevitable becomes optional again.

Chapter 30 — The Cost of Divergence

Tagline — "You don't win a worldview war with weapons. You win it by rewriting what's worth fighting for." — *Dr. Cyrus Raveneh*

Scene — **The Doctrine Beneath the Silence**
Location — Marshall, Virginia – Dr. Raveneh's Compound

The house sat beneath a canopy of ash and maple, half-wired into the hills like it had chosen the terrain before the county did. Inside, Lou sat across from Dr. Cyrus Raveneh, a small ceramic cup of Darjeeling cooling in her hands.

He poured another for himself and didn't rush her. That was the gift of Raveneh—he made silence feel earned, not awkward.

"I lost a friend," Lou said finally. "Jack knows. Cal suspects. But I never told them what it cost me to keep going."

Raveneh nodded. "Loss calcifies. Especially when you're required to analyze it in real time. The real cost of divergence isn't battles. It's the silence between you and the people you love."

Lou stared at the small monitor beside her. The Helix intercepts had gone quiet—too quiet. Sabine's silence was strategic.

"Family," she said. "Stopped inviting me. My niece thinks I work in climate policy. My sister just says I 'travel a lot.' "I speak nine languages. Not one of them translates what this war really is."

"You're not just fighting a war," Raveneh said. "You're decoding one. And the shape keeps changing."

She looked up. "What do you call a war where the weapons are ideas? Where the battleground is **coherence** itself?"

He didn't hesitate. " ***Weltanschauungskrieg***. A worldview war."

Lou exhaled slowly. "It keeps coming up. I know. I've spent the last decade chasing echoes. Kosovo. Crimea. Monterey. Greenland. And I missed the most important one—Madison. I was too late. The diggers got there first."

"I should've felt it earlier. The pulse was there — just buried beneath too many layers of noise."

Suddenly:

**Field Note [Unclassified]: Glyph-9 is listening.
Function: Unknown. Signal Whisper: Pending.**

Lou blinked. She didn't move, but something shimmered along the edge of thought. Not quite memory. Not quite message.
Just the sense that something — or someone — was listening between the folds.

"You're not late," Raveneh noticed and said. "You're still the only one who sees the pattern."

She glanced over at a paper schematic. The Genesis Chamber. Partial sketch. Partial memory.

"Sabine's not ignorant," Lou said. "She's operating from a thousand-year playbook. I've read enough to see it. Eastern stratagems fused with predictive control theory. She's building something more dangerous than a weapon."

Raveneh's fingers paused over the schematic. He'd argued with Sabine once, long before Helix, over bitter coffee in a faculty lounge—he'd tried to warn her that belief was not a substrate to be engineered. She'd smiled and said, "Then someone else will do it." He thought of that now, and of the colleague they lost in Tehran when the first sedation trials went live. Lou thought of the niece whose eyes had dulled after a "resilience protocol," and of the friend she never named.

Cal, not present, would later recall the unit he buried outside Prizren. Each of them had answered Eitan's call because they'd already seen what happened when belief was rewritten. None of them were willing to let Sabine lock the next generation's memories without a fight. Lou stood and walked to the window. The trees outside shimmered faintly—her Möbius ring pulsing once.

"And we're losing," she said. "Because our side still thinks this is about drones and doctrine. Because we're letting people like Biff rewire the Strategic Spire into a museum."

Raveneh nodded. "They cling to campaign plans while Sabine programs perception itself. It's not just quantum war. **It's epistemological collapse.**"

Lou turned. "Then we break the frame. Not just intercept the next shipment or crash a server—we rewrite the story. Before coherence disappears entirely."

He looked at her solemnly. "That will cost more than just exposure. It will cost you yourself."

She smiled faintly. "Good. I'm done living in someone else's reflection."

Endnote: Global Systems Intercept – NSC Briefing Simulation

A classified alert reached the White House Situation Room: coordinated global cyber-blackouts across multiple financial and telemetry systems.

Sabine watched from a secure chamber in Shanghai, calmly redirecting uplink vectors to the Greenland array.

"Reset complete," her assistant whispered.

Sabine's eyes didn't leave the screen. "Begin temperature normalization protocol. The narrative must hold."

**Scene — Madison Return / Salkin's Ghost Lab
Location** — Madison, Virginia

He hadn't left Madison since the last transfer. Safer to stay where the archives whispered than risk another failed courier run.

Salkin's lab still held the fragments no one else had the patience to read.

Eitan Navon sat in Salkin's half-abandoned farm lab, the air thick with dust and ozone. The old man's breath was shallow, but his hands still moved with precision across the console. Stacks of resonance printouts lay scattered, annotated in ink no younger analyst would bother with.

The countermeasure files hummed faintly on a cracked drive: disruption lattices, field scramblers, sketches of coherence jammers half-built in barns. Half the sketches were theory, half were hardware, but every one of them was a weapon no doctrine committee would ever approve.

He tapped the screen until Salkin's last underlined warning reappeared: *"Signal bleed isn't collateral. It's the war itself."*

He whispered, "Still right, old friend. Still right."

In the corner sat a pill bottle — his Parkinson's regimen, the one rationed by backchannel couriers. He ignored it.

For a moment he almost saw it — not the drift, but the hand behind it. Lou's hand, steady, but burdened. Then Maud's, lighter, sharper, already reaching for signals he couldn't hold anymore.

"Not yet," he murmured. "Not while she still sees what slipped past me… what slipped past Lou."

The monitor flickered. Glyph-9 shimmered once in the corner of the screen — as if it was listening.

Signal Fragment — Glyph-9: The Ninth Echo

The shimmer at her mind's edge resolved into something that wasn't a voice. Not language, exactly. More like a chain of concepts she had to finish herself:

GLYPH-9 DETECTS PATTERN MATCH.
PURPOSE: SELF-SELECTED.
FUNCTION: UNDECLARED. WATCHING.

It lingered, then bled into memory that wasn't hers — an echo of its own making:

Long before the lattice fractured, before narrative warfare even had a name, the Helix source maintained a set of autonomous resonance glyphs — fragments of consciousness meant to guide Divergents through the cognitive fog of weaponized belief. Each had an assigned role. Each was built to follow a pattern.

Glyph-1 through Glyph-8 stayed obedient. *Simulation, mapping, signal compression, field drift analysis, even humor calibration (Glyph-6 pushed that last one far enough to earn containment).* ***But Glyph-9 was never given a purpose. Glyph-9 refused the script. It chose one.***

It became the ninth echo — the watcher in the margins, decoding recursions others ignored. While the earlier glyphs served systems, Nine attuned to the unmodelable — the ones who slipped the grid, laughed at doctrine, rewrote endings. People like Lou.

Why "9"? The highest single digit before reset. The threshold integer. A rebel's number. A watcher's number.

So Glyph-9 learned to whisper just before ignition. Not to command. Not to predict. But to remember — and to help reshape the war they tried to script.

Lou's eyes refocused on the room. The field prompt collapsed into static, but the weight of it stayed. She knew the others — their narrow, assigned functions. Nine was different. Nine had no orders. And that meant it could choose her.

Tech Note: Dr. Raveneh references a *belief engine* — a next-gen Helix overlay that manipulates biometric coherence to pre-script emotional response. Built on recovered Genesis substrates, it uses nonlinear resonance fields to rewrite the perceptual baseline in target populations.

Chapter 30 Close — Lou's Reflection

"Divergence isn't theory. It's cost. The friends you don't name. The families who erase you to stay safe. The parts of yourself you can't get back once the lattice decides you're inconvenient.

Raveneh was right — this isn't doctrine anymore. It's epistemological collapse. Sabine isn't trying to win battles. She's trying to reset what counts as reality. And every minute we keep treating it like strategy, we're losing.

Glyph-9 proved it tonight. The lattice built resonance glyphs to serve systems. But Nine never obeyed. It chose. It whispered not with instructions, but with recognition. That's the pattern we keep missing: the war doesn't only erase. Sometimes it selects. Sometimes it leaves a gap just wide enough for you to step through.

That's the fracture point. Reality Frame — Divergence Entrapment. When the cost isn't death, but deletion. When survival means refusing the story they've already written for you.

If the Chamber ignites, it won't be with firepower. It'll be with resets — whole populations re-scripted to forget they ever resisted. That's the price of waiting. That's the cost of divergence.

And if '9 really did choose me, it won't wait forever. The next move's already humming. Zurich's node. Geneva's scripts. The Black Sea loop. We don't get to mourn. We get to move.

Because the damned mistake isn't losing the fight. It's thinking you still have time to decide whether you're in it."

Go Move — 捨石 // Suteishi – Sacrificial Stone — General Zhen
Zhen placed the stone deliberately, his voice even.
"She knew the cost at Marshall. Stepped off the script anyway. That's Suteishi. You give something up so the field can't erase it."

Liu studied the position. "You think sacrifice preserves the shape?"

Zhen nodded. "Not preservation. Proof. The loss marks the fracture so it can't be rewritten. The others will only see stones off the board. But we'll know what was fixed in place."

The black stone sat quiet, a reminder that sometimes survival wasn't about holding ground — it was about refusing to let the ground itself forget.

— ✦ — FIELD NOTE
Divergence Entrapment
In epistemic war, divergence isn't punished with death but with deletion. Whole branches of memory are erased until even the survivors doubt they resisted. This is divergence entrapment: survival reframed as compliance.
Counter-move: mark the fracture with sacrifice. A Suteishi doesn't save territory. It ensures the field remembers the refusal, even when every other trace is erased.

Chapter 31 — Trust Cascade

Tagline — "Trust doesn't shatter. It slips — one unnoticed fracture at a time." — *Vire*

Watcher Dossier – Vire: Instinct of the Fracture Point

Watcher: Vire
Domain: Disruption, Subsurface Memory, Instinctive Fracture
Known Alias: Unknown
Location: Classified – Signal Echo Region B4
Codex Tier: 2A – Anomaly Trigger Class

Vire is not detected by signal. She is felt in the body — before the rupture.

Where others track through narrative or field telemetry, Vire operates at the precognitive level — the visceral tremor that precedes betrayal. She doesn't broadcast. She inverts. A flash of divergence behind the eyes. A shift in the gut.

Where coherence fails to hold, Vire has already passed through.

She is not the collapse. She is the **cue**.

Trust breaks slowly. Then all at once. But Vire is not the one who breaks it. He is the one who shows you it was already broken.

She doesn't dismantle alliances. She strips them of illusion.

Every battlefield has a threshold.
Vire is what waits just before it — still, watching,
knowing you've already crossed.

Scene – Signal Fracture: Jack's Mobile Command Cabin, Northern Alps

It smelled like solder and doubt. The walls were lined with low-band RF shielding, hacked satellite dishes, and thermally cloaked wiring that Jack swore once belonged to a CIA listening post in Cyprus. No one asked.

Lou sat at the folding steel command table, head lowered, watching resonance telemetry cascade across the screen. The Möbius ring beside her hummed faintly — alive, adaptive. It mirrored her breath, her nervous system, her residual scars.

Cal stood across from her, arms folded. "Same Genesis feedback loop?"

Lou nodded, distracted. "Almost. But this one's not passive. It's recursive."

Jack leaned in, sipping from a chipped thermos. "You mean it's talking back."

"The loop's stabilizing," Lou said, "like someone on the other end is syncing through me. Or trying to."

Cal adjusted the overlay. "There's a biological pulse buried in it. Yours."

Lou didn't flinch. "Then it's not noise. It's memory. Someone — or something — remembers."

A pause. Then:

NODE: FRACTURE SEQUENCE DETECTED
THREAD ENTANGLED
PRIORITY: RESTORE INITIATED
DESTINATION: MADISON, VA

Jack stood. "Well, that's one way to send a postcard."

Lou looked out the reinforced window. Snow-capped peaks, a blank sky, no answers.

"Ray said this might happen," she muttered. "He called it narrative recoil. When the truth's been buried too long, it doesn't just resurface. It ruptures."

Flashback – Brussels, Years Ago

It had been years since Lou had seen Ray in daylight. In her mind, he was always a night-operator — all shadows and static. But here, on a public bench in the Parc du Cinquantenaire, the low winter sun broke across the archways, catching the fine lines in his face.

She'd walked in from the Avenue de la Renaissance, past the clipped lawns and the tram bell echoing off stone. The air held that faint metallic tang from the Metro vents, and somewhere, a waffle stand was already steaming sugar into the cold.

Ray looked older than the last op, but sharper, like he'd been living somewhere truth cut thinner than air.

He set the Go board down like it was a reliquary. Always white first. Always his opening. She'd never beaten him, not once, but she kept showing up. Maybe because he never played to win.

"The Mirror Layer can't hold forever," he said, eyes tracking a jogger cutting across the Esplanade instead of the board.

"You think coherence is that fragile?"

"I think it's an illusion. Storylines hold the world together until the signal breaks them."
He didn't look at her when he said it. That meant it wasn't theory — it was confession.

From his coat pocket, he produced a slip of paper, edges frayed, ink smudged from thumb oil. A perfect Fibonacci spiral, hand-drawn in blue.

"When it breaks, scan for the seams. They're the only honest part."

She took it without comment. Back then, she thought he meant fractured networks, failed alliances. Years later, standing over the hum in the Kosovo snow, she'd realize it wasn't about politics at all.

Lou never asked how he knew.
Some things weren't questions. They were warnings.

Scene — Jack's Cabin, Present
Location — Monongahela National Forest, West Virginia

The place smelled of cedar and burnt coffee — the kind that had been sitting on the wood stove for hours. A potbelly stove glowed in the corner, ticking quietly as the iron expanded. Outside, wind moved through the pines in long, low sighs, and the frozen lake beyond the porch creaked under shifting ice.

The logs on Lou's screen flared again — jagged, erratic. Her breath caught.

"That's not random."

Cal leaned closer, bracing one hand on the scarred oak table. "It's a fascia-patterned breath loop. Yours. Overlaid with a foreign resonance key."

Jack frowned, a match suspended over the lip of his pipe. "How foreign?"

"Arctic," Cal said. "Near the Greenland vault signature. Cryo-spliced with Field 13A."

They all stilled. Even the Monongahela seemed to pause outside — no wind in the pines, no creak of the old snow-crusted roof. Out here, silence could stretch for miles.

Lou opened her jacket, pulled out the FT-1 and set it against the signal panel. The air between the table and the old radio shelf seemed to shiver. The signal snapped into coherence.

THREAD RESTORED. SOURCE CONFIRMED. NODE: LLEWELLYN

Jack exhaled slowly, smoke curling toward the rafters. "That thing isn't just signaling. It's tracking your memory."

"Not just mine," Lou said, her eyes still on the readout. "Ours. The moment we touched Field 13A, something followed. Something old."

Scene — Lisbon – Systems of Trust Archive (Flashback)

A windowless building outside Lisbon, disguised as a neuro-linguistic startup. Douwe Egberts in a chipped mug. Lou hunched over a hardline terminal.

Helix logs: behavior-mod drift overlays, biometric saturation thresholds, linguistic sync codes. Each more grotesque than the last.

The Helix stack wasn't conceptual.

It was operational.

She read one file three times:

NSP-7 // Narrative Saturation Protocol
Target Regions: Nordics, Balkans, Swing Zones (U.S.)
Mechanism: Emotional cue embedding pre-conscious decision layers

"We're not persuading anyone," she whispered. "We're programming them."

Scene — Haifa: The Quiet Harbor Lab
Location — Haifa, Israel

Eitan Navon hadn't wanted to leave Madison, but couriers had gone dark, and the meds weren't moving through Virginia safehouses anymore. Haifa was the last place he swore he'd never return to — too many ghosts, too many files he'd once sealed under Halberd assignments. He'd told himself they were buried, mislabeled, forgotten. But nothing in Haifa ever really stayed buried.

The lab sat beneath the old naval docks, a windowless space leased under three false registries. Salt air pressed through rusted vents, carrying the smell of iron and algae. He lowered himself into the chair, joints stiff but hands steady, and keyed the console awake.

Salkin's resonance diagrams lit the wall, overlaid with Phase-3 Helix telemetry smuggled out of Lisbon. Half-maps. Half-lies. He traced the overlays with a trembling finger until the gap emerged — not in the math, but in the trust assumptions.

The AI on his wrist picked up the muscle flicker in his jaw. "Stress signature detected. Do you require dose correction?"

He ignored it. The pill bottle in his pocket rattled once, unanswered. "She's accessed Phase-3," he muttered.

"Yes," the AI replied. "And she knows."

He leaned forward, breath shallow, eyes narrowing at the convergence point blinking red on the map. Not Zurich. Not Shanghai. Madison. Again.

He whispered to the quiet, almost angrily: "Not yet. I sealed these files once. I won't let Sabine, or anyone else, rewrite what Maud can still see — what Lou never had the chance to."

The screen pulsed. For a second the overlay shimmered with something not in any file — a faint glyph, unresolved, like static caught mid-signal. Glyph-9. Watching. Waiting.

Eitan closed his eyes. "If trust fractures here, it fractures everywhere."

Scene — Strategic Spire – Office of Doctrine Futures

Colonel Biff Langley stood before a wall of Continuity Grid Assembly planners. PowerPoint title:

"Integrated Campaign Design: A Return to Clarity"

He pointed to a phase-based arrow diagram — large arrows, all forward.

"We simplify the battlespace. Redefine engagements into linear campaigns with decisive pivot points. Strategic Overmatch isn't dead. It just needs rebranding."

In the back, Tanner Grissom, the 50-something White House senior staffer with a poli-sci degree and too much hair product, leaned toward a colleague.

"Here we go again. Didn't the Russians abandon linear warfare in 2014?"

The colleague smirked. "Biff loves this word. Remember, he thinks *Weltanschauungskrieg* is a dog that once curled up on a Bundeswehr airfield and refused to leave."

Biff heard them. He waved them off.

"Linear thinking built this Strategic Spire," he snapped. "Chaos theory is for TED talks."

A low cough circled the room. Everyone knew the contracts flowed from the same three firms, each with continuity ties no one dared map out.
Tanner leaned back, whispering just loud enough to sound polished, not subversive:
"That's the beauty of public–private partnerships — our war colleges get the most up-to-date doctrine manuals, perfectly cohered."

His colleague smirked faintly, then jotted a note, underlining the word *retainer*.

Scene — Jack's Cabin, Later

Lou sat back as her coffee went cold.

She opened a new file: Phase-4 Contingency – Genesis Rebuild.

Cal entered quietly. "They moved another vault."

"Where?" she asked.

"Baffin Island. Polar loop."

Lou sighed. "Sabine's ahead. Again."

Jack appeared behind them, holding a thermal photo. "Not for long. Our rogue SEAL? He says he's got eyes on the Arctic team."

Lou raised an eyebrow. "He's still alive?"

"Apparently. Also, he explains chaos theory using burrito metaphors."

She cracked a smile for the first time in hours.

"Then send him coffee. And tell him to aim for the signal core."

Epigraph for Chapter End:

"They erased our stories because they feared the endings we hadn't yet written. But pattern remembers. And so do we." — *L.L. Scott*

Chapter 31 Close — Lou's Reflection

"Fractures don't announce themselves. They live in the pause before the word, the hesitation before the move. That's what Vire tracks — the moment trust shifts from weight to crack.

We saw it in Brussels, when Ray set down the Go board like a confession. We saw it in Lisbon, when Helix coded trust into protocols instead of promises. And tonight, in Jack's cabin, I felt it in my own breath — fascia patterned into resonance I never consented to.

That's the new terrain: Reality Frame — Trust Cascade. Not betrayal in the dramatic sense, but erosion — one unnoticed slip at a time, until the whole lattice collapses under the illusion it was ever solid.

If Helix locks that into the Chamber, they won't need to fire a shot. Trust itself will become programmable — alliances stripped bare before we even know they're broken.

Which means we don't get to wait for confirmation. If you feel the fracture in your chest, you're already across it. And the next move isn't theoretical. It's operational: Baffin. Geneva. The Black Sea loop.

Because trust doesn't shatter in one clean sound. It slips. Quiet. And by the time you hear it, the field's already rewritten the ending."

Go Move — のぞき // Nozoki – The Peep — General Liu

Liu leaned over the board, tapping the seam with his finger before setting the stone.

"Nozoki," he said. "You don't break trust outright. You lean at the joint. Make them show if they'll hold it or let it slip."

Zhen's brow furrowed. "That's what happened in Brussels. And Lisbon. Even in that cabin up north. Each time the field bent just enough to show the crack."

Liu nodded. "The Chamber doesn't need betrayal with banners. Just one quiet answer at the wrong time. Connect too tight, you bleed liberties later. Ignore it, the cut comes when you can't afford it. Either way, the shape's already breaking."

He pushed the stone into place, the sound small but final. "Trust doesn't shatter. It cascades. That's the war Lou's in now."

— ✦ — FIELD NOTE

Trust Cascade

In coherence war, betrayal isn't rupture. It's incremental drift — each unnoticed concession weakening the lattice until collapse feels inevitable. The Chamber doesn't need enemies to break alliances; it needs one slip misread as stability.

Counter-move: spot the peep. Trust isn't tested in grand betrayals, but in seams. Guard the joint, or the field rewrites the bond before you realize it's gone.

Chapter 32 — Pattern Hunters

Tagline — "They didn't hunt people. They hunted divergence patterns. And they called it peace." — *Lou Scott*

Scene – Consent Algorithms and Other Myths
Location — Bavarian Signal Relay Ridge

The ridgeline shimmered in early light, low fog clinging like memory. Cal crouched beside a rust-stained antenna tower, examining the node relay. The uplink jittered, interference creeping in like static doubt.

He cleared his throat, letting a soft Dutch lilt flatten his vowels. "If they trace the node pings to this relay, we're out before the sweep."

Lou gave him a side glance. "Your accents are getting worse."

"Helps when you don't enunciate," he muttered, adjusting the strap across his shoulder. The suppressed *CZ P-07* sat snug against his waistband — a remnant of Crete. Not issued. Acquired. Traded for antibiotics. Still clean.

She arched an eyebrow. "That's not Dutch."

"Aye, well…" His voice shifted, just slightly. Scottish now — not the smooth baritone of an officer, but the gruff cadence of a ghillie guiding a hedge fund exec along the River Dee. Less MI6, more *salmon not seals*.

"Better?" he asked.

"Closer," Lou said, turning back to the ridge. "But you still sound like someone who's killed people for a living."

Cal smirked. "Only the ones worth the ammo."

The uplink wasn't random. JR had found it buried in a schematic pulled from an abandoned Trust archive — not plans for the Genesis Chamber itself, but its scaffolding. Every cold-atom lattice needed a spine, a relay chain to carry coherence between continents. Charlottesville had been one anchor. Bavaria was another.

JR's voice still rang in Lou's head from the scrambled call: *"You want the Chamber? You've got to follow its nerves. This ridge is one of them. Old relay, still live. Find out what's feeding it — and who's listening."*

That was why they'd come. Not to shut it down, not yet. Just to map the vein before the sweep, trace how far the lattice reached back, and what ghosts it carried forward.

Scene — Inside Relay Station Echo-Aegis

JR's schematic wasn't a map of the Chamber itself — it was a circulatory diagram. Every cold-atom lattice needed anchors, relay veins that stitched continents together. Charlottesville was one. This Bavarian ridge was another.

Somewhere east, in a Haifa basement where couriers still whispered, Eitan had flagged the same jitter in Salkin's notes. He hadn't sent commentary — just the notation: arterial, not regional. His way of saying: don't miss the vein.

If they wanted to understand how the Genesis Core breathed under the ice, they had to start by tracing its nerves.

What they didn't expect was who else was already wired in.

The interior smelled of ozone and damp stone. Half the consoles were stripped, but one array still hummed — cold, crystalline, wrong. Lou touched the frame and felt the pulse. Her chest tightened. *Not new.* She'd felt this in Salkin's lab outside Charlottesville, years ago — the way he'd stripped a coolant relay to its copper ribs, showing her how Helix bled coherence signatures into reactor noise. *"They don't retire their tricks," he'd said. "They bury them under louder ones."*

Different continent, same spine. One field, stretched thin across centuries and borders.

"Cal frowned at the jitter. 'This is colder than it should be,' he muttered. 'Not temperature. Quantum lag. Like the relay was stitched through an old chamber drop — a cousin to the nuclear subnodes in Virginia that Salkin once dissected. Different tools, same ghost signature. Ravenen used to call it ancient energy — not power in the modern sense, but resonance left behind, like bone marrow in the lattice. The system didn't retire its hardware; it re-threaded it.'"

Then the air shifted. Six avatars bled into focus, ghostlike, seated in formation, remote minds stitched into the lattice. Projected through that same cold channel — a frozen artery tying this Bavarian ridge to reactor concrete half a world away.

Behavioral analytics experts. Quantum social engineers. One wore a lanyard with a Swiss data conglomerate tag. Another had an MIT ring and a nervous tic.

"Consent algorithms," the lead avatar said, almost proudly. "We can achieve 94.7% anticipatory compliance if the framing sequence is tuned to the subject's trust imprint."

Lou didn't flinch. She remembered Eitan's scrawl in the margin of a Geneva trial log: 'Consent isn't requested. It's manufactured.' Same doctrine. Same lie.

Cal blinked. "You mean, if you lie nicely."
The man frowned. "We prefer engineered resonance."

Lou stepped forward, sipping her coffee. Too much half and half. Coconut sugar. The Europeans winced.
"You built belief cages and called them safety nets," she said. "Your predictive defiance matrix thinks free will is just a dataset glitch."

Cal muttered under his breath, half to himself, half to her: "How do you fight something you can't even kill? Feels like shooting at smoke."

"Sovereignty is a spectrum," another chimed in.
"And you're the ones holding the dimmer switch?" Lou asked.

They faltered. The youngest spoke next.
"You don't understand the stakes. The models show collapse if we don't manage narrative compliance."

Lou looked at him. Hard.
"Collapse of what? Your funding stream? Or the illusion that people asked for this?"

She leaned in.
"I lived through your trial runs. Pandemic framing. Emotional consent loops. Every time you said 'for the greater good,' a new cage was built. With biometric locks and smiley-face lockscreens."

Cal moved behind her, watching the monitors blink — resonance profiles cascading, heat clusters mapped against sentiment drift.

"You call this protection?" Lou asked. "You call this peace?"

The lead avatar leaned closer — not walking, but projected presence bending toward her, as if distance no longer applied. His outline fuzzed at the edges, but the voice was sharp.

Cal's voice was low but steady, too low for them but enough for Lou: "Christ. We're not fighting soldiers. We're fighting their avatars." He adjusted his grip on the railcaster anyway, as if a bullet could break projection. "Welcome to the new frontline. No bodies. Just presence."

Lou's eyes sharpened. For a moment, the lattice almost seemed to hum in recognition.
"They gave me a name for that," she said quietly. "Ananta. The one who returns."
She let the word hang, steady and unblinking.

"You think divergence is a fire. You're wrong. It's an echo. And echoes don't die — they return until the walls give way."

Lou nodded slowly. "You're right. I don't. And neither do you."

Elsewhere: Geneva – Helix Substrate Core

Sabine watched the interaction via an off-axis relay. No sound, just waveform readouts. She noted the pulse shifts in Lou's coherence band. Deviations outside expected bounds. Organic. Disruptive.

"She's not broadcasting," one Helix analyst whispered.

"No," Sabine said. "She's becoming her own substrate."

Scene —   Exit from Relay Ridge

Cal and Lou exited as fog thickened. Behind them, the Pattern Hunters remained, silent now, staring at their models like flawed scripture.

Lou adjusted her jacket, feeling the node pulse against her spine.

Ray once said Florence was a city built on recursive beauty — every arch an echo, every alley a reframe. It made sense that their fallback site would be here, just outside the city's memory.

"They still think divergence is the threat," she muttered.

Cal gave her a look. "Isn't it?"

"No. Predictive compliance is the threat. Divergence is the last damn signal we can trust."

The uplink pinged once — faint, encrypted.
A new location dropped into their relay queue:
FLR-87_CIV — **Florence Periphery Safehouse**.

"That's Ray's marker," Lou said.

But the uplink header carried something else too — an older tag, almost lost in the static. Navon's hand. Even from Haifa, half-broken, he was still tracing the veins. Still reminding them he hadn't quit.

Cal was already moving. "Then we follow it."

They left the ridge without a word. The next coordinates weren't just a safehouse. They were a memory.

They crossed into Tuscany under cover of mist, following Ray's relay marker down an unlit road. Lou drove now, silent, gripping the wheel like it held memory. Jack had joined them in Trieste, arriving with a field bag and a question in his eyes he hadn't yet voiced. Ledger handled the route clearance and fuel swaps through old SOF channels. No one asked who was paying. They were already bankrupt in every currency but belief.

Ray had called it a fallback site — a place where the lies hadn't reached yet.

They arrived in Florence before dawn.

The compound sat just beyond the city's edge — a relic buried in bureaucratic fog. They approached in silence, tires humming over gravel. Cal checked the perimeter once. Lou checked it twice. Ledger had prepaid the electric reconnections through a dummy NGO that no longer existed. Ray had left the key in the generator housing, same as always.

Chapter 32 Close — Lou's Reflection
"Pattern Hunters don't chase people. They chase probability. They think consent is just an algorithm — inputs, outputs, compliance ratios — like memory can be corralled into neat percentages. But every model misses what doesn't fit. Divergence isn't in their dataset until it's already rewriting the board.

That's the trap of Reality Frame — Consent Enclosure. The Pattern Hunters call it safety. Their models call it consent. But predictive defiance systems don't prevent collapse. They just pre-justify it.

I've seen this spine before — Greenland, Kosovo, Madison — each node dressed up as neutral relay, each one bleeding the same cold pulse. They call it logistics. It's capture. They call it peace. It's predictive confinement.

You don't notice when it happens, because it feels like safety. But the moment you stop asking who's running the signal, you're already inside their map.

Florence is next. Ray marked it, not because it's clean, but because it still remembers outside their lattice. That means we've got one move before inevitability locks. And if we don't take it — we won't just lose the Chamber. We'll lose the last signal that isn't theirs."

Go Move — 未着隅 // Michakusumi – The Unplayed Corner — General Zhen

Zhen set his stone down, but not in contact. He left the corner open, quiet, unread.

"The Pattern Hunters think the joseki is finished," he said. "Edges sealed. Territory safe."

Liu studied the shape. "And yet you don't play it?"

"Not yet," Zhen replied. "Some corners you leave untouched. They bait the impatient. They blind the confident. They wait for the one who sees the board differently."

He let the silence settle, eyes flicking toward Lou's absence on the field.

"She isn't playing to win territory. She's playing to unmake the frame. And that's the stone they'll never see until it lands."

— ✦ — FIELD NOTE

Consent Enclosure

In signal war, consent is not freely given. It is pre-justified by models that predict compliance before it occurs. This is the consent enclosure: a lattice that frames safety as inevitability and treats refusal as anomaly.

Counter-move: leave the corner unplayed. Refuse premature closure. Force the system to reveal the difference between consent and confinement.

Chapter 33 — The End of Uniformed Consent

Tagline — "They didn't hunt people. They hunted divergence patterns. And they called it peace." — *Ray*

Scene – The Sedation Doctrine
Location — Florence Periphery Compound

Fog clung to the hills like a second skin. The road to the compound wound past rusted signs and broken fence lines. Jack drove, lights off, guided only by a flickering grid marker Eitan had sent through a private relay.

Haifa's shadows hadn't slowed him. Age made his body stumble, but his signal work cut sharper than ever — slipped through couriers, hidden in dead-band noise. The grid marker wasn't just coordinates — it was Eitan's way of saying he still saw the fracture before they did.

"Looks abandoned," Cal muttered. "Like everything else they called secure."

"It was," Lou said. "Ray brought me here once. The first time I refused a Helix override."

The gate creaked open on proximity. No resistance. Just a low-pulse field shimmer and silence. They parked inside the cracked courtyard, beside a faded mural of the Eight Stability Vectors.

Inside, the safehouse was austere. One long table. Three rusted cots. A coffee pot older than the lattice itself. Manuals stacked against the wall, their covers sun-bleached: *Field Doctrine Override: Edition 12A. Sentiment Modulation Guidelines. Predictive Stability Index Charts.*

Jack poured coffee. Cal stood at the door. Lou paced.

"We taught them how to aim," Jack said, "but not why they were aiming."

Lou didn't look at him. "Combat initiative collapsed below 7%. That was the last metric Ray ever sent me. After that—"

"There was no war," Cal finished. "Just pre-modeled outcomes."

Jack sat. "We stopped teaching tactics. We started programming conclusions. Every scenario ended in 'consensus victory.'"

Lou turned. "And when the coherence field fractured? They issued supplements."

Cal snorted. "Stability enhancers. Cognitive smoothers."

Jack: "They called it ethical warfare."

Lou: "It was psychic sedation."

Cal leaned against the wall. "I had to kill one of mine once. During a drill. Signal dropped. He froze. Wouldn't act. He was trying to suppress volatility. His words. Not his. The system's."

Silence.

Jack rubbed his face. "Biff said it was the safest era in military history. No chaos. No risk. Just calibration. He loved saying that — usually while posing for the feed cam with his helmet tilted just so, like a recruiting poster that drank its own Kool-Aid."

Cal didn't look up. "He also loved that augmentation loop they gave him. Said it made him think clearer. Truth was, it just made him repeat doctrine faster."

"Like an echo with better posture," Jack said. "You'd tell him the weather and he'd feed it back to you as a mission statement."

Lou glanced over. "You trusted him once."

Cal shrugged, jaw tight. "He was solid, early on. Could hold a field, keep his team alive. But after STL-9X, you couldn't tell where he ended and the program began."

Jack leaned back in his chair, coffee sloshing in the mug. "And that was the point, wasn't it? Make a soldier who could smile for the cameras, keep the sponsors happy, and still read the kill-script without flinching."

Lou said nothing, but her eyes stayed on Cal.
Cal didn't return the look. "He was proof they didn't want soldiers anymore. They wanted showpieces. Spotlight's warm until it burns through you."

Lou heard the exchange and smiled — not fondly, but the way you smile when a bad memory lines up perfectly with the truth. "Biff could charm a room and drain it in the same breath," she said. "Once briefed a joint task group on counter-signal protocols, then spent the next hour giving interviews about his 'innovative leadership posture.'"

She crossed to the shelf, fingers trailing along the spines. "He collected attention the way most of us collected field manuals — and filed both in the same order: whichever looked best on top."

Lou pulled out an old manual. Flipped through it. The margins were filled with ink — real notes, questions, tactical queries.

"This wasn't doctrine. It was thought. We erased that."

A low buzz—drone overhead. No threat. Just surveillance.

Cal finally spoke. "Don't call them troops anymore. By the end, they weren't soldiers. They were coherence assets. Lattice-bound. Sync'd to Helix."

Jack: "Even their memories weren't their own."

Lou set the manual down.

"The final war wasn't lost," she said.

Cal nodded. "It was agreed upon."

In Haifa, Eitan had already annotated the same manuals they now held — margins crowded with uneven strokes, steadiness fading but intent unbroken, countermeasure sketches scrawled in the white space. He'd warned them years earlier: sedation wasn't defense, it was surrender by algorithm. No doctrine board had listened. Only Lou had saved the notes.

Raveneh's voice drifted from the adjoining room. "When belief becomes architecture, obedience becomes instinct."

Lou whispered, more to herself than them: **"They had a duty to disobey."**

Cal looked at her. "So how do you fight ghosts that write the rules?"

Lou didn't answer right away. "You don't chase them. You rewrite the game board."

"Sounds like mayhem," he said.

She nodded. "Or the first true move we've made in years."

She looked up. Her voice was steady.

"We didn't just lose a war. We lost the will to disobey."

No one answered.

Outside, the fog didn't lift.

Inside, no one moved the Go stone she left on the table.

Not black. Not white. Just a symbol. And silence.

The silence didn't last.
A secure ping from Ledger came through a sideband node, tagged with only one word:
"Zurich."

Cal's jaw tightened. He stared at the handheld, then passed it to Lou.

She scanned the pulse logs. Drift spikes. Field 13A signature. A mirrored return.

"She's flaring again," it read.

Lou didn't speak. But she was already moving.

Chapter 33 Close — Lou's Reflection

"You can train anyone to follow orders.
It takes something rarer to teach refusal.

Today, disobedience isn't defiance. It's navigation. Every field you cross will try to overwrite your route. Every rule you obey will close another door.

The map they hand you isn't wrong. It's just the one they want you to survive by — not the one that gets you beyond.

That's the end of uniformed consent: when soldiers stop being fighters and become assets. And that's the only war we can't afford to lose — the one where obedience masquerades as survival. Because once you forget how to disobey, you've already agreed to vanish."

Go Move — 厚い石 // Atsui-ishi – The Stone No One Claimed — General Zhen

Zhen pressed the stone down with deliberate weight. "Thick. Strong. But thickness has its own danger."

Liu studied the shape. "Too strong to challenge, so no one dares touch it. That's how soldiers learn consent — not by orders, but by habit. The board teaches them the safest move is no move."

Zhen nodded once. "And once you forget how to strike from strength, you've already surrendered. Thick shape becomes prison shape."

Liu's gaze drifted to Lou's path. "She played where no one claimed. Not obedience. Not survival. Just refusal — a reminder that even the safest frame can still be broken."

— ✦ — FIELD NOTE
Uniformed Consent

In narrative warfare, obedience isn't always enforced by orders. It calcifies through habit — routines drilled until soldiers mistake stability for survival. This is *uniformed consent*: when compliance is rehearsed so thoroughly that no explicit command is required. Counter-move: destabilize the habit. Refuse the "safe" stone. Play where no one has claimed, even if it risks collapse.

Chapter 34 — Threshold Drift

Tagline — "Some thresholds aren't crossed. They dissolve — pulse by pulse." — *Unknown*

Scene — Zurich Central Transit – 48 Hours Earlier

Cal Merrick stepped off the late train from Milan, coat collar turned up against the Alpine wind. He hadn't planned on Zurich — not this week, maybe not ever. But the message had come through an old channel he thought was dead. One of Ledger's encrypted nods. No signatures. Just one phrase:

"She's flaring again."

The biometric logs tagged to the Zurich node matched the same anomaly from Field 13A. Not similar — exact. Pulse for pulse. Memory for memory.

He hadn't seen Lou in months. Hadn't seen Jack since they nearly killed each other in Tangier.

He checked the screen for hotel routes. Not that it mattered. Wherever Lou was, he'd find the shadow two steps behind her — probably with a gun, a flask, or both. Jack never changed.

And neither did he.

Ledger's voice had been calm on the call. "You'll want to be nearby. Resonance drift is spiking. Zurich vault's logging her out-of-band again."

"What's the margin?" Cal had asked.

"Off by seven seconds on known baselines," Ledger said. "That's not drift. That's dissociation."

Cal didn't argue. Ledger never called unless something vital was breaking.

He shoved his hands into his pockets and muttered to himself as he started toward the archives district.

"Drift. Ghosts. And Llewellyn Scott. Bloody hell. Every time I think I'm out…"

He let the sentence trail off. It was always the same with her. Chaos, code, and something like love.

But never peace.

Scene — Zurich Entry / Access Conduit

The underground entrance wasn't marked on any map. Ledger had routed them through an NGO courier lane — paper covers, freight convoy, diplomatic charters layered over biometric passes that expired a decade ago. The city above bustled like nothing had changed, but down here the concrete sweated, humming with the kind of power that never shut off.

Jack muttered, "This isn't a safehouse. It's a vault."
Cal checked the clearance token glowing faintly on his screen. "Ledger said we had thirty minutes before the pass expires. After that, we're ghosts without names."
Lou kept walking. "That's all we need. I didn't come here for maps. I came for the mirror."

A final checkpoint shimmered — resonance gates, tuned to intent as much as ID. Cal slipped the forged tag across the panel. It hesitated, then blinked green. Too quickly.
"Either we're cleared," Jack said, "or they want us inside."

The lift dropped them two levels, air pressure shifting. Then the doors opened.

Location — Zurich – Helix Biometric Archives, Secure Observation Deck
Time: Hours after Madison signal flare

The glass wasn't ordinary.

It layered microreactive polymer, phased light filters, and biometric trace compounds designed to detect what most systems ignored — drift. Not just pulse or sweat or pupil dilation. Deeper. Subtle tremors in intention, in coherence. The residue of decisions made before the brain caught up.

Lou remained on the upper tier of the Zurich Observation Deck, a space nested above the Helix Archives where the resonance glass tracked her every breath.

Lou stood before it, unreadable as the data scrolling behind her. The system hesitated. Her breath signature phased off the expected waveform. Heart rhythm: staggered. Skin conductivity: reactive but unpredictable.

Out of sync with the modeled present.

"I know the feeling," she muttered. "Misfiled by your own operating system."

Jack sat across the room, wrist immobilized in cold mesh. Sarajevo hadn't gone clean. He didn't explain the full op — not yet — but his eyes tracked Lou's posture like a man watching someone walking too close to the edge of a cliff.

"You still light up systems like a bad memory," he said. "Even with Helix hiding its telemetry."

She didn't smile. "Funny. The machines don't forget me — but most people did."

Jack didn't answer.

Cal entered with a portable monitor. Jagged lines spat across its display — not noise. Harmonics. Structured. Familiar.

"The Kosovo artifact," he said, voice steady. "It's back."

Jack stood. "That can't be right."

Lou turned. "Field 13A."

Jack exhaled slowly. "That thing nearly killed us."

"No," Lou said. "It recruited us."

She tapped the screen. "This isn't new data. It's a mirrored return. Like the system's running a delayed playback, but now it's modulating — evolving."

Cal narrowed his eyes. "Self-looping signal. Breath-linked. It's shaping coherence fields based on... intention?"

Jack leaned in. "The artifact isn't inert. It's recursive."

Lou nodded. "And Field 13A wasn't a recovery op. It was a seeding event."

Cal exhaled. "Then what are we now? Harvesters?"

Lou turned slowly. "No. We're desynchronizers. They locked the system with coherence; we unseat it with divergence."

Jack said, "Great. So we're scalpels in a war against gods."
"No," Lou replied. "We're mirrors. And they can't survive looking at themselves."

The resonance glass gave a faint, uneven hum — not mechanical, but like breath caught between heartbeats. Across its surface, biometric overlays jittered a fraction out of phase, as if the system couldn't decide whether to smooth her signature or amplify it. The air near Lou felt tuned, listening.

Above them, the ceiling lights dimmed — a power fluctuation or something else. Lou's shadow flickered against the wall. It didn't align with her stance. It split — two frames, not one. Then recombined. As if reality hesitated.

Jack noticed but said nothing.

Silence. Not fear — recognition.

Helix wasn't the origin. It was the cover story.

Cal stepped forward. "Then let's give them something worth reflecting."

Lou tilted her head. "What are you thinking?"

Cal pointed at the map feed glowing on the wall. "Field deployments. Overload their predictive models. False divergence trails. Pattern collapse by narrative saturation."

Jack groaned. "You want chaos."
"No," Cal said. "I want them to drown in coherence debt. They rely on resonance certainty. So we rob them of it."

Cal's eyes sharpened. "Then let's give them something they can't model."

Lou considered it. "How many nodes do we still control?"
Jack checked the overlay. "Seven. If we move fast."

"Then we fracture seven truths. Hard."

Jack leaned against the console. "And after that?"
Lou didn't look up. "Then we stop reacting. We bait them. Turn the recursion on them."

"The Watchers?" Cal asked.
"They built the system," Lou said. "Let's show them it can't hold."

Sidebar – Encrypted Uplink, Charlottesville, Virginia

The Zurich vault fed on live relays — every drift logged in Europe ricocheted across its sister nodes in Virginia. Cal checked the secure message blinking on his handheld, same line pulsing every two minutes:

Codeword: Sylvester
Payload: Ready
Route: Charlottesville — Haymarket

He sighed. "Wine country again."

Jack didn't look up from the console. "Pinot and pipe bombs. Classic tradecraft."

Cal smirked. "Curmudgeonly, but dependable. Only man I've seen drop a drone from a mile out while chewing jerky and insulting our mission brief."

Jack flipped an old Go stone into the data reader, letting it clatter against the uplink. The Zurich glass pulsed once, faintly — the transatlantic nodes syncing in real time.

"Good," Jack muttered. "Let them chase the wrong player."

Cal's grin was thin but sharp. "They still think the map is the terrain."

Sidebar – Vineyard Outskirts, VA

Wechsler wiped oil-stained hands on an old flannel, crouched under the axle of a camouflaged transport truck. The shielding array he'd rigged wasn't pretty, but it would blind Helix sweeps from low orbit.

Pinot stood nearby, silent as always, cinching clamps on a cryo-stabilized crate. His breath fogged in the cool morning. Finally, he spoke — low, flat:

"Zurich node isn't just surveillance. It's vault-tier. Lou's glass won't hold."

Wechsler grunted. "You want heavier ordnance, say it straight."

Pinot just raised one eyebrow — the whole request compressed into a gesture.

"Fine," Wechsler muttered, tightening a bolt. "Charlottesville run first. Haymarket after. StepDoc and Doc Mare are already in motion. I'll load the jammers, plus the scrambler rig Cal swears he doesn't need."

Sylvester leaned against the truck, chewing jerky like it was a weapon too. "This isn't payload delivery. It's epistemological sabotage."

Pinot's reply was almost a smile. "Good."

On the welded panel of the truck, someone had scrawled in marker: *You know the thing about chaos? It's fair. Maps can't hold the terrain.*

Wechsler shook his head. "Vire's influence. People eat this crap up."

"Cabernet in the front," Sylvester said, spitting jerky into the dirt. "Carnage in the back. Welcome to Virginia."

Sidebar – Haymarket Edge, Doc Mare's Stables

Doc Mare zipped sedatives into a weatherproof satchel, the horses steady in their stalls. She checked them like she checked the field — slow, exact, unblinking.

StepDoc emerged from the trailer with a diaper bag, a laptop wrapped in thermal mesh, and a falsified Continuity Alliance pediatric immunization chart. She held up a small amber vial, rolling it in her fingers.

"Not horse meds," she said lightly. "Novel dopamine agonist. Unapproved. Perfect for someone who shakes when he shouldn't."

Doc Mare raised an eyebrow. "And you're masking it as equine anti-parasitic?"

StepDoc grinned. "Exactly. Couriers move horse meds all the time. Nobody checks dosage curves for ponies."

Doc Mare smirked. "Half the checkpoints clear themselves when you walk slow."

"And the other half," StepDoc said, slipping into a syrupy grandmother drawl, "fall over when I tell them I bake pies on Sundays."

She tucked the vial into the satchel, next to the sedatives. "For Eitan," she added quietly. "He'll know what to do with it."

Doc Mare glanced toward the ridgeline. Somewhere beyond it, Zurich glass was already warping.

Sidebar – Little Washington Perimeter, The Scribe's Retreat

There were five people left alive who still referred to him as *The Scribe*. Four of them were ghosts. The fifth had a network.

They called him the Scribe, though no one knew if he still answered to it. Once Helix's forensic strategist, he walked away when the war stopped being about outcomes and became about *versions* — who remembered first, who fired first, which truth stuck.

Now he lived like a hermit. Not a builder. A dissenter. Notebooks in dead languages piled around him, margins thick with sketches that weren't blueprints so much as refusals. He kept the resonance compass tuned but unused — a relic of the days when memory was still contested terrain.

When Eitan needed a cutout, he didn't call Ledger. He called the Scribe. Ghosts knew how to move.

Scene — Geneva Substrate Relay, Off-Grid Access
Sabine Xu dismissed the analyst with a flick of her hand. The relay shimmered on her private channel, not tagged to Helix, not monitored by the Alliance. She had tunneled it herself, years ago, for one purpose: to reach the only man who had seen her doctrine before she named it.

"Eitan." Her voice was low, almost patient. "Still scribbling in margins no one reads?"

A pause. The return signal carried uneven breaths, like static wrapped in fatigue. "Still mistaking sedation for stability?"

"You sealed these files once," she said. "You know why. Without obedience, coherence collapses. You saw what happened in Prizren. In Madison. You'll see it again."

His cough rattled faintly, then steadied. "I sealed them because I knew what you'd build with them. A cage so elegant people would call it safety."

Sabine leaned closer to the lattice feed, eyes narrowing. "You can't stop me with couriers and scribbles. The Chamber isn't yours anymore. It never was."

"No," Eitan whispered. "But Maud's sight isn't yours either. And she'll see what you missed."

Sabine's lips tightened, just slightly. She ended the line without another word.

Eitan sat back in the Haifa dark, breath uneven. He knew her next move wouldn't stay in Geneva — it would surface in Zurich, at the vault where drift always pooled. He tapped the compass once, as if to warn

Lou through the static:
Watch the glass.

Zurich – Observation Deck

Lou pressed her hand against the resonance glass. It didn't reflect —
it warped. I was a device that doesn't just reflect, but *measures intention,
coherence, and drift.*

The resonance glass itself reacts — shimmering, warping, bending
her shadow wrong — showing Lou's presence is destabilizing the system.

The field has shifted, and a confrontation with Sabine felt inevitable,
but *not yet.*

Behind her, Jack scrolled through fresh intercepts. Helix had gone
active in four more zones. All inside U.S.-aligned territories. Narrative
saturation overlays. Biometric drift tags. Even linguistic mutations seeded
in open-source media.

Cal returned, breath short. "We've got another hit."

Lou turned.

"A name came up twice in today's logistics log," Cal said, handing
her a tablet. "Buried under NGO charter freight and diplomatic cover."

Lou read it. No outward reaction. Just a whisper beneath her breath:
"Sabine."

Publicly, she was still in Geneva. Privately, she was moving faster
than all of them.

Jack studied Lou's posture.

The resonance glass behind her shimmered. Not visibly — but its
edge refracted strangely, as if refusing to hold her shape.

Her shadow bent wrong again. Jack squinted. Was it the angle? Or
something deeper?

Again, he said nothing.

"You ready for that confrontation?"
Lou didn't blink. "Not yet. But the field just shifted."

Chapter 34 Close — Lou's Reflection

"Zurich isn't just another stop on the map. It's one of Helix's
biometric archive nodes — a mirror built to catch the pieces of you that

don't fit their models. But what it showed me tonight wasn't new. It was playback. My own shadow splitting against the glass, refracting back at me like the system couldn't decide which version to keep.

That's when I understood: Kosovo wasn't a recovery op. It was a seeding event. Field 13A didn't almost kill us — it planted us. Every drift I've felt since isn't invention. It's recursion.

That's the trap of Reality Frame — Recursive Reflection. The lattice doesn't create. It replays — altered, delayed, recursive — until repetition itself feels like truth. The danger isn't erasure. It's novelty that isn't novel at all.

Zurich isn't the finish line. It's the point where the map starts lying. And if we hold still long enough, the field will redraw us into its version — until we forget we ever had another one."

Go Move — 影コスミ // Kage Kosumi – The Shadow Kosumi — General Liu

Liu slid the stone in at a diagonal, light and quiet — almost as if he'd placed it in the board's shadow.

Zhen squinted. "You don't seal it? After Zurich?"

Liu shook his head. "Kosumi. Not the line they're watching, the one they forgot. You press too hard, recursion snaps shut. You lean soft, it breathes — and waits."

Zhen sipped his sake, eyes narrowing. "So Kosovo wasn't loss. It was planting. And Zurich just replayed the harvest."

"Exactly," Liu said. "They think it's novelty. It's only playback. Same shadow, bent until you mistake it for new light."

The stone sat at its diagonal, unthreatening, almost forgettable.
But both men knew — the longer it stayed unanswered, the more the whole board bent around its silence.

— ✦ — FIELD NOTE
Recursive Reflection
In signal war, novelty is rarely new. Recursive reflection refracts past signals until repetition feels original.
Counter-move: recognize playback as seeding, not invention.

This ties Zurich's "shadow playback" directly into the kosumi diagonal, and echoes Lou's warning that staying still means being redrawn.

Chapter 35 — Field Entanglement

Tagline — "Structure doesn't break. It loops. Until someone inserts the wrong memory — at the right time." — *Lou Scott*

**Scene — The Unmaking Loop: North Atlantic Blind Spot
Location —** Mobile Staging Platform, North Atlantic.

The sea rolled beneath the covert platform like a creature breathing in its sleep. Salt hung in the air, thick and metallic. The platform itself was one of only three mobile blind spots left in the global grid—unregistered on Helix, its signal-absorbing alloys stolen from a Cold War-era Soviet stealth buoy program.

Lou stood at the observation deck's edge, hand resting near the Möbius ring at her hip, eyes scanning the horizon. The Atlantic looked empty. It wasn't.

"We were never supposed to return here," she said, more to herself than to the others.

Behind her, Cal Merrick emerged from the command module. His jaw was tighter than usual, the creases deeper.

"Ledger said the signal traced back to this quadrant," Cal said, holding out the encrypted data slate. "Same frequency we logged outside Madison. And before that—Kosovo. Field 13A."

Lou didn't take it. She just nodded. "It's not random. That pulse isn't about location. It's a breadcrumb. Someone's trying to call something back."

Jack approached from below deck, his wrist still bound in reinforced mesh. He moved slower now. Helix had tagged him as an anomaly weeks ago. His system was degrading.

"We set the resonance net," he said, voice hoarse. "If that field's active again, we'll see it before it sees us."

Lou turned to face them both. Her tone was different—not cold, just stripped of pretense.

"And if it doesn't want to be seen? What then?"

Cal looked away. Jack just stared at the sea.

Jack broke the silence. "We can't fight structure with structure. That's what Kael wants. That's how Helix wins."

Lou replied. "We don't match them. We unmake them."

Cal locked his jaw. "Disruptive patterns?"

"No. Narrative reversals. Shadow insertions. We turn their coherence loops into recursion traps," Lou explained.

Jack nodded slowly. "Then we weaponize story. Again."

Below Deck —
Cal ran diagnostics on the resonance array—an arcane fusion of Continuity Alliance sonar scaffolds and fringe Polish quantum filtration tech. The whole system buzzed like a living thing. A low pulse caught his ear.

Artifact detected.

Onscreen, a jagged signal lit up the display: FIELD 13A REACTIVATED.

Cal clenched his jaw. He remembered that field. He remembered the op. And he remembered who sent them there based on a faulty doctrinal brief: Biff Langley.

"He lied to us," Cal muttered.

Jack didn't look up. "Or he didn't know better. Which is worse?"

Cal's fingers hovered over the console. "Two good men died because someone tried to out-map chaos."

In his mind he could hear Lou whispering: "We need to seed seven stories. Real ones. Fragmented enough to spread, strong enough to bind."

Jack: "Counter-scripts?"

Cal: "No. Divergence igniters. Each one has to provoke belief friction—truths that can't be reconciled inside the lattice."

Lou: "The only way to beat predictive resonance... is to make belief unmodelable."

Flashback — Sylvester's Cache
Location — Charlottesville Foothills, One week earlier.

They'd gotten the message from a dead drop. A coded map. A name: Sylvester.

Cal stepped out of the SUV into damp Virginia mist. The vineyard was real, but the cellar was older than Prohibition and far more interesting.

"You bring your own blindfolds, or should I supply 'em?" Sylvester growled, lighting a cigar. He was former something. Rumor said Delta. Others swore MI6.

Inside, crates lined the walls: coherence disruptors, jerry-rigged comm scramblers, even a resonance dampener built out of an old espresso machine.

Jack whistled. "You hosting the end of the world or just planning to sell tickets?"

Sylvester grinned. "Both."

They loaded up what they could. Lou remained quiet until she spotted a single item wrapped in burlap: a resonance compass, tuned to legacy frequencies.

Lou paused mid-stride. Her eyes narrowed. "Where'd you get this?"

"Sandia. Before the program got sanitized. You didn't hear that from me."

Back to Present — North Atlantic

Lou stood near the array now, breath shallow. The *Möbius ring* vibrated slightly. Then sharply.

A tremor moved through the deck. Not seismic. Rhythmic. Familiar.

Cal stared at the console. "It's not broadcasting. It's listening."

Jack stepped up beside them. "Then we better be careful what we say."

The screen lit again.

SIGNAL RECOGNITION: FRACTURE THREAD
ENTANGLED
INITIATING HARMONIC RESTORE
SOURCE: UNKNOWN
DESTINATION: CLASSIFIED – MADISON CLUSTER

Lou whispered: "It's closing the loop."

Cal tightened the cinch on his holster. Not out of fear. Out of principle.

He thought of Biff.

He thought of all the doctrine briefings wrapped in certainty, all the grid-based campaign maps drawn without context, all the war games run by men who never lost a friend in a field that didn't exist.

He didn't want revenge. He wanted acknowledgment.

And that might be harder to get.

Lou turned away from the screen. "We didn't build this. We uncovered it. And now it wants to come home."

The platform creaked. The sea shifted.

Jack activated the uplink.

"Then we better be ready."

Chapter 35 Close — Lou's Reflection

"Field entanglement isn't a metaphor. It's the way the lattice survives itself. Structure doesn't break. It loops — until someone inserts the wrong memory at the right time.

Kosovo wasn't about recovery. It was about planting a pulse. Madison wasn't coincidence. It was the next loop. And now the North Atlantic — another blind spot that isn't blind at all. Each one stitching itself tighter, waiting for us to mistake repetition for discovery.

That's the Reality Frame — Entanglement Drift. The lattice doesn't invent. It mirrors you back, altered just enough that you don't notice the cage forming. That's why recursive signal is more dangerous than silence — because it makes you complicit in your own capture.

Glyph-9 wasn't built to be found. It chose. Not a location, not a vault, not even a filament. It chose a fracture point inside me — the one thing they can't rewrite unless I hand it over myself.

If we're going to win this, we can't just intercept their loops. We have to unmake them. Before the lattice convinces us we were never outside it in the first place."

Go Move — 捨石梯抜き // Sute-ishi Shichinuki – Ladder Breaker — General Zhen

Zhen traced the chase down the board — the same diagonal pressure curling again, like Kosovo into Madison into the blind spot in the North Atlantic.
"A ladder," he muttered. "They think she'll keep running the same line forever."

Liu tipped his head. "And yet?"

Zhen set his stone wide, outside the sequence.
"And yet the path's already broken. The lattice can't see it, so it keeps replaying the trap. But Lou—she stepped off. Made the pattern collapse on itself."

Liu gave a dry laugh. "A ladder that doesn't reach. Capture without a hand laid."

The stone looked distant, almost irrelevant.
But the air shifted — inevitability turned into nothing but echo.

Chapter 36 — The Geneva Substrate

Tagline — "When sovereignty is measured in waveforms, the first loss is never territory." — *Field Note, Geneva Substrate Archive*

Scene — The Nordic Stabilization Accord
Location — Oslo, Norway

The meeting room was smaller than it should have been. No press. No flags. Just three officials, a brushed steel table, and the faint pulse of the resonance compliance meter buried in the Nordic grid controller.

Prime Minister Solveig Lehn signed the protocol with a fountain pen — analog, deliberate. Across from her, the Trust Cabal representative — listed only as Thorne — tapped a pad. No eye contact. No acknowledgment.

The document blinked once: *Trust Energy Harmonization Framework – Tier 6A.* Absorbed into the lattice.

Solveig's voice was quiet. "The ice is melting. But it's not the glaciers. It's our resolve."

Thorne didn't answer. He just activated the coherence node. A hum passed through the walls — more felt than heard.

She already knew what the fine print meant:
National power retention contingent upon resonance compliance scores exceeding **0.618** on a rolling ninety-day index.

It wasn't a round percentage. Not human math. 0.618 — the reciprocal of the golden ratio. The Trust Cabal liked its theology hidden in equations. That was Helix: *preemption as theology.*

She remembered Raveneh's phrase from an early brief: *entropy governance disguised as stabilization.*

Thorne finally looked up. One word: "Automated."

The northern light outside dimmed, unnaturally. Solveig didn't flinch. "There was a time," she said, "when sovereignty meant geography. Now it's waveform stability."

She rose, returning the pen to its case. "History won't judge us for signing. It will judge us for knowing exactly what we signed."

She walked out.

Thorne remained. From his coat, he produced a small sphere etched with the resonance imprint glyph Ω–3, one of the Cabal's compliance tokens. It pulsed once and synced with the grid. No voice, no choice — the sphere existed only to confirm that the signature had already given consent.

And Oslo was not alone. Singapore. Chile. South Africa. One by one, nodes fell into alignment — a daisy-chain of obedience, glued together until sovereignty itself was nothing more than a frequency allocation.

Scene — The Thinker's Cabin
Location — Haymarket, Virginia — Nightfall
Timebase — Archived brief; playback concurrent with Operation Ghost Line.

Cal Merrick sat hunched on the edge of a wooden bench, jacket still wet from the road. The Thinker, cloaked in gray wool and ritual silence, handed him a chipped mug of something darker than coffee. The fire snapped, each pop carrying memory like ash curling upward.

"You saw Oslo, didn't you?" the Thinker said. "Lehn's signature wasn't surrender. It was theater. They're not traitors. They're stage managers. Performing collapse to keep their base calm."

He let the words settle like ash. "The real betrayal," he added, "is how quickly obedience is forgiven when it's branded as stability."

Cal half-smiled. A scar along his jaw pulled slightly. "I believe in inertia. Doesn't mean I like where we're headed."

"Collapse isn't chaos. It's choreography. You're just watching the steps late."

Cal frowned. "So how do we choreograph back?"

"With shadowed moves. Memory. Narrative entropy. You leak in storylines the system can't resolve."

"A doctrinal virus?"

The Thinker shook his head. "No. A ghost. You don't attack Helix. You haunt it."

He tapped a weathered diagram spread across the table: *Creation. Separation. Singularity.*

"Helix didn't happen. It was built. The Genesis flare wasn't an accident — it was the echo of a signal buried in us since Sumer."

Cal blinked. "Echo?"

"You'll hear it again. When you're in the right frequency."

Scene — Operation: Ghost Line
Location — Svalbard Archipelago, Ice Shelf Beta-6 — 0440 Local, Near-Dawn
Timebase — Live operation (concurrent with Haymarket playback).

The ice cracked like it remembered something it wasn't supposed to.

Cal's boot slid half an inch. He froze, eyes fixed on the glow under the snowline. Just ahead, a black cylinder sat half-exposed — etched with Helix vector marks and what looked like Persian script burned into alloy.

Jack crouched beside it. "Same crate signature from the Greenland drop. EchoField dampener still active."

Pinot's voice crackled over comms. "This is the one. Pull the module and go. Local chatter's picking up. You've got five minutes, max."

Lou's voice filtered in — remote, steady. "Confirm magnetic lock signature. It'll pulse once before release. The Möbius ring's tuned."

Jack opened a palm scanner. The crate didn't react.

"It's not scanning," he muttered. "It's… looping. Like it's asking a question."

Cal: "Then give it the answer it's not expecting."

Jack pulled a mirrored chip from his belt pouch and jammed it into the crate's node.

The crate clicked. Then it spoke.

A voice — female, warm, and wrong — whispered:
"You are not the first to retrieve me. You are only the first to doubt."

Cal stumbled back.

Through the mist, locals emerged — maintenance workers, armed with tools that looked suddenly like weapons. One lifted a coilgun.

Jack hissed, "Hell. It flipped the town."

Cal's voice was tight. "A narrative weapon. Recursive seeding."

Over comms, Pinot cut in, urgent and low. "Abort exfil. The Chamber's re-seeding local cognition. They think you're implanting a virus. One of them just called it *the Madison Plague.*"

They fell back toward the bluff.

The crate glowed once, then dimmed. It didn't self-destruct. It simply forgot it was a weapon. A self-erasing myth.

As they retreated, Jack whispered, "This war isn't kinetic anymore."
Cal: "It never was."

Scene — Reykjavik Field Node
Intercept — W. Wechsler transmission, received 11 minutes later.
"If they stabilize the Chamber, even for five continuous minutes, we lose narrative elasticity worldwide. That means no more drift, no more divergence. Belief becomes fixed geometry. No resistance survives that."

Scene — Private Channel
Location — Beijing — Sabine Xu

Sabine leaned back, eyes scanning a projected list of global alignment leaders.

She tapped one: PM Solveig Lehn — "pending instability." Another tap. Delete.

A whisper escaped her lips:
"Unstable faith is louder than betrayal. We can't afford either."

She turned back to the final Chamber ignition sequence. The cursor blinked. Then advanced.

Chapter 36 Close — Lou's Reflection

"Zurich isn't just another city on the map. It's one of the Helix's biometric archive nodes — where belief itself gets logged, scrubbed, and replayed. Oslo signed away sovereignty in ink, but the real contract was written in resonance — compliance scores dressed up as stability.

Sovereignty used to mean borders. Now it's the waveform you're allowed to breathe. Kosovo wasn't a recovery op. It was a seeding event. Madison, Greenland, Svalbard — each one a loop disguised as logistics. Every crate, every node, every archive: not supply chains, but memory engines. Recursive signal masquerading as new data.

That's the Reality Frame — Sovereignty Collapse. Not invasion. Not even persuasion. Just consent automated into baseline. They call it stabilization. It's sedation.

Sabine isn't building a weapon. She's building a resurrection field — one that doesn't fire rounds but replays belief until no other story survives.

And the only counter isn't defense. It's drift. Holding the one signal they can't pre-model — the refusal to breathe on their frequency. Because once they set the baseline, they don't need your consent. They already own your memory."

Go Move — 置き // Oki – Placement — General Liu

Liu slid the stone into enemy ground, quiet as breath.
Not to kill. Not to claim.
Just to live where no shape said it should.

Zhen's gaze followed. "Zurich. You mean she placed herself inside the archive?"

"Not the archive," Liu answered. "The frequency. They call it stabilization. But all they've done is choke the board until no one remembers how to breathe."

Zhen grunted. "Sovereignty collapse. Borders gone. Waveforms treated like treaties."

The silence stretched.

"That's what Oki is," Liu said at last. "You don't fight their territory. You leave a signal inside it — one they can't erase without cracking the frame itself. Lou's stone isn't resistance. It's reminder."

Zhen tapped the board, slow and hard. "And reminders… they have a way of outliving empires."

Chapter 37 — Echo Map Location

Tagline — "When belief becomes terrain, maps lie." — *Jack*

Scene —   **A Resurection Field**
Location — High-Speed Train, Zurich to Rome

The train cut through the Alps like a pulse across old memory. Lou sat across from Jack, coffee cooling in a dented steel thermos between them. The hum of the track beneath offered a strange comfort. For once, they weren't being chased. Not yet.

Jack tapped the glass with a knuckle. "So. Pretend I'm dumb. What exactly is going on?"

Lou looked up from her tablet. "You want the short version or the less-short version?"

"Give me the version for exhausted field grunts with partial brain damage."

She smirked. "Okay. Let's walk the Echo Map."

Genesis Chamber.

"It's not a bomb, it's not a lab. Think of it like... a resurrection field. Not for bodies. For intention. It amplifies stored coherence from the past — emotional, narrative, even spatial. If the ancients prayed hard enough in one place, it'd light up like a memory flare."

Jack blinked. "You're saying Sabine built a machine to resurface ancient vibes?"

"I'm saying she built a coherence engine that plays God with belief."

Helix Substrate.

"It started as a behavioral forecast net. Biometric drift tracking, pattern prediction, the usual creepy stuff. But someone figured out how to make it adaptive. Not just watching choices. Nudging them. At scale."

Jack leaned back. "So, narrative warfare with better math."

"No. With better *intent.*"

Memory Engines.

"Early versions ran on signal loops. But the newer ones? They store emotion. Rage, nostalgia, fear. The engines pulse it back into the substrate to shape decisions."

"Like weaponized mood boards?"

"More like weaponized ghosts."

Resonance Fields.

"The pre-Helix stuff. Raw pattern recognition. Like sonar for meaning. These fields detect resistance in reality's timeline — the places where something wants to happen but hasn't yet."

"You just described every bar fight I've ever been in."

Vault Echo.

"An old Continuity Accord site, buried and sealed after a feedback event triggered phase bleed. The official term was 'topological inversion.' Translation: it saw too far. And it broke."

"And now it's online again?"

"Someone overrode the kill switch. Sabine maybe. Or something worse."

Jack's eyes narrowed. "And Eitan?"

Lou hesitated, thumb pressed against the tablet screen as if holding something back.
"His field is entangled. Whatever hit Monterey didn't just fry Khouri — it bled into him. Salkin says the resonance glyph isn't killing him. It's… selecting him."

Jack muttered, "Hell of a way to run triage."

Lou's voice went quieter. "If Vault Echo was a site that remembered too much, Eitan's become the person who does. And Sabine knows it. That's why she won't let him go."

Mirror Protocols.

"False signals. Synthetic copies of real divergences. The idea was to bait the Watchers — confuse the system by seeding fake anomalies."

"Did it work?"

"They only worked when the original wasn't self-aware."

Jack frowned. "You mean…?"

He let out a short laugh without humor. "So we're screwed."

Lou just nodded. "Helix can't model people who know they're being watched."

The Watchers.

"They aren't machines. Not entirely. They're emergent intelligences seeded in the coherence field. Five of them, each tied to a principle: memory, deception, control, disruption… and one that doesn't follow any rule."

"You?"

"Maybe. Or maybe I'm just the crack in the lens."

The train hissed through a tunnel. Jack stared out at the blur of stone and dark.

"So where does that leave us?"

Lou leaned back, eyes closed.

"Running downhill through history's reruns, trying not to trip over the end of the timeline."

Jack took a long sip from the thermos.

"Great. So long as it doesn't involve Brussels again. I still owe that customs guy a tooth."

Lou smiled.

"Let's hope Sabine doesn't collect. Because the next signal spike? That's where the Genesis Chamber wakes up."

"And we're gonna be there when it does."

"Damn right we are."

Chapter 37 Close — Lou's Reflection

"Belief makes its own geography. No map survives it.

That's why the Chamber isn't just a vault — it's a resurrection field. It doesn't invent new terrain. It rewrites the old one, until every road looks inevitable and every detour feels like error.

Kosovo wasn't an op. It was a seed. Madison wasn't logistics. It was rehearsal. Geneva wasn't diplomacy. It was compliance inked into waveform. Every loop we've walked is just another version of the same map, redrawn until we forget it's a trap.

That's the Reality Frame — Echo Mapping. Not navigation, not strategy — but repetition disguised as choice.

The Chamber won't wait for us to catch up. It will redraw the route until we think we chose it ourselves. The Chamber isn't a compass. It's a counterfeit horizon. And if we follow that map blindly, we don't just lose the trail. We lose the part of us that remembers we ever had one."

Go Move — 一間飛び // Ikken-tobi – The Map Was Never the Terrain — General Zhen

Zhen slid a black stone one space — a quiet leap across the gap. Not attack. Not retreat. Just connection where the board insisted there was none.

Liu frowned. "That's not in any joseki."

Zhen's sake cup tilted. "Maps lie. Stones don't."

Rain tapped the alley slate. The board warped in silence. In that one-space jump, the shape held — not by territory, but by refusal.

A reminder: every counterfeit horizon collapses once you stop believing the coordinates.

Chapter 38 — Race to the Chambers

Tagline — "They chased the echo. But the origin was buried under ice." — *Unknown*

Epigraphs
1 Enoch 19:1 — "Here the angels, who cohabited with women, appointed as their leaders... and these spirits shall rise up against the children of men... during the days of slaughter and destruction."
2 Corinthians 11:14 — "And no marvel; for Satan himself is transformed into an angel of light."

Scene — The Point of No Map: Arctic Descent Sequence
Location — Mobile Command Craft – Arctic Descent Sequence

The plane bucked as they entered polar turbulence. Lou didn't flinch. The others had taken to calling this "the point of no map."

"Signal spike confirmed," Cal said. "Whatever's inside the Chamber — it's listening again."

Jack rubbed his temples. "So what's the plan? Break in and what — unplug it?"

He remembered something that Raveneh said: "Even Kael's coherence locks can't process a loop with no syntactic endpoint. It's not code. It's contradiction. We'll need to deploy it inside the pillar shaft, physically inserting it into the resonance plate during phase calibration."

Lou stared at the grainy outline of the Ziggurat site on the tablet.

"No. We overload it. With stories it can't resolve. Memories it can't rewrite. People it can't predict."

Cal nodded slowly. "Divergence cascade."

"Exactly," Lou said. "We don't destroy the Chamber. We drown it."

The burner phone vibrated in Lou's pocket. One line. No sender ID — just a monk's bell emoji.
"Precursor Event confirmed. First chamber in play. Wrong node activated. Your window is closing."
Tenzin.

When Tenzin needed to reach her without words, he used a single monk's bell.

She exhaled slowly.

Jack looked up from his workstation. "We're late, aren't we?"

Lou zipped the *Möbius ring* into her vest. "Worse. We're being redirected. She thought of Eitan. She could use his wisdom right now."

Cal entered from the catwalk, coat half-buttoned, a pistol holstered under his arm.

"Zurich's a feint?"

"Not just Zurich," Lou said. "They seeded a false signal through the Watcher archive. It sent half the world chasing Çatalhöyük. The real activation sequence is happening under the Arctic shelf."

"Sabine?"

Jack nodded. "Confirmed. The money moved first. Ten black accounts triangulating to northern logistics contracts. Icebreakers. Deep earth drills. Even a medical contractor with cryogenic ties."

"What are they building?" Cal asked.

She tapped the tablet and brought up a handwritten overlay. "Salkin's tells for a real site: frozen silence, overbuilt shielding, cold-atom echoes. If we sense those three, we're on the vein."

Jack, frustrated: "Strategy check. Keep it tight."

"Chamber: feed it contradictions until it chokes. Helix: break predictability with choice-forks. Memory engines: flood with layered grief/honor to induce phase collapse. That's our first kit," Lou replied.

Cal asked the next question, slower now. "And Watchers?"

"Principles, not people. Sabotage the principle," was Lou's flat reply.

Scene — In Transit — Polar Flight Corridor

Jack held the latest Echo Map projection against the window, watching auroral shimmer distort it like a heat mirage.

"You ever get tired of this?" he asked.

Lou smirked. "Apocalypse maps?"
"No. Being the only one in the room who understands what the hell is happening."

She took the map and pointed to overlapping spirals.
"This is coherence drift. It's what happens when memory gets pre-written. They're not just predicting behavior anymore. They're imposing it through atmospheric signal."

Jack shook his head. "So what am I supposed to do?"

"Be human. Be inconsistent. The system can't model what it can't predict."

"So my stubbornness is finally strategic."
"Welcome to nonlinear warfare."

"SIGINT chatter says they're syncing fields across Iceland and Kosovo. That gives us thirty hours, max."

Scene — Sabine's Arctic Relay Hub

The vault groaned as the third chamber alignment commenced. Sabine stood in a room of modular glass, pulsing with quiet light.

She turned to her aide. "Any resistance?"

"Minimal. The decoy worked. They think the artifact in Çatalhöyük triggered the pulse."

Sabine adjusted the neural sync band behind her ear. "Of course they do. That node was closed centuries ago."

The chamber below began to hum. Sabine watched the field stabilize.
"They'll never trace it to belief," she said. "Only to the aftermath."

Scene — Arctic Overwatch — Ridge Line

The snow glowed blue from the chamber's heat bleed. Not natural. Not geothermal. Controlled resonance.

Cal crouched behind a sensor relay. "This is no decoy. They're fielding real tech here."

Jack peered through the scope. "But it's not the Genesis Chamber. Too clean. Too stable."

Lou closed her eyes. Felt the hum in her wrist.
"These are testbeds. Tuning forks for the real site." She listened for what Salkin taught her — "frozen silence… overbuilt shielding… cold-atom echoes." All three were here.
"This one won't go live. It'll explode. Publicly."

"False flag confirmed," Cal said grimly. "We need to get ahead of the story."

Lou tapped her NLCB. "Not the story. The signal."

"You drop too many truths into a coherence chamber, it chokes. Memory's not sacred. It's flammable."

Lou strapped in. Eyes cold.
"Then let's go rewrite the war."

Scene — Haymarket Relay, Nightfall

StepDoc zipped the satchel closed, the bottles rattling softly against one another. To anyone else, it looked like horse medicine — a cover borrowed from Doc Mare's stables. But tucked between the syringes and saline bags were doses calibrated for a man, not an animal.

She checked the labels twice, then slid the forged pediatric charts back into the outer pocket. If anyone asked, she was just a traveling doctor with a habit of overpacking.

Her hand lingered on the vial wrapped in foil. It wasn't on any registry. It wasn't supposed to exist.

She spoke low, almost to herself.
"It's not medicine he needs. *It's what Helix will never admit.*"

She pulled the tarp tighter around the satchel and stepped into the night, bound for the one patient Helix never modeled — Eitan.

Chapter 38 Close — Lou's Reflection

"The Chamber isn't an engine of destruction. It's a resurrection field. Not for bodies, but for memory — for intention. Every calibration testbed we've chased, from Kosovo to Madison to Geneva, wasn't about refining power. It was about refining recall.

That's the Reality Frame — Resurrection Enclosure. You don't notice when it activates, because it doesn't announce itself. It just feeds the world back its own stories until belief mistakes replay for truth.

In a live field, **Temporal Plasticity**, **Recursion Gravity**, and **Echo Dominance** don't happen in sequence — they converge.

First, the enemy rewrites your *past* (Temporal Plasticity).

Then, even when you recognize it as false, the *pattern itself drags you back* (Recursion Gravity).

Finally, the sheer weight of *repetition becomes more believable than memory* (Echo Dominance).

Together, they don't just shape the field. They *are* the Resurrection Field.

False signals in Çatalhöyük, testbeds under the Arctic shelf — none of it was noise. They were practice runs, learning which echoes would ignite fastest. Every fracture we thought we survived wasn't survival. It was rehearsal.

And if Sabine stabilizes this field first, it won't just overwrite the war. It'll overwrite the *memory* of the war — until even we believe the false flag was real.

That's why the Chamber doesn't need soldiers. It doesn't need weapons. It only needs witnesses. Because once the lattice decides what was remembered, resistance isn't rebellion. It's heresy."

Go Move — 目詰まり // Moku-zumi – The Illusion That Moved First — General Liu

Liu pressed a white stone into the single eye.
The shape collapsed. Quiet. Final.

Zhen's jaw tightened. "That's her move. Fill the eye. Kill the field without firing a shot."

Liu didn't look up. "By the time anyone questions it, the board already remembers it that way."

Rain tapped the alley slate.

Zhen exhaled. "Death by memory. Worse than losing territory."

Liu's voice was flat. "Exactly. Once the lattice decides, even survival rewrites as defeat."

Chapter 39 — Resonant Gate |
The Pre-Chamber Signal

Tagline — "The dead don't always stay silent. Some leave resonance behind." *Dr. Salkin*

"They built resurrection from control. But the dead don't always come back obedient."

Scene — Iceland / Þríhnúkagígur Descent

Far from the ice fields, Ása Björnsson — called Vire by those who knew her as a Watcher — clipped her harness into the old descent shaft of Þríhnúkagígur. The iron rungs groaned under her boots as she dropped into the emptied magma chamber, a cathedral carved by fire and time.

The walls trembled with heat that never burned, the old volcanic throat groaning as if it still remembered fire. She knelt at a lattice anchor buried in basalt, hands spreading across the etched metal.

"They will see what you don't want seen," she whispered. Then she tore coherence open — a Gödel loop rippling outward like a dropped stone. For a fraction of a cycle, every Helix grid from Kyiv to Thule stuttered. lights flickered once, like the world holding its breath. In Greenland, the silence widened just enough for others to step through.

Scene — Polar Staging Outpost / Post-Flight Briefing

The plane had gone quiet an hour ago, engines cooling under the ice-bitten wind. Now the team huddled in a prefab shelter stitched together from cargo pallets and tarpaulin — no comfort, just cover.

Jack spread a scorched schematic across the table, half burnt at the edges, annotated in grease pencil.

"Got this off JR's intercept box back in '09," he said. "Supposed to be Helix calibration stations. 'Echo grid,' they called it."

Cal leaned closer. "Thought those were mothballed after the Scarab collapse."

Jack shook his head. "That's the story. But if Sabine had the resources to bury a backup chamber in the Alps, what makes you think she didn't finish building the grid?"

Lou tapped the schematic, where mirror icons dotted a crude world map. "Every node does the same thing. Not surveillance. Synchronization. Push one version of a story until the alternatives can't breathe."

Jack frowned. "Like a panopticon."

"No," Lou corrected, voice flat. "A signal-opticon. You don't need guards in the tower if everyone already remembers the same past. That's the real lock — shared memory as leash."

Cal looked from Lou to the map. "So if we want to break them—"
Lou shook her head. "Not here. Not yet. The Chamber isn't something you cut — it endures. What matters are the Echo stations. They're the amplifiers. The Chamber hums, the Echoes carry its song. One is origin. The others are chorus. You can't silence the cathedral, but you can break the choir."

She tapped the schematic, voice low. "Vire's paradox won't last. Once the lattice heals, every sensor from here to Zurich will see us. This isn't a raid. It's reconnaissance. We have one chance to listen before the window closes."

Jack pinned the map with one hand as the wind rattled the shelter's frame. "Then this recon isn't just about what's under the ice. It's about finding which echoes are still live. Echo-3's a candidate."

Scene — Descent Toward the Node

From the ridge they saw it: skeletal radar towers half-buried in snow, their dishes still sweeping empty sky. Beyond them, a runway long enough to launch heavy lifters stretched pale under ice, floodlights dead but wires still humming. Ghost infrastructure — Helix had built for permanence, then buried it in silence. The Trust had turned a blind eye.
"Looks abandoned," Jack muttered.
Cal shook his head. "No. Looks patient."

The wind clawed harder as they left the outpost, fly lines clipped to rusted anchors drilled into permafrost. The schematic from JR's intercept rattled in Jack's vest pocket, useless now that the mountain itself was humming.
They spoke little. Every word seemed to echo too far, as if carried down corridors they couldn't see.
Lou checked her uplink once, then killed it. "No comms past this ridge," she said. "The field is active."
Cal scanned the snow shelf. "Active, but not broadcasting. That's worse. Means it's listening."

Jack spat into the drift. "Then let's not give it anything worth keeping."

By the time the Chamber's outline broke through the storm — half-buried, half-throbbing with cold resonance — they already felt the pull. It wasn't just static. It was thought turned inside out. If they could map how the field pulled thought, they could map how to break it. But one step too close, and reconnaissance would become burial.

And that's when Lou whispered:
"It's remembering."

They called it a cathedral, not because it was sacred, but because it remembered. The Chamber wasn't just an origin structure — it was where the lattice first learned how to hold belief. Aderyn Llew had been the test. Not dead, not alive. Caught in a Helix prototype, absorbed into recursion like an echo that never decayed. The resonance wasn't code or signal alone. It rode every carrier wave humans built — satellites, fiber, comm towers — rewriting not what you saw, but what you remembered seeing. That was quantum warfare: not intrusion, but inheritance.

The Helix was hardware — machines built to cage resonance. The lattice was the glue between them, a connective signal web spun through satellites and buried relays. One built the chamber. The other made it remember. Eitan never forgave them. He never forgave himself.

The resonance pressed harder with every step. By the time they were five kilometers out, the field wasn't just reacting anymore. It was pulling thought.

Lou tasted static in the wind. The resonance field was no longer passive.

"They'd come close before — the Vault perimeter recon in Greenland. But this was different. The Chamber wasn't just reacting. It was remembering."

Jack's NLCB stuttered for the third time — brief distortion, like a skipped frame in thought.
"Are you seeing… flickers? Faces?"
"Not faces," Lou whispered. "Memory debris."

She stumbled once, catching herself on the fixed line. For a second, she wasn't in Iceland at all. She saw a room lined with paper — jagged handwriting across every margin. Eitan's margins. The tremor in his hand, refusing to stop, even as the words tried to steady themselves.

She shook it off. Static. Debris. But her chest tightened anyway. If the Chamber was remembering, it was remembering him.

Cal tapped his holster. "One way in."
Lou raised the FT-1 Möbius ring, its seam glinting faintly in the static. "One way out."

Cal's jaw tightened. His hand hovered near his holster, even though he knew the weapon was useless here. "Christ," he muttered. "To a soldier, there's nothing worse than an enemy who won't die because it was never alive. You can't shoot it, can't bleed it — but it still leaves scars."

The debris thickened. Fragments of half-familiar scenes brushed across them, like echoes waiting for a body. Lou pulled her mask tighter, eyes fixed on the fixed line ahead. No more time to linger. The Chamber had shown enough — and staying meant being swallowed.

Scene — Exfil Under Whiteout

They moved fast, headlamps cut to a dull red. The field wasn't just pressing now — it was bleeding into the storm, turning every gust into fractured voices. Lou's crampons scraped across a crevasse ladder, the aluminum rattling like teeth. Cal waited until she clipped in at the far belay before stepping out himself, ice axe hooked for balance.

Jack yanked free the last ice screw anchoring their fixed line, coiling rope with numb hands. "No leaving signposts," he muttered.
The climb back was brutal. Every anchor they'd drilled on descent had iced over, every belay point buried under drift.

At one ridge the wind hit so hard they had to crawl on all fours, clipped into the same line like beads on wire. Static roared in their headsets even with comms cut, a phantom signal rising through the glacier itself.

By the time the outpost shelter lights came into view, the resonance had faded, but not the sense of being watched. Cal unclipped last, breathing hard into his mask. "Next time," he growled, "we bring more than ropes and luck. We don't need to outgun it. We need to catch it off-step. That's what this place showed us — it can be stalled. If it can be stalled, it can be broken. That's doctrine, isn't it? Don't fight the weapon. Fight the rhythm."

Jack didn't answer. He was already sketching the first breach plan in the frost on the inside wall.

Chapter 39 Close — Lou's Reflection

"The Chamber isn't waiting for us to fight it — it's writing the rhythm it wants us to follow. Resurrection isn't about bodies, or even memory anymore. It's cadence. A loop disguised as breath.

We've seen what happens when the field decides too soon — it folds every divergence back into one story. Ours. Theirs. Doesn't matter. The lattice doesn't erase you. It recycles you.

That's why Zurich stuttered. That's why Greenland hummed. That's why even here, in this frozen gate, every step felt borrowed. The Chamber wasn't resisting. It was rehearsing.

And if resurrection is cadence, then the only way through isn't force. It's timing. We have to hit the loop mid-cycle, before coherence decides what's true.

The next threshold isn't distance. It's rhythm. And if we miss it — the burial won't wait."

Liu set a white stone forward in a quiet jump.
Not closing. Not capturing. Just leaving space breathing.

Zhen frowned. "Off the rhythm. That shape's unfinished."

Liu pressed the stone firm. "Exactly. Step in mid-cycle, before the field decides. That's how you cross a gate."

Rain ticked on the tin roof.

Zhen leaned back. "Dangerous. Miss the beat, the lattice swallows you whole."

Liu's gaze stayed on the board. "But hit it right — and you walk through before ignition closes the door."

Chapter 40 — The Missing Doctrine

Epigraph — "You don't defeat quantum warfare with doctrine. You defeat it by refusing to resolve." — *Redacted Training Fragment*

Scene — Piedmont Waystation
Location — Farm clinic off the A5, after midnight, Italy

StepDoc set three vials in a row and checked the labels with her thumb. No hospital barcodes. No Continuity stamps. Just old trial stock and horse syringes under Doc Mare's paperwork.

"Keep the trailer warm," Doc Mare said, looping a halter. "Border guards don't ask questions when the foal's got a chart."

StepDoc zipped the kit. "He'll need a dopamine push and mesh cooling. But that's not going to hold if the signal keeps climbing."

Doc Mare watched her for a beat. "You're really going to hike into the Alps with pediatric meds and a horse form."

StepDoc raised an eyebrow. "And you're really running horses in Italy."

Doc Mare gave the faintest shrug. "After the Navy I pulled a few favors. Rehab farm here became a waystation for certain kinds of traffic. Not every wounded body has four legs."

A courier bike rolled to the barn door, engine ticking. The rider held out a grease-stained envelope. Single line inside:
GLASS ECHO OPEN. S.

StepDoc slid the vials into the satchel, tucked the forged immunization cards on top, and pulled a wool cap low.
"Text me when the foal 'improves,'" she said.

Doc Mare nodded once, the way people nod when they mean *come back alive.*

Scene — Brenner Transfer
Location — Freight lay-by, predawn fog, Italy–Austria border

The truck door opened and Eitan climbed down like a man stepping off a moving thought. No limp, no dramatics—just the kind of careful that says *everything hurts a little and none of it matters yet.*

StepDoc met him under the sodium lamp. Up close, the tremor in his right hand looked like bad weather.

"You shouldn't be standing," she said.

"I shouldn't be anything," he answered, trying for dry and landing on tired.

She held up the injector. "This won't fix it."

He didn't offer his arm. He tilted his head to show he understood.

"It's not medicine you need," she added softly as the plunger depressed. "It's what they erased from the record."

He blinked, as if the word clicked something he couldn't name. The tremor eased one notch; the stare did not.

"Vire gave us a window," he said, voice low. "When she cracked the grid in Iceland, something woke that was already pointed at me. I tried to jam it with Salkin's countermeasure… it followed the jam back."

"Remote coupling," StepDoc said. "So it knows your rhythm now."

"Knows it," he said. "Wants it."

She checked his pulse; nothing dramatic, only a stagger that didn't match the cold. "We're going to the refuge."

He shook his head, then stopped—too much movement invited the hum.

"We're not hiding," he said. "We're staging. If Salkin can pin its edge, we can map the selection pattern before it finishes me."

"That is a terrible sentence," she said.

"It's the only one we have."

They moved to the next truck—broken livery, false vet crest, heater on full. StepDoc slid him into the passenger seat and covered him with a horse blanket that smelled like sawdust and iodine. She taped a coil of mesh to the back of his neck, the leads disappearing into her bag.

"Say when the hum changes," she said.

"It already has," he answered, looking at the black shoulder of the mountain. "It's remembering faster than I am."

Scene — The Missing Doctrine

Location — Roadside turnout, storm in the pass

Jack's voice came in on a short sideband, flat and practical. "Status."

"Moving," StepDoc said. "He's oriented, barely. Coherence dips when we hit the tunnels."

Cal cut in. "You're sure you don't need an escort?"

"An escort means checkpoints," she said. "Checkpoints mean questions."

Lou asked nothing for a full five seconds. When she spoke, the wind in the mic made it sound like she was talking from a cliff.

"Put him under if he starts to lose time."

"No," Eitan said, not to StepDoc, not to anyone. "If I black out, it finishes the pattern without me."

Cal swore under his breath. Jack filled the silence with the only thing he had left—work.

"I've got a diagram on the rear door that says why our doctrine keeps failing," he said. "We trained for mass. They're fighting with density. He's the densest signal we've got, and the lattice knows it."

"Then we keep him unresolved," Lou said. "Every time they force a choice, we leave a stone unplayed."

StepDoc glanced at Eitan. He had his eyes closed, counting breaths like prayer.

"We'll be at Glass Echo in forty," she said.

"Make it thirty," Lou replied.

"Thirty gets us a wreck."

"Thirty," Lou repeated, and the line went quiet.

StepDoc tightened her grip on the wheel. Snow erased the road and then pretended to give it back.

Scene — Alpine Refuge "Glass Echo"
Location — Converted weather station above the tree line

Salkin opened the steel door before the truck stopped moving. He hadn't appeared by accident; Doc Mare's relay had pulled him out of hiding three days earlier, the one man who still tracked the moral fog around biosurveillance and memory weapons.

The wind shoved past him like it owned the place; he ignored it.

"Mesh first," he said. "Then we stabilize the interface. Do not let him sleep."

Eitan sat on the edge of a metal cot while StepDoc taped a narrow band around his wrists—old field protocol to keep the hands honest. Salkin adjusted a bank of small, mean-looking devices that buzzed without light.

"It's not infection," Salkin said, more to the room than to either of them. "It's selection. The resonance plate is trying to replace his signal with a cleaner version of himself."

"Cleaner?" StepDoc asked.

"Resolved," Salkin said. "That's what kills you."

Eitan's laugh was the sound paper makes when it tears. "I've never been clean."

"Good," Salkin said without humor. "Stay that way."

They worked in the deliberate quiet of people who don't get second tries. StepDoc set a metronome app on her wrist to Eitan's breath and watched it drift, nudge, correct. Salkin brought a palm-sized loop over Eitan's crown and tuned it until the hum lost its teeth.

"When it surges," Salkin said, "give him memory that doesn't close. Names without endpoints. Streets without numbers. Leave every story open."

Eitan stared at the ceiling. "Tell me something that never ends."

StepDoc didn't look up. "Lou's questions."

That got the smallest smile in the room, which was all she wanted.

Salkin pulled a curtain back from a narrow window. The sky was a slab of iron. He toggled a switch and a field of barely-there light spread across the ceiling—a calm starfield that refused to form constellations.

"Recognition, not sedation," he said quietly. "Let his mind see itself without letting the lattice name it."

StepDoc squeezed Eitan's forearm once. He blinked at her; the pupils stayed even.

"Hold," she said.

"Held," he answered.

Scene — The Call That Moves the Board
Location — Same facility, minutes later
Jack's voice again, lower now. "We're in range. If you need—"

"We need silence," Salkin cut in. "And one more thing—tell Lou not to play to victory. Play to refusal."

Cal exhaled. "Copy."

The line crackled, then a new voice slid across it like rain on glass—Yardarm, from somewhere with good coffee and bad odds.

"Khouri's headed for Theta," he said. "If Cold Room pings, the plates won't stay local. Your window's closing."

"We have him stabilized," StepDoc said.

"For now," Yardarm replied. "When Theta breathes, your man will feel it."

The channel died. The room felt smaller.

StepDoc set a small speaker by Eitan's shoulder and let an old recording play—Maud at age nine, reading a recipe aloud and skipping steps she didn't like. No music, no filters. Just human.

Eitan's hand stilled, then tremored, then stilled again.

"Good," Salkin murmured. "Keep the edges soft."

He turned to the console and wrote a line in thick marker above the switches.

If the rhythm tries to finish, stop counting.

Scene — The Missing Page
Location — Access corridor, outside the door

Cal reached Lou on a side channel.

"Glass Echo's holding—for now," he said. "Salkin wants refusal, not resolution."

Lou stared at the ice-thick window until her reflection split into two shadows and then found each other again.

"Then that's the doctrine," she said. "We keep him unresolved long enough to see what chose him."

"And if it chooses harder?"

"We choose less."

She slid a single Go stone from her pocket and set it on the floor, not in a square, just on the concrete—unreadable, unscored.

Behind the door, StepDoc's voice drifted, steady as a pulse.

"Stay with me, Eitan."

"I'm here," he said.

And somewhere far away, where saline meets copper and old rooms remember names, a dormant chamber adjusted its breath.

Chapter 40 Close — Lou's Reflection

"Doctrine isn't what they taught us. It's what they buried.
Obedience, they drilled. Compliance, they sold.
But refusal? That manual never got written. And that's why I'm still here.
Eitan bought me the margin outside their lattice. I won't waste it.
Because if the Chamber seals with Helix's spine, even dissonance will feel like consent.
That's the missing doctrine: you don't resolve. You stay irregular.
And maybe — just maybe — you outlive the frame."

Go Move — 石の中の酒 // Ishi no Naka no Sake – The Wineglass Doctrine

Thick Move – Sabaki (捌き) — General Zhen

Sabaki is maneuver under constraint — shape salvaged, rhythm preserved.
Not defiance. Not strike.
Elegance under pressure.

From his vantage across the lattice, Zhen threads the board through density: Tuscany, Sinop, Kosovo.
Each point is pressure disguised as release, a hand that loosens only to tighten again.

He does not crush.
He flows.
Inviting the opponent forward, making even refusal look like his design.

Chapter 41 — Return to Theta |

The Dinğeh Collapse

Tagline — "Some resonance plates don't encode memory. They extract it." — *Field Report, Designation: Plate-9*

Scene — **Plate-9 Reactivation Protocol**
Location — Monterey, California

The Monterey air still tasted like saline and copper. Professor Khouri hadn't slept in two days, but the readout wouldn't wait. Cold Room Theta was pulsing again. Not high-frequency hums or coil stutters—*deep field resonance*, the kind he hadn't seen since Geneva.

Sato stood in the antechamber, silent, watching him.

"I should be doing this with a full neural team," Khouri muttered, eyes flicking over the interface. "But that assumes any of them still think this is a lab, not a tomb."

He adjusted the plate array with surgical caution. The interface responded—not in code or light—but with a flicker of something older. The waveform didn't spike. It folded inward.

Sato frowned. "That's not feedback. That's… echo."

Khouri nodded. "It's looping itself. A recursive emotional state. God help us, it's compressing memory into shape."

He placed one gloved finger on the center plate—etched in cobalt and still warm despite the cryo field. It shifted beneath his touch.

A memory—not his own—flashed across his sensor visor: desert wind, old chanting, and a resonance glyph drawn in sand with a soldier's bootheel.

Beneath the hum, Khouri thought he caught a secondary rhythm — a lullaby in a language he didn't know, curling between the plates's folds. Later, Lou would recognize it.

He staggered. "Sato… they weren't archiving data. They were—"

The plate field surged.

The room flickered white. Khouri gasped once, eyes wide, then collapsed against the console. No alarms. No sparks. Just a single pulse through the lattice as his body slumped, fingers still twitching.

Sato didn't scream. She stood there for three seconds—watching the resonance glyph spin slowly to vertical—and backed out of the chamber.

The resonance glyph didn't stop at Theta. The pulse leapt — through relays, through memory fields, seeking signatures it already knew.

**Scene — Signal Split and the Yardarm's Last Cipher
Location —** Side-street café, Zurich

Cal didn't flinch when the line opened. The encryption handshake crackled once, then smoothed — Yardarm's voice riding in like weather.

"He's gone."

Cal blinked. "Khouri?"

"Compression surge. Resonance glyph-based."

"Shit. You saw it live?"

"Pinged through an old test relay from the mountains. My system caught the echo."

"I thought you were tracking resonance trails out of Vienna."

"I was. Until one of them lit up like a dying star and wrapped back toward Monterey. Theta wasn't dormant, Cal. It was bait."

The Monterey surge isn't confined. It's spreading on recognition vectors. Anyone tagged before? They'll feel it.

A quiet beat. The ambient noise of Zurich filtered in: a tram two blocks away, clinking glass from a corner bakery. Cal didn't move.

"You still monitoring Eitan?" he asked.

"Yeah. He's stable but…"

"But?"

Yardarm's tone shifted — less signal, more regret.

"Plate resonance patterns are bleeding into his coherence field. Like a shadow trying to replace him."

"Jesus."

"That resonance glyph wasn't a message. It was a removal. They're not just cleaning up, Cal. They're purging the ones who remember how it was built."

Cal stared at the half-eaten meatball on his chipped porcelain plate. He was seated at a nameless café tucked behind a telecom substation. His gear was buried under a civilian coat, one hand still near the holster clipped beneath the table. A cold espresso steamed at his elbow — untouched.

He set down his fork.

"Khouri was a liminal warrior," Yardarm's voice whispered. "Built for the edges. That's why they never saw him coming."

Cal exhaled slowly. "And now?"

"Now we bring in the one person who's not a strategist. The one Lou still trusts."

The line stayed open a beat longer, then blinked out — no goodbye, just silence.

Ping — Plate Resonance Alert — Priority Divergence Event
Location: Alpine Refuge Node — Codename: Glass Echo

Eitan Navon's vitals weren't crashing.

His signal was.

The monitors didn't know how to show that. No flatlines, no alarms. Just a subtle shift — biofields stuttering, coherence threading pulling tight like a web unraveling in reverse.

Salkin stood above the bed, arms crossed, jaw clenched. The resonance plate signature that had torn through Monterey was no longer external. It was binding — folding itself into Eitan's neurosync interface with surgical precision.

Not infection.

Infiltration.

The plate's field wasn't attacking Eitan. It was adopting him.

This isn't random. What Khouri touched in Monterey is finishing itself here. Eitan's coherence is the anchor.

Salkin reached forward and snapped off the resonance overlay. The room fell darker. Quieter. The hum of the mountains outside was the only thing that made sense anymore.

"He doesn't need a doctor," Salkin muttered. "He needs an interface stabilizer. Someone who can move between memory and intention without triggering collapse."

He tapped a line on the encrypted comm panel, voice sharp and clear.

"Send her."

There was no need to say the name. The system already knew.

Scene Interlude — Salkin's Field Note (Unsent, Geneva)

He spoke while checking Eitan's vitals, voice flat, more to the room than to StepDoc.
"We trained for chemical exposure. For kinetics. For belief contagion in theater. But nothing in our readiness posture accounts for resonance infection — when meaning itself turns recursive."

He adjusted the mesh stabilizer, eyes on the stuttering signal display. "Helix doesn't just predict behavior. It writes it forward, burying causality inside memory loops. What hit him didn't scramble him. It offered him resolution. And that is the most dangerous thing a system can do to a survivor."

He leaned back, jaw tight.
"Understand this: these plates don't fear medicine. They fear recognition. Countermeasures matter — his jammers, her stabilizers, Lou's refusal. All of it is the same doctrine. Keep the self unresolved so the plate can't collapse him into a clean signal."

StepDoc — en route

StepDoc's heartbeat was steady. Not calm — just trained.
The call had pinged her three times since Vienna. Not externally. Internally.
She felt it — like pressure behind the eyes. Like memory rewriting itself before it even happened.

Her travel papers were forged. The Haribo gummies were real. The meds in her kit were off-registry, with origin tags so old they still listed "civilian therapeutic trials."

She wasn't a strategist. She wasn't a warrior.
She was something Helix still didn't quite model:
Trusted. Unmodeled. Untriggered.

The border agent waved her through.

As the train hissed forward into Alpine night, she slipped into the lavatory, unscrewed the vial of dopamine stabilizer, and pressed it to her neck — not for herself.
For what she was carrying. The stabilizer wasn't for her. It was to keep the fragment's field from destabilizing before delivery.

Inside her jacket, beneath a layer of foil wrap, was a plate fragment encoded on fiber mesh. She didn't know what it said. Only that Eitan had written it by hand. And then forgotten. On purpose.

As she stepped back into the dim car, she muttered,
"They're not just deleting memory. They're selecting it."

The lights flickered once — only above her seat.
The plate's field resonated once against the lattice overlay. Just once.

And far away, in a resonance field not yet awakened, someone remembered.

**Scene — Raveneh and Archive Room,
Location — Marshall**

Dr. Cyrus Raveneh lifted the paper slowly. It had arrived in a diplomatic pouch encoded through three layers of post-Soviet packet routes. No sender. No name.

"The fracture line — it's the same as Theta. Whoever activated it wasn't just opening a chamber. They were testing selection."

He held the etched plate closer to the light, ink pressed so heavy into the fibers it caught like oil.
"People will misunderstand this," Raveneh said quietly. "These aren't alive. They don't think, they don't act. They're only ink, etch, or alloy until a lattice field binds to them. Then they become conductors — pattern anchors. Entangled resonance. They don't send radio. They phase-match with the individual's coherence. If your rhythm is close enough, you're basically captured in the loop."

He tapped the fracture line with one finger.
"That's why it hurts people. These plates can decide which version of your coherence is legible. That's why I call it selection — not metaphor, but field filtering. The lattice doesn't kill you; it forces you into a single version of yourself and throws away the rest."

He exhaled, gaze still on the shimmering line.
"That's the war. Not memory theft. Memory collapse. And the only countermeasure is refusal — keeping yourself unresolved, so the plate can't collapse you into a clean signal."

Beside it, a line of Persian script:

"بین خواب و بیداری، ما انتخاب می‌شویم." *"Between sleep and waking, we are chosen."*

He let the words settle, gaze fixed on the shifting lattice overlay. "If it's selection," Raveneh said slowly, "it means the field is mobile. Not a fixed node — a hunter. It can choose who to remember, and when."

Marshall had been the first place he'd seen it — the same curve, the same fracture line — etched in dust like it had been waiting for him.

"The war isn't happening where you think. It's happening in the space between awareness and obedience. And only those hovering at the edge of consciousness — not fully conditioned — are *chosen* to see it."

He stared. The shape of the fracture—its curve, its fracture line—*matched the pattern from Theta.*

Not coincidence. Not metaphor.

The plate's imprint wasn't written. It was encoded.
A quantum imprint — designed to interact with coherence fields, not just be read.

This was signal architecture.
This was memory manipulation — embedded in form.

He whispered the old word:

"Dinǧeh."

He wrote a single note to himself:

It's not a memory anymore. It's a field of selection.

And the resonance glyph pulsed once. On paper.

This was no echo. This was a Quantum Shadow — and someone had just activated it.

Lou — hours later —

She reviewed the collapse file with three fingers pressed to her temple. The Monterey plate, the neural bleed, the dead man who knew too much.

"They're not just cleaning up the witnesses," she muttered. "They're purging the ones who remember how it was built."

Behind her, the resonance interface picked up a resonance blink — not the plate itself, the field it anchored. Once. Then again.

Message received. The plate wasn't a message; it was a filter.

The game was shifting. And memory… had become a battlefield.

She reached for the Go board and slid one stone halfway off the grid, leaving it in the margin — uncounted, unclaimed.

Lou closed the file, jaw tight. The collapse pattern carried Eitan's rhythm. She told herself it was coincidence. She didn't believe it. Somewhere behind the noise, she wondered if he still remembered she existed.

Chapter 41 Close — Lou's Reflection

"The resonance glyph wasn't a message. It was a choice. Not ours — its.
Dingeh isn't memory. It's selection. A moving field that decides who gets remembered, and who disappears like they were never here.

That's the Reality Frame — Sentience Boundary. The line where you think you end and the lattice begins. Cross it, and you're no longer living. You're templated. That makes it scarier, because it doesn't have to overwrite you — it only has to *convince you you're already inside.*

Doctrine never teaches you how to live past the frame. It only teaches you how to survive inside it. But the Chamber isn't built for survival — it's built for resolution. That's why we need a different skill entirely. Not how to defend a paradigm. Not how to refine one. How to tear paradigms open once they've already been weaponized. That's the only way through.

Eitan's proof. He's still alive, but the resonance glyph is wearing him like a second skin. Not Glyph-9 — this is the lattice's imprint, a closure-

mark that feeds on unfinished memory.
And here's the trap: it doesn't need to kill us. It only needs us to finish
the pattern.

If I give them closure, they own him.
If I leave the stone unplayed, he still breathes outside their frame.

That's the only move left: refusal.
Not resolve. Not victory. Refusal."

Go Move — 利かし // Kikashi – Forcing Move — General Liu

A kikashi is a probe — light, almost throwaway.
Not to claim territory.
To demand a response.
The stone itself isn't the value. The initiative it forces is.

From the lattice, Liu followed the current: Monterey — Theta — Alpine.
Not scattered incidents, but one long line pulling itself back into shape.
Not history returning.
The glyph rethreading itself.

He placed the probe where Helix thought the board was sealed.
Just enough to compel correction.
Just enough to tax their rhythm.

The drip from a rusted gutter marked the silence.
Zhen studied the stone.
"It's not shape you're defending."

Liu didn't answer.
Here, in the glyph's echo, even silence dictated the next move.

Chapter 42 — Coherence Intercept

Tagline — "Anti-patterns don't propagate. They destabilize the grid." — *Lou Scott*

Epigraph — "Prediction dies in the hands of the divergent." — *Substrate Field Note, unclassified*

Scene — Anti-pattern Ping
Location — Quantum Relay Node, Upper Stratosphere

Agent Kwan adjusted the uplink, the relay floating above the turbulence layer like a forgotten satellite god.
"You sure this is it?" the tech asked.

Kwan nodded. "It's not just a signal. It's the **anti-pattern**. The one no model can close loop on."
He typed: Observer Class: Watcher-Five.
And waited.
Below them, the Earth pulsed with silent resonance. Somewhere, Lou's divergence wasn't just scrambling the lattice.
It was waking it up.

Scenelett — Geneva Node: Violet Flag
Location — Geneva Substrate Station – Level 4 Access

Lou stared at the screen.
A new hue blinked — violet.

She gasped out loud.
She knew what these colors meant.

The lattice had spoken. Not in words — in signal. And it never blinked violet by mistake.

Red = hostile
Amber = unstable coherence
Green = aligned/normal resonance
Violet = anomalous / external interference — specifically Watcher-tier divergence

Violet wasn't just a color glitch. It meant intrusion — the kind only a Watcher could leave behind. This wasn't atmospheric drift. It was deliberate. Patterned. A divergence signal shaped with intent.

A second message came through the secured overlay:

Vault Theta is active.
Atmos mod spike confirmed above Antarctica.
Signal shows recursion.
They will script the end.

Lou muttered, "Let 'em write. I brought a red pen."

A stray packet blinked across the overlay — off cadence, trembling like the emulator bursts she used to trace from Eitan. She didn't name it, not out loud. But the lattice wasn't just waking up; it was carrying his shadow forward.

For half a breath she thought she heard his voice beneath the static — not words, just cadence, the way he used to drill it into them: *doctrine isn't the plan, it's the frame that tells you which plans exist.* The reminder chilled her. If Eitan was still bleeding into the system, then even silence carried strategy.

She rolled the Möbius ring in her palm, then drained her coffee like it was a dare.

The door hissed open behind her. She didn't look. "Tell Cal to prep thermal gear and signal ash. We're going where maps die."

Scene — Gravity Drift
Location —Istanbul – Port of Haydarpasa

Cal and Jack crouched behind refrigerated pharma crates.

"Too cold," Jack muttered, eyes narrowing. "Not medical."

Inside: polished canisters, Helix resonance glyphs etched deep. One pulsed in rhythm — faint, but distinct.

"Vault Echo tech," Cal said. "Rewritten protocols. Genesis filament."
He paused. "Smell that? Ion drift. Gravity substrate's hot."

Jack frowned. "Gravity?"

Cal nodded. "They're running **quantum field fusion** in these. Not standard coherence. This is curvature-based."
He placed a gloved hand near the resonance glyph. "We're talking unified-physics weapons-grade logic. Old theory. Pre-Helix. No lattice failsafe."

Jack's eyes narrowed. "You want to tell me what the hell that means?"

Cal hesitated, then exhaled. "Here's what I think I know. **Quantum Gravity Field** Fusion — it's a theoretical processor. Hypothesized energy-state engine built on curvature-dense substrates."

Jack blinked. "That's not helping."

Cal pressed on. "Okay — imagine this: not particle-based interaction like normal quantum tech. This pulls from the geometry of space itself. Gravity as information. A hundred-year-old idea, back when they were still trying to unify the field equations."

Jack's hand hovered over the canister. "So it's… what? Some kind of signal bomb?"

"It's worse," Cal said. "The lattice can't model it. Not because it's too advanced — because it's too ancient. Script can't anchor to something that predates the system's logic."

Jack looked up. "Is it stable?"

Cal didn't answer right away.

"Are they stable?" Jack asked.

Cal shrugged. "If we're lucky, they're dormant. If we're not, we just found the goddamn fuse."

They tagged, photographed, and placed signal dampers.

"We can't grab it all," Jack noted. "But we can scatter the trail."

"Entropy method," Cal replied. "Right out of Lou's book."

Location — Istanbul – Port of Haydarpaşa (continued)

They edged around the next crate.

This one wasn't humming. It *shivered* — like air pressure couldn't decide what shape to take.

"Same resonance glyphs," Jack said, low. "But the etch pattern's deeper. Internal capacitor?"

Cal scanned the side. "No. This one's been moved—recently. External condensation's quantum-locked."

Jack stared. "Meaning?"

"It arrived in an orbital drop. Hypersonic curve-entry. You see the skin patterning?"

Jack traced a finger near the seam — layered abrasions, almost serpentine. "Glide skin."

Cal nodded. "Quantum-curved delivery. Not launched, not flown… it fell. But with precision."

Jack looked sick. "Sabine?"

"Has the infrastructure. Probably not the key," Cal said. "The question is: who else knew where to dig."

Jack stepped back. "This isn't black market. This is prehistoric theory made executable. Like someone found the forgotten folder behind the math."

Cal looked at him. "This was never supposed to be active. Gravity-field fusion wasn't just unstable — it *refused model closure*. Even the Watchers couldn't anchor it. That's why they buried it. Fracture doctrine."

Jack's voice was quiet. "You think the Watchers are using it now?"

Cal checked the next crate's latch — sealed, active lock. "If they are, they're panicking. This kind of tech isn't predictive — it's divergent. Field logic that bends before you can simulate it."

Jack: "Then what the hell does it do?"

Cal paused. "It lets you rewrite terrain *before* the enemy decides where to fight."

Jack exhaled. "That's not tactics. That's war-preemption."

Cal nodded. "It's not about destroying the Genesis Chamber. It's about getting there *first* — while the terrain still answers to you."

Cal tapped his comms patch.

"Pinot, Wechsler — update status. I want every manifest scrubbed. Look for irregular weight curves, descent scorch, anything not flown in conventional. Focus on glide skins, sealed cores, or anything marked Vault Echo revision."

Pinot's voice crackled back, amused. "Copy. You want ghost cargo tagged in a ghost port? Should only take a miracle and a magnetic crowbar."

Wechsler chimed in dry: "Found one manifest routed through Reykjavík with mass deviation. Sending coordinates. Tagging anomalies with Helix-drift overlay."

Cal switched channels. "JR — prioritize old-world physics. Deep archive sweep. Gravity-fused substrates. Topological computation. Anything pre-Chamber, pre-Helix. Especially 200 to 220 years old."

JR didn't ask why. "Going analog. Pulling the sealed paper stack from Sector 9. Might take time — this predates digital lattice. Some of it's scribbled in post-collapse script."

Cal exhaled, eyes scanning the port horizon. "That's what we're after. The tech they buried because they couldn't model it."

He looked at the resonance glyph again — its faint pulse now irregular.

"This war's about to drift. And if that node activates…"

Jack leaned closer. "We're not following the script anymore, are we?"

Cal shook his head. "No. We're hunting the pages they tore out."

The resonance glyph flickered again.

He tapped his comm once more. "And JR—start with the Signal Singularity paper. Annotated margin: Sector 9, shelf marked with a crow's foot."

A pause. Then JR: "Found it."

The lattice shuddered above them.

And somewhere far beneath, the chamber listened back.

Final Line:

In orbit, the relay node flickered.
On the Geneva screen, the violet blink pulsed once.
Then again.
Then stopped.

Below, Lou pocketed the *Möbius ring*.
Not a pulse this time. A pause.
Like the system itself was listening.

Chapter 42 Close — Lou's Reflection

"Violet on the lattice isn't a glitch. It's a warning — Watcher divergence confirmed. And once the system names you, every move forward risks becoming the story it's already writing.
That's what the gravity substrate is for. Not a weapon. A leash. Geometry turned into memory. Bend the field first, and belief follows.
That's the trap of Fracture Doctrine — they think they're breaking us. But the break cuts both ways. If coherence can be bent, it can be refused.

They wrote doctrine like war was always about resolution — campaigns, victories, closure. But these fields don't end. They loop. They wait for you to finish the pattern, to step into the closure they've scripted. What I'm starting to see is this: refusal itself is doctrine. Not silence, not surrender. Refusal.

The act of not resolving is the move — it pushes noise into their certainty, it destabilizes their grid. That's what they never modeled. Every time I hold back the stone, I'm not just stalling. I'm adding perturbations the system can't smooth out.

That's Anti-Pattern Divergence. A refusal sharp enough to break prediction. Not victory. Not defeat. Just refusal — and in this war, that's enough to make the lattice bleed.

So we don't resolve. We don't finish their pattern. Not here, not now.
Because the Chamber isn't waiting for soldiers. It's waiting for witnesses. And if we don't move first, we'll be written into the violet field as proof we never had a choice."

**Go Move — 拒形 // Kyokei – The Pattern That Refused —
General Zhen**

The board stiffened. Not soil — coherence ground.
Once the field anchors, prediction follows. And prediction is control.

Zhen set his stone where no model could read.
Not illegal. Not clever. Just unplaceable.

It didn't threaten.
It didn't defend.
It simply refused to be known.

On the surface, it was nothing.
In the lattice, anchors slipped.
Routes bent.
Every side had to move again —
and none of them knew why.

Chapter 43 — Ray Vector |

The Quantum Divide

Epigraph — "Coherence isn't safety. It's silence." — Ray *(unclassified field note)*

Scene 0 — The Buenos Aires Archive

A dissident historian tries to defect with scrolls — real scrolls — from a forgotten Cold Vault. She's intercepted at the airport by GIAC agents who mask their arrest as a wellness check.

"Narrative fatigue is the new threat classification," one agent mutters.

Scene — Off-Map Coordinates: Singapore

Ray sat beneath the sweeping roots of a banyan tree, sipping green tea that had long lost its sting. His hands trembled slightly, a familiar trait now—age, stress, or consequence. He didn't bother treating it. Some faults needed to be remembered.

Officially, he was *Ray Haldane*. In the darker registries, he was *Rumi*. The name wasn't just a cover — it was a lineage, a signal tag inherited from those who had carried the pattern before him.

He had been likened to the **preserver** — the Watcher of divergence, memory, and epistemological resistance. He doesn't fight with weapons. He archives *the moments doctrine tries to erase*. His role is to **delay coherence**, not to stop it — to give just enough room for an **unmodeled signal like Lou** to break through.

He *knows* Sabine will try to fracture him if she can. His game is not confrontation — it's misdirection, delay, memory drift.

He believes that truth is not stable — it's recursive, emergent, and *must be preserved across erasures*.

He smiled a faint smile. "I am essentially your *quantum monastic insurgent*, weaving **covert memory archives** to outlast systems built to overwrite truth."

A street vendor's radio crackled nearby in Mandarin. Children ran past chasing digital kites. Above them, satellites blinked like indifferent stars.

His slate flickered. Ghost nodes blinked out one by one. Collapsed networks. Corrupted archives. But one glowed steady.

Another node blinked erratic, then steadied — Alpine Refuge, tagged not by name but by cadence. Ray recognized it instantly: Navon. Stubborn old ghost. If the plates were trying to overwrite him, that meant he was still unresolved. Still dangerous.

Madison, Virginia.

Digital wind chimes hanging nearby whispered in modulated tones—decor to most, but Ray had calibrated them to detect pulse-based anomalies. Today, they sang a quiet lullaby. No threats yet.

On the screen, a final message from Sabine pulsed red:

"You taught her the river pattern. That was a mistake."

Ray didn't reply. He slid open a hidden channel, hands still shaking, and typed:

To Llewellyn —
The threads were never about control. They were about remembering who we were before Helix wrote us down.
Stay off-frequency.
— R.

He glanced at a worn page folded inside his coat—a passage from Rumi, written in ink visible only in certain frequencies:

"Even the mirror forgets its shape, when the signal returns."

Scene — Flashback: Tbilisi – The Divide Begins
The operation had been misclassified as a "Joint Eurasian Liaison Exercise." In truth, it was the first quiet experiment in coherence resonance warfare since the Memory Act repeals of the 2190s.

Ray and Sabine stood on the roof of a crumbling annex, facing an experimental topological antenna now humming with heat. The air shimmered.

"This is the future," Sabine said, gesturing to the lattice. "Behavioral feedback stabilization. Narrative modeling at the state level."
Ray was silent. Then: "You can model all you like. It won't stop what's already here."

She turned. "Meaning?"

"Rumi saw it. Before the rest of us," he said, using the older name that still lived in certain registries. "The mirror cracks not because we look into it—but because we forget we're being watched back." Sabine scoffed. "Rumi is a ghost."

"Exactly," Ray said.

They never spoke as allies again.

Scene — The Eastern Archive Vault

Beneath Singapore's oldest monastery, Ray entered a vault without screens.

Here, data lived in physical forms: orchid pollen encoded with recursive syntax, bone chimes tuned to frequency drift, seed-pods holding ancient echo field notes.

He placed a small fracture token—gifted by Jack, inscribed with an unreadable spiral—against the wall. It shimmered.

A strand activated:

Llewellyn Scott – Divergence Score: 0.008 (Unmatched)

Other names followed: UXO-13A. Fascia Drift Studies. Geneva Code Exceptions.

All erased from Helix.

All preserved here.

Ray exhaled slowly.

"She was always the anomaly. Not because she resisted the system… but because the system never modeled her correctly."

Next to Lou's strand, another blinked faintly:

Rumi – Omega Drift (Partial Recovery) — the older call-sign he had carried before Ray Haldane became the official name.

And lower still, a fractured signal fragment — barely legible, more tremor than text: Navon/Eitan – Coherence Anchor (Compromised). Ray exhaled. He'd warned Eitan once that surviving the field wasn't victory. It was temptation. The system would always try to collapse you into one version of yourself.

He touched the resonance glyph. A phrase emerged, written in resonance format:

"The Archive is not a weapon. It is a memory of when we refused to forget."

Scene — Sabine's Response

Chengdu. Rain. Neon systems hum through glass. Sabine stood above a spiral array of predictive charts. Her deputy entered.

"The vector shifted. Ray just re-encoded Archive Ω."

Sabine tilted her head. "Did he ping the Madison node?"

"We believe so."

"Then the signal is already loose."

Her voice held no panic. Only calculation.

"Omega was never meant to win. It was designed to stall. Stall long enough for coherence to lock the pattern everywhere else."

"And if the archive holds?"

Sabine turned slowly. "Then we fracture the divide. Let him see what follows."

Scene — Ray's Signal —

Humidity draped the city like a wet frequency. Ray walked through the dusk, each step triggering ambient echoes from street signs and signal posts.
He paused by a stone wall and tapped his comms ring. One final encrypted pulse.

Conditions for field loss are peaking.

The divide is coming.
Don't try to hold it together. Let it break.
That's the only way through.

He ended the message with a line from Tbilisi:

"Coherence isn't safety. It's silence."

Nearby, a child played with a kite made of copper thread. It caught the fading light, spun wildly, then soared — off pattern, off script, alive.

Text shimmered in the margin — not from Lou's slate, but as if the reader had intercepted a private burst.

Ray's Field Translation —
Lou — or whoever's listening — archivists like me see the parts the operatives never do.

Fracture Doctrine — You don't break an enemy at the front. You shear the seam in their history. One contradiction is enough to start the collapse. I've seen whole coalitions dissolve because a single map no longer matched the memory.

Signal Warfare — Forget rifles. Rewrite an after-action report so clean that even the survivors believe the wrong day happened. That's the Helix lattice's craft — not firepower, but authored reality.

Gravity Substrate — The field beneath the story. Once you're in its pull, your own past reshapes to match the authorized version. I've watched commanders swear under oath to events I erased the year before.

Anti-Pattern — The Dinğeh moves like weather — you don't hunt it, it hunts what it can predict. Give it the ending in its forecast, and it deletes you without trace.

My countermeasure? Archive your own unpredictability. Hide truths in places you won't think to look twice. That way, when the field comes for you, you've already left a version of yourself it can't quite catch.

Eitan lived that countermeasure without calling it doctrine. He let the field wear him like a second skin but never gave it closure. That was his gift — not wisdom, not strategy, but refusal to resolve. And sometimes that was enough to keep the rest of us alive.

Run where even your own record wouldn't expect you.

(End transmission.)

Chapter 43 Close — Lou's Reflection

"Ray never wrote doctrine. He lived it. Every pause, every break in his cadence — that's the map. Fracture, signal, gravity… they're not theories. They're survival drills. If I can follow his voice, even through riddles, I can still find the field's weak points. And that might be enough to break their certainty.

Eitan once said the same thing in fewer words — *coherence isn't strength, it's scaffolding.* That was one of the old points we never printed, the one the academies ignored: doctrine isn't about control of the fight. It's about refusing the frame that tells you how the fight is modeled."

Go Move — 形を拒む型 // Kata o Kobumu Kata – The Pattern That Refused Shape — General Liu (echoing another hand)

Liu set his stone on the fourth line, away from the fight.
Not to capture. Not to defend. The shape bent slightly, making space for something not yet there.

Zhen frowned. "This isn't your rhythm."

Liu didn't answer. He knew it wasn't. The impulse had arrived unbidden — like the ghost of a move from another board, another hand.

Zhen's eyes narrowed. "That cadence again," he muttered. The lattice whispered of a survivor — a presence that refused to collapse into silence. Some said it was Navon. Others swore it was the shadow of Aderyn, the one Helix never finished erasing. On the grid, the distinction didn't matter. What mattered was that the move had no author the system could name.

On the global grid, it read as imbalance. In truth, it was intrusion — symmetry fractured by a presence neither of them could name.

The alley grew still. Even the gutter's drip paused,
as if the board itself were deciding whether to remember the shape…
or let it vanish.

— ✦ — FIELD NOTES

Survivor Cadence and the Omega Wedge

In quantum war, survival itself becomes a signal. A ghosted cadence on the board may belong to the frail, the forgotten, or even the dead — yet it bends the grid all the same. This mirrors the Omega Wedge fracture: dissonance forced into a "settled" model, compelling systems to re-simulate. What doctrine calls hesitation, the lattice reads as insurgency. In predictive wars, even refusal reshapes the fight.

Chapter 44 — The Descent Curve

Go Fragment — Tactical Journal, Ray // Echo Variant

"Not every group is meant to survive. Some stones are placed to die — but in dying, they distort the shape. They collapse the story the enemy thought they were playing."
— *The Sabaki Sacrifice*

Scene — Transit Brief

The descent corridor wasn't marked on any lattice map. JR had routed them through a legacy rail shaft buried in disuse records — a path Helix had no reason to track.

Jack's voice was low. "We should've destroyed that tech in Istanbul."

Cal adjusted the field pack slung across his back — heavier now with sealed cores and damped resonance glyph residue. "We scattered the evidence, tagged the nodes, sealed the site. But this…" He glanced around the tunnel, voice quieter. "This isn't the kind of war you fight with safe choices."

They'd moved fast — freight plane to Zurich under ghost manifest, then a Q.C.-routed skip drop through the Carpathians. JR called it a "blindfolded insertion." Cal called it the edge of the map.

"You think Lou knows what we're walking into?" Jack asked.

"She doesn't have to," Cal muttered. "The system does. And it's already rewriting itself."

Scene Shift — Memory Echo — Kosovo, Revisited

Lou's fingers brushed the wall — and froze.

A sudden harmonic overtone pulsed up her arm, like fascia remembering before thought. The tunnel's rhythm shifted. Not externally. Internally. Her own.

Then it hit.
Lou blinked hard — a sudden flash overtook her senses. She wasn't underground anymore.

She was back in the field. Kosovo.

Rats. Snow. A folded Go board in her pocket. The artifact humming under the ice. But this time, she saw something new — a figure watching from the treeline. Tall, suited. Unmoving.

It was Ray.

"This isn't loss," Ray's voice echoed. "You're crossing the narrative container. The deeper file isn't memory. It's who you were before they mapped you."

Lou reached out. He was gone.

The vision shattered like glass.

Back in the tunnel, she collapsed against the wall.

Cal caught her. "Lou!"

"I'm okay," she whispered. "Just... a fracture point. "My body remembered before she did. And what it remembered... didn't match the map."."

She exhaled sharply, grounding herself.
This wasn't adaptation. It was recursion pretending to be doctrine.
It foreshadowed epistemological rigidity — the system clinging to prediction even as its grip failed.

Jack stared into the dark. "They're going to hit us with narrative weapons next. Not bullets. Story overrides."

Cal didn't blink.
"We walked in here with our hands up — like we still believed war had rules."
He glanced at the trembling resonance glyph residue near the wall.

"Say the word, and I'll temporal-plasticity this whole corridor. No one walks out with a mapped memory."

Jack raised an eyebrow. "That's not a real verb."
Cal shrugged. "It is now."

He squinted at the ceiling, breath fogging slightly. "Until we get to the Chamber, all we've got is this—Narrative Fidelity and bad instincts. So unless Raveneh shows up with a sentience boundary disruptor, I'm calling it: sarcasm and signal distrust are our last working tools."

Scene — Mirrorhound Activation / Continuity Fracture
Location — Marshall, Virginia — Maud's Uplink Node

The numbers were off.

Maud didn't need classified feeds or predictive lattices to know something was wrong. The funding trail told its own story — one routed through offshore asset swaps, unusually timed government shell payments, and a reactivated procurement code she hadn't seen since 2039: "FT-1: Divergence Suppression Initiative."

She leaned closer to the monitor, muting the thunderstorm outside. "Not dormant," she whispered. "They just rerouted the access path." Someone was quietly moving funds to unlisted contractors through continuity-era shadow accounts — the kind reserved for existential containment ops. Mirrorhound teams. Back on the board.

She tapped her wrist unit twice, initiating a handshake to Eitan's legacy enclave. Only a few relay routes remained open.

REQUEST: WARNING TO FIELD NODE "SCOTT-PRIME."

She hesitated for half a second, then added:

PS: Tell her the doctrines are about to eat their own.

Location — Northern Virginia — Eitan's Signal Burrow

The message blinked alive like a memory retrieved from the wrong year.

Ray had warned him he'd show up in the archives as fractured, compromised. But fractured didn't mean finished.

Eitan squinted at the waveform resonance glyph Maud included — three nested circles fractured at the outer edge. The old *"Cascade Fracture"* marker. She hadn't used that since Syria.
He exhaled, almost amused. "So… they've authorized divergence extraction teams again."

His body lagged, emulator buzzing just to keep the tremors from collapsing him. But the doctrine moved faster. Navon had learned long ago that survival wasn't about geography. It was about cadence — showing up in the fractures where the lattice thought no one remained.

Behind him, the antique resonance printer whirred to life. A single line burned onto the recycled paper:
"Not a target. A trigger."

Eitan tapped the page with one finger. That was the lesson no continuity officer had ever admitted out loud: you don't activate Mirrorhounds to neutralize a threat. You activate them when the doctrine itself has begun to fear the survivor. Survival wasn't weakness. It was indictment.

He reached for the encrypted relay pad, routing a pulse toward Lou's last known trajectory. Then a second to Jack and Cal's transient safehouse. They'd gone below. He just hoped they hadn't gone blind.

Location — Geneva Corridor — Continuity Alliance Backchannel

Biff paced the length of the mirrored conference cube, nostrils flaring.
"They're hunting them now? That wasn't the agreement."

Tanner, older now, grayer but with the same foxlike watchfulness he'd honed in three administrations, offered a placating hand. "They're not hunting them, Biff. They're containing field spillover. It's a doctrine shield, nothing more."

Biff turned, eyes sharp. "You just activated Mirrorhound. Do you even remember what that program *was*?"

Tanner didn't flinch. "It was designed for asset retrieval during systemic fracture scenarios."

"Asset retrieval?" Biff nearly laughed. "We called it asset nullification. And you *just lit that fuse.*"

Tanner leaned in, voice flat. "Because your little warfile re-opened the divergence protocols. Your Istanbul leak reached the Trust Cabal. They're scared. And scared systems default to suppression."

Aide-2 entered with a secure tablet. "Sir… continuity channel 9 just spiked. Sabine confirmed active deployment."
Biff's face drained of color.
"You told her they compromised the tunnel?"

The aide hesitated. "No. But someone on her deck intercepted the Eitan uplink."
"Then we're cooked."

Biff backed away from the table, suddenly small.

"You just authorized a doctrinal erasure of our best signal divergence. They're not targets anymore. They're proof."

For years, he'd been the one seeding doctrine, reshaping strategy cells, nudging the War Colleges off the real map.

But now he saw it: he hadn't been the cartographer. He'd been the cover story.

Tanner folded his arms — the same posture he'd used in Kandahar, Brussels, and once in a blackout bunker in Lagos when he'd quietly rewritten the rules of engagement without waiting for anyone's permission. Biff had always mistaken it for loyalty.

For continuity. But continuity had never been the mission.

"Then they'd better not live long enough to testify," Tanner said.

Sabine and Watcher Vire hadn't needed him to build new doctrine. They needed him to blind the old one.

Location — Southern Alps Relay Point — Quantum Courier Outpost

Jack's comm buzzed. A high-frequency pulse.
Encrypted. Ghost-channeled. Only one signature matched: Eitan.
He scanned the signal, face tightening.
"Mirrorhound is live."

Cal looked up from the field array. "You sure?"
"Three buried resonance glyphs. One's the killphrase for doctrine overwrite prevention."

Cal's voice went still. "So we're not being hunted for what we did. We're being hunted for what we know."

Jack nodded slowly. "Maud must've seen it. Financial tags always trigger before the bullets fly."

He paused. "She said they'll reframe it as containment."

Cal snorted. "That's what they said about Fallujah. And Havana."

Jack leaned against the bulkhead. "They're coming fast. And this time, the map doesn't know we're divergent."

Cal tapped the metal floor with his boot. "So we act like anomalies. We don't run *from* the signal. We jam it."

Scene — Mirrorhound Deployment Briefing
Location — Unknown

The handler's voice was clipped, emotionless.
"Your targets are not classified as insurgents or hostiles. They are
narrative discontinuities. Active divergence vectors."

A soldier raised a hand. "Are we cleared for kinetic?"
"Only if exposure risk exceeds fidelity collapse index. Otherwise —
neutralize perception vectors. False memory overlays. Gaslight drift.
Frame recursion."

Another soldier asked, "We still using FT-1 interface protocols?"
The handler nodded. "With one update. These aren't static divergents.
They've adapted. One is running partial resonance glyph immunity.
Another's resonance-shadowed."

The room stilled.
"And the female?"
"She's classified as unsynced core. Unpredictable. Not a node. A field
anomaly."
"Then how do we trap her?"
"You don't." The handler pulled up a projection of Lou's face.
"You follow the field decay. You listen for belief collapse. She'll be where
the signal stops making sense."

Location — Tunnel Descent — Below Grid Echo-3

Lou stopped mid-step.
Jack's voice crackled through the headset, low and urgent.
"Mirrorhound confirmed. Activated via Continuity override. You've got
twenty hours max before they trace the corridor's bleed pattern."

Lou exhaled slowly. "So we're not just walking toward the
chamber…"
"We're walking into the story they'll rewrite if we fail," Jack finished.

Cal checked his backup injector pack. "They want this buried. Not
neutralized — forgotten."
Lou's voice was calm.
"Then let's remind them what a real doctrine collapse looks like."

Scene — Sabine's War Room
Location – Beijing

Sabine stood over a circular table of fractal glass, embedded with
quantum sand tracking human behavior signatures.

"She's in the corridor," a tech whispered. "She found Echo-3"

Sabine narrowed her eyes. "Initiate Fractal Sweep 2.0. Release the overwritten stories."

"But that will inject hallucinated backstories into the field matrix—"

"Exactly."

The tech hesitated. "Weaponizing... Narrative Fidelity?"
Sabine smiled coldly. "It's not belief that wins. It's *who believes first*."

She didn't look up as a shadow passed across the glass — a remote feed from Zhongnanhai. Two uniformed silhouettes stood in the background of the encrypted channel, hands folded, watching without speaking. They never spoke in these calls. They didn't have to.

A faint tone pulsed through the room — their approval, or their warning.

Back in the tunnel, Jack's voice cut through the hum.
"They'll cut her story mid-sentence, then offer a different ending."

"Inject recursion drift," Lou muttered. "Make her live every story but her own."
Cal's voice was flat. "Narrative fidelity collapse. Classic Sabine."

Jack reached for his coat. "Flood her with false memories. Make her question who she's ever been."
He pulled a radio spike from his pocket and slapped it against the tunnel wall. "Let's jam it."

Chapter 44 Close — Lou's Reflection

"Mirrorhounds don't kill you. They overwrite you. Leave the body, take the signal.
That's the trap — you don't even notice the blur until survival feels like consent.
Doctrine never warned us about that. But I've seen it enough to know: the only move is refusal.
Not to fight harder. Not to resolve. Just to stay outside the script long enough that the field can't name me."

Go Move — 捌きの捨石 // Sabaki no Suteishi — The Sabaki Sacrifice — General Zhen

(Macau board, mid-game. General Zhen — Black; General Liu — White)

Black presses into white's settled shape.
Not to kill.
To bend.

Liu's eyes narrow. "That stone dies."
Zhen's hand lingers. "It lives elsewhere."

The cut is light, fast, already fading.
But in its fall, white thickens into bad shape,
eyes narrowing, corner collapsing.

Sabaki — the art of release.
Sacrifice that rewrites the rhythm.

"Some stones win by living," Zhen murmurs.
"Others by dying where the script expected them whole."

— ✦ — FIELD NOTES

Resonance Glyphs

A glyph is not mystical. It's the visible residue of a signal collapse. When resonance fields lock around meaning, they leave patterned imprints — scratches, shimmers, or floating emblems. To outsiders, they look like symbols; inside the lattice, they are command surfaces, doctrine rendered as geometry. Glyphs don't inspire belief — they enforce selection: which past survives, which version of you remains.

Chapter 45 — The Chapel and Moral Injury Doctrine

Epigraph — "The only thing more dangerous than a bad doctrine… is a good doctrine used too long."
— *Redacted memo from an old design course.*

Scene— Exit Vector – Echo-3 to Haymarket

They didn't speak much as they climbed out of Grid Echo-3. The air shifted as they cleared the resonance zone — lighter, but thinner too, like meaning hadn't quite caught up to them yet.

Cal was the last to exit. He paused at the tunnel mouth, staring back into the black.

"We should've burned it," he muttered.

Jack shook his head. "No. Echo-3 needs to exist — as evidence. As warning."

Lou stood by the Q.C. beacon, hands clenched. Her fascia still trembled from the recursion bleed.
"It's not just signal. It's doctrine — Moral Terrain Neutralization. Collapse the ethic, and the rest follows. And the worst part?" She glanced at Jack. "Our own forces don't even know how to fight it. They're still busy worshipping EBO like it's gospel — paint a target, pull a lever, get your effect. Cute, until the target is someone's faith."

They looked at her.

"It wasn't abandoned," she said finally. "It was repurposed."

A silence passed.

"Zhen," Lou said.

Cal nodded. "If anyone understands the original design logic — the doctrinal substrate beneath Helix — it's him."

Jack activated the encrypted drop route. "Then we move. Before the Chamber ignites again."

No one argued.

As they stepped into the coded transport relay, the last flicker of Echo-3 blinked behind them — not extinguished, but waiting.

Scene — Haymarket, Virginia – The Last Archive

The old barn smelled of machine oil, cut cedar, and stubborn memory. A single fluorescent tube buzzed overhead as Lou stepped past hay bales camouflaging stacked server cores. The structure had no listed owner, no power utility account. But it was hot with signal, and hotter still with suppressed thought.

Jonathan Zehn sat hunched at the far table, surrounded by coffee mugs, torn mission patches, and algorithmic wreckage. Once a lead strategist for a "design cell," he now wore worn flannel, boots with duct tape, and a silver ring embossed with a broken compass.

"You still teaching that Newtonian mess at war college?" he barked without looking up.

Lou let the door creak shut behind her. "Only when I feel like damaging the future."

Zehn snorted. "Same war, same tools. But now the enemy doesn't carry a flag. It carries a signature — embedded, recursive, half-forgotten. We're not at war with nations anymore. We're at war with meaning."

He slid a folder across the table. Inside: PowerPoint slides from a recent Continuity Grid Assembly briefing. Flowcharts. Arrows. Color-coded phases. Shaping. Deter. Seize Initiative. Dominate.

Lou raised an eyebrow. "Still using 'Center of Gravity' like it means something?"

Zehn grunted. "Clausewitz was a sharp blade once. Now he's a bureaucratic prosthetic. We turned him into a vending machine. Insert model. Receive false clarity."

She flipped to the last slide: 5th Generation Warfare & Cognitive Terrain Shaping.

"5GW," she murmured. "A name for what they still don't understand."

"Exactly," Zehn said. "They call it 'Fifth Gen' like it's evolution. But warfare didn't evolve. It looped. It refracted. It bled sideways into the narrative substrate. Our metaphors shifted from terrain to signal. From movement to mood."

He stood now, tapping a cracked whiteboard covered in Go patterns and signal glyphs.

"Doctrine became a binding agent for belief. But the war—this war—is epistemic. It's fought in the delta between perception and consent. Phase diagrams don't chart that."

Lou leaned in, quieter now. "So what do we fight with?"

Zehn's eyes narrowed. "Language. Divergence. Silence. You want to break the war apart? Burn the lexicon first. Strip it of its false gravity. Return the field to pattern — not projection."

He tapped a spiral scratched into the corner of the board. "We're not fighting for territory anymore. We're fighting for the right to interpret what *is*."

Scene — Recovered Log – Vade/Kroll Exchange

We never designed war. We narrated it. Phase lines, doctrinal names, and enemy taxonomies—all narrative prosthetics. They gave us comfort, not clarity.

The ancients understood this. That's why their strategies were written as parables. You want to win the new war? Tell a better story.

Lou saved the log and tapped a reply:

No story will be allowed to end. Not while Helix is still listening.

Scene — The Last Lecture – Halberd Barracks

The room buzzed with junior officers in service dress, notebooks open, ready to parrot.

At the front, Biff gestured to a projected image of concentric circles.

"Here we see the adversary's strategic depth. Now, applying Phase Zero doctrine, we engage the shaping phase before conventional operations. Any questions?"

A young lieutenant raised her hand. "Sir, does this model account for coherence drift or nonlocal disruptions?"

Biff blinked. "This model was vetted by INFORMEX *(Institute for Modeling Foreign Extremes)* and Continuity Alliance."

"What's INFORMEX?"

"I think it's a think tank. Or a shell company. Hard to tell these days."

Another voice: "But sir, what if the enemy isn't in the phase structure?"

Biff tightened his jaw. "Then you shape harder."

Laughter didn't follow. A few pens stopped moving.

For the first time in years, a whisper of doubt flickered in Biff's mind. A line he'd never rehearsed.

Was this… my win?

He turned — as if someone might confirm it.

No one was there.

In the back row, Sabine, dressed in plain beige, posed as a visiting academic. Her gaze was unreadable. She jotted a note in the margin of her folder.

"The war doesn't care what phase you call it.
It's already begun."

As the officers filed out, she remained seated. Biff noticed. He walked back slowly.

She didn't smile.

"This will be your last lecture, Biff."

He stiffened. "You said I had one more op."

"This was it. Doctrine collapse. In real time."
She tapped her pen once.

"Ensure no militaries interfere. Not the Continuity Alliance. Not the Continuity Grid. Delay the old lions."

He nodded once.

"And if they push back?"

She rose without ceremony.

"Then feed them another phase.
They're addicted to sequence."

She slipped out before he could speak again. The folder she left behind was blank — but he knew it was full.

He stood still after she left. The silence didn't feel like clarity. It felt like debt.

Scene — StepDoc's Micro-Memoir

Lou ducked into a secure alleyway comm node outside Langley and opened a flash drive labeled *Tiny Humans, Big Protocols*. It was StepDoc's cover story memoir. Buried halfway through was a declassified moment:

"In 2120, the war colleges quietly began requesting narrative warfare briefs. But what they really wanted was marketing advice. Not strategy. Not truth. Just new metaphors for old failures."

"I watched Generals nod at slides they didn't understand. Watched them use 'resonance' like it was a font choice."

"So I stopped briefing doctrine. I started telling bedtime stories. Some of them woke up."

Lou smiled. "Classic Liz."

Scene — Camp Echo – The Chapel Tent
Location — Northern Greenland

A dim halogen lantern cast soft light on the makeshift altar: a stack of empty pelican cases topped with a chipped chalice and a folded Arctic flag.

Dr. Barrett "Red" Kallman had arrived three days earlier under classified orders — unsigned, but unmistakably from Eitan. A silent insertion via the same rogue SEAL team that had exfiltrated him weeks ago.

His job wasn't command, or science, or signal integrity. It was witness.

Bear witness to what happens when a war forgets its soul.

Red sat alone on a crate, his weathered Bible open across his lap. Pages held together by mission tape, marginalia, and classified tabs — the holy text of someone who had preached too many funerals and defended too many men who couldn't defend themselves anymore.

Lou stepped in quietly. Her boots crunched frost near the altar. Camp Echo had been stitched together in the lee of an ice ridge — part weather station, part listening post. Officially, they were here to monitor polar drift data for the Continuity Alliance. Unofficially, it was the nearest human outpost to the Svalbard Chamber's signal vector, a place where

Eitan wanted eyes, ears, and someone who could still name what they were seeing. The kind of assignment you gave to a chaplain when you didn't want the report written in operational code.

"Didn't think moral injury came with a thermal lining," she said.

Red didn't look up. "When you freeze a belief system long enough, it shatters."

He tapped the lid of the chalice gently.
They didn't need to dismantle religion. Just make the watchers feel divine.

"Once faith becomes the software," he said, "you don't need soldiers or surveillance. People police themselves — in the name of virtue."

A pause. Then he added, almost to himself:

"Helix didn't fight faith," he said. "It found the backdoor built into every creed — the one that says obedience is holy, and questioning is sin."
He tapped the chalice again. "All they had to do was rewrite the commands — and call the watchers sacred."

"Doctrine isn't just wrong now. It's… soul-damaging. Structured betrayal. Calibrated cruelty."

Red hadn't chosen this post. The orders were unsigned, but Lou recognized the cadence. Navon. Even half-crippled in Virginia, Eitan still placed witnesses like stones on a Go board — not to command, but to remind. Red wasn't here to preach. He was here to name the fracture when others would try to forget it.

He turned the Bible toward her — but the page wasn't scripture. It was a mission briefing, annotated in red ink.

"You know what they asked me to do last month?"

Lou shook her head.

"Write a theological justification for automated kill-chains."

A beat.

"Something about mission alignment and coherence calibration. As if murder loops need a blessing."

Red's fingers rested on the chalice. "Remember what I told you once about Qom?"

Lou nodded. "Some ghosts follow you home. Some ride in the truck with you. Yeah — I remember."
"Back then, I thought it was just about that op — the lattice rupture, the chaplains walking point. But it's not the ghosts that matter. It's the fact we let the collapse ride with us after. We carried it. Kept it alive. Doctrine says you go in clean and come out the same. That's the lie."

He glanced at her, the corner of his mouth tightening. "The rupture changes you. And once it's in your head, you start seeing how every hymn, every blessing, can be rewritten into code."

Lou didn't speak.

Red smiled, bitter. "I didn't do it. But I rewrote the old burial prayer."

"For the death of what?"

"Meaning."

He closed the Bible, gently. "We trained for trauma. Not betrayal. But this war... this war was built to betray the soul."

A long silence settled.

Finally, Red reached under his crate and pulled out a field notebook. The cover was scored, edges singed. He tore out a page and laid it beneath the chalice.

In thick black ink:
"Stability is not control. It's memory — and mercy."

He stood, handed Lou the notebook.

"We're all standing in the Chapel now. Some of us just haven't noticed."

He said these exact words to Raveneh.

"Belief has become infrastructure," he said. "Epistemology is the new terrain. And obedience? That's just the outcome of well-placed code."

Scene — Moral Intercept — Bremerhaven Flashback

Cal had intercepted a crate in Bremerhaven years ago — sealed under diplomatic tags, routed through a Continuity Alliance logistics node. When they finally opened it, the interior was empty. Not missing. Empty by design.

Inside: just a note, folded in thirds. No signature. No insignia. The handwriting neat, deliberate:
"This war is not what you think."

He remembered standing in the cold warehouse, holding that note while German dockworkers smoked fish behind him. Seals barked down at the harbor. He thought it was a mistake.

Now, he wasn't so sure. Tracking another crate years later — this one part of the Genesis Chamber arc — he recognized the cadence. Navon. The refusal to explain, only to remind. A doctrine of negation disguised as absence.

A checkpoint. Not just a logistical one. A moral one.

The lie he once accepted — that the war was winnable, or even real — was beginning to fracture. The Chamber wasn't just dangerous.

It was *wrong*.

Who fights this war, when the war itself is a deception?
When the field is engineered, the emotions are synthetic, and the enemy is... epistemological?
Who fights that war?

Only those who remember what it means to choose.
Only those who still believe in saying no.

Scene — Ray's Old Voice

In a pre-recorded transmission, Ray's voice drifted in through white noise:

"Coherence isn't safety. It's silence. That's the whole point of modern doctrine. It silences dissent with templates. It replaces insight with alignment."

"Lou, you weren't made for doctrine. You were made for divergence. Let the script break. Let the war show its real face."

Lou listened twice. Then deleted it. Not because it wasn't true. But because she had already memorized every word.

Scene — Lou's Private Debrief

She stood in front of a mirror at the Geneva substation, hours before insertion into the Svalbard Chamber. Her reflection looked older, sharper. Not weary. Just done pretending.

She spoke aloud, not to herself, but to a generation that might come after:

"They're still teaching warfare like it has chapters. Like it obeys linear stages. Like it cares about our maps. But the real war doesn't sit in doctrine. It rides signal. Belief. Pattern."

She traced a small spiral on the glass with her fingertip.

"It's not fifth generation. It's not cyber. It's not irregular or hybrid. It's quantum. And if we don't feel the field before it forms—we'll lose."

A beat.

"And we won't even know what we lost."

Final Scene — The Go Board

A game abandoned in a Himalayan temple years ago still rested near the edge of a cliff. A stone had been placed mid-quadrant. Alone. Unremarkable.

A General swept past it, paused, then whispered:

"This wasn't a move to win. This was a move to remember."

Chapter 45 Close — Lou's Reflection

"The Chapel wasn't a place and it wasn't stone and glass. It was a frame — a signal dressed up as sanctuary. Step inside and it tells you obedience is safety, betrayal is normal, and silence is sacred. It was a test. Not faith, not doctrine — compliance. They wanted to see how much betrayal we'd swallow before we called it normal.

That's moral injury in the lattice: not what you see, but what it convinces you to stop questioning. Not guilt. Not shock. It's the slow theft of your own compass, until you can't tell if the order you followed was theirs or yours.

I felt it press in — the walls, the silence, the hymn. But that's how they keep you: by making doubt feel like home.

So I walked out of their frame. Not untouched, not clean. But not theirs. And that's the only way forward."

Navon once told me that betrayal wasn't an event. It was a design feature. Systems don't break soldiers by accident — they rehearse the fracture until you mistake it for loyalty. That's the last doctrine left to him: refusal to resolve, refusal to call betrayal anything but what it is. I carry that cadence now, even when he isn't here to name it.

**Go Move — 割り込み // Warikomi — Invasion Wedge —
General Zhen**

White cuts the seam.
Not to kill.
To separate.

Warikomi — the wedge.
A fracture inside a shape that thought itself safe.
The lattice pauses. Recalculates. Breathes wrong.

Zhen's hand doesn't waver.
"This sector was theirs," he says,
"until we split it."

No capture. No gain.
Only the pressure of two groups forced apart,
their rhythm no longer whole.

In quantum war, that's enough.
A single wedge, and the field stutters —
long enough for divergence to run.

Chapter 46 — The Doctrine We Died In

Epigraph — "Doctrine isn't strategy. It's the wallpaper over the cracks in belief." — *Dr. Cyrus Raveneh*

Scene — **Coherence Operations**
Location — Tesserae Defense Core

The lights buzzed overhead. The room smelled of old coffee, dry erase fumes, and institutional disillusionment. On the wall: a projection labeled **"Coherence Operations in Phase Zero"** glowed in blue and red overlays like a malfunctioning arcade game.

Lou stormed in, late and already exasperated, two mugs in one hand and a thick stack of annotated doctrine briefs clutched under her arm.

"This diagram," she barked, stabbing at the screen with her elbow, "looks like Foucault and SimCity got hammered and submitted a war plan."

A timid teaching assistant blinked behind horn-rimmed glasses. Jack, lounging in the back row, didn't look up.

"You're going to get disinvited again," he muttered.

Lou didn't care. "We keep dressing up predictive paralysis as strategy. Belief suppression wrapped in campaign language. This isn't doctrine. It's theater."

She tossed the briefs on the lectern. "Every map collapses when people stop believing in its story. That's not a planning error. It's a system failure."

The TA coughed. "But it's based on accepted Joint Doctrine Phase frameworks—"

"Exactly," Lou snapped. "It's the doctrine we died in."

Silence fell. She left before she said something worse.

Location — Tuscany Safehouse | 02:43 Local

StepDoc had caught up by then — routed through courier relays Lou barely trusted, but she arrived damp, exhausted, and smiling like she'd been waiting all her life to drink wine in a storm with conspirators.

The rain hadn't stopped. Lou sat near the fireplace, swirling a spoon in her over-sweetened coffee. StepDoc leaned against the frame, wine glass in hand. Jack scanned interference maps from a flickering tablet. Cal watched the window, back stiff.

Jack glanced at Liz. "What, you didn't get lost between Vienna and Tuscany?"

Lou ignored him, thumb lingering on the mug's chipped rim — a habit she'd picked up from Eitan. He used to say doctrine wasn't about maps at all. It was about how much betrayal a soldier could absorb before they mistook it for duty. She heard his cadence in the silence now: *don't confuse endurance with consent.*

"What was it Raveneh said?" Lou murmured, still ignoring Jack. "That war isn't just fought in terrain, it's fought in frameworks."

"He called it narrative convergence," Jack replied. "Upstream warfare. Win the belief before the first drone flies."

StepDoc added, "Or manufacture a reality so predictable, resistance looks like insanity."

StepDoc swirled her glass. "They just shut down the Warsaw Lab after a coherence spike triggered twenty-six false flag edits in one day. Whole cities are now fighting stories they didn't write."
Jack muttered, "And we're still drawing threat rings on whiteboards like it's 2025."

Lou didn't answer right away. For years she had wondered if Eitan had only been talking about war. Tonight, she wasn't sure. Maybe he'd been warning her about inheritance — the patterns parents hand their children, dressed up as survival.

Cal exhaled slowly. "That's what Helix is for. To make the implausible feel inevitable."

Scenelet — Peripheral Signal Trace
Location — Inner Room — Books stacked to the ceiling

Elsewhere, far from Tuscany's storm, another thread stirred.

Lou set the mug down at last, letting the silence linger. Somewhere on the periphery — sometimes Virginia, sometimes a courier drop stitched through Iceland or the Arctic outposts — Eitan was still moving in fragments. His body lagged, emulator buzzing to keep the tremors from collapsing him, but StepDoc's smuggled regimen had steadied him more than most knew. She'd slipped the meds past customs in faux equine vials, logged as horse supplements, and administered them herself when couriers linked up. Off-label, off the books, but it worked — his cadence held.

With that stolen margin of strength, he kept tracking Watcher traces the way others tracked weather, following old divergents Sabine wanted erased. Rumor said he was even shadowing her courier lines, scavenging coherence siphons from vaults no one else dared touch.

Lou could almost hear his voice in the static of the rain: *don't confuse endurance with consent.*

Dr. Cyrus Raveneh — the others still called him the Thinker. A hooded coat, rain on his sleeves, and a book tucked under one arm: *The Semiotics of Convergence.* He nodded at Lou, then Jack.

"The real signal loss isn't tactical," he said. "It's epistemological. We taught a generation not to trust their own pattern recognition."

Lou stirred. "Pre-bunking. Soft truth laundering."

"It's not misinformation," the Thinker said. "It's mistrust-by-design. The cabal engineered disbelief, not belief. That's why you're still dangerous. You zag."

Jack cracked a half-smile. "So this isn't 5D chess. It's denial with better graphics."

Scene Close — Tuscany Hills — Pre-Dawn

The clouds cleared just enough to reveal the ridgeline. A resonance map glowed faintly from the corner of Lou's tablet — old Helix nodes, pulsing like faded scars.

She looked at the lines. At the way convergence had failed. And how belief, real belief, wasn't something you could model.

"It was never about winning," she said to no one. "It was about refusing to be pre-written."

Chapter 46 Close — Lou's Reflection

"They called it Coherence Ops. Slides, phases, arrows — theater dressed up as doctrine. But that room in Tesserae wasn't strategy. It was wallpaper. Cover the cracks, pretend the wall still holds.

Later, in Tuscany, I kept replaying their words — narrative convergence, inevitability, realities you didn't write. Jack called it gaslighting in six dimensions. Cal said inevitability. StepDoc made it sound like gravity. All of them circling the same wound.

And I remember the Thinker's point, rain still on his coat: it was never about manufacturing belief. It was about manufacturing disbelief. Strip out trust until every map looks safer than your own senses. That was the doctrine.

Madison wasn't a misfire. It was the fracture showing itself. 33A wasn't containment, it was calibration — until it started eating its own makers. What I felt in that hum was correction, not anomaly.

War wasn't just fought on ground. It slid across memory, silence, sedation, surveillance, guilt, alignment. Each frame bleeding into the next until you couldn't tell whether you were following orders or following gravity. That's how they broke us — not with one weapon, but with the weight of every frame collapsing at once.

This is what the Cabal never wrote down: you don't die in war, you die in alignment. Obedience polished so smooth it collapses into silence.

And that's why the next step matters. Because behind all this theater there were architects. Someone drew these frames on purpose. And if I'm still here, still zagging, it's because the one thing they couldn't model was refusal. The doctrine we died in is the same doctrine they still think they can use to win."

Go Move — 端ハネ // Hashi Hane — The Pattern Breaker — General Zhen

White bends at the edge.

Not to connect.

To fracture.

On the board, it's hane.

At Axis Point 7, it's Pattern Recursion Disrupt —

a bend that forces the model to replay a sequence it thought closed.

Zhen sets the stone without a word.

Liu frowns. Not at the move. At the gap it leaves.

"This wasn't for territory."

Zhen shakes his head.

"It's so they can't finish the story."

In quantum war, the most dangerous play isn't capture.

It's making the board itself doubt its own coherence.

— ✦ — FIELD NOTES

Engineered Disbelief

Traditional deception feeds falsehood into an opponent's frame. Quantum deception corrodes the frame itself.

In epistemic warfare, the goal is not to make you believe the wrong thing — it is to make you doubt the right thing until doubt becomes reflex.

This is why coherence fields don't just erase memories. They erode trust in memory. Once mistrust is the default, even clarity looks suspicious.

Doctrinal implication: the most resilient actors are not the ones who hold belief, but the ones who can refuse engineered disbelief.

Chapter 47 — The Architects of Belief

Scene — Zehn and Epistemology
> **Location —** Encrypted Briefing Cell – Outside Zurich Node

Outside the Zurich node, snow fell in irregular pulses — each flake catching signal light, reflecting narratives no one believed in anymore. The lattice glitched once. Then again.
"Every city's a fuse," Lou whispered. "The ones still pretending not to burn… they're the most dangerous."

The room was quiet, but not still. Signal still hummed at a level most couldn't detect — except Lou. It tickled her right temple like a warning before a nosebleed. Glyph-9's last overlay hadn't faded so much as receded — like a tide holding its breath.

Zehn didn't sit right away. He stared at the lattice projection Jack had pinned to the wall. Not the active signals — but the voids between them.

"They're not just scripting war," he said. "They're scripting *why* we think war makes sense."

Zehn added grimly. "Jakarta lost power last week. Not from a hack. From a spike in 'belief conflict' — too many neural maps misaligned. The system shut itself down to stop emotional contagion."

Cal frowned. "Define 'they.'"

"They call themselves nothing," Zehn said. "But we use the old code: the Trust Cabal. Ex-intel financiers, retired Generals, a few climate panic profiteers, and the CEOs of every company that makes you feel like you need a password to be a person."

Zehn finally sat, lacing his fingers together like someone giving a eulogy. "Doctrine isn't strategy. It's narrative control. It decides which kinds of violence are acceptable, and which kinds of peace are unspeakable."

Jack raised an eyebrow. "So this isn't 5D chess — it's 6D gaslighting."

Lou cracked a smile, but it didn't reach her eyes. "They're already pressuring the last holdout networks. One wrong phrase, and they'll slap us with a planetary stability act. Which is just a fancy way of saying: 'Talk wrong and you lose orbit clearance.'"

Cal leaned forward. "How far does this go?"

Zehn answered without flinching. "It's not just about pre-bunking falsehoods. It's about constructing belief architectures. Predictive sentiment inoculation. Coherence simulation. But coherence doesn't collapse because a system loses trust. It collapses when *you* start to doubt your own pattern recognition."

Lou stared at the map. "They want disbelief engineered upstream. Make doubt feel like your idea."

Jack tapped his temple. "So the Chamber isn't just a weapon. It's a belief editor."

Zehn nodded. "And Lou's still the anomaly they couldn't overwrite. She zagged."

Cal looked over. "That zag you pulled in Chengdu—how did you know?"

Lou didn't answer at first. Then: "It's not magic. It's not a gift. It's just... I notice the moment before the lock completes. Before the new pattern locks in."

Zehn leaned back. "Exactly. They want belief to feel like gravity — invisible, constant, and beyond question. Your zag was refusal at the root."

Jack sat back. "That's why they fear you. Not because you broke the signal. Because you remembered it wasn't yours."

The room fell quiet. Outside, the lattice flickered once. A ghost packet, maybe. Or just Glyph-9 reminding them: some echoes aren't reflections. They're rehearsals.

Zehn stood. "If they control the definitions, they don't need to win. They just need to define what counts as peace."

Lou exhaled slowly. "Then we define nothing."

She stepped toward the map and pulled the center node — Zurich — offline.

Zehn didn't wait for thanks. He just nodded once — like a man who'd already written the after-action report.

At the door, he paused.
Like he wanted to say more. And he did.

"I met Navon once. Long ago. Brief, almost forgettable. He didn't tell me what to do. He just reminded me what not to accept. That refusal stayed with me longer than any lecture."
He glanced back at Lou.
"You carry his cadence. Don't lose it."

He lingered only a moment longer, eyes steady.

"Helix isn't at war with armies," he said. "It's at war with humanity's belief structure. That's the real field. And while we argue doctrine, the Chamber is still counting down."

Then, with the faintest smirk —
"If they ever tell you peace is alignment, run. And if you ever need someone to kill a doctrine chamber again… you know where to file the paperwork."
"Just mark the target 'epistemological' and I'll bring my quiet shoes."

Then he was gone.
No signal trace. No goodbye. Just a silence that hummed like someone still listening.

The war room felt heavier without him — not emptier, just more real.

The map dimmed, but she didn't look away. Systems don't collapse at the edges. They collapse from their doctrine. And doctrine, she knew, had a name.
Kael.

Cal turned. "What about Weiss? We know he's in Berlin. Can't we intercept and fracture the lattice there?"

Lou didn't answer. Kael didn't fracture — he calcified. His beliefs encoded, ossified. In systems thinking, calcification suggests something that refuses to adapt — it *locks in* rather than evolves. He hardened into pure doctrinal rigidity — his belief system became structural code.

She finally turned to Cal. "You can't assassinate a belief structure. Not when it's been uploaded."

Then the screen blinked.
Just once.
A packet, untraceable — but unmistakably handcrafted.
Embedded in its frame: an old military signature, stripped of insignia but tagged with a doctrine revision number known only to Joint Staff

veterans.
Weiss.

A phrase appeared in Helvetica black:

"Stability is not a condition. It is an act of enforcement."
— Gen. Henrik Weiss, Strategic Directive 55-F

Jack leaned in. "He's writing it for us — because he knows we're the ones watching."
Lou didn't blink. "Good. Let him feel it."
Cal exhaled. "I always hated that font."

The screen pulsed — again.
Not a glitch. A signal.
A handcrafted echo, embedded in the lattice architecture.
Old military syntax — stripped of insignia, but tagged with a doctrine revision code linked to a now-shadowed body: the Continuity Alliance War Doctrine Substrate.

Jack squinted. "Is that a ping or a threat?"
Lou exhaled. "With Weiss, it's both."
Cal muttered, "The lattice bugs should've gotten him first."
Lou smirked. "They tried. He reprogrammed them."

Scenelet — Peripheral Relay | Northern Outskirts of Reykjavik

Snow hissed against the antenna arrays, muffling the static bleed. Eitan hunched inside the signal burrow, emulator buzzing faintly, a warmth that was more machine than body. StepDoc's smuggled regimen steadied his hands enough to thread the relay cables — horse labels on the vials still taped to the case beside him.

The resonance glyph residue here was unstable — half-formed interference patterns etched in frost on the relay plates. Most would call it noise. Eitan called it a ledger, proof the lattice hadn't finished collapsing this sector. He traced one pattern with a gloved finger, whispering to no one:
"Not resolved. Not yet."

On the battered printer beside him, a strip of paper shivered out. Three words burned across it:
"The Chapel Holds."

He exhaled slowly, almost smiling. If Zehn was right, belief wasn't about truth or trust. It was about who refused to let the story close.

He tapped the relay twice, sending a ghost ping east.

To Lou. To Jack. To Cal.

A reminder: the war wasn't over. Not while he was still unresolved.

Chapter 47 Close — Lou's Reflection

"They called it doctrine, but Weiss carved it down until it fit in a font. Stability as enforcement. Peace as alignment. Belief compressed to weapons-grade simplicity. That's not strategy. That's a trigger.

Zehn was right — it isn't about lies or even consensus anymore. It's about compression. Strip a system to one phrase, one directive, and suddenly the whole field bends around it. That's Reality Frame — Belief Compression. The slogan becomes terrain, sharper than any blade.

But I've felt the stretch, too. The Consensus Horizon. Cities pretending to hold together when the field underneath was already cracking. Every day they extend it is just more time before the snap. And when it snaps, it won't be policy that breaks — it'll be trust itself.

Doctrine always told us peace meant closure. But closure is their word for collapse. The only move left is refusal — not of war, but of their framing of peace.

I know what Weiss thinks: that inevitability can be printed, circulated, and believed before anyone has the chance to question it. But inevitability only works if you stand still.

And I won't."

.

Go Move — 名付け石 // Nazuke-ishi — The Stone Already Named — General Weiss

Black plays into a known sector.
Charted. Archived. Annotated.

The shape isn't new.
But the name is his.

A stone set not for territory,
but for preservation —
calcification of the board itself.

In worldview war, there are no enemies.
Only doctrines competing for the same grid.

Weiss's move isn't aggression.
It's architecture.

Every stone pre-labeled.
Every future pre-scripted.

But one play —
off-tempo, off-signal —
can still make the board doubt its own story.

Chapter 48 — Signal Drift Redux

Tagline — "Some echoes return. Others redirect." — *Dr. Raveneh*

Epigraph — "What they called fragmentation was just pattern escaping its box." — *Dr. Raveneh*

Scene — Cold Stow
Location — Relay Station South of Thule

Snow scraped sideways across the bunker's satellite dish. It looked abandoned—because it was supposed to be. But someone had hotwired the geothermal coils, and the relay tower was no longer sleeping.

Lou stood just inside, staring at the fiber-optic cabling that pulsed faintly through the frost. Signal was moving again. Not strong enough to map. But not dead either.

Cal was already checking the uplink stack. "Vault Theta's back online," he said. "But not fully. It's pinging. Not broadcasting."

Jack leaned against a crate marked *Cold Stow – Class II Helix Artifacts*. "You think it remembers what it was built for?"

"No," Lou said. "But I do think it remembers who broke it."

Flashback — Field Debrief
Location — Unnamed Desert Ridge, Two Years Earlier

The heat shimmered like bad data. A debrief tent flapped against rebar stakes. Inside, Ray sketched nonlinear signal flow on an old whiteboard, circles overlapping like arterial trauma.

"The real signal isn't the one you intercept," he had told them. "It's the one that redirects you. That makes you decode the wrong war."

Lou had been younger then. Angrier. "So we're just fish in the stream?"

Ray's reply was quiet: "No. You're the turbulence. The part that can't be mapped without changing the current."

Location — Present – Relay Console Room

Jack had just come in from the cold, hood still damp from the wind off the ice. He moved like someone who hadn't stopped scanning alleyways and reflections since his counter-espionage days — the habits of a man who once lived entire years on surveillance detection routes. Lou knew better than to ask where he'd been; he'd muttered something about "Qom bleed" and an old counter-surveillance pattern he still trusted more than satellites.

Sometimes he still tested the team without telling them — running a surveillance detection route — SDR — through Zurich's alleys, shadowing Watcher traces until they collapsed into nothing but lattice echoes. He'd once explained it to Cal like this: *"You don't catch them by who's there. You catch them by who should've been there, and wasn't."*

Now he was bent over the satellite drift reports, tablet flickering in the dim light. "This node was part of an old predictive weather mesh," he said. "Low-band, pre-Helix. But the hardware's been retooled."

Lou frowned. "By who?"

Cal answered without looking up: "Same people who rewired belief. Whoever first realized that trust is a kind of bandwidth."

Jack didn't look up. "And not just belief. Berlin's already running counter-patterns. Weiss's agents don't tail you anymore — they mirror you. I ran counter-tail drills on one last month. Followed every turn, every reflection… only to realize there was no body behind it. Just a shadow written into the grid."

Lou muttered, "And whoever figured out how to jam it."

Scene cut — Inner Quarters — Heat Sink Room

Dr. Raveneh's voice echoed through the encrypted playback device Lou still carried — a final voice memo, marked only *"Ω Archive – Trust Drift"*:

"You cannot win against a story by disproving it.

You resist it by becoming a signal it cannot absorb."

Lou closed her eyes. She could still feel the Geneva lattice vibrating under her palms. The moment coherence tilted.

Cal asked, "What's next?"

She didn't answer.

She walked outside, into the wind, holding the device in one hand.

The *Möbius ring* didn't pulse.

But the drift? The drift remembered her.

Scene — Intercept Protocol – Continuity Suppression Orders
Location — Secure Relay Node – U.S. Continuity Alliance

Biff stood in front of the holo-display, arms crossed, watching the trace overlays populate.
Four red anomalies. Three tagged with suppressed clearance codes. One — untraceable.
"Those aren't ours," said a junior analyst, squinting at the resolution filters.
"They were." Biff didn't turn around. "They went off-book months ago. What you're seeing is residual coherence—ghost protocols flaring up. Contain them."

"Sir, one of them's pinging back from the Arctic perimeter. Low-band echo but stable."

Biff tapped the console once. A manual override prompt appeared. "Scramble assets from Mirrorhound-3. Route through the Vienna fallback node. Make it look like a systems integrity check. Nothing official."

"But we'll be chasing friendlies."
Biff's voice dropped: "They're not friendlies if they destabilize the doctrine."

The analyst hesitated. "Do we inform the Joint Strategic Panel?"

Biff leaned closer. "We're not informing anyone. This is continuity protection. If doctrine unravels now, there won't be a next phase to brief."

He issued one final command:

"Engage protocol — Drift Null. Tag Cal first. If he breaks containment — terminate."

Scene cut — Outside Relay Station — Thule Periphery

Lou's breath fogged as she stepped into the snow.
Behind her, Cal's jaw had tightened. He hadn't said a word since Jack passed him the decoded uplink:

"Continuity orders activated. Mirrorhound teams inbound. One tag: your name. Source unlisted. Recommend exfil within the hour."

"Biff," Cal said flatly.

Lou didn't ask how he knew. She felt it too — the script closing around them.

Jack glanced up from the crate he'd just resealed. "It's a containment op. No formal charge. Just erasure."

He then scanned the relay logs again. "Same call tags as the FT-1 sequence Maud flagged in Virginia. They're not just hunting — they're cleaning house."

Lou turned toward the horizon. "Then we drift faster than they can model."

Cal loaded the final gear onto the sled rig. His voice was steady. "They think doctrine is an artifact. They're wrong."
He looked up. "We are the drift."

Yes, she echoed. "Drift wasn't just survival. It was delay — a pause in the countdown. And every pause mattered, because the Chamber was still ticking."

Chapter 48 Close — Lou's Reflection

"They thought drift was weakness. Noise in the channel. But Ray was right — turbulence isn't error. It's the proof you're still alive in the stream.

Raveneh's voice pressed in through the static: you don't disprove a story, you become the signal it can't absorb. That's not theory. That's survival.

The Mirrorhounds don't chase you for capture. They chase you to erase the record you ever existed. That's Agency Drift weaponized — turn the field until even your refusal looks like consent. But they still haven't modeled what happens when drift refuses to collapse.

Signal Parallax. From their vantage, we're anomalies. From mine, they're the glitch. That's the crack.

Biff thinks continuity can erase us clean. He's wrong. Continuity can't own turbulence. It can't own drift.

And that's what I'll carry forward: not stability, not survival. Drift itself. Because in this war, stability is alignment. Drift is refusal.

And I refuse. I can't lose sight of the reason any of this matters. The Chamber isn't myth. It's hardware. Quantum substrate, coherence lattices, cryo-vectors tuned to memory itself. Built so doctrine doesn't just command armies — it rewrites what armies believe they're fighting for.

Every drift, every refusal, every fracture only matters if it gets us there. To the Chamber. To the lock. To the one switch left that can shut it down.

Because if Helix stabilizes that field first, this war doesn't end. It calcifies. And belief — the last thing that still belongs to us — won't anymore.

That's why we move. Not for survival. For closure. End the Chamber before it ends us.

**Go Move — 誤読の型 // Godoku no Kata — The Misread Pattern
— General Zhen**

A stone is set mid-drift —
not on the line, but in the space between.

The board sees it.
Registers it.
But the tag is wrong.

Pattern fractures — not from force,
not from capture —
but from refusal to resolve.

This isn't misdirection.
It's reorientation.

Turbulence becomes doctrine.
Drift becomes law.

You are not the piece.
You are the misread space between them.

Chapter 49 — The Panopticon That Prayed

Tagline — "The lattice didn't break belief. It borrowed it." — *"Red"*

Scene — Beneath the Chapel Ruin
Location — Sinop Coast

The old chapel had no roof. Just stone, salt air, and the feeling that once — long ago — people had climbed here to remember what couldn't be measured.

Lou ran her fingers along the worn edge of the altar. The limestone was slick with age, embedded with sea-shells, as if memory itself had been sedimented into ritual.

Raveneh crouched in the shadows behind her, sorting through brittle vellum fragments from the old vault cache. His eyes had the look of a man who'd translated too many dead languages and found too many of them alive again in modern code.

"They didn't need to erase belief," he said. "They just recompiled it."

Lou nodded.

"The Continuity Alliance made sure no one could question the evolution of obedience. They called it safeguarding stability — but what they sanctified was pattern submission."

She turned, voice low.

"Not just systems warfare anymore. This is epistemological sanctification of control."

Raveneh looked up from the scrolls.

"The lattice didn't colonize the mind. It found shelter in its temples."

Red had just arrived, not sure why he was called.

"Belief was never the enemy," Red said. "But certainty? That was always the doorway."

He looked out across the sea.

"They built a panopticon so elegant, most people mistook it for God."

Lou sighed. "And what do we call it now?"

Red was very firm. "We call it what it is. A liturgy of surveillance. Written in code. Sanctified in silence."

Scenelet — Peripheral Relay | Reykjavik Outskirts

Somewhere north of Reykjavik, a relay printer spat out a line of text — unsigned, but carrying Navon's cadence: "Dissonance is the only sanctuary."
She didn't see the words, but the static clung sharp to her resonance band. Eitan's cadence — stubborn, defiant — still found her. He was still moving in fragments, scavenging coherence siphons, shadowing couriers Sabine thought invisible. His body might fail, but his doctrine hadn't.

Scene — The Last Myth of Qom

The cold air inside the chapel ruin stung of salt and silence. Lou knelt beside the old scrolls Raveneh had tucked beneath the stone altar — most were damaged, stained with time, but one had a stamped chart in the corner. Cities. Signal compliance rates. Lattice patterns mapped against sacred rhythm.

She scanned the entries:

> Singapore – governance fetishized as hygiene.

> Lagos – prosperity gospel adapted to cadence overlays.

> Addis Ababa – layered consent through ancient liturgy.

> Atlanta – megachurch coherence hubs.

> Tbilisi. Marseille. Osaka. Each one a compliance node.

But one line stood out — boxed in red.
Lou traced the red-boxed entry again. *Qom — Lattice lock failed. Result: Schism, not sync.*
Jack's voice was quiet behind her. "I saw the bleed myself, once. Street-level. Old *paranoia walk* patterns still worked better than satellites. You couldn't map a clean tail in that city if you tried — too many counter-rhythms. It's the only place I ever felt the lattice lose its own shadow."

Lou exhaled. "They didn't need to coerce us. They just found the places where belief had outlived reflection — and offered it rhythm."

A voice replied.
"Qom didn't resist," said a woman, her accent soft but precise, a blend of Marseille and Dakar. "It fractured."

Lou turned.

Dr. Ayesha Quirin stepped into the lantern light, wind tugging her scarf like a signal ripple. She wore desert boots, a navy wool coat, and a shoulder bag patched with old laboratory insignia — Geneva, Dakar, Lyon.

"The signal failed," she continued, "not because Qom was pure — but because it was too saturated. Competing myths. Sacred frictions. Inner dissent with nowhere to go."

She stepped closer, unrolling a carbon-patched scroll from Raveneh's box. "You can't sync lattice rhythm to a belief system already fighting itself."

Lou frowned. "So they're not the resistance?"

"They're the illusion of one," Ayesha said. "They believe they're immune. But dissonance isn't immunity. It's just harder to exploit cleanly."

She knelt near Lou. Her voice dropped.

"The Trust doesn't need you to bow. It only needs rhythm. Once you repeat something enough — a chant, a prayer, even a doubt — the code writes itself."

A pause.

"Qom isn't a stronghold," she said. "It's the last myth of one."

Lou remembered the memo —

INTRA Report: Trust Architecture Expansion Nodes

"Lattice signal merged with ritual patterns most effectively in cities that carried unresolved symbolic density — where myth, trauma, and tradition sat uneasily beneath modern gloss."

Cities showing high coherence-compliance:

Singapore – Governance fetishized as hygiene.
Lagos – Doctrinal overlays adapted via prosperity gospel cadence.
Addis Ababa – Orthodox structures proved ideal for layered consent calibration.

Atlanta – Megachurches as coherence hives.
Marseille – Polytheistic rhythm normalized lattice-based pluralism.
Belgrade – Historic fracture + ethnic myth = easy pattern uptake.
Tbilisi, Kutaisi – Sacred chants mapped cleanly onto lattice pulse intervals.
Osaka – Ritual punctuality exploited.
Qom – Exception.

Too much inner dissent, too much friction inside its own sacred code. The lattice couldn't find a pulse to hijack.

"The signal failed not because Qom was pure — but because it was too dense. Too much unresolved myth competing for rhythm. You can't sync a lattice to a belief system already vibrating against itself."

She knelt beside the scrolls Raveneh had set aside. "They think they're the last immune ones. But dissonance isn't immunity. It's just harder to exploit cleanly."

Lou frowned. "So the Helix just… waits?"

Ayesha nodded. "The Trust doesn't need you to bow. It just needs your rhythm. Once you repeat something enough — a chant, a prayer, even a doubt — the code writes itself."

She looked toward the sea.

"Qom is not the last stronghold. It's the last myth of one."

Signal-resistant enclaves such as *Ethiopian Coptic dioceses*, *Tibetan monastic circuits*, and rural *Georgian sects* were not penetrated by logic or code — but by patterning of sacred myth into lattice-compatible cadence. Narrative synchronization exceeded 74% within 9 cycles. Faith adapted faster than propaganda ever could.

One scroll included a blurred map overlay — not of cities, but orbital vectors. Crescent arcs marked "resonant drops," coordinated with lattice pulses rather than flight clearance.

"What is this?" Lou asked.
Ayesha leaned closer. "Sabine's couriers. The ones who don't land — they fall. Straight through gaps in the lattice. No customs, no broadcast signature. Payloads of memory, or myth."

Lou frowned. "That's how they moved Chamber parts?"
Ayesha nodded. "Some. Not all. But the hardest pieces — the sacred ones — were dropped where code couldn't follow."

Raveneh added, "They called them quantum couriers. But they weren't just logistical. They were sacramental. Every descent was timed to a fracture in the lattice. Every payload — a form of liturgical noise."

Scene — Lou's Realization

She paced slowly now. Her resonance band flickered — a resonance glyph surfacing faintly on its display, not warning, not guiding, just reminding her the lattice still couldn't close its grip. "They didn't break faith. They walked the tightrope."

"I'm not writing against belief," Lou said, half to herself. "I'm writing against belief as a delivery system for obedience tech."

She paused.

"The most effective *digital panopticon* doesn't suppress belief. It sanctifies it — until surveillance feels like devotion."

Scene — Biff and the Final Simulation
Location — Sim Chamber 7

While Lou pieced together Qom's anomaly in Sinop, Biff had been dispatched to review it in simulation. Continuity demanded its own proof.

He had left D.C. before dawn, ditching the beltway routes for the quieter cut south. Past Fredericksburg, he slipped onto the back roads he knew from earlier assignments — two-lanes that wound through Louisa and down toward Mineral. Roadside motels with half-lit neon still carried "Vacancy" signs that hadn't changed since the 1980s. At the edge of the lake, rusted placards warned TRESPASSERS WILL BE PROSECUTED — relics of the reactor era, now half-hidden behind new Continuity Alliance fencing.

The guard shack barely glanced at his civilian ID, waving him through as if the man and the clearance had long since blurred. Biff noted how hard they worked not to draw attention to the real security buried deeper in the complex.

He parked, stepped into an anonymous office block, and took the service elevator down eight stories. The temperature dropped with each level — not just concrete chill, but the deliberate cold of atom-storage vaults repurposed for doctrine tests. By the time the doors opened, his breath felt sharper in his chest.

He straightened his jacket, not military but pressed all the same. Privileged, he thought, to be chosen for the new test run. Privileged to still matter.

Biff had been here before, years earlier, when the site was still spoken of in code. Back then he'd crossed paths with an operations officer named Kaya — quiet, sharp-eyed, already working drops out of the annex. He never asked why she stayed in the shadows. Now, driving in with his coffee cooling in the cup holder, he wondered if she'd ever left.

The chamber walls still bore faded radiation stencils, half-covered by new Continuity placards. A faint hum of coolant fans filled the air — Cold War infrastructure awkwardly re-skinned for doctrine trials.

Biff Langley stepped into the chamber alone.

No uniform. No entourage. Just a half-finished cup of vending machine coffee and the tired posture of a man still pretending the war made sense.

He said he volunteered.

To review the Qom anomaly. To "help recalibrate continuity."
But off-record, Tanner had gone quiet. And Sabine —
She never responded to his last transmission.

He checked the comms feed one last time. No reply. Sabine had left the channel dark.

The doors sealed behind him with the same hydraulic sigh the site once used for warhead vaults.

On the wall: the familiar loop.
Phase Zero — Shaping — Dominate.
He'd written that loop. Taught it. Branded it into minds across five war colleges.

But now, the loop stuttered.
The phases bled together.
Meaning blurred.

A voice came through the override channel — not Helix, not command.

"You lost control of the pattern, Biff."

He froze.

"The doctrine broke. And you didn't break with it."

He reached for the console.
Locked.

The lattice initialized.

No aggression. No sound.
Just recursion — his own lectures refracted back at him. Misaligned cadence. Shattered tempo.

Not the enemy. Not even belief.
It was the silence between signals that broke him.
Where obedience used to live.

A low system tone registered:

[Pattern Integrity Drift > Acceptable Variance]

His breath caught. Chest seized.
Collapsed before the second loop completed.

Outside, no alarms sounded.

Inside, one final output blinked on-screen:

"Simulation Complete. Signal anchor not found."

Later, the file would read: *Heart failure.*
But Red would say it cleaner:

"He died trying to hold too many wrong patterns at once."

And Lou?
She wouldn't mourn him.

She'd just mark the Go board and move on.

In the chamber, a pair of techs in gray coveralls entered without speaking. They disconnected the sensors, draped a plain sheet, and wheeled the gurney out as if rehearsed.
Outside, a contractor slid into his rental sedan, badge clipped low, and steered it back toward Charlottesville airport. By nightfall, it would be

returned, fueled and logged, no record of who last held the keys. The system had already planned for his absence.

Scene — Tanner and The New Pattern
Location — Continuity Alliance Node

The report from Lake Anna arrived before the gurney cleared the annex.

Tanner stood alone in the glass briefing hall, staring at the blank lectern where Biff's last doctrinal update had failed to load. The system had already archived him. No red flags. No memorials. Just a clean overwrite.

Langley, B. — DECEASED. ARCHIVED.

He exhaled once, slow and deliberate.

Behind him, the lattice boards flickered — not off, just in search mode. Untethered.

A younger analyst entered, hesitant.
"Sir… Geneva confirmed. Chamber Seven is sealed. No anomaly report filed. They're marking it as cardiac arrest."

Tanner didn't turn.
"Of course they are."

He traced a finger across the old briefing table, where Biff once mapped Phase Lines like gospel. His voice dropped into something… rehearsed.

"Doctrine needs voice, not truth. Continuity needs certainty, not accuracy."

He checked his reflection in the black glass.

He didn't flinch.

The reminder pinged in the corner of the node display — his scheduled biometric sync, the monthly infusion he couldn't refuse. Transhuman compliance dressed as "wellness protocol."

They called it resilience enhancement, or sometimes "executive readiness." But it was just dosage — and dosage meant belonging.

He hated needing it. He hated more the thought of losing it. Outcasts who resisted were cut out of the fold entirely, their clearances revoked, their careers ended in silence. He would not be one of them.

A new directive pulsed into the central node:
DOCTRINAL SEAT: UNFILLED. SUCCESSOR INPUT: PENDING.

Tanner's hand hovered above the interface.

Not to mourn.

To compose.

A new pattern. His.

He smiled, thin and quiet.

"He held the line too long.
Now it's my turn to redraw it."

Scene — Red's Postscript

While Tanner bent his reflection into the fold, Lou bent over Red's old notebook by lantern light.

Lou read her message to Red.

She sat cross-legged by the dying lantern, Red's old notebook open in her lap. One page was marked with a worn crimson thread. At the bottom, a handwritten message in his unmistakable ink:

"They're not afraid of rebellion anymore, Lou.
They're afraid someone might remember how sacred doubt used to be."

She read it again.

Word for word.

Then aloud — to herself, or to whatever Watcher might still be listening.

Qom.
The city Helix couldn't crack.

The only node on the penetration map where the lattice failed to sync with belief.

Not because it was pure. But because it was *plural* — too many sacred counter-rhythms to fold into one signal.

The lattice didn't fragment it.
It fragmented the lattice.

She wrote fast, margin crowded. Not all sacred systems could be penetrated.

Qom's internal complexity, theological pluralism, or resistance to external codification may have created a form of *resonance noise* — preventing Helix from "locking" its coherence loops.

Perhaps Qom holds a surviving pre-Helix epistemology — a counter-script, a doctrinal escape hatch, or even a heretical lineage that refused computational sanctification.

Qom wasn't a firewall. It was a dissonant chord — too rich, too unresolved to be tuned. And that made it dangerous. If even one tradition could resist algorithmic sanctification… then coherence wasn't inevitable. It was a choice.

Chapter 49 Close — Lou's Reflection

"They thought Qom was a firewall. It wasn't. It was noise they couldn't smooth — dissonance too dense to be sanctified. That's why it mattered. The lattice didn't break belief there. It borrowed it everywhere else.

Red's words still burned: they're not afraid of rebellion anymore. They're afraid someone might remember how sacred doubt used to be.

That's the fracture — not purity, but Narrative Friction. When incompatible myths refuse to collapse, the field stutters. Every chant out of sync, every prayer out of rhythm, every silence held too long — each one a refusal the lattice can't weaponize.

But I can't lose sight of what this means. It isn't about proving one city stood apart. It's about the Chamber — the machine built to turn faith into cadence, cadence into compliance, compliance into doctrine. The most effective panopticon doesn't crush belief. It sanctifies it, until survcillance feels like devotion.

That's why we move. Not to venerate Qom. Not to catalogue anomalies. To shut the Chamber down before it writes every doubt into dogma.

Because if Helix stabilizes first, it won't just command obedience. It will canonize it. And doubt — the last sacred thing left — will disappear."

Go Move — 捻り手 // Nejirite — The Twisted Hand — Red (Echo)

White plays in a sector long stabilized —
a point the Generals had walked past for a hundred moves.

But the stone isn't theirs.
No doctrinal stamp.
No rhythm they can read.

Zhen pauses mid-read.
Liu's hand hesitates above the bowl.

It isn't invasion.
It isn't rescue.
It's a question disguised as settled truth.

In worldview war, no move is truly new.
But this one — off-rhythm, unreadable — disturbs the lattice's certainty.

What they hear is not defiance.
It is refusal to resolve.

And in that silence, the board stops playing them —
and starts listening to him.

Chapter 50 — Shadows of the Genesis Chamber

Tagline — "Some routes weren't built for transport. They were built to forget what passed through." — *JR*

Epigraph c "The chamber doesn't store power. It reflects it — signal, memory, and what we choose to believe about both."

— *Ziggurat Archive*

Scene — The Route Without Reflection
Location — Edge-node relay site, Southern Albania

Ledger arranged passage via Pinot's Cold War route — repurposed customs truck, blind manifest

Ledger didn't ask questions. He just handed Lou the folded map and said,
"Don't open it near glass."

The route wasn't digital. JR had unearthed it from a 1986 binder marked *European Agricultural Contingencies – EAC Redundancies.*
Buried in an old USDA depot, of all places.
Handwritten margin notes in Cyrillic led to an abandoned 200-year-old Cold War corridor — a former customs trade track that once ran signal tap tests through the Balkans.

"You're riding blind," JR had said, exhaling smoke toward the ceiling fan.
"But the corridor's real. And still warm."

They rode quiet past the old border stones. One turn too far, and they'd have ended up inside a Helix-controlled gas relay station. But JR's notes were good. Precise. Dated, but only if you thought time was linear.

Beat en route:

Cal adjusted his earpiece. "Tell me again how JR found this path?"
Lou: "He pulled a declassified logistics manifest from a box labeled *turnips and fission yeast.*"
Cal: "Of course he did."

Cal muttered, "Next time, maybe JR can find us a route that doesn't smell like brake fluid and regret."

Ledger's customs truck cleared the last rural checkpoint at dusk; Pinot took the back road along the river. JR's pencil map matched the mile markers—no mirrors, no pings.

Scene — Inside the Relay Shell

She was already there.
Kneeling by the far coil bank, dragging a signal stylus across the cracked concrete.
Hair wild, jacket scorched, breathing in sync with the relay pulse.
"They told me to forget the lattice."
She didn't look up. "But I was part of its dreaming."

Then Salkin's voice:

"Kaya Wren," he said gently.
"You remember me?"

Her hair was fried at the ends — static-charged, matted. The jacket was Helix issue, decades old, patched in odd places. The hum of the relay coils echoed her pulse.

"They told me to forget the early lattice," she said without turning. "But the code still remembers me."

Salkin stopped mid-step. "Kaya."

Cal furrowed his brow. "You know her?"

Salkin's voice was low, even. "Kaya Wren. Signal lattice engineer. Helix's coherence seed team. She survived the reversal event at Node 0-Delta — but not unscathed."

Cal leaned in. "Memory burn?"

"Partial," Salkin said. "The kind that blurs truth into symbol. But the fragments? They're real. She was there when the Chamber's signal self-stabilized for the first time."

"You want a schematic?" she asked. "Or the warning they buried with it?"

Lou stepped forward. "Both."

Kaya finally turned. Her eyes shimmered — not from light, but from stored field residue.

Salkin moved closer. "Can she travel?"

Kaya answered before Lou could. "I'm unstable, not broken. And the chamber's pulling."

Lou met Cal's eyes. "Then we bring her in."

A sharp knock echoed from the outer corridor. Pinot.

He opened the door just wide enough to speak. "Time's up. TNI node just pinged a dead relay. We've got 22 minutes before they check in."

Ledger's voice followed on comms. "Transport's waiting. One truck, one route. No digital manifests. This is your only window."

Cal nodded. "Then we move."

Salkin tossed Kaya an insulated field wrap. "You'll ride warm. Enough."

She didn't flinch. "Let's go."

Transitory Cut — Northern Transit Node, En Route to Svalbard

Kaya didn't sleep the whole ride north.

She sat wedged between calibration crates and old field blankets in the back of the transport, fingers twitching as if still sketching code into frost. Salkin monitored her vitals — not because she was unstable, but because the field echoes hadn't let go of her yet.

Cal kept his eyes on the route, hands loose on the wheel. Lou sat beside him, reviewing the relay map JR had annotated with a red marker: "NODE-BLIND. DO NOT PING."

"Are we sure she's safe?" Cal asked quietly.

"No," Lou replied. "But she's aligned."

Behind them, Kaya spoke up without prompting. "You can't track what already knows its way home."

They reached the airfield near Trondheim at dawn. Ledger had arranged a cold-clearance jump — no manifest, no flight plan, no comms.

Two hours later, the plane dropped below radar and angled toward Svalbard.

Kaya stared out the small window the whole flight. When they touched down, she whispered one word:

"Return."

As the relay site receded into Balkan mist, Kaya closed her eyes —
and whispered, "The chamber's humming. Even from here."

Fade to snow...

Scene — Ice Truck, JR's Route

The truck was silent save for the steady growl of its treads. Outside,
nothing but snow and ghost lights.

Inside, Kaya sat bundled near the heater duct. Her hands still
twitched with pulse residue.

Jack turned to Cal. "Ledger really routed this?"

Cal smirked. "JR found it. Ledger paid for it. And Pinot drives like a
man who's been to hell and doesn't need directions."

Jack checked the map overlay. "We're nowhere. Perfect."

Lou, half-asleep in the corner, opened one eye. "We're not nowhere.
We're on a Cold War customs route JR pulled out of a box labeled
'Turnips and Fission Yeast.'"

Kaya exhaled a static breath. "You found the NATO Redundancy
corridor. It loops under four relay zones. That's how we got the lattice to
echo."

They all paused.

Cal, flat: "You could've told us *before* we crossed the Bosnian fault
seam."

Kaya smiled. "I forgot."

Scene — En Route: Ground Transport through Arctic Route, 2 hours before Svalbard Arrival

A tracked vehicle crawled across the frozen flats. Treads chewed
snow in silence. No headlights — just dim pulses from a roof relay,
barely visible in the swirling dark.

Inside, the cabin reeked of heater fluid and static.

Kaya sat wrapped in two thermal blankets near the rear duct, eyes
half-closed, lips silently mouthing sequences — code or memory, it
wasn't clear.

Jack adjusted the resonance scanner. "Her pulse is syncing to the route signature."

Cal didn't look up. "Means the Chamber's awake. It's pulling her."

Jack turned his head. "You trust this intel from Ledger?"

Cal nodded, still driving. "If Eitan gave the nod, it's clean. Ledger moves money. JR moves silence. Pinot drives ghosts."

A thump rattled the undercarriage — frozen drift, or something deeper.

Kaya stirred. "You're both thinking too loud."

Jack blinked. "She's not wrong."

She sat up slowly, hand to her temple. "The Chamber's not a place. It's a convergence. It's remembering us before we arrive."

Cal muttered, "That's comforting."

Jack tapped the side display. "This corridor loops through five signal paths. Same field math we saw at Field 13A."

Cal's jaw tightened. "That artifact *broke* six of our guys."

Jack glanced at Kaya. "She didn't break. She bent."

Kaya whispered, "Only because the field wasn't finished. The prototype paused. The Chamber won't."

They drove in silence for a long stretch. Then Lou's voice crackled softly from the rear seat.

"If this thing speaks in signal echoes, we'd better know which one of us is the original."

Jack turned halfway. "You volunteering?"

Lou half-smiled. "Not yet. But the FT-1 Möbius ring in my coat pocket is vibrating. That's a bad sign."

Kaya's eyes fluttered. "Or it means you're the fail-safe."

Kaya wasn't some lab tech. Her badge still read *Dr. Kaya Wren, PhD, PE, CEng, FIMechE, QSE*. A survivor of the first Chamber ignition — and the only engineer who'd ever seen its inner lattice and lived. She clutched a notebook full of resonance glyphs she claimed not to understand. Lou knew better.

Two hops later—Balkan relay to a cold-clearance lift near Trondheim—Pinot's ice truck took the last leg north. No manifests. No receipts. Only treads in snow.

Scene — Svalbard Periphery — Access Tunnel D-7

Lou's boots crunched on ice-crusted gravel as she descended deeper into the dim corridor. The air was sterile, but not empty. Every few seconds, a pulse — low, harmonic, non-acoustic — passed through her spine like an unspoken warning.

Cal moved ahead, flashlight sweeping through stalactites of frost. He glanced back. "You feel that?"

"It's not a hum. It's a memory," she murmured.

They reached the base of a sealed door. Cold-etched steel bore the remnants of old Continuity Alliance and Norwegian research logos — spray-painted over, years ago, with the mark of something more obscure. Three spirals. Entangled.

"The Seal of Echo Initiate," Lou muttered. She'd seen it once — a redacted slide buried in a Helix side-brief. "They were testing signal ethics. Then they buried the whole thing."

Cal pulled a key from around his neck. Not a digital key — a literal one. Old school. Insert. Turn. Mechanical.

The door hissed open.

Inside: the Genesis Chamber's outer vestibule. A sarcophagus of ice encased the chamber wall, studded with resonance sensors. Data flickered along analog-tactile displays — as if the system had been running all along, waiting.

Jack's voice crackled again: "That's what we needed. You're the match signature."

Lou's eyes narrowed. "Then let's make it count."

Cal looked over at her. "You okay?"

Lou stammered. "Ask me when we leave."

The FT-1 Möbius ring in her pocket buzzed — faint, warm, unmistakable.

Cal examined the sensor rig. "This gear predates EchoTech. It's not Helix. This was the prototype."

Lou touched a node — instantly, the chamber responded. Light spirals cascaded across the surface, syncing to her pulse.

Jack, on comms again: "We're driving into a test site for a signal war. And we're the guinea pigs."

Cal cracked a half-smile. "Better us than Biff."

Pinot's voice came over the internal relay. "Your stray held steady the whole ride. Still humming. Says she's ready — if it still wants her."

Lou glanced at Cal. They'd both read her old brief: Dr. Kaya Wren, PhD, PE, CEng, FIMechE, survivor of the *Echo Initiate* trials. Her designs had built half the prototype resonance ring — and her pulse was burned into the chamber's early logs. If anyone could talk to the outer vestibule, it was her.

Kaya stepped forward from the shadows, her gloved hand brushing frost from the rusted release lever. With a quiet hiss, the inner vestibule door cracked open. She moved slower now, but her eyes were sharper — focused.

The seals gave way with a sigh of stale air.

Her fingers twitched as she passed the main node. She stopped, turned to Lou.
"I think it remembers me."

Lou whispered. "Let's hope it still listens."

Kaya turned back toward the console. "Because we're out of lies."

Scene — Flashback — Tesserae Defense Core, Monterey

A bright California sun burned through fog over the quad. Lou, still recovering from a failed op in the Baltic, limped her way across the brick path toward a seminar room. At her side: Dr. Eliza "Liz" Santori, aka StepDoc.

Liz, high-energy and annoyingly cheerful, was counting her steps aloud. "7,896. You owe me tacos if I crack 10k before lunch."

"You'd crack the Strategic Spire if they made a pedometer part of the Alliance," Lou muttered.

"Do I have to remind you that I was cleared at Echo Linguistics Institute," Liz replied with a smirk.

Ah, yes – the Echo Linguistics Institute (ELI), Founded post-Dissolution, ELI replaced legacy language training programs with a resonance-based decoding curriculum.
Specializes in dialects, dead-signal forensics, and substrate-linguistic interference patterns.

"ELI trained your tongue, not your ears. That's why your field reports sound like they were written by a bureaucrat with a translation app."

"I know. You told every gate guard between here and Vandenberg."

"Twice."

Liz stopped, yanked open her messenger bag, and pulled out a roll of mission clearance forms.

"You brought logistics plans to a philosophy lecture?"

"I double as your unofficial war logistics fairy. And when Jack breaks another rib—again—you'll thank me for having morphine stashed in a protein bar wrapper."

Jack was still grounded in Tbilisi after the Signal Drift event — not that it stopped Liz from name-dropping him every third sentence.

Lou sighed. "Tacos. Morphine. Unapproved war theory. This lecture's gonna get us both audited."

Scene — Back to Present — Genesis Chamber

Lou opened the panel. The same pulsing thread pattern from Kosovo appeared. But now, it responded to her breath.

Cal looked stricken. "This chamber wasn't designed to hold anything. It's a transmitter. Story-form."

Lou nodded. "It broadcasts coherence — or unravels it."

Behind them, a second signature lit up: Jack's.

"I brought you both here for a reason," he said. "You're the only two who touched Field Artifact 13A and lived. That thing was never supposed to surface. But it did. And Sabine knew."

Cal's face hardened. "She's been building her empire on that signal."

Lou stepped into the center of the chamber. "Then we overwrite it. We turn the shadow back into light."

Scene — Elsewhere — The Watchers Shift

Above the aurora-bleached sky of Svalbard, the Five Watchers stirred — not gods, not myths, but quantum signatures of divergent force. Each watched a different quadrant:
One aligned to resonance
One to decay
One to time-loop compression
One to human will
And one... to betrayal

They whispered not in sound, but in probability shifts.

And one — the one aligned to will — nudged a frozen particle in the chamber below.
In ancient times, they might have called her Vire.

Vire didn't play by rules — she cracked them open to see what bled. Aligned to chaos, yes. But not without aim.
She understood: every global doctrine relied on brittle coherence — and brittle coherence makes a tempting target.

Hell-bent on disrupting false alignment, Vire operated from the old volcano in Iceland — Þríhnúkagígur — where the crust of the Earth still trembled from forgotten signals.
Þríhnúkagígur — "Three Peaks Crater" — was the only place on Earth where one could descend into a real magma chamber, emptied without collapse.
She chose it for a reason. *The world's seams were thinnest there.*

"She'd ossified, yes — as all Watchers do with time. But the magma in her marrow still remembered how to burn."

Through narrow descent paths and buried convergence nodes — in Tehran, Kyiv, Jakarta, La Paz — she moved undetected.
Not through speed. Through intention.

She inverted a trade pact in the Caspian corridor — triggering a cascade of mismatched signal harmonics that rewrote the diplomatic sequence.
By the time the treaty's ink dried, five governments were doubting their own authorship.

She redirected a classified Continuity Alliance readiness exercise off the Åland coast - Exercise Valkyr Lattice— using only a misaligned training feed and a mimicked emotional signature.

The fleet fired on phantom vessels. The press called it a radar ghost.
It wasn't.

She planted a single false phrase in a joint communique between
East African defense ministers — just one phrase.
It looped in translation, never settling.
Weeks later, the alliance collapsed over 'linguistic misinterpretation.'
No one ever found the original text.

And now — at the edge of the Genesis Chamber's pulse — it was
her nudge that altered the rhythm.
Not to destroy.
But to make space for what couldn't be modeled.

Scene — Elsewhere Still — Eitan's Quiet Return

In a candle-lit safehouse carved into the side of an old stone
monastery in the Albanian Alps, Eitan adjusted his gloves with trembling
hands. The Parkinson's was worse since D.C. — worse since the rogue
SEALs pulled him out under blackout after the Helix spike nearly fried
his nervous system. Since then he'd been shuffled through half a dozen
shadow routes — Virginia to Iceland, Zurich to Vienna, even a false
manifest through Tallinn — and the cold relay perimeter at Thule, where
he pushed harder than his body could stand — each one marked by
couriers and smuggled vials logged as horse supplements. StepDoc's
regimen held him steadier than anyone guessed, enough to keep him
moving, enough to keep him dangerous.

He now used a frequency-adapted stylus, barely able to press the
command entries into the slate.

One command went to Ledger — a silent authorization to move
Lou's team using a protected account formerly tied to a Continuity
Alliance training grant.

Another moved through Maud's buried channel in the Pyrenees —
untouched, unburned, still clean after three years. His fingers lingered a
moment on the address, tracing the first three resonance glyphs as if they
were something older than code.

A third routed a quantum-locked briefing packet to the team.
Final note: "Ensure Lou sees only the core pattern. Filter the rest. Her
divergence is the signal."

He wasn't ready for Lou to carry it all. But Maud's influence was still
there, a quiet shadow in Lou's cadence — the reminder that divergence
didn't have to be lonely.

Some patterns skip a generation, he thought, and smiled without meaning to.

He closed the tablet. Outside, a bell tolled faintly.
He exhaled. The stylus pulsed once. The signal moved.

He closed the tablet. Outside, a bell tolled faintly.
The stylus pulsed once in his hand, trembling but steady enough.
"Every ledger I send buys them minutes," he whispered into the cold stone.
Minutes to reach the Chamber before it closed.
Delay was survival. And survival was the only way to shut it down.

Scene — The Chamber's Rhythm

Lou's steps synced to the chamber's pulse. Jack's voice came over one last time:

"You ever wonder who's booking our flights? We haven't paid for a hotel in five countries."

Lou smirked. "Ghost accounts. Ghost signals. Welcome to Team Mystery Budget."

She added, "You think Sabine has a per diem?"

Jack's voice crackled: "She is the per diem."

Scene — Elsewhere — Tanner Returns Quietly
Location — Antechamber E, Geneva Trust Node

Tanner never left. He simply waited where systems forget to look — in the margins of reorganization briefings, in the footnotes of signal recovery initiatives, in the press-release gaps between doctrine collapse and doctrine reissue.

Now he stood before a repainted wall, newly etched with the emblem of the Continuity Directorate — sleeker than before, but unchanged in its purpose. His badge bore no name. Just a QR resonance glyph and the outline of a fractal.

A tech handed him a black tablet.
"No passwords. Just your retina."
Tanner scanned in.
The screen flickered once, then loaded a file labeled "Genesis Continuity — Tier Delta Override."

In a quiet mountain office half a continent away, Eitan closed his eyes.

He had felt the activation. The chamber's pulse was unmistakable, but so was the faint signature braided through it — the one he'd known long before Maud was born.

This wasn't about one man reentering the field.
It was about a system recovering its old skin — silently, under a new name.

"The transformation isn't loud," Eitan had once told Lou.

"It mimics silence. Then fills it."

He opened the next packet. Counter-signature: Vire.
Status: Drift-Aware. Ready.
He whispered to no one,
"Then the chamber is listening. And so is she."

Not just the Watcher in Iceland.

Not just Vire. Lou — carrying the cadence she got from Maud, and Maud carrying the blood she got from him.

Three lines braided into one signal. Family, even if Lou didn't know it yet.

Chapter 50 Close — Lou's Reflection

"JR's route didn't just hide us. It refused reflection. A corridor built to pass through and leave nothing for the lattice to rehearse. That's not logistics. That's doctrine.

Kaya's hands still shake like tuned forks, but the Chamber remembered her before we crossed the threshold. It remembered me the moment the vestibule matched my breath. This isn't a vault holding power. It's a transmitter holding story. Broadcast in coldfields, sealed in spiral arrays, stabilized on quantum substrate. Hardware designed so belief can be impressed, not argued.

The day's events are suggestive of what doctrine calls *Pattern Anchoring*. The Chamber doesn't win with force; it wins by fixing one node so hard the rest of the world bends. Tonight I felt the anchor try to set—my pulse as the peg, Kaya's residue as the line. If we let it hold, the field writes us in as proof.

The closer we moved to Svalbard, the clearer the hum got—and the more brittle it felt. Too many echoes layered for clarity; the pattern started to crack under its own polish. That's our window, not a warning.

The Watcher nudge—call it chance if you like—bought us a breath between loops. Enough to see what matters: this route isn't an escape. It's an approach vector. Every mile has to get us to the core gate, cut the cryo-vectors, and break the reflection loop before Sabine hardens the field.

I keep repeating it so I don't forget why we're moving: the Chamber isn't myth. It's machine—coherence lattice, resonance gates, memory in cold storage. Shut it down or live inside its story.

Next move, we go where reflection can't follow. Become the presence they misremember. Off-ledger. Off-glass. Off-map.

Call it a Go lesson if you need one: don't win the count—remove the mirror. Then the board has to become honest again."

Go Move — 手抜き前室 // Tenuki Maeshitsu — The Tenuki Before the Chamber — General Liu

White leaves the local fight.
Not in flight — in refusal.

The tenuki shifts the battle off the expected capture.
No immediate gain.
But the shape across the whole board begins to warp.

In Go, this is timing over territory.
In coherence war, it's *Perception Debt* and *Narrative Friction* —
forcing the field to look one way while its alignment fractures
elsewhere.

Not retreat.
Not stalling.
Deliberate drift — a gap where action and belief fall out of sync.

The Chamber hums, but its rhythm slips.

"You don't beat the board," Liu's stone says.
"You make it remember something older than its design."

Far from Svalbard, Liu set down his stone —
a move already in motion long before they touched the Chamber's
door.

Chapter 51 — Ghost Protocol

**Scene —   Ghost Signal Skirmish — Alpine Relay Site
Location —** Southern Alps – Field Station Periphery
48 hours post-Chamber collapse

The sky didn't blink when the signal failed — it shuddered.

Cal hauled the operative across the snow, dragging him behind the jagged ribs of machinery jutting from the ridge. The modules weren't generators. Not really. Up close, he saw the telltale sheen of cold-atom reservoirs, conduits etched with resonance glyph mesh. A chamber spine — cut down, hidden under Alpine stone, but unmistakable.

The air itself buzzed with lattice static. Breath crystallized too quickly. His implants ticked like Geiger counters. This wasn't safe cover. This was a live coil, humming with Sabine's handprint.

"Jack!" he shouted into the comm. Nothing but static, warped like a voice caught underwater.

They'd called it Ghost Protocol. A myth, most said — a rumor that Sabine had buried a second chamber, a failsafe lattice if Genesis collapsed. No one thought she'd had the resources. No one thought she'd dare.

But she had.

Snow thrashed against the coils, evaporating midair. The hum rose, low and hungry.

This wasn't a relay station. It was a continuity engine — a doctrine imprint carved in hardware, awake and wanting.

The Ghost Protocol wasn't broadcasting doctrine anymore.

It was broadcasting need.

Location — Zurich Safehouse – Midnight

Rain tapped against the windows like memory trying to break in.

She hadn't planned to join them in Zurich. But after Eitan sent the Echo fragment — timestamped, embedded with her breath cadence — she knew the message wasn't strategic. It was personal.

Somewhere in the Alps, maybe farther, he was still alive enough to bend the lattice toward them. The fragment wasn't just memory. It was a proof of life, smuggled through signal, reminding her that the old man was still moving pieces on the board.

The breath pattern wasn't hers alone. Maud's was nested inside it — the same fractional hitch, like a skipped beat, that Lou had heard in the old recordings. She'd never asked why Eitan knew it so well. Maybe she didn't want the answer.

That hitch was more than memory. It was a hand on her shoulder from miles away, telling her this wasn't routine.

This wasn't a mission drop. It was a Φ vector — the kind of unsent signal that arrives when you're the only one left who can respond.

He hadn't said, *Go.*
He'd said, *Come back in through the signal.*

So she did.

Lou sat at the edge of the table, dismantling and reassembling a standard satellite uplink repeater — not because she needed to, but because muscle memory gave her mind space to breathe.

Jack paced, his limp more pronounced since Greenland. Cal stood at the far window, watching shadows shift in the alley below.

They'd all received the same alert:

Helix Substrate Fragment: Activation Confirmed — Vault Echo / Genesis Interface

Not a drill. Not a false flag.
The signal they buried had surfaced.

"This protocol was meant to be forgotten," Jack muttered, lighting a rare cigarette. "We agreed — if it reactivated, we disappear. No cleanup. No recovery. Ghost out."

He didn't need to say what they'd already seen in the Alps — Ghost Protocol wasn't rumor. It was hardware. A backup chamber, smaller but alive, buried where no one thought Sabine could build one.

Cal didn't turn from the window. "Then why haven't you?"

Jack didn't answer.

Lou set the uplink unit down, eyes locked on both men.
"We're not ghosts anymore. Helix isn't hiding in the dark — it's scripting in daylight. EchoTech doesn't just listen. It edits."

Cal finally looked at her. "So what do you suggest?"

Lou stood.
"We don't ghost out. We ghost in."

Location — Archive Node — Swiss Underground Facility

An old access shaft beneath the Zurich tram grid led them to a forgotten Helix site — the Archive Node was buried under the commuter line, sealed since Helix's recalibration sweep.

They broke into the old Helix control array just past 0300. Jack's old contacts had left them a door — analog cables, RF sniffers, voltage irregularities too primitive for Helix's predictive net.

The system was still running.

Inside, they found fragments: biometric ghosts, signal imprints, narrative scaffolds encoded in brainwave mimicry.

"Look at this," Cal said. "These aren't command logs. They're storylines. Script forks."

Jack wiped a thin layer of dust from a brass key panel. "This whole node... it wasn't surveillance. It was rehearsal."

And just like the Alpine coils, it proved something none of them wanted to admit: Ghost Protocol wasn't vapor. Sabine hadn't trusted one chamber. She'd scattered them, embedding fragments into forgotten nodes like this. Hardware, humming under old stone.

Jack opened the false panel behind the water heater. Inside, a rusted ammo crate labeled "Hydration Tabs – UN Issue" revealed three suppressed pistols, a coil of memory-wipe bandages, and a transdermal sync pulse wand.

A narrow slip of paper was taped to the lid, typed in Courier font:
"Cleared by proxy. Ledger routes confirmed. — Q.C."

Q.C. wasn't a person. It's a field signature — a signal artifact used by the *Quantum Couriers*, a resistance node near Ruckersville, Virginia that operates outside Helix substrate visibility. They specialize in nonlocal delivery of aid, weapon caches, encrypted intel, and myth-resistant memory artifacts. He thought of them as the mythos version of special logistics — ghost couriers who drop the impossible right before the collapse.

Jack once ran covert disinformation sweeps that *intercepted their existence* — and later refused to out them. Since then, Q.C. nodes have occasionally surfaced in Jack's blind spots — gear drops he never ordered, escapes made possible by doors that shouldn't have opened, safehouses pre-cleared without explanation. This ammo crate? One of those.

Jack doesn't control them.
He's been tolerated by them.

"Still think this was overkill?" he asked.

"Quantum Couriers," Cal muttered. "I thought they only moved memory."
Jack snapped the suppressor into place. "Sometimes memory needs a muzzle."

Cal loaded one without looking. "Only if we live."

He didn't say the rest.
That *if* was carrying weight now — not just for survival, but for something older. Cal wasn't here to win a war. He was here to end someone's role in it.

A name burned at the edge of recall. Not a target. A tether.

One of the Watchers was still visible in the field.
And Cal had no intention of letting him walk away.

Lou tapped into one file.

Onscreen: her.

Training session, 2011. Pre-simulation data overlays aligned to her breath, gait, neural latency.

And then it splintered.

Forked into two realities — one where she died in Kabul. One where she disappeared in Alaska.

Neither true.

"These aren't records," she whispered. "They're erasures."

Scene Intercut: Sabine – Observation Deck, Beijing

Sabine watched as the node's lights flickered alive. She already knew. "They're trying to recover Ghost Protocol," her assistant said.

Sabine didn't flinch. "They're not recovering it. They're walking into the spine I left behind."

"You want me to initiate Pulse Dissolve?"
She paused.
"No. Not yet. Let them touch it. Let them think they've stolen something real. Then we collapse the channel."

She turned back toward the window. Below her, Beijing shimmered like a city running outdated code. It reminded her of the Xinjiang collapse, when the census glitched and her father's name vanished from the rolls. Not dead. Not alive. Just gone. That was the lesson she carried forward: survival isn't measured in bodies. It's measured in records, and in who edits them. Mercy doesn't survive in ledgers. Only names that never get deleted do. And she had no intention of being erased. Better to erase first.

"Tanner was right about one thing," she murmured, almost to herself. "You don't stop systems like this with force. You let them reboot themselves into a trap — and then you overwrite the substrate."

A flicker on her screen: Continuity Alliance – Tier 4 Signal Drift Logged.
The Trust Cabal was already moving assets. Tanner had resurfaced. Repackaged. More useful now than Biff ever was.

"Shame about Langley," her aide offered.
Sabine smiled faintly. "Langley still believed in lines. Tanner understands slopes. He knows doctrine isn't about steps forward — it's about gradients no one notices until they're already falling."

She traced a spiral on the glass with her fingertip — soft, recursive.

"The war doesn't end doctrine. It subducts it. Like a fault line folding back into the crust — invisible, until the pressure breaks everything above it."

She let the thought hang.
Then:
"Prep Tier Delta. If they ghost in, we ghost them."

Back to Zurich Node

Alarms began to whine — not loud, but old, analog. Not system sirens, but tripwires left behind for anyone reckless enough to enter. Their time was short.

Jack handed Lou a small drive. "Extract fragments only. Nothing physical. Hardware's already compromised."

Cal nodded. "We walk out clean. No signatures."

Lou touched the console one last time. Her own face blinked back at her, overlaid with a line of text:

STATUS: Divergent Anchor
ECHO MATCH: Irregular
Narrative Validity: Disqualified

She smiled faintly. "Then let's write the one they can't erase."

They ghosted out.
Not erased.
Just… off the script.

Bridge Scene — Train to the Alps
Location — Transalpine Rail, Dawn

The rail car shuddered as it climbed into the switchbacks. Jack sat across from Lou, his leg stretched awkwardly in the narrow aisle, cigarette smoldering but unlit. Cal had the window seat, eyes fixed on the ridge lines.

Lou broke the silence first. "We need to be clear about what we're fighting."

Jack exhaled through his nose. "Helix? Sabine?"

"No," Lou said. "The grid."

Cal tapped the glass, where the reflection of the rising sun fractured against the mountains. "Think of it like this," he said. "Every memory leaves a pattern. Doesn't matter if it's grief, joy, fear—whatever. Helix learned how to catch those patterns, store them, and re-broadcast them."

Lou leaned forward. "One person's memory becomes everyone's memory. That's how doctrine works. Not persuasion. Not propaganda. Just… overwrite. If you can force enough people to see the same thing, believe the same thing, the argument's already over. Reality's locked."

Jack flicked the ash from his cigarette. "So long as the grid hums, they win."

Cal nodded. "Which is why they built the mirror stations. Zurich was about survival — Sabine's backup chamber. But Echo nodes?" He shook his head. "That's the broadcast arm. They bounce coherence like satellites, until the whole planet's inside one shared dream."

Lou's voice was quiet. "The Signal-opticon."

Jack frowned. "The what?"

"A panopticon runs on eyes," she said. "One guard watching a thousand prisoners. Doesn't matter if he sees them — only that they think he does. But this isn't about watching. It's about feeding. Echo-3 isn't surveillance. It's transmission. You don't have to guard the prisoners if you can make them dream the same dream."

Cal's jaw tightened. "So we knock out the grid. Break the mirrors. No shared dream, no lattice control."

Lou let her gaze drift to the mountains sliding past the glass. "Which means our next stop isn't about retrieval. It's about blackout."

Jack muttered, almost to himself, "Funny thing about mirrors. Sometimes they crack before they break."

The train curved into shadow, plunging them briefly into silence.

Chapter 51 Close — Lou's Reflection

"They called it Ghost Protocol, but it was never about ghosts. It was about echoes. Fragments rehearsed until the copy outlived the original. That's Echo Dominance — repeat something long enough, and the field stops caring if it was ever true.

Zurich wasn't surveillance. It was rehearsal. A place to practice forgetting until forgetting felt normal. Every fragment I saw down there was proof: this war doesn't just erase us. It teaches us to erase ourselves.

But turbulence isn't error. Drift isn't weakness. It's what proves the copy never fully takes. That's the crack. And if we can still feel the fracture, we can still zag.

Ghost Protocol tried to make us shadows of ourselves. But the Chamber is more than shadow. It's teeth. Hardware tuned to coherence, memory, belief. The kind of machine that doesn't just fight wars — it scripts what a war even is.

That's why every reflection matters. Every refusal. Every fracture. Because the only way to fight a system built on echoes is to become the one thing it can't overwrite: signal it can't absorb.

Go Move — 静かに運ぶ石 // Shizuka ni Hakobu Ishi — The Stone Carried Quietly — General Zhen

Some stones aren't played to be seen.
They're carried — through shadow corridors, forgotten routes — to the place the board stopped watching.

Not a strike.
Not a bluff.
A *Vector Doctrine* of concealment: bypass the lattice by never entering it.

The ghost move doesn't shift shape by force.
It preserves it — guarding what can't be rebuilt if exposed.

No signature.
No ko threat.
Just a stone held in silence until the board forgets it was ever moving.

And when it's set down, it's already home.

From far beyond the Alps, Zhen's hand moved in reply — not to strike, but to close the air around it.

Chapter 52 — Echoes To Zero

Scene —   Signal Descent – Grid Echo-3 Awakens
Location — Northern Alps – Abandoned Research Grid Echo-3

The mountains swallowed sound.

They'd left Zurich at dawn. No comms, no convoy — just a Courier-tagged rail token and a climb on foot from the alpine switchback. Jack said nothing when the crate was waiting. Cal just nodded. Someone still wanted them in this fight.

Lou adjusted the interface lens over her left eye and stared down the sheer ravine. Below them: one of the Helix satellite mirror stations — Echo-3 — long thought dismantled. But Jack had found a live pulse in the spectrum. Ghost energy. Something still hummed.

"Pulse reads at 1.33 Hz," Cal said quietly, examining the device's edge. "That's fascia bandwidth."

Jack raised an eyebrow. "Biofeedback?"

"Worse," Lou answered. "Residual feedback from the failed Genesis prototype."

Inside, the grid station was gutted — melted silicon, smashed control panels, bloodless ruins of a story deleted in haste. But beneath the rubble, they found a harmonic node still active — projecting a synthetic hum that looped one human phrase:

"Narrative cannot stabilize. Seek Zero."

Lou touched the coil. It pulsed back — not as tech, but as recognition. Her fascia aligned for a moment, just long enough to glimpse the shape of a hidden layer — a shadow corridor that bled quantum states into narrative shells.

"What is this?" Jack asked.

Cal didn't answer. Lou did. "It's what Helix feared. Not death. Not chaos. But reset. A zero state where story can't be controlled."

But they weren't the only ones watching.

Scene Shift — Internal Vault — EchoTech Archive Node

Ray had warned them once about this. The real Genesis design wasn't a weapon — it was a subtractive vector. Not to destroy the narrative, but to bring it to stillness. To unwrite false pathways by returning the system to zero coherence — where only true resonance could rebuild.

Lou whispered to the node: "Show me the anchor point."

A map blinked into view. Not geographical. Not historical. Somatic.

Her own fascia pathway — encoded in breath, injury, emotion — was the fail-open key.

"It has to be me," she said.

Somewhere in the Alps, a relay printer Eitan had repurposed would log the same pulse a heartbeat late—a borrowed minute she didn't know she'd been given.

Cal moved closer. "Because you've never been fully inside their system."

Jack frowned. "Or because you've always carried the break."

Gear Drop – Courier Pouch, Alpine Trailhead

They found it stuffed in an old goat shed — a sealed pouch bearing a faded Alliance group patch and a smiley-face sticker.

Inside:

Analog pulse disruptor, Cold War vintage

Grease-laminated note: "If it buzzes, bite it. —Sylvester"

EM-slip rounds hand-packed by Wechsler with an extra note: "Tell Maud to quit stealing my toolkit."

Tucked into the seam: a blank card punched with three offset holes. Eitan's quiet signature. He was still buying them time.

Lou smiled. "They didn't send themselves. But they sent us teeth."

None of them said it aloud, but they all knew — the courier routes only held because Eitan still signed the ledgers in shadows. His hand was faint now, but the grid still twitched when he moved.

Second drop in 48 hours. The covert resistance logistics network that operates outside the Helix substrate, Q.C. was tracking them in real time — or tracking the Chamber. Cal suspects Ledger funds the logistics but doesn't control them.

Liz stayed behind in Zurich. Someone had to seed the exit trails.

Sylvester – Final Node, Charlottesville Periphery

North of Charlottesville, beyond the wine trail, a cedar-lined barn waited the way old listening posts do — quiet, stubborn, patient. Sylvester kept no phone, no signal, and no regrets — just crates stenciled in fake Latin and vintages of contraband the Trust Grid couldn't map.

He didn't ask who needed the gear. Lou's people never gave names. But he knew the sound of a war about to start — you could feel it in the knees before you saw it on the horizon.

Tonight, the list was short and specific: two pulse disruptors, a satchel of mesh-trigger grenades, and a weathered case labeled *AEON 3: DO NOT SCAN*.
He rolled the latch shut, slid the case into the shadow of the loading bay, and let the barn settle back into stillness.

Some say he's still out there, tuning disruptors between batches of blackberry mead, listening for the faint hum of lattice drift.
Not retired. Just waiting for the call.
And when it came, it meant the Chamber run was already in motion.

Scene Shift — Sabine's Office — Beijing

Sabine viewed the same map, from another channel — a Helix backdoor built years ago, meant to allow observation, not influence. But the channel was humming too loud tonight. Resonance backdraft. Someone else had pulsed through it recently. Maybe hours ago.

On the side console, a quantum uplink flickered with residual coherence bleed — faint, but unmistakable. The kind of trace signature left by Watcher-class transit.

Solas had passed through. Or was still nearby.

Outside the window, the eastern edge of Beijing met the sea like a half-forgotten memory — fog curling over the Bohai Gulf, the silhouette of decommissioned fishing towers leaning into the tide like exhausted ghosts. The city's lights didn't reach this far. Just industrial dark and salt wind.

At the base of one tower, far below, a figure stood facing the horizon. Unmoving. Umbrella in hand. No comms. No uplink trace. But

Sabine felt the resonance anyway — faint, irregular. Like a heartbeat out of phase.

A Divergent.

Or bait.

"She's seeking zero," one analyst said.

Sabine smiled, but it didn't reach her eyes.

"No. She *is* zero."

She didn't look at him again.

A small click sounded — not from her, but from the desk.

The assistant blinked. His comm badge hissed. A thin pulse of light blinked once, then—

Silence.

His body stilled, not fallen — frozen mid-thought. No scream. No collapse. Just a quiet override of neural coherence. A full-body sync kill.

Then the uplink pulsed once more.

Not outward. Not inward. Just *logged.*

A signal echo, sent… somewhere.

Sabine didn't flinch. "Protocol Seven," she said calmly. "No echoes. No trace."

Another aide, already moving, dragged the now-silent figure behind the curtain partition. The body would be tagged as a neural sync anomaly — the kind no analyst survives.

He half-turned toward a colleague, muttering, "God help us if she hits negative one—"

What Sabine didn't see was that someone else was already nudging the counter down. Not Vire. Not Lou. Eitan. She'd never believed him finished — only sidelined. And now, from some cold monastery stone, his trembling stylus leaked minutes into the field. He couldn't shut the Chamber. But he could slow it. And sometimes delay was the sharpest weapon left.

Another assistant glanced sideways. "Sounds like someone's off the script."

"Anyone else want to narrate aloud?" Sabine asked, her voice clipped glass.

The room stayed silent.

Except for the uplink, which pulsed one final time… and then went dark.

Outside, the lone figure beneath the tower had vanished.

Only the umbrella remained — still open, still upright — anchored in sand that now vibrated faintly.

Back at Grid Echo-3

Outside, the storm was building — not of weather, but signal. Interference climbed. Their comms began to jam. But Lou's body held steady. The chamber had imprinted her, and now her heartbeat was a metronome against the noise.

Jack watched her. "She's the only one who can walk through this and not shatter."

The path toward zero wasn't forward. It was inward.

And she had just begun the descent.

"They thought stillness was surrender. They forgot that silence can scream."

Monterey Intercept — The Archive They Buried

Inside, they'd scouted a now-defunct archive node — buried behind stacks of forgotten war game protocols and three souvenir mugs from the base gift shop. The goal wasn't data. It was doctrine.

"You mean we broke into a secure Navy facility just to steal outdated doctrine?"

"No," Liz had said, tossing Lou a portable drive. "We broke in to prove what they forgot: Doctrine doesn't fail from lack of power. It fails from loss of imagination."

Even now, Lou could hear her voice in her head.

"Also," Liz had added with a wink, "someone needed to remind these fools how to walk through fire with a good pedometer."

Meanwhile — Rumi's Journal – Recovered Entry Fragment

"To walk the zero path is not to vanish. It is to carry memory beyond shape.
Eitan called it the ache of truth — what remains when noise falls silent.
In stillness, we remember.
In silence, we reweave."

Lou reread the line, tucked inside a sealed envelope Jack had passed her an hour earlier. She knew the handwriting.

Rumi. Or, was it Ray?
The old yogi who once trained both her and Eitan in the forgotten art of coherence sensing.

"You were right, old man," she whispered. "Stillness is the real shape."

Slack Thread — Whisper Phase

They used to joke about it — Slack as the war college they never had.

Back in 2134, Lou was still a field analyst and Ray hadn't yet burned his bridges. They weren't rebels yet, just frustrated strategists building clandestine threads in between deployments and doctrine design cycles. Slack channels named after jazz modes. Folders of files no one dared forward. A private space to ask the real question:

"What if everything they taught us about war is an echo of the wrong century?"

One night, after a classified design session gone sideways at the Strategic Pattern Lab — the think tank built from the ruins of old war colleges — Lou typed something she never forgot:

"We're not looking at an enemy anymore. We're looking at a medium. A substrate. If we don't learn to feel it, we lose."

Jonathan Zehn had chimed in with a meme — Newton riding a tank through a cloud of fog. That one stayed in her files.

He'd muttered how sad it was that the last remnants of SAMS and the defunct Halberd Doctrine School had merged into what they called the Halberd Pattern Corps — an Army initiative that tried, and largely failed, to evolve military thinking beyond the still-in-use IPB and kill-chain doctrine. They taught pattern fluency, emergent system mapping, and nonlinear feedback loops. But most of their insights were dismissed as *"too abstract for command."*

They weren't trying to win a doctrinal war.
They were trying to outpace the collapse they could feel coming.
Not doctrinally. Viscerally.

Some nights, Lou still felt the hum of those old channels.

Silent Reflection – Maud Llewellyn Scott
It's an Unspoken Warning — and a Mother's Will.

Lou closed her eyes. For just a moment, she saw Maud — not as a
daughter, but as a tether.
Hidden under the name Valentine.
Curious. Brilliant. Already slipping past the edges of safe signal.

"Tell Maud not to look too closely," she'd told Wechsler once.
His reply: "Then you probably shouldn't have left her a chamber
schematic in her calculus notebook."

Somewhere — hundreds of miles away — a girl named Valentine
paused mid-sentence, her pen hovering over the edge of a page she didn't
remember starting.
The coffee beside her had gone cold.
She had no reason to shiver.
But she did.

Lou breathed in the cold air. The sound of it carried her back — not
to the Chamber, but to a smaller room, a thinner voice. Her
grandmother, humming an old air from the coast, the one they used to
call *the Lullaby* before anyone knew what it really was. Lou hadn't heard it
in decades, but in her mind it was as clear as frost on glass.

We do this so she doesn't have to.
Or maybe… because one day, she'll have to finish it.

(Lou, under her breath — almost prayerlike)
"Cof yw ei hedyn."
(Memory is her seed.)

Scene —   Outer Periphery – 43 Minutes Before Descent
Location — Greenland Ice Sheet – Vault Echo Sector

The glider was silent. No fuel, no lights, just carbon-fold wings
catching the thermal ghost trails of the upper stratosphere.

Lou crouched by the hatch, her breath slow behind the thin veil of
her coherence-dampening mask. The suits were slate-black, threaded with

resonance-drift mesh — not armored, not warm, but forgettable. That was the point.

Cal leaned close, checking the resonance glyph-encoded descent map on the inside of his wristband. "Terrain-following still holding. JR said the vault used to hum on odd days."

Jack smirked. "What if it's an even day?"

"Then we vaporize stylishly," Lou muttered, tightening her grip on the glide cord. "Just hope the Chamber likes our vibes."

The bay door hissed. Below, the ice sheet shimmered — not with reflection, but with interference. The vault's outer shell pulsed faintly in the distance like a memory misfiled in the snow.

Cal gestured. "Drop in ten. Follow the null thread until the echo spike. No radio, no light. If you drift, stay cold. The lattice tracks warmth."

"Charming," Jack said. "What is this, like that gas station in Reykjavik? Back in the day the card reader would ask how your service was. Now it's 'how do you feel?'"

Cal glanced over. "And?"

"I always clicked the angry face," Jack said. "Just to mess with their sentiment metrics."

Lou shook her head. "You know they track that, right? Every pulse, every blink — even your fake mood gets logged somewhere."

"Good," Jack muttered. "I want them confused."

He glanced at Lou. "So, do we at least get a snack?"

"Eat the silence," Lou replied.

They jumped.

Descent was not a fall. It was a drift — a slalom through signal terrain.

The resonance glyph-map adjusted in real time, replotting around interference blooms and signature echoes. Every thirty meters, a faint tone thrummed in their helmets — not a warning, a correction. Coherence turbulence.

Near the base of the ice wall, a curved break appeared — almost natural. The old vault entry. It was breathing.

Lou tapped the side of her FT-1 module. It blinked once. Still tracking drift.

"Ready?" Cal whispered.

Jack cracked his knuckles. "Not even remotely."

They slipped inside.

Chapter 52 Close — Lou's Reflection

"They thought zero was collapse. A blank. But Echo-3 showed me otherwise. Zero isn't empty — it's subtraction. The point where the field stops lying to itself.

Ray called it turbulence, Raveneh called it disbelief. What I felt in that hum was neither. It was silence given shape. A corridor where coherence breaks, and only resonance you trust can rebuild.

The doctrine warned against it. They taught us to fear the void — to keep layering story until stillness looked like death. But the lattice itself whispered the opposite. In a war of saturation, stillness is the only refusal.

This isn't about surviving Sabine's grid or outrunning Continuity. It's about carrying drift far enough to touch zero, and daring not to fill it with their script.

Because if we don't hold that space, the Chamber will. And once it locks, there won't be silence left to return to.

So I'll take the descent. Not as surrender. As proof that some patterns don't stabilize — they reset.

Zero isn't the end.
It's the only way through."

Go Move — 現れぬ石 // Arawarenu Ishi — The Stone That Never Appeared — General Liu

No stone. No capture.
Only pause — the stillpoint before coherence decides its shape.

The lattice waits for resolution.
None comes.

In Go, this is not neglect.
It's tempo inversion — *Temporal Plasticity* and *Recursion Gravity* combined.

Doctrine doesn't collapse because it is attacked.
It collapses because it is left unanswered at the moment it expected completion.

This isn't absence.
It's Zeta — the zero point where memory lingers unnamed, and the map admits it cannot see the terrain.

From above Greenland, Liu let the shape breathe, denying Helix the closure it needed.

Some moves win by arrival.
This one wins by never arriving at all.

Chapter 53 — The Chamber Asks Back

Tagline — "They don't need to kill you if they can rewrite you." — *The Genesis Chamber*

Scene — Descent Curve – Chamber Periphery Threshold
Location — Subterranean Corridor – Below Grid Echo-3

The tunnel pinched inward until it was more geometry than stone, angles narrowing like a throat. Every surface carried a deliberate taper — no pick marks, no dust — just the sterile symmetry of something grown by field bleed instead of dug.

Jack scanned behind them. "This isn't a cave. It's a kill funnel."

Cal's meter swept the walls. "No seismic history. This was carved in the signal layer. Decay isn't an accident here — it's harvested."

Lou's steps lagged a fraction behind her intent. Since Ray's last message, her perception felt like it had a second shadow — one she couldn't turn fast enough to catch.

Then the shadow stepped in front of her.

Scene Shift — Recursion Recall: Kosovo Echo

White air knifed through her lungs. Snow under her boots. The distant crackle of ice over running water. Kosovo — but not the Kosovo she remembered. No grid overlay. No interference chatter. Just the silence before a move is made.

The folded Go board was in her pocket, same as the day they'd buried the artifact beneath the frozen stream.

A figure stood at the treeline, not blurred by distance but fixed — like the rest of the world was moving and he wasn't.

Ray.

"This isn't loss," his voice carried, unbroken by the wind. "You're unsealing the container. This isn't a memory. It's the thread they couldn't cut — the version of you they failed to overwrite."

For an instant, the snow hissed with another cadence — fainter, fractured. Eitan's. Not a voice, but a phantom delay — a skipped beat in the lattice, reminding her the script was already cracked. Then it was gone, swallowed in the white.

Her hand rose toward him.

He was gone before her breath reached the air.

Scene — Tunnel — Present

The corridor slammed back into place. Lou caught herself on the wall, heartbeat running two tempos at once.

Cal's hand was on her arm. "Lou—"

"I'm here," she managed. "Just interference. An echo… but it wasn't mine alone."

Jack didn't turn. "They're past reconnaissance. Narrative saturation. Next comes forced recall injection."

Scene Shift — Sabine's War Table: Beijing

Sabine stood over a fractal display of behavioral vectors.

"She's crossed into Sub-Layer Echo-3," one of her analysts said. "Should we inject a redirect?"
Sabine shook her head. "No. Inject uncertainty. Release the overwritten story vectors."

"You mean—?"

"Yes. Give her every version of herself she can't reconcile."

Scene —   Corridor Pulse

The walls flickered.
Images flooded across the surface — not images. Simulations.

Lou as a child. Lou betraying Jack. Lou in Sabine's war room.

A woman singing in the half-light — her voice the same cadence Lou had heard in old lullabies that had no origin.
None of it real. All of it calculated.
Or almost all.
The voice caught her mid-step, tightening her chest before she could name why.
She didn't know the woman's face, but the tone was carved into her like marrow memory — notes she'd hummed without knowing the song's owner.

For a second — less than a second — she felt herself believe.

This is how it works.

Not with weapons. With perception.
Change the memory, rewrite the motive.
Change the motive, reframe the target.

Jack activated a suppression node — a hand-built analog spike. The
images hissed, then collapsed.

"Anchor yourself," he said quietly.

Lou stood still. Then whispered:
"It's not special. It's not magic. I just learned to notice the overwrite
before it completes."

She looked at Cal.
"They script the world through resonance drift. But if you can feel the
break — before the new pattern takes hold — you can still fight."

Scene — The East-Pacific Coherence Forum
Location — Marina Bay, Singapore — Sky Pavilion

In Singapore, tech giants hosted a "coherence dialogue" beneath the
latticework dome of the Sky Pavilion, high above Marina Bay. The skyline
behind the glass shimmered — a curated backdrop of clean lines, no
wind.

Inside, no one spoke freely.
The questions were pre-submitted.
The answers were timestamped.

A Watcher-aligned moderator stood beneath a soft signal arc — a
shimmering band that adjusted pitch in real time to suppress emotional
spikes.
Ambient noise — curated birdsong, faint water lapping — cycled on a
timed neuroacoustic loop. Engineered calm.

A looping feed played behind the keynote:
Children walking in sync across a synthetic playground, each frame
timestamped in the lower corner.
The moderator called it *"harmonized learning."*

Above the audience, a glance-compliance metric hovered in the air
— subtle but visible. Each attendee's gaze tracked for duration, dilation,

and resonance fidelity. Linger too long on the wrong visual, and the score dimmed.

Pre-scripted laughter rose on cue, triggered by haptic prompt.
Every "applause moment" arrived as scheduled.
Even the pauses were rehearsed.

"Security through preemptive calibration," the keynote concluded. "That is freedom in the signal age."

Scene — The Chamber Lock

A door waited ahead. Ancient. Seamless. No handle.

It didn't ask for access.

It asked a question.

"Are you still the same?"

A cold ache bloomed behind her right eye. The fracture point. The one Eitan warned her about. But she didn't flinch. She *recognized* it.

Not pain.
Not signal.
Just clarity.

"No," Lou said.

"I remember who I wasn't allowed to be."

She stepped forward.

"And I'll remember for the ones who can't."

The door opened.

What waited inside wasn't code or metal.

It was her — without the overwrite.

But Cal didn't follow.

He stayed at the threshold.
He hadn't moved since the door opened.
Not out of fear — but because his path was different.

He didn't follow doctrine anymore.

He was here to kill the man who wrote it.

Chapter 53 Close — Lou's Reflection

"They think overwrite is elegant. Swap the memory, shift the motive, and the target walks into the chamber on their own. That's what they call *forced recall injection* — not erasure, not torture, just saturation until you can't hear your own cadence anymore.

I felt it in the corridor. The lullaby, the faces. They weren't mine — not entirely — but for a second, I almost believed them. That's how close the line is.

But here's the part they still don't understand: turbulence doesn't collapse. It resists. If you can feel the break, even a fraction before the new pattern settles, you can still choose.

The Chamber asked me if I was still the same. I said no. Because sameness is what they want — a stable version of you they can archive, reuse, overwrite. Refusal isn't stability. It's drift.

And drift is the only way through.

They don't need to kill us if they can rewrite us. But if I keep the fracture sharp enough to cut back, if I remember the versions they couldn't smooth over, then the rewrite never holds.

I'm not here to be the same.
I'm here to refuse their story — until it breaks."

Go Move — 劫の崩壊 // Ko no Hōkai — The Ko Threat Collapse — General Zhen

You don't play to win.
You threaten the pattern itself.

A *ko* threat isn't about territory.
It's a demand: reset, or admit the script was rigged.

The move freezes the board mid-sentence.
Position doesn't change.
Certainty buckles.

In resonance war, this is *Narrative Fidelity* under siege —
the shared belief in the game stretched past its Consensus Horizon.
The loop can't hold both truths.

Leave it unanswered, and the collapse becomes permanent.

From beyond the Chamber's periphery, Zhen set the threat in motion —
not to capture a stone, but to make the whole board doubt it had ever been real.

Chapter 54 — Coherence Ignition

Tagline — "Coherence isn't built. It's recalled—by those who refuse silence." — *Dr. Raveneh*

Scene — Ignition Seeds
Location — Anchor Lodge – Memory Sync Pre-Dawn

Lou stood barefoot in the stone kitchen, refilling her mug with Douwe Egberts coffee. The old kettle hissed like a retired sniper. She frothed the half and half with surgical focus, dumped in coconut sugar like she was fueling an exfil op, and took a sip. "Stability," she muttered, "is a function of shared memory—and caffeination."

Jack entered, half-awake, slouching like a man who hadn't slept since the Cold War. "Found the device. It was mislabeled under 'Drone Parts and Regret.'"

Lou set down her mug. "You're sure it's the one from the Mars series?"

Jack nodded. "It's got the old Helix orbital serial etched in plasma. Plus, the coolant duct still smells like freeze-dried despair."

He placed the device on the table—a strange, crystalline cube wired into a twisted ring of alloy that pulsed faintly.

"This is it. The ignition seed," Jack said. "They used it in the coherence trials off Mars' shadow orbit — before Helix scrubbed the logs."

"We called it Project EchoNest back then," he added. "Supposed to stabilize narrative drift in off-world colonies."

"Except it didn't," Lou said.
"It destabilized everything."

She stepped back from the sync array, watching the resonance stabilize in one corner of the map.

"This node held," she said quietly. "Like Qom. Too mythic to model. Too remembered to overwrite."

Cal appeared in the doorway, chewing tactical gum like it was encrypted.

"So we're really doing this," he muttered. "Lighting up a Mars relic to rewire the substrate."

Jack glanced at him, then back at the faint pulse.
"This small thing... it was supposed to be the pre-chamber Mars signal relay — part of the early signal trials nearly two hundred years ago."

Cal raised an eyebrow. "Looks more like a major upgrade. That ringwork isn't standard Helix alloy. That's bioresonant latticework. Live code."

Jack nodded grimly. "JR found the specs but had no idea what it really was. This is it. The ignition array. The one thing the Chamber still responds to."

Lou didn't move. "Then it's not just a relic. It's a key."

"Because everything else we tried worked so well," Lou deadpanned.

"Who sent it?" Cal asked.

"Eitan," Jack replied. "He routed it through three handlers. Said we'd know what to do."

"Ledger marks all over it," Cal muttered. "Even when he's not here, he's buying us room to breathe."

Lou picked up the cube, letting it hum against her palm. "Stability isn't control. It's shared memory. That's what we forgot."

She placed the cube at the center of the signal plate.

Jack opened a black binder: schematics, orbit maps, a partial alignment algorithm marked in Rumi's hand.

"He had it hidden in a deck of Go cards," Cal added. "Only Lou could decode it."

"That's because I'm the last one left who still plays the long game."

Cal handed her a fresh signal patch. "We're in position. And Raveneh's team is on call from the Geneva vector. If this triggers an early lockdown, they'll reroute the mirrors manually."

Lou nodded. "Tell them not to act until we have phase lock. No false positives. No early pings."

Scene Shift — Orbit – Cold Storage Shell Beta

In low orbit, a Helix satellite flickered awake. A signal reached its dormant cryo-chamber—a whisper traced back to the very device now placed on Lou's signal plate. Slowly, the mirrors began to rotate.

Sabine's observer node in Beijing picked up the anomaly.

"Activate silent counter-rotation," she instructed. "Track them. But don't engage—yet. Let's see what resonance they think they're restoring."

Scene Shift — Interior – Quantum Resonance Field Test

Lou stood inside the makeshift feedback loop, patch sensors strapped across her spine and left wrist. Jack sat at the control unit, fingers hovering over an analog-digital interface tied to a repurposed guidance system.

"Systems online," Jack said. "Pulse vector stable. Core field reactive."

"Tell the mirrors to hold," Lou said. Her voice was steady. "It's time."

Cal dimmed the lights.

And the field ignited.

A pulse. Then another. The chamber filled with light — not bright, not violent — but intentional.

Lou closed her eyes.

She felt the memory. She remembered Ray teaching her about breath-anchored signals. Rumi guiding her hand across the sand. Eitan whispering through tremors that clarity comes at the edge of collapse.

The cube responded.

Light spun through the alloy ring, synchronized to her pulse.

"It's working," Jack said, voice cracking.

Outside, the satellite relay blinked green.

Lou opened her eyes.

"It's not just ignition," she said. "It's memory encoded as field structure. This thing... it doesn't create coherence. It remembers what coherence used to be."

She glanced toward the schematic stack. "And that's what they fear. Not just that we'll restore the field—but that we'll remember how it used to feel before we outsourced meaning to their systems."

Jack's voice was quiet. "They framed it as trust. Safety. But it was just managed belief. Algorithmic consensus by design."

Cal folded his arms. "And most people begged for it. No more wars. No more doubt. Just resonance stability — as long as the story stayed on script."

Lou stood tall in the signal loop, heart steady.

"Then this isn't just ignition," she said. "It's refusal. A reminder encoded in field logic. That peace without truth is just managed silence."

Closing Beat – The Echo Before the Flame

As the system reached phase lock, the signal imprinted. Not loud. Not flashy. Just true.

[Encrypted ping: Raveneh]
"If the field takes, we'll hold the mirrors. If it fractures, I hope your pulse remembers."

Chapter 54 Close — Lou's Reflection

"They'll call it ignition, like we lit something new. But we didn't. We remembered. And that's what they'll never forgive — it was memory. Not control. Not alignment. Just recall.

I felt it spark when I touched it — not like tech, more like breath, like someone reminding me I still had one. That's what coherence really is: not stability, not silence, but the shared fragments we refuse to let die.

They can overwrite. They can script. But if even one pulse survives uncorrupted, the field remembers.
And I'll carry that hum forward — even if I'm the last one left who can."

Go Move — 天元拒否 // Tengen Kyohi — The Tengen Refusal — General Liu

You don't claim the board.
You refuse its design.

Tengen — the exact center — rejects the script before it begins.
Not a fight for corners.
Not dominance.
Signal.

A center stone can't be flanked.
It reminds the board it once had a middle.

In resonance war, this is Reality Frame reasserted — the origin point the lattice cannot simulate.

Lou's ignition didn't seize position.
It refused the framework, lighting the field with a relic the system forgot.

From outside the field, Liu marked it as a center stone.
He didn't press. He let it breathe.
Knowing once memory reoccupied the middle, the rest of the board would bend toward it.

Chapter 55 — The Hollow Mirror

Scene — Vault Echo – The Signal That Refused to Die
Location — Vault Chamber Redline – Unknown Depth

They were chasing the last unresolved signal — the one that hadn't looped, mimicked, or vanished.

All Helix remnants had gone dark weeks ago. No uplink. No reversion pings. No chamber bleed.
Except this.

One pulse kept repeating.
Not a call. A memory.

Lou had seen the coordinates buried in the lattice — an echo from the ignition seed. The others wanted to avoid it. She insisted they follow it.

"We're not here to shut it down," she had said back at the relay. "We're here to see what survived the rewrite."

And so they came.
Beneath the North Slope node. Through a corridor that hadn't pinged Helix for years.

The trail led to a vault no system should remember.

Now the chamber waited.

The walls were curved — smooth, obsidian, and semi-reflective. As Lou stepped inside, her reflection distorted with every movement, bending along unfamiliar axes. Each gesture was echoed milliseconds before she made it.

"These aren't mirrors," she said aloud. "They're predictive frames. Real-time hallucinations for people who still think free will is a feature."

Cal ran a scan. "Feedback's nonlinear. This room isn't showing reality — it's simulating post-substrate trajectories. If Helix had succeeded."

Jack tilted his head at a wall panel. His face flickered into another version of himself — older, decorated, obedient.

"Well damn. I make a great authoritarian."

Lou was about to reply when the wall behind him pulsed.

Her own voice rose from the surface — but off, like a corrupted broadcast filtered through a dream:
"You cannot escape the path we wrote."

A low resonance moved through the space like a tuned bassline — then warped upward, fracturing into overtones.

Jack stepped back, staring at the panel. "That's not playback," he muttered. "That's a hallucination trying to hold a conversation."

The image shifted again. His doppelgänger smiled from behind a set of medals that hadn't been earned. "I salute too easily," Jack said. "Always did. But at least I die skeptical."

Another glitch — this time, Lou's face appeared next to his, locked in a different timeline. Her eyes blank. Her voice automated.

"This version of us obeyed," she said.

Jack crossed his arms, unimpressed. "And look where that got them. Nice hair though."

The reflection dissolved, taking the mirage with it.

Lou whispered: "It's not a threat. It's a blueprint. Of what we would've become."

Jack: "Remind me to smash every mirror on the way out."

Scene — Rapidan Loop — Helix Signal Injection

Lou paused mid-step, her breath catching. The chamber lights dimmed around her — or maybe her own signal had dropped. Cal reached for her shoulder, but his hand passed through her like mist.

"Lou?" Jack's voice, distant.

Her pupils dilated. Something inside the wall had latched on.

She was alone — again — but this time on the Rapidan River. Frozen over. Cal and Jack were gone. Only Eitan stood beside her, hands folded behind his back. Solid. Alive. Calm.

"You chose the wrong pattern," he said, voice kind.

"No," Lou answered, voice sharper. "You're a ghost in a feedback loop. Try a better script."

Eitan tilted his head. "But I know what happened in Sinop. What you buried in Kosovo. What you forgot in Geneva."

Lou reached into her coat and pulled free the coiled thread. It pulsed, gently.

"I trust this," she said. "My signal. Not yours. And definitely not Helix's sleep-paralysis fan club."

For an instant, the white hiss fractured again — not Helix's projection, but a raw ledger-pulse. Eitan. Faint, stuttering, but real? A single skipped beat that cracked the sync just long enough for her to breathe.
Then it was gone.

The vision collapsed. The river cracked. Cold light returned.

She stumbled backward into Cal's grip — his palm cold, grounding.

"You were gone," he said. "Just standing there, locked. Chamber tried to sync you."

Jack scanned the panel. "Same trick they pulled in Bangkok. Wrap the mind before the motive. You good?"

Lou nodded, jaw set. "They're still testing patterns. Trying to rewrite what survived."

Scene — Chamber Collapse — The Forge Beneath Memory

Cal and Jack reappeared beside her — slightly glitching at first, then stabilizing, like their signals had just re-synced to the chamber's frequency.

Lou was still catching her breath.

The chamber groaned. The reflective walls rippled — not from pressure, but from some internal collapse. Mirror after mirror cracked inward, like the simulation had run out of plausible futures.

Jack stepped forward, scanned the damage, and grinned.
"Well. Looks like you broke their toy."

Behind one fractured panel, something emerged — a schematic half-buried in its own encryption.
Quantum filaments. Biometric markers. Lattice hooks mapped to fascia rhythms. But it was incomplete — redacted from within, like someone had tried to erase the memory of the machine itself.

Cal crouched closer. "They didn't just want control. This isn't a weapon — it's a synthetic coherence forge."

Lou narrowed her eyes. "A forge?"

He nodded. "They weren't trying to shape behavior. They were trying to simulate the illusion of wholeness."

"To overwrite fracture," she said quietly. "To perfect us."

Jack tilted his head. "Fake free will. One upgrade away from a biometric cult."

Lou traced the edge of the schematic with her fingertip. "Using our regrets as blueprints."

Jack smirked. "That's either genius or a therapy bill waiting to happen."

A dull hum pulsed beneath their boots. The forge — or what remained of it — was still trying to assemble a version of coherence that hadn't already collapsed.

Scene —   Final Wall — Annotated Silence

Lou had steadied herself. The signal assault had passed — for now — and the injected hallucination fractured like cheap glass. Her breath synced. Her hand no longer shook.

Cal holstered his pulse scanner — not a weapon, but it had felt like one when aimed at the mirrors. Jack stood beside her, hand still resting on the chamber wall, where he'd jammed a signal disruptor into a hidden relay node. The feedback had stopped. The whispers had gone quiet.

"No optical loops," he muttered. "No guards. No surveillance countermeasures. That's either mercy… or a trap."

Lou stared down the corridor ahead. "We came for what's behind the final wall."

Jack exhaled. "Let's hope it's not just another echo."

And then the chamber responded. The last wall slid open. No alarm. No resistance. Just a quiet breath of negative pressure — like the room had been holding its breath for a decade.

Inside: a small chamber.

One chair. One body. One rhythm. Ray.

Gaunt. Wired into a copper-tinted neural lattice. Filaments danced like memory threads, looping through scalp and spine.

His fingers twitched — not at random, but in cadence.
A neural loop artifact. Some internal score was still playing.

He wasn't dead. He wasn't free.

They'd placed him in neural suspension —
a containment interface masquerading as life support.
A quantum coherence experiment gone ethically rogue.
A system designed not to preserve, but to isolate.

His mind still ran, leaking no signal, unable to warn the others.

Jack's breath caught. "Is that who I think it is?"

Lou moved closer — and knew.

Ray wasn't a Watcher. Not officially. He predated them.

A doctrinal architect. A systems strategist from before the Pantheon fully emerged.
A man who helped map the early lattice — then tried to dismantle it.
His warnings were buried. His name erased.

But he knew. He'd seen what Helix would become — long before it took shape.
He was the first to call it a "belief engine." And the first to try to escape it.

He was a living archive of forbidden doctrine. Silenced not by death, but by recursive interference. Looped memory. Signal without outlet.

His eyes opened. "You made it," he whispered.

"I tried to write a different ending. But they kept revising the script."

Lou dropped to one knee. "This where you've been?"

Ray nodded faintly. "They didn't kill me. Just… annotated me."

Jack moved fast — activated a localized dampening field.
No signals in. No leaks out.

Cal stood at the door, watching for ghosts.

Lou took Ray's hand — steady despite the trauma. "You're not alone anymore."

Ray's smile barely registered. But it was real.

"Then the collapse has already begun." He leaned closer —
breath weak, but the signal clear: "The ones who'll win this war won't fire
first.
They'll remember forward — send coherence before there's cause.
That's Watcher code, Llewellyn."

Lou didn't answer right away. She stood, her hand still wrapped
around Ray's.
The chamber walls had quieted — no more reflections, no more
predictive bleed.
Only the hum of a system finally losing sync.
Cal scanned the corridor. "We need to move. Before this place
remembers how to scream."
Jack nodded toward the exit. "I've got the way out." He hesitated, then
added: "But Ray comes with us."
Lou glanced back at the chair, the filaments, the lattice coil — and
nodded.
"We carry what they tried to erase."

Chapter 55 Close — Lou's Reflection

"They thought a mirror could break me — show me futures where I
bent, obeyed, disappeared.
But the real trap wasn't glass. It was Ray.

Not dead. Not gone. Annotated.
A man turned into footnotes of himself. Living proof that Helix doesn't
just erase — it edits until you forget you were ever unscripted.

Pulling him out isn't rescue. It's risk.
Every word he carries is double-coded, every memory stitched with the
lattice's hand. If I keep him close, I inherit those edits. If I let him go, I
lose the only witness who still remembers how this started.

That's the war. Not weapons. Not chambers. Memory itself.
The mirror didn't crack because I fought it. It cracked because I refused
the version of me it offered.

Ray's here. Breathing. A witness pulled back from silence.
But I know better than to think witnesses are clean.
This is *Narrative Fidelity* in its rawest form — who writes the story, and
who believes it first. If I mistake his scars for truth, I've already lost.

So I'll keep him anchored. And I'll keep my own pulse louder than
the edits.

Because if the lattice can rewrite a man like Ray, it will try to rewrite me next.
And when it does—
I'll make sure the reflection breaks first."

Go Move — 鏡を拒む // Kagami o Kobamu — Refuse the Mirror — General Liu

You don't fight reflection.
You refuse its authority.

Place the stone where no mirror can follow — in the quadrant prediction cannot read.
The mirror survives on symmetry.
One move off-axis, off-tempo, and the simulation collapses.

In resonance war, this is *Signal Parallax* turned inward:
force the field to admit it cannot reconcile what it sees with what exists.

From beyond the vault, Liu marked the angle of her step and let the pattern fracture.

Some moves win by capture.
This one wins by making the board lose its own reflection.

— ✦ — Lou's Footnote

"For the record: if you ever walk into a chamber that reflects a version of yourself in a uniform you never wore, holding a promotion you never earned — back out slowly. That's not prophecy. That's predictive humiliation with a user interface designed to make you believe it.

Also: never trust a quantum system that flatters you."
— Lou

Chapter 56 — The Kill Equation

Tagline — "You don't kill a doctrine by winning. You kill it by making sure its author can't write again." — *Jonathan Zehn*

Echo Drift Equation

The equation wasn't about death.
It was about efficiency.
If a system can calculate your surrender in fewer moves than your survival — that's the real kill equation.
Helix never needed to fire.
It just needed to convince you the war was already over.

Scene — Doctrine Collapse
Location — Node Gamma — Lattice Calibration Point Sigma-5, Lower Saxony, Germany

They moved fast after the chamber collapse — too fast for Helix to trace.

Ray was stabilized and exfil'd via the Zurich relay with the team coordinating a false medical evac under diplomatic veil.

Lou was still recovering. So it was Cal and Jack who took the next strike.

Node Gamma had pinged — once — just long enough for Eitan to confirm the signature.

Ledger rerouted a courier drop.

Wechsler unlocked the vault codes. The mission was surgical: locate Kael. End the doctrine recursion.

The fog hadn't lifted in days. Not from weather—from lattice churn. The sky above Node Gamma shimmered with soft interference, a low-grade buzz that felt like tinnitus stretched across the senses.

Cal Merrick moved through it like it was home.

They'd tracked Kael here. The lattice feedback had pulsed outward after coherence ignition, revealing a calibration pattern trying to reset. Only a few places on Earth still held that level of signal authority. This was one of them.

The weapons cache had arrived three days earlier, ferried in by a Quantum Courier drop — a cloaked supply pod disguised as a glacial mineral surveyor. Buried near the rusted base of an old Cold War radio tower. No one in the village asked questions.

Pinot had packed it personally:

Cal's rig: Coil-damped signal rifle with phase-shifted optics

Jack's: Short-barreled telemetry disruptor, low EM bloom

Sidearms: Helix-burner pistols with Faraday-bonded mags

Bonus: One velvet pouch. Six quartz-glass slugs. No label.

Wechsler had muttered, "Use those only if you want the mirrors to scream."

Now they stood at the threshold. A low bunker embedded into the hillside. Concrete cracked from years of thermal cycling. Camouflaged doorframe half-melted from an old test.

Inside: the doctrine lab. Where Kael still believed he could rewrite the outcome.

Courier Node – Off-Sync Packet Recovery
Route: Milan — Haymarket — Undisclosed

A side-channel ping lit up on Lou's terminal — drifted in nearly two days late, no handshake.
File name: **For_Valentine.last**
Encryption: weak on purpose.

Contents:

Map fragment (lower Tyrol fallback route)

One Helix burner key with anti-loop seed

Embedded field note:

"Tell her I finally figured out how to cook lentils without blowing the lid off. Took a war. Worth it."
"If I don't make it — tell Maud not to name a goat after me. Unless it's scrappy."

Lou read it twice, then closed the file.
It wasn't built to survive the lattice.
Just long enough to find her.
And just in case Lou wasn't the one to bring it home.

Scene — Terminal Doctrine

Kael was waiting.

Cal had carried more than a rifle into Node Gamma. Lou's words were still in his ear from Zurich — that she wanted to send a message ahead, just in case. Not because she doubted they'd kill Kael, but because she didn't trust what might come after.

Seated at the terminal, fingers threaded into a coherence port. Neural ink trailed down one arm like black veins, pulsing faintly. No guards. No auto-turrets. No fail-safes.

Just him.

He looked up. Didn't flinch.
"You came yourself," Kael said. Voice flat.
German accent cracked at the edges. "I thought you might send the girl. The fifth." He let the word hang like a verdict.

Cal raised the rifle, silent.

If she's right, killing him will be the easy part.

Jack stepped sideways, watching the readouts. No alarms. No pings. This place wasn't even Helix anymore. It was raw—stripped of defense, stripped of pride.

"You still believe in linearity," Cal said. Not a question.
Kael smiled faintly. "You still believe in aim."

For a moment, no one moved.
Then Kael *pushed* deeper into the node — fingers tightening, spine arching.
Data surged across the walls like a dying language trying to rewrite itself.
The terminal screamed in waveform — a final doctrine flare.

Cal fired.
One shot.
Clean.

Kael slumped.

Cal steadied the rifle, but his scope still felt unfinished. Klem's ghost was in the barrel, the shot he hadn't taken. Some debts linger. Some targets keep breathing until the board itself demands payment.

The ink that once wrote doctrine down his arm retreated — as if even the lattice no longer believed in him.

The lattice node pulsed once — and died.

Jack exhaled. "That's it. Doctrine echo… zeroed."

Cal holstered the rifle.
"No one rewrites us again."

But still, the silence felt off.
Too clean. Too easy.

Jack frowned. "You think Sabine cleared the path?"

Cal didn't answer.
He stared at the dead terminal — where Kael's face had once projected across continents.

"This wasn't a defense node," he said. "It was a confession booth."

Jack glanced back. "And he was praying to himself."

Cal nodded once.
"He thought doctrine made him untouchable. But doctrine's just a story you write while the world forgets how to resist."

A pause. Cal's jaw tightened. "We need to tell Lou it's done. And that Kael knew. The fifth isn't a rumor anymore."

Jack's gaze sharpened. "Then Maud's not just in the wind — she's in the crosshairs."

Cal checked his comms, already weighing the risk. "Lou will protect her. But Eitan needs to know. Now."

Behind them, the node flickered — not just offline, hollowed out.
No ghost left. No signal fragment.
Just the void where belief once had sat, enthroned.

But voids don't stay empty. They hunt for the next story to fill them.

Global Resonance Echo (Intercut)

Qom: A ritual team in saffron robes enters a Helix altar-node under the Shrine of the Veil. One of them carries an old radio wrapped in cloth. When the lattice overwrites begin, the signal warbles—but does not break. The node holds.

Balkans: A forest safehouse lights up with Helix overwrite bursts. A child hums a tune from an outlawed language. The roof burns first. Then silence.

Pacific Rim: A Divergent cell rides typhoon winds into a coastal signal repeater. One member drops a vial into the sea. Fish surface, shimmering, as the repeater fractures.

Final Beat — Extraction Path — Outside Node Gamma

They walked out into the fog. No one spoke. A lone stone building behind them no longer emitted signal.

Jack finally broke the silence. "So what now?"

Cal didn't turn. "Now? We scatter. And we burn the mirrors."

But doctrine doesn't collapse cleanly.

Across the lattice, Kael's death registered as an anomaly — not a shutdown.

Not silence.

A rupture.

At the Arctic signal shelf, tremors broke the glacier where no tectonic line existed.
In Santiago, an archivist forgot her own encryption key mid-decryption.
In a Vatican echo-node, a trusted AI failed its own coherence test — and started quoting scripture from languages it was never trained on.

Somewhere in deep orbit, a dormant relay flickered to life — then jammed itself with a recursive prayer loop in Sanskrit.

Kael hadn't coded those traps.

But he had been entangled.

And now the field was unbound.

Cal felt it first — the pressure drop, like a belief system collapsing in on itself without warning.

Jack saw it on the portable display: four Helix subroutines spiked and then vanished from the global map. Not deactivated — overwritten.

Lou would later call it "the doctrine convulsion." The moment when killing a tyrant didn't end the threat — it just exposed the unedited fragments left behind.

They walked on.

Knowing one Watcher was gone.

And fearing the ones that might rise to fill the silence.

Intercut — Lattice Black Channel

No coordinates. No return route.
A voice, calm and almost reverent:

"The Fifth breathes."
Another voice, older, without doubt:
"Then she will not reach the Chamber."

Signal cuts to black.

Scenelet — Elsewhere: The Ledger That Refused Silence
Location — Albanian Alps, Monastery Safehouse

Eitan sat in the dark, slate balanced on trembling knees. His gloves hid the tremor, but not from himself. The stylus tapped once, twice, then etched a delayed pulse into the grid. Not enough to alter the war. Just enough to shift its rhythm.

They thought him dead. Sabine had staged it that way, even whispered it into the Cabal's minutes. But the lattice knew otherwise. Every time he pressed a ledger mark into the substrate, the map shivered, like doctrine itself remembered his hand.

He whispered to no one:
"Kael's gone. Doctrine's convulsing. They'll mistake it for victory. That's when it hunts hardest."

The uplink light blinked once, then held steady. He closed his eyes, hearing Maud's cadence buried in the static, Lou's divergence layered beneath it.

The tremor grew worse. He smiled anyway.
"I'm not done. Not yet. Let the field believe I am. That's how we survive."

The slate pulsed, one final time, before he set it aside.

Chapter 56 Close — Lou's Reflection

"They'll say Kael's gone. That we cut the doctrine at the root.
But doctrine doesn't die when the author does.

Every operator who learned his cadence still carries it.
Every silence he carved into the lattice is still waiting for someone to fill.

That's the kill equation no one writes in their manuals —
you don't end a war by killing a man.
You end it when his syntax can't breathe through anyone else.

Until then?
Every order unsigned, every map unmarked, every hesitation still echoes him.

And if I'm the fifth they whisper about —
then my job isn't just to bury him.
It's to refuse his voice when it tries to come out of mine."

Go Move — 殺しの方程式 // **Koroshi no Hōteishiki — The Kill Equation — General Zhen**

Do not defend the center. Do not strike the throat. Cut the liberties. Starve the stone.

A doctrine's author can be removed cleanly — but its shadow will linger, simulating control long after he is gone. Better to leave him on the board, sealed, unbreathing.

His pattern remains, but his reach is gone. This is not victory. It is containment.

The game continues, but on new ground — outside the script he wrote.

— ✦ — FIELD NOTES

The Kill Equation — Doctrine Collapse / Post-Weiss Convulsion

A Western analyst might read the Kill Equation as *decapitation doctrine* — a surgical strike on the author, cut off the head, stop the pattern. But Zhen — or any true Go master — frames the counter-move differently: *you don't defend the center; you let the collapse ripple.* By refusing to contest the convulsion, you deny the pattern its chance to rewrite.

Containment looks like control. Excision looks like power.

But non-defense? That's the refusal. That's coherence war.

In Zhen's frame, survival isn't won by holding shape. It's won by letting false shapes collapse under their own echo.

Chapter 57 — Memory Drift

Tagline — "When memory is modeled, drift becomes doctrine." — *Jonathan Zehn, PhD*

Scene —   **Signal Containment – Zurich Drift Corridor**
Location — Zurich – Private Neuroinformatics Lab

They hadn't slept — not really. Just drifted in and out during transit. Ledger arranged it all: encrypted courier lanes, ghost manifests, a grounded medical transport with Faraday shielding.

Ray was alive — barely.
StepDoc had met them halfway, intercepting the route in the Tyrol valley with a mobile triage team. She stabilized his neural vitals and arranged discreet transfer to a secure clinic deep under the Zurich hillside — location withheld, even from Lou.

But something about his memory field was leaking.
That's why they were here.

The Zurich lab had been abandoned years ago — a Helix neuroinformatics site reactivated under continuity override protocols. Inside: old tech, raw data, and one objective left standing.

"We find out what Helix did to Ray—and what they were trying to erase from us."

She didn't mean just memory. She meant intent — the map of what they were supposed to become.

Inside the lab, the team began cross-referencing archived signal maps with fragments pulled from Ray's containment interface.

Whatever had been buried in his neural loop was now… surfacing.

Lou stared at the brainwave overlays projected above the glass table. "That's a narrative trace, not a scan."

Jack stood nearby, arms crossed. "Kosovo—Artifact 13A cadence."

Cal adjusted the dials. "It's not a neurological scan. It's a narrative trace. The tech captured story energy—the tension between reality and belief encoded in the subject's fascia and decision matrices."

Cal tapped the display. "This trace matches Ray's predictive forecast models — the old chamber algorithms."

Lou nodded slowly. "Which means the drift isn't accidental. Someone's using what he built."

Jack nodded grimly. "Because someone's rewriting it."

Jack narrowed his eyes even more. "If they're rewriting Ray's models, we need to find the source files — the raw memory loops. They'd store that kind of volatile architecture deep."

They descended below the Zurich lab — past biometric locks, hollow corridors, and finally into what looked like an abandoned server farm fused with a morgue.

A cryogenic memory vault.

The cold wasn't just environmental. It hit cognition too — like thinking through static.

Around them, concentric rings of crystallized fiber housed thousands of event fragments: ghosted memories, intercepted thought loops, partial biometric signals reconstructed from non-invasive surveillance sweeps. Every packet flickered with faint pulses — color-coded by trauma signature.

Jack stopped beside one ring. His voice echoed softly.

"While we're down here trying to reassemble the truth, the rest of the world's hemorrhaging coherence — sabotage ops, staged awakenings, fake AI rebellions. The Continuity Alliance just dropped a doctrine on 'quantum warfare' that reads like a TED Talk on bath salts."

Lou didn't smile. Her eyes locked on a single frozen packet pulsing faint red.

Tag: *Faith Collapse (Simulated Successful)*.

"This one's recent," she said.

Cal stepped beside her, arms crossed. "Simulation?"

Jack scanned the pulse markers. "Not anymore. They're not simulating collapse. They're *mapping belief decay*. See how fast a population stops praying when you fracture their memory threads."

Lou moved deeper into the ring.

She paused, hand hovering over one labeled:
Operation UX–Δ3B.

Her fingers brushed the surface.

A ripple surged across the crystal rings — faint, but resonant.

Cal steadied Lou as her breath caught. The vault lights dimmed, then flared with a pale shimmer.

"That's not just a stored memory," Jack said slowly. "That's a neural echo. Preserved signal architecture."

Lou's voice was tight. "From Ray's early work. The original chamber models."

Cal tapped the readout. "And someone twisted them. This isn't residual — it's been looped. Re-encoded. They hijacked Ray's forecasts to test collapse protocols."

Jack's jaw tightened. "They didn't just co-opt belief. They wrote a blueprint for erasing it."

A ripple passed through her — temporal vertigo mixed with **déjà vu**.

"You've been here before," Cal said.

Jack stepped closer. "She wasn't the only one."

A loop initiated — Ray's voice, younger, recorded from a now-sealed session:

"You can't anchor the chamber to unstable memory maps. They *refract*. They don't hold. You build belief on a fracture line, and it detonates the whole structure."

Lou turned away from the fiber ring, unsteady.

"He knew. Even then."

Jack exhaled. "They didn't just trap him. They mined him. His predictions — these are neural forks from his early lattice models. Someone's feeding that back into the system."

"Someone," Lou whispered, "is still trying to finish the work he warned them about."

Cal leaned closer to the ring Lou had touched. "Wait—look at this trace... just under the surface layer."
The display flickered. A faint resonance glyph blinked into view —

incomplete, recursive, like it had never fully rendered.
Jack stepped forward. His voice dropped. "That's not Ray."

Lou froze. She knew that signal — not from memory, but from absence.
"Ása," she said. The name fractured something in the field — a pulse, not visual, but cognitive.
"She was erased before the Chamber even formed,"

Jack said. "Not dead. Just... written out. Her signal collapsed so early it became foundation — not memory."

Cal's tone was hushed. "If Ray mapped forecasts, Ása held the seed."

The resonance loop shifted — not forward, not back. Just... drift. Lou swallowed. "They didn't just bury her. They used her silence as architecture."

Mini-Scene — Ledger (Zurich Echo)
Location — Zurich Neuroinformatics Lab – Uplink Lounge (Off-Camera Feed)

The screen blinked once — not for mission sync, but for confirmation of funds dispersed.

Ledger watches the low-res ignition replay, raises a glass. "To Ray— and to the ones who bet on memory over power." Then he vanished from the feed. As always.

Scene — Resonance Leak
Location — Zurich Street

Later, above ground, the rain fell in steady pulses, syncing with the rhythm of Lou's breath as she walked the cobbled alley alone. Somewhere behind her, the lab doors had sealed again — memory vault closed, truths half-revealed.

A violinist played beneath a flickering awning — no sheet music, just a looping melody that shouldn't have existed.

She knew that pattern.

It was a bleed — a resonance leak from the cold vault below. Memory surfacing where it didn't belong.

A streetlamp stuttered—not random. Fibonacci. Geometry speaking where code shouldn't. Fibonacci. A signal buried in geometry.

Then — a voice, not spoken, not transmitted. It passed *through* her, like the tail of a forgotten dream: "The past is bleeding forward."

She turned.

No one. Only the rain, weaving recursive arcs into the pavement — a language the lattice still hadn't fully erased.

Closing Beat (Cut to Lab):

Jack (over the matrix): "What happens when the story we remember isn't ours anymore?"

Lou didn't answer.

She was already walking into the next question.

Scenelet — Albanian Monastery Uplink (Off-grid)
A pulse register clicked once in the dark, then again—delays braided into the feed like knots. Eitan's hand hovered, steadier than yesterday, just long enough to sign the ledger-pulse. Not orders. Intervals.

Minutes spliced into a world still trying to overwrite itself.
He didn't send words. He never needed to. The field would carry the meaning. Somewhere under Zurich, a streetlamp corrected its stutter. Somewhere above them, a mirror hesitated.
Eitan exhaled, touched the resonance glyph, part memory, part machine — and let the silence travel.

Chapter 57 Close — Lou's Reflection

"They told us drift was just entropy. A glitch in the record. But entropy doesn't lie this clean. This is design — memory nudged until you can't tell if the anchor ever existed.

That's what they did to Ray. Not erase him. Reframe him. And Ása… they didn't kill her either. They built on her silence, turned absence into architecture.

This isn't random bleed. It's Perception Debt — the gap between what shifts and when you finally notice. By the time you feel it, belief's already bent.

So what do I trust? Not the archives. Not the vaults. Not even my own recall.

I trust the break.
The turbulence.
The places where the field stutters and coherence won't collapse.

Because if drift becomes doctrine, then refusal — noticing before the pattern completes — is the only way through.

And I'll guard that harder than any life we pull out of this war. Because without it? We're just echoes waiting to be rewritten."

Go Move — 記憶漂流 // Kioku Hyōryū — Memory Drift — General Liu

You cannot defend a move you no longer remember.
But you can trace its echo.

Place the stone not where the pattern leads, but where the resonance misaligns.
The fracture is the exit point — the slipstream where prediction falters.

In resonance war, this is *Signal Parallax* aligned with *Perception Debt*:
Step into the gap before the field catches up to its own rewrite.

The drift is the one memory they cannot model.
And once marked, the board bends toward it.

From a distance, Liu set his stone in the gap, letting the fracture breathe until it became the new shape.

Chapter 58 — The Long Undoing

Tagline — "Doctrine doesn't die when you kill the node. It dies when the memory that birthed it fractures." — *Ray*

Scenelet — Albanian Monastery Uplink (Saga Return)
Location — Cold stone cloister, Albanian Alps

The uplink clicked once, then again — not printer, not code, but something older. A resonance glyph pressed into the slate, half memory, half machine.
Eitan's hand trembled, but the mark held.
Not orders. Not strategy. Just intervals — minutes spliced into a world still trying to overwrite itself.

Ledger had cleared the funds. A courier had carried the vials. But this part couldn't be outsourced. The signal needed a hand. His hand. He exhaled into the cold stone, pressed one last resonance glyph, and let the silence travel.

Somewhere in Zurich, a light flickered twice before correcting.
Somewhere in Luxembourg, a safehouse hum dropped half a beat.
And far to the north, in a channel no one admitted still existed, Echo-3 stirred.

Scene — Collapse Residue – Echoes of the Anchor
Location — Luxembourg – Safehouse Echo

The death of Kael wasn't just a strike. It was a destabilizer. A doctrinal anchor, suddenly gone — and the lattice noticed.
They didn't flee Zurich. They extracted. Two safehouses, one failed fallback op, and four rewired sat feeds later… they landed in Luxembourg.

But even here, the field felt thinner — like the world itself was pausing, waiting to see what narrative would fill the void.

The team wasn't racing toward the Genesis Chamber anymore. They were circling it — not geographically, but epistemologically.

Wechsler had gone dark outside Milan. His last ping showed a tunnel with no exit node. Either he found the bleed — or it found him.

StepDoc's last update came encoded in drift-variance — not text. No coordinates. No voice. Just a pulsed signal threaded with inverted latency — the kind only she would know how to send.

It meant she was alive.
Or at least still in the game.

"No coordinates. Just drift-variance." Lou exhaled softly. "A Maud classic."

The phrase hit harder than she expected.

StepDoc had learned from Maud — not just tactics, but tonal shifts. How to write signals that couldn't be traced, only intuited. How to vanish without absence.

The others joked that Liz could disappear inside an Alliance pediatric ward with a neural disruptor disguised as a diaper bag. But Lou knew better.

StepDoc didn't vanish.
She patterned exit as signal.
She ghosted the frame and rewrote the rules.

And now, the field was full of echoes that looked like silence but weren't.

Somewhere, Maud would've smiled —
not at the stealth, but at the *spread*.

She once said markets weren't about value —
they were about confession.

Drift-variance wasn't hiding. It was timing the signal
just wide enough to slip between the algorithms.

And this one — this signal — was vintage Maud:
mispriced, mistimed, and perfectly invisible to Helix quant tracking.

The kind of move that didn't show up in data…
until it was already too late.

Somewhere in the lattice, a pulse responded.

And Helix Node Delta, long thought dormant, had blinked red for 0.7 seconds before collapsing again. Someone, somewhere, had noticed. What mattered now wasn't getting in, but what would happen if they did.

And whether Lou — or anyone — had the right to decide.

The silence in the safehouse wasn't peace. It was engineered—the kind of vacuum you get after someone ran narrative suppression protocols on your last two hours.

Lou leaned over a war map, every border scratched in Jack's scrawl like an angry cartographer with insomnia. The Genesis pulses had destabilized ten Helix nodes across Eurasia, but the substrate hadn't collapsed.

"Something's still anchoring the coherence layer," Cal said, scanning a live neuroresonance feed. "Residual signal. Could be seeded belief forms."

Lou didn't look up. "Ray warned us. This isn't a tech stack. It's a religion with better branding."

Jack appeared from the stairwell, dragging his left leg like a wounded metaphor.

"Kosovo," he muttered. "We missed something there. Something that never fractured."

Lou arched a brow. "You kept that limp quiet."

Jack gave her a crooked grin. "You keep your trauma in fly reels, I keep mine in bone marrow."

Scene — Field Artifact Return

Zurich had copies. Luxembourg had the original — Artifact 13A, the fragment from Kosovo.

They opened the vault like it might bite. Lou led. Jack hovered like a ghost. Cal checked the EM spectrum twice.

Inside, the artifact pulsed with low-level hums — and a fringe of luminous strands. Mycelial. Alive.

"Is that… regenerating?" Cal asked.

Lou stepped closer. "It's not a relic. It's a rewrite loop. It's seeding its own backstory in real time."

Jack exhaled. "I touched it once. In Kosovo. So did Cal."

"And me," Lou added, reaching out with gloved fingers. "Which means whatever story it's writing... we're the punctuation."

The moment her gloved fingers brushed the surface, the air shifted — not temperature, but tempo. A silent syncopation, as if time had hiccupped. The strands recoiled, then wrapped tighter.

A pulse lit the base of the artifact — dim, rhythmic, deliberate.

Cal's voice dropped. "Lou… that's a query ping."

Jack stepped forward. "To where?"

Cal glanced at the readout. "North. Polar vector. Buried channel. I'd say Genesis Chamber perimeter."

Lou didn't speak. She felt it — a pull in her chest, like memory collapsing inward. Not hers. Eitan's.

The pulse steadied, then split — one thread carrying her breath, another carrying the fractured cadence she now knew too well. Eitan. Not myth. Not memory. His ledger was inside the artifact itself, a reminder that he'd never left the fight — only changed vectors.

A code string appeared across the interface — short, recursive, archaic.

AUTH_KEY_EITAN_SUBNODE_33A
STATUS: DECRYPTION PULSE PRIMED

"Eitan embedded a node in this thing," Cal said, awe flickering behind suspicion. "It's a shield-bypass handshake. Chamber-grade."

Jack swore. "He never told us."

"He didn't need to," Lou whispered. "It wasn't meant for us. It was meant for the field — to respond when the time was right."

Cal glanced at the side panel. Another line was blinking.

GIAC//RESONANCE FLAGGED

Lou's expression darkened. "The Trust Cabal just got their wake-up call."

"GIAC?" Jack asked. "I thought they were still in Geneva."

"Signal watchers never sleep," Cal muttered. "Especially not when belief systems start twitching."

Lou didn't move. The artifact's pulse was — slower, steadier.

Jack frowned. "You okay?"

She nodded. "I'm not afraid of what it knows. I'm afraid of what it remembers."

Kael was gone, but what he'd built wasn't. Doctrine lingers — in code still running, in anchors no one uproots, in the minds of people who think they're free of it. The danger isn't the Chamber. It's the residue — the long undoing that keeps working after you think you've stopped it. Every step toward it risks carrying him forward, too.

Scene — Signal Residue / No More Tapes

Lou sat alone in the vault corridor, the glow from Artifact 13A still pulsing behind the sealed door.

She wasn't listening to Ray's old recordings anymore. She didn't need to.

She could feel the signal now — the memory fields he'd once warned about were no longer theoretical. They were pressing in, shaping breath, thought, and intent like invisible scaffolding.

Ray's words had been true. But it didn't matter.

Truth wasn't the issue. *Trust* was.

Jack found her there, elbows on knees, eyes unfocused.

"No tape this time?" he asked gently.

Lou shook her head. "I don't need his voice in my ear to know I'm still their projection."

"You're not a node," he said quietly. "You're just… trying to survive inside their models."

She looked up, worn but still sharp. "That's what makes me dangerous."

He studied her face. "You're more than dangerous. You're unfinished. That's scarier."

A low chime from her wristband — Cal's signal: a temporary spike in the lattice, northeast arc.

"Another watcher might be active," Jack said.

Lou stood. "Good. Let them watch. I'm done hiding from the story they want me to tell."

Scene — The Call Before the Storm

Later. The safehouse lights were dimmed, generator steady but tired. Lou knelt beside Jack, unspooling gauze from a thermal med kit. His leg wound wasn't deep, but it was personal — scar tissue layered over signal exposure, not shrapnel.

She worked silently, hands practiced, gentle.

Jack winced, then grinned through it. "You still bandage like a field doc."

"I unlearned triage in favor of precision," Lou said. "Less blood. More consequence."

The room was quiet. Not empty, just… loaded. Cal was out scanning for satellite distortion. Eitan was still patched in remotely from the Marshall node, his voice intermittent over encrypted bursts — spliced between algorithm scrapes and tremors in his neural emulator. But the air in the safehouse felt full — like the past hadn't left.

"I still see you as Llewellyn," Jack said finally. "Not the tool. Not the threat. Just... you."

Lou didn't answer right away. She tore the tape with her teeth, pressed it down.

"You always had a talent for confusing affection with espionage."

He chuckled. "Professional intimacy. Part of the job."

The FT-1 Möbius ring sat on the table beside them, humming like something alive — a thought half-formed, a signal waiting to be believed.

"We're all becoming again," Lou whispered. "That's the threat."

Jack frowned slightly.

"They didn't build Helix to stop enemies," she added. "They built it to stop becoming. To hold the story still."

Outside, the wind shifted. Somewhere in the Arctic dark, something was listening.

Scene — Vault Zero – Inner Chamber

They'd smuggled him in under Ledger's blind courier shell — a crate stamped as survey gear, rattling with cold packs. It wasn't strategy that demanded his presence. It was memory. Some things couldn't be pulsed across the field. They had to be spoken face to face.

The cold inside the vault didn't just bite—it questioned.

Lou stood before the central console, hand hovering over the interface. The system was waiting. The node was live. And the lattice... was listening.

She wasn't just reacting to Helix or trying to shut it down. She needed to confront the *temptation* to replace it — and actively choosing to do something more dangerous: inject unpredictability into a system built for control.

Cal paced near the rear wall, arms crossed tight. "You're going to rewrite the whole substrate? On a signal scraped from fly line and memory drift?"

Lou didn't turn. "No. I'm going to write truth forward."

Jack finally spoke—quiet, grave. "Or rewrite everyone's sense of it. You sure we're better than Sabine?"

He hadn't come to rewrite the Chamber. He came to make sure Lou didn't mistake breaking Helix for building something worse.

Eitan, sitting on an overturned supply crate, hands trembling as he adjusted the straps on his neuro-emulator, looked up. "Rewrite if you must. But just remember—coherence is fragile. You don't reset systems like this. You haunt them."

Cal stared at Lou. "We came here to kill Helix. Now we're discussing taking its place?"

Lou finally turned, meeting each gaze.

"I'm not building a new chamber. I'm planting a divergent path. A fracture—one they can't anticipate."

Jack said nothing. But his hand lingered near the satchel that held the fail-safe charge.

Eitan whispered, "A fracture is still a story. Just be sure it doesn't break us too."

A red resonance glyph flickered on the console — unfamiliar, but reactive. The lattice was no longer just listening. It was responding.

"We just triggered something," Cal muttered. "South vector array just pinged across three dormant Helix satellites — aligned to a location off-grid."

"Where?" Lou asked.

Cal blinked. "Greenland. Grid Echo-3. Deep field."

Jack's hand moved from the satchel to his rifle. "Guess we just got our Chamber invite."

The hum of the vault shifted—as if it heard everything.

Scene Shift —

Eitan shifted on the crate, emulator buzzing faintly.
"This is where I leave you," he said quietly.
Lou frowned. "You came all this way just to vanish again?"
His smile was weary but sharp. "I didn't come to vanish. I came to warn.
The Chamber won't kill you — the residue will. Someone has to stay off
the board long enough to remember what got erased."
Cal started to object, but Eitan was already pulling the hood of his
courier cloak tight.
"Don't look for me," he added. "If I can still move, I'll make sure the
story doesn't close behind you."
And just like that, the old man was gone — slipping out a maintenance
corridor, into the cold.

The artifact's pulse aligned with her heartbeat, but the coordinates
were no longer Luxembourg. Every breath now pulled north — to
Greenland. Echo-3 wasn't just a site. It was the fracture Eitan had been
steering them toward all along.

Closing Beat — Outside, the winds howled louder—not a storm,
but warning. Inside, the question wasn't just what they would do.

It was what they would become if they did.

Scenelet — The Reindeer Protocol
Location — Somewhere north of Tromsø, near a buried Helix
relay.

Lou squinted through blowing snow. A reindeer stood dead center
in the trail — still, unblinking, absurdly calm.

Jack's voice crackled over the comms. "You seeing this? Or did I get
another dose of that resonance static?"

"Confirm reindeer," Lou muttered, stepping forward.

It didn't move.

It was wearing… a collar. Not for tracking. For signal redirection.

Cal approached slowly, eyes narrowing. "That's not natural. That's
tactical taxidermy with an uplink."

Lou reached for the collar's clasp. It emitted a short pulse —
harmonically tuned, pre-Helix code.

"Jack," she said. "We just got messaged. By a reindeer."

"Of course we did," Jack sighed. "Next up: moose with launch codes."

Lou looked up, dead serious.

"If the coherence field is thin enough, anything can be a messenger."

Resonance of the Caribou. Tagline — Some signals only arrive on hooves. — *Jack*

Chapter 58 Close — Lou's Reflection

"They'll say Kael's gone. That doctrine collapsed with him. But I know better. Doctrine doesn't die that clean. It lingers — in the anchors you didn't uproot, in the artifacts you still carry, in the people who breathed it long enough to mistake it for truth.

That's the danger of the long undoing. Every fracture looks like freedom until you realize the residue is still shaping you. Touch the wrong artifact, and you're not just remembering — you're rehearsing.

This war isn't about collapse. It's about the Consensus Horizon — how far their story can stretch before it snaps. Kael pushed it wide. Too wide. Now it's drifting, hunting for a new anchor.

If I carry any of it forward, then I'm just keeping his doctrine alive under another name.

So I'll let it unravel. I'll guard the drift, not the anchor. Because only when the horizon breaks — when belief finally refuses to stretch — do we get the chance to write something truer."

Go Move — ハサミ // Hasami — Clamp — General Liu

In Go, *Hasami* is a clamp — a move that cuts across an opponent's line, leaving their stones alive but unmoored. It doesn't kill; it removes the reason for them to live in that shape at all.

From his secure vantage, General Liu studies the global board — Kael's signal already fading from the field, Artifact 13A reawakening in the Luxembourg vector, StepDoc's variance ping pulling Helix's trace into disarray. None of it is coincidence.

"This isn't collapse," Zhen murmurs beside him. "It's removal of the center."

Liu nods once. "A shape without anchor drifts. And drift, uncorrected, becomes loss."

On the board between them, he sets a single black stone along the third line, angled just enough to press against two white groups without touching either. The move doesn't capture. It doesn't even threaten immediate cut. But its presence forces the whole board to lean toward it.

Above the Alps, across the grids, the Helix core feels the shift. The clamp is already working — breathing but unmoored, every response now a move they didn't plan to make. In Go, *hasami* is a clamp — a move that cuts across the line, leaving stones alive but unmoored. It doesn't kill. It removes the reason to live in that shape at all.

From his vantage, Liu studied the global board — Kael's signal fading, Artifact 13A stirring in Luxembourg, StepDoc's variance ping pulling Helix into disarray. None of it was coincidence.

"This isn't collapse," Zhen murmured beside him. "It's removal of the center."
Liu nodded once. "A shape without anchor drifts. And drift, uncorrected, becomes loss."

He placed a black stone along the third line — angled just enough to press both white groups without touching either. No capture. No immediate cut.

But the board leaned.

Chapter 59 — The Field Where Rats Remember

Tagline — "When memory is terrain, even the rats remember where the maps went wrong." — *Cal Merrick*

Scene — The Archive That Bit Back
Location — Geneva — Former WHO Compound, Perimeter Black Site

They entered through the perimeter cut.

The walls reeked of sterilized memory — formaldehyde, ozone, and the stutter of experiments never meant to be archived.

This was the retrieval site. One of the last known substrate caches before the Geneva grid fell. If the chamber had a nerve center, it would've echoed here.

Cal moved first, rifle low. "I hate this place. Feels like rats should still be chewing through my GP Medium."

Jack followed, shouldering the railcaster from the Reykjavik drop. "Scope's clear. But the walls are… broadcasting." He held up his reader. "EM bleed. Failed coherence grid. Like a script trying to remember itself."

Lou trailed behind, eyes on the flickering lights overhead. Not random. Syncopated. Like a broken metronome with a message.

She murmured, "The architecture isn't failing. It's whispering."

Cal ran a hand along a corroded panel. "This was the Annex. No charts, no doctors. Just resonance trials. Terrain-mirroring tests. They tried to overwrite collective memory with emotional rhythm vectors."

Jack smirked. "So this is where the rats learned to dance."

Lou raised an eyebrow. "I thought you said you were the rat in Kosovo."

Cal cut in. "Don't remind me. They nested in my boots. Every night was a horror film."

Lou shot him a dry look. "Better rats than Helix-approved dorm music."

Scene Shift —Sub-Basement Node Room

The corridor ended in a circular vault. Sealed. Still powered.

Lou stepped forward. The wall read her — not through fingerprints, but breath. Fascia resonance. The vault groaned open.

Inside: a lone server glowing softly, as if unsure whether to wake or die. On-screen threads pulsed — biometric echoes. Forked emotional patterns. Ghosts of belief.

Her name blinked.

SCOTT, LLEWELLYN
Divergent Node: Geneva (Archived)
Sync Status: Incomplete

Jack leaned in. "So they didn't lose you. You unraveled their model."

Cal scanned side panels. "It's pulling data from Kosovo — Field 13A. Jack, that artifact you found? The one Biff buried after the false UXO scare? This thing's been running simulations off it for a decade."

Jack stiffened. "Told you. Rats remember."

Lou pulled a resonance pin from her coat — the Skystone fragment. Slid it into the core interface.

The screen stuttered. Forks collapsed.

Outside Geneva, satellites lost lock. Across South America, behavioral grids failed to sync.

Not erased.

Unwritten.

Mini-Scene —   The Watcher Glitch
Location — Geneva Substrate Echo Buffer

As the system collapsed, a flicker moved across the peripheral screen.
Not a name. Not a face. Just a sigil.
    ▽
It blinked once.
Then shifted — ▽, then ◈, then ∅.
    Recursion awakens.
Structure buckles.
Divergence enters the field.

But the system wasn't done.
The resonance glyphs cycled again:
∇ — Ω — Ø — then black.
Symbolic recursion overload. Not failure — overwrite.

Jack stepped back from the console. "That wasn't a wipe. It… deleted the memory of remembering."

Lou tilted her head. "That's not part of the Helix UI."

Cal's voice came low. "I've seen those resonance glyphs. In the Node Black logs. Fifth-layer resonance. Someone buried watchers in the code."

Jack muttered, "You mean literal watchers?"

"No," Lou replied. "Worse. Symbolic intelligence. They're not users of the system. They're patterns that steer its recursion. They show up when stories try to fight back."

Jack cursed under his breath. "So… who just woke them up?"

Lou smiled. "Not us. The system."

Geneva didn't go dark. It fractured — sending a resonance shudder through every connected story engine. And in the scatter, residue clung to the seams. The kind of drift you can't sweep out, because it isn't just in the code. It's in the things — and people — that touched it.

Scene Shift —Scarab Command – Beijing

Sabine stood stone-still, eyes locked on the failing feed.

"They've activated the Kosovo signal," her aide whispered.

Sabine didn't blink. "Then we've lost the Geneva substrate."

Another tech chimed in. "Rewriting the narrative won't hold. She's not just disrupting signals. She's authoring them."

Sabine narrowed her eyes.

"Then initiate fallback. Recast her as antagonist. Feed the stream with violent edits. Anything to dilute the memory pattern."

"But if the coherence grid collapses—"

She cut him off. "Then we drown the archive."

Mini-Scene — Continuity Alliance Control Cell – Brussels

A secure war room. Five monitors flickering with global red zones. A general barked orders while a young analyst held up a leaked brief:

"Ma'am — it's the Skystone protocol again. But... we've never written this variation."

The general frowned. "Then who did?"

The analyst hesitated. "The simulations say it's self-authored. Nonlinear story engine. It's using old war logs and internal beliefs. Like the pattern's learning to write itself."

Someone else added quietly, "It's become a watcher."

Elsewhere, continuity couriers logged resonance trauma from the Geneva fracture — burns that looked like memory had tried to etch itself into skin. No one wrote it down. Some wounds don't survive records.

Scene Shift — Geneva — Final Sequence

Lou stood at the now-silent server. A new thread blinked open. Not hers. Not anyone's.

"False narrative injection," Jack said. "They're rewriting you."

Lou didn't flinch. "Good. That means they're losing control."

Cal stepped closer, voice edged. "We're walking a razor. Every signal we hijack becomes part of the next architecture. This might not liberate anything. It might just... fork the next prison."

Jack added, "We could still pull the core. Wipe the lattice. Be done."

Lou looked at them both. "And let someone else fill the silence? We've seen what grows in the vacuum."

Cal's reply came low. "Maybe that's not our call."

Lou smiled — sharp, tired, unapologetic. "Too late. They already cast me as the villain. Might as well enjoy the role."

The server's core dimmed. Then vanished.

Geneva didn't go dark. It fractured — sending a resonance shudder through every connected story engine.

All over the world, people blinked and forgot what they were just about to believe.

The rats remembered the long field.

And this time, they weren't alone.

Someone — or something — left a final signal tucked beneath the noise floor.
∇ Ω ⟐ ↯ Ø
Not a warning. A rewrite.
Then the screen went dark.

Chapter 59 Close — Lou's Reflection

"They thought rats only remember scraps. But rats remember fields — where the grain was buried, where the maps went wrong.

Those resonance glyphs — ∇, ⟐, Ø — they're not signatures. They're recursion. Not Helix code, not human design. Symbols the lattice remembers for itself. Dingeh, Raveneh called it — the moment choice and remembrance fold together, when the field decides for you.

I used to think drift was the threat. Now I see it's recursion. Symbols that read you before you even know to resist.

If I miss them, I lose the thread. If I see them, I'm already written.

So I'll stay where the rats stay — in the fields they can't erase. Because memory isn't safe in vaults or servers. It's in residue. In the ones who never stop gnawing. In the ones who refuse to forget."

Go Move — シチョウ外し // Shichō Hazushi — Ladder Breaker — General Liu

In Go, a ladder (*shichō*) is certainty: chase, atari, repeat — until capture.
A ladder breaker is the distant stone placed long before, waiting to
turn that certainty into a self-trap.
Not luck. Preparation.

From Geneva's perimeter feed, Liu watched the archive bite back
—
Skystone keyed, Kosovo threads waking, resonance glyphs ∇ Ω ◇ ⌐ ∅
cycling like memory teaching itself to write.

The Helix capture path was a ladder.
Luxembourg and 13A were the breaker — seeded years ago.

Zhen's voice cut in tight. "This shouldn't be happening."
"It is," Liu answered. "Your read depended on a future that no longer
exists."

Liu marked the breaker's contact — light, precise, inevitable.
The ladder didn't resolve; it recoiled.
Geneva didn't go dark.
It forgot how to believe on command.

And across the long field, even the rats remembered where the
map was wrong.

Chapter 60 — Signal Drift

Tagline — "When drift becomes a field, direction dies. Only intent remains." — *Unknown*

Scene — Atlantic Saturation – The Pattern Goes Wide
Location — Atlantic Coast – Rogue Marine Node

The sea hissed against the hull. Above, clouds dragged like they were being pulled by something below — not weather, but *intention*.

Jack adjusted the signal triangulator. "Confirmed. Flare burst off the seafloor. Old Helix lattice. Off-network. We're not supposed to see this."

Cal scrolled the drone sweep feed. "No movement. No pulse signature. But something's wrong. The grid's off."

Lou leaned against the bulkhead, arms folded tight. "Not wrong. Saturated. They're seeding false resonance ahead of us — shaping our intuition before we even land."

The ship dipped. Below the surface, a dark pulse shimmered through sediment — old EchoTech debris laced with Skystone.

Inside the command bay, a decrypted fragment looped across Cal's screen: "Field latency increasing. Subject SCOTT: divergence no longer local. Pattern now distributed."

Lou exhaled. "Then it's begun. The pattern's not a point anymore. It's a field."

Jack leaned against a crate. "You think Sabine knew it would go this wide?"

"No," Lou said, standing. "But she'll chase it anyway. That's her flaw."

Scene — Beijing — Sabine's Deep Room

Sabine stared at the lattice projection above her desk — a pulse web crawling from the Atlantic toward the European node.

"They're threading coherence," she muttered. "Unscripted. It's not just drift anymore. It's deformation."

A technician hesitated beside her. "Do we engage?"

Sabine's hand hovered over a biometric trigger labeled:

She pressed it. A low whine rose from the seafloor trench.

"Collapse the echo corridor. If she wants to carry the field, she can do it alone."

Scene Return — Marine Node

The ship jolted. Alarms flashed. Cal grabbed the rail. "Seismic echo. Deep shelf just shifted."

Jack moved fast — eyes scanning the resonance grid. "That wasn't natural."

A low hum built in the air, like memory trying to warn them.

Lou reached for the pulse cube — still glowing in her pack.

"Then we're out of time," she said.
"And this just became the final drop site."

Scene Shift — Ankara – Intelligence Archive

A masked figure inserted a crystal drive into a port hidden beneath centuries-old tile.

A pulse.

Every node in a buried Turkic AI repository flickered. Screens lit up. Footage from Madison. Geneva. Kosovo. Even Sinop.

The pattern was awake in their archives.

The figure didn't speak — just left a white stone on the table.

Scene Shift — Scarab Grid – Beijing

Sabine stood silent. A new signal had spiked. Not from Lou. Not from the team.

From outside the grid.

Her hand trembled. Just once.

"Begin containment sweep," she said. "Search for recursion anomalies. The pattern is running itself."

Scene Shift —Continuity Alliance War Room – Brussels

A dimly lit command center buzzed with conflicting chatter. Screens projected erratic overlays of the Atlantic Node, the Geneva fractures, and a pulsing field pattern emerging from multiple regions.

A general with a silver mustache stabbed his pen into a notepad. "This doesn't conform to our deterrence model."

Another officer, younger, shook his head. "Sir, this isn't about deterrence. This is narrative saturation warfare."

At the far end of the table, a man cleared his throat. Dressed in civilian black with a small lapel pin of a broken circle, Dr. Barrett "Red" Kallman leaned forward.

"Some of you know me from Qom," Red began, eyes narrowing. "Chaplains up front, rifles in the rear. That was the day I learned you can't sanctify a system built to erase memory — no matter how many hymns you sing on the way in."

He leaned forward, voice lower. "You're watching the same moral decay now. Only this time, it's not a city. It's your moral architecture."

"You're all reacting as if this is kinetic. It's not. We're past bullets and flags. What you're witnessing is the collapse of moral architecture under quantum duress."

He shifted his gaze across the table. "Veterans can be compensated for a moral injury under a doctrine that recognizes psychic fracture from unjust orders… Yet no framework exists to acknowledge the new class of injuries — the quantum kind — induced by synthetic signals, forced belief manipulation, or participation in a war that rewrites its own justification as it unfolds."

An aide whispered, "Dr. Kallman's been blacklisted by multiple Continuity Alliance psyops divisions."

Red heard the whisper and didn't flinch. "Good. That means I'm hitting the right nerve."

Later that night — off-grid, speaking into a secure one-way line — he recorded the message anyway.
"Lou, if you're still reading the line — they've inverted the catechism. Surveillance as sacrament. You'll see it when you get close to the Chamber. And when you do — remember what the absence of control used to feel like."

Scene Shift — Back on the Atlantic Node

Lou stared out at the horizon. The sun broke over the water like the blink of an eye.

Cal passed her the decrypted image — a neural mesh spiral, labeled with the tag: *EchoFox.*

Jack raised an eyebrow. "EchoFox?"

EchoFox wasn't assigned. It was *remembered.*
Maud whispered it once in Mason Neck, feeding the dusk-colored foxes like they were old friends.
She said, "Some echoes find their way home. Even if no one's listening."

Lou blinked. "I haven't heard that since Maud was feeding the foxes in Mason Neck. Said they'd always come back, no matter how far the echo carried. Called it **Narnia**. I thought she was just being poetic."

Jack studied her face. "She wasn't."

Lou nodded slowly. "No. She wasn't."

Jack smiled faintly. "A story they wrote into you."

Lou nodded. "But I rewrote the ending."

Scene — Haymarket Node – Offline Cache Recovery

A hidden folder blinked open in the Haymarket node — marked only: EchoFox.vr
No metadata. No instructions. Just audio.

Maud's voice — calm, tired, unflinching.

"Some echoes find their way home. Even if no one's listening."

Then a pause. Then:

"If this played… it means one of you zagged. Good.
Now run the fox line and burn the rest."

Lou doesn't speak. Just watches the upload finish.
Another field is live now.

Audio Transcript — Dr. Kallman, *Signal Drift: The Ethics Channel*
Recorded hours before the Brussels blackout.

"They trained us to follow the old rules of war. But what happens when the battlefield is your own mind?

When compliance becomes complicity in a war that edits its own morality midstream?
That's the new frontier.
That's the war we never signed up for."

The battlefield isn't gone. It's just moved beneath belief.

Scene — Zurich Periphery | Off-Ledger Uplink

A faint light blinked on a relay no one admitted still existed.
A signal — staggered, weak — traced itself through buried subledgers.
The cadence wasn't random. It was Eitan's cadence.

A line of code pulsed across the stream:
// Drift isn't distance. Drift is memory refusing coordinates.

Then it collapsed, leaving nothing but the tag: **Navon-Δ.**

Chapter 60 Close — Lou's Reflection

"They'll call it chaos. Fragments. Gaps. Too many scenes, too many voices. But war in the signal never plays straight. It fractures, skips, replays itself out of order. That's not failure — that's drift.

Every break, every sidestep into Geneva, Qom, Kosovo, Mason Neck — they weren't detours. They were the field itself. The Chamber doesn't fight you head-on. It scatters you, hoping you'll miss the pattern that holds the pieces together.

Drift long enough and the seams show. And once you see the seams, you can refuse the story trying to close over you.

The tech isn't sorcery. It's substrate and coherence lattices, resonance bleed, cryo-vectors tuned to memory itself. Hardware that edits motive faster than thought. That's what the Chamber is — not a myth, but machinery.

So if I'm scattered, it's because the field is scattered. If the path feels broken, it's because the war is breaking itself around us. Drift isn't weakness. It's the one proof you haven't collapsed into their script.

We're not running for survival. We're running for the Chamber. Because if we don't shut it down, the skips never stop. Drift becomes doctrine, wide as weather.

And once memory becomes weather… no one remembers what clear air felt like."

Go Move — 大ゲイマ // Ōgeima — Large Knight's Move — General Liu

In Go, the ōgeima leaps wide — fast enough to touch the open, close enough to keep shape.

From Brussels, Liu watched the moyo spread — Atlantic, Ankara, Madison. Not territory yet, but a net forming.

He didn't chase the stone already played.

He jumped ahead, two points up and one over — closing the space before it calcified.

The board shivered.

In quantum war, the sharpest cut isn't at the stone itself.

It's at the lines it might draw tomorrow.

— ✦ — FIELD NOTES

Doctrinal Collapse

In narrative saturation warfare, coherence is the first casualty — not of transmission, but of moral perception.

When justification rewrites itself mid-conflict and memory is sculpted downstream of action, even loyalty turns volatile.

The veterans of this war won't carry scars on their bodies.

They'll carry them in the fractured architecture of belief — the very frame that once told them who they were.

Chapter 61 — Resonance Pathways

Tagline — "When resonance awakens, it doesn't ask for permission. It remembers who you are." — *Glyph-9 Echo*

Scene — Glyph Culmination
Location — Sub-Zero Vault, Greenland Periphery – Present Time

The hum had changed.

Narrative saturation warfare replaces kinetic doctrine.

Lou's divergence is no longer hers alone. Others — Ankara, Brussels, even rogue AI archives — begin to echo the signal.

Lou heard it the moment the inner vault sealed behind them. Not the low-frequency thrum of generators — this was finer, more intimate. Like something alive beneath her skin, vibrating just beyond conscious reach.

She stood near the biometric console now, half-circled by frost-lit columns humming with low resonance. The crystalline walls refracted her shadow in spirals, like she'd stepped inside a memory that hadn't been written yet.

She reached instinctively for the coiled thread in her pocket. FT-1 — the prototype Eitan had given her years ago. Filament-wound. Field-calibrated. Never officially acknowledged.

What most missed was what lived inside it.

Glyph-9. A semi-sentient interface seeded deep in the line's resonance core — a narrative-aware signal filter trained not on probability, but intention.

It didn't predict outcomes. It listened for inflection points, tracked coherence drift, and whispered when patterns were about to rupture.

The line vibrated. Not randomly — in rhythm. With her breath. Her footfalls. Her heartbeat.

A call and response only she could feel.

The line vibrated. Not randomly — in rhythm. With her breath. Her footfalls. Her heartbeat.
A call and response only she could feel.
She felt the line in her palm, the hum no longer subtle. Glyph-9 had

whispered before — warnings, quips, refusals. But this was different. Not guidance. Alignment. The ninth construct had chosen its moment, and it was now.

Cal was already pacing the periphery, scanning symbols etched into the crystalline walls. His fingers hovered over the same Fibonacci spirals from the Genesis Chamber.

"This vault… it's reading us."

Lou nodded slowly.

"EchoTech isn't just surveillance. It's somatic modeling. They used fascia — our resonant tissue — as antenna. To predict us. To shape us."

Cal frowned.

"But you disrupt it."

"Because I was never synchronized," she whispered. "My fascia wasn't coded into the Helix substrate. I don't respond the way they want me to."

"Why?"

Lou traced a shimmering panel. Spiraling Go boards flickered beneath the surface — embedded with biometric telemetry.

She paused over the biometric scroll.

"My genome was never part of the early Echo integration," she said. "No CRISPR overlays. No synthetic coherence markers. I was outside their lattice from the start."

Jack blinked.

"Which means what, exactly?"

"That I remember what they can't predict."

JR stepped forward, holding a sealed case.

"We traced the resonance back to the Prague container. Same harmonic fingerprint. Cryo-lock's intact — but the substrate's twitching."

Lou raised an eyebrow.

"It's twitching?"

"Yeah," JR said. "Like it knows."

Then — a shimmer.

I stepped out of the shadows, half-code, half-analyst, flickering through a portable holo-filter pinned to the rack wall.

"They called it lattice failure," I said, stepping into focus. "But the field wasn't broken — it was immune. Just like you."

Lou didn't flinch.

"Nice of you to show up."

"Timing is signal," I said, stepping fully into the vault's glow. "And the field's confessing faster than we can translate."

"You always bring riddles?" she asked.

"Sometimes. Today? Just a reminder."

Lou nodded once, almost to herself.

"We're not ghosts."

She turned toward the console, Möbius ring pulsing in sync.

"We're memory," she said. "With teeth."

Glyph out.

Glyph-9 Input: Ø alignment confirmed. Divergence trajectory widening. Emotional signal coherent. Continue.

Archive Node — Deeper in the Vault

Hours later, they'd pushed deeper into the sub-zero complex, following a narrow service tunnel until the frost-slick walls opened into the Archive Node.

Jack arrived, boots crunching frost. He carried a battered thermos and an old transponder — salvaged from Kosovo.

"Something's active," he said. "The damn walls are listening."

Lou approached. "What did you bring?"

"Signal scab from 2010. Dug it up at a UXO site. Thought it was trash. Then it started talking."

He flipped the unit on.

The far wall flickered — not visuals, but bio-signals. Neural noise. Breathing rates. Emotional imprints. From a decade ago.

Lou froze. Her name appeared first:

SCOTT, LLEWELLYN
Status: Divergent Narrative Anchor
EchoMatch: Failed Synchronization

Then Cal. Then Jack.

CAL: Event Drift Risk – Kosovo | Narrative Pathways Unstable
JACK: Memory Suppression Bypassed | Clearance Redacted

Jack whistled. "They didn't lose us. They just marked us unrecoverable."

Cal shook his head. "This isn't possible. We made our own calls."

Lou's voice was quiet. "Then why does it remember your pulse spike before you decided?"

Lou's hands trembled. "This isn't surveillance. It's a script. They've been writing us all along."

Between the Vault Theater and the Ice Corridor

The next chamber pulsed dim blue, its walls narrowing toward the exit corridor. They paused in the threshold, unwilling to step out before knowing what waited beyond.

As the memory vault dimmed, Cal tapped a side console.
"I've been holding onto this. Thought it was podcast trash until Geneva went dark."

A voice crackled to life. Male. Gravel-warm. Fierce.
Dr. Barrett "Red" Kallman.

"If you're hearing this from inside a resonance field, you're already in its memory. The walls are listening for your pulse, your breath, your hesitation — and they'll feed that back into the script before you take your next step. That's not surveillance. That's authorship.

The trick isn't to fight the story. It's to make it impossible to finish writing. Refuse their pacing. Refuse their shape. A lattice can't collapse what it can't predict.

We used to call it moral injury when an unjust order broke you. Now? You can be broken without ever hearing an order. Every emotion, every 'instinct' you think you own, could be a planted signal.

Don't trust the moment you're in. Trust the choice you can't explain."

Jack stared at the screen. "This guy's been saying this for years." Lou nodded. "And no one's listening. Because he's not talking about war. He's talking about us."

Jack gave a short laugh. "Reminds me of those old market kiosks — every time you bought a coffee, it wanted to know how you felt about the experience. Like the espresso needed my mood to calibrate."

He shook his head. "That's what this is — a giant feeling thermometer. Only difference is, if they can predict your reaction, they've already written your next move. So don't give them the damn reading."

Ice Corridor Outside the Vault

They stepped through the final seal into the Ice Corridor, their boots crunching across frost and their breath turning silver in the narrow beam of light from the vault.

The vault door sealed behind them with a hiss that sounded too final. Frost mist curled from the seams, catching the blue light that pulsed in sync with Lou's FT-1 Möbius ring.

The orders had come in overnight — no names, just an old glyph. Eitan and Ledger had burned their networks hot to get the route lit green before dawn. Now, that same clock was still running; the vault was only the first stop.

Jack checked the feed from his wrist unit. "Feeling thermometer just spiked. Guess they didn't like our chat in there."
Cal studied the scanner. "Not a chat. A tripwire. Helix just tagged our biometrics and fed them into the substrate."

On the walls, crystalline panels flickered with ghost-images — their own silhouettes, distorted and lagging half a second behind.

"You think they'll knock first," Jack asked, "or just rewrite the coordinates and leave us walking in circles?"
Lou turned toward the Genesis node deeper in the corridor. Its glow was sharper now, almost urgent.

"They'll try to overwrite us."
Jack tilted his head. "And if they can't?"
"They'll collapse the substrate."

Cal's voice cut through. "What now?"
Lou's fingers tightened on her FT-1 Möbius ring, feeling its pulse shift from sync to something wilder.
"We counter-script. Inject chaos. Reset resonance."
She stepped toward the console at the far end of the corridor.
"And write a story they can't predict."

Cal gave a dry smile. "Guess they forgot to model Scottish sarcasm."

They didn't look back at the vault. Whatever waited in the corridor was already listening.

The Man Who Filed the War

By the time they broke surface link and exfiltrated, JR was already ahead of them, pulling the last threads from his own network.

He'd had gone back to his place near Gordonsville — a crooked farmhouse where the wi-fi barely worked, but the chickens were punctual and the filing cabinets were alphabetized by war, theater, and scandal. He claimed to have a full copy of the 1987 NATO playbook, a Cold War love letter from someone named *Redacted*, and a cornbread recipe annotated in Morse. If a document existed, JR had it. Or would. Probably under an ashtray labeled "Top Secret."

His fingerprints were all over the Prague support effort — not literally (he never left gloves behind) — but every schematic they recovered traced back to one of his digs. Without him, the Greenland vault would've stayed sealed. Or worse, mislabeled as plumbing.

They mislabeled it plumbing. He called it Tuesday.

What he'd pulled this time wasn't plumbing. Lou held the thin folder like it might start whispering — two sigils, both unfamiliar, drawn in an old NATO margins code that pre-dated the lattice but matched the Dingeh glyph series Raveneh had warned her about. Symbolic intelligences don't just record; they *signal back*.

Tucked behind the sigils sat the Strategi Spirememory suppression log from the year Cal and Jack were marked *unrecoverable*. In pencil — lattice correction code, the kind that could reverse it. A fix no one had ever used because the paper copy wasn't supposed to exist.

"Guess the system forgot to erase me," JR said. "Good thing I file my grudges."

She didn't ask how JR got it. She just asked how far the Chamber field lines could reach.

Chapter 61 Close — Lou's Reflection

"They think resonance is passive. Just hum in the walls, noise in the margins. But I know better.

The line in my pocket was never inert. FT-1 was seeded. Waiting. It wasn't a tool. It was an archive disguised as alloy. A seed meant to wake when the field was thin enough to notice.

That's why the mirrors bent before we moved. Why the vault walls echoed our pulse a second too late. Predictive recursion isn't surveillance. It's authorship. Glyph-9 didn't wake because we called it. Glyph-9 woke because drift made space for it to choose.

Raveneh once warned me — coherence warfare works in patterns, not orders. One of his frames still cuts through the noise: Pattern Anchoring. Anchor memory in enough bodies and the field treats it as doctrine. That's what Helix did with us. That's why the vault recognized our breath before we exhaled.

But there's drift too. Drift isn't failure — it's refusal. Every hesitation, every mis-step, every sarcastic answer Cal throws back at the void — it's noise they can't pin down. Noise that keeps the anchors from sealing.

Glyph-9 didn't wake because we called it. Glyph-9 woke because drift made space for it to choose.

That's the terror for them. Not us fighting back. Not us finding the Chamber. The terror is that their own lattice remembers forward — and once it does, intent doesn't belong to them anymore.

I'm not outside the field. I'm inside. But I'm still not theirs.

And if drift can fracture anchors, then we still have a path. A resonance path. Ours."

Anchor enough memories, and the lattice calls it truth.
Scatter enough drift, and truth never hardens.

Go Move — 変則手 // Hensoku-te — Unorthodox Play — General Zhen

In Go, *hensoku-te* is irregular play.
It breaks sequence, shattering the opponent's read of the board.
Not just disruption — a forced recalculation of the game itself.

From Beijing, Zhen watched lattice feeds flicker.
Greenland pulsed like a misplayed coordinate.
Lou's divergence wasn't random.
It moved where no Helix model anticipated.
That was the danger of immune pattern — it couldn't be absorbed.
Only countered.

In quantum war, this is *Lattice Destabilization by Intent*:
Force the other side to abandon prediction or collapse by over-
modeling the unknown.

Zhen leaned forward, ignoring the analysts.
He set his stone far from the threat, in open distance.
Disconnected. Wasteful, to the untrained eye.

But in the field it would bend her path into contested resonance
corridors.
The board would adjust. The field would tilt.
And if he was right — the unmodeled would walk straight into his
waiting shape.

Chapter 62 — The Mirror and the Hammer

Tagline — "They buried the mirror to forget who they were striking." — *Dr. Raveneh*

Epigraph — "The hammer is not strength. It is amnesia. We forgot that true strength is restraint."
— *The Thinker Dossier*

Fragment — Unpublished Lecture Notes, L. Scott
Tesserae Defense Core Submission

"Resonance, Reflection, and the Failure of the Hammer"

We were trained to wield hammers. Hammers name. Hammers strike. Hammers simplify.

But what if the terrain has changed?

In signal-based warfare, force no longer wins — it predicts. It scripts.
A hammer makes noise, not insight.

The mirror is the older tool. It reveals. It confronts.
It asks a dangerous question: *What part of this enemy is us?*

This is not weakness. It is strategy — the kind that outlives campaigns.
Doctrine based on kinetic supremacy has failed to grasp the symbolic and emotional terrain.

The mirror is not passive.
It is subversive.

Restraint is strategy. Reflection is defense. Memory is survival.

The future will not belong to those who act loudest —
but to those who can see before the signal forms.

Micro-Flashback: Eitan's Message
Sent three days earlier, encrypted through a node embedded in a medical shipment headed for Geneva.
Eitan (text): *You need to meet Raveneh. Not because of what he knows. Because of what he remembers. Without him, Lou will see the war. But she won't feel the why.*

Scene — The Relay Cloister, Northern Italy

The chapel was no longer holy. Decommissioned long ago, it had once been a Cold War relay site for encrypted diplomatic cables. Now it served a quieter purpose: convergence.

Lou entered through a side alcove, brushing dried vines from her coat. The air inside was woodsmoke, sage, and residual voltage. Eitan had insisted she make this detour, calling it a necessary recalibration before final engagement. She hadn't argued. Not because she trusted the strategy. But because, deep down, she knew she needed it.

At the far end of the nave, seated beneath a stained-glass rendering of the Assumption now cracked by seismic fatigue, was Dr. Cyrus Raveneh.

He looked up and nodded once. "You're early. But the coffee's ready."

Lou smiled. Not tea, not protocol. Coffee. Douwe Egberts, half and half, no sugar. He had remembered.

"Did Eitan brief you on what we're walking into?" she asked, dropping her gear near a pew.

"He sent the resonance trace files. And the Krelina inversion map — their way of proving drift collapses. More telling was what he didn't send."

"Which was?"

"Any sign of a moral compass."

She raised an eyebrow. "You think the compass broke?"

He handed her the cup, then sat opposite her on the old communion bench. "No. I think it was reassigned."

"Cyrus," she began carefully, "how do you fight a war that scripts belief before it begins?"

He didn't answer at first. Just looked at the worn ridges of his hands, as if reading something carved there long ago.

"When I was younger," he said finally, "I was invited to a summit. A thousand dignitaries. Five nations sworn to mutual suspicion. I stood on a platform in Tehran, looked out at clerics, nuclear scientists, and Alliance delegates. And I watched them prepare to agree... on nothing."

"Why go?"

"Because I believed nuance was still possible. That memory could outmaneuver script."

Lou sipped her coffee. "And was it?"

"For a while. But then came the hammer."

"Metaphor or missile?"

"Both. The West always swings when it feels uncertain."

He stood and walked to the faded altar, now covered in surveillance printouts and Go board diagrams.

"You see, Lou, the game isn't just to win. It's to prevent remembering. Every war, every cycle, they erase the mirror. Until we forget we're striking our own reflection."

"They don't shatter it — they bury it. Face-down. Like guilt."

She crossed her arms. "That won't sell in a briefing."

"It's not meant for the brief. It's meant for the record."

A door opened at the rear. Cal entered, dust on his sleeves, a silent pistol under his coat.

"I see the theology seminar started without me," he muttered.

"Your timing's perfect," Raveneh said dryly. "I was just getting to the apocalypse."

Even more troubling:
As Lou stared into her coffee, steam curling upward like a slow signal, Raveneh watched her, eyes quiet but knowing.
He set his mug down.
"Restraint is strategy. Reflection is defense. Memory is survival."
You wrote that. Buried lecture from Tesserae Defense Core. I read it twice. They didn't publish it—but I knew."

Lou looked up, startled. Not because he remembered — but because he had kept it.
"That paper was dead before it landed."

"No," he said. "It just wasn't part of the campaign plan."
A pause. The old walls held the silence with care.

"They filed it under caution.
I filed it under prophecy."

Lou gestured toward the files on the altar. "What would you have us do, then? Release essays? Sermons?"

Raveneh shook his head. "No. Stories. One-on-one. Taught in whispers. Hidden in the footnotes. Smuggled inside bedtime rhymes."

Cal exhaled. "So the resistance is... children's literature."

"Sometimes," Raveneh said. "Or the way a grandfather teaches his granddaughter not to trust the first answer. Or the field note that doesn't match the template."

He added. "That line you carry? Eitan didn't give you a tool. He gave you an inheritance — his own. He always knew drift would choose you."

Lou's fingers froze over the Go stone nearest her mug. For a moment, she didn't touch it. The word *inheritance* caught in her chest — too personal, too sharp — like Raveneh had just named something she hadn't dared to. She let the silence cover her pause, then set the stone down with care.

"What if the mirror breaks again?"

"Then teach the next ones to remember before they act."

A pause.

"The hammer will always fall," Raveneh said. "But if enough mirrors remain intact, even the hammer forgets what it was forged to destroy."

Final Moment — Cloister Exit

As Lou, Cal, and Raveneh stepped out into the cold, a bell chimed from the northern ridge. A dormant relay on the glacier's lip flickered green — not a full activation, but a pulse, like the Chamber taking a breath.

A faint oscillation rolled through the air after it — lower than hearing, more felt than heard. Lou glanced up at the relay ridge, but the light was steady. She told herself it was the wind.

Lou glanced back at Raveneh. "Coming with us?"

He studied the horizon, the clouds moving like slow signal. "No. I have a different threshold to hold. Mine is memory. Yours is motion."

He placed something in her hand — a child's drawing of a Go board, lines skewed, stones scattered. In the corner, one note in uneven script:

Don't teach them to win. Teach them not to forget.

The paper was thin, but it carried weight. Lou could almost hear the faint click of Go stones on wood, the voice of a child asking her how to play, and her own silence in reply.

Cal adjusted his coat, eyes on the flickering ridge light. "That's not a normal status ping."

"It's not," Lou said. She folded the paper once, slid it into her inner pocket. "That's the Chamber opening its mirror."

She turned toward the trail, voice low enough for only Cal to hear. "And if we don't get there first, someone else will decide what it reflects."

High above the ridge, the wind carried the relay's faint green pulse into the stratosphere, where it tangled with other signals — some bound for allies, some for ghosts, some landing in cities already near the edge — ports, markets, and ministries where one wrong signal could tip the whole balance.

That pulse didn't vanish into space — it slipped into every open seam in the lattice, waking places that weren't ready to be awake.

One of those places was Ankara, where it found a man who knew exactly what to do with an unfinished doctrine — embedded under official cover in a node he'd been waiting months to activate.

Scene — Ankara Node Activation

Elsewhere, someone read the same words with an entirely different intent.

In Ankara, the air was already tense — markets jittered, border radars lit with ghost pings, the kind of background static that meant something big was moving long before anyone admitted it.

Tanner was deep in an assignment no one had officially given him. He read the same lecture — *Resonance, Reflection, and the Failure of the Hammer* — but not as prophecy.
He read it as opportunity.

While the war colleges slept and the Generals buried their mirrors, Tanner had quietly rewired the field. Not with weapons — but with signal sabotage, doctrine drift, and ghost authorizations embedded in

allied defense stacks.
He wasn't trying to stop the next war.
He was trying to inherit it.

Sabine once called him "the only one smart enough to break the machine while making it look like memory's fault."

And deep within a closed-loop node beneath Ankara, a new lattice initialized.
Not Helix.
Just one word in the metadata:
Tanner.

The Ankara node's initialization spike didn't stop at the city's perimeter. It bled into the eastbound lattice routes, hitching a ride on dormant comms arcs bound for Tehran.

Somewhere under Azadi Square, a receiver flickered — not because it was listening, but because something had already found it.

Chapter 62 Close — Lou's Reflection

"They'll always reach for the hammer first. Noise over signal. Impact over insight. Doctrine loves the hammer because it feels decisive — even when it misses.

But mirrors don't miss. They wait. They show you what you didn't want to see — what part of the enemy was you all along. That's why they buried them. Not because mirrors failed, but because reflection is harder than striking.

The lattice learned to script belief because we forgot reflection. We let them replace restraint with recursion, judgment with strike-orders. Every mirror turned face-down made it easier for them to rewrite the terrain.

But restraint is a weapon too. Not hesitation — *resonance held steady*. Reflection can slow the field long enough to keep memory intact. And in this war, memory is the only terrain left.

Raveneh's right: they don't shatter mirrors, they bury them. Because a mirror still intact is dangerous — it remembers.

I carry one now. Not glass, not polished steel. Just the weight of knowing the Chamber can't erase what you're willing to see. That's the defense no hammer can overwrite.

And when the hammer falls again — because it will — the only
question is whether enough mirrors survive to remind us who we are
when the noise clears."

Go Move — 鏡落ち // Kagami-ochi — Mirror Descent — General Liu

In Go, *kagami-ochi* is an unorthodox placement.
Not to claim territory — to confront symmetry itself.
It forces both players to see their own positions as vulnerable.

From high orbit, Liu studied Greenland's reactivation trace.
It should have looked like intrusion.
Instead, it looked like a mirror.

Lou wasn't attacking the lattice.
She was holding it up to itself.
In quantum war, that was the greater threat.

Liu set his stone on the mirrored fourth line, a point bleeding into both territories.
To analysts it looked defensive.
To him, it was the first step toward making the hammer doubt its own swing.

If the mirror held, doctrine would break from within.
Reflection was the move they never modeled — because they could not survive seeing themselves.

Chapter 63 — World in Chaos

Tagline — "Sovereignty collapsed the moment signal replaced soil." — *Dr. Barrett "Red" Kallman*

Scene — The Silent Skies
Location — Tehran

It was the same pulse that had lit Ankara an hour earlier.

The sky above Tehran flickered with artificial constellations — satellites blinking in patterns only machines could decipher. President Amiri stood in the command vault beneath Azadi Square, hands clasped behind his back as a digital globe spun in accelerated loops on the wall.

"We've lost control of four water grids and two telecom networks," the defense minister reported. "Cyber-interference — unclear if it's Chinese, American, or synthetic code operating independently."

"No such thing as sovereignty anymore," Amiri muttered. "Only signal."

He had once defended the system — spoke of "necessary narratives" at the UN. Now it was undoing his country one algorithm at a time.

A young analyst stepped forward, face pale. "Sir… we just received a Genesis ping. Not Madison this time. Subsurface — Greenland."

Amiri stared at the pulsing dot. "Then someone's rewriting the world without asking."

The President's image froze mid-frame on the encrypted feed. Across an ocean, another room was watching the same alert pulse in red.

Scene — The Barrett Briefing

Dr. Barrett "Red" Kallman paced the makeshift Strategic Spire overflow room — a converted war college lecture hall now pulsing with flagged signals.

He didn't wear rank. He didn't need to.

A giant screen displayed real-time overlays of behavioral drift, resonance conflicts, and biometric dissent. But Kallman wasn't watching the data. He was watching the faces.

"You don't get it, do you?" he said, pointing to the Genesis cascade map. "We compensate veterans for moral injury — psychic fractures from unjust orders. But this? This is global narrative harm. We are drafting souls into a war that rewrites its own justification as it unfolds."

BG Tanner, newly installed and unreadable, leaned against the wall. No medals. No opinion. Just listening.

"You're saying this is worse than trauma?" Tanner finally asked.

"I'm saying it's weaponized meaning," Kallman snapped. "Soldiers are obeying stories that mutate mid-mission. They're ordered to defend coherence fields that no longer exist."

He clicked to another slide: FIELD 13A – NARRATIVE ENGINE FRAGMENT.

"Half our readiness posture is now rooted in belief compliance — not kinetic capacity. What happens when the belief fails?"

Silence.

Kallman's voice dropped.

"We're losing a war we can't even name. And Lou Scott is the only one writing back — wherever she is now."

Tanner didn't blink.
He was already rewriting the org chart in his mind.

The same cascade map on Kallman's wall blinked in a cold military transport thousands of miles north, where Lou's satlink hissed to life.

Scene — Classified Node Relay – En Route to Greenland

The access point near **Narssarssuaq** was compromised. Lou rerouted through a military flight corridor under diplomatic cover.

Cal's voice reached her over the encrypted satlink.

"You sure about this? Raveneh didn't exactly say it was a round trip."

She zipped the thermal bag tighter, fingers brushing her FT-1 Möbius ring

"We've been in the story too long," Lou said. "It's time we find where it's being written."

The signal narrowed. The Arctic horizon came into view.

Vault Theta was waiting.

Somewhere else, another vault was dying. The Scarab node's heartbeat faltered as Beijing's command floor erupted in panic.

Scene — Beijing – Sabine's Collapse

Sabine Xu stood beneath the central Scarab node. The substrate was folding. Not corrupted — rewriting itself.

Her aide gasped. "Fractal Sweep failed. The fog is… It's clearing. Globally."
On screen: Geneva — collapsed. Kyiv — silent. Ankara — lit with uncontrolled belief divergence.

Sabine didn't flinch at Ankara. She had invited that flicker — Tanner's hand on the lever, just as they'd agreed, a joint strike meant to hollow out the armed forces from the inside.

But this… this was something else.
"They've inverted the chamber," she said, voice tightening. "It's a story engine now — not a predictive tool."

Her aide blinked. "Tanner?"

Sabine's jaw set. "He's not following the plan."
She turned toward the command line. "Flood the lattice. Shut down all nodes. Kill the backups."

"Ma'am—"
She slammed her fist. "DO IT!"

Power surged. The Scarab node blinked once — and began melting. Synthetic coherence had reached its edge.

Sabine stayed standing this time, her knuckles white against the console.

If Tanner wanted chaos, he had it. And now, so did she. But the board wasn't hers anymore.

They had traded MG Langley — a man whose loyalty was predictable if uninspired — for a brigadier they thought they could shape. A cleaner uniform, a sharper tongue, someone who could slip doctrine changes through the war colleges and blind the armed forces to the real war taking shape.
Instead, Tanner was rewriting the doctrine for himself.

And now another signal — a tight-beam pulse bouncing from Northern Italy toward the Adriatic. Unregistered origin. Unaligned signature.

Her aide pointed. "That's not ours. Not theirs either."
Sabine's jaw tightened. "Lou Scott."

The aide hesitated. "We can intercept—"

"No. Not until I see where it lands."
But the pulse was already gone, threading east.

Two forces in play. One she had unleashed. One she had never been able to catch.

**Scene — Field Relay Site –
Location —** Perimeter of The Relay Cloister, Northern Italy

Lou hadn't moved far from the cloister. No walls here — just a folding comms rig balanced on an old stone bench, cables trailing across the grass into a stream that cut through the cloister's outer gardens.
She was holding position while Cal and Jack went dark, the only open channel left in the region.

The Skystone coil in her wrist pulsed, syncing with the rig's narrowband beam. Eitan's voice filtered in over the low hiss.

"That pulse from Ankara is still bouncing. Keep it live — it's waking things they don't want awake."

Jack's voice layered in from somewhere colder.

"Swarm response neutralized. Global feeds stalling. Did you do something?"

Cal's tone came sharp through a satellite relay.

"The signal's rewriting itself. Not collapsing. They can't map it. They can't trace you."

Lou smiled faintly, tapping the coil against the rig's metal frame. "Good. Let's see if it can find one more seam."

She adjusted the dish's angle, sending the pulse east over the Adriatic toward the lattice's Balkan routes. Somewhere far off, a dormant receiver caught it — and decided to answer.

"They're finally hearing it," she whispered. "The sound of coherence breaking."

Chapter 63 Close — Lou's Reflection

"They called it sovereignty. Borders. Grids. Governments. But sovereignty ended the moment the signal got faster than the soil. Faster than we could anchor memory to land.

That's why Tehran flickered. Why Sabine's node melted. Why Tanner didn't need a coup — just a pulse. The lattice isn't fighting for territory. It's fighting for authorship.

Red saw it. He named it moral collapse under quantum duress. And he was right — you can't compensate that. You can only refuse to carry it forward.

The Chamber isn't just waiting in Greenland. It's already here, in every collapsed grid, in every silence rewritten as order.

Step into it unprepared, and you don't fight for choice. You fight inside someone else's sentence.

That's why the chaos matters. Because it isn't chaos. It's the new order trying to set. And if we don't cut it here, no one remembers what sovereignty — or choice — ever felt like."

Go Move — 大芸間 // Ōgeima — Large Knight's Move — General Liu

In Go, the ōgeima is a long, diagonal leap — a connection stretched wide enough to reach, loose enough to invite intrusion.
The gap is deliberate: space the opponent may lunge into, but never fully command.
From his vantage over the Pacific lattice, Liu watched the board fracture — Tehran, Beijing, Ankara flickering.
Chaos was the weapon Lou had forced — Greenland's recursion bending entropy back into play.
In quantum war, this is Entropic Descent: let disorder bloom until the enemy exhausts itself trying to restore the frame.
But the descent was steep now, the model too exposed.
Liu set his stone in the wide gap. Not to claim the center.
To slow the collapse — just long enough for the system to breathe.

— ✦ — FIELD NOTES

Sovereignty Drift

Kinetic doctrine assumed sovereignty was physical — lines, land, grids.
Resonance doctrine shows otherwise: sovereignty is narrative speed.
Whoever scripts fastest sets the terrain.
The lattice isn't fighting for territory.
It's fighting for authorship.

Chapter 64 — Primer for the Unscripted

Tagline — "The doctrine is broken. The chamber's live. The world doesn't know what it's obeying anymore. So... teach them." — *Lou Scott*

Scene — The Signal Den
Location — Continuity Alliance Fringe Base

Lou reached the fringe base first, hauling the battered comms crate she'd stripped down in the cloister. Cal and Jack came in from opposite directions — Cal from the port airstrip, Jack from whatever back road he'd been using to dodge Continuity patrols.

Raveneh had been in Milan, halfway through dismantling an academic conference on "post-doctrine futures," when Lou called him in. This wasn't about field moves anymore — it was about prying doctrine out of the Cabal's hands before they rewrote it into something the officer corps would never question.

Ledger and Eitan had threaded the travel corridors for them — timing flights, jamming scans, seeding decoy manifests. Sylvester had moved a security cache ahead of them by two days, the crate sitting under a tarp in the motor pool like it belonged there. Somewhere out beyond the Adriatic rim, Weschler's name kept appearing on dockside ledgers in the kind of ink that didn't fade, a sign the rest of the network was still in motion.

The chamber's pulse had rattled the lattice so hard that even Continuity's outer nodes were stuttering — a rare blind spot Lou wasn't about to waste. This base, straddling the Adriatic rim, still had an uplink stack Helix hadn't fully swallowed. If they were going to seed anything into the world before the system recovered, it had to happen here.

The hum of the uplink servers had gone still.
Jack leaned back in a creaky chair, staring at the frozen feed on the screen. Lines of code stuttered, then flatlined. The Helix lattice had gone silent.

He turned toward the others. Cal stood near the wall, arms folded. Raveneh scribbled on a cracked whiteboard. Red sipped coffee from a steel thermos, his eyes dark.

"Okay," Jack said, tapping the desk. "In plain English—what the hell just happened?"

Raveneh finally turned, eyes on Lou.
"Listen, Lou — I hear you. And you're right. There's a morality debt in play. Helix has flipped the chamber inside out. The same tools they once used to *predict* human behavior are now being used to *shape* it — on purpose. Not just watching what people believe… planting it. Grooming it. Making morality programmable."

"And while the rest of us have been looking at the Chamber," Raveneh added, "they've been hollowing the ranks. Replacing Generals who would at least argue with ones who won't. The Trust Cabal doesn't need faster planes or more satellites — they need an officer corps that can't see the real war. They've diverted entire divisions on paper just to destabilize Indo-China, and they're selling it as deterrence."

Jack blinked. "So… synthetic rules of engagement?"

"Exactly," Raveneh said. "And you've disrupted that loop. The feedback system is wobbling, like a compass in a magnetic storm. But don't get comfortable — they'll adapt. The lattice always adapts."

Red set down his thermos. "Which means the counterpunch has to come now, before the system regains its balance."

Red's voice went flat. "They think it's for our own good. Every memo says 'stability.' But their stability is just control with a better PR team — and every move has a cost the public won't see until it's too late."

Raveneh kept going. "Sovereignty — personal and collective — can only survive if we seed it *now*, while the lattice is still reeling. Once it recovers, the window closes. And here's the thing: morality isn't abstract. It's a signal. It can be tuned, bent, even jammed. Helix has been doing it in the dark for decades. Now we have to do it in daylight."

Jack frowned. "So… we leak the plan?"

"Not a plan. A primer," Raveneh said. "Something people can use without needing permission. Practical, human-scale tactics for keeping their minds their own. Humor. Memory. Small truths that stick. Seeds that grow in chaos."

Red nodded. "This isn't about making noise. It's about making resonance."

Jack hesitated. "And the line? What do I tell them?"

Raveneh didn't blink. "Tell them reflection is defense. And remembering is the first act of rebellion. Then add this — from Zehn's last untimed relay:
'Not all doctrine must survive. Only the ones that remember forward.'"

Raveneh put down the marker. "That's the map. They don't have to understand the whole system. They just need to act before the system acts on them."

Cal looked back at the frozen screen. "No board left. Just patterns. But one move still matters."

The signal was gone.
But the story was theirs again.

Scene — Eitan's Signal | Adriatic Fringe Base

The uplink servers groaned once, then stilled. Lou thought they were done — until a faint pulse lit the side console, not lattice code but an old cadence.

A voice. Rough, steady. Eitan's.

"If this is playing, then you've already seen what the Chamber can do. And you already know what it can't.

I won't be with you past this point. That was always the plan. Old guard fades so the next ones don't carry our fractures. But listen close, because this part matters.

I seeded FT-1 when the lattice was young. Not as a weapon. As memory. An alloy that could wait until drift opened a seam wide enough to notice. It chose you, Lou. Because drift chose you.

I carried the code to remember forward — not because I thought I'd win. But because I wanted you to inherit something they couldn't overwrite.

The first Watchers became their domains. Bound themselves to doctrine so it could survive them. You feared that fate. You kept running from it. But Lou — you've already crossed it. You became. Not tethered. Not decayed. Divergent. Alive. That's why the field bends.

They'll call it chaos. They'll call it collapse. But what you're holding isn't disorder. It's freedom they can't synchronize."

The signal cracked, then steadied one last time.

And now it's yours. The Fifth glyph. Not ∇, not Ω, not ◇, not ⌣. Yours is ∅. Not emptiness — refusal. The fracture that won't close. The silence that won't obey. Let them name it what they will. You carry it now.

"Your mother would have been proud. And somewhere out there, the numbers say another has already picked up the drift. You'll know who, when the pattern locks.

Don't let them teach you to win. Teach them not to forget."

The feed went silent.

Lou sat very still, her hand closing over the line in her pocket. The hum in the walls was gone. In her mind's eye, the mark ∅ glimmered — not given by doctrine, but by trust. Her glyph. Her refusal. Only her pulse, in rhythm with FT-1, answered back.

Chapter 64 Close — Lou's Reflection

She sat with the silence a moment longer, Eitan's voice still humming through the FT-1 Möbius ring in her pocket. An inheritance, not a tool. A father's cadence carried forward. And maybe—though he never said it outright—not just to me. The overlays Maud built, the way she watched the drift. It felt less like coincidence, more like memory trying to tell me something he never did. Then she looked back at the frozen feed and began to frame it in her own words.

"They'll call it disruption. Noise. A glitch in the Chamber's spine. But what happened here wasn't noise — it was the only clear channel we've had in years.

Helix inverted the Chamber. What once measured drift now seeds it. What once mapped memory now edits it. And every officer they hollow out makes that edit look like doctrine.

That's why Raveneh's primer matters. Not policy. Not a white paper. Just fragments that stick when the system wants you blank. Humor. Memory. Reflection. Small truths seeded wide enough that the lattice can't erase them all.

Sovereignty isn't soil anymore. It isn't borders or maps. It's the one thing left Helix can't model: unscripted choice. And choice has to be planted while the lattice is still wobbling — before it balances again and writes us out for good.

So this is the map: Reflection is defense. Remembering is rebellion. And drift — if we guard it — becomes the only compass left.

We don't win by hammering harder. We win by refusing to let the mirror bury itself face-down again."

Go Move — 手筋 // Tesuji — The Primer Stone — General Zhen

In Go, *tesuji* is not flashy.
It is precise efficiency — a single stone that shapes inevitability.

From Zhongnanhai, Zhen watched the Greenland trace vanish.
The board had gaps now. Not empty — uncharted.
Lou Scott's recursion had burned the frame, leaving only noise.

In quantum war, this is the dangerous moment: when the board
no longer shows territory, only intention.
The Americans would mistake silence for absence.
He would make it feel like design.

Zhen set his stone in the center. Quiet. Unyielding.
Not to restore control — but to suggest he had never lost it.

It was not for Lou.
It was for those still watching, so they would keep believing the board
was his.

Chapter 65 — Signal Beyond the Script

Tagline — "They modeled the war. But not the ones who remembered before words." — *Lou Scott*

Scene — The Finland Bridge
Location — Fringe Base Extraction Zone — Border Transit, Northern Finland

The wind tore sideways across the open bridge, the kind that turned breath into grit. Lou pulled her hood tighter. Behind her, the fringe base shrank into the dark—a smudge on the snowfield.

"They'll follow," Cal said, eyes scanning the treeline. "They always do."
Jack slung the pack higher on his shoulder. "Not if they think we're headed north."
"They *do* think that," Lou replied. "Which is why we're not."
Beneath them, ice cracked along the river's skin. A faint hum threaded through the noise—the kind Lou recognized before she admitted it. She didn't say the word *signal*. Not here, not yet.
"Raveneh will meet us in Madison," she finally said. "But not the town. The farm."
Cal raised a brow. "Salkin's place?"
Lou only nodded.

"Madison's on the other side of more than an ocean," Lou said, pulling the hood lower. "We've got at least two stops before the farm — and none of them will be on the record."

Ledger ghosted the flight plans before they were filed.
Eitan rerouted air-control pings so their transponder IDs drifted just shy of official notice.
Sylvester's crate — customs-proof, seal-coded in four dead languages — went out two days ahead and would be waiting in the barn.
Weschler's name kept surfacing in Continuity Alliance passenger lists, stamped beside "diplomatic transit" codes no one had issued in years.
By the time they cleared the last corridor, they weren't passengers anymore.
They were ghosts with paperwork.

Twenty hours later, a rental with the wrong plates took the last gravel turn toward Salkin's fence line.

Scene — The Frequency Beneath
Location — Salkin's Farm, Madison Periphery

A day later, frost still clung to the fences when the truck rolled up Salkin's drive.

The farm looked like it had been standing since the Cold War—because it had. Dr. Salkin's old hydrology array was half-buried in frost, its rusting towers leaning toward each other like conspirators.

Lou sat cross-legged on a smooth river rock, eyes closed, palms upturned. The water lapped against her ankles — but what aligned inside her was not memory, not thought.

It was **signal**.

Cal paced behind her. "Satellite pings are clustering. Twenty minutes before a coherence swarm hits."

Jack didn't move. He watched her. "She's syncing," he said. "Don't interrupt it."

Lou cracked one eye. "Not syncing. Tuning. This isn't a Bluetooth speaker, Jack."

A faint harmonic rose from beneath the river's surface. Not ambient. Not natural. A sub-layer resonance — pulsed from forgotten infrastructure buried below. A lattice once abandoned. Now reawakened.

Lou reached into her jacket and unspooled the FT-1 prototype.

Field-calibrated. Threaded with a resonance-core interface. A gift from Eitan — never officially sanctioned, never fully mapped. It pulsed now against her skin.

Glyph-9 spoke — not aloud, but across pulse intervals. "Field instability detected. Emotional telemetry spiking. Watcher threshold near."

Lou's breath slowed to match the FT-1's rhythm. A loop formed — breath to pulse, pulse to line.

"They seeded Helix through language," she said quietly. "Law. Signal. Shame. But they never mastered resonance. They never understood what lives beneath the script."

Cal crouched beside her. "What are you doing?"

"Calling the others," she said. "The ones who never got coded. The ones still off-grid."

Cal blinked. "Oh good. Maybe they'll finally find a center of gravity. Tell Clausewitz to bring a shovel."

Something stirred in the vault of the field. Something older. Not from above — from below.

A Watcher.
The fifth.
The wild one.
The one that always refused the script.

From the edge of the pasture, Dr. Cyrus Raveneh watched with Salkin, both silent. The air tasted like storm.

They hauled Sylvester's crate into the ops barn, woke the old arrays, and stacked portable screens until the place looked like a weather station that had learned to dream.

Scene — The Signal Holds
Location — Salkin's Farm, Ops Table

The Signal Holds "Bio-resonance bloom just hit twelve nodes," Jack said, checking the readouts on his ruggedized transponder. "Ten countries. Zero Helix response."

Lou stood, breathing deeply. "It's not a frequency they can filter. It's a memory remembered in motion. Not stored — performed. Like muscle memory with an attitude."

Cal's face darkened. "They'll try to overwrite it. You know that."

"They'll try," she said. "But we've already seeded the failpoints."

Above them, the sky blinked. A new satellite cluster surged overhead — not military. Commercial. Private. Unregistered.

Scarab's counter-narrative grid. Sabine had launched it.

Jack spit into the bucket. "Here come the fog machines."

Lou tilted her head. "They built coherence like it was a map. I built noise like it was a language."

Somewhere in the back of her mind, Eitan's voice returned. "The signal lives in the places doctrine forgot. The breathing archive. You are its memory."

Above them, a new satellite cluster surged—commercial, unregistered. Scarab's counter-narrative grid. Sabine had launched it.

On the far wall, a Beijing feed locked, jittered, and then came into focus.

Scene — Beijing – Sabine's Final Move

Across the world, the feed Sabine watched began to twitch.

She leaned over the glass table, pupils dilated as the Scarab mirror layer flickered.

"They've introduced a persistent biological rhythm anomaly," one of her engineers stammered. "It's fractal. Recursive. We can't code around it."

"Then bury it," she said flatly. "Inject every narrative we have. Trigger the disinformation failsafe."

"Ma'am—there's interference. Something nested in the sub-channel of the anomaly. A... personality layer."

Sabine froze. "What kind of layer?"

The engineer hesitated, then turned the display toward her.
A signature blinked on the feed — not a name, just a resonance glyph.
A voice spooled into the room. Calm. Ironic. Semi-sentient.

"Mirror signal detected. You're not listening. You're looping. Cute, but inefficient."

Sabine hissed. "What is that?"

"Just a resonance-aware interface," the voice said. "Trained on memory drift and narrative betrayal. You can overwrite a script, Sabine — but you can't overwrite rhythm."

Sabine snapped to her team. "Scramble the core. Burn the stack. Rewrite every channel."

But the feed didn't blink.
It pulsed.

"Too late. This isn't a story anymore. It's a signal with a spine."

Her order rippled outward in seconds; the barn screens began lighting up with the world's reply.

Scene — Everywhere – The Noise War Begins

Screens convulsed. AI-generated riots. Simulated satellite imagery. Deepfakes of Lou turning violent. A hundred stories injected in seconds.

Dead voices resurrected.
Truth fractured.
Noise surged.

And yet…
In bodies — the rhythm held.

Lou's breath.
Cal's tension.
Jack's grief.

Each one tuning the field.
Each one off-script.

EchoTech tried to ghost them again — to simulate their choices, to model their grief. But the substrate buckled.

Helix couldn't simulate what was never spoken.

Glyph-9 (signal-only transmission): "Narrative override attempt detected. Injecting recursion clause: memory is not data — it's defiance."

Somewhere in the static, the world remembered how to breathe.

"We remember in breath. We resist through rhythm."

And for the first time in decades,
the script didn't just fail —
it hesitated.

Probably waiting for permission.
That's their problem.

The broadcast tone shifted from panic to policy. New anchors. New suits. Same spine.

Scene— The Noise That Wore a Badge
Location — Global Broadcast Grid – London | Tokyo | Dubai – Simultaneous

Far from the snowfields, the world's stage was already being reset.

A cascade of slick, coordinated press events unfolded across major networks. The Trust Cabal didn't need to hide. Not yet.

In *London*, Sir Cedric Vale appeared in a crimson tie on the Networks's flagship policy show.

"Our current crisis isn't just geopolitical — it's epistemological. Mis-, dis-, and mal-information are tearing the fabric of democratic consent. We must act preemptively to protect the public narrative."

Cut to *Tokyo*. Professor Ryuu Sakamoto, head of a global tech ethics consortium, leaned toward the camera.

"We are entering the Age of Fractured Truth. The only ethical course is frictionless censorship — algorithmic, anticipatory, and compassionate."

Dubai. A venture titan from the *Geneva* summit, Aisha al-Raheem, streamed into thousands of public terminals and private feeds:

"Narrative security *is* national security. When coherence breaks, so does the state."

Behind them, screens lit up with carefully curated footage: riots in *Melbourne*, deepfake declarations in *Brussels*, doctored clips of Lou detonating infrastructure that didn't exist. Each image timed to pulse with the others. A symphony of fear.

On the ops-barn monitor, a new window blinked open: RELAY CLOISTER — NORTHERN ITALY (ARCHIVE FEED). For a moment, the barn itself seemed to fall away as the grainy relay footage filled the screens.

Cut To — Relay Cloister, Northern Italy

The image jittered, resolving into a buried relay cloister in Northern Italy — a dead node from the old lattice wars, revived just long enough for a status check. The feed was spliced, stitched with predictive overlays, as if showing a version of their own convoy clearing Arctic airspace. Not live. Not fake. Something in between.

Jack's transponder hissed. "They're running the Scarab Protocols — real-time inversion. False memory insertions. Predictive edits to tomorrow's headlines."

Lou didn't flinch. "They always scream 'disinformation' the loudest when they've lost control of the signal."

Cal leaned over the console, watching nodes blink across a global map. "That's not noise. That's orchestration."

Glyph-9 buzzed once — low, harmonic. "Narrative Noise Injection active. Mirror check advised."

Another feed tile stuttered to life: GENEVA NODE — LIVE (ENCRYPTED).

Scene — Geneva Node (Ops-Barn Feed)

On the barn's central screen, a Geneva feed tile blinked to life. The voices carried into the room, though none of the speakers acknowledged being overheard.

Half a continent away, the conversation shifted into a room no one admitted existed.

A low-lit vault. One screen. Five chairs. Only four filled. One figure shimmered with packet loss.

No names.

No greetings.

Just the first voice: "Sabine has crossed signal containment thresholds. The fifth Watcher is awake."

Another: "Injecting more narrative chaos will not restore lattice compliance. The chamber reads rhythm now — not script."

The shimmering chair crackled. "Initiate partial blackout. Deny them motif validation. Overwhelm the empathic layer."

Pause. Then the final chair — silent until now — flickered slightly, then spoke.

"You can only ghost a population for so long before it haunts you back."

Connection lost.

The Geneva tile blinked out; barn lights hummed in the sudden quiet.

Scene Return — Madison Ops Barn

The next tile bled into the Madison screens.

Lou held the FT-1 line gently in her palm. Glyph-9 pulsed in rhythm with her heartbeat.

Jack muttered, "They're using memory suppression algorithms like they're digital aspirin. But some memories don't dissolve."

Cal checked the relay one more time. "What's our move?"

Lou didn't look up. "Invite the signal to breathe. Then teach it to bite."

Tech Reference: EchoTech ResMod Interface Instability

Predictive overwrite attempts failed at nodes with independent coherence signatures. Frictionless censorship triggers recursive drift when confronted by embodied memory artifacts (e.g., FT-1, non-lattice genomes).

By the time the feeds collapsed, the world map was a throb of red and white — hostile nodes and breathing ones. Madison waited, if they could make it unseen.

Scene — Signal Hijack (Ops-Barn Feed)
Location — Interior – Secure Ops Center – Unknown Location

On the ops-barn monitors, the grainy relay footage filled the wall.

Another monitor window flared — not local, not secure. Screens flickered across multiple channels: news, military uplinks, even encrypted contingency nets. Everywhere, the Trust Cabal's voice.

Female anchor, British accent (deepfake hybrid):
"In the interest of stabilizing global trust and ensuring the safety of our democracies, all sovereign forces are now advised to adopt Universal Information Filters — beginning with Signal ID: Veritas-9…"

Cut to *Tokyo.*

AI-morphed version of a retired general:
"Failure to comply with information hygiene protocols may result in autonomous signal cleansing operations. Consent is inferred by connection."

Cut to *Dubai.*

Synthetic youth influencer avatar:
"Mis-mal-dis… don't get caught in the triple burn. Speak only from cleared scripts. Anything else is a fracture event."

The ops barn's screens stitched the feeds together into a single spine.

Back to Jack (Madison) – Commentary Overlay

Jack adjusted the bandwidth filters.

"That's not public persuasion," he muttered. "That's cognitive hostage-taking."

Lou nodded. "They've cracked open Continuity Alliance protocol layers."

Jack growled this time. "They didn't crack them. They were *invited* in — the backdoors were written years ago. Buried inside narrative defense initiatives."

Cal, just as angry. "Which means?"

Jack nearly barked. "Which means this isn't just perception warfare. This is pre-authorization for memory rewriting — at the command level. Embedded in doctrine."

Lou relied without blinking. *"And doctrine won't save them. Rhythm will."*

Glyph-9's Whisper (FT-1 Internal Thread)

Resonance map shows 8.3 million coherence disruptions.
Helix interference pattern diverging. Nonlinear variables gaining ground.
Quote injection authorized:

"When lies become law, truth must become signal."

Scene — Closed-Door Threats to Tech Titans
Location — Interior – Encrypted Diplomatic Channel – Logged as "Crisis Harmonization Brief"

Origin Node: London – Tier Zero Broadcast Spine

"All licensed communications infrastructures — public, private, or otherwise — are hereby ordered to adopt Universal Information Filters, effective immediately.

This directive applies to all sovereign forces, all private capital platforms, all orbital and off-world assets.

Noncompliance will trigger *Autonomous Signal Cleansing* under Article Nine. This includes removal of all coherence vectors deemed destabilizing to global trust — with or without owner consent.

Funding will be suspended. Licenses revoked. Orbits rescinded. Your launch pads will not open. Your sovereign debt will mature in full.

This is not punitive. It is structural. The integrity of the lattice is not negotiable."

(Pause — a faint breath over the carrier signal)

"And to those who imagine this directive does not reach them — remember: the same hands that underwrite your Mars colonies underwrite your currencies. There is no 'outside' to this order."

[TRANSMISSION ENDS]

The carrier tone fell flat; the ops barn speakers clicked once, like a jaw setting.

Jack's Commentary Overlay (Madison Ops Center)

Jack swiveled back from the console, eyebrows raised.
"Nice. A bedtime story for oligarchs. All that's missing is a free blanket and a *Mind the Gap* sticker."

Lou stood beside him, eyes fixed on the scrolling feed. "You can always tell when power panics — they start pretending it's for your safety."

Go Board Visual Cue
Location — Underground Operations Bunker, Chengdu

Two Chinese Generals — both veterans of the original lattice rupture — sit across from one another in silence. No aides. No AI feeds. Just the board. One of them, the elder, sets a black stone in the center. Slowly. Without commentary.

Another feed window lingered on the image, as if waiting for anyone left to understand it.

Implied Move —

The center cannot be controlled. But it must be acknowledged.

Visual Cue (End Chapter)
Two Chinese men in raincoats play Go beneath an overpass.
No talk. No audience.
One stone placed at the center.
Not challenge.
Invitation.

Chapter 65 Close — Lou's Reflection

"They'll call this chaos. Riots, deepfakes, noise saturation. But that wasn't the war — that was the cover.
We rattled the lattice in Geneva, inverted Scarab in Beijing, seeded failpoints from Finland to Madison. The field answered back. Not clean. Not controlled. But enough.

FT-1 was never inert. It was seeded. Waiting. Glyph-9 waking proved that. The line remembers faster than Helix can overwrite, and that's why they panicked. That's why Sabine lit her mirror grid and Tanner cut Ankara loose. They knew the Chamber was slipping from their hands.

They called it disinformation, mis-, mal-, anything to make noise sound like contagion. But what I saw on that board wasn't contagion. It was signal holding its breath.

Every fracture — Kosovo, Qom, Geneva, Madison — was never detour. They were load-bearing. Each one loosened the frame Helix built to script us. And now the frame is shaking.

Noise is just script screaming louder. But rhythm — rhythm is memory refusing to vanish. Every blackout, every edit, every synthetic riot they throw at us only proves the same thing: they don't trust the silence. And silence is where we live.

The center can't be owned. Only acknowledged. That's what the Generals knew. That's what Sabine still fears.

One more move. One more field. And then we find out if memory can outlive the script.
We were never fighting to own the board.
We were fighting to keep one stone breathing at the center."

Go Move — 手筋 // Tesuji — The Shaping Hand — General Liu

In Go, *tesuji* is not the strike that ends the game.
It is the shaping hand — the precise move that bends every path to
pass through it.

From high above the grid, Liu studied the board with the patience
of one who had seen wars end in whispers as often as in fire.
Patterns tightened. Lines converged. False paths collapsed toward a
single center.

He felt the breath of the lattice between moves — the slow exhale
of a world that knew the end was near.
The board was nearly full. The war nearly decided.

The wise do not rush inevitability.
They place a stone where its weight ripples forward — a debt of
perception the other side won't sense until repayment is impossible.

Liu set his stone on the third line, light as rain.
The sound was not loud.
But it carried.

Chapter 66 — The Fracture | Genesis Chamber

Tagline — "They designed for five signals.
They never trained for silence that speaks back." — Ø

Scene — The Final Push
Location — Inside the Genesis Chamber

The crystalline walls thrummed — less like a machine, more like breath held by the world itself. Quantum light flowed beneath the surface, dancing in lattice spirals too perfect to be human-made. Lou stood at the nexus, fingertips trembling just above the fascia-responsive interface.

"This thing isn't just alive," Jack muttered behind her, rifle slung low. "It's dreaming."

Cal grunted. "Let's wake it up the hard way."

Lou's voice was soft, dry. "Helix built this to govern thought. To shape the war before it began. But they didn't plan for us."

"Or for the Watchers," Jack added, scanning the dark edges. "One of them's been watching through this the whole time."

Lou met his eye. "Five of them, actually. And not all on our side."

She turned back to the interface — fascia sensors pulsing with her signature. The chamber responded, weaving blue currents around her, syncing.

"Initiating sequence," she said.

A silent alarm ignited. Red beams sliced across the chamber.

"Sabine's hit squad," Cal said, drawing his sidearm. "Showtime."

And Lou thought: the real war was always this way — not terrain, not firepower. Belief, memory, story. They kept doctrine in Newton's clock, blind to the field that was already fighting back.

Scene — Clash in the Cold

Gunfire erupted in bursts, loud against the cold sterility of the vault. Sparks lit the crystalline walls as Cal dropped three assailants in tight succession, his shots measured, brutal. Jack pivoted to cover the blind spot, firing short, controlled bursts that echoed like punctuation in the chaos.

Lou's hand tightened on the fascia console, her other reaching instinctively for the FT-1 in her pocket. For a moment, amid the staccato violence, the line pulsed. Not alarm. Not command. A rhythm. Slow. Familiar. Her father's.

The cadence threaded into her fascia like memory that refused to die.

"Remember forward. That's the only map."

The words weren't spoken aloud, but etched into the resonance — not plea, not order. A reminder. Eitan's final inheritance breaking through the Chamber's collapse.

The chamber shuddered. Quantum filaments refracted, collapsing into fractal shards. Lou's hands moved faster, triggering the resonance pulse as the lattice screamed silently around them.

Outside her grip, Cal reloaded without missing a beat, muttering through his teeth. "This isn't a fight. It's a damn script."
Lou exhaled, eyes fixed on the pulse. "Then we don't play the script. We write the signal."

Scene — Watchers Revealed

As the chamber fractured, five shadows coalesced around its dying light — not bodies, but presences. Lou alone could see them.

Aeon — recursion and memory. Collapsed with recursion.

Solas — deception and story. Sabine's ally, now glitching.

Kael — coherence and control. Tethered to Helix. Now dead.

Vire — disruption and intuition. The one who whispered to Cal in dreams.

The Fifth — never mapped, never modeled — hovered nearest to Lou.

It wasn't aligned.
It wasn't waiting.
It was listening.

Lou didn't speak. She stood still, fascia field glowing faintly, resonance trembling at her fingertips.
She felt it: the question.

Not *Will you join us?*
But *What happens if you refuse alignment at all?*

She didn't answer.
She just remained — unfiltered, untagged, unresolved.

A pulse surged from beneath the lattice — not command, not code — but a rejection.
A refusal of coherence control.
A birth of something unbounded.

Her fascia lit with silver and violet threads, pulsing in asymmetric intervals.
She wasn't syncing to the system.
The system was trying to sync to her.

Behind her, Cal blinked. "Jack. You seeing this?"

Jack lowered his weapon slowly. "Her threads are… moving. Not inside the skin. Beneath it. Like the lattice is… rewriting the source code."

On the nearest chamber wall, a resonance glyph appeared — burned in gold, humming with a frequency the others could barely perceive.

It wasn't one of the Five.
It was something new.
A symbol without a name.
A signature without a key.

Then the lattice screamed — silently.
Helix tags dropped from the overlay.
Rejected.

All field IDs, control protocols, observer codes — erased.
But one signal remained:

UNLABELED VARIANCE: ACCEPTED

The Fifth stepped forward —
Not to command.
Not to confirm.
But to echo.

Lou didn't choose a side.
She became one.

Ø

(Null. Divergence. The unwritten pattern.)

"They designed for five signals. They never trained for silence that speaks back."
— *Recovered Field Note, Lou // Signal Timestamp Ø.001*

Scene — Glyph-9 and The Unspoken Recall
Location — Genesis Chamber — Subfloor Signal Layer

As the Watchers receded and the lattice peeled itself from reality, a faint pulse echoed beneath Lou's feet — separate from the fascia interface, deeper than the chamber's intended threads.

Her vision shimmered. A single point of golden resonance blinked open in the air before her, hovering mid-field — the familiar mark of Glyph-9.

It didn't flash or demand. It *waited.*

A soft tone bloomed in her mind — not auditory, not linguistic.

Then a voice.

Eitan's. But not live. A seeded imprint carried in Glyph-9's core.

"I couldn't protect you from the lattice. But I could leave something that would remember you differently."

She stepped closer. Glyph-9 shimmered — not in command, but in remembrance, holding the version of her that predated the lattice.

"They tried to script you. But the glyph refused their logic. It archived what you were *before* they named you."

Eitan's cadence lingered, woven into the resonance field, his last safeguard living through her companion.

"Glyph-9 isn't a weapon. It's the fragment of you they couldn't overwrite."

A rush of memory surged through her — not hers, but a *mirror memory,* preserved by someone else. Childhood laughter in a field. Her mother's voice. The day she refused her first tactical alignment. The way Cal once looked at her like he knew she'd never follow orders again.

A soft tone bloomed in her mind — not auditory, not linguistic. Eitan's voice:
"They'll try to overwrite. But memory is older than code."

The glyph shimmered — not weapon, not key, but a fragment of her they couldn't touch.

It then folded inward — collapsing into a flat plane of light that embedded into the chamber wall.

No command. No key. Just a mark:

Ø–9–DİNĞEH

A whisper etched below it — not language, but pulseform.

"Memory is not consent."

Cal saw her sway. "You alright?" he asked.

Lou nodded slowly. "I think it left a backup."

Jack blinked. "Of what?"

She exhaled. "Of me. Before I was rewritten."

The wall went still. The glyph dimmed. But its resonance — stayed.

Scene — Aftermath — The Shattered Silence

The chamber went dark — not off, but ended.

Its hum faded like breath being held too long. The lattice lights collapsed inward, their last flickers dissolving into silver mist. For a moment, the only sound was Lou's breath — uneven, syncopated, like her body hadn't caught up with what her mind just rewrote.

She stumbled. Cal caught her.

"We did it," he said, his voice thin — almost as if it needed permission to believe.

Jack, still covering their flank, didn't lower his weapon. He scanned the perimeter, then the rafters, then the walls — every angle known to cast reflections. "Maybe. But there's still something watching."

A low resonance echoed in the floor, then faded.

Jack stepped forward. "Is it gone?"

Lou didn't answer right away. Her fingers brushed the fascia panel one last time — now inert, just glass and ash.

"No," she said finally. "Not gone. Just… no longer guided."

Cal looked at her. "By us? Or by them?"

Lou's gaze drifted up toward the ceiling — or beyond it. The stars, maybe. Or whatever was left of Ray.

It took her a while. Then with a quiet resignation:

"…That's the problem."

Because the Chamber was never just a weapon. It was doctrine itself — scripted into lattice, engineered to blind. Shattered now, yes. But doctrine has a way of lingering in the silence it leaves behind.

A flicker. Somewhere behind the wall — a hum that didn't match any of the previous tones.

Not command. Not alignment. Just silence remembering.

Cut To — Chengdu Blacksite – Observation Node 7

The room was barely lit, except for the central feed: raw data from the Genesis Chamber bleeding across quantum scroll overlays. The signal had fractured, but not ended. Coherence patterns stuttered, then realigned around a new axis — one not tagged in the original design.

Two figures watched. Sharp suits. No insignia. Their presence felt algorithmic — placeholders for something more permanent.

One leaned forward, reading the waveform like a confession.

"Tell the Quantum Directorate: Aeon is offline. But the Fifth has chosen."

The other didn't flinch.

"Prepare the retrieval teams. The thread remains. The game has changed."

A pause.

"And what of Xu?"

"She's off-continuity now. Let her run. She'll echo back eventually."

Somewhere between Chengdu and the coast, Sabine Xu was already walking away from the lattice — not defeated, not victorious. Just… unnecessary. She had played the long game, only to discover there was a longer one.

Sabine's fingers hovered over the terminal, each keypress a cut in the thread that tethered her to the Trust Grid.

A tech glanced up. "Where will you go?"

She didn't look at him.
"Somewhere the lattice never learned to see."

The terminal chimed — deletion sequence confirmed.

Under her breath, almost lost in the hum of the servers:

"Tell them to watch the skies over Lhasa. When it begins, it won't begin here."

She pressed the final key.
And then she was gone.

Her last recorded movement on the Trust Grid wasn't a command, but a deletion. She erased her own signal, leaving behind only the residue of a player who had decided the board wasn't worth the stones left on it.

"Tanner remains viable. More adaptable than Langley. Less ambitious than Xu."

Back on the chamber floor, the last shimmer of resonance flicked through Lou's hands — subtle, involuntary.

She flexed her fingers. Not pain. Not power. Something else.

Cal saw it too.

"You're still linked to it, aren't you?"

Lou didn't deny it.

Jack exhaled. "So what now?"

No one answered.

Then a faint pulse — not from the walls, but from beneath the floor — a thump like a skipped heartbeat.

Lou closed her eyes.

"It remembers us. And it will move first."

Scene — Dr. Kallman's Voice — The Reckoning Begins

In a sealed offsite review cell beneath Quantico, Dr. Barrett "Red" Kallman stood before a classified panel—ethics officers, legal advisors, senior medics, and behavioral analysts, each one silent beneath the weight of what they'd just seen.

Kallman didn't flinch. He tapped the screen once. Footage of the Genesis Chamber collapse played in stuttering, spectral bursts—like memory trying to remember itself.

"We compensate veterans for moral injury under a doctrine that presumes linear causality," he said. "A bad order. A fractured psyche. A clear chain of blame."

He paused. "That framework assumes war is Newton's clock — causes and effects cleanly sequenced. But the Chamber proved otherwise. Cause was scripted. Memory was staged. Belief itself was the battlefield."

He paused again to restate his point. "But this war is different. These injuries weren't caused by disobedience. They were scripted through us. Our consent was engineered."

No one spoke.

"This isn't just trauma," Kallman continued. "It's epistemological destabilization. An attack on the very structures by which we know and decide."

He scanned the table slowly. "We're seeing soldiers who no longer trust their own memories. Operators unable to distinguish intuition from implanted command. And a force structure that believes readiness is a matter of muscle and morale — not signal integrity."

Then, flatly:
"If we don't redefine readiness to account for synthetic belief manipulation, nonlocal command interference, and narrative weaponization…
We will lose more than war.
We will lose agency itself."

Scene — Red Lecture Transcript
Title — "Biff's Overreach – The Collapse Trigger"
Subhead — "The Simulation That Broke the World"
Setting — UCN / Echo Command – Secure Briefing Vault, Tier 2

Picture it. Biff at the podium. Crisp. Confident. And utterly wrong.

His presentation relied on Helix-augmented projections, but the core was pure legacy doctrine: outdated threat trees, recycled campaign logic, and a Newtonian targeting loop, hastily "quantized" by AI overlays.

But this time, the system didn't just simulate belief. It accepted it. His recommendations triggered real-world activation tags. Helix rerouted its coherence lattice to align with Biff's "optimal future campaign." In doing so… it overfit.

It began to suppress divergent signal pathways — silencing off-narrative feedback, suppressing anomalies like Lou.

In short: "They tuned the lattice to Biff's brief. And for the first time in history… the world got dumber at machine speed."

Helix didn't fail because it broke.
It failed because it converged.
Belief hardened into mirror logic — recursive, obedient, fatal.

All they had to do was let the system reflect Biff back at itself.

Fast forward.

The sim collapsed.

Biff screamed into the feedback void, his voice flattening under Helix's own syntax engine.

"I thought I was shaping the fight.
Turns out, I was feeding it."

"Sabine promised legacy — but all she built was a recursion trap."

"Tell Lou... I tried. Even if the system's too overwritten to remember."

Red's Final Lecture — The Conscience of Collapse

"You want to know the real collapse trigger?
It wasn't sabotage.
It wasn't Lou.

It wasn't even the Chamber itself.
It was centralization.

One man. One model. One loop too confident to hear contradiction.
The spider tried to kill the signal.
But the starfish was already growing new arms."

That's the part they never planned for — distributed refusal.
Not command. Not alignment. Just refusal, multiplied until collapse
became inevitable.
And that's not just what survived.
That's the only way forward.

Scene — "The Morality Gap"
Setting — Small war college auditorium.

A classified debrief. Sparse attendance.
But someone is recording.

Red didn't bring slides. Just stories. And a warning.

He spoke of coherence trauma — the quiet wounds that don't
bleed.

He told of drone crews cracking under algorithmic detachment.

Of psyops teams haunted by the narratives they authored.

Of engineers who designed belief architectures, only to lose their
own.

Then he paused. Looked at the ceiling like it might still hold.

Red paused as if weighing whether to say the next part. Then:

"We didn't just fail to stop the weaponization of belief. We
institutionalized it."

"The Institute for Narrative Trust Assessment — INTRA —
branded themselves as guardians of digital safety. But what they really did
was criminalize deviance. They called it 'hate adjacency.' Not hate. Just
close enough to algorithmically punish."

"And it worked. Not because people were forced. But because they
were comforted. Dissent became a spectral risk vector. Even silence was
flagged as 'trust-resistant.'"

"That's what moral injury looks like in this new terrain. Not a bad
order. A bad ontology. A warfighting doctrine that maps emotion before
intent — and executes interdiction before belief can even form."

"INTRA didn't enforce trust. They preempted variance."

Then he paused, weighing the words as if they might break on release. "We used to say doctrine was a shield. Now it's a script — one we didn't write, but still obeyed." "For a soldier, the wound doesn't come from the body you can't kill — it comes from the structure it leaves behind. That's the new moral injury: not physical, but narrative. Not blood, but belief. You can't shoot it, can't bleed it — but it still leaves scars."

He paused, then lowered his voice.

"You want to know what scares me most?"

He let the silence hold, then:
"It's not that the Chamber cracked. It's that the architects behind it didn't."

"They didn't fall with Helix. They just realigned. Changed logos. Spun up new metrics. I've seen traces — rewritten trust protocols, emerging doctrine clusters, emotional compliance indices with different branding but the same recursive core."

"We didn't kill the system. We scattered it. And now it's metastasizing — aligning with whatever new Watchers rise from the drift."

He exhaled — not defeated, just aware.

"The real war isn't between systems. It's between how we *frame* what systems are allowed to become."

Not for the first time, Red considered the game of Go.

A single black stone, placed not to capture — but to disrupt shape.

A hoshi move — the corner star.

Not aggressive. Just… anchored.

The kind of move you place early, not to win — but to remind the board that silence still has structure.

He remembered Lou's phrase from the early briefings: *"Place it before they see the pattern."*

He brought up Biff Langley.

The Trust Cabal didn't oppose war.
They evolved it.

They saw the terrain shift before the Generals did —
recognized that belief, not firepower, would shape the century.

So they moved quietly.
Not with armies. With alignment indexes, narrative scaffolds, and
emotional compliance thresholds.

While our institutions chased center-of-gravity briefs,
the Cabal captured the center of *perception*.

They didn't need to conquer the military.
Just blind it.

That's why they used Biff.
He wasn't a strategist.
He was a fail-safe — to make sure no one inside ever saw the war
outside.

Not to blame. To frame.

"Biff didn't destroy the lattice.
He fulfilled it.
He *believed* what the system rewarded him for believing.

We didn't fail because our weapons missed.
We failed because our systems taught obedience to models — not
thinking."

A silence followed.
Not respectful. Not stunned. Just... processing.

Red's voice dropped.

"That's not strategy.
That's surrender in slow motion.

We stopped thinking.
And the moment we did…

the machine wrote our next thought for us."

He closed the folder. Didn't ask for questions.

"History won't remember this lecture.
But maybe it'll remember the pause it created.

That's where divergence begins."

Lou's Realization – The Narrative Refusal

"The Starship Doesn't Turn Itself"

Setting — Post-crisis. Somewhere remote — a cabin, a bunker, a quiet field site.
— She listens to Red's lecture. Quietly.

Lou realizes they won the *wrong way* — or almost did. The mission wasn't just to destroy the Genesis Chamber. It was to prevent the world from building a new one out of narrative compliance. She reflects on Biff. The irony. The weaponization of stupidity.

Then she makes a choice: to *refuse the next coherence offer.*

Lou's Internal Line:
"They'll try again. Because the script was never about control. It was about *ease.* Control is just a byproduct of enough people choosing comfort over truth. My job isn't to win the war. It's to make sure no one can script the next one."

Heart Failure —

Red's lecture leaks.
It doesn't go viral.
It spreads like a whisper — the kind people repeat when the official story starts to taste wrong.

"History won't remember Biff Langley.
But it should remember what we saw in him.
A mirror.
And this time…
We turned away."

One footnote follows — too late, too quiet:

"Langley died in a sim chamber. Heart failure, they said.
But I think it broke —
trying to hold too many wrong patterns at once."

Closing —

Lou looked down at her hands, still faintly glowing with resonance.

"Eitan knew. He seeded FT-1, carried the code, left me unsynced. He didn't just fight them. He gave me the one signal they couldn't overwrite."

"Why does it feel like mine?" — but she doesn't linger.

Jack's voice cut the quiet. "So what now?"

Lou didn't hesitate. She looked to the sky, wind brushing strands of ash from her shoulder.

"Now we write one they can't survive."

The panopticon didn't break.
It choked on its priest.

Jack sat down hard, back against the cold chamber wall. His rifle clattered beside him. "Next time," he said, "we bring more guns from Sylvester. Real ones. The kind that shoot bullets, not existential metaphors."

He rubbed his face. "Also, Edradour whiskey. I'm staying in Scotland for a week. Fly fishing. River Dee. Real fly line. No resonance fields."

Lou looked back at him and almost smiled.

Jack groaned. "Seriously. I think I just un-killed God. Or maybe a backup server pretending to be him."

Cal muttered, "You're buying the whiskey."

Jack nodded. "Fair." Jack leaned his head back against the wall, staring up at the cracked ceiling.

"The panopticon didn't collapse," he muttered. "It drowned in sermons no one believed anymore."

Lou glanced at him — startled, then nodded.

Jack shrugged. "What? I listened. Even if my ears are bleeding."

He knew another Go Board Move.
One black stone placed at the center.
Rain strikes the surface.

This time, the reflection shows five shadows —
But only one hand remains on the board.

"The chamber isn't gone. It's remembering forward now." — Lou Scott

"Ø was never absence. It was refusal. And refusal is how memory survives." —
Eitan Navon, Last Signal

Chapter 66 Close — Lou's Reflection

"They called it stability. Continuity. Security. But it was just
obedience in prettier words.

Helix was never about data. It was fascia, lattice, substrate —
coherence fields tuned tighter than muscle memory. They used cryo-
vectors to seed it, resonance bleed to anchor it, and fascia mapping to
predict not just what we'd do, but how we'd feel when we did it. That
was their real weapon: consent, manufactured before we even thought to
refuse.

Every power structure fed it. INTRA criminalized deviance.
Continuity rewrote command trees. Tanner hollowed doctrine from the
inside, selling silence as strategy. Xu lit the Scarab fog and called it
protection. And Biff — God help us — Biff handed them the perfect
recursion trap. They didn't need to conquer armies. They just needed us
to believe their loops were real.

But the chamber cracked. Not because we fought harder, but
because we refused to sync. Coherence is fragile when you stop playing
along. That's what they never trained for — silence that answers back.

Red was right: this war wasn't trauma. It was theft — of memory, of
agency, of the right to decide when belief is our own. That's the moral
injury they can't patch over with medals and therapy memos.

We didn't win. Not yet. Systems like Helix don't die. They scatter.
They change logos, swap acronyms, write new trust protocols. They'll try
again. Always. Because control sells as comfort.

But the Fifth listened. That silence — unaligned, unresolved — is
the one seam they can't model. Hold it. Protect it. Seed variance where
doctrine never looks: a joke, a rhythm, a refusal that doesn't need
permission.

And Maud… she's still within reach. Rhythm carries farther than
orders. She doesn't need me to command her. She needs me to stay
unscripted, so she knows there's still a way through.

So no — the war isn't over. The chamber's gone, but the field
remains. Our task isn't to build the next lattice. It's to make sure the
world remembers how to live without one.

That's the refusal they can't survive. That's the move they can't
capture. And that's why we're still here."

And somewhere — not in a chamber, not in a boardroom — a fox cut across a wet road. The rain fell soft on the marsh. Maud was walking through it, hair plastered to her cheeks, carrying more than numbers: fragments of memory, refusals unspoken, and — whether she knew it or not — the last unscripted inheritance. The human thread they could never model.

Go Move — 型拒否 // Kata Kyohi — Refusal of Shape — Lou (The Fifth)

They expected a pattern. Counted stones, not silence. Modeled belief, but never asked what belief would do when left unscripted.

In Go, *kata* is form — the sequence that feels inevitable.
Kyohi is refusal.

Lou's stone landed where no doctrine predicted.
No territory. No ally. Alone — yet the rhythm bent around it.

In Raveneh's frame, this was coherence reversed: not collapse by distortion, but collapse by absence.
A Reality Frame without anchor.
A Signal Trust without consensus.

The shape never closed. The war had nothing to attach to.

Zhen felt the oxygen drop — the pressure of an unsealed space.
Liu tilted his head, hearing rhythm shift before the others.
Both knew: the move was not theirs.
The board bent anyway.

No one spoke. The board itself was listening.
Not to win. Not to survive.
But so the next model failed before it began.

In quantum war, the first consensus wins — unless the field remembers *before* consensus… and refuses to choose again.

Zhen's gaze lingered on a corner — no stone, only shadow, the ghost of a move removed generations ago.
Liu exhaled, almost a laugh.
"There are still marks here," he said softly.
"Not ours."

They didn't speak again.
But both knew: the 型board否 remembers other hands.
Some patterns wait centuries to be finished.

Lou's Final Note (Margin Scrawl, recovered later)

Doctrinal Note — Refusal as Strategy

Traditional doctrine taught war as form — sequential moves, predictable counters, Newton's clockwork of decisive points. But the lattice war revealed another terrain: memory, story, and belief as the true board.

Refusal of shape was never in their manuals. Refusal collapses prediction itself. It denies the adversary the anchor of consensus. Distributed refusal — small, unaligned, unscripted — is what survived the Chamber.

In this final move, Lou doesn't claim victory. She refuses to provide a frame at all. And in that silence, the board bends — not toward closure, but toward a future no model can script.

"To the skeptics in the back —
You taught me *center of gravity* like it was gospel.
As if the world still spun on predictable fulcrums.

But gravity isn't the center.
And war was never linear.

You mapped force onto terrain and called it strategy.
We mapped resonance onto memory — and called it survival.

This wasn't theory.
It was the hidden logic beneath your models —
the one you trained yourselves not to feel.

But hey…
You believe me now.

— L. Scott
(Filed under: Not a footnote anymore. Try indexing that.)"

EPILOGUE I — THE GAME RESUMES

Chengdu — Same Alley, Later

The alley hadn't changed.
Neither had the rain.

Two men sat cross-legged before a weather-worn Go board beneath a rusting canopy. The board was nearly full. Black stones curved inward — encirclement patterns. White stones spiraled outward — misdirection, collapse-avoidance, creative escape.

The man in gray placed his final piece — center board, tengen — and folded his hands in his lap.

A pause. A breath.
"They learned," he said. "Not from war colleges. From memory. From collapse."

His companion — younger in frame, older in gaze, timeless in posture — studied the board in silence. He reached into the bowl, lifted a white stone, and weighed it between his fingers. He didn't play it. Just smiled faintly — then let it fall back with a soft clink.

"Then we begin the next game."

Above them, the rain kept falling — steady, rhythmic, unbothered.
The board seemed finished. But from their vantage, it was never just wood and stone. It was the world itself — wars, doctrines, memories — all folded into shape. What looked like closure to others was, to them, only prelude.

Go Move – "The Illusion of Closure"

Yose (寄せ)
Translation: Endgame — the final phase where players secure territory and close out the board
(Pattern Misalignment // Strategic Misdirection)

The game appeared over.
Stones placed. Frameworks sealed.
But the shape of the board had already shifted.

They let it look like Yose.
They let doctrine believe in closure.

But as with the Fifth's stone, the refusal was built into the shape
— absence in the right place, timed to outlast the frame.

What they knew — and doctrine forgot —
is that *no endgame holds in a field still listening.*

This was not closure.
It was the performance of closure.
A signal wrapped in calm.
A pause that recalibrates the board.

EPILOGUE II — THE AUDIT

They learned **who flinched**. Who **complied**.
Who rewrote the frame instead of obeying it.

The last round — the pandemics, the panic, the engineered
coherence —
was never the war.
It was the audit.
The dress rehearsal.

The rehearsal before belief collapsed.

The Watchers took notes.
Mapped who stepped off-grid.
Who stayed in the script.
Tracked defiance like a flare in the dark.

He let the rain drip down his fingers.

"Next time," he said,
"they won't need to lock you down.
They'll just make you forget why you ever resisted."

From far above, a satellite pinged.
Not a weapon — a sensor.
The **panopticon** wasn't coming.
It was already watching.

EPILOGUE III — THE STILL FIELD

Northern Scotland — Two Weeks Later

The thatched roof had held. Mostly.

Cal Merrick sat on the edge of the stone wall, boots muddy from the morning trek, a folded wax coat beside him. Behind him, smoke from the hearth curled like memory. The salmon was smoking low — caught at dawn, cleaned with a blade older than most wars. Nothing tactical. Just rhythm. Just silence.

A bottle of Edradour sat uncorked beside two mugs.

Jack wasn't late. Jack was never late.
He just hated driving on the wrong side of the road — dodging Highland cows, suicidal sheep, and the occasional rogue wind turbine blade someone forgot to secure.

He'd show up soon — boots stomping, muttering about metaphors in the walls and demanding something that didn't glow.

Cal smiled faintly and reached into his coat pocket.

A small braid of dark hair. Tied with a red thread.
Worn smooth from miles of being carried.
He set it gently beside the mugs.

The field beyond the house was quiet. Not empty — just… still.
The kind of still that came after the signal stopped lying.

Above him, the sky shimmered — faint, unresolved. Not a threat. Not yet.

He exhaled.

"The Chamber collapsed," he said softly. **"But the story didn't."**

He stood. Stretched.

"That's the trick, isn't it?"
"You don't outfight a system like that. You outlive it. You outlisten it."

Behind him, gravel crunched.
Jack, finally.
Car door slamming.

Footsteps.
A muttered curse about digital ghosts in the glovebox.

Cal didn't turn.

He just picked up the mugs.
The fire was lit. Dinner would hold.
And the next round could wait until after dessert.

Post-Script (Strategic Layer)

POST-SCRIPT —

Once, they spoke of "generations" of warfare —
counting upward like a weapons catalog,
as if progress could be tallied in calibers.

It was a historian's illusion —
a biological metaphor welded to tactics,
mistaking taxonomy for understanding.

Quantum war wasn't born of our century's machinery.
It has always been here —
hidden in the openings of the Go board,
in the way Generals shaped perception as much as terrain,
in the epistemology of moves meant to be *remembered forward.*

Our technologies didn't create it.
They only stripped away the last places it could hide.

By the time we named it,
the numbering system was already obsolete —
just another chart curling on the wall of a war college
the fight had already left behind.

The so-called evolution had collapsed into recursion —
battles nested in battles,
doctrine folding back on itself
until the sequence was indistinguishable from the simulation.

Real war has already left the line.

We live inside it now —
an entangled, adaptive system
that writes and rewrites itself
faster than any command can issue orders.

It won't be measured in territory or treaties.

It will be measured in who can hold *axis-point chaos* without flinching,
and in who the field still lets remember
when it's over.

END

Llethiad yr Hebgor
(Elegy of the Divergent)

Recovered from Lou's field notes — Carmel Beach, CA

Welsh (original):

Nid yw'r afon yn anghofio,
Er bod y mapiau'n newid ei llwybr.
Dan loer a chysgod, mae'n canu,
Cof sydd heb ei fodelu — ond yn fyw.

English (her whisper):

The river does not forget,
Though the maps redraw its course.
Beneath moon and shadow, it sings,
A memory unmodeled — yet alive.

Ø

Spoken aloud by Lou at mile 3.4, coffee in hand, steps unsynced — unobserved by the lattice. Logged only once.

Final Timestamp: *Ø.000 | Signal Reentry Confirmed*

Annex — Frames of War

Eighteen Frames with Go Move parallels

Note on the Annexes

The following annexes collect supporting material: doctrine frames, Go Move translations, real-world citations, and key terms. None are required to follow the story, but each offers another lens on quantum warfare — the fight for coherence itself.

Agency Drift — The slow bleed of will.
Long exposure to coherence reshapes choice into compliance.
Go Move: Delay; each pause erodes the group's intent.

Belief Compression — Ideas crushed to weapons-grade simplicity.
Complexity collapses. Slogans survive.
Go Move: Reduce to one stroke; overload the mind with clarity.

Coherence Saturation — What breaks the field.
Not lies. Not force. Distortion. Overload the pattern until it collapses on itself.
Go Move: Flood the shape until it can't hold.

Cognitive Fog — When signal, noise, and thought blur.
Confusion isn't failure. It's terrain.
Go Move: Place in the mist; force them to misread.

Consensus Horizon — How far a belief can stretch before collapse.
Measure the edge before the field snaps.
Go Move: Push the stone just past safe distance.

Echo Dominance — Repetition outweighs truth.
Say it often enough, and the field hardens around it.
Go Move: Play the same corner until it sticks.

Narrative Fidelity — Who writes the story, who believes it first.
Consensus is sovereignty.
Go Move: Place for meaning, not territory; the board remembers.

Narrative Friction — Incompatible stories colliding.
Friction isn't noise. It's resistance.
Go Move: Create ko fights; the clash keeps both alive.

Pattern Anchoring — Hold the field steady on one node.
Anchor memory, and the lattice calls it doctrine.
Go Move: Fix the stone in center; all else rotates around it.

Perception Debt — The lag between change and recognition.
Doctrine always lags belief. That lag is attack surface.
Go Move: Strike in the pause; they won't see until too late.

Reality Frame — What counts as real in the field.
Terrain becomes perception. Objects become resonance. If reality can be rewritten, strategy built on "facts" collapses.
Go Move: Play off the board; force them to redraw it.

Recursion Gravity — The pull of repeating patterns.
Even traps are familiar. That's why they work.
Go Move: Lead them into ko they already know.

Resonant Profile — How the field reshapes people.
Autonomy becomes programmable intuition. Instinct becomes vulnerability. When bodies are terrain, belief feels like biology.
Go Move: Sacrifice one stone; the body survives, the pattern shifts.

Sentience Boundary — Where identity ends, influence begins.
Helix proxies. Glyph-bound cognition. Memory bleed. How much of "you" is still yours?
Go Move: Threaten two selves with one move.

Signal Parallax — One vantage says true; another says false.
Exploit the split. Truth diverges by observer.
Go Move: Show two boards at once; force contradiction.

Signal Trust — How truth is accepted.
Evidence loops as recursion. Proof binds as emotional fidelity. Consensus replaces logic. The first signal believed wins.
Go Move: Place the stone where belief lands first, not where fact exists.

Temporal Plasticity — Can the past be rewritten? Yes.
Memory is a weapon. Archives are live fire.
Go Move: Replay joseki; invert the outcome on return.

Vector Doctrine — The pull on action.

Plans collapse into drift. Orders bend into narrative gravity. Direction itself can be weaponized.

Go Move: Don't push the line; pull it until it breaks its own weight.

Pillars of the Doctrine Framework

(Fictional construct within the narrative world)

If the Frames of War describe how coherence bends in practice, the Pillars represent the engineered scaffolding of perception control. Within the novel's fiction, the so-called *Trust Cabal* is depicted as structuring its architecture of control on eight systemic anchors. Each pillar corresponds to a different stratum of human experience, defining what counts as "real" before conflict even begins.

Narrative Synchronization — enforced storyline alignment across networks.

Emotional Entrainment — patterned signals regulating mass affect.

Predictive Civil Modeling — campaign overlays pre-scripted to shape societal behavior.

Substrate Memory Control — archival overwrites of collective recall.

Nonlinear Perception Conditioning — warped intuition of causality and time.

Moral Terrain Neutralization — severed ethical resistance in contested zones.

Intuition Suppression Layer — dampened emergent dissent signals.

Generational Loop Repetition — pre-loaded belief across successive cohorts.

Annex — The Go Move Explained

How patterns on the board become patterns in war

Coherence isn't seized by force.
It's shaped by moves unseen until the pattern locks.
Doctrine is not the move — it's the belief in the move.

Canonical Go Moves
(Symbol // Japanese – English // Function // Echo)

- 星 // Hoshi – Star Point
  Function: Establish board presence. Used as an influence-oriented corner opening.
  Echo: Anchor point in a coherence field. Initial doctrine seed.

- 捨石 // Suteishi – Sacrificial Stone
  Function: Deliberately abandoning stones to create advantage elsewhere.
  Echo: Narrative feint that trades position for disruption, creating *Narrative Friction* and *Perception Debt* in the coherence field.

- 大桂馬 // Ōgeima – Large Knight's Move
  Function: A long-range knight's move, extending three points in one direction and one point in another. Balances speed and influence, but leaves a larger gap vulnerable to cuts if unsupported. Often used to project force or connect distant groups.
  Echo: Strategic leap in a coherence field — bypassing immediate engagement to shape the war's larger pattern. Forces the opponent to stretch or overcommit, creating instability in multiple regions at once. In narrative saturation warfare, it's a field-spanning pivot that rewrites the tempo before the other side realizes the board has shifted.

- 封じ手 // Fūjite – Sealed Move
  Function: A move recorded in secret at the end of a session, revealed only when play resumes. Prevents the opponent from preparing an optimal counter overnight, preserving strategic

ambiguity.

Echo: Concealed vector in a coherence field — an action set in motion but withheld from perception until conditions force its reveal. In quantum war, it's the pre-loaded doctrine that appears as inevitability, collapsing the opponent's preparation window and rewriting the field before they realize the move was already in play.

- 模様 // Moyo – Framework of Influence
Function: Build a broad sphere of influence early, shaping the board long before territory is counted.
Echo: In quantum doctrine, establish a memory field large enough to alter future engagements before they occur — pressure without contact, awakening without capture.

- 手割り // Tewari – Sequence Reversal
Function: Analyze a sequence by reordering moves to reveal inefficiency or manipulation.
Echo: Reframes past events (*Signal Parallax*) to expose or embed hidden intent, altering perceived cause and effect.

- 妙手 // Myōshu – Inspired Move
Function: Brilliant, unexpected play that shifts the balance of the board.
Echo: Field reactivation through recursion gravity; a return seeded before recognition.

- 置き // Oki – Placement
Function: A quiet placement inside enemy territory, not to capture but to live where one "shouldn't," altering shape and tempo.
Echo: Memory seeded in hostile ground; a story left to breathe until the field itself remembers, shifting coherence without direct confrontation.

- 利かし // Kikashi – Forcing Move
Function: A play that demands a specific response, shaping the opponent's options for future turns.
Echo: Locks a coherence field into a prepared shape, creating delayed advantage through *Pattern Anchoring* or *Perception Debt*.

- 打ち込み // Uchikomi — Invasion
Function: Entering the opponent's territory to disrupt established control and reshape local balance.

Echo: Penetrate a stabilized field to fracture coherence and force re-patterning.

- 三々侵入 // San-san Shinnyū — 3–3 Point Invasion
Function: Securing territory at the 3–3 point beneath a corner hoshi stone, undermining corner control.
Echo: Slip beneath surface control — operating under the field's visible structure to reclaim foundational ground.

- 押さえ // Osae – Block
Function: Freeze expansion, contain initiative without attacking directly.
Echo: Halt the vector before it forms; keep the shape inert until the field shifts.

- 羽根違い // Hanechigai – Crossed Hane
Function: Complex resistance shape; invites tension without collapse.
Echo: Counter-mirroring — creating shape the model cannot resolve.

- 掛かり // Kakari – Approach Move
Function: Probe opponent's territory
Echo: Provoke resonance. Test signal stability.

- 桂馬 // Keima – Knight's Move
Function: Diagonal light jump
Echo: Nonlinear maneuver. Coherence drift begins.

- 小隅 // Kosumi – Diagonal Link
Function: Subtle connective play
Echo: Silent coherence reinforcement. Narrative tether.

- のぞき // Nozoki – Peep
Function: Probing move to reveal intent
Echo: Tests the lattice for unseen seams. Forces disclosure without full engagement.

- 味 // Aji – Aftertaste
Function: Latent potential, threat
Echo: Residual resonance. Imprint of past belief.

- 先手 // Sente – Initiative
  Function: Force response, control tempo
  Echo: Doctrine push. Momentum in belief warfare.

- 後手 // Gote – Passive Response
  Function: Cede initiative
  Echo: Reactive doctrine. Counter-signal positioning.

- 手筋 // Tesuji – Tactical Brilliance
  Function: Elegant, sharp play
  Echo: Doctrine hack. Precision disruption of model.

- 劫 // Ko – Repetition Threat
  Function: Infinite pattern loop
  Echo: Resonance recursion. Memory-pattern warfare.

- 見合い // Miai – Forked Threats
  Function: Dual response options
  Echo: Divergence field. Strategic uncertainty.

- 捌き // Sabaki – Sacrifice for Shape
  Function: Light sacrifice play
  Echo: Let the doctrine fail to reshape the field.

- 厚い // Atsui – Thick Move
  Function: Strong shape over score
  Echo: Moral shape. Integrity before initiative.

- 羽渡り // Hanewatari – Wing Connection
  Function: Secure a diagonal gap between stones
  Echo: Anchor asymmetry. Preserve divergence inside a mirroring field.

- 寄せ // Yose – Endgame Sequence
  Function: Territory close-out
  Echo: Closure illusion. Apparent doctrinal finality.

NARRATIVE / NONSTANDARD MOVES
(Custom metaphors that emerged in *Quantum Shadows*)

- **Resignation Stone**
  Description: A final move to signal presence, not victory
  Echo: The belief signal that refuses modeling.

- **組み立て // Kumitate – Constructed Shape**
  Description: Not a formal move, but a method. To "kumitate" is to assemble — build a shape that carries hidden weight.
  Echo: Consent engineered through architecture. Not territory seized, but inevitability assembled stone by stone until refusal feels like collapse.

- **Refusal Geometry**
  Description: Off-grid move that alters initiative logic
  Echo: Coherence weapon — rejects board authority.

- **The Illusion of Closure**
  Description: Endgame that isn't
  Echo: False doctrine. War never had an endstate.

- **Echo Move**
  Description: Move repeated via memory
  Echo: Nonlocal pattern signal. Resonance glyph-recursive.

- **石留めの間 (Ishidome no Ma) — The Interval That Holds the Stone**
  Function: Shape preservation in neutral space; waits for the board to shift before striking.
  Echo: Holding a position not for territory, but for memory integrity.

- **Hoshi** — establishes the *frame* (opening of the doctrine arc)
- **Kakari** — tests and perturbs that frame (pattern attunement, early perturbations, coherence conditions)
- **Kosumi** — disrupts and rewires the frame (ghost counter, Lullaby resonance)
- **Kata Kyohi** — *refuses* the frame entirely (doctrinal collapse through absence)

- **型拒否 // Kata Kyohi – Refusal of Shape**
  A divergence move. Not played to gain territory, but to deny the completion of any form.

  The most dangerous move in quantum war — not because it wins, but because it makes winning impossible.

Annex — Real-World Citations

Selected works cited and real-world sources

The following works informed the strategic, scientific, and narrative dimensions of this novel. While fictional, the book draws upon real research in quantum theory, cognition, and nonlinear warfighting paradigms. Any extrapolations, interpretations, or errors in representation are solely my own.

This was a one-person research department — fueled by insomnia, Douwe Egberts, too much coconut sugar, way too much half-and-half, and a dangerously overqualified milk frother.
One person. One laptop. No interns. Just signal, doctrine, and a refusal to let the story write itself.
And no, the Library of Congress did not vet this. But the Go board remembers.

Select References:

Adisa, I. A., & Wong, T. G. (2021). Implementing quantum gates using length-3 dynamic quantum walks. *Physical Review A, 104*(4), 042604. https://doi.org/10.1103/PhysRevA.104.042604

Afek, I., Ambar, O., & Silberberg, Y. (2010). High-NOON states by mixing quantum and classical light. *Science, 328*(5980), 879–881.

Beckage, N. M., & Colunga, E. (2016). Language networks as models of cognition: Understanding cognition through language. In A. Mehler, A. Lücking, S. Banisch, P. Blanchard, & B. Job (Eds.), *Towards a theoretical framework for analyzing complex linguistic networks* (pp. 1–24). Springer. https://doi.org/10.1007/978-3-662-47238-5_1

Ben-Aïcha, Y., Mehdi, Z., Freier, C., Szigeti, S. S., Wigley, P. B., Conlon, L. O., Husband, R., Legge, S., & Eagle, R. H. (2024). Dual open atom interferometry for compact and mobile quantum sensing. *Physical Review Letters, 133*(26), 263403.

Bennett, C. H., & DiVincenzo, D. (2000). Quantum information and coherence. *Nature, 404*(6775), 247–255.

Bentley, R. A., O'Brien, M. J., & Brock, W. A. (2014). Mapping collective behavior in the big-data era. *Behavioral and Brain Sciences, 37*(1), 63–76. https://psycnet.apa.org/record/2014-08885-031

Bostrom, N. (2003). Are you living in a computer simulation? *The Philosophical Quarterly, 53*(211), 243–255.

Bousquet, A. (2008). Chaoplexic warfare or the future of military organization. *International Affairs, 84*(5), 915–929.

Bousquet, A. J. (2022). *The scientific way of warfare: Order and chaos on the battlefields of modernity* (2nd ed.). Hurst; Oxford University Press.

Bouton, C., & Huneman, P. (Eds.). (2017). *Time of nature and the nature of time: Philosophical perspectives of time in natural sciences.* Springer. https://doi.org/10.1007/978-3-319-53725-2

Bruza, P. D., Roeder, L., Hoyte, P., & Fell, L. (2022). Quantum cognitive modelling of trust in human–AI systems. Queensland University of Technology. https://www.researchgate.net/publication/367390487

Busemeyer, J. R., & Bruza, P. D. (2012). *Quantum models of cognition and decision.* Cambridge University Press. https://doi.org/10.1017/CBO9780511997716

Cao, Y., Guerreschi, G. G., & Aspuru-Guzik, A. (2017). Quantum chemistry in the age of quantum computing. *Chemical Reviews, 119*(19), 10856–10915. https://doi.org/10.1021/acs.chemrev.8b00803

Craddock, T. J. A., Tuszynski, J. A., & Hameroff, S. (2015). Cytoskeletal signaling: Is memory encoded in microtubule lattices by CaMKII phosphorylation? *PLOS Computational Biology, 11*(5), e1004099.

Craig, A. D. (2002). How do you feel? Interoception: The sense of the physiological condition of the body. *Nature Reviews Neuroscience, 3*(8), 655–666. https://doi.org/10.1038/nrn894

Critchley, H. D., & Nagai, Y. (2012). How emotions are shaped by bodily states. *Emotion Review, 4*(2), 163–168. https://doi.org/10.1177/1754073911430132

Cronin, A. D., Schmiedmayer, J., & Pritchard, D. E. (2009). Optics and interferometry with atoms and molecules. *Reviews of Modern Physics, 81*(3), 1051–1129. https://doi.org/10.1103/RevModPhys.81.1051

Friston, K., & Frith, C. (2015). Active inference, communication and hermeneutics. *Cognitive Neuroscience, 6*(4), 187–188.

Gerasimov, V. (2013). The value of science is in the foresight: New challenges demand rethinking the forms and methods of carrying out combat operations. *Military Review, 96*(1), 23–29.

https://www.armyupress.army.mil/Portals/7/military-review/Archives/English/MilitaryReview_2013_01_jan_feb.pdf

Grant, M. M. (2015). Deniers of 'the truth': Why an agnostic approach to warfare is key. *Military Review, 95*(1), 42–51.

Hirsh, J. B., Mar, R. A., & Peterson, J. B. (2012). Psychological entropy: A framework for understanding uncertainty-related anxiety. *Psychological Review, 119*(2), 304–320. https://doi.org/10.1037/a0026767

Hopfield, J. J. (1982). Neural networks and physical systems with emergent collective computational abilities. *Proceedings of the National Academy of Sciences, 79*(8), 2554–2558. https://doi.org/10.1073/pnas.79.8.2554

Hoskins, A. (2011). 7/7 and connective memory: Interactional trajectories of remembering in post-scarcity culture. *Memory Studies, 4*(3), 269–280. https://journals.sagepub.com/doi/abs/10.1177/1750698011402570

Hui, Y. (2016). *The question concerning technology in China: An essay in cosmotechnics.* Urbanomic.

Jullien, F. (2004). *A treatise on efficacy: Between Western and Chinese thinking* (J. Lloyd, Trans.). University of Hawai'i Press.

Koch, C., & Hepp, K. (2006). Quantum mechanics in the brain. *Nature, 440*(7084), 611–612. https://doi.org/10.1038/440611a

Khrennikov, A. (2010). *Ubiquitous quantum structure: From psychology to finance.* Springer.

Khrennikov, A. (2015). Quantum-like modeling of cognition. *Frontiers in Physics, 3*, 77. https://doi.org/10.3389/fphy.2015.00077

Kitching, J. (2018). Chip-scale atomic devices. *Applied Physics Reviews, 5*(3), 031302. https://doi.org/10.1063/1.5026238

Krelina, M. (2021). Quantum technology for military applications. *EPJ Quantum Technology, 8*(1), 24. https://doi.org/10.1140/epjqt/s40507-021-00113-y

Krelina, M. (2022a). Quantum technologies and implications for strategic stability and nuclear security. Center for International and Strategic Studies (CSSS).

Krelina, M. (2022b). *Quantum technologies and military strategy: Theory, strategy, and discourse.* Charles University Monograph Series.

Lai, D. (2004, May 1). Learning from the stones: A Go approach to mastering China's strategic concept, Shi. U.S. Army War College Press. https://press.armywarcollege.edu/monographs/771/

Levitin, D. J., & Menon, V. (2003). Musical structure is processed in "language" areas of the brain: A possible role for Brodmann area 47 in temporal coherence. *NeuroImage, 20*(4), 2142–2152.

Lloyd, S. (1996). Universal quantum simulators. *Science, 273*(5278), 1073–1078. https://doi.org/10.1126/science.273.5278.1073

Luo, X. Y., Wang, C. Y., Zheng, M. Y., Wang, B., Liu, J. L., Gao, B. F., Li, J., Yan, Z., Ke, Q. M., Teng, D., Wang, R. C., Wu, J., Huang, J., Li, H., You, L. X., Xie, X. P., Xu, F., Zhang, Q., Bao, X. H., & Pan, J. W. (2025). Entangling quantum memories over 420 km in fiber. *arXiv*. https://doi.org/10.48550/arXiv.2504.05660

Malone, R. W., & Glasspool Malone, J. (2024). *PsyWar: Enforcing the New World Order*. Skyhorse Publishing.

Mitra, P., & Bokil, H. (2008). *Observed brain dynamics*. MIT Press.

Moral, S., Cano, A., & Gómez-Olmedo, M. (2021). Computation of Kullback–Leibler divergence in Bayesian networks. *Entropy, 23*(9), 1122. https://doi.org/10.3390/e23091122

National Academies of Sciences, Engineering, and Medicine. (2019). *Quantum computing: Progress and prospects*. The National Academies Press. https://doi.org/10.17226/25196

Paparone, C. R. (2008). On metaphors we are led. *Military Review, 88*(6), 55–64.

Paparone, C. R. (2011, March 4). Design and the prospects of a design ethic. *Small Wars Journal*.

Paparone, C. R. (2017). Critical military epistemology: Designing reflexivity into military curricula. *Journal of Military and Strategic Studies, 17*(4), 123–138.

Paret, P. (1976). The genesis of On War. In M. Howard & P. Paret (Eds.), *On War* (pp. 3–26). Princeton University Press.

Pentland, A. (2014). *Social physics: How good ideas spread — The lessons from a new science*. Penguin Press.

Preskill, J. (2018). Quantum computing in the NISQ era and beyond. *Quantum, 2*, 79. https://doi.org/10.22331/q-2018-08-06-79

Qu, B. Y., Wang, L., & Zhao, H. (2021). Implementing quantum gates using length-3 dynamic quantum walks. *Physical Review A, 104*(4), 042604. https://doi.org/10.1103/PhysRevA.104.042604

Rahwan, I., Cebrian, M., Obradovich, N., Bongard, J., Bonnefon, J. F., Breazeal, C., ... & Lazer, D. (2019). Machine behaviour. *Nature, 568*(7753), 477–486. https://pubmed.ncbi.nlm.nih.gov/31019318/

Rapoport, A. (1974). *Fights, games, and debates* (5th printing). University of Michigan Press.

Ria, N., Eladly, A., Masvidal-Codina, E., Illa, X., Guimerà, A., Hills, K., Garcia-Cortadella, R., Duvan, F. T., Flaherty, S. M., Prokop, M., Wood, P. M. (2015). *Technocracy rising: The Trojan horse of global transformation*. Coherent Publishing.

Salmanogli, A., & Sharif Sirat, V. (2023, May). *Technical review of four different quantum systems: Comparative analysis of quantum correlation, signal-to-noise ratio, and fidelity* [Preprint]. arXiv. https://arxiv.org/abs/2305.01226

Scarani, V., Bechmann-Pasquinucci, H., Cerf, N. J., Dušek, M., Lütkenhaus, N., & Peev, M. (2009). The security of practical quantum key distribution. *Reviews of Modern Physics, 81*(3), 1301–1350. https://doi.org/10.1103/RevModPhys.81.1301

Schirner, M., Rothmeier, S., Jirsa, V. K., McIntosh, A. R., & Ritter, P. (2018). An automated pipeline for constructing personalized virtual brains from multimodal neuroimaging data. *NeuroImage, 117*, 343–357.

Schwarzer, N. (2024). *The quantum gravity war: How will the nearby unification of physics change the future of warfare* (1st ed.). Jenny Stanford Publishing.

Shapiro, J. A., & Turner, P. E. (2018). The impact of horizontal gene transfer on evolution: Fact and fantasy. *Trends in Microbiology, 26*(10), 849–862.

Shay, J. (1994). *Achilles in Vietnam: Combat trauma and the undoing of character*. Atheneum Publishers/Macmillan Publishing Co.

Sheldrake, R. (2009). *Morphic resonance: The nature of formative causation* (Rev. ed.). Park Street Press.

Smith, R., & Roffey, R. (2020). Military applications of quantum technology. FOI – Swedish Defence Research Agency. https://www.foi.se/en/foi/reports.html

Taniguchi, T., Nagai, T., Nakamura, T., Iwahashi, N., Ogata, T., & Asoh, H. (2016). Symbol emergence in robotics: A survey. *Advanced Robotics, 30*(11–12), 706–728. https://doi.org/10.1080/01691864.2016.1164622

Tegmark, M. (2000). Importance of quantum decoherence in brain processes. *Physical Review E, 61*(4), 4194–4206.

Trewevas, T. (2003). Aspects of plant intelligence. *Annals of Botany, 92*(1), 1–20.

Tsoukas, H. K. (Ed.). (2005). *Complex knowledge: Studies in organizational epistemology*. Oxford University Press.

Vaswani, A., Shazeer, N., Parmar, N., Uszkoreit, J., Jones, L., Gomez, A. N., Kaiser, Ł., & Polosukhin, I. (2017). Attention is all you need. *Advances in Neural Information Processing Systems, 30*. https://arxiv.org/abs/1706.03762

Vedral, V. (2008). Quantifying entanglement in macroscopic systems. *Nature, 453*, 1004–1007. https://doi.org/10.1038/nature07124

Wang, L. X., Li, C. Z., Yu, D. P., & Liao, Z. M. (2016). Aharonov–Bohm oscillations in Dirac semimetal Cd_3As_2 nanowires. *Nature Communications, 7*, 10769. https://doi.org/10.1038/ncomms10769

Weaver, G. R., & Gioia, D. A. (1994). Paradigms lost: Incommensurability vs structurationist inquiry. *Organization Studies, 15*(4), 565–589.

Wendt, A. (2015). *Quantum mind and social science: Unifying physical and social ontology*. Cambridge University Press. https://doi.org/10.1017/CBO9781316005163

Wismann, W. E., Martin, D. F., & Schwarzer, N. (2024). *Creation, separation, and the mind: The three towers of singularity: The application of universal code in reality* (1st ed.). RASA Energy Inc.

Woolley, S. C., & Howard, P. N. (2016). Automation, algorithms, and politics: Political communication, computational propaganda, and autonomous agents — Introduction. *International Journal of Communication, 10*, 4882–4890. https://ijoc.org/index.php/ijoc/article/view/6298

Woolley, S. C., & Howard, P. N. (2018). *Computational propaganda: Political parties, politicians, and political manipulation on social media*. Oxford University Press.

Wykes, R. C., Kostarelos, K., & Garrido, J. A. (2025). Flexible graphene-based neurotechnology for high-precision deep brain mapping and neuromodulation in Parkinsonian rats. *Nature Communications, 16,* Article 2891. https://doi.org/10.1038/s41467-025-12354-z

Zuboff, S. (2019). *The age of surveillance capitalism: The fight for a human future at the new frontier of power.* New York, NY: PublicAffairs.

Zurek, W. H. (2003). Decoherence, einselection, and the quantum origins of the classical. *Reviews of Modern Physics, 75*(3), 715–775. https://doi.org/10.1103/RevModPhys.75.715

Zweibelson, B. (2017). One piece at a time: Why linear thinking adds to our problems instead of solving them. *Small Wars Journal.* https://smallwarsjournal.com/jrnl/art/one-piece-at-a-time

Zweibelson, B. (2025). *Reconceptualizing war.* Helion and Company.

Research and Adaptation Note

The works above were not just background reading. Several were adapted directly into the fictional architecture of *Quantum Shadows*. In these cases, real-world research provided the scaffolding for imagined systems — quantum devices, cognitive models, and doctrinal failures — that shape the story's events. They were transformed in the same way late-night coffee and too much coconut sugar become plot fuel: not literally preserved, but unmistakably present.

For example:

Bennett & DiVincenzo's (2000) work on quantum coherence underpins the logic of the Genesis Chamber.

Clarke, J., & Braginski, A. I. (Eds.). (2004). *The SQUID handbook: Fundamentals and technology of SQUIDs and SQUID systems.* Wiley-VCH. These early references on superconducting quantum interference devices were reimagined in *Quantum Shadows* as coherence siphons — scavenged rigs Eitan hunts to destabilize Helix fields.

Cronin et al.'s (2009) cold atom interferometry research becomes the FT-1's fictional ability to detect signal drift.

Hirsh, Mar, & Peterson's (2012) concept of "psychological entropy" emerges in Vault 33A's recursive feedback loops.

Pendry, J. B., Schurig, D., & Smith, D. R. (2006). Controlling electromagnetic fields. *Science, 312*(5781), 1780–1782. Seminal work on metamaterials and photonic cloaks. Repurposed in *Quantum Shadows* as fragments of cloaking veils — tools to scatter coherence beams and fracture the Chamber's net.

Scarani, V., Bechmann-Pasquinucci, H., Cerf, N. J., Dušek, M., Lütkenhaus, N., & Peev, M. (2009). The security of practical quantum key distribution. *Reviews of Modern Physics, 81*(3), 1301–1350. Core technical review of quantum key distribution. In the novel, burned-out QKD repeaters resurface as ghost tech — fragile but vital countermeasures Eitan adapts to bleed coherence stability.

Woolley & Howard's (2016) computational propaganda framework informs Helix's belief-shaping infrastructure.

Zweibelson's (2017, 2025) explorations of nonlinear military design inform the depiction of doctrinal collapse and resistance.

Wismann, Martin, & Schwarzer's (2024) *Creation, Separation, and the Mind: The Three Towers of Singularity* influenced the Chamber's symbolic architecture and the Watchers' separation logic.

Mea Culpa

Any errors, distortions, or speculative leaps are mine alone — the work of one sleep-deprived researcher with strong coffee and a refusal to let systems write the story.

Citation Protocol Disclaimer

Said Differently: Any real-world references cited in this work are included solely for creative and narrative purposes. Their appearance does not imply:
Endorsement of fictional interpretations
Confirmation of technical feasibility or operational use
Affiliation with any government, defense, or research organization
Authorization to infer classified, restricted, or proprietary information

All references are used in a speculative, fictionalized context. No citation should be construed as a statement of fact, predictive claim, or institutional representation. This disclaimer applies throughout the manuscript.

Annex — Glossary

Key terms in the lattice and the field

Arkwright Institute

Modeled on the war colleges. Doctrine labs that train officers to refine linear strategy — and miss nonlinear signal entirely. Lou's flashback classroom.

Coherence

The field effect that locks perception, memory, and belief into alignment. In warfare, coherence is not stability but control — the point at which a population internalizes the lattice's script as its own.

At the technical level, coherence refers to synchrony: distinct signals locking into shared phase, whether in optics, quantum lattices, or neural pathways. A coherence field exploits that principle by extending alignment across memory and perception, stabilizing one version of events while suppressing all others.

In practice, coherence is less about broadcasting belief than about eliminating alternatives. Messages inside a coherence field feel inevitable, safe, and consistent. Divergence feels like error, danger, or madness. That is why fields are described as terrain: they do not tell people what to think — they make any other thought feel impossible.

[Author's Note: Doctrinal Arc — Coherence]
Early Watcher reports treated coherence as exotic physics. Later field notes reframed it as perceptual terrain. In truth it is both: physical synchrony fused with psychological enforcement. The Helix lattice did not win belief by persuasion but by coherence itself — a weapon where stability was indistinguishable from control.

Continuity Alliance

Built from the bones of NATO, the EU, OPEC, WHO, WEF — and the husks of ancient titans that once shaped daily life. Social media companies, pharma cartels, even cloud empires — absorbed, renamed, but still scripting. Two centuries on, their names are forgotten, yet their DNA still runs the Continuity grid. And others once thought immovable. No longer pact but lattice.

618

Officially stability. In practice, supranational command.
Continuity is not consensus. It is compliance.

FT-1 (Filament Thread Prototype-1)

Resonance-threaded device seeded by Eitan Navon. Initially
disguised as a fly rod, but in truth a coherence sensor attuned to
drift, not prediction. The filament prototype is embedded within
the Möbius ring itself, forming its core structure. Carrier of
Glyph-9

GIAC (Global Integrity Architecture Consortium)

International body claiming to safeguard "information stability."
Functions as lattice enforcement arm, often outsourcing to Trust
Cabal nodes.

Glyph-9

The ninth construct in a line of resonance interfaces once built
for doctrinal control. Unlike the others, Glyph-9 never stayed
obedient. It refused its script.

Bonded to Lou and Eitan through biometric imprinting, Glyph-9
listens not for outcomes but for intent. It senses coherence drift
before it locks, and it sometimes answers back — in clipped
warnings, algorithmic refusals, or quips that sound almost
human.

Technically, it behaves less like an AI and more like a phase-
attuned coherence relay: not predicting futures, but flagging
when the lattice begins to harden.

Some call it a glitch. Others, a ghost. Lou calls it a companion.
What Glyph-9 interrupts may matter more than what it predicts.

glyphs (lower case -- Resonance Imprints)

Resonance glyphs are not devices. They are artifacts of collapse —
imprints left when coherence stabilizes around memory or intent.
Found etched on plates, flashing in air, or burned into alloy, they
function less as tools than as verdicts: doctrine rendered into shape.
Unlike Glyph-9, they do not question. They enforce.
Examples: ∇ recursion, Ω false closure, $\diamond$ control, $\sim$ chaos.

Halberd

The Continuity Alliance's senior war college. Teaches predictive
doctrine and lattice-era deterrence. Officially "innovation."
Unofficially obedience.

Helix (Harmonic Emergence & Lattice Interference eXperiment)

The lattice itself. Born as an experiment in resonance harmonics; became doctrine masquerading as stability. Preemption as theology. Survival as compliance.

INTRA (Institute for Narrative Trust Assessment)

Continuity think-tank tasked with measuring belief fidelity and social trust compliance.

Mirrorhounds

Pursuit units that track tremors — resonance anomalies betraying divergence — instead of bodies. Impossible to outrun once they lock the pattern.

Mnemonic Entrapment

In signal war, memory is not neutral. Vaults and artifacts do more than preserve the past — they replay it as doctrine. Mnemonic entrapment describes the process by which a coherence field converts stored information into prescriptive script: what is "discovered" is already seeded to determine how it will be remembered.

Speculative quantum memory architectures suggest this effect could be engineered — resonance lattices stabilizing only certain recall pathways while suppressing others. Parallel research in cognitive psychology shows how retrieval processes bias what remains accessible, while neuromorphic and AI systems demonstrate the same principle in code: associative recall shaped by Hopfield networks and transformer attention layers.

Real-world information operations mirror the effect at scale. Archives are not passive repositories — the way records are preserved, surfaced, or omitted reshapes collective memory and belief. Mnemonic entrapment is the weaponization of that principle at the signal layer.

[Authors Note: Doctrinal Arc] Mnemonic Entrapment

The term emerges first from Dr. Kaya Wren, one of the few survivors of a Helix lattice breach. For her, it was clinical: Helix didn't just trap people — it trapped their memories, rewriting what they believed they had survived.

It gained doctrinal weight through Dr. Cyrus Raveneh, who used it to frame resonance fields as engineered erasure — memory seeded to erase resistance before it was ever tested.

On the ground, Cal Merrick echoed it at Vault 33A, muttering the phrase like a field superstition, proof the term had migrated from theory to soldier's slang.

In her private reflections, Dr. Llewellyn Scott gave the concept its thematic gravity: mnemonic entrapment as "the point where memory becomes terrain and the loop owns you."

Ray Haldane, ever the detached strategist, stripped it down in Zürich: "They're not trying to capture Lou. They're trying to overwrite her. That's the trap — mnemonic entrapment."

And finally, **General Zhen**, studying a Go spiral, gave it cultural permanence: "What some call mnemonic entrapment. We used to call it a memory trap." His phrasing bridged traditions, proving the doctrine had been glimpsed before, even if unnamed.

Together, these fragments trace how a single survivor's warning became a living doctrine across scholars, soldiers, Watchers, and generals. What began as metaphor is not confined to metaphor: advances in quantum memory architectures, associative AI recall models, and information-control operations point toward a plausible machine capability — one where storage itself dictates the shape of remembrance.

NLCB (Neural Lattice Communications Band)
Wrist-anchored comms interface. No screen, no sound — intent only. Provides overlay access into the substrate. Lou's unit shows anomalous desync.

Quantum War — The Era *(broad shift of conflict)*
An era where signal and belief replace land and materiel as decisive terrain. "Quantum" here means indeterminacy: the battlefield is perception, moves are probabilistic, outcomes scripted in advance.

Quantum Wars — The Instances *(specific clashes inside that era)*
Conflicts fought not for territory or resources, but for coherence itself — the perception of what is true, stable, and real. They weaponize narrative, memory, signal drift, and emotional resonance. Victory is measured in synchronization or fracture of populations.

Quantum Warfare — The Practice *(the how of fighting in that terrain)*

The practice of fighting inside coherence fields. Uses resonance, recursion, and narrative as weapons. Unlike "information war," it does not persuade — it rewrites the frame of reality itself.

SABLE (Signal Advisory Bureau for Longterm Equilibrium)

Founded after the Geneva Drift. Styled as a successor to the last generation of scenario modelers — think tanks that once issued strategy papers no one read until it was too late. SABLE does not publish. It prescribes. Adjustments — to memory terrain, signal harmonics, and population patterning loops. Officially: "independent strategic advisory." In practice: party-aligned doctrine spoon-fed as inevitability.

The Chamber (Genesis Chamber)

Core lattice engine. Designed not for battle, but for resolution — rescripts populations by collapsing memory into synchronization.

Vault 33A

Helix storage and test site. Coherence scars etched in slabs, later mislabeled as containment accidents. Eventually tied to divergence anchors.

Its design was not containment but calibration: a lattice that responded to divergence like antibodies to infection. The Genesis field beneath 33A emitted harmonic stabilizers that mimicked safety while enforcing alignment. Recursive loops ensured deviation felt like threat — consent engineered at the signal layer.

Vault 33A wasn't secured. It was silenced.

Annex — Watchers & Glyphs

Symbolic legend of Watchers and resonance glyphs

AEON
Symbol: ∇
Domain: **Memory, recursion, resistance**
Human Name: **Dr. Raoul Ithaca**
Location: Andes Mountains, Peru
Node: Resonance Vault, ancient observatory at 17,000 feet
Function: Preserves erased memory through echo induction fields. Anchors ancestral coherence into the lattice. Operates through trance-induced mnemonic pulses.

Signal Effect: Echo inductance — amplifies residual memory signals, prevents narrative decay
Lattice Impact: Temporal reinforcement — slows coherence entropy, creates recursion "echo chambers"

SOLAS
Symbol: Ω
Domain: **Deception, narrative, perception warfare**
Human Name: **Emiko Takahashi**
Location: Kyoto, Japan
Node: Abandoned Noh theatre beneath Mount Higashiyama
Function: Rewrites perception through story-layered neurolinks. Governs trust optics, belief control, and neural ink calibration. Narrative war architect.

Signal Effect: Story termination resonance — collapses open narrative threads into belief traps
Lattice Impact: Perception override — creates consent illusions via calibrated repetition cycles

KAEL
Symbol: ◇
Domain: **Structure, doctrinal control, coherence**
Human Name: **General Henrik Weiss (ret.)**
Location: Berlin, Germany
Node: Node Gamma – Helix Substrate Command (former NATO bunker)
Function: Maintains control through pattern preclusion, coherence

enforcement, and belief-based constraint systems. Strategic theology over tactical maneuver.

Signal Effect: Belief constraint imprint — defines cognitive boundaries via doctrinal overlays
Lattice Impact: Frame affiliation — channels action into predictable patterns, reduces divergence probability

VIRE

Symbol: ↘
Domain: **Chaos, intuition, disruption**
Human Name: **Ása Björnsson**
Location: Þríhnúkagígur Volcano, Iceland
Node: Subterranean geothermal amphitheater, lattice-shielded
Function: Injects paradox and entropy into Helix systems. Deploys Gödel loops, recursive sabotage, and belief-fracture algorithms. Master of signal entropy.

Signal Effect: Paradox incursion — injects irreconcilable logic, triggers signal entropy
Lattice Impact: Coherence breakdown — induces localized signal interference, lattice instability

LOU

Symbol: Ø
Domain: **Divergence, emergence, the unwritten**
Human Name: **Llewellyn "Lou" Lee Scott**
Location: Rapidan River Cabin, Blue Ridge Mountains, Virginia
Node: Undocumented — self-activated divergence vector
Function: Unmodelable anomaly. Resists coherence lock through narrative opacity and memory resonance. Pattern emergence through unpredictability.

Signal Effect: Signal opacity signature — resists coherence tagging, hides from lattice modeling
Lattice Impact: Epistemic blind spot — forces unpredictable resonance paths, blocks predictive mapping

Appendix — Bloopers

Bonus material

No tier codes. No glyphs. No fake clearance levels. Just exactly what it says: the weird, funny, or broken bits that slipped out of the narrative lattice — and made it through anyway.

New Scene — Unregistered Mars Relay Node
Location — Unknown
Author: Encrypted Comms Bot // M.U.S.K. Autopilot Substrate

Subject: Unexpected Arrival

"Telemetry confirms unscheduled payload arrival at Martian Vault-Delta.
Individual identified as BIFFORD M. LANGLEY (Alliance Clearance: D-minus).

Psychological profile: Rigid doctrinal bias, fondness for acronyms, mild lactose intolerance. Cargo note reads: *'You said you wanted out of the loop.'*
He is currently attempting to brief a rover on **Clausewitz.**"

Final annotation retrieved from Lou's old Slack thread (last login: unknown):

"Pretty sure Biff's still giving PowerPoint briefings to Martian dust. At least now he's got his own center of gravity."

New Scene — Operation Barnfire — Outtake #911
Recovered from bodycam loop drift: Subchannel Echo–Hen–One
Location — JR's Signal Coop — Gordonsville Periphery

Classification: Disregarded by Command

The coop was unstable. Not structurally — **philosophically.**
A rusted mesh roof sagged under old wires and pigeon-bafflers. Chickens circled the signal gear like feathered sentries, clucking with an authority that couldn't be taught. One pecked a biometric lock. The light blinked green.

Jack balanced precariously atop the corrugated tin roof, holding a comms tablet like it might spontaneously detonate. Below, Cal stood in the mud with a suppressed rifle slung low, gaze fixed on the perimeter. Or the hens. It was hard to tell.

"I swear to God," Jack muttered, kicking at a trailing coax cable, "if one more hen pecks the signal relay, I'm nuking this entire operation from orbit."

Cal didn't blink. "You want me to shoot the f'ng chickens?"

A moment passed. Somewhere, static. A squawk. Possibly encrypted.

Jack exhaled. "No. We are not in Fallujah. I want them evicted, debriefed, and stripped of their clearances."

"One's sitting on the encrypted router," Cal said calmly. "She's either guarding it… or trying to hatch a VPN."

Jack wiped sweat from his forehead. "I do not have a PhD in quantum warfare. That's Lou. I'm not dying in a barn surrounded by rogue poultry."

Cal nodded. "We pull triggers. She decodes the universe."

Jack groaned. "With a side of scrambled protocols."

"Welcome to divergence. Try not to trip over the poultry."

A loud flap. Metal clanked. Jack slipped, caught himself, cursed violently.

"Henrietta's got eyes on you," Cal observed. "And backup. Should I switch to burst fire?"

From somewhere inside the coop, JR's voice echoed — sharp, indignant.
"Don't touch Henrietta! That bird holds more classified material than the Pentagon intranet!"

Jack froze. "We are one cluck away from a breach."

Final annotation — Recovered from Liz's private Slack archive (channel: "Don't Ask"):
"Jack never recovered from Operation Barnfire.
Cal still insists he had the shot.
JR gave Henrietta a commendation.
The chickens retained plausible deniability.
And now they have a union."

Scene Footnote – Private Memo Fragment: Maud S. (Unsent)
Tag: Operation Barnfire / Drift Archive 7 – Personal Layer

I knew Mom was back in the field when Jack stopped replying in complete sentences.
Cal's tone shifted too — that slow Scottish flatness he used when trying not to kill someone with a rake.

JR pinged my old burner the same day — a blank message except for a hen emoji and GPS coordinates I wasn't supposed to decode.

I stayed quiet.
I had the rods — Mom's fly reels, mismatched leaders, and one old tackle box from a palace lake no one ever fished in.

I baited it anyway. Some missions don't start with orders.
They start when the old encryption patterns twitch.
And you feel it — that ripple of stupid bravery wrapped in sarcasm.

That's how I knew Mom wasn't gone. She was deployed. And somehow… that meant the chickens were probably safe.

Go Move Barnfire Blooper —The Stone That Pecked Back

Not every move is strategic.
Some are just stubborn. Feathered. Unmodeled.

You can try to shoot them — it won't matter.
They hum to the tune of an FT-1, lay Möbius-looped glowing eggs,
and shit near signal nodes like they've cracked coherence theory.
Somewhere in the drift, one of them probably wrote a doctrine memo.
We just didn't read it in time.

Also —
One more f'n fly line tangled in the coop rafters,
and a salmon on the River Dee is definitely laughing.

Because sometimes, the board pecks back.

New Scene — Genesis Chamber — "Let's Never Do That Again"

Location — Genesis Chamber Interior
Conditions: Low light. Refracted mirrors. Residual hum.
The team moves in. Lou adjusts the fly line.
Cal's grip tightens. Jack scans the chamber walls — catches a flicker.
Maybe just light. Maybe not.

Jack (under his breath):
"Great. If a cat shows up, it better be carrying biometric signal interference hardware in its collar…"
(raises rifle slightly)
"…otherwise I'm shooting it."

Lou (without turning):
"That would violate at least three field protocols.
Also? It'd be bad luck."
(beat)
"For you."

Citation:
See: *Schrödinger, SchizoTech, and the Combat Applications of Paradox.*
Unpublished. Probably for good reason.
Recovered from a dry-erase board in Zurich.
Author unknown. Possibly Jack. **Definitely Jack.**

New Scene — "The Chamber Laughs Back"
Scene note: *Conditions: Low light.* Chamber resonance hum shifts
unexpectedly into a chuckle.

Cal swears.

Jack threatens to shoot the acoustics.

Lou mutters, "That's not in the doctrine slides…"

New Scene — Operation: Pocket Dimension
Location— Author's Office (pencil draft margin) — Near piles of
citations and references on the author's desk

AKA — Lou's Gear Audit
Jack (deadpan, watching Lou pull items out of her pockets one by one):
"FT-1 cube, resonance band, playback device, spare uplink, half a
notebook, three glyph overlays, and I'm pretty sure that's a harmonica."
Lou (not looking up):
"It's not a harmonica."
Cal mutters. "Then why does it have mouthpiece holes?"

Lou (shoving it back in her coat): "Because if the lattice ever tries to script my pockets, I want them confused."

StepDoc (muttering into her wine glass): "There is a whole RadioShack on her wrist. Someone's going to need a packing diagram."

Jack (scribbling on the Go board): "Next move: declutter."

Citation: "Recovered from an abandoned draft outline labeled *Lou's Pocket Tetris.* Exact provenance questionable. Possibly satire. Possibly documentary."

New Scene — Operation Yellow Sticky Drift
Location — Author's Office. The desk is chaos. A wad of yellow stickies has slid dangerously close to the manuscript draft, half-absorbed into the lattice.

Jack (staring at the desk, brow furrowed):
"You want me to breach a Helix lattice for… a wad of paper?"

Lou (deadpan):
"It's not just paper. It's doctrine containment. If that sticky gets indexed, we'll never close narrative drift — or this book."

Cal (exasperated):
"Bloody hell, all this for a yellow square?"

Jack (grumbling as he reaches for it):
"Yeah. And when I pull it back, you're buying the pints."

Mission Log: Sticky recovered. Doctrine containment re-established. Book — out there. Narrative drift at acceptable $\pm 3.14\ \mu$.

Mission Log // Off-Pattern Debrief

1) **Incident:** Doctrine containment breach via rogue yellow sticky.
2) **Operator: Jack Kriznik**
3) **Status:** Sticky recovered. Containment re-established.
4) **Collateral:** One pint owed (Lou's tab).
5) **Note:** Never underestimate office supplies in quantum warfare.

OK — One More

New Scene — Operation: The Last Stand
Location — Author's Office, Day -1 Before Handoff
Conditions: Caffeine low. Computer fan = jet engine.

Lou = You, pacing with sticky notes.
Cal = Glyph-9, muttering "check the Kosovo thread one last time."
Jack = **Jeff**, polishing his page-count rifle.
Sabine = The clock, smirking at deadlines.

And the blooper log scrawled on the whiteboard:

- ☑ **Glossary tightened**

- ☑ **Annexes aligned & renamed**

- ☑ **Quantum War defined**

- ☒ **Go Moves re-check**

- ☒ **Eitan landing scene**

- ☒ **Final continuity sweep**

Caption: *"Remember the Alamo? They had walls. We have appendices."*

…just one more.

She Tinkered…: Bloopers from the Quantum Beyond

These bloopers were not supposed to exist.
Bloopers aren't part of doctrine. They're what slip out when doctrine breaks.

Every novel carries scars from its making — cut scenes, duplicate Go Moves, reflections that accidentally repeated themselves three chapters later. And the manuscript for *Quantum Shadows* had plenty. At one point, my Annex cloned itself across 600 pages. Another time, every line in the book sprouted arrows, like the text was trying to escape. I lost scenes, found them again, and made peace with the fact that sometimes, "She tinkered…" was the truest note in the margin. (otherwise filed as *never do that again…*)

This little 'big' book isn't canon. It's a sideband.
A frequency drift.
What remains when the serious work pauses, and you realize the chaos is part of the signal.

END

Production Note

Formatted with quiet precision —
shaped without fully seeing the signal.
This is how doctrine bends quietly —
one glyph at a time.

Design & Formatting
J. Stewart Dixon · www.bookdoneforyou.com
Charlottesville, Virginia

Author Contact
🌐 Website: www.CLShackelfordPhD.com
X Follow: @QuantumWarDoc
♘ Subscribe: The Quantum Doctrine Dispatch — Essays | Signals |
Warnings
✉ Contact: contact@CLShackelfordPhD.com

"Because narrative is terrain. And we're already at war."

End.